FEATURING SIMON BESTWICK, GARY

THE BE

TOMES
OF THE
DEAD

VOL. 2

WWW.ABADDONBOOKS.COM

An Abaddon Books™ Publication
www.abaddonbooks.com
abaddon@rebellion.co.uk

This omnibus published in 2011 by Abaddon Books™,
Rebellion Intellectual Property Limited,
Riverside House, Osney Mead, Oxford, OX2 0ES, UK.

10 9 8 7 6 5 4 3 2 1

Editor-in Chief: Jonathan Oliver
Desk Editor: David Moore
Junior Editor: Jenni Hill
Omnibus Cover: Luke Preece
Original Covers: Mark Harrison
Design: Simon Parr & Luke Preece
Marketing and PR: Keith Richardson
Creative Director and CEO: Jason Kingsley
Chief Technical Officer: Chris Kingsley

ISBN (UK): 978-1-907992-17-9
ISBN (US): 978-1-907992-18-6

Printed in the US

TIDE OF SOULS

BY SIMON BESTWICK

To Judith and Roger Bestwick, my parents.

INTRODUCTION

MIGHT AS WELL be honest about this. Without Jon Oliver, this book literally wouldn't have happened.

Back in 2008, Jon gave me the opportunity to pitch a novel for Abaddon's *Tomes of the Dead* line. I don't actually write that often about the staple genre monsters – vampires, werewolves, etc. – but I do have a soft spot for zombies (largely because of the dozens of shlocky zombie films I watched back in the '90s).

Note to other writers, though: if you pitch a zombie novel to Jon, don't just shoehorn the walking dead into an old idea from your bottom drawer. He'll notice. But he did like certain things: an apocalyptic flood, and an army of aquatic zombies.

I started jotting down ideas about situations and characters – and then, from nowhere, came the words *my name is Katja Wencewska...* and the first of the novel's characters began telling her story. The plot worked itself out from there.

Jon phoned a few weeks later.

JON: 'So, would you like to write a zombie novel for me, then?'
ME: 'Well, I dunno actually – I've been thinking of writing more Jane

Austen style romances... hey, there's a thought. *Pride and Prejudice...* with zombies!'

I swear to god, that's actually the truth. I do my best not to let Jon forget he turned that one down.

Tide of Souls was my first published novel, and it made more of a splash (no pun intended) than I'd dared hope it would. I set out to make it personal to me and to write something I could be proud of, and in the end I did. Hopefully the zombies are also genuinely frightening, but you'll have to make your own mind up about that.

Which is probably the best place to leave you. On with the story. And don't forget your life-jacket.

Simon Bestwick
Lancashire
March 2011

PART ONE

Storm's Edge – The Boatman's Call

I looked upon the rotting sea,
And drew my eyes away,
I looked upon the rotting deck,
And there the dead men lay

Samuel Taylor Coleridge,
The Rime of The Ancient Mariner, Part IV

CHAPTER ONE

Katja

THE RISING OF the dead was the best luck I'd had in years. A godsend, even. I was lucky to survive, of course; my owners showed exactly how they valued me when they left me locked in a Cheetham Hill brothel to drown. I was lucky they kept me upstairs; I heard the women on the ground floor. I heard them die. Heard their screams of panic, choked off as they drowned.

At least, at the time, I thought they had drowned. Hours later, clinging to a rooftop, holding a gun with one bullet left in it and trying to decide which of us to use it on, I wasn't so sure.

MY NAME IS Katja Wencewska. Although my family is Polish, I grew up in Romania. It's a long story, none of it relevant to this. I will tell you what is relevant.

I am twenty-seven years old. My father was a military officer. Special forces. A good, brave man, always very calm. Tall, as well. A tree of a man. An oak. My mother, in contrast, was like a tiny bird – very bright, excitable. I loved them both dearly. I was their only child. They were proud of me; in school I won prizes in Literature, the Arts and Gymnastics. I have two degrees.

None of that helped when they died. A stupid man, driving drunk, late one night. Their car went off the road, into a ravine. My father died instantly; my mother took several hours. The idiot responsible was cut out of the wreckage with barely a scratch. I wanted to kill him, and could have. Papa had often shown me how. He knew the world was full of predators, and taught me to protect myself against them.

I was studying for a PhD at the time, but of course that had to be abandoned. Bills had to be paid, but there was no work to be found. Then I heard of a job in England. For a fee, strings would be pulled, things arranged. A teaching job.

I spoke good English. I thought I would work hard, make money. Eventually I planned to come home – when things were better there, when I had money saved.

I thought I was so clever. I was well-educated and, I thought, streetwise. I could kill with a blow after all, if I was forced to. But the thought never crossed my mind. I had heard of people-trafficking, of course, but you never think it will be you. Predators would be so easily dealt with if they came to us as predators.

I was a fool.

You can guess the rest. My passport was taken. There was no teaching job. I was to service men for money. When I refused, I was beaten and raped. Worse than rape. Other things were done to me. I will not talk about those things: they are not relevant, you have no need to know them. After this, I felt defiled and wretched. I did not refuse again. It was made clear to me – to us all – that if we were too much trouble we would be killed. We were expendable: easily disposed of, easily replaced.

I was kept at a brothel in London at first. After six months they moved me to another, in Manchester. I spent the next eight months there. Being able to kill with a blow means little when there are always more of them, when the doors are always locked, the windows always barred, when you have nowhere to go.

I think that is all I need to say about myself.

I was woken that morning by screams and blaring horns.

I got to the window and squinted through the bars. On Cheetham Hill Road, people were leaping onto the roadway to avoid something pouring over the pavement. At first I thought it was water – dark, filthy water – but when I pushed the net curtains aside I could see it flowed uphill. And over the screams and traffic noise, even the horns, I heard it squealing.

They were swarming rats.

It was raining heavily; water gushed down the pavements and the road into the gutters. There'd been a lot of that lately.

There were rats on the road too – all on one side, the lane for city-bound traffic, which was deserted. The road out of Manchester, on the other hand, was jammed solid. I could see the people in the cars – wild, terrified faces, fright and fury mixed, fists pounding windows, dashboards, steering wheels, making their horns blare and blare and blare.

The rain intensified until the road blurred. I stepped back from the window, let the curtains fall back into place. My stomach felt hollow and tight.

We had a television there, but I hadn't seen the news in months. We weren't allowed, and besides, we only wanted to watch things that would take our minds off our lives. I had no idea what had happened, or was happening; only that something was very wrong.

Soon, I heard banging on the brothel's front door. I looked outside. It was Ilir, our owner. One of his sons came out of the door; he'd been left in charge. Ilir's black BMW was in the traffic jam, doors open. Ilir dragged his son to it. They slammed the doors; Ilir pounded the horn, but the traffic didn't budge. After a minute, they pulled into the deserted city bound lane. Other cars started following their example, and for a short time the traffic moved forward, but then locked up again. So many people, all trying to leave. Some of the other girls had started screaming, pounding on the doors. They'd abandoned us. They hadn't even turned us loose, just left us here.

People were running along the pavement, clutching their belongings, their children. Their eyes were wild.

An hour or so after Ilir and his son left, the answers started coming. Below Cheetham Hill are the Irwell and the Irk, two of the three rivers that run through Manchester. None are very deep; all have high banks. But water was washing *up* the street. Lapping up in slow, relentless waves.

Even then, I didn't really get it. It only really sank in when people started abandoning their cars.

It happened very quickly after that. Water washed around the wheels of the cars and rose higher. It lapped round their skirts. It poured over the pavements. Across the street, water flooded under the front door of the kebab house and across the floor. People were wading the torrents, and then began climbing on top of the cars.

For a few minutes, I just watched. None of it felt real. It was like watching some bizarre art-house film. But nothing had felt real in that place for a long time. You couldn't let it, if you wanted to stay sane.

The water now started pouring over the crest of Cheetham Hill, and the rising waters now became a surge. A middle-aged Asian man fell over and was swept along, screaming for help. His arms flailed, and a toupee slipped off his head. I heard myself giggle; it was a jagged, ugly sound. I clapped a hand over my mouth. He went under and didn't come up.

Then I heard the girls downstairs begin screaming in earnest, and I realised the waters were entering the brothel.

We were all locked in our rooms overnight. Each one had an *en-suite* sink and toilet; for convenience, not comfort. The windows were all barred, so there was no escape. Even if the waters didn't flood the upper floors, I could still look forward to starvation.

My father had shown me how to pick a lock. I could've escaped my room easily enough before now. The difficult part had always been what I would do then. There were two front doors, inner and outer, the inner triple-locked. And even if I'd got clear of that, where would I go with no papers, no passport, no way of getting a legitimate job?

But now the rules had changed.

I started searching, trying to find something I could use. The women downstairs were screaming. People on the street were screaming. I blocked it out. It didn't help me to hear it, wouldn't help me do this faster.

I tipped up the wastepaper basket. There were used condoms in it, slimy to the touch.

Ignore them, Papa said.

At last I found a paper clip.

I knelt by the door and set to work. It was a slow job. Trial and error. My fingers got sweaty and slipped on the metal.

I realised the girls downstairs had stopped screaming; all but one. Then she too was choked off. And there was only silence from the ground floor.

Outside the street was silent. I went to the window. Stopped, and stared.

Most of it was underwater. Brown, dirty water had covered almost all the cars. The roofs of a few vehicles showed. There was a double-decker bus opposite, the top deck still above water. A dozen people were there, slack-skinned faces gazing into mine. Here and there, on the water, I saw reddish stains, dispersing slowly in the current.

There were two other women upstairs in the brothel – Marianna, who was about my age, was praying over and over in the next room. Marta, the youngest of the girls, was sobbing helplessly across the landing. She was only fifteen. A child. Tiny. Dark. Like my mother had been.

I ran back to the door, back to the lock. My fingers shook. I took a deep breath.

Panic is a choice, Papa used to say. *You can decide not to be scared, not to panic. You can decide who's in charge.*

So I chose to stay calm. I could still hear the rain pelting down outside, but I didn't look to see if the waters were still rising. I couldn't think about that. I had to act as if time was not a factor. I just kept working. Even when the thin carpet I knelt on grew cold and wet.

Marta was sobbing and screaming as well now. From next door, Marianna's prayers had blurred into a rising jumble of sound, fast turning into a wail.

The tumblers clicked.

I got the door open. Water filmed the landing, welling up from the flooded staircase. There was a fire extinguisher on the wall. I could smash the locks on the other girls' doors.

Then there were fresh screams. From outside.

I don't know why, but I went back to the window. I suppose I thought the worst of it was past: the door was open, and I had time. Or, perhaps, there was something about the screams that alerted me.

When I look back, I believe going to the window probably saved my life. It forewarned me – just a little, but enough. Even so, as with much else, I wish I hadn't seen what I saw.

It was the double-decker. The waters were still rising, but the top windows and the people inside remained visible. They were scrambling away to the back end of the bus.

Someone was standing up in the water at the front end, near the staircase. At first I thought he was just fat. Then another figure rose up out of the water and I almost screamed. The bus passengers weren't so restrained. I could hear them from where I stood.

The second shape – its flesh resembled well-cooked meat, falling off the bone. I could see the bone of one arm showing through, and when the thing swivelled sideways for a second, showing its back, I saw the flesh coming away from the spine on each side, baring it like a moth's body when its wings are spread. Then it turned my way. *God. God almighty. That face.* Grinning because so much of the flesh was falling from the skull. And looking at me. The sockets of its eyes were empty. They glared; a greenish-yellow glow, bright. It started forward, the fat shape following – I saw now it wasn't fat, just bloated, from its drowning. And then a third figure rose up into view, climbing up the bus's flooded stairwell, and a fourth... all with those glowing eyes.

The passengers were still. There wasn't really anywhere to go in any case. The rotting thing seized one of them, a woman in her twenties, and bit into her neck. I heard her scream. The bloated figure grabbed her too and they pulled her down; blood splattered the windows.

It was over for them very quickly after that. Sometimes I think they were the lucky ones.

I just wish, before I turned away, I hadn't seen the child, hands and face against the glass, screaming...

But there was nothing I could do.

*   *   *

I GRABBED THE extinguisher off the wall and smashed the lock on Marta's door. She stumbled out, then shrieked again as she saw the flooded stairwell.

"What are we going to do?" It came out in a wail.

I pointed to the hatch in the ceiling. "Get into the loft, then out onto the roof."

Luckily I didn't have to tell her everything; she clambered onto the landing rail and I caught her legs, boosted her up. She pushed the hatch up, grabbed the edges and started wriggling up into the loft. I ran to Marianna's door and smashed the lock there too.

Marianna was on her knees praying. I dragged her to her feet and out onto the landing. The water was ankle deep now.

"Climb!" I shouted to Marianna, and started clambering onto the banister. Marta reached down to grip my hands. Then her gaze drifted past me and her eyes widened.

I looked.

Wished I hadn't.

Down in the dark water, in the flooded stairwell, I could see movement. And lights. Pairs of yellow-green lights, rising towards the surface. And then I could see their faces.

CHAPTER TWO

"Marta!"

Her eyelids fluttered. The tranced state broke and she focussed on me again. She gripped my wrists tightly, then pulled me up through the trap door.

The first dead thing rose out of the water. The top part of its face still clung to the bone, matted hair hanging from the remaining pieces of its scalp. Marianna, frozen on the landing, stared down at it. A second corpse, equally decayed, emerged a second later.

"Marianna!" She looked up, then scrambled onto the banister. The dead thing seized her legs just as I caught her outstretched hands. Screaming, she fell sideways into space, almost pulling me through the trap after her; Marta caught me around the waist.

My grip broke. Marianna fell back onto the dead things, and all three of them crashed into the brown water. Another dead thing rose. A woman, in jeans and t-shirt like my own. Her skin was blue, but she was unmarked. Except for the eyes; the empty sockets were filled with that green glow, and what looked like dried candlewax clung to her cheeks. Her face was blank and slack.

Marianna screamed my name. Not her mother's or father's, or even

God's. Mine. Because I always knew what to do. But there was nothing; already she was beyond help.

They didn't kill her, not outright. That was the worst part. They weren't interested in that. They could hold her down, hold her still. The blue female gripped Marianna's arm at wrist and elbow, then leant forward and sank her teeth into the flesh. She shook her head back and forth, like a terrier with a rat. Marianna's shriek was the sound of a drill going into bones. I'd heard that, once. Ilir arranging a punishment, on someone who'd crossed him. He'd made us all watch, so that we would understand.

Thick blood began pouring out, down Marianna's arm, down the dead woman's chin as she pulled her head back.

Skin stretched and split, then the muscles and tendons underneath, as Marianna's drilling shriek rose ever higher. I heard them tearing. Blood spurted out in a vivid, unrelenting spray. I glimpsed white through it. Bone. Something ragged hung from the blue woman's mouth.

The water in the stairwell was red. The other two dead things held Marianna's legs, heads shaking to and fro as they bit. Her free arm flailed about, until a fourth pair of hands seized her wrist. A head lunged out of the water and sank its teeth into her breast.

I pulled Marta away from the trapdoor. Marianna's screams faded, became moans. Shock setting in, numbing the pain. There was that much mercy left, at least. But nothing would take away the sight of those things eating her alive. Perhaps, if she was lucky, she was beyond understanding it now.

But I wasn't.

There were other noises, too. Grunting and tearing. A sound like ripping wallpaper. *Skin.* A wet splatter, like piss on stone. *Blood.* And the chewing sounds.

They were eating her. There was still flesh on her bones.

Panic is a choice, Papa said again.

While they were eating her, they were not eating Marta, or me.

Marta – she'd wriggled away, across the bare loft floor, huddled in the angle where it met the wood panelling. Her breath was hitching, rapid. Whimpering. So was mine. Faster and faster. My heart, hammering.

I closed my eyes, breathed in deep, then slowly out. In. And out again. Made myself count to ten. Just thinking about the numbers, not about the things eating their way through Marianna's body or what they would do when they'd finished.

Eight. Nine. Ten.

I opened my eyes. Marta was still huddled and whimpering.

I could get further, move faster, alone. Papa might have done the same.

But I chose not to. I cannot quite explain why. Perhaps because she was a child. Perhaps it was something in myself I refused to abandon.

Or perhaps because, small, dark and birdlike as she was, she was very like my mother; it might have been that simple.

I dragged her to her feet, shook her, slapped her face.

"We have to get to the roof. Quickly. Before they" – I hesitated, then said it – "before they finish eating Marianna."

She gulped a weepy, shuddering breath, face twitching. I touched her cheek. "Take deep breaths. You have to stay calm."

I looked around the loft. Any exit to the roof would be behind the thin plywood panelling. Was there a window? I'd never seen the front of the building; on the rare occasions I'd left or entered the brothel, I'd been bundled through a door at the back.

From below came ripping and munching sounds, and the gristly pop a chicken leg makes when wrenched free of the bird's body. Marianna was silent. Hopefully dead.

There was little time. Too much had been wasted already.

The window would be in the middle.

I prodded the wood panelling. It gave easily. Thin. I stepped back and drove a kick at it.

The plywood split. I yelled and kicked again. On the third kick the panel gave way; splinters stung my ankle and shin.

I grabbed at the edges of the hole I'd made, and pulled. "Marta! Help me. Quickly." She saw what I was doing and ripped at the panelling too. Chunks of it tore away. Behind it, wooden planks were nailed across something.

Thankfully the wood was old and soft, the nails pulling free of the brick work.

Please let there be a window behind this. Please.

There was. A casement, a couple of feet deep, and two panes of grimy glass.

I had to crawl into the casement feet-first to get at the window itself. I kicked out twice, with both feet, smashing the glass. Two or three short jabs knocked away the jagged edges.

It was almost silent. Almost. From below, there were still faint chewing sounds. And things breaking. Hard things. Bones.

Soon there'd be nothing left of Marianna.

The best I could hope was to keep us alive as long as possible. When there was no other option, I would find a way to end our lives. Marta I could finish with a single blow, could twist her neck. For myself I would need a weapon of some kind. Better that than a death like Marianna's.

"We're going to climb up onto the roof," I told Marta.

"What... Katja, what do we do *then*? They'll just come after us. They –"

"*Marta.*" I put all the authority I could into my voice. It didn't feel like very much, but she stopped talking. "We'll deal with that when we get up there. Okay?"

"Okay."

"Good," I said, and told her what I wanted her to do.

THE BIGGEST DANGER is loss of nerve. When I slid into the casement, I had to go head-first, on my back. Just as I was about to put my head out through the window, I pictured the water below, teeming with dead things reaching up for me. You can't stop to think in a situation like that, except about your next move, or it will paralyse you.

If I stuck my head out, it would be grabbed, seized in rotting hands. If I was lucky they would twist and tear, and my head would be ripped from my shoulders. If not, they'd drag me out and pull me into the water, where I'd feel their ragged nails ripping away my clothes to get at the flesh underneath, their teeth tearing pieces of my body away...

...while Marta...

"Katja?"

...while Marta was left on her own, waiting to be devoured. Unless she killed herself first.

I hadn't saved Marianna. But I'd been locked in my room to die, and I hadn't. I'd been treated as a piece of meat, but I wasn't. I was alive. Marta was alive. I'd got us both this far.

I was meat to Ilir, meat to the punters; now I was meat to these creatures. Only the appetite was changed.

Ilir – Ilir was probably dead already. Trapped on the flooding roads, in those infested waters.

But not me. Or Marta. We were alive. Now Ilir knew what it was to be meat.

I started laughing. Even to my own ears, in that space, it was an ugly, jagged sound. But I couldn't stop. It was so funny. Ilir was the meat now, and I wasn't. Not yet.

"*Katja!*"

Do it, Papa said. *Now.*

I stuck my arms out through the window and reached for the top of the casement. I wasn't meat now, but I would be if I didn't move.

Nothing grabbed me. I began pulling myself up and out, still laughing. Hands grabbed my legs. I kicked out. Still laughing.

"Katja!"

"I'm sorry. I'm sorry." But still laughing.

The casement jutted out from the slope of the roof. The top of it was flat. With Marta behind and then under me, holding my feet and boosting me up, I was able to climb up on top of it. Then I turned and grasped her wrists as she reached up towards me.

The water lapped around the windows on the floor we'd lived on.

Where would it be in our rooms now? Shin, knee, waist deep?

Something bobbed at the edge of the water. A mass of small objects, bristling with brown fur. Rats. Drowned rats. Hundreds of them. Beyond them, the water was full of faces, crammed together, glaring up with dull, impersonal hostility, eyes glowing. Live rats scurried, squeaking, over the roof tiles and guttering.

Water, the deep brown of drinking chocolate, rolled down Cheetham Hill Road and down side-streets and alleyways, frothing and eddying around lampposts and the bus. The bus's windows were steamed up bloody. Handprints. Shadowy figures moved inside. Eyes glowed behind the windows.

I leant back, pulling on Marta's wrists. She wriggled out of the window and braced first one foot, then the other, on the frame.

Fresh pairs of eyes flickered into life below; new faces swam up through the murk. They were gathering. I mustn't look, mustn't think about them.

Marta was composed now, focussed on the task in hand. I was proud of her. I pulled on her arms, and she walked up the sides of the casement, got a foot up onto the top of it. Then the other. And then she slumped down onto her knees and sobbed, and I stroked her hair and whispered things my mother had said to me when I was little, on long and sleepless nights when I saw monsters in the dark.

The casement roof creaked under us. If it broke...

I couldn't hear anything from below. No movement in the attic.

When I looked around and across the street, I saw that others had done the same as us. All the roofs were occupied. Scores, maybe even hundreds, of people. Men, women, children. Babies. Grandparents. All huddled on the rooftops. Some clung to the sloping roofs, trying to hold on, feet wedged in the buckled guttering.

All that remained of Cheetham Hill Road were the rows of buildings that had flanked it, steadily sinking from sight as they descended towards Manchester. A mist was gathering; I couldn't see the city, or whatever remained of it.

It was almost peaceful. The only sounds were the lap and splash of the water, and the low, muffled weeping washing in from the rooftops. I looked back down. The faces were still there. Now and then there'd be a faint splash as arms broke the surface. They were treading water.

So far, we were safe. Safe. That was funny. I giggled. Marta stared at me. I made myself stop, forced a smile.

Above the casement, the roof sloped upwards another two or three metres. Just to our right, there was a chimney stack.

"Marta?" I pointed. "We have to climb."

The roof was sharply angled, the tiles wet. One slip... she looked down.

I caught her by the shoulders. "Don't look at that. Don't think about it. Now, listen to me. You're going to go first –"

"I can't –"

"You're going to go first because then I'll be right behind you. If you fall, I'll catch you. And when you get to the top, you can help pull me up. Okay?"

At last, she nodded.

"Alright. Go on. *Now.*"

From below, there was a thumping sound. Marta let out a terrified squeak.

"Don't listen. Just climb."

She spread herself out across the tiles, dug in her toes and pushed upwards. Sobs made her back shake.

From below – *thump, thump.* Something had flopped into the attic space. It was moving around. The thumping got louder. *Closer.* I wanted to look around, but I did not. Would not.

Marta fumbled for a purchase on the tiles. Her hands slid. "Katja!"

"Don't use your hands like that. Spread them flat and press down. Use your feet to climb."

"How?"

"Bring one leg up. Get a grip with your trainer. Then push up. Then with the other. Yes, that's right. Quickly now." I kept my voice as level as I could.

Panic is a choice. Panic is a choice. Panic is a choice.

From below, the thumping grew louder still. I ignored it, had to. Watched Marta climb. *Oh please, God, let her make it.* I hadn't prayed in years. I would say a prayer for Marianna when we got up there. Even though I did not believe. She had. And she had been a friend. Or a colleague. Something to me, anyway.

Marta was sobbing. She was just a child. A child. Still. Despite everything she'd already gone through. Now this. No child should have to see this. Nor any adult.

She will never make it. Too young, too small; too fragile, too afraid.

"Keep climbing, darling. You can do it."

She was almost there now, close enough to reach out and grab the apex of the roof. First one hand, then the other. As she did, her feet slipped, and her whole weight fell on her hands. She screamed. Her feet scrabbled and kicked desperately, sliding off the tiles. When I tried to catch them, she nearly caught me in the face.

"Marta, stop kicking. *Stop kicking.*" I heard my voice rise. Sweat trickled down my back. How long could she hold on? If she fell, could I catch her? Would I? Or let her fall?

So easy to let her go. On my own, I could take better care.

Responsibility, Katja, Papa said. *She is one of yours. And besides, she looks so like your mother.*

I lunged out and grabbed her ankles. She screamed again, twisted her head around. Thank God, her grip didn't break. "Marta, keep still!"

This time, she listened to me, and obeyed. I shifted my hands so they were braced under her heels. "I've got you. Alright?"

"Oh, God."

"Sh. It's alright, little one." My mother called me that, as a child. "I've got you now. I'm going to push you up. You pull with your arms, and get one leg over the rooftop. Okay?"

"Yes."

The thumping was very loud now. "Go on!"

I pushed, and Marta hauled herself up, pulling herself astride the roof. "Katja!"

And the thumping stopped.

Marta grinned down at me, stupid with relief. It lasted for a barely a second. Then she was staring past my shoulder. "Katja?"

I turned. A head stuck out of the window. It was the blue woman. Her glowing sockets stared up at me. Drool welled up in her mouth like blood from a wound. It overflowed and mixed with the blood around her mouth. Marianna's blood. Her hands fumbled at the casement's top edge. Two fingers were without nails.

None of this could be happening. Perhaps my mind had finally given way and in reality I lay on my bed in the brothel, unmoving and unaware, a piece of meat at last. What would Ilir do? Probably take me out and bury me in some unmarked grave. Peace of a kind.

"Katja, climb up!"

Marta. She needed me. If this *was* real, and I gave up, she had no chance. Perhaps that was really why I saved Marta. To save myself.

But I couldn't look away from the blue woman. We stared at each other – for how long? Seconds, perhaps even minutes. It could have been hours, from how it felt. I waited for her to drag herself the rest of the way through the window. But she didn't. She let go of the window's edge and slid back inside the attic.

I stared at the space where she'd been.

"Katja, come on!"

I turned around, spread myself flat against the roof, and started to climb.

IT WENT WITHOUT a hitch. I pulled myself astride the rooftop and pointed to the chimney stack. We shuffled along until we were against it. I huddled behind Marta, trying to share body heat. We only wore jeans and T-shirts, and it was still raining. After all this, dying of hypothermia would be ridiculous, but entirely possible. Life has a sense of humour; this much I know. That jagged, ugly laughter bubbled up in me again, and I bit my lips until it passed.

A wind had risen, thinning the mist enough to reveal what remained of Manchester. I'd seen the city once before, from a distance. A private party that Ilir hired us out to. They'd taken us out back, bundled us into a van, told us to be nice, to pretend we were having a good time and happy to be there, happy to be doing this. One of the men must've said something good to Ilir, because he'd been kind to me. Kind for Ilir, anyway. He'd driven me into Manchester. Taken me shopping, bought me shoes and a dress. Taken me to a restaurant, bought me dinner. Then taken me back home to his bed, because he'd bought me.

The city wasn't there any more. All I could see – almost all – was water. Higher buildings stood clear of it, like strange, tall islands, the walls like cliffs. There was a towerblock nearby. A tiny stick figure stumbled out onto a balcony. I wondered if it was alive or dead. It stumbled back inside.

In the city proper I could see the CIS tower, sticking out high above the waters, but not the Hilton building; I had no idea what had happened to it. Other towers stuck up. A few tree tops, some of the taller lampposts. But that was all.

The rooftops were crowded. People huddled atop them like pigeons, clinging to each other. The rooftop beside ours was very crowded. A group of Asians; there must have been at least twenty, of all ages. They were trying to spread out along the roof, towards ours. One woman held a baby in her arms. Someone was shouting. Panic in his voice. Some sobbed, others prayed. I remembered my promise to Marianna and mumbled to myself, something like a prayer. It started with 'God' and it ended with 'Amen,' anyway.

The sky was black and empty. Rain streamed down. Lightning flashed, a crack of thunder crashing down from almost directly overhead. Thin, bleating cries drifted from the rooftops. I looked for planes, helicopters. Surely the government would send help? They might deport me, I realised, when they realised who I was. But that was for later. I couldn't think that far ahead. Staying alive. That was all I had. Me and Marta. My little family of one.

The creatures seemed to be staying in the water and inside the buildings. They weren't coming out into the open air.

Not yet.

But until they did, we had some rest. Sort of. But that meant time to think as well, and it was all crashing in on Marta. On me, too. I felt sobs hitching in my throat. I had to stop. I couldn't let go now. I had to keep control.

How long ago had I woken up to this? How long had it taken? From getting out of the room, breaking Marta and Marianna out of theirs? It couldn't have been much more than fifteen, twenty minutes. Fifteen or twenty minutes in which to lose a friend and run for my life – or climb for it anyway – from things that could not but did exist.

I had to stop crying, had to stop crying. I took deep breaths. Counted to ten. It didn't help. Not at first. But I kept doing it, and eventually I felt calm again.

"Get back! Get fucking back!"

I looked up. Then I heard the gunshot.

Marta gave a tiny gasp. Screams from the neighbouring rooftop, a thud. A body flopped and slid down the tiles, smearing blood over them. A woman, middle-aged. Still alive. She hit the guttering, scattering half a dozen squealing rats, then dropped.

Instantly the water erupted into churning froth. The woman screamed; the water turned red.

I couldn't see much more than that, but I saw enough. Arms, flailing and clutching; eyes, glowing. The water heaved – they were swarming. Like piranhas. The woman's screams were cut off and for a moment a scrum of bodies heaved on the surface – some rotting, some bloated, some freshly dead – then sank, but the water continued to heave. And the red stain deepened and grew.

"There, you see? That's what happens. That's what fucking happens. You keep away from me, you Paki bastards. Fucking keep *away*!"

I peeped round the edge of the chimney stack. A man was crouching at the near end of the neighbouring rooftop. He held a gun. The others on the rooftop were trying to move back from him. One man jostled another. The second man shoved the first. They fought, and then they both fell. A woman was knocked loose as they went. Oh, God. It was the woman holding the baby.

I didn't look. I heard the splashing as they landed, and then the screams. The screams. And the other sounds. But I didn't look.

The gunman inched backwards. I couldn't see his face. He was white and wore a leather jacket. It looked expensive. He pointed the gun at the knot of people.

"Stay where you are. Don't fucking move."

His voice sounded ugly, ragged and high-pitched. A man with a gun who'd panicked. Nothing more dangerous. How had it started? Who was he? Someone like Ilir, most likely. None of it mattered now. All that mattered was the gun.

That, and one other thing; he was backing towards our chimney-stack. What would he do when he found us? I pushed myself up into a crouch.

"Kat –"

"Sh." I put my finger to Marta's lips.

The gun would come in useful, if those things came out of the water. Even if it was only so that I could save myself and Marta from a death like Marianna's.

"Don't fucking move. Back. Back."

Someone moved. I didn't see who, I was watching the gunman. But he fired again. There was more screaming. Another body – no, two bodies – fell. I saw them from the periphery of my vision. Then I focussed again. It was the man I had to watch.

I crouched and lifted my hands. One would have to grab the gun. The other...

Papa had shown me all the different ways a man could be killed with a single blow, but I'd never used any of them. I'd spent the last year as a slave, not daring to even think of striking back. But now... I didn't feel the same. It hadn't been long, since I'd broken out of that room, but I felt different. I felt like somebody who could use what Papa had taught me. Who could deliver one of those killing blows. I hoped I was right. There would only be one chance.

He was inching back along the roof. His foot slipped. He yelled, flailing for balance. Was he going to go over and save me the job? No; his free hand grabbed the rooftop and he steadied himself. He was shaking. I didn't know if it was fright or fury. Then he was backing up again.

I could hear Marta's tiny, whimpering breaths. I forced myself to shut them out. And the screams of the poor frightened bastards further down the roof. And the sounds from the water. I just focussed on the man with the gun.

He was almost at the chimney stack now. I could hear his breathing. It was wild and gulping and hoarse.

"That's right. Stay where you fucking are. Don't fucking move. Don't –"

He'd reached the stack, grabbed at it with his free hand. Then he stiffened and whipped round. He had a thin face, sandy hair. Pale eyes wide in shock and rage and madness. He was only in his twenties. He might have been younger than me. But he had the gun. And then the gun whipped up towards my face –

I hit the inside of his wrist with the edge of my left hand. The gun was knocked sideways and fired, perhaps twenty centimetres from my ear. Marta shrieked. The gunshot felt like I'd been punched in the side of the head. I boosted myself to my feet, driving my right hand upwards, heel-first. I knew the exact spot I was aiming for, at the base of the nose.

Papa had taught me this; a blow there, from underneath, can smash the bone up into the brain. Result: instant death.

The angle of the blow had to be just right. If I missed, or got it wrong –

Pain shot down my arm. I felt the give of the breaking bone, and sickness burned the back of my throat. The jarring pain of impact as my hand slammed against the skull. The hot, sick spray on my hand and face as his nose exploded into blood and tissue. The gunman's head rocked back and he dropped the pistol. It slid past us.

He toppled backwards, face splashed red, his nose pulped – blood coming out of his eyes – sliding down the far side of the roof and off the edge.

A dozen pairs of green lights gleamed in the brown water where the narrow backyard had been. As the faces began resolving themselves through the murk, he crashed into the water.

I swayed, off-balance. Marta caught hold of my arms and steadied me. He'd been dead before he hit the water. The heel of my hand was bruised and throbbing.

From the backyard, I heard the waters churn and splash, heard things tear and break.

Marta was wide-eyed and crying.

"It's alright," I told her. "It's alright."

The gun had come to rest on top of the casement. Marta saw where I was looking. I looked back at her. "We need it," I said.

I thought she was going to argue, but she didn't. After a moment, she just nodded. She was starting to look less panicked now. Good. It would be easier if she was able to think for herself a little. Not too much. Not so that she started arguing with me or brooding, but enough that I didn't have to explain everything.

It went smoothly enough. When I reached the casement, I felt it creak under my feet, and tensed, afraid it'd give way. I listened out for thumping sounds in the attic, but there weren't any. I crouched and picked up the gun. Found the safety catch and put it on. Thrust it through the waistband of my jeans. And started to climb again.

By the time I reached the top I was shaking. Delayed reaction. And the cold. I managed a smile anyway. Marta smiled back.

And we settled down to wait.

CHAPTER THREE

THE RAIN HAD slackened off; the waters had stopped rising, for now at least. The creatures were nowhere in sight. Now and again there was a gleam of green light. No more than that.

Cold was the enemy now. My teeth chattered. Marta's too. We huddled together for warmth.

With stiff, awkward fingers, I tugged the pistol from my waistband and slid out the magazine. Nine rounds. A tenth in the chamber.

I'd hold them off as long as I could. If they could be killed again. Ten bullets. Eight for them. Two for us.

I put the magazine back in and put the gun back in my waistband. I still shook occasionally. Some of it was the cold. Some was what I'd just seen. The rest was what I'd done. I kept reliving the blow, the feel of the man's nose driven back into his brain. He'd pointed the gun at me, yes, but I'd planned to kill him from the first. I would have done it no matter what, because he was a threat.

Was it like this for you, too, Papa, the first time?

Marta stirred and mumbled. I nudged her and her eyes opened; she moaned, glaring at me for disturbing her. But we had to stay awake. It was too easy, in the cold, to drift off and die. On the other hand, perhaps that way wouldn't be so bad. A warm, toasty feeling, then sleep, never waking again. Peaceful. But...

But if *they* came for me while I slept, only waking when they bit into my flesh like a ripe peach...

I shook my head like a dog shaking off water, forced myself to sit up straight. I looked up, praying for an aircraft. Some sign of life. Rescue.

But I knew there'd be none. Manchester was many miles inland. If it was underwater, what of the rest of the country? London was on an estuary. London would be gone. And the government? If they were anywhere, it would be in a bunker, keeping themselves safe, jealously preserving what they had. Wherever you went, that didn't change.

And still the cold, pelting rain fell. Marta moaned faintly again, straightening up. "Easy," I said.

"I'm cold," she said.

"Me too, little one."

Nothing else to say or do. Sit here and slowly freeze. Nowhere to go. I looked up Cheetham Hill Road, the people huddled on the rooftops, hunched on the sloping sides. Most were Asian, women in bright saris, men in shalwar kameez, but I saw people of all colours, in smart dress and casual. But the rain, the cold, the terror made everyone more and more alike. A woman caught my eye, middle-aged and plump, in bright sodden clothing, like a half-drowned tropical bird. She forced a trembling smile. I forced one back, then looked away. Little customs. Etiquette. None of it meant anything now. No help would come. We'd been abandoned.

Nothing I wasn't used to.

There was higher ground than this, somewhere. Further above sea level. Relative safety, if we could only get there. But even if we crawled along the rooftops, even if we found a path through the huddled crowds there, sooner or later, there'd be nowhere to go but the water. And in the water...

Eyes open or shut, I kept seeing Marianna, pinned down and torn apart.

So far, they'd stayed in the water, or the flooded buildings. They hadn't come out into the open air, onto the roofs. Were they afraid?

What if Marianna came back as well? Could I aim a gun at her, and fire?

Not that it seemed likely. There would be nothing left of her. Nothing that could move. In a way, that was almost worse. I imagined pieces of Marianna – a severed head, a string of vertebrae – bobbing in the water lapping out on the landing, empty eye sockets filled with green light.

Someone screamed. I forced my eyes open. The group to my left. The Asian family. A small, chubby man with a long white beard was pointing downwards.

I rubbed my eyes and looked again. I wasn't sure what I was seeing. My vision must be blurred. But I looked again, and I saw the same thing.

The water below, filled with points of glimmering light. Green light. Dozens, even hundreds of pairs. All staring upwards. At me.

I DON'T KNOW how much time passed. I tried not to look, but every so often my gaze would shift, wandering down to the water, and they'd be there. Once or twice I saw new sets of eyes appearing, blinking on like electric lights.

They were gathering.

My fingers were wrinkled from the damp. Marta was very pale. Perhaps hypothermia *would* get us first. I almost willed it on.

My right hand still throbbed, despite the cold. The heel of the hand. If I fired the gun, that was where the recoil would hit. Christ, that would hurt.

All we could see were their eyes, watching. There were so many of them. And they were already dead. We wouldn't stand a chance. *What are they waiting for? What?*

When the attack came, it was almost a relief.

A face broke the surface, little more than a collection of holes in a clump of greenish-black sludge. Two hands rose, either side of it. More faces appeared. First in ones and twos, then by the dozen and the score. A forest of faces, jammed together. Rotted, grinning ones. Bloated ones, like maggots with glowing eyes. One was little more than bone. And others that hardly looked dead at all. Except for the eyes.

They reached out of the water, clutching at brickwork, drainpipes, shop-signs – anything that gave them a handhold – and started to climb.

There were screams now, like steel on glass. Deafening. A terrible, helpless sound. But I had the gun. I had the gun.

That made the panic go away; I felt numb, inside and out. Marta clung on to me. But she wasn't screaming. Or crying. I think she'd realised the same as me – with the gun we could cheat the dead things, if nothing else.

I watched them climb with an odd, dull sense of detachment. I wasn't afraid, not then. It had gone out of me. The shock, perhaps. Or perhaps there is only so much a person can sustain before something gives way.

They moved slowly, stiffly. When they brought their arms up and over to grab each handhold, it was like watching an old, clockwork machine, badly rusted and winding down.

But with purpose in spite of it all, relentless and inexorable. They climbed over each other – not jostling, not fighting. That was the worst part. They were an army, acting as one. They used one another to advance as a mass. Towards us. A wall of dead, rotting flesh, studded with glittering green eyes.

Hands groped out of the casement, clutched the edge of the frame. A head and shoulders followed. The blue woman.

Dragging herself out, she leant her weight on her arms, and hauled herself onto the casement top. A clumsy lunge landed her on the slope of the roof. Crawling on all fours, she began to climb. Her eyes didn't leave my face. It would be easy, if I just kept staring into them. I mightn't even feel anything.

Marta was shaking me. "Katja. Katja. Use the gun."

Screams shrilled across the street. The creatures had reached a rooftop. Brutal, simple tactics. One lunged out, seized hold of someone and pulled. The first brought half a dozen people down with it. Falling, they dislodged others. Pebbles in an avalanche. Three careered straight down the roof's slope and off it into the water, which exploded into churning froth as they were borne under. Others clung to the roofing, tried to stop sliding and climb back up, but more dead things closed on them. A teenage boy slid, screaming and scrabbling, until a dead thing grabbed his arm, twisting it up towards its jaws. Others scrambled in to join the feast.

A dull thudding, behind us. The ones in the back yard. They'd be climbing too.

The blue woman crawled on. Her face opened in a hissing snarl.

"Katja!"

Marta grabbed for the pistol, and I was awake again. I slapped her hand away and pulled the pistol out, took the safety off, fingers stiff and clumsy. The blue woman's hand rose up, clutching and clawing at the air, slapped down on the tiles.

Papa taught me to shoot. So long ago now. I hoped I could still remember.

Aim with both hands, one steadying the other. At the chest, the centre of the body's mass; squeeze the trigger slowly and gently – pull it hard and you'll spoil your aim.

She looked at the gun and cocked her head to one side, almost quizzically.

The gun's bark, jagged in the cold still air. Pain jolted up my arm as the butt recoiled into my bruised hand; I almost dropped it. A brass shellcase tinkled down the roof-slates, and the blue woman reared backwards and fell. Her body slid and rolled until it hit the casement, a hole gaping in the centre of her chest.

Good shot.

The dead things climbing behind her stopped, staring at her. I held the gun ready, smoke drifting from its barrel and breech.

The blue woman's head rocked side to side. She rolled over, showing the ragged exit hole in her back, and started climbing again.

The screams gathered in close, pressing down on my ears like hands. The blue woman's eyes expanded, filling the world.

I aimed at her forehead. If that didn't stop her, I'd turn the gun on Marta and myself, while there was still time for a quick death.

I hardly felt the recoil this time. A small, neat hole dotted the woman's forehead. Dark matter flew out in a spray from the back of her head, like a flock of scattering crows. Her mouth formed an O and she went completely still.

Then her eyes... faded. Like dying lamps. The glow in the empty sockets dimmed, and was gone.

Her limbs locked her in her crouch, then slackened and tipped her backwards, sliding. She thudded to a halt against the guttering, lolling over the water. The dead things around her, around us, stopped climbing. One reached out and prodded her. They stared up at us. Then back down at her.

I almost felt a sense of loss. At least the blue woman had been an enemy with a face.

"Katja, behind us," Marta whispered.

It was crawling up the other side of the roof, from the backyard, a tangle of bones and rags clotted with green-black mud that had once been flesh. It suddenly accelerated as if in a speeded-up film, scuttling up towards us like a putrid spider.

I brought the gun across and fired. One eye-socket blew out like a shattered bulb as the bullet snapped its head round. The remaining eye dulled and was extinguished. The remains cartwheeled down the roof, flying apart as they went. They fell into the water and sank. But other faces were filling the flooded backyard.

The blue woman lay where she'd fallen. The other dead things still surrounded her. Then they stepped back and slid down into the floodwater, the lights of their eyes dimming in the murk before disappearing.

WHEN I LOOKED back down at the yard, that was empty too. They didn't come near us; they left us alone.

Just us.

Perhaps if anybody else had been armed... but they weren't. The roofing in the neighbouring building caved in suddenly, collapsing under their weight. The white-bearded man lost his balance and fell in. The rest of his family shrieked. He screamed too. The dead things crawled out of the hole; the ones who weren't busy devouring him. They swarmed up towards the survivors... and just threw themselves forward, bowling the whole mass of them, living and dead, down the far side of the roof. The shrieks were swallowed up, lost in the churning and thrashing of water, the tearing of flesh and the splitting crack of bone.

I had to look away. Even if it cost me my life, I couldn't look. But I could still hear.

I tried to shut it out. Maybe I succeeded. I can't quite remember when I realised the screaming had stopped. At first I thought I'd gone deaf. But then I registered the hiss and splatter of falling rain, the slap of floodwaters against the buildings. The squeak of rats, the patter of their paws. And the wind; I felt it chill me, and I heard it moan. But there were no more screams.

I had no idea what sounds the dead things might make. Did they breathe? They were dead, after all.

I knew when I looked up, they'd be standing around me, silent and motionless, waiting for me to see them, so I'd *know*. Perhaps if I didn't look up they'd let me live.

"Katja?"

"Yes?"

"Do you think they've gone?"

"Who?"

"Those things. Whatever they are. They could be all around us."

Great minds obviously thought alike.

"What do you think?" she asked.

"I don't know."

"I think we should look."

We were going to die anyway, if not by the dead things then by cold, starvation, or disease, or just falling off the roof when we fell asleep. If we looked now there might be time to use the gun. "I think so too."

"Okay, then."

"Okay." I opened my mouth to count to three.

"They're gone," said Marta.

I looked along the rooftops, across the street. The dead things *were* gone. So were the living. Rats scurried along the gutters; two bedraggled pigeons alighted on an abandoned rooftop. But there were no people. None.

Blood splashed the brickwork and tiling; here or there a child's doll lay in a gutter, or a handbag, a shoe, lay on the tiles. The bus's windows, still cracked and blood-smeared, were no longer steamed. The top deck was empty. Anything living had either been eaten or got up and walked, living no longer.

If those things killed us – if we weren't devoured completely – would we become like *them*?

And where *were* they?

"Where have they gone?" Marta whispered.

I had no answer.

* * *

WE GREW COLDER and colder. Soon we could barely move.

Perhaps this was their plan. We were dangerous, so they'd retreated, leaving the cold to do their job for them. Just waiting.

The thought was almost appealing. I knew I wouldn't be able to keep awake much longer.

Marta's lips were tinged blue. Her teeth chattered.

"So cold," she whispered.

There was a thumping sound from below.

Tiny lights blinked on in the water.

They'd decided not to wait after all.

I tried to count the shots I'd fired. My brain felt thick and slow. Two at the blue woman, one at the other creature. That was right, wasn't it? Ten rounds. Minus three. Ten minus three. What was ten minus three?

Seven. Seven bullets left.

Five for them. Two for us.

Thump. Thump.

The ones in the water weren't moving, just watching. There were others, coming up through the brothel. Would they smash up through the roof beneath us? We wouldn't stand a chance.

I drew the gun, fumbled the safety off, looked across at Marta.

"Don't let them get me." Her voice was hoarse and gravelly; she sounded impossibly old. "Please."

I smiled and touched her cheek. Both felt like someone else's movement. "I won't."

Hands groped out of the casement window. They looked normal, not rotted or discoloured. It was only when the rest of the arms groped out, showing big, ragged scallops of flesh missing from the forearms and biceps, that all doubt went.

It pulled itself free of the casement. I aimed at the head. Aimed. Aimed. Couldn't focus.

"Krysztyna?" said Marta.

Krysztyna. She'd been Polish. Blonde, tall. Very beautiful. Punters often asked for her specially. Less beautiful now. She'd been on the ground floor. Her eyes had been blue. They were still there, but clouded and opaque, lit green from within like grimy bulbs.

She crawled up the roof towards us. After her came Elena. She'd come from the same part of Romania as my mother. A village not far from Timisoara. Her eyes had been dark. Not anymore.

Glass smashed behind us. Down the back of the building, another girl was dragging herself out. Anya. And after her, Sonia, and Hana.

Krysztyna was closing in. My hands shook, the gun barrel jerking to and fro. *Shit. Shit. Shit.* She was close. I pulled the trigger.

Shaking too much. Missed her entirely, clipped Elena's shoulder instead. She reared back, arms pinwheeling, then began climbing again. Below, another pair of hands emerged. Gabriela. She was the last one. Unless it was Marianna, but surely there couldn't be enough left.

I aimed again. Krysztyna reached out, her hand coming towards my face.

The bullet hit her just left of her nose, and the back of her head blew out. Her eyes went dark and she flopped forward, then slid down the roof to block Elena's path.

I turned around. Anya reached for my dangling foot. I pulled it back and fired again. The top of her head blew off. She dropped, bounced off the guttering and crashed down into the water in the yard. The surface glittered green.

How many shots now? Three had been fired. That left... that left...

Marta was moving, trying to get up. "What are you doing?"

"Standing up. If we hold onto the chimney... they can't grab our feet."

I nodded and stood. Down in the water, they were rising.

This was it, then.

I perched both feet on top of the roof. Marta got an arm round my waist, another round the chimney stack. I gripped a chimney pot's rim. I'd have to shoot one-handed.

Four left. Four.

They were closing in on both sides. Sonia one side, Elena the other. I'd liked Elena more. So I shot her first. End it for her.

Too low. It blew off the bottom of her jaw. A muffled, strangulated moan came out of what was left of her mouth. I aimed at her nose this time. The bullet punched a hole in her forehead.

I watched her fall.

Two rounds left.

Tears swam in Marta's eyes. Mine too.

"Do it," she said, voice calm and clear. She tilted her chin up. *Ready.* She closed her eyes.

I put the gun against her temple.

I pulled the trigger.

CHAPTER FOUR

Click.

Marta's eyes opened. "What?"

"Misfire." I pulled back the slide. The bullet clattered down the roof. Sonia was closing in. I aimed down at her.

No.

One bullet.

I looked at Marta.

One bullet left.

Sonia, Marta or me?

I could kill Marta with a blow. I would have to, if I wanted to spare myself a death like Marianna's. I nodded; first Marta, then myself.

I put the gun through my waistband and said: "Close your eyes." Marta did. "Put your head back."

She did, biting her lip, shivering, eyes tight shut. I thought of a young girl about to make love for the first time – how I'd been, the first time. Terrified. The bruised heel of my hand throbbed. I drew back my arm to strike and –

Something wet splashed my legs. A second later I heard the shot.

Sonia slid back down the roof, the top of her head gone. Hana half-turned to look behind her, and blood and matter sprayed from the side of her head too. The shot echoed out as she toppled after Sonia.

The mist was closing in, but something was moving through it. Something long, dark and low.

A narrowboat drifted towards the building. A man crouched in the bow, a rifle at his shoulder. He aimed again.

Marta yelled. Gabriela had seized her ankle. I started to aim at her as she pulled herself towards Marta. Her head came up over the point of the roof and the rifle cracked again. A hole appeared between her eyes and the back of her head blew out, and she slid back down towards the water.

Whoever the man on the boat was, he was a good shot.

The boat came in over the flooded backyard. The man shouted something, then ran back inside the cabin.

It wasn't going to stop, I realised. I threw both arms round Marta and the chimney stack, trying to make my fingertips meet.

The boat thumped into the side of the brothel. The building shivered. I kept hold of Marta, and the chimney stack. *Don't break. Don't break.*

It didn't.

When I looked, the man had climbed back into the bows. He'd slung the rifle across his back; now he carried a shotgun. Another dead thing mounted the brothel's roof; he fired and blew its head apart, pumping the slide to reload.

"Get on board!" he shouted. He was about forty or fifty, with a beard and greying reddish hair. A pot belly, too. An unlikely rescuer; he hardly looked the stuff gallant heroes were made of. Not that I was complaining.

He stepped back, thumbing fresh shells into the shotgun. I jumped into the bow, turned, arms out to catch Marta, but she'd already jumped too, and cannoned into me. We hit the deck.

The man grabbed my arm and pulled me to my feet. The shotgun was shoved into my hands.

"Take this. I've got to get us off here."

He took a pistol from his belt. A lot of guns. Not easily done in this country. Not legally.

Then he ran back through the boat towards the stern. As he did, a dead thing slid down the brothel roof and into the bow. I threw the gun to my shoulder. Papa had taken me hunting when I was a girl. My mother had disapproved, but...

I aimed low. The gun kicked back hard. The dead thing's head came apart and it collapsed against the guardrail. I pumped the slide. How many rounds were left in the gun?

The engine revved. Three more dead things sliding down the rooftop towards the boat. A hand flapped under the port guardrail, scratching at the decking.

The water, full of them. Full.

I walked towards the prow. Marta screamed my name. They landed in front of me, reached out. I fired point-blank, stumbling from the recoil, but at that range two went down. *Pump the slide. Aim. Fire again.* The third fell back over the side, headless.

The boat juddered backwards, turning.

Slap. Slap. The dead thing in the water was hauling itself under the rail. I drove the butt of the shotgun down into its skull. Bone crunched; I felt sick as I felt it give way. But the dead thing went limp and fell away.

Heads poked out of the water, green eyes glimmering. Then the boat turned, and the mist swallowed them.

WITH THE BOAT moving straight ahead, the man leaned out from the stern and waved to us. I stumbled to the rail, and peered down the cabin's side at him. Marta's fingers were tight little claws on my arm.

"You look half-dead," the man called.

I nodded.

"Get yourself in. I'll join you in a minute."

We used the door at the bow end. We stumbled through the galley and a narrow corridor, then out into a wider space at the stern, a cabin about two metres wide. There were curtains on the windows. A carpet. A couch. Ornaments. In the corner, a wood-burning stove.

I collapsed onto the couch. The man's footsteps thumped on the steps.

A PILLOW AGAINST my cheek, a blanket on my skin. I was warm. It felt good.

Awake in my old familiar bed at the brothel, if not safe and sound there. But I was glad, actually *glad* to be back there. After that nightmare. So *real.*

It wouldn't last, of course. By nightfall, I'd be wishing it was real; at least there I could kill some of my enemies, before they –

The blanket.

I opened my eyes.

The blanket was rough, coarse on my skin. My *bare* skin. I was naked. I never slept nude. Stripped for the customers, yes, but at night, when I crawled into bed, I always wore something.

The carpet. My bedroom carpet was a faded blue, nearly worn away. This was thick and cherry-coloured.

There were curtains on the window above my head; bright, floral patterns. A woman's room, surely?

The room rocked gently, side to side. Sick. Dizzy. This wasn't my room. Had Ilir taken me somewhere? A private party? That must be it. Taken to entertain some clients.

The room lurched and I nearly fell to the floor. I yelped, grabbed the edge of the bed. Pain shot up my arm. My hand. My hand hurt. Why did my hand hurt?

"Easy."

I squawked, before I could stop myself. There was someone in the room. The blanket had slipped down. I grabbed it and pulled it back over me.

"It's alright."

Someone sat against the wall. A bench seat. He reached up the wall. *Click.* A lamp came on above.

Fortyish, gingery hair going grey, a beard, balding... a big burly man... a little overweight...

I knew him, but where from?

"It's alright," he said again. "You're safe."

My hand... It was wrapped in bandages. Bruised. How?

"We're out in open water now," he said. "It's far less dangerous."

Danger. Glowing eyes. Anya and Krysztyna, shot in the head. Sonia too. And Hana. Hanicka, we used to call her. She hated it – she said it was a name for a little girl with her hair in bunches – but we loved to tease her. Affectionately though. She'd been a friend. Marianna... Marianna was dead too. But not shot. Something else. Something worse. *Eaten?*

No, that couldn't be it. Stupid. That was stupid –

Marta. I'd put a gun to her head. No. Not Marta too?

Too?

I'd killed the others. Had I gone mad? What had I done?

"Katja?" He leant forward. "That's your name, right, lass? Katja?"

Speak. Speak. "Yes."

"I'm Derek. You're on me boat. The *Rosalind.* Called it after my daughter. The little one's at the tiller. Taking a turn steering. I showed her how. She caught on fast. Seems to be enjoying it." He gave me a smile; it was quite sweet really. Shy. Awkward. "S'pose it takes her mind off all of this."

"All of what?"

But then I was shaking my head, trying to reject what I was remembering. But no such luck; it all came back. The flood. Picking the lock. Breaking the doors down. The loft. Marianna... Marianna dying. Torn apart. Eaten. *Alive.* By...

I don't know what name to give the kind of sound I made. A strangled cry, a yelp, a sob, a scream... it was all of these things at once, and wholly none. My hand was on my face, trying, too late, to silence it.

Derek started out of his chair, then thought better of it. "Easy lass. You'll be alright. You're safe now. Got thee out of there."

The boat, smashing into the side of the brothel. Derek picking the dead things off with his rifle, then the shotgun. "I'm... you undressed me?"

He nodded. "You were half-frozen. Nowt I've not seen before."

I remembered *that* part. "Thank you."

"You're welcome, lass. How you feeling?"

My fingers were still stiff, and the bruising still ached dully through the bandages. But I wasn't numb anymore, not shaking. "I feel okay."

And of course, I was still breathing, and nothing had been bitten out of me by something that should've been dead.

"Do you want another brew?"

"Another?"

"We managed to get some sweet tea down your neck before. Do you another if you want."

"I'd love a coffee."

He grinned. "Milk and sugar?"

"Just milk. Thank you."

"Mention it." He moved down the living room, through a narrow passage towards the galley. I could see him, fussing over the gas stove. "Let me know if you need another one, or just help yourself. For now, anyway. Got to keep warm. But after that – well, this is all we've got, so don't go overboard." He grinned again, a boy once more. "No pun intended."

I could feel the tea he'd mentioned clamouring for release. "Is there a toilet?"

"Mm? Oh aye. Loo's through here, first left. Cabin's on your right. My daughter's room. That's for you and the lass when you want to get your heads down."

I held the blankets awkwardly round myself as I went in. When you're naked, you feel like easy meat. I did, anyway. Hence never sleeping that way. Derek seemed harmless enough, but still...

When I came back, Derek had moved a small side-table over to the bed and sat a large, steaming mug on it. He looked away as I passed him. The bed... it had been a couch before, hadn't it? I looked closer – it had folded out. Tidy.

Derek talked about the boat. The *Rosalind* had 'all the mod-cons,' as he called them. A generator gave heat and lighting, although it would have to be conserved from now on, as there was only limited fuel. "And we've a long way to go," he added. The wood-burning stove could run on salvaged driftwood, left to dry on the cabin roof. Weather permitting.

We sat in awkward silence. Finally I asked: "Do you have my clothes?"

He grunted. "Stuff you were wearing's fit for nowt. I've some you can wear. Claire – the missus – she were about your size."

"Was?"

He nodded.

"I'm sorry."

He shrugged and looked away, blinking fast. "I'm alright, long as I don't think about it. We used to go out on the canal at weekends. I were moored up at Castlefield when this all started. Best place to be, as it turned out. Just slipped moorings and... floated. Pretty choppy." He looked back at me; his smile was tight and stretched. "Tell you, when the waters get rough, boat like this, you don't half feel it. Flat-bottomed, you see. Every time it goes up and down in the water... makes your teeth rattle, I'll tell you."

I smiled back at him.

"Most of the time, I just had my work cut out not going under. Christ alone knew where I'd ended up. Once I could, I started trying to get my bearings. Lucky I'd got a compass aboard. Tend not to need them on a narrowboat, since you just stick to the canals. Then I saw you."

"From that distance?"

"I wasn't far off. Looked through my binoculars. Used to like birdwatching. Not be much of that anymore. 'Cept for ducks and the like, eh? Got the rifle and that out, and... well, you know the rest."

I nodded.

We sat in silence for nearly a minute after that. Then he slapped his thighs and got up. "You'll want them clothes," he said.

I WORE JEANS and a sweater. And underwear – large white briefs – and a standard, sturdy bra. Once I would have considered them dowdy, but after two years of thongs and g-strings, push-ups and peepholes, they were a blessed relief. (If you're a man, you'll just have to take my word on this.) My trainers were still usable; he'd dried them out.

I joined them at the stern. Marta held the tiller; he'd found her a stripy jersey, several sizes too large, and an old sailor's cap. She grinned at me, eyes bright. Like a kid out on a day-trip. But that's all she was, a kid. I shouldn't be surprised.

All I could see, when I looked out into the gathering mist, were bits and pieces – tree-tops, the occasional part of a house. "Where are we going?"

Derek slipped a cigarette into his mouth, then offered me the packet. I took one; I'd been trying to give up, not that there'd been much motivation in the brothel. Some of the girls had been on heroin, after all.

"Can I have one?" Marta asked.

"No you bloody can't!" Derek choked on a lungful of smoke. "You're too young. And if I were you, I wouldn't start."

"I've been smoking for two years," she protested.

Derek looked as if she'd just slapped his face. "You bloody *what*?"

"I have," she said, shifting uncomfortably. The way he was looking at her told her she'd made a mistake.

I tried to intervene. "Derek, it's alright."

"Is it hell."

"We both smoked. It was better than what some of the other girls had." I realised he might not realise what we were – had been. "It can't do any harm."

"No harm? Are you mad, woman? Bloody lung cancer and everything?"

We'd be lucky to live so long. I opened my mouth to speak again, but he held a hand up. "No. And that's final." He took the tiller, shouldering Marta aside. "I'd best steer a bit. Get yourself in, lass. You'll catch your death."

She blinked, looking more childlike than ever. "But..."

"Do as you're told, love."

Marta looked at me. I gave a small nod. Something made her hesitate at the cabin door and look back. "I'm sorry, Derek."

He nodded. "Alright, lass. Now get yourself in."

The door clicked shut. Derek kept his hands on the tiller, looking straight ahead. "You shouldn't encourage her."

"Encourage her?"

"Smoking. It's one thing for you, love, but she's just a kid."

I was closer to Marta's age than his, but didn't argue the point. Men tend never to grow up, in my experience; I was a grown woman, and that would tend to erase the age gap as far as Derek was concerned. But Marta was so obviously so young. Part of the appeal she'd had for some punters. Of all the girls at the brothel, I'd been fondest of her. It had been nice having someone else to worry about and fuss over from time to time. Fondest of her, and more worried about her than anything else.

I thought for a second, chose my words carefully.

"Derek... do you know what it was we did? What that place you rescued us from was?"

He didn't answer, just kept staring straight ahead.

"Derek –"

"*Yes.*" His eyes squeezed shut, then reopened. "Yes, I bloody know what it was. I talked to the lass." He thumped the tiller. "Bastards."

I didn't answer. I looked out over the dull brown water. Something bobbed in it. A horse. Dead. Its belly bloated, legs jutting stiffly up, horrible and ridiculous all at once. No people, though. None that I could see. They would be below the water.

Derek seemed likeable enough and – the biggest point in his favour – he'd saved both our lives. But there was something... something not quite right about him, but I couldn't tell what yet. And anyway, I could hardly leap overboard and swim for it.

When I felt enough time had passed, I looked back at him. I started to speak, but he cut me off.

"I know... what you were. Both of you. But it's *were*. That's the one good thing about this. You don't have to be that anymore. Do you?"

I didn't want to think too far ahead; didn't want to consider what might be necessary in order to obtain food and shelter in the future. We only had one thing to sell. Unless I could hire myself out as a mercenary or something like that. Perhaps I could teach Marta how to kill people. God knows what Derek would make of that.

"What?" he said, but he was smiling.

"Mm?"

"You're smiling."

"So are you."

"Because you are."

He looked directly into my eyes when he said that. I looked away.

"Sorry."

"It's alright," I said. "I was only smiling... because I was thinking you were right." *Hoping* would have been more accurate.

"Aye. We can start again. No baggage. So you can leave all the shite behind. And that includes smoking." He looked at his cigarette – still hanging, unlit, between his fingers – with distaste. "Should bloody quit myself and all. Doubt I'll have much choice before long anyroad."

That was true too. And not just luxuries like cigarettes or alcohol. Vital things. Medical supplies – antibiotics, antiseptics, even plasters and bandages. I looked at my bandaged hand, the cuts there. The floodwater was filthy. Full of silt, effluent. Certainly unfit to drink. Teeming with germs. Full of the dead, walking or not. I thought of the dead horse. Was it only humans who were coming back to life? If it *was* life? Either way, a mouthful of the water could be lethal. A minor cut could get infected and there'd be fewer and fewer things to treat it with. I remembered what I'd thought before – there would be no rescue. Still...

"Is there... do you know if there's anyone else out there?"

"Not seen anyone save yourselves," he said. "Can't pick up owt on radio, either. I can get police and military frequencies and all." He raised his eyebrows. "And there's nowt. I reckon we're on our own, lass."

"I thought the same thing." But there'd have to be other survivors. And the government – they'd have kept themselves safe. In their bunkers. Sooner or later they'd stick their heads out again, if only to get their power back. The only question was how long that would take.

Then I remembered the question I'd wanted to ask. "Derek, where are we going?" He didn't answer. "Do you know?"

"Straight to Hell in a handcart, lass." He saw me staring at him, and laughed. "Figure of speech. No, we're aiming north."

"North?"

He nodded. "Further north we head, more higher ground we're likely to find. Better chance of making landfall. Can't keep boating around forever. Lot of farming country that way too, so more chance of finding food. We've tinned stuff here and bottled water, but it'll not last forever. Besides – up that way, it's not very heavily populated, you know?"

I gestured at the water. "Will anywhere be heavily populated, after this?"

"Not by the living, lass."

"Oh." Of course. How stupid could I have become?

"Far as I can tell, they're staying put. Not following us. Sail in among the buggers they might try and climb aboard, but otherwise –" He shook his head. "Further away from the big cities we get, the better."

I nodded. "That makes sense."

He barked a laugh. "Glad you approve."

And I did. But trusting him was a different matter.

CHAPTER FIVE

As we headed north, the wind rose. The mist began thinning out and the visibility improved, but the waters grew choppier, white streaking the brown surface as it crested and heaved. The narrowboat rose and fell; the deck swayed underfoot.

"Better get inside," Derek shouted over the noise. "Get down, hang on to summat."

I nodded and stepped to the door.

"Just one thing."

I looked back. "Yes?"

"Do us a favour? Just put any loose stuff away. There's a cupboard. It's just – some of it was the wife's. I'd miss it."

"Of course."

I went inside.

Marta huddled on the couch; she looked pale, scared and ill. I'd forgotten her. "Are you alright?"

"No!"

I ruffled her hair, grabbed the couch as the *Rosalind* lurched. "It's alright. It's just a squall." I hoped that was the right word. I hoped I was right.

"It's not that."

"What, then?"

"I'm scared of him."

I looked back at the door. "I think he's okay, Marta. He's just a little – messed–up. We all are."

Her voice rose. "No. There's something wrong with him."

I held her shoulders. "Marta. We don't have anywhere else to go right now. So stay –"

"Stay calm! Stay calm!" She pulled free. "I know. I know." She dropped her voice to a whisper. "But something's wrong with him."

"Okay." I nodded. Privately, I agreed, even though I wasn't sure why right then.

Her eyes narrowed. "Don't talk to me like I'm stupid."

"I'm not."

"I'm not stupid. I'm scared, that's all."

"Me too. You did well back there."

"I didn't."

"You were scared at first –"

"I still am."

"But you got yourself together. You watched my back, you kept your head. I'm proud of you."

She scowled, but I could tell she was pleased.

The boat lurched again. A china figure flew off a shelf and hit the carpet. Luckily it didn't break. I wasn't sure how Derek would react if it had. But why hadn't it broken before? Had he put everything away when the floods came? Or before?

There was something wrong there, niggling me. But there was no time now.

"Help me put this stuff away," I said. "Let's keep him happy."

We PACKED AS much away as we could, then climbed onto the couch and grabbed hold.

The boat heaved and bucked, juddering each time it came down in the water; once we were nearly thrown clear across the room. I don't know how long this went on, but finally the storm eased. The boat bobbed and rocked gently in the water, but I could stand, although my legs shook.

Marta looked shakier still, and queasy. I guessed seasickness was kicking in. My stomach felt a little tender, but nothing bad. I guessed I had good sea legs. That was the English term, if I recalled.

"I think it's calmer now," I said.

She nodded weakly. "I hope so."

I parted the curtains. Outside, brown water slopped against a few protruding treetops, and a thin mist gathered. Without the wind, it would soon thicken again.

THERE WAS A cabin, with a double bunk. Apparently it had been his daughter's room.

"He said they used to go out on the canals at weekends," said Marta, pulling off her shoes and socks. "Him and his family. Sometimes a friend of his daughter's."

"Sounds nice."

"Yes." She slumped onto the lower bunk and pulled the covers over herself. "But I still don't trust him."

I went back up on deck. Derek glanced down at me. "Y'alright there, love?"

I nodded.

"How's the kid?"

"Seasick, I think."

"Ah. Poor love. I've some tablets for that, somewhere. Break 'em out later."

I stood next to him in silence. I wasn't that eager for conversation, and I doubted he was, either. But I wanted to see where we were going as best I could. It gave me, at least, the illusion of control. "Where are we now?"

"Hard to tell at the minute. At a guess, I'd say somewhere between Bury and Rochdale. But I could be way off."

They were just names to me, in any case. "How far along are we?"

"Along?"

"Towards where we want to go?"

He shrugged. "Not sure, love, to be honest. All I can think at the minute is keeping on northward. Like I said, further we get from towns and cities and the like, the safer we'll be. Best thing'd be a good stretch of land well above sea level, preferably in the middle of nowhere. But at the minute it's pot luck. Just got to keep going long as we can."

"And hope we sight land?"

"Pretty much."

I didn't ask what would happen if we didn't.

Something loomed ahead. It came out of the mist; a church steeple. Near the top, a woman was clinging to it. Her face was pale, eyes tight shut.

"Derek –"

He gripped my arm. "Shh, lass."

"What?"

Too late. The woman had heard me, or us. Or the chug of the engine. Whatever the cause, her eyes flicked open. They were sunken and ringed with darkness; we were close enough now that every detail of her face seemed to jump out. "Oh, thank God... help me, please. Please!"

But Derek just gazed straight ahead.

"*Please!*"

"Derek, what are you doing? We can't just leave her."

He glared at me and spoke through his teeth, lips drawn back from them. "How much food do you think we have? How much bottled water? And extra weight means we'll use more fuel. How much of *that* d'you think we've got?"

He kept staring at me, without blinking, until I looked away. I could've asked why, in that case, he'd rescued Marta and me? But perhaps I didn't want to go down that road. He might start to regret his decision. Or I might find out why he'd really rescued us. I didn't believe it was simple compassion. My sense of something badly wrong with him had deepened.

I might be better off knowing the truth, but I didn't think Derek wanted to get into that, anymore than I did. I'd heard a phrase in a song once – 'comfort-lies.' It's not just men who have those, it's all of us. Or almost all. Perhaps people like me, or Marta, had none of those because we couldn't afford them. Or was that a comfort-lie in itself?

Whatever the case, there's nothing more dangerous than a man stripped of his comfort-lies. And I believed Derek had them, about what he'd done and why. As long as he had to keep believing he'd rescued us out of kindness, we had a degree of safety. But if I made him admit his real motives, that would be gone – and so far I didn't know what his real motives even *were*.

And there was something else.

Derek was right. There would be others like this woman, like us. People who'd climbed onto rooftops or church spires. People on hilltops or little knobs of ground just clear of the floodwaters. None of them safe for us to stay. But all of them begging us to take them on board. Derek's Ark.

That horrible jagged laughter bubbling up in me again; a scream broken up into a kind of manic stutter to stop me going mad. But if I started laughing now I'd never, never stop.

Yes, we could take this woman on board. But what about the next, and the next? There would always be good reason to take another on board, until the boat wallowed low from the weight... running more slowly from it too... using more fuel... the food rationed more and more... and the water too... until very, very soon there was none left at all...

So yes – Derek was right. But that didn't mean he was safe. And it didn't make the woman's screams, increasingly desperate and forlorn as we moved away from her, seeming to get more loud with the distance and not less, any easier to hear.

We heard them for quite a long time. I don't know if we just moved out of her range or if she gave up. I think the latter; for a while I was sure I could hear sobbing. But that could just have been my conscience.

For some time after that, thankfully, we didn't see anything. Just unbroken brown water. The mist was thin and distant, but the light was starting to dim. Visibility, though, was reasonable for us. Neither of us spoke.

I wondered how much food or fuel Derek had on the *Rosalind*. Probably a lot. He seemed prepared for a crisis. Or he'd always expected one. The guns, for instance. Why all these guns on a boat kept for weekend breaks? Yes, we were only alive because of them, but what did they say about Derek?

Still, I could hardly pick and choose. Derek might be paranoid, but so far that paranoia had kept me alive, in comparative safety, with food, water and some degree of protection. Better than the poor woman on the steeple had or was likely to. I would have to cope as best I could.

"You can go below if you like," Derek said after a while. "Getting nippy out."

"I'm okay."

He shrugged. "Whatever. I could murder a brew, though. Tea'd be good. If you wouldn't mind."

I made my way through the boat and ran the wood-burning stove. There was coffee as well as tea; I found I was cold as well, and made myself one. He only had tin mugs, and no tray. The heat seeped through the metal as I carried them through; I gritted my teeth against the pain.

"Ta, lass."

I cradled my own in my bandaged hand; the gauze gave some insulation. "What time is it?"

"Getting on for four, me love. We'll need a place to moor before long. No point travelling by night. Could go straight past dry land. Or hit something."

I nodded. *What if it gets dark and we can't find a place to moor?* I didn't ask. There were too many questions like that, with no answer. Or no answer I wanted to hear.

The mist parted and I saw something dark. "Derek, look –"

"Aye, love, I see it."

The boat wasn't built for speed. It took time to reach the island.

Island. Before today it would have been a hill. Now it was a low hump of land, twenty metres square and maybe three, four metres above the surface at its highest point. Tiny, stick-like figures moved atop it.

At first I thought they were trying to hail us and my stomach clenched, imagining what would follow. The woman on the steeple all over again, only worse. But they weren't hailing us; I don't think they'd even seen us then. They were screaming. And minutes later, I saw exactly why.

Eight or nine men and women and two or three children were huddled together on the top. They were the only people on the island. But they were not alone.

The dead things ringed the shoreline, the water lapping around their ankles. Most looked newly dead. Some had pieces missing, bite wounds. One had a dangling arm that was mostly bare bones with a few chunks of meat still clinging to it. They just stood there, staring up at the humans. Eyes glowing. I flinched, and actually drew closer to Derek. I hate that feeling, of dependence on another. Especially for protection. I didn't need a man for that. The ones who'd claimed they were doing so – Papa aside – did anything but.

Derek lifted the edge of his sweater, and I saw the butt of a revolver, tucked into the waistband of his trousers.

I realised something; didn't know how I could've missed it. My gun – when he'd undressed me, Derek had taken it. There'd only been one bullet left, of course, but even that was better than none. The pistol he had wasn't mine, so where was it?

But the dead things didn't move. They gave no sign of having seen us. They just stood there, looking up at the tiny, frightened huddle above them.

Then one of the women on the island saw us and screamed, pointing. The next moment, they were all shouting.

"Fuck," Derek hissed. I didn't say it aloud, but I was thinking the same. I already knew we wouldn't – couldn't – help them. And I hated them for expecting us to. For shouting and pointing and drawing attention to us. For doing exactly what I would have. I hated them for wanting to live.

As the boat passed them, it seemed at first that the dead things hadn't noticed us. Too fixated on these survivors to notice. How long had they been there? Minutes? Hours? I remembered, at the brothel, the long pauses between attacks. As if they were advancing, taking a piece of territory, then consolidating, regrouping, planning the next move. They had plenty of time, after all. The water belonged to them, and there was so little land left. Just as they must outnumber the living.

But then one turned. Just one. It turned and stared, directly at us. Not the boat, but Derek and I.

No. Not at *us*.

At *me*.

I was sure of that. It stared straight at, *into*, me. I had no idea what was behind those eyes. But I knew what it would want to do.

The ring of the dead around the island began drawing in. With those jerky, tottering steps they advanced up the slopes. All of them, except one.

The one who'd been staring at me – it'd been a man once. It wore a smart suit, and I could see the glint of gold on its wrist. He turned all the way round to face us and walked forwards, into the water. Soon he was swimming, a sort of convulsive dog-paddle. The water splashed and churned white about him, but only his head stayed above the surface, his hair – doubtless once neatly coiffured – now a grotesque, straggly bird's-nest.

"*Fuck,*" said Derek again.

The people on the hilltop were screaming as the dead closed in. There was nothing else they could do. Nothing anyone could do – not even us, if we'd been so inclined. They had nowhere to run and no weapons, except for some kind of wooden post one of the men was brandishing at them. Two of the things seized one of the women and bore her down as she shrieked. Another woman ran in and tried to pull her free, but another of the dead things seized hold of her, biting into her shoulder. Two more lumbered in, grabbing her arm and catching her around the legs, and she went down.

The two nearest the man with the pole slowed down, lifting their arms to grapple, and he swung at them. One retreated, and the other lunged forward. A second swing drove into its skull; even at that distance, over the screams, I heard the crunch of bone. The dead thing went down and didn't rise, but the other lunged forward, in one of those sudden, jerky bursts of speed. It seized the pole, and as they struggled for it, three others fell on the man.

I saw a child snatched up by a dead thing and held high. Other dead hands thrust skyward, groping for it. It shrieked and shrieked until the thing holding it thrust it groundwards and they descended.

The other humans went down very quickly after that. I say 'went down,' not 'died.' Because they didn't die quickly. They kept on screaming for a long time.

They were still screaming when Derek drew the revolver from his belt and leant out over the railing. The head bobbing in the water, growing slowly closer to the boat, was no longer alone. Four, no, five more were now bobbing in the water behind it. As I watched, a sixth appeared.

"Take the tiller," Derek said. He aimed two-handed, steadying the revolver. There was a dull metallic *click* as he thumbed the hammer back. I took hold of the tiller, but I kept looking back.

For a long time he seemed to stand like that, unmoving, while the bobbing heads drew silently, relentlessly closer.

Then he fired. The gunshot was so sudden and loud I have to admit I almost wet myself. But didn't.

Water spewed up in a short-lived geyser, about half a metre from the dead thing's shoulder. Derek cocked the gun again. This time, when he fired, a shower of dark fragments flew up, back and out from the dead thing's head. It stopped moving forward and I saw its eyes flicker and fade, leaving it a dark featureless lump in the dying evening light, that slowly sank from view.

The other heads stopped advancing. They were treading water. They didn't follow us; one by one, as the boat moved away, they turned and swam back towards the island. I saw the first of them climbing out of the water onto dry land, dripping heavily, as the mist closed around them. Moving in to join the others at their feast.

A feast whose screams we still heard long after they were lost to sight.

CHAPTER SIX

ABOUT HALF AN hour later, with the mist growing thick and the light failing in the east, we found a place to moor.

It wasn't much – the top of a pylon – but there was nothing else man-made in sight. There was no buzz of electricity from it; the power stations were long dead, drowned by the flood.

"With any luck, we're a way from anywhere inhabited," Derek said. "We'll moor here for the night. Not exactly recommended practice, but it'll do."

He'd replaced the revolver's empty cartridge cases with fresh ones. I wanted to ask if he had a spare – in fact I knew he did, he'd carried an automatic earlier, and he still had mine too – but I could guess his response. It made sense we should both be armed, and perhaps Marta too. He'd given me the shotgun without a second thought at the brothel. But that had been then; this was now. He wouldn't have any answer for not arming us, except that he didn't want to. And I didn't want to provoke a direct confrontation as yet.

I watched him clamber in among the pylon struts to tie the mooring ropes. Watched very carefully. I needed to know how to run the boat without Derek, if I had to. Something might happen to him. Or might need to.

He jumped back into the well-deck in the bow and stood facing me, his eyes suddenly empty. Then he smiled. "That's that then," he said. "Who wants dinner?"

I WOKE MARTA up; she'd managed to sleep not long after collapsing into the cabin bunk. She'd been lucky enough to sleep through the encounters with the other survivors.

Derek set up a folding table in the middle of the boatman's cabin and stationed chairs around it. He turned off the lights and lit candles on the table. "Need to save energy anyway," he said, and grinned. I found myself smiling back. Cooking smells wafted from the galley. A microwave pinged.

"Just some frozen stew," said Derek. "But it'll do the job. Might as well use the frozen stuff up first. I've a lot more in tins and suchlike but they'll keep. Fridge takes up gas, so the sooner we get shot of it the better."

The stew came in bowls, with hunks of brown bread. "Eat up," Derek said. "Keep up your strength. Been a long day."

I felt the jagged laughter bubbling up in me again. Yes. A long day. The world as I knew it had ended, I'd seen one friend torn apart and eaten alive in front of me, killed a man with my bare hands and shot several other friends because they'd turned into walking corpses. But I wasn't a whore any longer. I had that much. One good thing. I might be fighting for my survival on a day to day basis, but now that made me no different from almost anyone else. I probably had a better chance than most – not stuck on some isolated lump of sodden turf waiting for the dead things to come out of the water.

Derek poured me a glass of wine, plus a Coke for Marta. He ruffled her hair as he set it down before her. She glowered at him and he laughed. I admit it, so did I. She looked like a kid again, a real kid.

The stew was excellent. Beef, garlic, mushrooms, potatoes, broccoli, carrots, a rich gravy. Probably the best meal I'd had in a long time, except for the time Ilir had taken me to the restaurant; the usual quality of the food in the brothel was lousy. Cheap takeaways and cheaper frozen dinners.

I took a glass of wine, but drank sparingly. I wanted to keep a clear head. Finally I pushed the bowl away. "That was great," I said. "Thank you."

"Mm," said Marta. She was picking over hers. Maybe still a little queasy from the seasickness before. Her glass was already almost empty though. So her stomach couldn't be *that* tender.

Derek smiled and inclined his head. A good shot and a good cook. He definitely had his points. For the first time, I thought I might be wrong about him. Who wouldn't be damaged after something like this? The flood, the dead things, the loss of his family...

His family.

The one subject Derek had avoided. What *had* happened to Claire and Rosalind?

Maybe he hadn't wanted to talk about it. Maybe that was how he kept control. But even so... a dead wife and child? And the ornaments...

That was it – what had niggled me before. Before, when the squall hit – he'd asked me to put the ornaments away. His wife's things. I remembered wondering why they hadn't been damaged before. He'd said the waters had been rough at the start: *"When the waters get rough, a boat like this, you don't half feel it. Flat-bottomed, you see. Every time it goes up and down in the water... makes your teeth rattle..."*

So where had his wife's things been? Packed away already? They had to have been. And one startling absence, now I thought of it. No pictures. No pictures of them at all.

"Katja?" Marta slid her bowl away from her, still half full. Her glass of Coke was almost empty. "Katja? I feel..."

She slumped forward.

"Marta!" I rose.

"It's alright, love," said Derek. "Let the kid rest up."

The Coke glass – I picked it up. There was some kind of sediment at the bottom. "You bastard, what did you –"

"Take it easy, love. No need for that language." Sweat glistened on Derek's forehead. "Just summat to help her sleep. She's been through enough today. Needs her kip."

I put my fingers to Marta's neck. Her pulse was there, regular and fairly strong.

"She'll be fine, Claire." When I looked at Derek, he was smiling tenderly. "Why don't you put the little 'un to bed? Then we can get an early night."

HE FOLLOWED ME as I carried Marta to her cabin and laid her on the lower bunk. I pulled off her trainers, but left the rest of her clothes on. I could feel his eyes on my back. He stood a couple of metres away, just out of easy reach, and I knew the revolver was still in his waistband.

I pulled the bedclothes over Marta. She looked younger than ever now; I could have taken her for twelve. I touched her cheek. It occurred to me that she was the nearest thing to family I still had.

"There you go," said Derek. "She'll be fine. Now stop fussing, Claire. Come on."

I turned on him. "Katja. My name's Katja." There had to be some way of reaching him. Had to be.

But he only smiled, his eyes glassy. "Whatever."

"My name is Katja."

"It doesn't have to be," he said reasonably. That was the worst thing, how casual he was sounding, as if we were discussing what brand of toilet paper we bought. "I told you before, love. Fresh start. We can all try again."

He waved me out into the passageway, took a key from his pocket and locked the bedroom door. "Keep her safe," he muttered, and looked over at me. "Got to keep them safe, haven't you? Always got to keep them safe."

I didn't know what to say.

"I was a good husband," he said. "And I were a good dad, and all. Whatever that stupid bitch said."

"Who?" Keep him talking. Try to reach him.

"Claire. Not you, the other one. Stupid bitch I was married to. Dumped me and ran off with some bloke. A fucking *travel agent*. Ran off with him. Took Ros as well. Don't even know where they are. Well, didn't. I know now."

"You do?"

"Full fathom five. Full fathom fucking five. Know Shakespeare, do you?"

"*The Tempest*, yes?"

"That's the one. 'Full fathom five thy father lies, of his bones are coral made. Those are pearls that were his eyes, nothing of him that doth fade but doth suffer a sea-change, into something rich and strange...'"

His voice choked and trailed off. "Only, I'm not the one who's dead, am I?"

"They could still be alive," I ventured.

"Tripe!" His lips curled back from his teeth. "The bitch moved without telling us. Can you bloody believe that? I couldn't even see my little girl. Claire – fuck her, she'd made her choice and buggered off and I don't give a shit what happens to her now. But Ros... No. That's what hurts. She's dead. She's dead and the stupid bitch killed her." He touched the cabin door gently. "But now... Now I've got a family again."

He came towards me. "First time I saw you, on that rooftop, I knew. It was fate, Claire. *Fate*. Bloody fate." He reached out and touched my cheek. I did my best not to flinch away. "If you could see how like her you are, how like both of them you both are. I wasn't going to do owt. But I got my binoculars out and took a closer look, and there you were. It was just you and the girl left by then. I had to think it over. Must've sat there nearly an hour trying to make up me mind. Started getting all your things back out again. Trying to find summat to do. Helped me think."

An hour? Perhaps just out of sight in the mist? All that time, watching us cling onto the rooftop...

"Then they started coming out of the water, and I had to make me mind up. Piss or get off the pot, as they say." He shook his head. "I had all me guns, of course. Shouldn't have 'em on board... shouldn't have 'em at all, really. But fuck that. Knew this was coming. Well, not this. Fucking dead men walking? No-one'd've believed that. But knew it'd all hit the fan one day. The Pakis, global bloody warming – something, anyway, it'd all kick off. So I got everything stocked up. Better on a boat anyroad. You can always move around if things get bad. See? Got it all planned out."

"Yes, Derek. You did."

He advanced, waving me down the passage towards the boatman's cabin. "Come on, love. Let's get to bed."

"No. Derek. Please." I hated hearing the begging sounds come out of my mouth. Why didn't I kill him then and there? Because half of me pitied him? Because I'd already killed today and every time I remembered the awful crunching feel of his nose under the blow I felt sick? Because if Derek was dead, how would I run the boat? Because if I failed and he killed me instead, then what would happen to Marta?

For all those reasons, I hesitated. And the moment passed. Papa's voice again, coming back to me: *These are not children's games, Katja. To take a life is a grave thing. But once you know you must – do it quickly. If you hesitate, the moment passes, and may not come again.*

"Get in," Derek said.

"Please don't –"

He seized my arm and yanked me bodily into the cabin. I stumbled and broke free, brought an arm up to strike –

The revolver was in his hand and aimed at my face.

"Go on, then," he said. "Try it."

Slowly I let my arm drop.

Derek stepped into the room. I moved back. He kicked the door shut behind him. Dragged the table aside. Pulled the couch back out. Fumbled with it until it folded out.

"Well, then?" he asked.

I knew what he wanted. I had no choice. I peeled my t-shirt over my head, then began to unbutton my jeans.

AFTERWARDS, I SUPPOSE, I could have killed him. When he'd finished – grunting and heaving on top of me before collapsing and half-crushing me with his weight – he rolled over and was asleep. The gun was still in his hand, tucked under his body where I couldn't reach it.

But I could have done something. If I'd been quick...

But if I'd got it wrong, if he'd woken, with the gun...

But it wasn't even that. I felt... defiled. Disgusted with myself. Much as I'd felt after I'd first come to England, after Ilir and the others raped me. I felt worthless. All too often this is the way. The rage and the hatred do not go outward, where they belong; they turn inwards, on yourself, and they fester there.

I got up. I was sore. Men often wanted to start before a woman was ready. If you were their lover, you could explain these things, work at a common pace, but a whore has no such choice. We have tricks of course, to prepare ourselves beforehand so it doesn't hurt, but he'd given me no time for them. Another reason it felt like the aftermath of Ilir's punishment.

I could feel his stuff dripping out of me. Thank God, he hadn't locked the cabin door. I made it into the passageway and then the bathroom, shutting the door behind me.

I had to clean myself, to get him out of me. But before that, my throat was clenching, my gorge rising –

I reached the sink just in time, before the beef stew and wine came back up.

I coughed and retched and spat, then turned on the taps to rinse the mess away.

I rinsed my mouth with water again and again. After the first couple of times the taste of bile was gone, but it took far more attempts than that before I could no longer taste the sour flavour of his mouth and tongue.

When that was done, I ripped tissues from the toilet roll and used them and the water to clean away all traces of him. I flushed the tissues down the toilet and then sat on it, thrust my hands in my mouth and began to cry for the first time since the end of the world.

CHAPTER SEVEN

I WENT BACK to his bed, afterwards; where else could I go? I slid slowly and carefully between the sheets so as not to wake Derek.

He'd made me a whore again. He talked about fresh starts, of new beginnings, but they only applied to him. Marta and I were just clay to make a new family with.

Outside the grimy cabin window it was still dark, thick mist swirling. One of us should be keeping watch. Derek was probably right; we were far from any populated areas, there'd be few if any dead things to contend with, but what if he was wrong? If they boarded us in the night, we'd have no chance.

So? So they would eat me alive, like Marianna. So what? Marianna hadn't been given false hope, a promise of freedom, only to have it betrayed by the same person who'd offered it. It'd be the same ending as hers, only she'd have suffered less. What were all my skills and strengths worth, if that was all the good they did?

But Marta – Marta would die, too...

Even then, I didn't care. Not at that moment. I said I would be honest. I'd said she was the closest thing to family I still had, and I'd meant it. But right then, that meant nothing. I only wanted an end to this. By a bullet, by my own hand – by one of the dead things even, if it came to that.

I looked across at his sleeping bulk, his flabby bare back, pale as a grub. So easy to do something to him – if I could find the weak spots under the fat. It was worth a try, if only to save myself from a repeat performance next time he woke, if that came sooner. Surely if I looked I would find something, a weapon. One sharp thing would be all I'd need.

But I did nothing. I lacked the will. I only wanted the world to go away, however briefly, and leave me alone. So I curled up, my back to him, making sure his greasy, sweaty skin didn't touch mine, and closed my eyes.

As a piece of long-overdue mercy, sleep came.

THIN LIGHT STUNG my eyes and I woke. The cabin window was white with mist.

At first I just stared at it. I felt leaden and numb. I told myself to go and look. But my limbs felt so heavy. Moving them was too great an effort.

Then I heard Papa's voice again. It would be nice to imagine something more mystical, something with a little more hope involved, but more than likely I was only imagining what he would have said. If you know someone long enough, you can imagine almost exactly what they'll say.

Get up, Katja. You don't give up. You're my daughter; surely I taught you better than that?

Oh piss off, Papa. Go away and leave me alone.

Don't speak to your father that way.

Oh, just fuck off, will you? You never had to deal with this. You were never raped.

You're right, of course, I wasn't. But I faced things as bad as this; ugly things that brought me to the point of despair.

And you always overcame them, didn't you Papa? Were you ever fucking human?

Always, Katja. Another way to look at it is this: you were in this situation before, and you survived.

Yes, but –

But nothing. You thought you'd escaped; it turns out it's not so simple. But this time it is not the same. Think on it and you'll see you're not so helpless. He is only one. He has no sons, no gang of thugs to help him. And you don't have to worry where to go. This place can be your sanctuary, this boat.

But I don't know how to run it!

You're in a safe mooring – you and Marta have time between you to learn. Kill him quickly and be done with it. Don't waste the next opportunity. He is insane; the next opportunity could be your last.

I didn't have an answer for him. I'd never had an answer for him; sooner or later I always ran out of them.

You can do this, Katja. You know you can. But first, look out the window.

And so I got off the couch-bed. I was still sore, between my legs, but it had faded from a raw burning pain into a dull, persistent ache. I would remember this.

I looked back at the white hump of Derek's body, and started to feel a new sensation, breaking through the cracking pack-ice of my despair.

Anger. It was only a small flicker, a spark amid embers, but it was there to be nurtured. It was like being stranded in an arctic wasteland. Without a fire to warm you, you would die. So you kindled a spark, and you bent your strength to keeping it alive, making it grow.

I felt rage, and I felt humiliation. All the ugly feelings rose. I could have shut them out, retreated from them, into some warm place where I could grow numb again. But I did not, would not. Not this time.

I picked up the bra and knickers and put them on. That was a little better. Only a little, but better. I found my jeans and my T-shirt and I put those on as well. My socks were nowhere to be seen, but I found my trainers and pulled them on, lacing them up as I watched the heavy shape in the bed.

Now I was fully clothed. I felt better still. No longer naked. But he was. And he was asleep. I had a position of strength. I realised how easy it would be. I could see at least two spots where a single blow would cause instant death. He'd never wake. It would be better this way. Simpler.

But first –

I looked out of the window.

The mist was still there, but it had receded, far enough that I could see for quite a distance. The brown water lapped around the pylon. Further along I could just see the top of another one, but nothing beyond that. There was only the wide brown sea, and the mist –

And something else.

Even now, I'm not sure if I really saw it. It registered for a second and then was gone. A brief, momentary gap in the mist? Or an illusion?

Whatever the truth of it, for a second I was sure I saw a low dark hump in the distance. Something that could only be land.

Only for an eyeblink, then gone.

Even if I'd imagined it, there would be land somewhere. There had to be. The seas hadn't, couldn't have covered everything.

But even if they hadn't, the dead things would find it. I'd seen that already. The circle of dead things around the island, closing in. And if anyone was passing by, they'd keep on going. Just as we had. *I'm sorry,* they'd think, *but better you than me.* Just as we had.

One problem at a time, Katja. Deal with each situation as it arises. Now, kill that man.

Yes. While he was still asleep. Quickly, while I had the will –

"Morning, love."

Shit.

I turned. Derek blinked and smiled sleepily at me. His face was kind again. Like any loving husband's, waking up to see his wife's face. "Up already, are you? Seeing as you are, fancy getting us a brew?"

I COULD HAVE killed the Derek of last night without a second thought. But this was the original Derek. The one who'd saved Marta and me. Did he remember what he'd done? Probably, but not as I did. He'd remember me coming to him of my own free will. He'd have erased the parts that didn't fit with that.

In the galley, I boiled water for the coffee. There was no sound from Marta's cabin, but I could hear Derek thumping about in his. In a moment, he'd be through.

He would be awake and armed. I needed a weapon. And I had little time.

He'd put something in Marta's drink. Where would he have kept that? No, I'd never find it in time.

A knife. There'd be cutlery. Something sharp – a steak knife maybe. I pulled the top drawer open.

"What you after, love?"

Derek lumbered in, barefoot in jeans and t-shirt. The butt of the revolver in his waistband.

Last night I'd had the opportunity, but not the will. This morning it was the other way around. I had to focus on the anger, keep it bright. Wait for my chance and take it without hesitation.

He looped an arm round my waist and kissed my cheek. "After a teaspoon? They're in there."

The gun nudged my hip.

There.

He'd made it so easy.

Now.

I went for the pistol, but for a big man he was quick. I didn't catch him off-guard; it was as if he'd been waiting. One hand caught my arm; the other swept out in a backhanded arc. My lower lip split and I crashed against the cooker.

"Stupid bitch!" he spat at me as I slid down. He drew the gun. "Stupid, ungrateful bitch." He grabbed a fistful of my hair, half-lifting me from the floor; I yelled at the pain, clutching at his wrist. "I fucking saved your life!"

"Katja?" It was Marta. Her cabin door was rattling. "What's going on out there? Are you alright? I can't get out."

"It's alright, love," Derek called out. His flushed, sweaty face twisted back and forth between the rage of a second ago and the kindly rescuer we'd first seen. Trying to be two people at once. "Mummy and Daddy are just messing around, that's all."

"*Katja!* Leave her alone, you mad bastard!"

"Shut up!" Derek half-turned to scream at her. He kept his grip on my hair and it felt like I was being scalped, but he'd given me an opening and I took it; I hit him in the groin with everything I had.

He screamed and doubled up, but the gun was swinging towards my face. I grabbed it with both hands, trying to wrestle it away. It fired once; the report was like a blow to the head and for a second I thought I'd been hit. But I hung on.

He let go of my hair. And then clenched his fist and brought it down, in a brutal, clubbing blow to the side of my head.

I vomited. I let go of the gun and fell to the galley floor and I vomited. There was a shrill whining tone in my left ear and through it I heard the bang and rattle of the cabin door and Marta screaming my name.

"Bitch!"

Derek staggered to his feet above me, aiming down. I was on the floor, woozy. I tried to wriggle away. He turned the gun towards me. I kicked out with my right leg, driving the heel out straight. It slammed into his kneecap; I felt the bone crunch, and heard it even over Derek's shriek. He fell, and the revolver clattered from his hand. He was howling and sobbing in agony. He lashed out at me blindly and started crawling away.

The gun. I reached for the gun. Picked it up. Managed to stand. My neck was throbbing. God, what had he damaged? He was crawling up the steps, towards the bow door, dragging his ruined leg behind him. One hand fumbled in his pocket –

"Derek!" I screamed, aiming at his back.

He kept crawling. I pulled back the hammer. Aimed. And then fired.

The recoil drove me back, the gun flying up towards my face. I pulled my head aside just in time; the barrel clipped my ear nonetheless. The back of Derek's t-shirt ripped, blood flying out. A bright, vivid crimson fan of it exploded up the steps. There was a splintering crack as the bullet ploughed into wood. Derek's body jerked and fell forward. His legs tremored and kicked, and then he was still.

"Katja?" Marta's voice had grown strangely calm. "Katja?" Now it was small, despairing and forlorn.

"I'm alright," I called out. Probably louder than I needed to, but my ears still rang from the gunshots. "I'm alright."

I LET HER out of the room. But first I checked on Derek. I had to make sure he was dead.

I was almost certain he was long before I checked his pulse; there was a stench coming off him; shit and piss. A dark wet stain was spreading out from between his legs, dripping down the steps, mixing with the blood. The galley stank of it, of the blood; it overwhelmed the rest. I had to walk into it to get close enough. It squelched underfoot, and my trainers began to stick.

I put the gun behind his ear and cocked it, then reached down and felt for a pulse in his neck. There was nothing.

I uncocked the gun and stepped back. His hand had come out of his pocket, holding a bunch of keys. It took several tries to unlock the door of Marta's room, but soon she was out.

She didn't cling to me, or cry.

"You're okay, then?" she asked.

I nodded.

She looked down the corridor towards Derek's body. Her face stayed calm, like a Madonna. She turned and looked back at me and nodded.

"I told you," she said. "I told you there was something wrong with him."

I put the gun in my waistband and held her. She was stiff to begin with, like wood, but finally she hugged me back. "That's right, little one," I told her. "You did."

WE NEEDED TO find out where everything was. The bullet I'd fired into Derek had been soft-nosed; it had expended most of its energy on him and embedded itself in the step beneath. The other round had punched a hole out through the galley wall.

We went through the boat to take stock. In the gas locker beneath the well-deck, we found a rubber dinghy, complete with oars in unscrewed sections. Obviously Derek had liked having a getaway option.

The guns were there too. Two pump-action shotguns, the rifle, the automatic pistol he'd carried and the one he'd taken from me. Both pistols were the same calibre, so I could reload mine.

When I'd done that, I dragged Derek's body onto the well-deck and propped him against the bow. His head lolled back over the gunwales. I tried to tilt it forward but it kept falling back.

I stepped back and drew the revolver. Aimed. Clicked back the hammer.

Now he was dead, my pity for Derek resurfaced. He was no longer a threat, just a man who'd lost too much and been unable to cope with it. He'd saved our lives, even if it had been for distorted and insane motives. We were alive because of him.

And so this was as much to ensure death was the end for him, and that he found whatever peace there was to be found, as for mine and Marta's safety.

So I told myself, at least, as I pulled the trigger.

CHAPTER EIGHT

WE RESTARTED THE engine and cast off. I left Derek's body in the bows until we were moving, then heaved it overboard, just in case he brought anything to the surface. He didn't sink, just bobbed face down in the low brown swell as we pulled away. The mist swallowed him before he could sink.

"Where do we go now?" asked Marta.

It might have been a trick of the light, an optical illusion, or my worn-out brain seeing what it wanted, needed to, but it was the only clue we had, and we had to go somewhere.

"That way," I said, and pointed.

"Why?"

"Because I think I saw land out there this morning."

"You think?" We just looked at one another. Then Marta broke out in what sounded all too much like the mad, jagged laughter I'd been fighting off. "Why not?" She squeezed my shoulder. "Let's go."

MORNING BECAME AFTERNOON and the afternoon wore on in turn. We passed through flat, featureless brown waters, endless and still. At least there were no winds yet, no storms.

"Jesus Christ!" Marta was staring over the guardrail, she looked sickened and fascinated, all at once. "Have you seen this?"

I looked over the side and felt my stomach perform a slow roll. The boat was cleaving its slow, steady way through a thick, matted brown mass. At first I thought it was sewage, but then I looked more closely and saw the fur. More; I saw paws, tails, tiny faces twisted in a last agonised snarl.

Rats. Thousands, *millions* of drowned rats. They piled up around the bows of the boat and against the sides, rolling back and down into the water. Their legs stuck stiffly out, bellies bloated, huge as if massively pregnant.

Marta turned away, grimacing. The smell was foul. I saw other debris mixed in with them. A broken chair. A tyre. Plastic bottles. Twigs and branches. Clothing, snarled up amongst it.

Clothing?

It was nearly ten minutes later – the boat still forging a path through the matted tangle of corpses – that it hit me.

Where would all the rats have come from? Rats live among people. In a city, someone told me once, you're never more than three metres from a rat.

Please let them have drifted. Let them have drowned somewhere far away.

"Katja?"

Marta was pointing out to starboard. I looked.

The dead rats spread out for metres on all sides of the boat. The surface was lumpy and irregular. But there was something under it, where she was pointing.

Two somethings, to be precise.

Two somethings that glowed green.

As I watched, the surface broke. Rats and water streamed and tumbled away from a dark figure with glowing eyes.

Then another appeared, and another. I whirled, stared down the sides, towards the stern. A head bobbed in the stretch of dead water behind us. Two others rose behind it.

"Shit." Marta was looking portwards now. "They're over there as well."

She had Derek's automatic; I had my gun. "Marta?"

"Yes?" She was still looking to port, hypnotised. I caught her arm. She started, turned and stared at me, face white.

"Get the shotguns," I said. "And spare ammunition." To port and starboard I could see dozens of the dead things now, rising all around us, watching – just watching, for now. "Plenty of it."

*　　*　　*

THE SEA OF dead rats never seemed to end. We had to be over a population centre. A good-sized town, at least. I hoped that was all it was. At best, it meant hundreds of the dead things; at worst, thousands. But if we were over a city...

I stayed on the tiller, the shotgun slung across my back. Marta had climbed up on the cabin roof to scan for danger ahead.

The engine growled, the only sound. And all around there were heads in the water. None of them moved, other than bobbing up and down. Treading water. And watching.

They weren't mindless. They might look it, but they weren't. It might just be an animal cunning, but that was dangerous enough; they had huge superiority in numbers, after all.

They seemed to prefer it in the water. They ventured out of it only when they had to. And they seemed to know when their victims were helpless. I remembered Derek shooting the dead thing that swam after us; the others had retreated. Staying in their territory. Back at the brothel, when I'd killed a couple of them – was killing the word, when they were already dead? – the others had retreated. They'd killed everyone else, the unarmed ones, but left us alone.

Briefly. Then they'd come back, attacking in force.

At least with the boat, we had the advantage of being mobile. The swimming ones had let us go; once we'd left their territory, we were of no interest. Which meant that –

"Katja!"

I looked up. Marta was grinning over the edge of the cabin roof. "It's clearing up ahead! I can see it!"

I craned my neck to see ahead. Marta was right. Perhaps another twenty or thirty metres, and the drifting mass of rats came to an end. The open waters beyond seemed empty. *Seemed.* It could be a trap.

How much intelligence are you crediting them with, Katja?

I didn't know. But better to be cautious than otherwise. Would we be any safer when we reached land, or would we have just painted ourselves into a corner? But Derek had said himself, there was only so much fuel. Sooner or later, we would have to stop for good.

But for now, we were moving, and the dead things weren't. They were just watching. And soon we'd be clear of them, I hoped, and then –

The dead things were shifting in the water. I wasn't sure, but I thought their eyes had brightened.

The engine. Its steady puttering growl had begun to falter and cough.

I looked at Marta. Her face had gone white, the blood draining.

The *Rosalind* jerked in time with a couple of particularly violent coughs from the engine. No more than twenty metres left to go. They were up ahead, but moved aside as the boat passed. Shouldered aside by the bow wave. Behind us, they were moving too; closing in to fill the gap the boat had made in their ranks.

The engine whined. And died.

The boat jerked and jolted once, and then stalled. It cruised forward under its own momentum a little further, but it wasn't enough. Not enough to take us clear.

We were between ten and fifteen metres from the clear water. With the motor gone, the only noise was the slap of waves against the boat's sides. The world was so silent now.

I unslung the shotgun. "Marta?"

"Yes?"

"Get in. Shut yourself in a cabin."

"What about you?"

"Do as you're told!"

Careful, Katja; don't panic. Remember, panic –

Panic is a choice. Yes Papa. I heard you the first time.

"What are you going to do?"

I pumped a round into the shotgun. "Hold them off."

Marta pulled back the 'pigeon box' on the roof and dropped in through the skylight. I didn't like giving her a gun. Perhaps, after this, I'd show her how to use one. The heads just watched me. The blue, bloated faces of the lately drowned; the oozing, rotted ones of those longer dead.

A muffled thumping came from forward. The bows.

I scrambled up onto the cabin roof and ran. It was the best place to be. Exposed and vulnerable, but it gave the best vantage.

Three of the dead things were clinging to the bow. Their hands thumped on he hull as they clutched for a hold. One was hauling itself over the gunwales. I aimed down and fired.

A shotgun isn't a marksman's weapon, but it didn't need to be at that range. The full charge hit the back of the dead thing's head and blasted a gaping hole in the skull. It teetered and then flopped forward across the gunwales. The second of the three was heaving itself up, mouth agape. A low hiss escaped, like gas from a punctured, bloated corpse. I pumped the slide and fired again, blowing away everything from the eyes upwards.

The last one looked from the second thing's body in the water to the first's draped over the gunwales, then back up at me. I pumped the slide again. Hissing, it let go and slid back into the water.

I stepped back, looked around. The heads in the water had closed in around the *Rosalind*. They were all staring at me.

Reload while you can, Katja.

Yes, Papa.

I was wearing an old coat of Derek's, pockets stuffed with shotgun shells. I pushed two fresh rounds into the gun.

Marta, down below. Derek's death had done something to her, hardened her somehow. Whether this was a good or a bad thing, I couldn't decide. Should I have kept her with me? Had I underrated her? But she was still just a child. She should be still in school, getting her first boyfriend, swapping kisses and gropes in sweet secrecy. Not this.

And I should be teaching English. And the ground should still be above the water. And the world should be fair.

None of them were making any move to attack yet, but it was surely just a matter of time.

Bows, stern, starboard. I could cover all three at once. Nothing moving. Nothing moving –

Thump.

Behind me. The port side.

I whirled, but I was too slow. Rotting hands grabbed hold of the shotgun. I fired, the blast smashing into the dead thing's side, blowing it back off the cabin roof. It tore the shotgun out of my hands. But the gun was still slung around me. I crashed flat on the roof, sliding forward. The dead thing hissed. The parts of its face that hadn't been eaten were blue and mottled with decay. It wore a baggy top and tracksuit bottoms and its hair was a slimed mess; I had no idea if it had been male or female. It reached up for my face. Two more were clutching at the gunwales below.

The revolver; the revolver was in the back of my waistband. I pulled it out, pressed it to the rotting forehead and pulled the trigger. For a horrible moment I thought it wouldn't let go of the shotgun and I'd be pulled out after it, but then its hands opened and it fell away. I shot another dead thing as it climbed; I fired too fast, without aiming properly, and caught it only in the chest, but the impact knocked it back into the water. The third one I got in the forehead.

"Katja!"

The second shotgun roared. I scrambled over and dropped into the stern. Marta was clambering up the steps from the boatman's cabin. The shotgun's recoil had thrown her back down them. A dead thing bobbed in the water off the stern. Four more were clambering over. I fired the shotgun again and again until it was empty. No sooner had they fallen than another pair of hands began clutching at the bottom of the guardrail.

"Back!" I grabbed Marta and dragged her inside the boat, slamming the door shut behind us and locking it. Hands began pounding on the wood. Through one of the windows, behind the net curtains, I saw another body drag itself up into the starboard gunwales. Its free hand pounded against the window.

Thumping came from the port side too, and from the windows forward.

"Oh Jesus," Marta was whispering. "Jesus, Jesus, Jesus..."

"Reload," I said, pushing shells into the shotgun. She was wearing one of Derek's coats against the cold. She looked tiny in it, more of a child now than ever in her fright. "Marta! Reload your gun! Now!"

She dug out shells and thumbed them in. I broke open the revolver and replaced the empty shells.

A blow rattled a window. Marta turned, raising the gun, but I caught her arm. "Don't. If you shoot out the glass, it's easier for them to come through."

"So what do we do?"

"We wait until they start breaking in before we open fire." I thought for a minute. "You go forward. Cover the galley. I'll deal with them here."

"Okay."

"And remember, if it goes quiet –"

"Then reload. I know."

"Good girl."

"Don't be so bloody patronising."

I had to smile, although I didn't let her see it. A teenager is still a teenager. "Okay. I'm sorry."

Up at the bow end, glass shattered.

"It's alright," said Marta. "Oh, God. Oh, God." But she walked towards it.

The banging on the stern door, now savage and loud. The port window smashed, a hand lunging through, sliced bloodlessly by the glass. I wheeled and fired. In the confined space the explosion reminded me of an old cartoon I'd seen, where a character's head is slammed between two cymbals. It was less a sound than an impact on the ears. After it, a long bell-tone sounded. The dead thing flew back, headless.

I chambered another round. Marta fired.

Glass breaking – the galley.

A dead thing climbing through the window. The recoil slammed me against the doorframe when I fired; its head evaporated across the walls and ceiling. The bell-tone rang in my ears. What if I couldn't hear where they were coming from next?

Marta kicked in the bathroom door and fired. The recoil drove her back into the far wall. She pumped the slide, stepped through the doorway. A dead thing hung in the window frame, half-in, half-out, one arm dangling limply and half-severed. She aimed at its head, keeping her feet wide apart, bracing herself for the kickback, and fired straight into its head.

Wood splintering. The stern door. I ran towards it, working the slide. Behind me more glass broke – the galley again. But no time. "Marta!"

I heard the shotgun fire behind me and shouldered my own gun, aiming at the door. It splintered in the middle from the blows. A hand reached through, skin hanging off it like rotten wallpaper, and groped for the lock.

Marta shouting behind me. I could hardly hear it over the bell-tone and my heart's pounding. To my right – I wheeled towards the port windows and fired.

Marta screaming.

I turned, ran aft. A dead thing scrambling through the galley window. Marta's shotgun on the floor. Reaching for her pistol as she backed away.

Another dead thing lurched between us, grabbed at me. The shotgun was useless at that range. Too close. I let it go, pulled out the automatic. The dead thing still had both its eyes; they were clouded and lit from within, like misted lightbulbs.

Marta screamed again. This time it was different. The thing had grabbed her left forearm and sank its teeth into the flesh. Its head shook side to side.

The dead thing forced me back against the doorframe, hands clutching at my throat and shoulders. I fired into its chest, twice. It stumbled back into the galley. I shot it in the head.

Marta screaming.

Aim two-handed. Steady. A breath. Then fire.

The top of the dead thing's head blew apart, and it slumped. Marta screaming and sobbing as she tore her arm free of it. The ragged bite wound gaped in her slender arm, marring her flesh. Blood poured down in a slick. She grabbed the shotgun off the floor and blasted the corpse.

There was a crash as the stern door gave way. I shouted. No words, inarticulate. All I had time and space for. Ran astern. The door hung off one hinge, splintered and smashed almost in two. A nightmare thing staggering through, its face half-eaten, the rest discoloured, its scalp reduced to mangy patches by scavengers. One eye a gaping, glowing socket, the other clouded and glowing.

Aim and fire. Watch it fall. Pivot left, shoot again. Then right. Marta not at the port windows. Scream for her. Seeing her out of the corner of my eye, stumbling and firing.

I can't remember the next few moments with any clarity. It couldn't have been much longer than a handful of minutes, but the fight seemed endless.

The shotgun emptied and there was no time to reload. I let it hang on its sling, relied on the automatic.

We tried to get them as they crawled through the windows. We left them where they died; if they were blocking the windows, it took that much longer for the next dead thing to drag the carcass out of the way.

I felt small, hard things crunching underfoot. I could hear the sound of them faintly, through heart-thunder, screaming – Marta's and mine

– and the bell-tone. When I looked down – during a brief second where nothing seemed to be trying to break in – empty cartridge cases littered the floor. Shotgun shells. Pistol cartridges. Surely I couldn't have fired so many? I didn't remember reloading. But when I checked my pockets, one of the three spare magazines were gone. One lay empty on the floor.

There were two shots from Marta, then silence. I watched the windows and the shattered doorway. Nothing. I safetied the pistol, shoved it through my belt, then unslung the shotgun and started thrusting fresh shells into it.

Something fell against the stern doorframe, lurched into view.

Derek.

His clouded eyes glowed dully. The top of his head flowered open; something clotted seethed in the ragged, gaping wound. A flap of torn flesh hung down under his chin from where the bullet had gone in.

I'd thought by shooting him through the head I'd spare him this. I thought I'd owed him that, if nothing else. But I hadn't spared him anything.

He let out an almost plaintive moan and shambled forward, hands clutching at the doorframe. Did he know? Did some vestige of memory remain, to tell him this had been his home? That I wasn't just food, but his killer?

I didn't bother asking. I shot him between the eyes.

He toppled backwards, crashed against the tiller, and slumped.

And after that, finally, there was silence.

"Katja?" I heard Marta's voice through the bell-tone. My heart was no longer thumping quite as hard as it had been. "Katja, are you alright?"

I looked at Derek's body, nodded without speaking.

"Katja?"

"Yes."

"Glad to hear it," she said. "I'm not. How about some help?"

I turned. She was sagging in the galley door, face less white than grey, blood puddling under her torn, dangling arm.

I caught her just before she fell.

THE ATTACK HAD stopped, for now. The only dead things in sight were truly dead now. At least, I hoped so. I'd thought Derek was, but...

I tried not to think about it as I cleaned the ugly, ragged hole in Marta's arm. She whimpered as I sponged the raw flesh with antiseptic. I made no comment. She'd earned the right to whimper at least once. Besides, a teenager is a teenager...

Once I'd done all I thought I could, I bound a gauze pad over the wound and bandaged it tightly, but I was still thinking about the bodies scattered around the boat. Was the headshot only a temporary stopper? Were they all going to come back anyway?

They showed no sign of doing so, but how long had it taken for Derek to wake up again? We'd gone some way from where we'd dumped him. That was it; he must have followed the narrowboat. He'd said they tended to stay where they'd died. Their homes, their familiar surroundings. But then, it had been different for him; the *Rosalind* had *been* his home.

I fought back that crazy, jagged laughter again.

So he must have revived quickly, to catch up with us. I looked at the dead things; they remained still.

"Can you move your fingers?" I asked Marta. She waggled them.

"There's that at least," I said. "As long as we can keep it clean of infection, it should heal up okay."

I hoped I sounded more convinced than I felt.

I GAVE MARTA some painkillers and went astern to try the engine. It sputtered and coughed, but it didn't start.

I lifted the hatch near the tiller. The propeller shaft was almost lost to sight amongst chopped, crushed flesh and bone. Twisted and bent, the fingers of a human hand stuck up when the hatch rose, and moved. An accident? Or deliberate? How much intelligence should I credit them with?

There would be another attack. Just as there'd been at the brothel. We'd killed some of them, and the rest had retreated. But before long, they'd come back.

As for the propeller, I wouldn't know where to start.

I went back to Marta.

"It's fucked, isn't it?" she said.

I nodded and sat beside her on the couch.

"We're fucked then, too."

I didn't answer. I wanted to tell her *no*, but I couldn't.

Marta took the gun from her belt. At first I didn't realise what she was doing, until she brought the pistol up to her head.

"No!" I grabbed the barrel.

She glared at me. "I won't let that happen to me, Katja! I'm not going to let them eat me. Like they did to Marianna. I don't want to die like that."

"You won't. Marta, you won't."

"Of course I bloody will! They're going to come back again! And then again, and again, and again! Even if they don't get us next time, they will the next, or the one after that. Don't you get it? They aren't going to give up."

What could I say to her? The boat wasn't going anywhere. And it wasn't like there was another –

"Marta?"

"What?"

I let go of the gun. "I've got an idea."

WE FETCHED THE fuel cans from the locker. Most were full. Next we pumped up the dinghy – or I did while Marta kept watch. She fetched bottled water and provisions when I took my turn on lookout. The open water seemed hardly any distance at all. Ten, fifteen metres. The kind of distance that can be tiny, or huge.

A head broke the surface, eyes glowing. Then another. And another. It wouldn't be long now.

I uncapped a fuel can and poured it over the port side.

Marta came back up. "I brought the first aid kit too."

"Good thinking." We were also taking one shotgun, the rifle, plus the two automatics. There wasn't room for more.

Marta poured a can over the starboard side. We poured some over the stern too. Can after can, very quickly, before it could evaporate. Everywhere except over the bow.

When the fuel was gone, I lit the first spill. We'd made them from the pages of a book we found in Derek's cabin. I threw it over the stern rail. For a second, nothing happened, and then the fuel caught.

Whumph.

Blue and orange flames rushed outwards. There were muffled explosions as the bloated bellies of the rats burst.

The water churned and splashed. The dead things were flailing about. They were retreating from the flames.

"It's working!" I shouted. Marta threw a spill overboard.

I threw another off to port, and ran back through the narrowboat to the bow.

The water frothed and churned as the dead things retreated. Heads vanished under the surface.

"Now. Quickly."

Marta nodded. She was pale; sweat studded her forehead. I'd give her more painkillers later. When it was safe.

A narrow strip of clear water led off from the prow. We lowered the dinghy over the side. I climbed down, crouched there and reached out for Marta. She flopped into the dinghy and it almost capsized.

I grabbed the oars. I felt hairs shrivel on my arms from the heat. The dinghy would start to burn soon as well.

I rowed and kept rowing, hauling on the oars. I was in the bow, facing the boat, my back to whatever was coming up ahead. Marta sat in the stern, her automatic in her lap.

I felt the solid mass of rats fouling and clotting the oars. At any moment I expected something to seize one or other of the oars and tear it out of my hands, but nothing did.

"We're almost there!" Marta's voice was high. Spots of colour stood out now in her pale cheeks. I took it as a good sign.

Where would we go after this? How long would our supplies last? What chance did we have?

More than we did here. Here, we had none at all. Perhaps, like this, we'd be too small to be noticed. Perhaps.

The oars suddenly moved more easily. I looked down. No rats.

I rowed fast and hard. Would they come after us? I could see their heads emerging from the waters now – from the clear waters around the boat. Their eyes glowed. They watched us. Were they going to follow?

Marta managed to shift herself round in the dinghy. She held her gun ready in both hands.

But they didn't follow. One by one, the heads disappeared below the surface. I kept rowing. Nothing happened to us. The boat receded into the distance; by now it was on fire. There was a muffled bang from aboard it, and flames spurted out.

It didn't sink, not that I saw. Just burned. It receded as I rowed, slowly. Gradually the faint mist thickened around it, and it was gone.

CHAPTER NINE

WE'D BEEN ROWING for about an hour before I dropped the oars and let out something between a gasp and a cry.

Derek had had a compass. And I'd forgotten it. The most obvious thing of all. It'd probably been in his pocket when I'd put him over the side. Might still have been when he'd come back. With it, we could have got a bearing on the land I thought I'd sighted. With it, we'd have known which way to go, and if we were still going there. A forlorn, threadbare hope, perhaps, but better than this.

There were no landmarks; only the bare, spreading water which in any case was disappearing into the encroaching mist. All I could do now was to keep rowing, and hope we were still pointing the right way.

I would have suggested that Marta and I take turns rowing, but it's not easy to change positions in a dinghy. If we capsized, then even if the dead things didn't take us, we'd lose our supplies of food and water, maybe the guns too. To say nothing of the risk if the filthy water got into an open cut.

And in any case, Marta was in no fit state to row.

She'd grown pale, and groggy. When I gasped, she stirred and forced her eyes open.

"Katja?"

"What is it?"

"I don't feel well at all. I feel... I think I'm going to be sick."

"Aim over the side."

"What if there are... things in the water?"

"I don't think they'll be interested in vomit," I said, trying to smile. She tried too. I don't think either of us made a very good job of it.

The water slapped against the dinghy, which rocked and bobbed. Marta gave a faint moan; the dinghy listed badly as she leant over the side. I looked away as she threw up.

Maybe it was just seasickness. She'd been ill on board the *Rosalind*, at first. On the heels of that came a second thought; what if we met another storm? We wouldn't stand a chance in an inflatable.

I didn't let myself think about it. Or how easy it would be, in the mist, to row straight past the land I'd seen. If it had been real.

If we were heading the right way.

All I could do was row.

Out of the frying pan. Into the fire.

"KATJA?"

"Yes, little one?" I spoke gently. She was white now, dark rings around her eyes, swaying slightly.

"I feel horrible. I need to lie down."

"Okay." I stopped rowing. "Careful now."

She nodded weakly and wriggled round. She rested her head in my lap and propped her feet over the edge of the stern. I tried not to think about dead hands lunging up to grab them. Her forehead was burning not.

I gave her some water and painkillers, hoping they'd take the temperature down. Were there any antibiotics in the first aid kit? I needed to stop and look properly. I needed some solid ground under us. But there wasn't any.

Something scraped the dinghy's hull, rocking it, and I let out a yelp. Marta moaned in fear. Then I looked astern and saw thin, limp twigs and drooping leaves, just breaking the surface. A tree.

A tree.

"Higher ground," I whispered.

"What?" Marta's voice was a croak. I held the water bottle to her lips. "Not too much," I whispered. Supplies were finite. If we had to drink the muck around us, the dead things might offer a quicker death.

"It was a tree. We might be close to somewhere. Land. There might even be other people."

Perhaps even a doctor. I didn't dare say it aloud. This wasn't seasickness. The fever, the nausea, the weakness: they all spelled one thing.

Infection.

The dressing on Marta's arm was still relatively clean, but that was no indication of what might be under it. I didn't want to look, not yet.

The first aid kit lay next to my left knee. I picked it up and opened it. Antiseptic creams, TCP. More painkillers. Plasters and bandages. Surgical tape. No antibiotics. "Katja?"

I touched her hot cheek.

"I'm scared."

So was I. "Just hold on, baby." My voice wouldn't stay steady. "We'll get to land. We'll get you help. Just hold on."

I began to row again.

I KEPT ON for another hour, with brief pauses. Finally I had to stop. My arms were throbbing. Marta's eyes were closed, and her breathing was shallow. I looked at her arm.

My breath caught. The bandage was stained an ugly yellowish-green. The flesh on either side of it was livid and swollen.

The kit held a small pair of scissors. Marta let out a faint moan as I snipped at the bandage, and I stopped, but her eyes didn't open.

I peeled back the bandages. The gauze pad was stained and wet, and the thick stench of the wound was nauseating. I'd smelled something similar once, a staphylococcal infection. But I'd never seen one develop so *quickly*.

The wound itself oozed pus, but the flesh around it was, if anything, worse. It was black and green, like something rotten.

I threw the stained bandages over the side, poured TCP onto a cotton-wool pad and pressed it to the wound. It was all I could think of to do.

Marta's faint, sick cry was worse than a shriek. Either she was too weak to even give proper voice to the pain, or the damage was already so bad she had almost no feeling there.

Antibiotics. We needed antibiotics. Nothing else would give her even a chance of survival.

This was how it began, I realised. The second wave of deaths. After the flooding, after the dead things. Deaths from lack of clean water. Lack of food. Lack of medicines. Deaths inconceivable only the day before. That is how quickly it can go – how quickly it *had* gone.

Even Ilir, if Marta had been this ill, would at least have called a doctor. He might dispose of her if she'd suffered something too expensive or troublesome to treat, but antibiotics wouldn't have been a problem. But now even the water was a precious, limited reserve. I rinsed my hands with some of it, and rubbed antiseptic cream into the wound. Then I gauzed and bandaged it, and secured it tightly with surgical tape.

That was all I could do.

I could see the blue tracery of veins on Marta's eyelids. Her lips were parted and dry, already starting to crack, her breathing hoarse and shallow. Soon, she would be thirsty. When she woke – *if* she woke – she'd have to drink.

And there was only so much water.

It might be better if she never woke up.

If it's just you, there's less weight. You'll go further. If it's just you, there's more water. You'll live longer. If it's just you, there's more food. You'll be stronger.

The worst thing about the voice that said all this? It was my father's.

Marta was my friend. More than that. She was a younger sister, or a child. The difference in ages was such she could have been either. And she looked so like my mother.

Marta was all the family I had.

And she is dying, said Papa.

No. We could get help.

What help? The authorities are either in hiding or they've been wiped out too. Even if they had any intention of providing help, do you think they'll have the means?

But a village, high on a hill. We might find that. There might be a doctor's surgery there. They would have medical supplies.

Perhaps. And if they do, why should they give them to you? It is survival now, Katja. The others who've lived through this may even now be fighting amongst themselves for dominance, for control of resources.

If they were divided, it would be so much the easier to take them.

But you will be on your own. What then? How will you establish yourself in such a community, if *you find one? Why should they share what they have with a stranger?*

I have food and water. I have guns and ammunition.

Without which, you are dead.

I have my body.

Hours after killing Derek for what he'd forced me into, swearing I would never do such things again, I thought this quite calmly.

I have my body.

And if you offer that, what then? They'll expect more such favours. And when you give yourself to them, how will you stop them overpowering you, taking your guns? You will be where you were before the floods came. And Katja – Katja, look at her. She is beyond help. This infection has taken hold so swiftly and savagely. She will be dead before you reach land.

"No!"

Marta moaned at the shout. So, this was it. Madness at last. Drifting in a boat with a dying girl, arguing with a ghost. No, not a ghost. A figment of my imagination.

Katja, you admit yourself that she is dying. There is no choice here.
"No."

Triage, Katja. Advanced *triage. You know what that means.*

And I did. Triage was how you graded the severity of injuries – decided who would cope with little or no treatment, whose treatment could be delayed, whose treatment was required now.

But advanced triage...

Oh Papa, you've taught me too well. I don't need these things in my head.

Without them, Katja, you'd already be dead.

And now I was conversing with a ghost in rhyme. Final proof of madness. That crazy, jagged laughter, climbing in my throat again.

Advanced triage.

In advanced triage, patients with no or small chance of survival may not receive advanced treatment. Painkillers, nothing more. At most.

I didn't have much more than painkillers anyway.

But the rationale – where there aren't the resources to spare, where there's no chance, you let them die.

I looked down at Marta.

She is dying, Katja. You cannot help her. Anything else is a delusion.

I shook my head. Dimly I became aware that I was crying. Tears splashed Marta's pale face, like tiny drops of rain.

You were ready to kill her before, at the brothel. When the alternative was an agonising death, you were ready to kill her quickly to spare her. Do you want to see her die in such agony now?

I shook my head. "Shut up," I whispered through my teeth.

Katja –

I grabbed the oars and jerked them savagely, smashing the surface of the water into froth. A petulant child, throwing a tantrum in response to a truth she wouldn't accept. "Shut up! Shut up! *Shut up!*"

Marta moaned and opened her eyes. Her lips were bloodless. "Katja?"

"It's alright, darling." I touched her cheek, bent to kiss her forehead. Both burned to the touch. "It's alright. We'll soon be there."

"You've... found somewhere?"

"Not yet, little one. But we will. It's close. I can feel it."

I grabbed the oars again and began rowing. Her eyes closed again.

Stop crying, my father said. *Stop crying.*

"I'm not crying."

You are. Stop crying. You have to be strong, Katja. You have to be strong.

But it was so hard to be strong, watching this.

My father's voice faded as I went. I never heard it again.

One other loss, amongst so many.

*   *   *

MY ARMS ACHED terribly. I took two of the painkillers at long last. I had to keep going. Had to. There was no alternative.

Had to find land. Had to find land.

A dank, chilling mist lay thick around us, reducing visibility to a few metres. The redness had spread up to Marta's shoulder now. Her hand was a bloated claw. Around the edges of the bandage was a rim of black, green-tinged flesh. The veins on the arm around the wound were visible. They too were black.

So much easier to kill her. To finish her before it got worse.

It would be bad. I knew that. It would be bad. But I could do it.

But that would not be the worst.

Because even if I killed her with a bullet to the head, even then –

She would come back. She would come back and *I would have to do it again*. And I could not do that. *I could not do that*.

But if she died anyway, died of the infection –

If that happened she would come after me anyway. And it would be kill or be killed.

So it was very simple. Marta was not going to die. She *could not* die. It could not be allowed to happen. Could not be countenanced. It became my mantra, as I rowed. I may have mumbled, or spoken, or screamed it aloud. Marta could not, must not, die.

It was as simple as that.

I had to stop at last. Gathering my breath. Painkillers or not, my arms were throbbing.

Marta's face was grey. Shallow breaths hissed in and out through her lips. Her forearm was black from elbow to wrist. Her small, swollen hand had gone green; so had about half of her upper arm. The bandage I'd secured was already sodden.

She's dying.

No. No.

I took the oars up again. It felt like I was trying to lift and move tree-trunks.

Something hit the side of the boat. I yelped, released the oars and grabbed my pistol.

Something in the water.

I actually had the gun aimed at it, finger tightening on the trigger, before I realised what it was.

A treetop. Beyond it there were more, vanishing into the mist. And then I saw the roof of a white, half-submerged house. Another building beyond it. A chimney.

I looked around. A dark mass to starboard. *Land*. A wind began to rise, thinning the mist, and up ahead, I saw a bridge. Something else, through it all. I heard voices. I was sure of it.

I looked to port. A road rose up out of the water, bordered by a stone wall and a half-submerged tree. The road rose to the bridge. I thought I saw a rooftop, up on the dry land.

I rowed the dinghy past the white house. We passed a window, through which I could see a bedroom. A figure stood, its back to me. It started to turn.

As the mist dispersed I saw peaks. Hills. All around us. I hadn't seen them in the mist, and my frenzy to keep moving. Because I'd never really believed we'd reach land. I'd hoped – I'd *had* to believe – but deep down, I'd known. We were fucked.

I twisted slowly around and looked aft.

Rooftops. Hills. One in particular, tall, wide and sheer, rising to a steep crest. It looked like a huge wave, but it was made of rock and earth. A sheep's bleat drifted towards me.

"Marta?" I whispered. "Marta, we've done it. We're here. I can see land. It's right there. People."

She didn't answer. I turned, put my hand on her shoulder. Stopped.

Her face so grey.

No sound of breathing.

"Marta?" I shook her. "Marta!"

No. Nothing. No. No. No.

I kept shaking her, until finally her head lolled sideways, lips slack.

I felt her throat for a pulse. There was nothing. I kept trying. This time there would be something. This time. But there wasn't.

I blew air into her lungs, spat out the sour taste of her dead mouth. I pushed down on her chest, tried to pound her heart back into life. The dinghy rocked and tipped, nearly throwing us both out.

Nothing.

I don't know how long it was before I gave up. I slumped back, away from her. Nothing. All for nothing.

I sat there. Again, I have no idea for how long. Time was meaningless now. Marta was dead. The last of my little family was gone.

The swelling was going down, I noticed, and let out a wave of that jagged laughter. Her arm, paling, was regaining its normal size and shape almost as I watched. I couldn't stop laughing. All this way, and for nothing. A hundred metres from land and any point to continuing was gone.

Except it wasn't. *I* wasn't dead. There was one thing I could still do for Marta: get to land. Try to survive.

And if she rose, put her back down into the earth.

I forced myself to pick up those heavy, heavy oars.

And rowed.

Her head was still in my lap. I looked down at her face; I'd turned her head back upwards so I looked down into it.

Suddenly, there was movement. Had something hit the dinghy? No. The movement was coming from within it.

From Marta.

The infected hand was twitching. The arm shuddered. The small, delicate fingers flexed, opened and closed. A leg kicked.

I knew what it must be. How could I not? But if we excel at one thing, it's self-deception. For one, precious moment, I thought I was wrong, that she wasn't dead, that she was coming back...

And then I saw her eyes.

Through her eyelids, I saw a flickering, greenish glow.

Oh, God, oh no, oh fuck...

Dim at first, the glow was strengthening, flickering, pulsing.

Brightening.

And finally blazing.

Her arms thrust outwards, fingers hooked and clawed, shuddering. Her legs kicked and shook. Her lips peeled back from bared, snarling teeth. Thin spit jumped through them. An eye burst; warm, thick fluid spattered my face. I screamed then.

The other eye opened, the eyeball clouded over, glowing from within. The empty socket blazed. With a gagging, choking noise, Marta's jaws yawned open. A hissing, croaking howl escaped her dead lungs.

The boat rocked, water splashing over the gunwales.

Her head rocked side to side. Then stopped. She stared up at me, the burst eye congealing like wax on her cheek, and lunged up at my face. I tried to pull back and overbalanced, toppling into the water.

The shock... I'd heard the shock of icy water could stop a heart. In that second, I believed it.

Marta sat hissing in the dinghy, a vaguely baffled expression on her slack, empty face.

And when I'd killed the blue woman, I'd mourned the loss of an enemy whose face I knew...

There could be more in the water. The road was near. I struck out for it and Marta lunged after me.

Kill her, Katja.

Was that a last fading echo of my father's voice? I didn't think so. It was my own. Perhaps it always had been.

Kill her. If you care for her, finish it. This is not Marta, just a dead thing that looks like her. A puppet made of her body by something vile. An obscenity. An insult to Marta, and you. Destroy it.

And give her rest.

But I couldn't, because it *was* still Marta, and if I pulled the trigger, I'd be killing her, again. As I already had, by not reaching land in time.

You did everything you could.

But it hadn't been enough.

She swam closer, eyes glowing above the waterline.

I reached the road's edge. Clutched at the wall. Pulled myself clear. So heavy, so slow. She'd grab me any second. I flopped over, onto the tarmac. My feet slid but I was on dry land at last.

When I looked back, Marta was scrabbling over the wall, a thin arm reaching out, eyes blazing in the fading light, hair matted and straggling, face grey and slack and full of hunger. She slithered and fell in the mud.

I began to run. Hills rose through the mist. A big grey building. A sign on it: The Pendle Inn. A row of houses.

The wet splat and slap behind me of her feet.

Kill her or she kills you.

It wasn't her anymore.

Turn around, look into her eyes – they aren't really her eyes now anyway – and blow her brains out. End it for her. Kill a part of me too, of course, but...

I reached into my waistband for my gun.

It was gone. I must have lost it in the water.

Marta suddenly flying forward, in a manic, thrashing burst of motion. I went backwards, tripped. Fell.

The bullets hit her with a wet, sickening thud. Holes exploded in her chest and stomach; pieces of meat, cloth, bone and clotted blood flew out of her back. More bullets whipped past, buzzing like angry hornets. They cracked and whined as they hit stone.

Marta stumbled, but didn't fall. She stared up to my left, and hissed with a kind of drunken, baffled rage.

Her right hand – so tiny, so delicate – flailed through the air. A bullet, or bullets, hit it and blew it apart. A forefinger and a thumb remained, twitching.

Another half-dozen rounds hit her torso. One must have shattered her spine; she dropped to the ground and lay hissing and thrashing.

And still the bullets came. One whipped past me; two more hit the ground centimetres away. I think I screamed.

"Cease fire! *Cease fire!*"

A man ran down the road.

"*Cease fucking fire!*"

Tall, reddish hair, a soldier's lean hard build. A military uniform and a pistol in one hand, pointed at the ground away from his feet.

He brought the gun up, two-handed and aimed past me, to where Marta lay. He fired once.

The hissing and snarling and the drumming sound of thrashing limbs on the ground stopped. A long, rattling sigh from Marta. And then silence.

The solider pivoted, and pointed the gun at my face.

The muzzle of a gun looks so small.

Except when it is pointed at your face.

For a second I thought my bowels would fail, but I held onto that shred of dignity at least, although when he shot me they would open anyway. Like Derek's had when he'd died.

Then he stepped in closer, gun still aimed. "Were you bitten?"

He had a harsh accent I hadn't heard before. "Answer me! *Did she bite you?*"

I shook my head. "No," I said at last. "No."

He looked me over – in case I was lying, in case there were any wounds a casual glance might have missed – then nodded, stepped back, pointed the gun upwards and shouted "Clear!"

Other voices echoed the cry. "Clear... Clear... Clear..."

The soldier uncocked and safetied his pistol, then holstered it. He held out a hand. "I'll no hurt you. Come on."

I took his hand; he helped me to my feet. "Don't look back," he said. But of course I did. Marta was a stained, ragged bundle of cloth. I pulled free of him and went to her.

I didn't cry. I just stood there, looking down. There was nothing I could do. I didn't want him to see a frightened woman. I was more than that. I had strength. I knew that now. It had its limits like everything else, but I was still alive, and I wouldn't have been otherwise.

If I could have, I told her silently, *I would have saved you too.*

Her mouth hung slackly open; her clouded eye and empty socket – both now lightless – gazed blindly upwards. A neat hole starred her forehead; fragments of skull, scalp and brain littered the road behind her. I'd get no answers there. Neither accusation nor forgiveness. If Marta was anywhere now, it wasn't here.

The soldier came up behind me. I turned sharply; I don't like it when people do that. Never have. "You can do nothing for her," he said. His voice was as close to gentle as he could make it.

At last, I nodded. He nodded back. He motioned me forward and I followed him up the road. I kept my back straight, tried to show nothing with my face. No weakness. No fear. No helpless woman. I vowed as I followed him that I would never be helpless again.

PART TWO

Storm's Eye – Floodland

None wears the face you knew.
Great Death hath made all his forevermore.

Charles Hamilton Sorley, 1895-1915.

CHAPTER TEN

McTarn

THE TIME: APPROXIMATELY 0600 hours, November 7th. That day, of all days. If there was someone up there, He, She or It really had a twisted fucking sense of humour.

The place: a briefing room at Fullwood Army Base, Lancashire. Eleven soldiers, including me, plus one RAF commissioned orifice – sorry, officer.

Outside, the rain beating down, and a gathering storm. Inside, Squadron Leader Tidyman telling us it was the end of the world. And worse.

I COULDN'T SLEEP that morning anyway. My first clear memory is shambling, fully dressed, around my home just before dawn.

Home was a small detached house just outside Preston, Lancashire. Rented, obviously. Since leaving the service I'd bounced between security jobs and the dole queue. Doesn't make bank managers reach for the mortgage applications.

I finished up in the front room. Threadbare carpet. An old sofa, a pair of armchairs – one leaking stuffing – and a vintage '70s coffee table with heel marks where I'd put my feet up. Kept forgetting to clean my trainers when I came back from a run.

I didn't bother switching the lights on. Grey pre-dawn light played on the wall, shaped by the rain trickling down the front-room window.

I paced. Flopped onto the sofa. Tried not to think of the six-pack of McEwan's in the fridge. From outside, a soft hiss of rain. It'd been pissing down for the past week, non-stop.

For the first time in over a week, I switched on the TV. Flooded streets. Houses half-underwater. Odd words came out of the babble: *emergency; death toll; evacuation; army.*

Army. Teams of squaddies – not even remotely blending into the landscape in their camo gear – piled up sandbags, got old dears out of flooded houses, wheeled in food and blankets for all.

See the nice soldiers. Here to protect you.

Sand blowing across a dirt road. Blood on my hands. Blood on my face.

I switched it off. I looked at my hands. They shook.

Outside, dawn breaking. What the fuck; sun was over the yardarm somewhere. I fetched a can of McEwan's and popped the tab.

These days, this was as good as it got for me. I wasn't complaining.

I deserved a lot worse.

I took a deep breath, and then a sip.

Someone knocked on the door.

Churchill said you're in a free country if, when there's a knock on the door at five a.m., you know it's just the milkman.

But I got my milk from the corner shop.

I turned, looked at the door. They knocked again.

I parted the curtains. Two men in combats stood outside. Redcaps. Big. Pig-faced. Pig-eyed. Shaving rashes. Practically fucking clones.

One had a moustache, one didn't. Tweedledum and Tweedledee.

I opened the door. No security chain. I'd been meaning to get around to that.

"Robert McTarn?" said the one with no 'tache. Tweedledum.

"No, pal, I'm the fucking Tooth Fairy."

He didn't like that. He tried to push in through the front door. I didn't budge.

"Fucksake," said Tweedledee.

"Are you Robert McTarn?" Tweedledum asked. He was very pale. Looked ragged round the edges. Something was very fucking wrong. Something clenched and curled in my guts like a cold worm. I think they call it dread.

"Aye, that's me. What do you want?"

Tweedledum took a deep breath and pointed to the Jeep parked outside. "Need you to come with us, Robert."

Old habits die hard. Despite it all, I nearly did as I was told.

Nearly.

"You can get to fuck," I said, and shut the door.

On his foot.

Tweedledum just looked at me.

"In case you hadn't heard, I was discharged. I am no longer a serving soldier in the Armed Forces. So with respect, fuck off."

"You're still on Reserve List B, Sergeant McTarn. They've called you up." I wondered how many of his teeth I could knock out with one punch. "So please, come on. Let's not make this difficult, eh?"

I wondered just how difficult these two grebs thought they could make it for me. "If I've been called up, where's the telegram?"

They always do that – I don't know any other buggers who even send telegrams anymore. Except HRH, of course, when you make the century.

"Telegram?" Tweedledum looked at Tweedledee, who shook his head. "Have you *watched* the fucking news lately, mate?"

"No. It just depresses me."

He pulled something from his pocket and shoved it at me. "*There*. Okay?"

I opened it. Read it. *Bollocks*.

"Now will you get a bloody shift on please, Sergeant? We have a national emergency. *International*. And you're needed. So – *please* – while I'm still in a good mood, stop dicking us around and get your fucking coat."

"Gonna tell me what it's for?"

"You'll be fully briefed at base."

"You mean you don't know either."

His eyes narrowed; his mouth compressed. "Sergeant, I am not going to ask again."

Jesus. That was it. I'd been trying to pin down the look in his eyes. He was scared. Both of them were.

No-one likes the redcaps; they have a habit of turning up and spoiling the fun while you're beating up your platoon commander. But they're not complete girl's blouses. *International emergency*. The cold worm writhed in my guts again. I was thinking *crisis*, I was thinking *war*, I was thinking *fucking mushroom clouds over Britain*.

"Alright."

"Good boy."

DRIVING FAST. AVOIDING certain main roads. Sandbags stacked at the roadside. A huge wash of water blown outwards by the wheels as we passed. The wipers beating hard to clear the view ahead.

I sat in the back. Tweedledee looked back at me, offered a cigarette. I took it with a grunt. He lit one up, as did Tweedledum.

"Don't know the details," Tweedledee said, "but there's a major crisis on and they needed to put together a reinforced section PDQ. Someone's got you down as a good section commander. Any truth in that?"

"Used to be."

Translation into plain English for non Army-speakers: a section is eight men. A reinforced section is ten men.

"There's a Chinook coming in from the Sneaky Beakies to lift you out. You'll get the full brief on arrival."

Sneaky Beakies: Special Ops squadrons.

"'Fraid that's all I know."

"Thanks," I said at last.

"Mention it." He turned to view the road. Brought the cigarette to his mouth. Hand shaking as he did.

I finished mine. Stretched across the backseat. Closed my eyes. Might as well put the time to good use.

I dreamed of the desert road. When they woke me on arrival, I was glad of it.

"Sergeant McTarn?"

RAF uniform, shoulder pips. Thin. Pale. Clipped moustache. Old reflexes; I snapped to attention, Tweedledum and Tweedledee on each side of me. "Sir."

"Squadron Leader Tidyman." Sweat on his brow. "This way. We haven't much time."

"Sir?" Tweedledum. "Beg pardon, sir, but what do we do now?"

Tidyman looked back at him. "Make whatever preparations you think best for yourselves." He turned away.

I looked at the redcaps. They'd both gone white.

Poor bastards.

"Good luck," I said and turned away before they could react. I've no idea what happened to them.

"There's a set of combats for you in there. If you can change into them during the briefing I'd be obliged."

"Sir."

"We're loading the remaining kit aboard the transport. I'm in overall command, but on the ground you're in charge. Understood?"

"Sir."

"Good." He opened a door. "After you."

Ten chairs, all but one of them occupied. Lights off. Heads turned our way. They were in uniform, but some had bundles of civvy clothes at their feet. A plasma screen on one wall, a laptop on a table. Thick, stale air; cigarette smoke, sweat.

"This is Sergeant McTarn. He'll be this section's ground commander."

"Robbie?"

A wiry little man with a corporal's stripes, grey hair and a leathery monkey's face. "Chas?"

"Good to see you."

Chas Nixon. We'd served together.

The girl turning back to look at us. The look on her face. Incomprehension and grief.

"We need to start." Tidyman waved me to my seat. On it, folded combats and a pair of boots. I sat. I didn't want to touch them. And yet I did. I touched the fabric, felt the coarse weave.

Fuck. And they wanted me to lead these men? Didn't they know? I couldn't do this, not anymore. A wave of anger and resentment. Stupid bastards. They'd get them all killed. *I'd* get them all killed.

"You okay, Rob?" whispered Chas. I nodded.

"Alright," said Tidyman. "We'll come to the mission details in a moment, but first..."

I spotted someone else I knew: forty-something, six foot tall, still a private. Alf Mason. Not the brightest, but good at your back in a fight. We exchanged nods.

The plasma screen came on.

"This footage was shot in London earlier this morning."

Not much earlier. It's the same grey half-light I was wandering about in before dawn. They put this together fast.

Filming from a helicopter. The buildings nearest the Embankment are *gone*. Aerials and chimney pots, the occasional roof – nothing else stands clear.

The streets are awash. The water looks like stewed tea. But you wouldn't be drinking this. Sediment from the river bed, maybe raw sewage as well.

Further out, buildings are only half-submerged. Abandoned buses and lorries are visible on the roads, roofs just above water.

Fuck, it's bad. I look around the room, at people's faces. I see the same looks on theirs too.

Still, least it doesn't look like nukes.

The screen changes. Satellite pictures. I could tell that much; see the banks of shifting cloud and the shapes of sea and land through them. Beyond that, they meant nothing.

"Anything you've seen on the news in the last week is just the tip of the iceberg." Tidyman smirked. "No pun intended."

"Dicksplash," Chas Nixon coughed into his hand.

I suppressed a grin. Tidyman ignored him, a flush rising up his neck. "There's been a media blackout. Here's why. These pictures were also taken this morning. This is the Greenland icecap. This" – the picture changed – "is the Antarctic." Tidyman looked round to make sure he hadn't blinded any of us with science yet.

I unbuttoned my shirt.

"What you've been seeing on the news isn't restricted to the UK. It's global. Virtually every country on the planet is experiencing, or about to experience, flooding on a catastrophic scale."

"Good news for the Africans," said a goatee-bearded soldier with a Liverpool accent. The one black soldier in the room – Akinbode – gave the speaker a killing look.

"Parfitt," snapped Tidyman.

"Sorry, sir."

Tidyman carried on. "We have no idea what's caused the rapid melting of the ice-caps."

"Not global warming, sir?" Akinbode.

"Unlikely. No predictions concerning global warming have suggested anything happening at this speed. If the current rate of meltdown continues, we're looking at a rise in sea level to seven hundred and twenty feet within a matter of *days*."

No-one looked any the wiser. I could almost hear Tidyman reminding himself he was briefing a gathering of thick-headed squaddies.

"If that happens, almost the entire British Isles will be underwater."

Gasps, cries of "What?" Somebody even said "the *fuck*?" and then ducked down – a small, wiry soldier of about twenty with cropped, light-brown hair. I read his tag – Mleczko. Trying to pronounce that was going to be fun.

"Multiple storm fronts are also appearing. The first storm surge is expected to hit London within the hour. Another five, possibly six, are expected by the end of today, all over the coast. And that'll just be the start."

My stomach hollowed out; nothing inside my ribcage but echoing space. Looked like I'd never be going home now. I didn't have much there – books, a few souvenirs. But what was there was mine.

And there were photos. Mam. Me and Jeannie. Aw Christ, I didn't have any with me.

Focus, Robbie. Couldn't do anything about that now. The Army had been my family. Like it or not, I was back in. *These men depend on you, Robbie. Focus on that.*

Shirt off. Trousers and shoes off. I dressed without looking.

"We have contingency plans for incidents like this."

Grab all the top wankers and put them somewhere safe.

"The central government has already been evacuated from London. The capital's flood defences have already failed. We're broadcasting what information we can to the public, but the harsh truth is it's hopelessly inadequate to the task. Nothing on this scale was ever anticipated. There's virtually nothing we can do for the bulk of the population. We don't have the resources."

They never do.

"Central government will hand over power to regional control centres, as they would in the event of nuclear attack. They will do what they can to control the situation."

Probably fuck-all except sit tight.

"Teams such as yours are being sent to retrieve key personnel to secure locations."

Like I said, grab all the top wankers.

"Because of the nature of the crisis, I'm afraid we've been caught somewhat on the back foot. So some teams – like this one – have been put together at short notice. We've had to pull in people from the reserve lists." Another smirk. "Sorry for any inconvenience."

"Wankstain," Chas coughed. Sniggers broke the tension.

"Nasty cough, Corporal Nixon."

"Sorry, sir."

"I know this is a lot to take in, but I'm afraid there's more." Tidyman licked his lips. What could worry him worse than the floods? "We'll get to your mission in a moment. But first, I'm going to show footage shot by a team sent in to investigate reports from London earlier this morning. It was emailed over in the last hour." Deep breath. "This is the part we've *really* kept the lid on, men. It's easiest if you see for yourselves."

AN OFFICE BLOCK. Bottom floors submerged, but the top two are clear. The 'copter hovers, then descends.

It touches down. Soldiers de-bus across the flat roof. Moving fast, keeping low. M-16 carbines. SAS issue. The cameraman follows.

A door on the roof opens onto a stairwell. A soldier aims down, shouts "Clear." Another soldier runs down the steps. The cameraman moves to the door. The steps are dimly-lit – the power's out.

"Clear."

The rest of the squad shoulder past the cameraman. The picture bounces. Then down into the dark.

Out into a corridor. Torches clipped to the rifle barrels pick out bloody handprints on the walls. Thick muddy stains on the carpet. Dripping red arcs on the walls: arterial spray. On the ground – a handbag, a shoe. Dark lumps, mercifully not identifiable.

A hand.

Fuck.

(Tidyman's not looking at the screen. Seen it already. He wipes his mouth with the back of his hand. It's shaking.)

The hand is female. Slender, rings, painted nails. Not cleanly severed; strings of torn meat trail from the stump, and a jagged end of bone.

They move on. Open doorways. Empty offices. Overturned desks and tables. Blood on windows.

Then down the stairs.

Two flights down the stairs vanish into murky, lapping water. Torch-beams play over the surface. An empty drinks can, twigs and leaves, a dead rat.

Voices:

"The fuck?"

"See that?"

"Where?"

"There. *There.*"

The beam plays over the water again.

"*There.*" And clicks off. Now we can see it. The camera zooms in.

Beneath the surface, glowing through it – two green lights. Like eyes –

They brighten. I realise they're moving up just before the head erupts from the surface.

("Shit!" Half a dozen people yelp it together, in the film and in the briefing room. Nervous laughter, choked off before Tidyman says a word, as –)

The head's rotten. Greenish skin. Sunken cheeks, with holes showing the grinning teeth beneath. The eyes are ragged holes. They glow.

A hand rises from the water. Skin hangs down in flaps. Bones and ligaments work inside. It slaps on the wall, scrabbles. The rest of the body rises after it. It sways and lurches, like a drunk. The hair is a collapsed, bedraggled mess.

A second figure rises. A woman, in her twenties. Skirt, suit jacket, smart blouse. This one is fresher, hardly looks dead at all. Apart from the wounds. A chunk of her neck's missing. The wound's open and raw, but doesn't bleed.

They lurch forward; behind them a third nightmare bursts out of the water.

Someone fires. Full-auto. In a confined space, not very clever. The water erupts into spray. The three figures jerk and stagger. Pulped bone and meat hit the walls behind them. The rotted one and the third nightmare – a skeleton hung with rags of skin – fly back into the water. The woman's hit in the arm and falls against the wall, but doesn't show any pain.

Someone steps into shot, aiming at her. He blocks her from view, so we can't see what happens, but suddenly she's on him, clawing at his face. He screams, fires. She's thrown back into the water. The gunner doubles over, clutching his face.

The other two nightmares burst out of the water and seize him. The woman's up too – her blouse gapes open. Her breasts are out; one's been torn apart by the bullets.

She throws herself on the gunner too, and before anyone can shoot, they all crash into the water together.

Bullets blast the water into froth. The water's red.

And suddenly also full of pairs of glowing green eyes...

Something screaming in the water. An arm flails, missing a hand and spurting blood. The nightmares don't bleed. The gunner. Must be, but I can't be sure. He's got no face.

"Pull back! Pull back!"

The camera's all over the place, catching random glimpses – steps, walls, ceiling, soldiers running back up, one firing a burst from his carbine until someone screams at him and he runs too.

Up the stairs. Back into the corridor. Shouts. Turning back. Drunk-looking figures lurch into the corridor. Dim light – it's a dull day out, with all the rain. Can't make out much. Shadows. Silhouettes. The glowing eyes stand out. They lurch forward. Slow, clumsy, but relentless as machines.

Half a dozen automatic weapons fire. It sounds like a single blast, an explosion lasting five seconds. The nightmares dance back, trying to keep their balance; they hit the walls and drop, but then they get up and lurch forward. More come shambling into the corridor.

Then it happens. I don't know if it's luck or deliberate, but one of the nightmares – I think it's wearing a skirt, I think it could be the woman – takes a headshot. Head snaps up and back. Dark stuff flies up and out from it.

It drops to its knees.

Its eyes stop glowing.

And it falls. Doesn't get up again.

The other nightmares stop. Look down at it. Look back up.

Someone shouts: "Go for the head." More gunfire. Two more nightmares go down. The others – they blunder back through the doors, and they're gone.

Nobody goes after them.

They go over to the woman. She's face down. The back of her head is just a hole.

Kicked in the side. She doesn't move. They flip her over. Yup, it's her. She definitely looks dead. Then again, she did when she was still moving.

"Let's go. Go, go, go!"

And cut.

(The screen goes blank except for the DVD logo. No-one says a fucking word. Just dead silence, except for the hiss of rain outside, bringing all our deaths closer.)

THE SILENCE STRETCHES on and on, until Tidyman breaks it.

"Before anyone asks, yes. It's exactly what it looks like. They're dead. But they're moving. They kill and eat the living. And the only way to put them down is to destroy the brain. Questions?"

The medic's hand went up – a young Asian guy, tall and wide-shouldered. Hassan.

"Other than what's causing it."

Hassan's hand went down. A few people laughed.

A klaxon blared. Tidyman shouted over it.

"Your destination will be north-east Lancashire –"

The briefing room door burst open. A Flying Officer, forty-something, stocky and bald on top. He looked scared. He opened his mouth to speak.

"Knock before entering!"

"Sorry, sir."

"Well?"

"Floodwaters entering the compound, sir."

Tidyman took a deep breath. "Alright. Let's wrap it up."

"Probably got about ten minutes, sir."

"*Thank you*, Cannock." The airman ducked back. Distant shouting, feet thudding. Splashing. In water.

A man's face flashed up on the plasma screen. Long black straggly hair, streaked grey. Thick beard. Gaunt face, deeply lined. Reddened, bleary, staring eyes.

"Your target," Tidyman said. "Dr Benjamin Stiles."

"Fuck's he gonna tell us?" muttered Chas. "Apart from the best brand of White Lightning to get your brains fucked on, I mean."

"Pack it in, Chas."

"Alright, Sarge. But you must admit."

I knew what he meant. The poor bastard looked a total train wreck.

Still, I didn't have anything better do, so I sat back and listened.

CHAPTER ELEVEN

Fullwood Army Base, 0630 approx, November 7th.

Outside the building, wet spray hit my face. On the airstrip, a Chinook HC2 transport helicopter. A Flight-Sergeant stood at the back-end, beasting the ground crew as they backed a short-wheelbase Landrover aboard. The heavy rotors at each end were whirling, whipping up the water on the tarmac. It was already ankle-deep.

Stupid thought number one:

Fuck me, they weren't kidding.

Dr Benjamin Stiles. Ben to his friends. Assuming he had any left. When they think you're a mentalist, the friendships tend to dry up.

From the photo, I'd've put his age around fifty.

He was, according to Tidyman, thirty-six.

Stiles' area was marine biology. Five years ago, he'd been in a diving accident. Tidyman skimmed the details, but in a nutshell the poor bastard was physically fucked and in constant pain. And naturally, he could forget about diving again.

His career had fallen apart. The drinking hadn't helped. Probably to deaden the pain. Alcohol's good at that. But there was more. Obviously.

He'd started spouting doomsday predictions. Oceans rising, floods, the end of the world.

Not that unusual. Not enough to end a career.

That'd come when he'd started predicting the rising of the dead.

Tidyman skipped the details there too. Not relevant. What it boiled down to:

The powers that be wanted to pick whatever brains Stiles had left.

Location: A village called Barley. North-east Lancashire.

WE RAN ACROSS the strip. They were trying to shore the sandbags by the main gates but already the water was gushing through the gaps and they gave way as I reached the chopper. Akinbode and Mleczko went sprawling in the surge of brown water that rushed across the compound towards the strip like a breaker from a dirty sea.

"Move it! *Move* it!"

Back five minutes and it was like I'd never been away. Akinbode pulled Mleczko to his feet and they scrambled aboard. The water washed around us, shin-deep. Shouts and screams.

I jogged up to the Flight-Sergeant. He turned around and we eyed each other up. Any transport 'copter – Sneaky Beaky or otherwise – has a loadmaster. The pilots decided where we flew, but just as I was in charge when we hit the ground, the Loadie was God when it came to deciding what went on or off the chopper. "McTarn."

"Lomax."

"Anything I can do to help, Loadie?"

He shook his head. "Just get your arse in there before you drown."

I didn't need telling twice with it pissing down like that. Cannock was at the controls. The co-pilot, a thin droopy-moustached type called Hendry who looked as if his cat'd just been run over, stood in the cockpit doorway, staring out. "That everyone?"

I looked out of the main doors. The rain was rods and bolts, the sky black. Two last runners coming in: Nixon and Tidyman. "Couple more."

"Tell 'em to get a shift on, or we'll be flying underwater."

"Move your fucking arse, Nixon!"

I wasn't beasting an officer. I'm not *that* stupid.

Chas put on a burst of speed and jumped for it – pretty limber for a man near fifty. "Nice to have you back, Jock."

"*Sergeant* Jock to you, grotbag."

An old joke, but still a good one.

"That's the lot!" Lomax shouted. The loading ramp at the back closed up and he dropped into a seat.

"Everybody sit down and buckle up!" That was the co-pilot. "If we're going, it's fucking well now."

"Room for one more, I hope." Tidyman climbed in.

The co-pilot went red. "Sir."

Tidyman pulled the door shut. "Whenever you're ready."

I looked Tidyman over as I strapped myself into my seat. The Chinook lifted, rocking in the wind. Tidyman seemed at ease. In his comfort zone now.

My old CO, Lieutenant Alderson – he'd seemed decent enough as officers went. But the orders he'd given me...

I hoped Tidyman didn't give me orders like that.

Because I couldn't obey those orders again. I could not. Fuck.

Why put me in charge, you stupid bastards? Why? I'm not fit for it. Not anymore.

I look out of the porthole. The waters were flooding the compound now. The men ran back and forth. Like ants.

Had they been told they'd be evacuated too? Must have been, to stay at their posts like that. Or maybe it was duty. I used to believe in that.

"Everybody hang on," Cannock shouted. "Winds up here are a nightmare."

Nightmares in the water, nightmares in the sky, and the ground all washing away...

So who the fuck am I?

Robert James McTarn. Born and bred: Easterhouse, Glasgow. Age thirty-six. Only child of:

Rose Frances McTarn. Wife, mother, drudge, part-time cleaner and full-time punching bag for:

Douglas Robert McTarn.

My father. Six-foot-three, equal parts lard, muscle and bone. Very little brain. A dozen tattoos, one professionally executed – the Red Hand of Ulster, on his chest – the rest homemade: Rangers FC, No Surrender. He kept vowing to get a full-scale depiction of the Battle of the Boyne emblazoned across his back but never, to my knowledge, fulfilled it. Too busy pissing the weekly wages from his builder's job up the wall. He worked like a bastard, I'll give him that.

He battered my Ma, and he battered me. No plea for sympathy here. Just a simple statement of fact. That stopped at seventeen; I blocked one of his punches and dealt a few back. Not many. Not enough. He was down on the floor spitting blood and teeth and still it wasn't enough.

And my Mam, pounding my back with her fists, scratching my face, screaming at me to 'get away from her man.'

I went out the door and kept on walking. I didn't stop until I'd reached the recruiting office. Too young to drink, too young to vote – Christ, I wasn't even old enough to put my name on a direct fucking debit. But old enough to sign my life away.

I armed myself up, built muscles and combat skills. None of it kept out the real pain. My father might be a bastard (and was), but he was the only one I had. My mother might've tried to scratch my eyes out, but she was still my Mam. If you don't like it, go take a long hard look at your family, and then come back and start preaching.

I came back home exactly once, for Mam's funeral. We'd exchanged a few awkward letters in the decade since I left. Never talked about it. Never would now.

As the chopper flew north-east, I hoped she was too long-dead and rotted away to ever come back for me.

THE WINDS PICKED up as we flew. The pilot kept us above the cloud cover wherever he could, for why I don't know. Not as if we had any enemy aircraft to worry about, not unless the nightmares could fly Harrier jumpjets.

I wasn't even going to *think* about that.

We tooled up in mid-flight.

Tidyman, Cannock, Hendry and Lomax all carried pistols – Sig-Sauer P226s, with the extended twenty-round clips.

Most of us 'other ranks' carried Army-standard SA80A2 rifles. I picked one up and it felt like coming home. Some put their faith in Jesus, and that's well and good, but he can't deliver 610 rounds per minute on request. We had a reinforced section, which in our case meant three snipers. There was Akinbode, who I'd met already; the other two were called Andrews and Levene. All three carried Parker-Hale L96 rifles. High-quality, bolt action. Lovely bit of kit. Andrews was thirtyish with short dark-brown hair and a goatee; Levene was a few years older with dark, grey-flecked hair and a droopy walrus moustache, and seemed permanently half-asleep. Neither said much, but snipers can be a funny bunch.

We were also issued with two Minimi M249 light machine guns – box magazine or belt-fed – as support weapons – along with a GPMG (general purpose machine gun), and a blooper (Mk19 grenade launcher.) All that and two Landrovers to mount them on.

They'd also issued us with combat knives, although quite frankly if the nightmares were *that* close in we really were fucked.

Still, in for a penny...

*　　*　　*

FOR ALL I know, my dad's still alive. Only the good die young.

He was at the funeral. I was pretty sure I'd given him the cauliflower ear. Maybe the skewed nose, too. Although Dad was never shy of battle scars.

We didn't speak or approach each other. A truce. Neutral territory. He stayed with his cronies and I stayed on my side of the church, in my lonely pew. I waited until they were all gone from the Crematorium, him and his pals from the boozer and the football terraces. Someone brayed a laugh as they went, I'm pretty sure it was him.

I never saw him again. If I had, I might have killed him. Mam was the only thing that stopped me.

I'd barely made it to the funeral in time. The flowers were from the corner shop down the road. I left them in the Garden of Rest and spent the rest of my leave and what money I had in London drinking, whoring and punching out any bastard who could stand in for my father for long enough.

In between leaving home and coming back, of course, I'd seen action. It saved me from thinking. When I wasn't doing that, there were always boozing sessions with the lads and trips to the red light district. That last one stopped when I met Jeannie.

More or less.

There'd be nights before a mission. The kind I mightn't come back from. All the boozed-up camaraderie can't help with that, but a woman can. And Jeannie might not be in reach on nights like that.

I wasn't the only one. I never told her. She never asked. She was an army wife. She understood these things.

She did.

That wasn't what broke us up, anyway.

That came later.

Maybe it'd been building up for a while. All the things I'd done for Queen and Country, never asking, never questioning. Maybe it was only a matter of time. The invasion just brought it to a head.

The Army had been my new family. The invasion was where that ended.

LIGHTNING FLASHED THROUGH the portholes. The thundercrack followed seconds later.

I glimpsed the ground through rain and clouds. Streets turned into rivers. People huddled on rooftops. Waiting for help. Maybe they heard the Chinook over the storm, thought it was coming for them. Poor bastards if they did.

Only glimpsed them; no time to interpret. To see if anyone was looking up. Screaming for help or deliverance. Held up children like we were a friendly eagle come to snatch them away. Screamed in terror because they'd seen eyes glowing down in the water or their owners crawling out.

Imagination's a curse for a soldier. Never thought I'd had one. Probably got it around the same time as a conscience, and a mind of my own.

The woman screaming at us. Bastards, murderers – I could tell the meaning without knowing a word of her tongue...

Blood on my hands, blood on my face, blood I could never wash clean...

"You okay, mate?"

Chas, sat next to me, leather face furrowed. "Fine, Corp."

"You look stressed." The look in his eyes said: *Talk to me.*

I lowered my voice. "Don't know if I can do this, Chas. The fuck were they thinking?"

"That you were a fucking good section commander. That's what. You've done this before."

"That was before –" Before the desert road. Before all that.

"Yeah, I know, mate. But you did it once, you can do it again. It's not like then. Not now. You've gotta do it. For the lads."

"I know. I know."

"I've got your back, Robbie. You need help, you got me. Alright?"

I nodded, bumped his shoulder. "Thanks, Chas."

"No probs."

We managed to stay above the storms. To stop myself thinking about how much I fucking hated flying, I started matching names to faces. Well, you want to know what to call the soldier you're commanding, don't you?

Chas, Alf, Mleczko, Akinbode, Parfitt, Hassan, Andrews, Levene – I knew them already. That left two. There was one with greying hair, but who couldn't have turned thirty yet – that was Joyce. And the other one, a skinny girl with short blonde hair who barely looked old enough to join up – that was Parkes, the 'Sparky' (radio op in plain English). Chas, the Corporal, was section leader, with Joyce, carrying a Lance-Corporal's stripe, as 2IC. I ran the names through my head as we flew.

When Cannock finally took us down, closer to the surface, almost all we could see was open water. Sea. It looked close enough to touch.

The water was mostly empty, stewed-tea brown, churning sluggishly as it poured further inland. Further ahead, as the ground rose, the roofs of houses were visible. Telegraph poles. Treetops. Street lamps. Debris clotted in thick swirling clusters on the surface. I looked out towards the horizon. Rain spattered against the porthole. The sea looked calm.

"Any idea how much further, sir?" I felt like a kid, asking *are we there yet?* but couldn't help it.

Tidyman shrugged. "Weather's been slowing us down, but I think the worst of it's behind us. At a guess, we're about halfway."

Only half?

Tidyman seemed to read my thoughts. "Don't worry too much, Sergeant. Making better time now. Should be there within the hour."

"Thank God."

Tidyman smiled, but it looked fixed. Sweat glittered on his forehead. Well, we were all wound tightly at the minute. I felt like the last man who should be in charge when we hit the ground. I wasn't sure if I still had the skills, or if I'd want them back. What would being a soldier again do to me?

All the same, I'd seen men look like that before. It was never a good sign.

FURTHER NORTH, THE ground rose higher, and land broke the surface. Just hilltops at first. Little islands, some with a few bedraggled sheep grazing. I wondered what they made of it. My knowledge of sheep psychology was a little vague.

Hendry had taken over; he flew in low and at low speed.

A larger hilltop. A farmhouse near the water's edge. A man, a woman, a couple of kids ran out. Waved up at us.

I felt like flinging open the door and screaming, *we're not here for you, we never were.* But didn't.

Same old shite. The powers that be give the orders, move the chess pieces. Poor bastards on the ground suffer and die.

This trip brought all the memories back. But it's like the end of a marriage. All sorts of things aren't the same. First kiss, the first time you said *I love you* – they're all tainted by it being over now. The pain of that.

The same here. The camaraderie, being among men who understood what it was to be a soldier. I'd missed that. But I couldn't love it as I used to.

Whatever. Truth was, I was a fucking Sergeant again, like it or lump it. I was responsible for my men.

Hills, rising clear of the water. The Chinook wove between them.

"There it is," Hendry called out.

A road came up out of the water. There was low ground on either side of it, flooded and overflowing it. The top storey of a large white house stuck up above it to the right, and ahead of that a tall chimney and the upper story of what I guessed to be a converted mill. On the left were only the tops of trees.

"Barley Road," said Tidyman. "The village should be dead ahead."

And it was, perched on the edge of the floodland, where the road branched off into a Y-junction. The one on the left led higher up the neighbouring fell; the one on the right led through a short row of houses before curving off into the distance.

"That's Barley, there," Tidyman said. "Stiles' last known location."

One street. A pub. Fields. Meadows. Farm buildings further out, as the ground rose, sloping steadily up towards a big, wide hill like the fin of the biggest fucking shark in the known universe. For a second, it looked like a huge wave coming in at us.

I got a good long look at it, as the Chinook wheeled about.

"Pendle Hill," said Tidyman.

Cannock took us over the village, found a flattish field on the lower slopes, began to descend. The grass flattened out from the downdraft.

"Sarge?" Chas Nixon waved me over to his porthole.

I looked. A dozen stick figures were clambering over the drystone walls and into the field. They didn't have the staggery, drunken walk of the nightmares in the video. That was a plus. On the other hand, they were all holding shotguns and rifles.

"This could get interesting," I murmured at last.

"You're not wrong, Jock," Chas murmured back.

"Sergeant to you," I murmured back, "grotbag."

CHAPTER TWELVE

THE CHINOOK'S WHEELS bumped the ground. The chopper rocked, finally settled. The rotors wound down. As the machine fell silent, the whistle and howl of the wind came, and the patter of rain on glass.

I got to my feet: "De-bus!"

First order given. That was easy enough.

Doors open – the wind's bitter bite came through and the men baled out. They moved fast, forming a circle round the Chinook, dropping to one knee, guns facing out. Lomax leant against a bulkhead and watched with folded arms, giving every appearance of being deeply unimpressed.

"Stand by for take off at short notice," Tidyman, unbuckling. "We're not bloody stopping for long."

"With respect sir, we might have to," said Cannock. "Looks like there might be another storm coming in." He pointed. Out to 'sea,' a black stain was sweeping in across the sky. "Flying in that'd be suicide."

"I'll be judge of that, Cannock." Tidyman's voice rose; his face was very white. "Just remember who's in command here."

"Sir."

"Best get a move on, either way," I chipped in. "Take it I'm clear to go, sir?"

Tidyman nodded irritably. I decided to leave them to it and hopped out, then turned back. "Sir?"

Tidyman stuck his head out of the cockpit. "Sergeant?"

"Where do we find Dr Stiles, sir?"

"We don't have an exact address. He sort of dropped off the grid."

Off the grid. So, not a private house, then. A squat – some tumbledown cottage or barn? A tent? A static caravan, maybe...

"Sarge?" Chas pointed at the group of men moving in on the chopper. "What about them?"

"Fire on them, man!" shouted Tidyman.

"Beg pardon, sir, I'm pretty sure they're civvies."

"So am I," Tidyman said. "I'm also sure we've got a military helicopter, along with weapons, medical supplies, and food. Which they'll want. This isn't a relief mission. We're here to locate Dr Stiles and get him out. Nothing more. That is our priority. Nothing can be allowed to stand in the way." Flecks of spittle had gathered at the corners of his mouth.

I felt my hand drop to the butt of the SA80. I'd been somewhere very like this before. Some orders must not be obeyed.

Luckily, Chas Nixon stuck his head back in through the doorway before I did something stupid. "With respect, sir, they're not showing any hostile intent. No sense in starting a fight yet if we don't have to, is there?"

I stepped in. "He's right, sir. You said yourself I was in charge once we were on the ground."

"But I retain overall command, Sergeant."

"Not in dispute, sir –"

"Better not be!"

Sent to retrieve a fucking mentalist, and now it turns out the CO's one too. Any chance of some sanity round here?

Looked like I was the best bet for it. God help us all.

Pull it together, Robbie. You're not at home now. No time to go on your fucking guilt trip.

"Actually, sir, I was thinking of asking them where Stiles is. Sooner we know, faster we can finish, right?"

Tidyman's mouth twitched violently. "Very well. But the first sign of hostilities..."

"Sir."

Our lads were watching the locals and the locals were watching us. Nobody actually pointing their guns at anyone yet, thank Christ.

"Thanks, Chas."

"No probs."

"Keep an eye on Tidyman. Don't for fucksake let him kick anything off."

"Will do, Sarge."

A thought occurred to me. "Sir?" Tidyman leant out of the chopper. "You have a photo of Stiles?"

"What? Oh. Yes. Think so."

He disappeared back inside the Chinook, emerged a moment later with an eight by ten glossy. The same shot we'd seen in the briefing room.

"Thank you, sir." I turned to Chas. "I'm going to have a chat with the natives. Watch my back."

"Will do."

I slung the rifle across my back and started walking, hands out from my sides.

The apparent leader was a tall, wide-shouldered man in his late fifties, maybe early sixties. He had a thick full grey beard and wore a heavy coat with the hood pulled up. The rest were a mixed bag, aged between eighteen and fifty.

The big man had a shotgun. A Franchi SPAS-12. More of a combat gun than something you'd use to clear the rooks off the cornfield, but oh yes, very, very nice. I felt a twinge of Shiny Kit Syndrome. Every soldier gets that when they see a nice-looking bit of equipment. If it'd been loose, I'd've tried swiping it for myself. Unfortunately, the big man was holding it.

He looked me over. His eyes were pale and cool. Wolf's eyes. Rain spat down between us. The ground squelched underfoot.

I closed the distance and nodded at the other men. I didn't get any responses. They looked surly, more than anything else.

I held out the picture. "We're looking for him."

The big man looked down. His bald crown gleamed in the rain. "What you want him for?" A Lancashire burr ran the words together.

"We're not after giving him any trouble."

"What'd he do, you're coming out for him in all this? Did he start it all off or summat?"

For all I knew, he had. "We need his help. Believe it or not, he's a scientist."

"Bugger can barely tie his own shoelaces."

I'd known men like him before. Mam had had family in the countryside, farming folk. Used to long hard hours of back-breaking work and nothing but scorn from the 'townies' who'd have starved to death without them. They'd been hard folk, tough, giving little away. The kind of men I'd want on-side in a fight. What would Stiles have been to him? Pitiable? Ridiculous? Both?

He shrugged, pointed out towards the Hill. "Lives out near there. Caravan in the field. Foot of the Hill."

"Any chance you could show us?"

He shrugged. "Aye."

"Good."

I glanced at the shotgun. Lovely bit of kit there; take a nightmare's head off like a fucking dream. "Bring that with you."

"I was going to, lad."

WE TOOK THE Landrover with the mounted GPMG and got it onto the main street in Barley, Pendle Row – no way of driving straight up from where we'd landed. From there it was a short journey up the hill-roads to the base of Pendle itself. Alf Mason took the wheel; Mleczko crouched behind the Gimpy in case any large numbers of nightmares showed up. Akinbode sat in the back with his rifle. The big man sat in the back with us, the SPAS-12 across his knees. He only spoke to give us directions.

We went round the back of the Hill. The floodwaters had come in pretty close at that side too. Alf parked as close to the base of the Hill itself as we could get; we left him with the Landrover and sprinted round to the Barley-facing side. The big man loped along without breaking a sweat, while Mleczko, on point, was outright bounding ahead. Me, I was feeling the effects of letting myself go. I was still in halfway good shape, but too many beers, too many takeaways and too many cigarettes were taking their revenge on me now. Still, at least overindulging wasn't likely to be a problem in the immediate future.

Akinbode brought up the rear, making sure we weren't followed. Thank fuck, there was no sign of the nightmares.

The farmhouse was a big, solid-looking square building, built from blocks of yellow-brown stone. Shapes moved behind the windows, and I glimpsed a gun. Shotgun or rifle, again. Probably no threat, more scared of us than anything else. But fear could be bloody dangerous. You never assumed anywhere was safe.

Behind us was the Hill. A flight of steps made from biscuit-coloured rock led up a slope that was as close to vertical as you could get without needing ropes and climbing irons. Thank fuck we didn't have to climb *that*. You see, there's always a silver lining, if you look hard enough.

"What now, Sarge?" Mleczko looked flushed and almost happy from the run. I felt like giving the little sod ten laps around the Hill on general principle.

"Check the house, front and back. The rest of you, with me."

Another drystone wall marked out their front garden. I cut round it, keeping low, until I had the meadow in plain sight.

They'd left it lying fallow. Thick tufts of grass and weed sprouted up. Good cover for the approach, but the ground could be uneven. The caravan was tucked away at the far side, close to a thick hedge and under a heavy tree shedding leaves all over its roof. The caravan had to be twenty, thirty years old, the kind you saw on the roads when I was a kid – short and rounded at the ends, with a set of wheels in the middle. I stopped at the wall's edge and lifted a hand as the others came up behind me.

I looked at the others. Mleczko jogged up. "Clear, Sarge."

"Good work. Alright; Akinbode, you cover us. Mleczko, you're with me. Spread out across the meadow. Stay low, use the cover. Clear?"

"Clear, Sarge."

"Sarge?"

I glanced at Akinbode. He had a narrow face and quick eyes. Looked like he might have a brain. Always handy. "What?"

"Thought this guy was a friendly."

"Briefing said psychiatric problems. We don't know his mental state, and for all we know he's armed. So we take no chances. Questions?"

"If he does fire on us?"

"How good are you?"

"Good enough, Sarge."

"We want him alive, so if you do have to, shoot to wound."

He nodded. Christ. Almost sounded like I knew what I was doing. Step back. Assess the situation. Take action. Keep it simple. Forget whatever memories it threatens to bring back.

"Any more questions?"

Akinbode shook his head. Mleczko said nothing; he'd never had any questions to begin with. "You stay here with Akinbode," I told him. "Watch his back in case anything tries sneaking up."

He grunted.

We spread out from the wall, into the low grass, Akinbode spreading himself prone on the ground by the gate and aiming on the caravan.

"Remember to spread out, Mleczko."

"Copy, Sarge."

"Go!"

I ran in a crouch with my head down, picturing Stiles in there pointing a Kalashnikov through the window.

No gunfire. Reached the caravan. Mleczko appeared in the grasses at the far end. I belly-crawled to the door. Reached up and knocked on it. Ducked back, expecting bullets to punch through it. Nothing.

"Dr Stiles?"

No answer.

"Dr Stiles?"

Still nothing. Fuck.

"We go in," I said. I motioned Mleczko to get the door, moving back to cover him.

Mleczko pulled the door wide. The stink rolled out; I smelled piss, shit, stale sweat, rotten food.

"Stiles?"

Still no answer. I leant in through the door. This end held a kitchenette. Filthy 1970s lino with old food smeared and trodden in. A sink piled high with filthy pots. I climbed up and stood.

Bathroom at the end, door ajar. Stench making me gag. A faint buzz of flies.

In between the two, the main room. An old TV set in one corner, the screen smashed. A couple of chairs. A small table lying on its side. Threadbare carpet with scattered ash from the table, plus old beer cans, dirty plates, pizza boxes and the like. And a divan.

A man was sprawled on it, on grimy sheets. Even in the grey light coming through the curtains, I could see they were dark and wet.

"Fuck!"

I moved forward.

"Sarge?"

"Stay put."

I went to the divan. It was Stiles alright. Eyes shut. Face grey. An empty whisky bottle in one hand, a knife in the other. The dark stains were round the hand with the bottle. He'd cut the wrist, but clumsily – gone across, not up the vein.

Stiles' wrist was still oozing blood. Still alive, then. Small mercies. I pulled out a field dressing, bound up the wrist. He let out a weak moan, then coughed and puked out a thin stream of bile.

"Mleczko, get in here!"

WE DROVE BACK fast. Stiles lolled in the back, head propped up on a blanket roll. He threw up twice more. Joy of fucking joys.

The wind blew harder as we went, and the spray of rain was heavier. When I looked up, the sky was black overhead. Lightning flashed. Thunder rolled in with deafening cracks.

Some of the locals were still in the meadow, huddled by the nearest drystone wall. Keeping watch. If it came to an all-out fight I doubted they'd stand a chance. Then again, they could take a few of us with them. Chas still had the rest of the men around the Chinook.

And the rain poured down, and the wind flicked the long coarse grasses of the meadow to and fro.

The storm hit full-force as we reached the Chinook, displaying some truly perfect timing. There were two, three strokes of lightning, almost directly overhead, and the rain became industrial in force, hammering into us like machine gun fire. When it drove into your face, you were practically blind.

"Medic! Medic!"

"Jesus Christ!" Tidyman jumped down from the helicopter as we ran up. "What the hell did you do to him?"

Hassan leant out of the helicopter and looked down at the limp body. "What happened?"

"Found him like this. He cut his wrist."

"Just the one?"

"Aye. He'd put a lot of whisky away, too."

Hassan shook his head sadly. "Get him in here."

Mleczko and the others bundled Stiles inside. Tidyman clambered back into the Chinook, and I went after him. Hassan was spreading a blanket out on the floor. "Put him down here."

He checked the throat pulse and airways, unwrapped the dressing on the wrist wound. "Will he be alright?" Tidyman demanded.

The medic didn't look up. "Can't say for sure just yet, sir. Let you know as soon as I can."

The wind picked up into a roar and the Chinook rattled from the force of it. Muffled curses came from the men outside. "Let's get airborne," Tidyman shouted over the tumult. "Get out while we can. We can get him better attention at a secure location."

"Beg pardon, sir." It was Cannock. He stepped out of the cockpit. "We can't fly in this. Just look at it."

Tidyman didn't. I'd already seen it. Even without looking, I could hear the rain hitting the bodywork. It sounded like a platoon of drummers going flat out. Like machinery. Like machine guns, all firing together.

"Stop contradicting me," said Tidyman. His eyes had a fixed, unblinking look to them now, and he spoke through his teeth. They were bared, like an animal's.

"Sir, we have to wait out the storm. It's all we can do."

Tidyman's gun was in his hand. I hadn't expected him to move so fast. The Sig-Sauer was lined up with Cannock's face before either of us knew what'd happened. All of a sudden, Tidyman looked very calm.

"You can take the bird up yourself," he said. "Or I shall do it for you. I'm quite capable, you know." I don't know if he meant flying the Chinook or blowing the pilot's brains out. I guessed at both. "Now which is it to be?"

"Sir, if we try taking it up in that –"

Tidyman cocked the Sig-Sauer. "Is that your final answer?"

"Sir!" Lomax called out, but he was frozen. His eyes met mine. The same thought passed between us both: *Fuck.*

I leaned in. Reason wouldn't work. Use a language he'd understand. "Sir, I understand we have to complete the mission. I know. But if we attempt to fly in that, the chopper will go down. If that happens, we die. You die. And most of all, so does Dr Stiles. And the mission will have failed."

A bead of sweat – or it might have been rain – ran down Tidyman's temple. His eyes flicked over to me. I had his attention anyway. "But if we wait out the storm, sir, we can fly out when it's clear. We get Stiles where he needs to go, and the job's done."

After a moment, he nodded, and lowered the Sig. "Alright," he said. "Carry on, Cannock."

Cannock swallowed hard, looked at me, then back to Tidyman. He nodded quickly and went back into the cockpit. His hand hesitated on the door as if to pull it closed. I wasn't surprised if he wanted to, but then maybe that would set Tidyman off again.

I looked at Hassan and the others; they were all staring at us. They quickly looked away again.

"Sergeant?" I turned back to Tidyman. "Alright. If we're staying here, here's what we do. I want you to send the men out and confiscate all firearms."

That weight in the belly. Something dropping away.

This is the moment. The order I cannot obey. I just know it. "Sir?"

"*All* firearms, Sergeant. This is a potentially hostile situation. Leaving them armed is insanity."

I fought to keep my voice level. "How are they supposed to defend themselves if those things attack, sir?"

"That's not our problem, Sergeant. Anyway, as long as we're here, they don't have to worry, do they?"

"We'll be returning them on departure, sir?"

He stared at me and his mouth opened, twisting into an aborted laugh. "Don't be ridiculous, Sergeant. We'll be abandoning them to those things. If they have weapons, you can guarantee they'll fire on us. It only takes one lucky shot."

The man shouting, holding out his hands. The pleas. But I'd had my orders. Hands reaching out. The shot.

He had a point, perhaps. There might be a good reason. Just as with the plans to pull all the key players back and leave the common herd to drown. There might be a good reason, but guess what? There is *always* a good fucking reason. Whoever gets left to die, whoever gets the bombs dropped on them. Someone, somewhere, always has a good reason why that has to be done.

Tidyman was carrying on. "We will confiscate the firearms and we will take them with us."

Watching them walk away down the road, through the plumes of sand blowing across. Carrying their dead. Trying to call them back, screaming it, but they kept going.

"If we do that, sir, these people will have no chance of survival." I tried to keep my voice level.

Tidyman leant close. His breath was sour and rank. "For the last time, Sergeant, *that is not our problem*. We have our priorities. Civilian rescue is not one of them. I will not put the mission in jeopardy over a few minor qualms about a handful of surly yokels."

"You are sentencing these people to death, sir." My voice sounded hard and flat. I said it without thinking. Sometimes something kicks in, some override. Emotion. Something. Makes you helpless. Your actions seem to belong to somebody else. You hear your voice, see your body move, but they belong to someone else. That was happening now.

Tidyman's face was white with rage. "I am giving you an order, Sergeant. Now get out there and take those guns off those people if you have to shoot every single one of them to do it."

"No, sir."

For a blissful second, I thought Tidyman was about to give himself a stroke and save us all the trouble. "What did you say?"

"I said, I will not obey that order. Sir. They're giving us no trouble and we can cross that bridge when we come to it if they do. We can't fly yet and we may face attack from those things. If that happens, they have weapons and they have local knowledge which will come in pretty damned handy."

"I am in command here!"

"And I am in charge on the ground, sir."

"*Were*." His head swivelled. "Corporal Nixon –"

I stepped in close. "The Chinook has the carrying capacity to take most, if not all, of the local residents with us sir, and no hassle. Doing so will not jeopardise the mission in any way, shape or form. And I'll be quite happy to tell them that, not to mention your little plan of leaving them behind to be eaten alive. *Sir.*"

His mouth snapped open. Sound came out. A sort of screeching. He might have been planning for it to turn into words, but there was no time to find out. The gun was out of its holster again, and coming up.

I caught his wrist and twisted. Tidyman screamed, dropped the Sig, and kicked out at me, catching me on the thigh. I blocked a punch, then caught his hand as he tried to scratch my face and nutted him as hard as I could.

Another thing I hadn't done in a while, but it wasn't a bad job. A good Glasgow Kiss is supposed to hurt the other guy more than you. On those grounds, I did pretty well. My forehead smarted a little, but Tidyman's nose crunched under the blow and warm blood splashed my face.

Blood on my face, blood on my hands. Grained into the skin. Still there. Still there now. Impossible to shift. Always carried with me. The blood. The guilt. My guilt.

His head snapped back. His eyes crossed and rolled up and the weight of him sagged. I lowered him to the ground. He let out a weak groan.

Everyone was staring. Hassan, Mleczko and the rest had all frozen over Stiles, and Cannock and Hendry were in the cockpit door. Chas was at the main door of the craft, looking in. He looked down at Tidyman and then up at me.

Shit.

We looked at each other for a few seconds that lasted a lot longer for me. Chas had been there too, that day in the desert, outside the city. He'd seen what I'd seen, been part of what I'd been part of. He understood. But at the same time, he'd stayed in when I'd left. Maybe he was just a tougher nut than I'd been, I don't know. Or maybe it was just that he'd been in too long; had nowhere else to go.

After a moment, he nodded and turned away.

Lomax stood there watching, about as easy to read as the fucking Sphinx. After a moment, though, he nodded too. I breathed out. Then I picked up the P226 and unbuckled Tidyman's gunbelt, strapped it round my own waist. Well, he wasn't going to need it now. Shiny Kit Syndrome again.

Cannock looked from me to Tidyman and back again. "Thanks for before," he finally said.

"Don't mention it. Chas?"

"Sarge?"

"See to the Squadron Leader, if you would. Get Hassan to look him over once he's finished with Stiles. In the meantime, better place him under restraint."

"Copy that. What about the men?"

I wiped my face. It felt cleaner, but traces of blood were still on my hand. "Stand them down for now. We're in the same boat as the locals. Better off pooling resources."

"Makes sense."

I stepped out into the rain and looked across at the farmers as Chas barked out orders. The big man with the shotgun gave a slight smile and nodded. I nodded back. Finally a response. I wondered how much he'd seen.

Chas drifted up. "He's in cuffs for his own good, but he's still conscious and he's coming round. My guess is he'll be breathing hellfire and damnation. Want me to give him a little tap on the head?"

Tempting, but perhaps not. "Maybe later, Corp."

"If you say so."

"I do. Want to see how Hassan's doing with Stiles?"

"Not particularly," sighed Chas. He half-turned away, then turned back. "You know, Sarge, you probably could've disarmed him without smashing his hooter like that."

"What's your point?"

Chas grinned. "Good to have you back, Robbie," he said, and moved off. Time to talk with the natives again.

I made my way over. Most of them had drifted away by now, but the big man was still there.

"Looks like we'll be staying here for a while," I said at last.

He grunted. "I could have told you that, lad."

"Aye, well. We'll not be a bother to you."

"Come in handy, having you lot around. If those bloody things come back."

"Things?"

"Don't piss about, lad. You know what I'm talking about."

I nodded. "We're better off co-operating."

"What I thought. You want to get your lads in out of this?"

"Where did you have in mind?"

He gestured. "Pub's down at the end of Pendle Row. They can still pull a decent pint, even in this. Might be the last chance to get one in for a while."

I nodded. "Just keep 'em away from the optics to be going on with."

"We'll manage, I'm sure." He offered his hand. "Ged Wynn."

"Robbie McTarn."

I headed back to the chopper. "Chas? Move the men into the pub. Just leave whoever we need to keep watch on this." I gestured to the Chinook.

"You mean Tidyman."

"I mean both." I climbed aboard. Stiles was still out. Tidyman too. "Thought he was waking up again."

"Had a bit of a dizzy spell," said Chas. One thing about Chas Nixon, he could keep his face admirably blank if he wanted.

"That'll give us some peace." I pushed through into the cockpit. "Sir?"

Cannock and Hendry looked up. "Either of you know where it is we're supposed to be going?"

Cannock shook his head. "Not exactly."

"Not *exactly*?"

Hendry chipped in. "It's in the Cotswolds somewhere, Sergeant. That's all we were told. The only one with the exact location is Squadron Leader Tidyman."

I took a deep breath. "Please tell me we have a contact frequency."

"Yes. And a call sign for them. Windhoven. Twice a day – oh-nine-hundred and twenty-one-hundred."

And we were nowhere near either. Fuck.

"I suggest we get on the radio, and see if we can raise anyone else – army base, airfield, anything."

"Good thinking."

"Aye. Parkes!"

"Sir." Parkes showed her face at the doorway. She looked terrified.

"Work with the pilots. See if you can raise anyone who can point us in the right direction." I looked over at Cannock. "Do you want to see if you can get anything helpful out of Tidyman when he's a bit more awake?"

Cannock nodded. "Will do."

"Sergeant?"

Lomax. "Aye?"

"We'll need to secure the chopper. I mean *physically* secure it, in this storm. There's some tarps and guyropes in back. Am I okay borrowing a few of yours?"

"I'll see to it."

"Thanks."

I clapped Chas on the shoulder and we stepped down. Ged Wynn was still standing by the drystone as we approached, the broken shotgun over one arm.

"Haul three of the lads in to help Lomax. Get the chopper secured and then all we've got to do is sit tight 'til the storm clears."

"What about Tidyman?"

"Think the aircrew'll back me up. Frankly, Chas, as long as we're not leaving these poor sods completely fucking helpless I'll be happy facing the music. Worst comes to the worst, you just followed my orders."

He grinned. "Might be a plan securing a perimeter out here."

"Could be right. But we're not near a major population centre. Bit of luck, all we need to do is sit out the storm."

"Ged! *Ged!*"

Someone was running up the footpath.

I felt my hands moving of their own accord to slip the SA80 from behind my back, closing round the barrel and pistol grip. My thumb was on the safety catch.

Ged ran towards the newcomer, catching him as he almost fell. We reached them a few seconds later.

"Billy!" Ged shook the lad by the shoulders. "What's up?"

The lad was about nineteen, at a guess, with a round pallid face. He looked from face to face, like a scared kid half his age. "They're coming," he said. His voice sounded thick, slurred, as if something was wrong with his mouth. "They're fucking coming."

"You were saying, Sarge?" muttered Chas.

"Chas?"

"Yes, Sarge?"

"Shut up."

"Yes, Sarge."

CHAPTER THIRTEEN

CROUCHED IN THE doorway of the Tea Rooms, halfway down Pendle Row with Ged and Chas, dozens of the nightmares massing already at the Y-junction at the bottom of the road, all facing our way. Slack, empty faces; glowing eyes. All I saw at first. But looking closer, the details sprang out – clothes, hairstyles. Men, women, and – *aw, Christ* – children. Some as young as five. A woman held a baby to her breast, its arm waving. It couldn't be alive. It couldn't be.

If it didn't have teeth, maybe I wouldn't have to shoot it.

The child kneeling in the dust. Baba. Baba.

Ged stared past me at them, white lips pressed together, breathing deep, eyes wide and bright. Billy was across the road behind a parked car, rocking slightly, humming faintly. Pale. His lips twitched. Poor bastard looked ready to piss his pants. What was his mental age? Eleven, twelve? If that, from what I'd seen of him; he'd lolloped back down to Pendle Row with us like a kid off to play soldiers. Retarded or not, though, they'd given him a 12-bore over-and-under shotgun. Please God, they'd taught him to use the damn thing properly.

Up ahead, a stocky, short-haired woman in her forties knelt behind a 4x4, aiming a deer rifle at the nightmares.

"Some of them came out before." Ged's voice wasn't completely steady.

"Yeah?"

"Aye. 'Bout an hour or so before you got here."

The nightmares stood, watching us. The rest of the locals from the meadow were with us, in doorways or behind walls or parked vehicles. Everyone else was scrambling for higher ground.

"Chas!"

"Sarge?"

"Get Joyce and Mleczko down here." I looked around. There was high ground each side of Pendle Row, one to our right, behind the farm opposite the Tea Rooms to our left, the other near the junction with Barley Road. I pointed there first. "I want Mason up there with the Minimi, Andrews and Levene up there." Behind the farm. "You and Akinbode get the blooper round the other side of the Hill just in case."

"Copy that."

"Get as high up as you can. They might come from more than one side. Keep the rest of the lads on standby with the other Dinky. Copy?"

"Copy."

"And Chas? Headshots only, single rounds or short bursts. No wasting ammo."

"Got it."

Water sluiced over my boots. The stream running down from the Hill had overflowed. My feet were cold.

"Been pissing down all week." I looked at Ged. His breath puffed out white as he spoke. "Just thought it were more of the same. Flood warnings on telly. We rounded the sheep up. Stayed in. Didn't want to get caught out in this.

"Then telly went off-air. Then the radio. Then the electricity went. Nowt we could do but wait it out. Then..." He pointed down at the Row. "We just saw it pouring into the valley. Heard folk screaming, but there was nowt we could do. What's been bloody happening out there?"

I told him. Classified, of course, but I was past caring.

"Dear Christ." He shook his head. "We knew it was bad, but... so it's everywhere?"

"'Fraid so."

"Bugger." He nodded down the street. "Should've guessed when those things bloody turned up. There were only a dozen or so that first time. Shot a couple. Rest just fell back."

I nodded. Retreat and regroup, then attack again. "Looks like they've brought friends this time."

Ged gripped his shotgun. "Hard to tell, state they're in now, but... that one there – think that's a bloke called Hargrave. Runs a farm about half a mile down the road. And that one... looks like..."

He stopped. I decided not to push it. At least I wasn't likely to meet anyone I knew. Although I wouldn't put it past Dad to swim down just to take a chunk out of me. Vindictive old bastard.

The young woman holding the baby might have been pretty once. She had dark blonde hair, bedraggled and rat-tailed. Her eyes were clouded and glowing green. Something had bitten a chunk out of her face. The baby was in a romper suit, a small hand beating the air.

I pulled back the bolt on the SA80.

Beside her stood a tall man, long hair hanging limp and wet. Goatee beard, pasty skin; he would have looked satanic even alive, with or without the Slayer T-shirt under his open cardigan. If you wanted a poster boy for the carnivorous walking dead, there it was.

Behind them was another man, taller still, at least six-three and built to match. Another long-hair. Thick full beard. Looked like a Viking. They seemed to be sticking together. Maybe they'd been friends.

Don't focus on any of them like that. Don't see the people they used to be. See the target. The enemy. The monster.

For once, at least, there was no thought at the back of my mind about the enemy being some mother's son.

It didn't help.

Levene and Andrews were in position. Alf ran past, down one of the little yards branching off the Row, hopping the fence at the end and scrambling for the top.

"Alright, everybody. Don't panic. Remember you need a headshot."

"Sarge." Mleczko didn't look like a joker any more. His face was hard and tight.

I spoke into my personal communicator. "Levene, Andrews, make sure none of them get past you, and keep them out of the buildings."

"Copy, Sarge."

"Alf – what's Barley Road looking like?"

"Chocka, Sarge."

"Alright. They start moving, aim for the head. Sweep across, try and whittle them down before they get here."

"Copy that."

I turned to Ged. "If I were you, I'd get behind us. We've got more range. Your shotguns'll be handier if they get in close."

Ged shrugged. "You want to put yourself between them and us, you're more than bloody welcome."

I moved towards the riflewoman. "You want to move back too?"

She glanced at me. A wide, impassive face; a small gold ring in each ear. "Not particularly." She turned back to watch the nightmares.

"This is gonna kick off any minute, hen."

"Why do you think I'm here? And don't call me hen."

"Fair enough. Can you can shoot straight?"

"Just watch me."

I studied the back of her cropped head. "Were you in the army?"

"No. Why?"

"Should've been."

She glanced back, grinned.

"Sarge!" Joyce. "They're moving!"

I shouldered my rifle. "Pick a target, lads. Fire on my mark, not before."

They lurched drunkenly along Pendle Row, dressed in a sodden array of coats and colours. Farmers in their Barbour jackets. Hikers in boots and cagoules, some still wearing backpacks. Caught out on the fells, trapped in their cars, up to tour the Witch country.

I sighted on the blonde girl. I didn't want her to get closer. I might see the child properly.

Her eyes glowed. I was looking right into them. That strange glow. It was fascinating. You could look at them all day long, somehow, wondering how they worked.

Keep staring at them right up until –

"Pick your targets and... fire for effect!" I yelled, and pulled the trigger.

Even when you think you're a hardened bastard, however many times you've killed, some deaths stay with you, and always will.

The rifle butt driving back into my shoulder. The bolt snapping backwards. Smoke darting from muzzle and breech, brass cartridge cases jumping out and to the side. A perfect three-round burst.

The woman's head snapping backwards as a shot took her through the left eye, rat-tailed hair flying wild as the bullet exited the back of the head, tearing the ear loose to dangle from a skin flap.

She dropped forward and lay still. I let out the breath I'd been holding and snapped back into the real world.

The noise crashed in on me first, gunfire erupting left and right. I'd almost forgotten just how fucking *loud* a gunshot is. Falling shellcases tinkled on the wet ground, hissing as they hit the water. Eight nightmares down. A couple staggered – hit in the neck or scalp – but kept coming.

I aimed for the satanic-looking one.

And then the nightmares *charged*. A sudden scuttling burst of motion, jerky but fast, like a bunch of horrible wind-up toys.

"Fuck!"

Focus, Robbie.

Satan-boy was weaving. Not intentionally – at least I didn't think so – just the convulsive, flailing way they moved. I fired and missed, catching the Viking in the shoulder. Didn't slow him for a second.

I fired at Satan-boy again, but he was almost on top of me. A bullet tore off an ear, but he kept coming.

I jumped back, fired again. This one hit him in the face. The Viking knocked him aside as he fell, lunging for my throat.

I got the rifle up to block him and we went down together. I shoved the barrel crossways into his mouth. His teeth gnashed at it, eyes blazing inches from my face.

"Shiiiit!"

The chattering of an automatic weapon.

"Control your fire!" I roared out. A villager ran in to help, but one of the nightmares leapt on him. He staggered, screaming, and two, three more fell upon him. Blood sprayed up.

The Viking hissed and snarled round the metal of the gun, pushing me down. Beyond him, more nightmares were lurching forward. But a heap of them were on the ground too.

A gun butt smashed in to the side of the nightmare's head. It juddered and collapsed as Alf Mason stood over me, put the Minimi to his shoulder and fired another automatic burst, sweeping left to right at head height. Almost the whole front row of nightmares went down, and most of the ones behind. Behind us, another volley of gunfire rang out. Two more nightmares, nearly on top of me now, jerked and dropped.

I rolled the dead nightmare off me; Alf helping me up. "You okay, Robbie?"

"Thought I told you to get the bastards on the road."

"They've stopped coming out of the water. You seemed to need the back-up more."

"Alf!" Another nightmare seized his arm and sank its teeth in. Alf bellowed. I shot it through the top of the head.

Four of them were still snarling and tearing at the fallen villager. He wasn't screaming anymore. The woman ran forward, shot one in the head, swung the rifle to crush another's skull, but the third seized the weapon and grappled for it. Then Mleczko was there, Billy stumbling in his wake, and blew its brains across the nearest wall. The fourth nightmare lunged towards him, and he swung back and shot it. Billy fired first one barrel, then another, flinching from the fire and smoke; another nightmare fell. Then he was falling back with Mleczko and the woman.

Maybe twenty nightmares remained, staring at us with those glowing eyes. I put the rifle to my shoulder and aimed.

Then one by one, they turned and started walking away. One by one, they walked back down Barley Road towards the deep water.

Alf had slumped to his knees, cursing and groaning. I made for the fallen villager. Blood splashed out around him, steaming. Chunks of flesh and organs lay in it. I walked on, pleading to the God I didn't believe in that the poor bastard *was* dead. He was. One prayer answered today.

Something was wriggling out from under the blonde woman's corpse.

Something small, wearing a romper suit. It hissed. The small cowled head turned. I glimpsed a tiny, snarling face, two empty sockets blazing with green light.

Oh, Jesus, no.

A thundery, rolling *boom* and its head exploded. The rest of the body, torn and mangled by the shot, twitched and was still.

Ged pumped the shotgun slide. The cartridge case clattered on the ground. His hands shook. He dragged a sleeve across his eyes, then turned away without a word.

Alf's face was grey. Mleczko wrapped a field dressing round the wounded arm. "Get him to Hassan," I said.

Billy stood staring down at them. "D'you want any help?"

"Er, yeah." Mleczko took Alf's bad arm. "Giz a hand here, yeah?"

"Yeah. Yeah." Billy was nodding as he looped the other arm about his shoulders. "Upsi-daisy!" He grinned.

The woman clapped Mleczko's shoulder. "Cheers for before."

"No worries." Mleczko and Billy marched Alf off, almost dragging him.

Past them, Ged was trudging up the Row, head down. "Is he okay?" I asked the woman.

She looked savage. "What do you think?"

Ask a stupid question.

She let out a long breath, closed her eyes, pointed at the dead girl. "See that?"

"Yeah."

"That was his daughter. Clare, her name was. Nice kid."

I looked at the bloodied rag doll beside her. "Was that..?"

"Yeah."

"Fuck."

"He'll be okay." I looked at her. "Well, not okay. But he'll cope."

"What I thought."

She cleaned her rifle butt on Satan-boy's T-shirt, then offered a hand. "Jo."

"Robert. Thanks for your help. You did a good job."

She half-grinned. "Cheers mate. You weren't so bad yourself."

She offered me a cigarette, lit her own, leant back against the 4x4.

INSIDE THE CHINOOK, Stiles lay on a blanket with another pulled over him. Tidyman likewise, only cuffed. Hassan had splinted his nose and secured it with a bandage across the face. Sadly he was conscious now.

"What happened?" he demanded. I ignored him. "Sergeant?"

Hassan unwound the dressing from Alf's arm. Electric lamps inside the helicopter shed a cold, antiseptic glow. "Shit. That's a mess."

Hassan started cleaning the wound. Alf bellowed. "Fucking twat!"

"Sounds more like it," I said, and managed a grin. But Alf was crying with pain. Shit.

"I'll give him a shot." Hassan swabbed Alf's forearm and jabbed a morphine ampoule in. Alf grunted, closed his eyes.

Hassan inspected the damage. "There's a whole chunk missing. Best I can do is pack the wound. What happened?"

"What do you fucking think? One of those bloody things took a bite out of him."

"He was bitten?" I looked round. Tidyman was sitting up, staring at me. He had a brace of beautiful black eyes too, I noticed. A Glasgow kiss can do that. "Sergeant, you have to listen to me. Was he bitten?"

"Yes. Okay? He was bitten. *Sir.*"

"You have to kill him."

"You fucking what?" I scrambled over, shoved Tidyman up against the bulkhead. "What did you fucking say, you arsehole?"

"You've got to kill him!" Tidyman screamed it, all composure gone. "You don't understand. You have to kill him."

Focus, Robbie. Get control. Breathe in, count to four; breathe out, count to four. "Why?"

"The bite. It's poisonous. Everyone bitten by those things dies. Every one of them. There's no cure. Antibiotics won't stop it. Nothing will. And when they die, they come back as one of them."

"Fuck off."

"It's true. Why should I lie about it?"

Good point. "Then why didn't you tell us?"

"There wasn't time."

"Lying bastard."

Tidyman tried to wriggle away from me. "It wasn't my choice. It was decided that if the men knew, they'd be less likely to get the job done."

"You fuckers. You fucking fuckers."

I let him go and turned away.

"You've got to kill him, Sergeant. It's the most merciful thing you can do."

Alf was out for the count, by the look. Thank heaven for small fucking mercies.

"Flying Officer Cannock?"

The pilot didn't answer.

"Cannock?" Tidyman demanded again.

"Sir?"

"Can we take off yet?"

Cannock looked at me.

"Flying Officer Cannock? Why are you looking at that man? He is not an officer in Her Majesty's Royal Air Force. I am. I am your *commanding* officer. Answer my question. Can we take off?"

Cannock cleared his throat. "Not yet, sir. We've secured the Chinook against the weather, but we'll have to wait out the storm."

Tidyman's face worked, but finally he got himself back under control. "Alright, Flying Officer. But I expect to be told the moment we're able to fly. I don't intend to wait here any longer than I have to."

Prick.

"And in the meantime, you can let me out of these cuffs." He held his hands out. "Immediately."

Cannock looked over at me.

"Cannock!" It was a scream. A fleck of spittle hit my face. "Stop looking at that man! He has no authority here! I am your commanding officer and *you will let me out of these cuffs immediately!*"

Cannock didn't move.

"Flying Officer Cannock!"

I moved towards Tidyman. He shrank back. "Sir, I suggest you calm down and be quiet. You're staying as you are."

Tidyman was trying to stay calm. "Alright, Sergeant. Now, I accept you had to do what you did before. I overreacted. But I'm perfectly alright now. So please let me go."

I shook my head. His face whitened with fury. "We have to get out of here. That man is vital."

"Stiles? Why? What is it he knows?"

Tidyman compressed his lips and gave no answer.

"I'll make a deal with you, sir. You tell me why Stiles is so important and I'll consider undoing the cuffs."

He spoke through his teeth. "It's classified."

"So they didn't tell you either. Need to know only, right?"

"Sergeant McTarn. I am giving you a direct order."

"Tell you what," I said. "Give me the location of the Cotswolds base and we'll see."

He blinked at me – he almost looked surprised – then smiled. "I don't think so, Sergeant."

"What about this all-important mission of yours, sir?"

"I don't trust you to carry it out, McTarn. Anymore than I do to keep your word and let me go. No," he leant back, "I have something to bargain with here, don't I?" An odd smile twisted one corner of his mouth. "We'll see who cracks first."

I turned back to Hassan. "Do what you can, okay?"

He nodded.

"What shape's Stiles in?" I asked. I could almost feel Tidyman's ears pricking up.

"He'll be okay," Hassan said. "My guess would be he decided to kill himself – perhaps because of all this – but had to get drunk to do it." He smiled. "So drunk he passed out before he could cut anything vital."

I had to laugh. "Well, thank fuck for that. It'd put the bloody tin lid on it if we'd come all this way for nothing."

I LEFT HASSAN at the helicopter with Hendry and Tidyman. And Alf. I was trying not to think about what Tidyman had said. I didn't want to believe it.

I stationed Parfitt on Alf's former position with the other Minimi, kept Levene where he was and moved Andrews to an upstairs room at the Pendle Inn. Guard and lookout duty would rotate hourly. I posted Joyce and Akinbode on top of the Hill.

We moved the booze out of the Inn to one of the nearby farmhouses. It was a large place and empty, so it would serve as a billet, meeting place, and if necessary an informal boozer. The Landrovers were stationed outside, ready to be mobilised at a moment's notice. Chas had put the one with the grenade launcher to good use earlier – the nightmares had been coming out of the water on the far side of the Hill towards Clitheroe, but a quick fusillade from the Mk19 had put them to flight.

I allowed myself a small tipple, the Inn had had some decent single malt in. Isle of Jura; not bad at all, although for me it's really got to be one of the Islay malts like Laphroaig or Lagavulin, but I wasn't going to complain. There wasn't much chance of me tasting a good whisky in the future. I tried to remember how far above sea level the Inner Hebrides were.

Besides, the spirits might be a lot more useful for other purposes – Molotov cocktails, not to mention for a steriliser if Hassan needed it.

The rest of the section congregated in the front room, along with a few of the villagers. Lomax leant against the wall and sipped a Coke, surveying the proceedings with a fine disdain. Mleczko perched on the arm of the sofa, with Billy sat on the floor beside him, gazing up with what looked suspiciously like hero worship in his eyes. Jo sat on the sofa next to Chas. They were chattering away nineteen to the dozen; he said something and she not only laughed, but reached out and ruffled his hair. And Chas Nixon – as the God I don't believe in is my judge – actually fucking *blushed*. Now I *knew* it was the end of the world.

"Lads!" Heads turned. "Just wanted to say – well, I think we can safely say no-one else has *ever* had to deal with anything quite like we have today." That got a few grim chuckles. "You all did bloody well. I'm proud of you." The words felt false, like any of this still mattered. "One beer apiece. Everyone takes a turn at watch tonight." Groans. "Corp?" I gestured towards the kitchen. Chas nodded and got up. "Parkes, you too."

"Sorry, Corp," I murmured as we went. "Hate to break up the romance."

"Piss off, Jock."

Ged, Cannock and Hendry were waiting in the kitchen. I took a sip of the Jura, resisting the temptation to gulp it down. Outside the wind howled, dashing rain against the windows.

"Situation's this," I said. "For the time being we're stuck here. Big question is where we go when the storm clears."

Ged was watching me closely. So was Chas.

"According to Tidyman, there's a secure location we're supposed to take Stiles to. Problem is, only he knows where this fabulous place is, and he won't talk unless I let him go. Which I don't fancy."

"He wants to get out of here, doesn't he?" snorted Chas.

I nodded. "Thinks he can wait us out. Meantime, we've a contact frequency for them, and designated times to try them." I turned to Cannock again. "Just how much fuel do we have for the Chinook?"

"Enough to get to the Cotswolds, certainly; even enough to spend some time searching for the base. But from what I understand, Windhoven is an underground bunker, and, obviously, hidden from plain sight. We could search forever and not find it."

I nodded. "So unless we can scavenge further fuel supplies, we've got one shot."

"You got something in mind, Rob?" Chas.

"I have. For the minute, we're going nowhere anyway. We can't fly in this, and we don't know what the national situation is. Parkes?"

The radio-op looked up from a pint of Foster's she didn't look old enough to legally drink. Not that that mattered anymore. "Sarge?"

"Any luck?"

"None, Sarge. But the electrical storm's playing hell with our comms."

"I thought we had top of the line sat-comm equipment."

"We do, Sarge, but it's not much good if you can't connect with the satellite. Again, our best chance will be when it clears."

Pretty much what I'd expected. "So we can't fly, and even if we could, we wouldn't know where to go. On top of that we don't know what Windhoven's status is, or that of the regional control centres. For all we know, those things have overrun them all. So 'til we know better, we're on our own." I looked over at Ged. "While we're here, we can help organise the defence of the village, search for other groups of survivors. Then, when we do fly out, you're not all left completely in the lurch."

Ged nodded. His face was expressionless, and he had a large brandy – triple or quadruple at the least – on the go. Was making pretty good headway with it, too. I didn't think he'd said a word since the fight on Pendle Row.

"If anyone's got any better ideas, let's hear them."

No-one did.

"Alright. Light 'em if you've got them. Unless anyone has any objection?"

Ged shrugged, the faint memory of a smile curving his lips. "Never liked that fucking smoking ban anyway."

CANNOCK WENT TO mind the chopper around twenty-one hundred, taking Parkes with him, to try Windhoven again.

The storm was still raging. Fresh cracks of thunder rolled in every few seconds. Ged told me there was a local saying that if you could see Pendle Hill it was about to rain, and if you couldn't, it was already raining, but even by local standards it was fucking well pissing it down.

Then the first shots rang out.

"Oh shit."

I snatched up my rifle, pulled back the bolt. My PC crackled. "McTarn."

"Sarge? Joyce. They're coming out of the water, over."

"Shit. Location?"

More shots. "Just looks like a localised attack. Near the two pools."

The pools were just north-east of the Hill, on a wide flat stretch of open ground beneath a wooded slope.

"On our way," I said.

"Don't think there's any need, Sarge." A few last shots, then silence. "Looks like that was the lot."

I sat back down. "You mean you woke me up just for that?"

Muffled laughter.

"Keep us posted, Joyce."

"Will do, Sarge. Out."

I looked at Chas and grinned.

Then more gunshots. From right outside.

I BROKE OUTSIDE, into the pelting rain, Chas at my back. Ged and Mleczko followed, Billy stumbling after.

"Sarge! Sarge!"

Parkes. She ran towards us fast, head down.

"What? What is it?"

"Tidyman, Sarge. Got loose somehow. Knocked Hassan out, maybe killed him. Shot Cannock. And –"

"What?"

"Private Mason, Sarge. He shot him in the head."

"Bastard." I unslung the rifle, passed it to Chas. "That'll be no good where I'm heading." I drew the P226.

"Need any back up?" He asked.

"We start firing rifles at the Chinook, we could fuck our ticket out of here."

"Copy that."

"But we need to keep Tidyman occupied. Get a couple of the lads to the chopper and bang a few off, but for fuck sake aim high."

Chas nodded. "Mleczko?"

"Sarge?"

I thought of how he'd done back on the High Street; a man you'd want with you. "Can you use a pistol?"

"Yeah."

Hendry and Lomax had joined us. "Mind if Mleczko borrows your gun, sir?"

Hendry, face pale, nodded, and handed it over.

"Thank you, sir. Mleczko, you're with me. Priority's keeping the Chinook in one piece. Tidyman's gone apeshit, so if you have to, drop him."

Mleczko nodded. He didn't seem to have a problem with that. If anything, he looked pretty bright-eyed at the prospect. Then again, that could've just been Shiny Kit Syndrome, at getting his hands on the pistol. He handed his rifle to Chas.

"Need another body?" asked Lomax.

"Always handy. You're a good shot?"

"I can hit a barn door."

There was a coughing sound from the Chinook. "Just don't hit anything important. Chas, ready to fire. Mleczko, Lomax, move your arse."

Shots rang out behind us as we ran low across the field. A bullet whined and buzzed past my ear. Too fucking close. Sparks flew from the cockpit canopy.

"You do know," Lomax huffed as we went, "the Chinook's got two Gimpys mounted in there?"

I did, but I'd been doing my best to forget that. Hopefully Tidyman would content himself with Hassan's rifle.

Something lay in the grass outside the helicopter. It was on fire.

The rotors were turning.

Shit.

But thank fuck, the side door was ajar. I ran faster.

Then the door flung wide. Tidyman stood in it. He was holding a SA80. Probably Hassan's.

Oh shit.

The rifle's muzzle spat flame, and I dived. Bullets whined overhead.

I brought up the P226, fired three rounds. Tidyman ducked back.

I got up and ran. Lomax's heavy boots pounded the turf behind me. Tidyman popped back up, fired again. Lomax cried out, and a body hit the ground. The rifle arced towards me, but Mleczko fired first; Tidyman screamed and dropped the rifle on the ground.

I was almost at the chopper now. Tidyman was clutching at the door, trying to drag it closed. I fired at his hand as I ran; the bullet spanged off the door, and he scrambled back inside.

I dived through the door as Tidyman fired a pistol at me from the cockpit. Cannock's, I guessed. Blood had splattered the inside of the cockpit canopy; Cannock himself was slumped forward in his seat.

Tidyman aimed for another shot. I fired twice, a double-tap. More blood splattered outwards across the cockpit canopy. Tidyman fell back across the instrument panel, staring at me, then dropped to his knees and fell forwards.

Alf Mason lay where I'd left him, only with a neat bullet hole behind his right ear and the left eye forced half-out of its socket. Stiles was unmarked, but still unconscious. Hassan was crumpled against one of the bulkheads; alive or dead, I couldn't tell.

The Chinook was rocking. Mleczko scrambled in. "Sarge?"

"I'm fine. Fine. Get Hendry. We need to shut this fucker off."

I went to Tidyman. I put my foot on his Sig-Sauer and slid it away, out of his hand. His head was turned to one side, eyes open and sightless.

Dead, but will he stay that way? Now there's the question.

I checked Cannock. He hadn't been shot; Tidyman had smashed him in the head with the rifle butt. Made no difference in the end – the blow had shattered his skull. I closed his eyes for him.

Then I remembered Hassan. No bullet wounds. Just a lump the size of a chicken's egg behind one ear. I checked the carotid pulse. He'd live.

Stiles too. Still completely dead to the world. Whatever he'd been drinking, I made a mental note to get myself a bottle if the opportunity ever presented itself.

Feet thudded on the grass outside, then clanged on metal. Chas, Mleczko, and Hendry scrambled aboard. Hendry stepped over Tidyman's body and gently moved Cannock's to one side. The coughing roar of the engines died and the rotors quickly wound down.

Lomax sagged against the doorway, clutching his arm. "You okay?" I asked. He was white.

"I've been fucking shot, you Jock dickhead."

He was okay. I inspected the wound. "You're lucky. Just a crease." For the second time that day, I broke out a wound dressing. "Get Hassan to take a look when his brain's unscrambled."

He nodded. Lightning flickered through the cockpit canopy, followed by a roll of thunder.

"Fuck," said Mleczko at last. "What a cunt of a day."

We all stared at him for a moment, and then I began to laugh. It was a wild, hysterical sound. Chas was laughing too, even Parkes. Only Hendry didn't join in; he just looked at us over the bodies of his friend and of his CO, and we fell silent.

"Sorry, sir." I said at last.

He just shook his head and slumped into the vacant seat beside Cannock.

I smelled burning. I remembered what I'd seen outside and suddenly I knew. I leapt outside and stamped on it.

"Fuck. *Fuck!*"

"Sarge?" Mleczko was jumping down, followed by Chas.

"Robbie?" Chas came over. I'd fallen to my knees beside the remnants. "What's up?"

"I'm an idiot," I said. "A total fucking idiot."

"What?"

Despite the rain, only a few charred scraps were left. Paper.

Tidyman's face earlier when I'd asked him about the location. Surprised, as if I should've known. No fucking wonder. "He had this all along. Probably in his pocket. And I didn't even think to look."

Chas clicked. "Oh, *shit!*"

"What?" Mleczko looked from one of us to the other.

"Windhoven's location. Just my guess, but I'd put money on it. It was right under our noses all the time."

A mad part of me was glad of it. Opt out, drop out, fuck them all off and piss on their chips. But that couldn't be allowed, not now. For better or worse, like it or lump it, I was a soldier again. I was back in command.

There was a groan from inside the Chinook. Stiles sat up, rubbing his head.

"Fuck..." he said faintly. "Anyone got an aspirin?"

"Obviously, sir, you're in overall command here now."

Hendry's fingers fidgeted around the glass. I sat with him, Chas and Ged in the farmhouse kitchen.

"Squadron Leader Tidyman put you in control on the ground, Sergeant. Until we're airborne, I see no reason to change that. Quite frankly, I wouldn't know where to start."

"Thank you, sir." I turned to Ged. "We can set up barricades on Pendle Row – slow them down if they come back in any numbers. And all around the island" – because that was what it was now – "as well."

Ged nodded.

"For the time being, I've posted lookouts, and the Landrovers will make regular sweeps of the area. We'll get stuck in tomorrow. We'll need to evacuate the houses on Pendle Row, move the occupants elsewhere, maybe use some of the farmhouses –"

"Make yourself popular," chuckled Ged.

"I can live with that. Pendle Row's the front line. We'll use the Inn as an OP, put one of the Minimis there. Install a permanent lookout on the Hill – that way we can monitor the whole area for signs of attack. We'll need help from your people too – there's a lot of ground to cover. We'll give you fellas some basic training on the SA80s and Minimis."

"You sure that's wise, Sarge?" Chas's eyes flickered to Ged. "No offence, mate."

Ged shrugged.

"We need any defenders able to use any available weapons. We'll keep the Gimpy and the blooper mounted on the Dinkies –"

"You what?"

"Sorry, Ged. The general purpose machine gun and the grenade launcher mounted on the Landrovers. We keep them in reserve at a central location, so if the shit hits the fan, they can go straight in to do some heavy fucking duty back-up. Make sense?"

Ged nodded. After a beat, so did Chas. Hendry sipped his drink.

We talked a bit more, and that was it. Ged rose, nodded and made for the door. Hendry got up to follow, then hesitated. He waited until the door had closed behind the big man, then glanced from me to Chas. "Er – a word, Sergeant?"

"Sir."

"In private?"

Chas shrugged. "I'll be through there." He went through into the front room.

I turned to Hendry. "Sir?"

"Sergeant... I just wanted to say, my report on what's happened here..."

Fuck.

"I'm going to put in it that Squadron Leader Tidyman was killed in action. By the creatures."

"Sir." Something more seemed to be called for. "Thank you."

"I don't know if any of his family will have made it. They all lived in London, you see. His wife, their children, both his parents."

"Christ."

"I know he didn't... handle the situation well, but I served with him, and he was a good man. Better than you saw. He deserves to be remembered... well, you know."

"Sir." It wouldn't be the first time a few white lies'd gone in a report. And if it kept me clear of a court-martial, I wasn't complaining. "Appreciated."

Hendry nodded and went out. Chas came back in. "What'd he want?"

I told him. Chas picked up the whisky bottle, waved it at me.

"Go on, then."

He passed me a glass. "You reckon they'll be back?"

"What do you think?"

He pursed his lips and nodded. "I think they'll be back."

"Aye. Me too." We clinked glasses. "So what do you think?"

"I think we can hold out here a while. 'Til we can get out to Windhoven. Wherever it is."

"And if it's still there."

"That too."

"You don't sound too enthusiastic about it."

"I don't like the idea of leaving the villagers in it."

"Think I do?"

"But you'd do it."

Chas leant forward. "We have a job to do, Robbie. You know that. Like it or not."

"Yeah."

"Look, it's not like... it's not like that time."

Sand blowing across the desert road. The fading echo of the rifle shot.

"No?"

"No. We'll be training them up, maybe even leaving them some kit. They're not gonna be left in the lurch. They'll make out."

"You reckon?"

"Yeah, I do." But he didn't meet my eyes. Then he looked up and grinned. "Did a good job today though, anyway, Jock."

"Sergeant Jock to you, grotb –"

Outside, there was a shout, then a panicked yell, and then a shot.

"Fuck!" I bolted for the door. Behind me, Chas yelled my name, feet thumping on the floor.

I burst outside and nearly cannoned into Hassan. A body lay at his feet, the top of the head gone. It wore combats, although you could barely make them out under the filth.

"The fuck happened here?" I heard Chas yell.

"Just came at me, Corp –"

I flipped the body over. Alf Mason stared back up me with dead, clouded eyes.

We'd buried him in a grave at the far end of the meadow – him, Tidyman and Cannock. But here he was.

The other two had stayed where they'd been put. For them, at least, it was over.

CHAPTER FOURTEEN

THE NEXT AFTERNOON.

Parkes had been trying to raise Windhoven on both the contact and distress frequencies, but got only static in response. The sky was thick with dark cloud. The storm had passed for now, but a couple of times lightning flashed far off in the distance, and a faint crack of thunder would roll in.

Stiles was huddled in a corner of the farmhouse's living room with a microwaved lasagne, a dismembered bread roll, and a can of Special Brew, avoiding eye contact and rocking to and fro. He hadn't spoken, except to request food or alcohol. If I'd expected a fount of wisdom, I'd be disappointed. But if the powers that be had been convinced about him, they'd have a sent a full platoon, maybe a company. More likely some senior brasshat or MOD bod had thought of him at the last minute.

Still, I did my best. "Dr Stiles?"

He took a gulp of beer.

"Doctor, I need to know what's happening. We were sent to fetch you. Please. What is it you know?"

He took another gulp of beer.

I kept trying. After a while he started to hum tunelessly. He wrapped his arms around himself and rocked again. Sweat slicked his forehead.

When I tried to speak, he hummed louder. I gave up. After a few minutes, he stopped, unwrapped his arms, and drained the can. Then he breathed out, looked into my eyes and said: "Can I have another one, please?"

The food situation wasn't so bad. As well as having stocks in the village, we were in farming country, with plenty of sheep, chicken and cows, plus wild rabbits. Most of the animals had survived, so we weren't looking at starvation just yet. And we had provisions of our own.

For now, though, the locals were using up frozen food before it went off. Result – large amounts of stews and casseroles were being knocked together. So at least it'd be a while before the freeze-dried Army rations came into play. I still had nightmares about the shepherd's pie. In the first Gulf War, the Yanks had called their rations MREs. Officially, it stood for 'Meals, Ready to Eat,' but the troops preferred 'Meals Rejected by Ethiopians.'

I decided to climb the Hill and scope out the terrain. Tidyman had had a pair of field glasses, which I'd appropriated (Shiny Kit Syndrome again). Besides, it might be fun.

JESUS FUCKING CHRIST!

If I'd thought I was out of condition before, I knew it beyond doubt after making that ascent. The path up the Hill facing Barley was practically vertical.

The climb took me twenty minutes. By the end of it, my leg muscles were howling and my lungs felt sandblasted. I sat down at the top to enjoy not being in agony for a minute or two, then stood and got out the field glasses.

Visibility wasn't great, with a thick mist rising off the water spreading out in all directions. Fells rose clear of the surface, a scattering of islands. How many were populated? I remembered the folk waving to us as we flew in. Did they have guns? Would that be enough?

If I hadn't already killed Tidyman, I would've by now for not warning us about the bites. Alf might not be dead if we'd known that. Taken precautions. At least we knew now.

Still, now we knew it took more than just dying to turn you into a nightmare. It was the bite; the bite or the water.

God knew *what* in the water. I looked down towards the meadows. In the distance, I could see the nearby reservoir. It should be usable. All the same, I'd given instructions that all drinking water be boiled before use.

But what about the water the animals drank?

Not a productive line of thought.

Still, in a way I was starting to enjoy myself. Other people's problems are always easier to deal with than your own.

I looked across the hilltop, saw someone standing by the thick white stubby plinth of the trig point. I was reaching for my P226 before I realised who it was.

I walked over. "Levene."

"Sarge."

"Anything to report?"

"No, Sarge." Stupid question; if there had been my PC would've been quacking like Daffy Duck.

I handed him the field glasses. "These might come in handy."

"Thanks, Sarge." He looked out towards the village. "Sarge?"

"Yes?"

"Something to report."

"What?" My hand on the gun again.

"There's a boat out there."

"A fucking what?"

"A boat. There, see?"

He passed me the field glasses. I focussed in. There it was. Small. A dinghy. In the waters off Barley Road. Two occupants. Both women. One was rowing hard, wrenching at the oars, her back to me. Trimly built, chestnut hair in a bob-cut. The other lay slumped across the floor of the dinghy, feet propped on the stern. I couldn't see her face. She was very small, slender. A child?

Also, very still.

The dinghy shifted in the swell, turning side-on. The girl's head lay in the other woman's lap. I zoomed in. Her face was grey. There was a crudely-dressed wound on her arm. Then the other woman was turning the dinghy so her back was to me and the girl's face was hidden once more.

I felt something cold move inside me. "Got your radio?"

"Sarge."

"Alert them down in the village."

BY THE TIME I reached Pendle Row, I could hear screaming. As I ran in, gunshots rang out. Fully automatic fire. Parfitt, with the Minimi. Mleczko and Hassan running from the Pendle Inn, Billy in their wake. Andrews and Akinbode ran down the Row – later they told me they hadn't been able to get a clear shot at the girl through the hedgerows along the roadside. I waved them all back.

The dinghy bobbed, abandoned in the water. The woman lay huddled near the top of the road, crying out as bullets ricocheted about her. Behind her, the dead girl thrashed on the tarmac. I yelled up at Parfitt.

"Cease fire! Cease fire! Cease fucking fire!"

I ran in. The dead one was still making sounds. I aimed at her. She stared back, frothing blood, eyes ablaze. She was just a kid. Had been.

One shot. Dead centre in the forehead. Her head snapped back. Her body went still, a last, rattling breath escaping in a sigh.

I remembered the live girl and spun to aim at her. Checked there were no bites. Safetied the gun and helped her up, led her back towards the village.

Not straight away, though; the woman insisted on stopping to look at her friend's body. Never a good plan. Just gives you bad dreams.

Believe me.

WE TOOK HER back to the farmhouse. Hassan checked her over and pronounced her in reasonable health; Jo sorted her out with a change of clothes.

She wove a little as she went, still cold and shivering, and I reached out to steady her. She shrugged me off. "I'm fine. I'm fine. I don't need any help. Which way is the toilet, please?"

She went off fast, not looking back. There was an outbreak of sniggering from Hassan and Parfitt at the bottom of the stairs, who'd wandered in to cop an eyeful, not to mention Billy, who'd wandered in after Mleczko, gawping and giggling. I ignored them and got some stew reheated for her.

Stiles was still rocking in his corner. Now and again he'd grimace, as if at a twinge of pain, or cock his head as if he'd heard something. He was cradling a bottle of gin and taking nips from it. When not doing that, he'd roll another cigarette from the tobacco tin he'd dug out of his filthy jeans.

When she came down, her face was scrubbed clean and her hair tied back with an old shoelace. She mumbled a *thank you* when I handed her the stew. Otherwise she didn't speak.

Parfitt and the others were still eyeing her up. "Shouldn't you be at your posts?" I demanded.

"Sarge," said Mleczko.

"Well shift your bloody arses, then. Now."

The door bumped shut in the wind, Katja looked up. Glanced sideways at me, and smiled for a second. I felt a warm flutter in my chest.

"Try to eat something," I said to her quietly. "Keep your strength up. You've been through a lot."

Her head snapped up. "How the hell do you know what I've been through?"

I noted her accent for the first time. Eastern or Central European. I had to admit, I liked it. Her jaw was clenched, her eyes bright, her hand shaking.

I leant back in my chair. "I think we've all been through a lot, last couple of days."

She glared a moment longer, then nodded. "Of course. I'm sorry." She said it awkwardly, looking away, chin up. I thought of a cat, proud and territorial.

"Forget it. I'm Robbie McTarn." I didn't give my rank. Time was, it'd've been second nature. I stuck out my hand.

She saw it and smiled, maybe despite herself, then shook. Her skin was smooth and soft, but her grip stronger than most women I'd known. "Katja Wencewska."

"That Polish?"

Her eyes narrowed. Shit. Maybe she'd been an illegal before the flooding. "Just asking," I said. "One of ours is called Mleczko. Polish family."

"Ah." She nodded. "It's Polish. I grew up in Romania. A long story."

And clearly not one she planned to tell. Fair enough. It hardly mattered now.

She ate. At first she was forcing herself but before long she was doing it with real hunger. I wasn't surprised. I didn't know how long she'd been rowing for when I'd first seen her, but from the speed and fury she'd been putting into it, it must have taken its toll.

There was only silence in the room, except for her eating and the odd little noises from Stiles's corner. So as she ate, I told her my story. Some of it anyway. I didn't tell her about the desert road. I don't tell anyone about that. But I told her about the redcaps coming to my door, why we were here, and what had happened – Tidyman, the nightmares attacking.

Katja put down her fork and looked over at Stiles. "What is it that he knows?"

"Search me, hen. No-one saw fit to tell us, and he's not talking." I felt anger flickering up in me suddenly. "One of my men is dead, plus one pilot" – I didn't mention Tidyman because I couldn't care less about the sod – "and the whole reason for the operation sits on his arse stuffing his face and getting pissed. Isn't that right, Stiles?"

He flinched. He'd been looking in our direction; now he looked away. "Please don't."

I looked at Katja. "It's not his fault," she said. "I know it's difficult, but he didn't ask you to come."

"Difficult? You don't know the half of it, hen."

"I know more than you might think. My father was a soldier. Special forces, yes?"

I nodded.

"So I know something of it."

"And what about you?"

"What about me?" She met my gaze full-on.

"What happened to you?"

She didn't speak for a few seconds. Then she shrugged and forked more food into her mouth. "I survived," she said. "Just me. That's all."

Stiles had stopped fidgeting. He was looking over at us both. At *her.*

As I turned back to Katja, he spoke.

"They're calling me," he said.

"Who?" I asked. He didn't react. He was staring at Katja.

She glanced at me, then back at him.

"Who?" she asked.

"The voices. The souls. All the dead."

He wouldn't say anymore than that. He just stared at her, and her back at him. I don't know what he saw there – more than just a pretty woman, I'm sure of that – or what she saw in him. But after a moment, she went to sit with him. Waiting for him to say more.

Chas slipped in, sat beside me. "All quiet," he murmured.

"Good."

He saw Katja and Stiles. "What's this, then?"

"Fucked if I know."

"Not bad-looking, is she?"

"Shut up, Nixon."

"Robbie?"

I looked at him.

"Don't go falling in love now, for Pete's sake. You're bad enough without getting blue balls."

"Piss off. What about you and Jo?"

He reddened coughed. I stared. "Don't take the piss, Robbie, eh? She's a nice girl."

I shook my head and looked back at Katja and Stiles. I could see Stiles's lips moving, but I couldn't make out what he said, and afterwards, Katja wouldn't tell.

CHAPTER FIFTEEN

"I want to help."

Katja: hands on hips, hair cropped raggedly short, head cocked back to look me in the eye.

Joyce, Parfitt and Akinbode climbing aboard the Chinook. Hendry at the controls, Lomax guarding the entrances like fucking Cerberus. The rest were staying to guard the village.

"If you want to help, see if you can get anything more out of Stiles."

Folding her arms; looking pissed off. "Stiles talks when he wants to."

"But he's more likely to want to talk to you than anyone else."

A shrug. "I can do more than that."

"How?"

Nodding towards the Chinook. "Let me come with you."

"What for?"

"You need everyone you can get."

"These men are professional soldiers."

"So was my father. And he taught me a lot."

I still didn't know exactly what she'd gone through, but it couldn't have been easy. I remembered her eyes when I'd first seen her, after the initial terror. They'd been dark and staring somewhere far past me.

She'd seen Hell, or something damned close to it, and she'd survived. She'd kept her head.

"Can you handle an automatic weapon?" I asked her.

"Give me a rifle and I'll show you."

I looked into her eyes; she didn't flinch.

Some things break under pressure. Others grow stronger.

"Okay."

OUR THIRD DAY at Pendle.

We'd hooked up with the occupants of the other hamlets immediately around the Hill; Newchurch-in-Pendle, Sabden, Spen Brook. No further attacks. Nothing on the radio.

Too fucking quiet for safety. We were soldiers. Needed to be doing something.

Needed to see what was out there.

THE ROTORS CHOPPING at the air. The sound beating through the hull. The sky outside still dark. Rain peppering the cockpit canopy. Least they'd managed to scrub Cannock and Tidyman's brains off it.

Katja sat, rifle across her lap, in a spare army jacket two sizes too big. It, and the Browning pistol in her belt, had still been in the dinghy. The pistol had been Marta's – I'd got her friend's name from her, if nothing else. The rifle was an old US Army M-14, firing 7.62mm NATO rounds. They packed a punch. The 5.56mm rounds in our SA80s wouldn't even slow a nightmare down unless it was a headshot, but a 7.62 would knock it flat, dead or not.

The men huddled in their seats, smirking. Probably thought I was cunt-struck. But the smirking stopped if she looked their way. There was nothing comic about her, outsize jacket or no. Her face was hard, expressionless, her jaw set.

We touched down on the fell we'd passed on our first approach, a broad shoulder of grass and rock. The men de-bussed, surrounding the chopper. Katja went with them and fell into place, gun held ready.

"Akinbode, stay with the chopper. You and Lomax man the guns."

"Sarge."

"Rest of you, with me."

The farmhouse was near the water's edge. No-one in. The only other life visible on the fell were a dozen or so sheep, cropping the grass.

The rotors wound down and fell silent. A thin wind keened across the fells and the sea. I heard the faint lap and suck of waves on shore. A sea sound. It didn't belong here.

A sea.

Sometimes it takes that one final detail to bring it home. To make it real. It was all gone. Waterstone's and Starbucks, Tesco's and the Co-Op, Boots the chemist, multiplex cinemas, McDonalds, Burger King, KFC, Pizza Hut. All the totems and trademarks of the world we'd lived in. All gone.

Glasgow. The street I'd grown up in. The house I was born in. Gone.

London, Manchester, Birmingham, Paris, Berlin, New York, Washington, Pretoria, Harare, Brisbane, Melbourne...

Gone.

This huge sea, in place of them all.

Focus.

There are different kinds of silence. The kind that's all charged up with something about to happen. The hush before something breaks.

Or the kind that says nobody's home. When you walk into the married quarters and you know she's gone. There's more space in the house suddenly.

This was the second kind of silence.

A sheep bleated. An ordinary countryside sound. Like the lapping of the water, it made the loss more real.

It would be so easy just to stand here and try taking in the scale of it. The people we knew who'd be dead by now. That we *couldn't* believe might have survived, because the one thing worse than certain death was false hope.

So easy.

Mustn't let it happen.

"Parfitt?"

"Sarge?"

"Round up the sheep."

"Sarge?" He looked like I'd just told him to piss out his ear.

"Round them up. We could use the meat."

"Fucksake."

"What was that?"

"Yes, Sarge."

I grinned as he scooted off. Lomax would probably say a damn sight worse when we started herding old McDonald's farm aboard the Chinook.

"What if there's still someone here?" whispered Katja.

"That's the big question, isn't it? Joyce?"

"Sarge."

"Check round the back." Joyce nodded and moved off. I turned to Katja.

"Alright, hen. I'm going in."

She covered me as I went down the slope. The door had been smashed in. Most of the windows were gone as well.

Joyce moved round from the other side of the building, keeping out of Katja's line of fire. "Clear, Sarge."

"Okay." I motioned to Katja and she followed us in.

Chairs knocked over. An old child's Peter Rabbit mug – probably the mum's or dad's, handed down – on the table. A congealed, half-eaten plateful of bangers and mash with flies crawling listlessly on it. Potted herbs on the windowsill. A Welsh dresser surrounded by broken crockery.

Spent shotgun shells on the floor. Buckshot spatters on the walls.

Three bodies, the waxy remains of their eyeballs crusted on their cheeks below the empty sockets. Nightmares. They'd each been blasted in the head.

Another nightmare lay in the hallway by the smashed front door, head gone above the eyebrows. Arcs of blood on the walls. Arterial spray.

When had it happened? During the storm, maybe, when the nightmares had attacked Barley. I hoped so. Because then we couldn't have saved them. It wouldn't be my fault. No need to feel guilty.

Only, I did.

The bodies in the sand, staining it with blood. The women and children, carrying the dead away. The girl looking back.

I shook my head. Focus, you prick.

The dining room. Untouched. The battle had never spread there. The table was set for some special occasion that'd never arrived. It could come and pass unmarked now, with no-one to observe it or even know what it was.

The living room.

Katja went in first.

There were bloodstains on the living room carpet. Chunks of shrivelled flesh. A couple of severed fingers. A hole blasted in the ceiling. Shotgun.

I found the shotgun itself in the corner, broken open. A shell loaded into one barrel, the other empty. An unfired shell on the carpet. Like a painting – the composition tells the whole story. I picked it up, pocketed the shells.

Katja was staring at a photograph she'd found. When she saw me looking, she put it face down on the mantelpiece and moved away. I lifted the picture; a husband and wife, three kids, the youngest not much more than a toddler.

We checked upstairs and in the cellar. There was no-one else, dead, alive or anywhere in between. There was blood in one of the bedrooms. A child's nursery. Arterial spray on walls and ceiling.

Messy eaters.

There were cured hams and flitches of bacon stored in the pantry. Cans. Jars. Some fresh. Cabbages and lettuces. Boxes of shotgun shells. We took them all.

Parfitt had herded the sheep onto the Chinook. Lomax didn't look happy about it. Neither did Parfitt. Or the sheep, come to that. When not thrashing or nipping, the sheep retaliated by shitting everywhere.

Akinbode seemed to think it was hilarious. If looks could have killed, the one on Parfitt's face would have finished him on the spot. Meantime I told them to help Joyce load the provisions.

Katja and I picked up the last load. We were about ten yards up from the farmhouse when Akinbode pointed down the slope and shouted.

They stood in the shallows below the farmhouse. It lapped around the knees of the two adults and the waists of the two older children. The toddler clung to the mother. They stared up at us with their slack, empty faces and glowing eyes, but they didn't move.

"Shit!" I dropped the cans and fumbled for the rifle. Katja was already on one knee, the M-14 shouldered.

I don't know why we didn't fire straight off. But we didn't. The father turned his head to stare at the farmhouse; he cocked it to one side, as if trying to recognise it. The children stayed close to their mother, who clung to the toddler. All of them staring up at us.

"They're all around us, Sarge," Akinbode shouted. I managed to look away from the family. Heads broke the surface here and there. Not many. After the other day, there couldn't be that many left in the area. But they were in the water around us, watching.

"Fall back to the Chinook," I shouted, "and fast."

I walked backwards. They didn't move. Maybe they could tell they were outgunned. There weren't enough of them to rush us.

Not yet.

The doors slammed. The rotors churned. The chopper lifted.

I peered out of the window. The family stood where they'd first appeared, watching us go – except for the father, who still stared towards what had been his home.

Katja was looking down at them too. I touched her arm and she whipped around.

"You did good back there," I said.

"I know," she said.

But a small, crooked smile touched her lips.

BACK AT THE farmhouse, we opened a few tins in the front room. Stiles was in his usual corner with another bottle of gin. His eyes brightened when he saw Katja. She went over and sat beside him.

The rest of us sat on the far side of the room, drinking in silence. It was Parfitt, in the end, who said it.

"You reckon they remember anything, Sarge?"

"What?"

"Those fucking things."

"Why should they?" Akinbode's fingers brushed the small cross at his throat. "They are dead. They are just... corpses. Things made to walk around. What could they remember?"

"The fuck should I know?" There was an edge in Parfitt's voice; Stiles and Katja both looked up. He glanced at them, took a deep breath, calmed himself down. "I mean... come on, Aki, you saw them too. You and all, Sarge. It was like they knew the place. Like they remembered it'd been –"

"Shut up," said Akinbode. "Just shut up, Mark."

But I knew he had a point. We all did, even Akinbode; he just didn't want to accept it.

When they were just nightmares it was easy enough. They were monsters. They weren't human. You pointed a gun and you shot and their brains flew out and they were dead. Like they should've been to begin with.

But the way they'd stood in the shallows. The way the father had looked up at his old house. The way the dead mother held her dead baby...

I'd felt fear, yes. But something else. Almost... pity.

"Doesn't matter," I said. "Doesn't change anything. We've seen what –"

"They don't remember," said Stiles.

We all turned around and looked at him. Even Katja was staring at him. I looked at his drawn, prematurely aged face, the bleary, reddened eyes.

"They don't remember," he said, "but the Deep Brain does."

"What the fuck is the Deep Brain?" I asked.

His face tightened in pain, and he looked down.

"Stiles? Stiles, what's the Deep Brain?"

He didn't answer. Katja laid a hand on his arm, looked up at me and shook her head. She leaned in closer to him and spoke softly, but his head kept shaking, although after a while I heard murmuring too. I shrugged and turned back to my beer.

We finished our drinks and the others went off, they all had work to do. So did I, but fuck that for now.

Stiles had slumped over in the corner. Katja looked up. "Passed out. Can you help me get him back?"

"He was lucky to survive," she said back at the caravan, looking down at him sprawled on the filthy divan. "He was in agony, after the accident. Still is. Not as bad, but he's still in constant pain."

Just for a second or two, the hard mask slipped, and I saw – something. Sorrow, perhaps.

"Poor bastard. But it's not much use to us. No fucking relevance at all that I can see."

Katja put her finger to her lips. "I think there *is* a link," she said outside. "But I don't know what. I also think he wants to tell us. Or me, at least."

"Did he say anything useful?"

She shook her head again. "Odd words and phrases. The Deep Brain, the voices, the souls. They're calling him. Over and over again."

"Word salads."

She gave a short laugh. "That's a good phrase. I like it. Otherwise, he talks about his childhood, his adolescence, his first girlfriend, university, going diving. He wants to make sense. But he can't. It's like..."

"What?" We started walking back down, close, almost touching. Not a date, exactly. But a man could always hope.

"He's afraid."

"He can join the fucking club."

"Do you have to swear so much, Robert?"

I was tempted to say *aw, fuck off,* just for the hell of it, but that was lost in the realisation she'd just called me by my first name. For that, I'd even sign the pledge.

Well, hang on. Maybe not that far. I'm not fucking *demented.*

"Sorry."

She shrugged. "No, I am. Stupid really, with everything that's happened."

I didn't say anything. Sometimes women want you to agree with them and sometimes not. Buggered if I ever know which it is.

Probably why I know what a married quarters feels like when you go in and you know it's empty, and she's gone.

Jeannie.

Christ. Don't start thinking about her, Robbie.

The blood in the sand, the bodies, the women walking away.

No, she wasn't there. But she was part of the casualty list, even so. Part of the fallout.

Death, murder... the cost is limitless. Like ripples from a rock. The damage it does knocks on, in ways you never expected. It can come back and damage the murderers too.

No more than I deserved.

But still it fucking hurt.

"You said he was afraid. Stiles, I mean. What's he afraid of?"

"I think..." She looked up at the hillside, bit her lip and shook her head, then looked over at me. She really had beautiful eyes. Big and dark.

Christ, Robbie, you're falling. Don't fucking do it. Just don't.

"I think he's afraid that if he talks about it – whatever it is he's so scared of, this Deep Brain thing... he's afraid it will know and come for him."

"What the fuck is the Deep Brain, when it's at home?"

She didn't tick me off over my language this time. "At a guess, whatever controls the dead things."

"Controls them?" That would make sense. I mean, there had to be a reason that the dead started waking up. Didn't there?

"The 'Brain' part would suggest a controlling intelligence, yes? But what it is, and where..."

"That's what we need to know." The thought of the 'Deep Brain' made things better and worse at once. Worse because it was bad enough when the nightmares were just shambling flesh-eaters. The idea of something directing them...

But if there was such a thing, it could be found. Perhaps destroyed, if there were some submarines left. Torpedoes punching through soft grey brain tissue and exploding, blowing it into scraps of fish food. The nightmares keeling over, the lights going out in their eyes.

Give me an enemy I can fight, and I'm a happy man.

"We're so in the dark, with this." Katja sat on a drystone wall. "We don't even know what his theories *were*. He could be insane. Or only half-right. Which could be just as disastrous."

"Well, keep trying. You're the only one he seems to talk to. Maybe he's in love."

She didn't answer.

"Sorry," I said.

"What for?"

"I shouldn't – I mean, I wasn't – I didn't mean to take the piss."

"You think you can offend me?" She looked up. "You will have to try harder than that. Do you know that there are mornings when I give thanks for the flood, even for the dead things? Do you know what I was, before this? What was done to me? I was fucked by a dozen, twenty men a day. Sometimes so sore I *bled*. Fucked in the arse so I could barely *walk*. Treated as a piece of *meat*. You think a *joke* will hurt me?"

My face was burning.

"But," she carried on, "you could be right."

"What?"

"Stiles. Perhaps I remind him of someone. Perhaps I'm just the first pretty girl who doesn't laugh at him or look at him in disgust. Either way. He wants to make contact with me. He just doesn't know how. And I don't know how to help him."

I looked at her and I wanted to kiss her. I wanted to ask if I could kiss her. Been a long time since I've done that. I've slept with hookers. But Katja wasn't one, not anymore, and God help any man who treated her as one. And even then –

I didn't just want her. I wanted her to want me.

I had no idea where to start with *that*.

"When are you next going out?" she asked.

"Tomorrow. We'll scout west."

"Can I come?"

"Aye."

"Thank you."

"Just be careful."

No-one else could get shit-all out of Stiles. If she died, we'd know nothing. Always assuming there was anything to know in the first place.

If I was honest, that was why I didn't like him – apart from the obvious one of him being mad. I'm not comfortable around mental illness, can't handle the idea of it finding a home in me. I laugh at nutters out of fear – fear I might become one of them. Because I've come too close to it. So I laugh, because I'm still on the rails and they're not. Ugly but true.

But it wasn't just that. It was Katja.

I was jealous.

WE FOUND SURVIVORS in nearby villages that had survived the flooding – Blacko, Roughlee, Downham. More often than not, we'd see the nightmares, lurking in the shallows. They didn't attack, just watched. We never had to fire a shot.

For the first time, an uneasy hope began to blossom. Perhaps they'd leave us alone.

After all, they were dead. And dead flesh rots. Tendons and ligaments parting, the skeleton falling apart. And bodies in water, salt water most of all, rot away fast.

If we could just wait them out. If we could just hold on long enough, then nature would do the job for us.

About a week after that first flight out, I was in the farmhouse front room, drinking with Mleczko and Chas. Billy sat by Mleczko – there was no shaking him, which got Mleczko ribbed unmercifully – while Jo and Chas sat together on the sofa, holding hands like a couple of kids. Nobody took the piss, and not only because Chas'd make their lives hell if they did. It was – never thought I'd say this about Chas Nixon – sweet. Good to see something going right.

Katja and Stiles were talking in their corner. I took a large swallow. Stupid to be jealous of Stiles anyway. She wasn't with him out of love.

Katja got up, left the room.

Mleczko nudged me. Stiles was coming over, hunched and moving stiffly, grimacing at the pain each movement brought. Poor bastard.

He had Katja. Lucky bastard.

Stop snivelling, Robbie.

"It isn't over."

I looked up at him. "What?"

He gestured round with a free hand. "You think it's all over. Don't you?"

"They think it's all over," Billy sniggered. "It is now."

I ignored him, and so did Stiles. He just stared at me. His eyes were incredibly bloodshot, the irises snared in red webs of tiny broken veins. Dad'd had eyes like that.

"It hasn't started yet," said Stiles. "The Deep Brain. It's watching and waiting. The ocean. The voices. The souls. It's coming."

"What is?" I asked.

Stiles' eyes screwed shut, as if against a sudden jab of pain, lips peeling back from his clenched, yellowed teeth. Then he sucked in a breath and opened his eyes again. "It's coming, Sergeant," he said again, and then turned and limped back to his corner.

"What is?" I asked. He didn't answer. I stood up and shouted. "What fucking is?"

The whole room was silent. Movement at the corner of my eye; Katja, stood in the doorway, watching.

Stiles did not turn around. "Death," he said. "Death is coming."

Then he sat back down, picked up the bottle he'd been working on, and said no more.

Katja went over to him. I sat back down.

"Fucking lunatic," muttered Chas. Jo huddled closer to him, as if for warmth. It was the closest to frightened I'd seen her.

"Apeshit," Mleczko agreed.

"Yeah," Billy echoed, "apeshit."

"Yeah." I grunted.

I saw them sat together. I wanted to look away, but didn't.

He was holding her hand. And Katja... Katja wasn't just *letting* him hold her hand. Do you understand? She was squeezing his hand back, stroking the knuckles with her thumb. She was responding. Of course, it could have just been like a whore's kisses – faking it to please the customer.

But I could see how she looked at him. I could've handled pity. Even lust, hard to imagine though that was.

But this was something else. This was the look I'd wanted to see in her eyes when she looked at me.

She realised she was being watched. She looked up. I turned away before she met my eyes.

"I need some fucking air," I said, standing. I went outside.

"You okay, Robbie?"

"Aye."

"Rob –"

"Chas, I'm fine."

I felt the cold wind on my face, breathed out. The clouds had broken briefly, letting moonlight gleam on the dark waters beyond. Scratching the surface, shedding no light on the depths. And all I could think was:

Death, Sergeant.

Death is coming.

CHAPTER SIXTEEN

THE NIGHTMARES MADE a brief, vicious attack on Blacko a few days later. They struck in numbers, but they were driven off. If something was controlling them, it was new to tactics and slow to learn. Humans have been killing each other for years, on the other hand, so that gave us an advantage.

Almost too easy. Almost like a testing of our defences.

Parkes and Hendry tried every day, almost religiously, to contact Windhoven, but there was only ever the hiss of static. I had to believe they were still out there. Had to.

Katja had been staying with Ged. He never put a foot wrong with her, she assured me. A widower. Better things to do. He'd sit up late into the night, cradling a photograph of his daughter, her boyfriend and their kid. She reckoned he liked having her round. Reminded her of his daughter. For some reason I didn't understand at the time, she didn't seem to like that.

Anyway, she moved in with Stiles. That's right. Into that filthy hole of a caravan. Not that it stayed filthy for very long. When she was done, the caravan was unrecognisable. Scrubbed clean.

And yes, I have to admit, that burned. But I turned away, blanked it out. Got on with my job. At times, I was glad to be a soldier again.

*   *   *

"THERE'S A LOCATION not far from here," said Hendry. "An army base, pretty new, but with landing facilities and some fuel supplies. We were told we could use it as a temporary stopover if we couldn't fly straight out to Windhoven."

"You didn't mention this before, sir."

"We tried contacting them just before we flew out, but..."

"What?"

"They were being overrun. God knows how: they were on high ground, well-defended; they should've been able to hold off any attack, especially in the early stages."

"But they didn't?"

Hendry spread his hands helplessly. "I don't know the details. We got a few garbled messages, enough to tell us what was happening without saying how and why. Right then it didn't seem particularly important."

I nodded. "But the base itself?"

"Should be intact."

"And those things?"

"Again, no way to tell. All we can do is... go and take a look."

"What kind of supplies are we talking about?"

"Avgas for the Chinook. Plus army rations, medical supplies, weapons, ammunition..."

"Christmas come early, you mean."

"It's not far off, anyway," Lomax put in. "Christmas."

Jesus, he was right. Well, at least if I lived that long, I wouldn't be spending Christmas alone. I could thank the nightmares for that, if nothing else.

"What?" said Lomax.

I realised I was smiling. "Doesn't matter. Alright then. Let's go take a look."

THE CHINOOK FLEW over Nelson; as we went, we could see what was left of the town, the tops of taller buildings and a few of the higher-up streets poking clear of the water.

Another thing I noticed as we flew.

The waters were clearer.

They'd lost that shitten, stewed-tea look they'd had. Under them, we could see houses, buses and cars, streets.

It was, for the record, a weird fucking sight.

I was glad when the chopper veered away from it and homed in on a flat-topped hill nearby.

High fencing ringed the base. A watchtower. At one end the perimeter was partly submerged.

The compound itself was a cluster of unremarkable prefab buildings on a concrete floor. Probably still in its early stages.

We flew over a couple of times. No sign of life. On the other hand, if we kept flapping around overhead, then anything lurking in the water might notice. And I wasn't keen on having a welcoming committee when we touched down.

"What do you think?" asked Hendry.

I took a breath. "Let's chance it."

On board we had Joyce, Hassan, Parfitt and Akinbode, along with Lomax and Katja. Also a couple of villagers, Neil and Steve. 'Villagers' was probably the wrong term – they were both tourists who'd been trapped in Barley by the floods. Steve was in his forties and had had a potbelly, which had disappeared in the two weeks they'd been with us. He and his wife had been celebrating their anniversary with a hiking tour of the fells. Neil was in his late twenties, rangy and outdoorsy-looking. He'd been down for 'a spot of bird-watching'. Both could handle a gun, and carried hunting rifles.

"Alright," I said. "Our main priority's the Avgas, followed by medical supplies. We've already got guns and food, though extra supplies would be useful. We go after them later, if we've time and room. Clear?"

"Sarge."

Lomax pointed at one of the buildings. "That'll be the QM store. Pretty much everything we're looking for should be in there."

And what else, I wondered?

"Akinbode, you're on lookout. Lomax, Joyce – take the Gimpys. Neil, Katja, Steve – we're looking for fuel. Hassan, Parfitt – find the medical gear. Any sign of trouble, raise the alarm and fall back. Do not, repeat *not*, engage unless absolutely necessary. I'll decide if we start a shooting match or not. Any questions?"

There were none.

"Right. Let's go."

EXACTLY WHAT PURPOSE the base'd been meant to serve even Hendry didn't know. A support base for the regional control centres, perhaps, although the floods hadn't been recognised as a major threat until only a few days before November 7th. This hadn't been built *that* quickly. Of course, there were any number of dangers the authorities could've had in mind, not least its own citizens.

* * *

WE LANDED THE Chinook broadside-on to the storehouse. Joyce manned the Gimpy in the rear doorway, aiming at the half-submerged end; Lomax covered the side of the compound opposite the storehouse with the other one. Akinbode stood by the cockpit with a Minimi, watching the far end.

The rest of us de-bussed, formed a perimeter. Neil and Steve'd been briefed on what to do, and they fell into step pretty well for civvies.

Wind moaned across the concrete.

"Sarge?" asked Parfitt.

"Go."

The door wasn't locked. I stepped back, rifle shouldered. Katja, Hassan and Parfitt followed suit. I motioned to Neil and Steve to open the doors.

Inside was dark silence. I moved forward to the doorway, sighting left and right, quarter-turning the sight to activate the night vision.

Rows of steel shelving and a big central aisle. Nothing moving.

"Clear. Parfitt, Katja – go."

They moved forward, rifles aimed. "Clear."

"Okay. Get looking."

The Avgas was near the back; behind it was –

"Sarge! Check this out!"

Two more Landrovers. "Very nice, Parfitt. Shouldn't you be looking for the medical supplies?"

"Sorry, Sarge."

He found them; luckily they were very portable. Which freed him and Hassan up quickly for the next job – rolling drums of JP-4 Avgas on board the Chinook.

"Alright. Let's move."

"What about the other stuff, Sarge?"

There'd been Gimpys, SA80s, Minimis and a shedload of ammunition back there, not to mention the Landrovers and at least one Mk19. "No room for it. We'll come back."

WHEN WE RETURNED, everything seemed as we left it. A good sign.

THE WEAPONS WERE crated up, so we moved them out fast. Just as planned. All running smoothly. *Thank you, O God I don't believe in.* Not a hitch.

"Sarge!" yelled Joyce.

Fuck.

JUST OUTSIDE THE perimeter fence, up to its thighs in foul water, was one of the nightmares.

I threw the rifle to my shoulder and sighted. It didn't move. From the chopper I heard Joyce cocking the Gimpy. "Hold fire!" I yelled. If there were more, a shot could open up a whole new world of grief.

It wore the remains of an Army uniform; much of its face was eaten away. The jawbone yawned, almost unsupported, the cheeks hung like tattered flags, and half its nose was gone. But there was still flesh on its limbs, and the empty sockets of its eyes blazed green.

"Shit," I heard from behind me, followed by a rifle bolt snapping back. "Hold fire, Parfitt."

As I watched, the water beside the first nightmare stirred, and a fretted scalp, clumps of skin and hair still clinging to the skull, broke the surface. Its face was greenish coloured – there seemed to be something furring it up – but otherwise more or less intact. Its eyes were whole, glowing like dusty bulbs, and I could even make out a moustache. It stood beside the first nightmare, a few short yards away, and watched us.

Another rose beside that, upper half canted sideways. Its face was badly torn, hanging loose off the bone on one side. It straightened up as it neared the fence. They all wore Army uniforms.

"Another around here!" Katja was aiming her M-14 round the side of the store. "In the water."

"I've got some too," Lomax called. "By the fence."

"Hold fire!" I shouted again.

"What the fuck?" said Parfitt.

I stared at the three nightmares. Their eyes were... pulsing. The glow brightened to a blaze, faded, then brightened again. All in perfect sync.

"I've never seen this before," Katja called. "But I don't think it's good."

When was it ever? "Hold your fire!"

They stood there, eyes pulsing. Then it stopped.

A few seconds later they turned and sank back down into the water.

"Sarge?" Parfitt again. "What the fuck was that?"

"Fucked if I know," I said. "Let's get out of here."

BACK AT THE farmhouse.

"We saw maybe a dozen, Chas. Not exactly an army."

"Yeah. But what if they've started inviting their mates?"

"Aye, I know. There's the rub."

But the Landrovers, more weapons... that grenade launcher, which we'd forgotten in the rush...

Chas shrugged. "No point doing the job if you *don't* take a risk now and then, is there?"

*　　*　　*

THIS TIME WE circled the base twice, and saw nothing. Everything exactly as we left it.

"Okay, let's move." Lomax and Joyce manning the Gimpys again. The rest of us were heading straight for the store.

"Let's go, let's go. Get the doors open."

Steve and Neil pulling the doors open. The darkness within.

The stench rushes out to meet us, and the green glow of eyes in the darkness.

And the dozens of leering, rotted faces.

And their outstretched, rotting hands.

Death, Sergeant.

Death is coming.

Parfitt's closest, doesn't stand a chance. Gets off one scream as they lunge forward, one biting into his face, two, three others falling on top. Can't get a clear shot. He's screaming. Blood spews out in a jet. The screaming stops.

Fall back and fire – me, Katja. Steve and Neil already hightailing it back to the chopper. A few go down.

"Go!"

Akinbode's Minimi firing, more of them coming out of the other buildings in the compound. They're fucking *everywhere.*

The Gimpys hammering. They're in the water at the far end.

Thinking as I run: *they were waiting for us. They were fucking waiting for us.*

A trap.

They set a fucking trap.

"Akinbode! Move your arse, you bastard, *now!*"

Akinbode frozen, seeing the nightmares rushing in on our tail. Then he blinks and runs for the side door.

Too slow. One leaps on his back – two more throw themselves in.

Akinbode screaming.

Drawing the pistol. Firing. Three headshots. Three down. Akinbode scrambling up as –

"Down!"

Lomax, running in, firing his Sig-Sauer over my head. "Come on!"

More nightmares rushing inwards, teeth bared and arms reaching out. I blow the face off one, then I'm backpedalling.

"Akinbode! Get on the fucking Gimpy! We're leaving!"

He scrambles aboard the Chinook.

"Sarge!"

More of them rushing in, no time to aim, oh, fuck –

Rat-a-tat-a-tat-a-tat.

Joyce on the tail GPMG, raking the submerged end of the compound and the dead figures coming out of it. Three, four go down. Akinbode firing the door gun.

"Move, move, move! We are leaving! We are very fucking leaving!"

And then the kind of scream I never want to hear again.

"McTarn!"

Lomax on the ground. Pinned flat. Still alive, but already they've started eating him, tearing chunks off his hands, arms, legs, face. The look in his eyes, the fucking horror in his eyes.

I aim at Lomax. I see his eyes close.

And I fire.

"Robert!" Katja. "Come on!"

I run for the chopper. I look back.

Bad idea. Just ask Lot's wife.

The nightmares are still coming.

And shouldering through the crowd, a fresh one. Mangled, bloody. A hand, reaching out towards me. Two fingers missing.

The torn, ruined face, slack in death. The eye sockets empty and glowing. Clumsy. Shambling. Parfitt's jaws gape open. And he gives out the hissing snarl I've come to know so well.

"Aw, fuck."

A hole appears in his forehead and the back of his head blows out.

Katja, lowering the M-14. "Come on!"

The Chinook's rotors thundering, beating at the air. Hands pull me aboard. We're lifting. Not even time to close the door.

The nightmares are running for the chopper. One jumps. In through the fucking door. Lands on its feet, rocking and swaying for balance.

Scrambling back on my arse, fumbling for the P226, knowing there's no time, it's glaring down at me –

Claws reaching down –

The side of its head blows out and it falls sideways onto the deck.

Katja lowers her pistol.

I am really fucking glad, for the record, that I let her tag along.

Airborne. Looking down. The nightmares gathering below, glaring up.

All across the compound, glaring up.

And as we fly out, I see more of them.

They're swimming up through the waters, towards the surface.

Heads breaking water. Staring up. And they're moving.

They're moving after us.

But we're faster. We're leaving them behind. Not fast enough for me, though. Never fast enough.

Joyce moves to the dead nightmare, face white. He grabs its ankles to drag it clear. Dump it.

"No," I tell him. He stares at me. "No."

I'm looking at it, and something is different; something is definitely different. I need to know, we need to know, *what*.

"We're taking it with us," I say. "Time we got a proper look at one of these things."

"Oh, God!"

Akinbode.

He's cradling his left arm. He's staring at it.

Oh shit.

Even from there I can see the wound in his forearm. I can see it very clearly, because there is white bone gleaming through the mess.

But worse. Oh, worse.

Far worse.

His hand is swollen. Horribly swollen. He's cut the sleeve open with his knife. The flesh all around the wound is already black and green.

"Oh, no. Oh, fucking no."

Feeling my hand drift towards the P226 at my belt.

And Akinbode's suddenly on his feet in the doorway, holding his rifle one-handed, and the muzzle whips towards my face, then away, towards Katja's.

And then he puts the barrel in his mouth.

"Akinbode!" I yell.

He pulls the trigger.

He drops down into space.

He hits the water below, and we watch it churn into a bloody froth.

It recedes fast, into a pale, fading spot on the water.

Until Katja stumbles over and pulls the door shut.

Click.

HASSAN HAD SET up a temporary hospital in a barn. A trestle table rigged up; the dead nightmare laid out on it. He didn't have much else to do. That was one thing about fighting the nightmares – there wasn't much middle ground. You were either unscathed or you were dead.

"Sarge." He looked up as I trudged in. Tired, gaunt. Dark rings around his eyes. Stubble thickening on his cheeks.

"Hassan. You okay?"

He nodded. "Not enough sleep, that's all."

"What can you tell me?"

"I'm just a medic, Sarge, not a pathologist."

"Give me your best guess."

"The body's not bloated. And the skin... I'm not sure what that green stuff is. Some kind of algae, or mould. If I had to guess, I'd say it's protecting the skin somehow."

"Protecting?"

"From the water, Sergeant. Bodies in seawater decompose very quickly."

"But this hasn't."

"No."

It hasn't started yet.

"So when we hoped they were just going to rot away..."

Hassan nodded. "I don't think they're gonna, Sarge." He rubbed his face. "I don't understand how it works. I mean, the water must get into body cavities, in through the mouth. It should rot them from the inside out. Unless it coats them on the inside too. But then..." he trailed off.

"Like you said, you're not a pathologist. But there is one thing you might want to consider."

"What's that?"

"We're dealing with something that makes the dead get up and walk. That's against pretty much every fucking law of nature I ever heard of. If it can do that, rustproofing the bastards shouldn't be much of a challenge."

It.

The Deep Brain.

Neither of us could add much to that. I didn't know what he was thinking as I trudged back out into the night, but I could guess.

Death, Sergeant. Death is coming.

I SAT IN silence in the bar of the farmhouse kitchen.

Alone. Unless you counted that bottle of Isle of Jura.

I didn't want anyone to approach me. No-one did. Maybe they knew how I felt and respected it. Or maybe they just wanted to keep away from me. Blamed me for it. My fault.

Death is coming.

Parfitt going down under a rush of nightmares. Parfitt, now a nightmare himself, staggering forward. Parfitt falling, brains blown out.

Akinbode. The terror and the despair on his face. His arm rotten and necrotic in fucking *minutes*. The gun in his mouth. The eyes popping out of their sockets as he blew off the top of his own skull. Dropping back out of sight. And gone.

Akinbode's arm. Alf Mason had quickly fallen ill, had passed out. Katja's friend, Marta – the bite had taken time to kill her. In a rare moment of openness, Katja had described the state of the girl's arm, but it had taken hours to get to that state. Akinbode's had been turning green and black in the time he'd been taken on board the helicopter and into the sky.

It's working faster. Getting more poisonous.

I poured myself another shot.

"Robert. How are you?"

I looked up.

"Can I join you?" asked Katja.

I shrugged. "Free country."

"Is it still?" She gave a thin, tight smile. Good point. God knew what kind of country it was anymore. Whatever was left of it.

She sat. I lifted the bottle. She nodded, and I poured a shot.

"Are you okay?" she asked.

"No. I'm not."

"I didn't think you would be." Her eyes were very dark, very frank. "There's nothing you can say, is there?"

"Not really, no."

"When Marta died. I was responsible for her. I felt like I'd failed her. For a while I felt as though I shouldn't be alive."

"Still feel that way?"

"No." A small shake of her head. "But it still hurts. I don't let myself think of it often. One day, I'll be able to. It'll never *not* hurt. But it will be bearable."

"In time."

"Yes."

"That what you came to tell me?" My voice sounded sharper than I meant it to. She drew back a little. When she spoke again, her voice was more clipped. "No." She looked at me. "Stiles wants to see you."

I stared at her. "He does?"

She nodded.

"That's a switch."

"I don't think it's good news."

"When is it ever?"

"Just go easy on him, okay?"

We walked up towards the Hill.

"I've been going easy on him ever since we got here, hen," I said. "I can't afford to anymore. He said death was coming. Remember?"

"Yes."

"Has he said anything to you?"

She nodded, her eyes lowered.

"What?"

"Something happened last night," she said. "How much do you know about him?"

"Got a basic bio before the mission. I don't know his shoe size or anything."

"Size eight English, forty-two European. I read it on the label." She smiled crookedly. I couldn't keep away a little pang of jealousy.

She knows his shoe size, if he snores or talks in his sleep. All those little things lovers know.

Focus, Robbie.

"Does the name Ellen Vannin mean anything to you?" she asked.

I ran back through the briefing in my head. "No. Why?"

"He woke up screaming it."

"Oh." Maybe a nightmare that *didn't* relate to this? It could still happen. Maybe.

"Early hours of this morning. He woke up screaming her name. All he said was 'It's Ellen. Ellen Vannin. She's found me.'"

Tears gleamed in her eyelashes. I put my hands in my pockets, because all I wanted was to reach out and touch her. "You love him, don't you?"

"Yes." A whisper.

"I'm sorry."

"I'm not. I'm not sorry I love him. But..."

"What?"

"He cries, you know? He looks at me sometimes, and... he just... cries. I think... I think it's that he knows I'm going to die soon. We all are. That's why I'm crying, Robert. I don't want to die."

"None of us do."

"Stiles... he said that we all die alone. And he's right, isn't he? However you die. Whoever you're with. In the end, it's always alone."

I nodded. "Yes." I'd seen men die often enough.

"And I don't want to. Do you know what the strangest thing is? I'm happy here. Meeting him has been the best thing to happen to me since I lost my parents. And it wouldn't have happened without this. Do you ever think that perhaps there is a God, and that he has a very cruel sense of humour?"

"Only explanation that ever made sense as far as I'm concerned."

Katja began to laugh, and she wiped her eyes. She looked around at the fells, the meadows, the woodlands, even the sea that surrounded us, and seemed to see it, really see it, for the first time. "It is very sweet, isn't it?"

"What is?"

"Being alive."

And it was. And to be savoured and treasured and lived, and all of that. And if this had been a movie I would have swept her into my arms and kissed her then and there, rather than go my grave not knowing it. But I didn't. It would have been wrong.

But she took my arm as we walked the rest of the way to the caravan, and I savoured every minute of that. It was as close to her as I was ever going to come.

*   *   *

"THANKS FOR COMING," Stiles said, forcing a smile.

Even for Stiles, he looked pretty ghastly – pale, sunken-eyed, his hands shaking. Two bottles of own-brand vodka stood by the rickety chair he perched on.

Katja sat on the divan, her knees pulled up to her chest. Stiles was breathing, fast and shallow.

"Sorry," he said. "Just... some pain. That's all."

I sat on the other divan. I kept still and didn't speak. I could see the effort he was making, and finally started to realise what he was up against. But I mustn't speak. Mustn't give him the chance to back out. He needed to talk and I needed to listen. Silence was the only help I could give him.

"I know... you came here to find me," he said. "And I know that you don't really know why. And you've a right to know. I'm afraid, though... it won't make much difference."

I felt my stomach hollow and tighten.

"The thing is... the Deep Brain... whenever I think about it... I can always hear it, you see. The voices. The souls. I can always hear them. It's like a screaming in my head, a roaring. Drowning out my thoughts. It's always in my head, Sergeant – never far away. But when I think about it, *talk* about it..." His voice had risen. His fingertips touched his forehead.

"Ben –" Katja, a hand outstretched. I touched her wrist. Wordlessly, I shook my head.

For an instant, there was fury in Stiles's face. Then it cleared. He straightened up and nodded. He uncapped one of the bottles and took a big gulp. He leant back in the chair, face screwing up, tightening, flushing a violent red, and let out a long, explosive breath. After a few seconds, he opened his eyes again. Forced a smile.

"Takes away the pain, a little."

Swaying slightly, he leant forward again, breathing quick and ragged. He swallowed hard.

"As I said... when I talk about it, the pain gets worse. I'm still not sure... not even now... if it's trying to silence me, or... if it just becomes more aware of me at those times."

I waited.

"Would it surprise you to learn, Sergeant, that I was predicting what's happened as long as five years ago?"

"No," I said at last.

"I suppose not. You're not stupid, after all." He gave a sudden, almost boyish grin. "Not a Nobel prizewinner or anything, but you're not stupid."

"Was that a compliment?" I asked, feeling my eyebrows go up.

Stiles grinned again. "After a fashion."

After a moment, I grinned back.

"Ben." Katja, cutting in on the male bonding. "There isn't much time."

Stiles nodded wearily. "The alcohol's just a temporary aid," he said, "and it's getting less and less effective. The Deep Brain is the only name I've got for what we're facing. I've been aware of it for several years now."

"Since the diving accident?"

"Yes." He pulled a sheaf of stained, rumpled papers out from under the divan. "It's all here. I've managed to write it down, just about. Katja will tell you – I've been up late writing these past few nights. Mostly drunk out of my skull."

I looked at Katja. She nodded. Stiles reached out and took her hand. "Only way I could manage it. Very difficult. Painful. But, this will give you some idea of why you were sent... but as I say, I don't think there's anything we can do to stop it."

"That bad?" I asked. Stupid question.

"How do you fight the sea, Sergeant? Men have been trying for millions of years. And it's always won. And now it's starting to move against us in earnest."

A chill ran over my skin. Pretty much what I'd suspected, but now it was confirmed, in black and white, so to speak.

"I don't think there's much you can do with the information, to be honest. But I thought you had a right to know."

I nodded my thanks.

"The dead rising was only the beginning. When it had enough control, enough strength, it found ways to preserve the bodies it controls. Also, the waters were thick with silt after the floods. Impossible to see very far. The walking dead are the Deep Brain's eyes and ears. It's split itself apart, a tiny fragment of its consciousness in each reanimated corpse, each independent but linked into a greater whole. It can't keep track of them all at once – imagine having a billion eyes, each moving independently – but it gathers information steadily. And now, with the water clear, it can move in search of survivors."

"Why didn't you warn us when we went to the army base?"

"Would you have listened? Besides, you might have escaped without incident. And it was inevitable we'd need supplies. The same with any other group of survivors. Sooner or later there'd have to be a clash."

"Clash?" What he was describing sounded more like genocide to me.

Stiles sagged, deflated. "It's a word for it. Not a very good one, perhaps. Anyway..." He took another gulp of vodka, his throat working. Squeezed his face tight as the booze hit; he flushed again. "I'm afraid we may be at a particular disadvantage, because I'm here. It wants *me*, Sergeant, most particularly."

"Why?"

"It's all in my notes. Perhaps if you killed me, you might have a better chance."

"Ben!"

"It's true, Katja. On the other hand, it might attack even harder out of rage. Or you could fly me out, far away from here, abandon me on some far-off scrap of land."

"Ben, don't talk like this."

"If it gives the rest of you a chance of survival, Katja, then it has to be done. I'm tired of hiding. I'm tired of being a coward."

"You're not, Ben."

Stiles turned to me. "I've told you pretty much all I can. I don't know any way to fight it, or destroy it. I'm sorry, Sergeant."

"So am I." I got up. There really wasn't much more to say. Stiles wasn't looking at me, but Katja was. Her eyes were bright. "You're tougher than you look, Stiles. I'll say that for you."

He looked up and forced a smile. "Was that a compliment, Sergeant?"

I forced a smile back. "After a fashion."

KATJA WALKED PART of the way back with me. Stiles had said he wanted to be alone for a while. The fields and the meadows spread out before us; beyond them the glitter of the water that would bring all our deaths.

A thought occurred to me. "You don't think..."

"What?"

"Stiles. You don't think he might do something stupid?"

A moment's unease, then she shook her head. "I don't think so. Not yet. I think he'll wait until the end. When he's sure there's no hope. It'd be stupid – wouldn't it – to kill yourself only to find out you were wrong?"

"You think he is?"

"I wish I did."

So did I.

"What about you?"

"Me? I think, yes, I'll kill myself, rather than let them take me. I don't want to die like that. And I don't want to be one of them. But I've been here before."

I waited. She told me how it had begun for her. Trapped on the brothel's roof with Marta.

"I fought as long as I could, until I was sure there was no more hope. Then I was going to kill myself. Marta too. But we were rescued." She told me the rest then. Her voice faltered once or twice, when she talked about what had happened on the narrowboat. "We went through all of that, just to die here. Hardly seems fair, does it?"

"Life isn't fair."

"I knew that," she said. Of course she did. Even before the floods, she'd known that. "But still..." She shrugged. "Well, I'll do the same. Hold out until I'm sure there's no more hope. Until then..."

She shrugged, looking off into the distance, towards the sea.

"Katja?"

She looked at me.

"I don't want to die either."

She smiled. Then leant forward, put her hands on my shoulders, and kissed me once, very softly, on the lips. I tried to respond, but she pushed me back, shook her head. "To remember me by," she said. Then she looked away. "I'd better get back."

I watched her walking back up to the farmhouse, to Stiles' caravan. The kiss still tingled on my lips. It lifted me, a little, but there was a cold hard weight in my stomach, and it wouldn't go away. I think they call it doom.

I've read Stiles' notes. Not an easy task. His handwriting's not brilliant, and the pages are a mess; creased, crumpled, stained – spilt booze, spilt coffee. And what he's got to say is pretty wild. Craziness on craziness. Except that I can't say it doesn't make sense.

It gives me some idea of what's coming, and why. But it doesn't help.

I've been writing this last thing at night, first thing in the mornings. I know Katja's done something similar. Seemed right to leave a sort of record, for the future.

Except there isn't one. Not for any of us.

I was called away. We've just heard.

Dear God. Already.

It's started.

CHAPTER SEVENTEEN

WE'D LEFT A radio with each of the groups of survivors we'd found. Each morning, Parkes hailed them to check their status.

That morning, the survivors at Roughlee didn't reply.

Hendry, Parkes, Mleczko and Joyce flew over in the Chinook. Doors stood open. There was only silence. No-one came out to greet them.

They made a landing, Parkes handling the Gimpy while Mleczko and Joyce searched the houses.

All empty. Blood on the walls. Torn flesh. Fragments of bone.

They'd hit, and hit hard. No warning, no alarm raised. And everybody gone.

No defence is total.

And for all the advantages that technology, training and equipment give you, numbers always win in the end.

IN THE EVENING, just before the light failed, Parkes got a transmission from the survivors at Blacko, nearby. The nightmares were gathering in the waters around the village – dozens, scores, finally hundreds. Standing in silence, with their glowing green eyes.

They were massing, but had made no hostile move. Yet. If I sent the Chinook for them, would that trigger an attack? Unknown. But if we waited until they *did* attack, we'd never reach them in time.

I sent the Chinook, with Mleczko and Parkes. Just them. We weren't there to fight. It was an evacuation, pure and simple.

The Chinook returned just before dawn. The villagers disembarked, pale and shaken and out of place; people with nowhere to go, reliant on the kindness of strangers. The shell-shocked look of people who'd had what security, what stability, what home they'd had, snatched away. I'd done some peacekeeping duties in the former Yugoslavia; I knew that look. Refugees.

No violence. None of the nightmares had emerged from the water or attacked.

Mleczko stepped off the Chinook and came over; he looked grim. "They were in the water," he muttered.

"We know that."

"Not around Blacko. As we flew back here. Sarge, I think they were on the move."

As DAWN CAME and light stole across the landscape, Parkes' radio came to life again.

Hendry flew out to the other communities. As before, it was an evacuation, not a fight. Any food, fuel or weapons available were cleared out and brought back.

As Hendry flew in, the Chinook wobbled in its flight, the engine sounded an irregular, coughing and spluttering note. The rotors were skipping beats.

He brought it down in the meadow near the Hill, where Stiles' caravan stood. He came out to meet me as Parkes and Mleczko shepherded the evacuees clear, the rotors winding down.

His face was pale, lips moving soundlessly.

I said it for him. "It's fucked, isn't it?"

He nodded.

"Can you fix it?"

"I don't know."

"Shit!"

"I can try, Sergeant. That's all I can say. We'd never be able to move everyone, anyway."

"We could at least get some of them clear."

"Where to?"

"Right now, anywhere but here would probably be good." We looked at each other. "Just do whatever you can, sir."

A few minutes later, my PC crackled; the first of the nightmares had been sighted in the waters round Pendle.

IN THE FARMHOUSE, we held a brief council of war.

Joyce was in charge of the men while we talked. Jo was working with him to co-ordinate with the villagers. Katja, meanwhile, I'd put in charge of the refugees – we had close on a hundred of them. She was finding places for them to stay – hunting up tents or anything that could be used to jerry-rig them, spare rooms in farmhouses, abandoned buildings – while at the same time trying to pick out potential fighters. We needed to mobilise everybody capable of using a gun.

Around the table: me, Chas, Ged and Hendry. Parkes was on the Chinook's radio, trying desperately to hail Windhoven.

Hassan was clearing space in the abandoned barn, a couple of local women as impromptu nurses. Not much he could do for anyone bitten, but there was still the risk of injury from shrapnel, stray bullets, falls.

The sky was darkening. A thin, mizzling rain had started to fall.

"Focusing," I said.

"What?" asked Hendry.

"What Stiles said. Imagine having a billion eyes, all working independently. You couldn't keep track of it all. Drive anybody mad." An insane controlling intelligence? Fucking hell, it just kept getting better. "But as it becomes aware of survivors, it focuses on them, one by one. And it gathers its forces... and marches."

"And keeps attacking 'til they're all gone," said Chas.

"I think so."

"Lovely. Got a cig?"

I threw him my packet. "The attack this morning... testing its strength. Seeing how we'd respond."

"Are you trying to say they're using tactics?" Hendry looked at me as if I'd just dribbled on my shirt.

"I know how it sounds, sir. But according to Stiles, there's a controlling intelligence. Primitive, only recently conscious. But if it's aware, it can learn."

Hendry leant back in his chair.

"But now we've pulled back, sir," said Chas. "We're not gonna be trying to defend scattered, isolated positions, just one. And we've got high ground, a lot of warm bodies on the deck, weapons and raw materials to build defences. And we've had a lot more combat experience than it has."

"Question is," said Ged, "how does that help us in long run?"

"Well," I said, "that's the big question, isn't it?"

"Fair enough." Ged toyed with an empty glass; probably wishing there was something strong in it, but resisting the call. Getting blootered now helped nobody. "What the hell can we do?"

"One, Parkes is on the radio, trying to hail Windhoven –"

"Done us bugger-all good so far."

"She's also hailing on all other frequencies. If there's *anyone* else out there, they might be able to help."

"Or they might be as stuffed as we are."

Christ, I didn't need Ged cracking on me. "We're not dead yet. Any progress with the Chinook, sir?"

"Not as yet. Engineering's not my area. I think I might know what the problem is, but fixing it –"

"Understood, sir. Just do whatever you can, requisition whatever you need. What I'm thinking is this. We set up defences fast. Pull everyone who's not actually going to be fighting those things to the most central location we can."

"The Hill, most likely," said Ged.

"Aye. So we block all approaches to that location with anything spare – any barbed wire left over?"

"Might be a roll or two."

"Break it out. We've got the Landrovers and their armaments. We've also got farming vehicles – tractors, mechanical diggers. We can use them to run over the bastards."

"What if Parkes can't raise anybody?" Chas spoke quietly. I looked at him. His eyes were wide. He was thinking of Jo.

"We're not dead 'til we're dead, Chas. The important thing is to get the Chinook airborne again. If we can do that, some of us can hold the ground here while we fly the rest out, then it can come back for us."

"Fly out? Where to?"

"Any stretch of land that's not occupied or surrounded. It's taken them time to get here. They've got to march like any other army. So, we put distance between us. It buys us breathing space."

Chas nodded. After a moment, so did Ged. I was relieved to see he looked a little more energised.

"We build concentric lines of defence. They break through one, we fall back behind the next. The longer we hold out, the better chance we've got."

Hopelessness folded round me, like pressure at depth. But I wouldn't, couldn't, *must not* give way. Don't think about the long game, Robbie, 'cause we all lose that in the end. Just think about the next problem. Except, like the nightmares, they just kept coming. No matter how many of them you dealt with there were always more, and bit by bit they wore you down. By sheer weight of numbers.

Because numbers always win in the end.

"If we can do them a lot of damage in that first engagement," I said,

"From what we've seen, they'll pull back to regroup and reinforce. So the harder we hit them, the more time that buys us 'til the next attack. We need to show this Deep Brain it's got a fight on its hands, and we will not go down easily."

"Sounds great," said Chas. "How?"

"Simple. We invite them in."

WE HAD SA80s, Minimis, sniper rifles, several Gimpys and the blooper. Plus some C-4 explosive and personal communicators from the army base. We still had a good supply of ammunition for each weapon, plus each man carried two frag grenades. The exceptions to that were Hassan, who had none, and Chas and myself, who carried three – frags, smoke, white phosphorous.

There were also shotguns, rifles and ratting carbines – .22 revolvers with ridiculously long barrels and wire-framed stocks. Not in the same league as what we had, but all it took to turn a nightmare's lights out was an accurate headshot.

Those who couldn't fight were put to work erecting defences. Barbed wire, furniture, farm machinery, unneeded cars. Anything that could block a path was dragged across it.

We had stocks of Molotov cocktails. Torn bits of fabric, old bottles – add something flammable and Bob's your uncle. Fuel siphoned from vehicles, bottles of spirits. Any spare reserves were now pressed into service to make more; I saved the last of the Inn's Isle of Jura for myself.

Katja was on lookout on top of the Hill. The Dinkies were back at the farmhouse, to be deployed where they were needed.

On the higher slopes, we'd set up fougasses, for when – *if* – we were pushed back. A kind of improvised mine. Take one fifty-five gallon steel drum, readily available on any farm. Pack explosive at the bottom – C-4, fertiliser mixed with petrol – and pack the rest with pieces of metal, stone chips. Anything that would do damage. Bury in the earth with the open end sticking out, and then you just had to set it off and watch your enemies blown to shreds.

Chas was on Pendle Row, Jo round the opposite side of the Hill.

As well as guns, everyone carried a hand weapon of some kind. I had a hatchet tucked into my belt; others carried old police truncheons, baseball bats and pick-axe handles and spades and shovels, axes and hatchets, pitchforks. Even knives lashed to broom handles as crude spears. No-one was completely defenceless.

God help us if it got to that stage. We weren't special forces, knew nothing about hand-to-hand fighting. If a position was overran, you fell back and fired again. Hopefully driving them back.

But there were so many of them.

And we could only fall back so far.

JUST NORTH OF the Hill, the road leading towards Downham vanished into the sea; beside it lay a stretch of flat ground containing the two pools where the nightmares had attacked, the night Tidyman died. The space was wide open, up to the encircling drystone walls, and below a wooded slope. From the water, all they'd see were two men with rifles – Mleczko and me. Not even a Minimi in sight. Short of putting up a sign saying *picnic area*, there wasn't a clearer invitation.

Behind the wall, however, Ged crouched with his shotgun beside me, and Billy with his beside Mleczko, gazing up adoringly. Mleczko did his best to pretend he wasn't there. Beyond them was a long line of villagers and soldiers with rifles and crateloads of Molotov cocktails.

The rain intensified. A slow, low hissing from the blackening sky. A white fork of lightning left floaters in my vision – red, gold and green.

"Brace yourselves," I said. "Any minute now."

"How do you know, Sarge?"

"Storm's coming in, Mleczko. Heavy rain'll cut visibility and give them a better chance."

I could see the question in his eyes: *You really think they're smart enough to plan like that?*

Maybe not, but the Deep Brain is.

Stiles was in his caravan. Katja said he'd been brooding, silent. She didn't say she thought he might have an idea to save us, but I read the hope in her eyes. She was afraid to think about it, let alone give it voice.

The lightning flashed again, dazzling me. Mleczko sucked in a breath; in the murky distance, shadowy figures stood in ranks at the water's edge.

The thunder rolled in. The rain was driving down now with merciless force, pounding and hammering on my skull. Water danced on the ground, in puddles and on any hard surface. Splashing into my eyes. Hard to see through it. The thunderheads were almost directly above.

Then a sound.

Like a huge breath, let out through a phlegmy throat.

Like a thousand hissing snarls, unleashed as one.

And the nightmares came for us.

Hundreds of the bastards. Closely packed. No room to manoeuvre.

"Hold on," I said to the men around me. "Hold on," I repeated into the communicator.

The nightmares staggered forward, forward, forward. Mleczko and I began firing. Some fell. But the army came on. Closer. Closer. So close I could see their faces.

"Sarge?" Joyce's voice crackled out of the communicator.

"Wait for it."

The front row of nightmares erupted into a run.

"Now!"

The men hidden behind the wall stood and fired, fast volleys. Two GPMGs laid down sweeping arcs of fire further down the wall, tearing into the nightmares still swarming out of the water. The nightmares were falling. But there were so many more.

Aim and fire.

Got one in my sights. God, that *face.*

The empty sockets of the eyes, round and pale and glowing.

I pulled the trigger. Its head snapped back, spraying dark matter. It fell. Another in my sights.

Aim.

Fire.

Gunfire all around now, almost lost in the roar and the drum of the rain.

The panic burning, gnawing at your control. The urge to fire wildly, pray you hit something, anything, to hold back the tide. So many of them, and for each one you dropped, ten more still surging forward.

Bodies jerking under the bullets that hadn't hit the mark, then carrying on. Bullets hit chests, stomachs, legs, arms – hit and changed nothing.

But enough shots hit home. Retain control. Panic is a choice. I remembered Katja saying that. Her father had said it. He'd been a soldier too. "I think you would have liked him," she'd said.

I wondered if he'd have liked me.

Heads snapped back, brains flew, glowing eyes went out. Bodies toppled and crashed to the ground, trampled by the ranks behind them.

Firing. Firing. A SA80 rifle holds a thirty round magazine. The bolt locked back. Empty.

Pulling out the magazine. Steam floating up from the barrel and breech as the rain hit it.

Ram the fresh clip in. Lightning flashed. Thunder rolling in and down.

And on they came, in rags of clothing, rotten and torn. Some naked. Maybe they'd died that way; maybe the clothes had rotted off. Irrelevant now. Some male, some female. Some showed signs of their former youth or age, under the green moss. But you hardly noticed now. Death, the great leveller.

A poem I'd read once – *Great Death hath made all his for evermore.*

If he hadn't yet, he was bloody well working on it.

Bodies piled on bodies like sandbags.

So many soldiers, expendable, uncomplaining, to be flung into the meatgrinder, again and again and again. I'd once seen a film about Stalingrad. The Germans kept on driving into the fray, the Russians too.

Each more afraid of their own leaders than the enemy. Or drunk on their own propaganda.

But the living tire. Even the most professional soldier, or the most fanatical, runs out of steam. Not the nightmares. A General's wet dream. They'd never complain about inadequate equipment, never crack under the constant threat of destruction or seeing their comrades fall, never question the morality of their task.

Like I had.

After the desert road.

Baba. Baba.

Another face in the sights. Aim. Fire.

Now.

"Wall of fire!"

The Molotovs started flying. Two-person teams – one lit the cocktail, the other threw. The Molotovs hit the nightmares' front rank and erupted into sheets of flame.

Nightmares blundered through, aflame head to foot. No pain, but blinded. And the flame eating through soft tissues. A skull burst in the heat.

But there were always more.

They thought – the Deep Brain thought – there were still the numbers to push through our weak spot.

Which was the whole point.

I grabbed the communicator. "Joyce. *Now.*"

From the wooded slope above came the roar of engines.

Rotting heads turned.

They surged down the slope towards the nightmares. Tractors and mechanical diggers, scoops and ploughs extended. They drove into the nightmares' left flank.

The mechanical diggers' scoops scythed bodies in two, shattered skulls. Caterpillar treads rolled over what remained, leaving lifeless pulp.

The tractors smashing nightmares aside; the heavy wheels crushing, flattening.

They went down in droves. Severed limbs flew free. Survivors writhed and thrashed on the ground, still 'alive' but helpless.

Each driver had at least one armed man in the cab, who picked off any undamaged nightmares trying to attack. And from behind the drystone walls, still we fired.

Because there were plenty left.

The farm vehicles roaring in towards us. The men stumbling back from the walls. Me yelling to Mleczko to move a dozen men further down, towards the water, and hammer any still emerging or trying to retreat. Hitting the ground as a tractor grates to a halt inches from my position. Joyce looking sheepish behind the wheel. "Sorry, Sarge."

The bodies, piled up across the once-green field. Well, it's still green, I suppose. Except where the nightmares had been burned black. Not the same kind of green, not the kind I wanted to see.

Scattered shots and bursts. Twenty nightmares left now. A dozen. Dropping like flies. Heads exploded as high velocity bullets smashed into them. Blood and brains, spilling over the grass and the dead in the rain.

A last one standing, weaving, twisting this way and that from threat to threat.

Half a dozen guns fired as one, and it toppled.

And then there was only the guns' fading echo, the thunder's distant rumble, the rain's relentless sound as it rinsed the clotted slurry of blood and brains into the clogged quagmire of the ground.

The ground was empty. Forty or fifty still stood in the water, silent, watching, but made no move towards the land.

I aimed. We waited. The gun's barrel hissed, steam rising; the rain beat down so hard I could only see the glow of their eyes.

Then, as one, they turned and walked back into the water.

"Yeee-hooo!" whooped Billy, in what he doubtless thought was a rebel yell. He leapt over the wall, danced a clumsy jig. Mleczko, jogging back from the water's edge, shook his head, grinning wearily. "All fucked off, Sarge."

"Good work."

A ragged cheer went up. Rifles and shotguns shaken in the air. From the distance came firing, scattered shots, but they died away.

"Chas? Jo? What's your status? Report. Over."

"Clear, sarge. Over."

"Clear," said Jo. "Over."

"Good work."

The farm vehicles were parked up. Joyce climbed down, staring out over the torn, broken corpses.

Ged glanced over, smiled slightly, and began reloading the SPAS-12.

I could still hear cheering, through the whining in my ears, as Joyce's men waded in, finishing off the crippled nightmares with blows from rifle butts. A couple of shots rang out; Joyce's sandpaper voice, berating whoever wasted the ammo.

"Yee-haa!" Billy skipped and gambolled round the still-flaming patches of ground, in among the bodies, kicking at a torso here, a severed head there, waving his over-and-under shotgun in the air. "Got them! Got the smelly fuckers! Ha-haaa! All fucking dead! Got them!" He whirled back towards us, waving the gun in the air. "Got them, Danny! We got them all!"

"Billy!" I heard Mleczko scream.

On the ground lay a nightmare; everything gone from the waist down, guts trailing in the dirt, an arm and half its face torn away. But one eye still glowed, and one arm remained.

And jaws. It still had jaws.

The nightmares could move incredibly fast when they wanted, even in a state like that. Only in short bursts, but that was all it needed to grab Billy's ankle, yank itself forward, and bite into the meat of his calf.

Billy screamed, first in panic, then in pain. Mleczko yelled something and ran past me, dropping to one knee as the nightmare's head reared away from Billy's leg, torn meat hanging from its mouth. Blood spurted from the wound. Mleczko fired, and the nightmare collapsed.

Mleczko ran towards Billy. I followed; Ged too.

Billy was wailing, clutching his wounded leg with both hands. Blood streamed through his fingers.

"Ow, fuck! Fuck!" Fright stole over his face as it dawned. "*Fuck!*"

He looked up at Mleczko. "Help me. Please, Danny, help me!"

"Alright, mate," Mleczko said in an older, wearier voice than I'd ever thought to hear him use. "Alright."

Billy was crying. "You can make it better, can't you?"

No-one spoke. Like I said, he was simple. Not the full shilling. What Mleczko later told me they called a 'not-right' where he'd grown up in Salford.

"You can, can't you?" His wide, wet eyes darted from face to face. "You can make it better." Poor bastard was blubbering openly, now. "Make it better, Danny, please. I don't want to die."

"You're not gonna, mate." Mleczko crouched beside him, squeezing his shoulder. "We'll get you right again, no worries. Not getting out of twatting those fuckers that easy."

I opened my mouth to speak, but Ged put his hand on my arm.

Billy was grinning, however tightly, through the tears. "You're gonna be fine," said Mleczko. "I hadn't shot the fucking thing, it'd've died from biting you. Fucking hell, I've been there when you've let one rip. Poison fucking cities, you could."

Billy was laughing, even as he cried. Mleczko patted his shoulder again. "You'll be right, pal. Just hang on. I'll go get Saddam to take a look at you."

"Saddam," giggled Billy, as Mleczko walked away from him. "Saddam. That's fu –"

The three-round burst blew most of his head apart on impact; the rest flew clear of the body.

I leapt back from the blood; with his head gone, it hosed and splattered the ground. The body dropped forward onto the churned, blackened turf.

Mleczko stood over him for a moment, as if computing whether he'd need to shoot again, then lowered his rifle.

Ged went to him, reaching out a hand; Mleczko twisted away with a warding-off gesture, and walked off, brushing by Joyce like he wasn't there.

BODIES CHOKED PENDLE ROW.

The nightmares lay on tarmac and pavement, draped over the cars blocking the road, crumpled against the walls where they'd fallen. Scattered down Barley Road, too. Spent bullet cases crunched underfoot.

The bay's surface looked flat and innocent.

Chas came towards me, face furrowed and sombre.

"We lost four," he said. "All locals."

"Shit."

"Could've been a lot worse."

"Aye."

The rain hissed down between us. "Want me to clear this lot away?"

I shook my head. "They could be back any minute."

"Thought you said we'd keep them away longer like this."

"That's the plan, but they might have a different one."

Chas nodded. "Well, best get ready for them then, hadn't we?"

"Besides, we leave their bodies where they are, it'll slow them down. More to climb over."

"Every little helps. So what do we do about the next one, Sarge?"

"See if we can get 'em again."

"Same trick?"

"Aye."

"Think they'll fall for that twice?"

"We'll see."

"Same place?"

I shook my head. "Thought you could give it a try."

Chas looked dubiously up and down the Row. "Where'm I supposed to put a bunch of tractors?"

"The Newchurch Road. They can sweep down and hit them here at the junction."

"Try anything once. Stiles said anything?"

"He's out for the count. Checked before. Drank himself stupid."

"Maybe he's got the right idea."

"Fucksake, Chas."

"Sorry, sarge."

"I need you of all people with your head screwed on right."

"Yeah, I know. Sorry." He grinned. "Fucking hell, Jock, I thought *I* was supposed to keep *you* on the straight and narrow."

"*Sergeant* Jock to you, grotbag."

*   *   *

THE RAIN KEPT driving down, harder than ever before.

Still was two hours later, when they attacked again.

The second try...

God, just thinking about it...

The Deep fucking Brain.

It's learning fast.

They threw a big load at the Row, or so it looked.

Chas and his men did as we had, hid the main force and left a skeleton crew visible, then hit them hard with heavy fire and Molotovs before whistling the vehicles down. The nightmares falling back.

And then the second wave came out of the water.

They hit the farm vehicles. Overran them. Jamming the wheels and tracks with sheer weight of numbers – pushing, rocking – a tractor keeled over, a mechanical digger reared up and crashed to the ground like some weird beast in its death throes. Most of the drivers got clear. Not all.

And then they overran the Row. Andrews, about twenty other defenders – all killed.

They fell back, laid down heavy fire. But they kept coming.

And next I knew, the call was coming out.

"Robbie! Robbie!"

Rapid, muffled explosions in the distance. "Chas?"

"They've taken Pendle Row. We couldn't hold them off. They've broken though onto the lower slopes behind it. Need help *now*."

"On its way."

JO GOT THE Landrover with the Mk19 onto the open ground behind Pendle Row. The nightmares staggered through in droves, but Chas scrambled aboard and opened up on them with the launcher, hitting them hard.

I brought Joyce, Mleczko, a good thirty defenders with me, all with SA80s, and it didn't look anywhere near enough.

The survivors of Chas's team were running back to us. Just him and Jo left on the Dinky, covering their retreat, Chas firing the blooper into the nightmares' ranks, blasting fragments of them skywards, until –

It stopped firing. Chas grappled with the blooper. A jam.

And that was when the nightmares, milling closer, broke into a run.

Jo gunned the engine, trying to turn.

The nightmares smashed into the vehicle, tipping it over.

Jo was on the ground rolling, scrambling to her feet with rifle raised as I screamed for covering fire.

Chas landed under its shadow as it toppled towards him.

Scrambling clear – almost made it – almost –

Almost.

The Landrover crashed down, belly-up to the sky, the full weight of it coming down on his right leg, just above the knee.

And Chas was bellowing, scrabbling at the earth, tearing his nails to bloody pulp. Jo beside him, firing this way, then that. One nightmare fell, then another – but never enough. There were always more.

Blood seeping out from under the Landrover. Chas yelling at Jo. Jo shouting back, shaking her head. He yelled again. She ignored him.

Leave me. Save yourself.

No.

Almost automatically, as if my hands were moving of their own volition, I found myself sighting on Jo. Her first, then Chas? Or the other way around? If she was going to stand her ground until they got her too, it'd be a mercy.

Chas tearing the WP grenade from its harness, pulling out the pin.

Jo staring back at him.

Click. I couldn't've heard it over the gunfire, the screams, the explosions, the dying, but I'd swear I did.

Click.

As he released the handle, it fell away and the fuse began to smoke.

Jo screaming.

Chas shouting at her to *go, go, go.*

Jo running – nightmares barring her path. Mleczko firing, and me too, cutting them down.

But I didn't sight on Chas as he lay there, the grenade smoking as the nightmares rushed in on him and –

Mleczko pulling me down. A vivid sheet of flame, then the explosion, followed by several others as the remaining grenades in the Landrover, the Dinky's fuel tanks, all went up.

I scrambled up. Flames. A gouged, blackened crater. The Landrover's wreckage crashed back down into it. Of Chas Nixon, nothing remained.

Jo lay on the ground, unmoving.

The nightmares pouring through. Mleczko yelling in my ear, wanting orders.

Joyce running forward, shooting. Nightmares leaping up at him, pulling him down.

Focus, Robbie.

The voice sounded almost like Chas. Except that he'd've said *Jock,* and – no. Don't think of that now. I aimed on one of Joyce's attackers and fired. Mleczko too. Joyce scrambling free, slinging Jo over his shoulder, staggering back, a wound gaping in the side of his face – half his cheek torn away. But he kept going, until other hands took the woman from him and carried her away, and then he turned and walked out to meet the nightmares, firing on them until the gun was empty and they pulled him down.

But before they could finish him, I did. I did what I'd been going to do for Chas, what I should've done for Billy. I sighted on his head and fired a burst that tore through his skull and that of one of his attackers. They both went down and the others swarmed all over Joyce, biting, tearing, chewing...

Aim and fire. Aim and fire.

I glanced left at Mleczko. His SA80's barrel moved this way, then that, shellcases jumping from the breach. Too fast, it seemed. He was firing wild. But when I looked, I saw a nightmare go down each time.

Fucking hell, he's good.

Aim and fire. Aim and fire.

The bolt locked back. The nightmares, yards away, wading in, jaws yawning open.

"Fall back. Fall back."

I heard myself screaming the words, but felt oddly calm. Everything moved slick and easy. The SA80's empty magazine sliding free as I ran. The replacement clip sliding neatly into place.

Turn to face them. Two nightmares closing in. I dropped the first, tracked right, fired again. The second one fell too.

But still they came.

"Grenades!"

I was already overarming the first one. Mleczko sent another sailing in. Then everyone dived to the ground and tried to burrow into it.

The two explosions sounded so close together it was like a single blast. I felt an intense wave of heat and could see the explosion even through squeezed-shut eyes.

"Fall back! Fall back!"

AND SO WE did. We fell back up to the next line of defence and dug in.

And we waited.

But for now, they didn't come.

For now.

JO SAT IN a corner of the farmhouse living room, blank-faced, rocking to and fro.

She'd dived for the ground before the blast went off. Knocked unconscious, but barely scratched. Hassan said she should be fine. But she hadn't spoken a word.

I crouched beside her. "Jo?"

No answer. Just rocking.

"Jo?"

Rocking.

"Joanne."

Endlessly rocking.

"Fuck you, then."

A blink, a reaction; reddened eyes focussing on me.

"That all you're gonna do for Chas? Sit in a corner crying? That what he died for? Him *and* Joyce? What a fucking waste of two good men."

Her whole face flared, and her hand flew out. I caught it at the wrist – just. The fury, vibrating in her muscles, trying to tear free to try again.

"Better," I said.

Her voice was thick. "Bastard."

"Aye. I'm a bastard." I knew I was. But this had to be done. "I need you, Jo. I need your help. You'd've made one fucking hell of a good soldier. I can't afford to let that go to waste."

Eyes wet and bright; a shuddering breath. Then a sob and she pitched forward. I gripped her tight.

"I loved him," she whispered.

"Me too."

"I would've died with him. I wanted to."

"My best mate."

"I should've stayed. When he took the grenade out. I should've died with him."

"He gave his life."

"That's what you do if you love someone."

"That's what soldiers do."

"I should've stayed, but I ran."

"That's what he wanted. Jo, hen, I'm gonna need you to stay alive a wee bit longer."

I let her go. She sat back, looking at me. "What do you want?"

"I need someone to take care of the other survivors. The ones who can't fight."

"Katja –"

"I've other plans for her." She looked at me, and I lit her a cigarette. "You're to keep them alive long as you can, if those things break through."

"When."

"If." I felt like the prize fool of all time for not just owning up and admitting the truth, but if I didn't act like we'd make it, who bloody would?

She opened her mouth to argue, then shrugged.

"If there's no hope left, it's your judgement what you do."

She nodded. A silence. "That everything?"

"Pretty much."

A knock at the door. "Who is it?"

"Mleczko, Sarge."

"One minute." I turned to Jo. "You up for it?"

"Alright."

"Get going." She nodded and stood. "Can you tell Katja I'd like to see her?" She nodded again. "Come in, Mleczko."

He stood to attention as the door closed behind her.

"You wanted to see me, sarge?"

"Aye. At ease."

"She okay?"

"What do you think? Take a seat."

I uncapped the bottle, poured two Isle of Juras.

He grimaced, but choked it down. Strictly a lager man, Mleczko. Not like Chas. I almost smiled. Almost.

"Sarge?"

Focus, Robbie. Focus.

"I need a new Section Leader, Mleczko."

"Sarge?" Then it dawned. "Serious?"

"Seriously. Consider yourself promoted. Assuming you want it."

His face lit up. "Yeah, sarge. Won't let you down."

"I know. You'll need a 2IC."

"Got anyone in mind, sarge?"

"I was thinking of Katja." His eyebrows rose. "Any problem there for you?"

"No, sarge. She's good. I'd've gone for her myself."

"I'll bet." He was still young, after all. "Just keep your mind on the job, okay?"

"'Course, sarge."

I nodded. "Get your head down, Corporal. Dismissed."

He got up, saluted, went out.

"What do you reckon, Chas?"

No answer; he was dead.

"You reckon he'll do?"

No answer; he was dead.

"I reckon he'll do."

No answer; he was dead.

"Fuck, Chas. What the fuck am I gonna do without you?"

No answer; he was dead.

"Fuck."

CHAPTER EIGHTEEN

THE NIGHT HAS passed, thick with rain, lit only by lightning and dying fires.

They haven't come back yet. But they will. You can put money on it. It's the one inevitability left. Death isn't as final as it was, and taxes – well, there's always an upside.

I'm going to give this to Katja when I'm done. It's going in a safe place, along with her account and Stiles' notes.

Maybe they'll be of some use to someone. Maybe someone else will read them all one day. Someone from Windhoven, maybe.

Maybe this will just be a curiosity by then. Maybe the nightmares will be gone, or at least contained. I like the idea that this will run its course, and the dead'll be dead again. At last. Permanently...

Focus, Robbie.

I haven't much time. I want to explain something.

I want to talk about the desert road.

7TH NOVEMBER. WINTER back in Scotland, but in the desert, it was still hot.

I read somewhere that a breakdown isn't normally down to one single traumatic event. It's cumulative, like erosion – one thing after another.

Maybe it'd been building for a while. I'd helped fight enough dirty little wars, after all. Sooner or later, questions get asked. If only in the silent places at the back of your mind.

The city had been under insurgent control from around the middle of the year, with the civilians caught in the crossfire. Rumours circulated: civilians with white flags fired on, ambulances fired on. We dismissed it as lefty propaganda. Civvies didn't understand war.

So the coalition forces were going in.

But I wasn't involved in any of the fighting. I heard the reports. But I can't say for sure what happened in there.

What I can say is this:

On the afternoon of November 7th, I was stationed on a small desert road leading out of the besieged city.

With me was a section of eight men. Among them Chas Nixon. My CO, Lieutenant Alderson, had given me my brief. No males 'of military age' were to be allowed to leave the city.

"Military age being, sir?"

"Under forty-five, Sergeant."

There was no lower age limit.

"These orders are specific, Sergeant. They're to be turned back. Not detained or held at the checkpoint. They could end up massing and pushing through the roadblocks."

Fuck. That'd been the plan forming in my head. Not letting them through, but not forcing them back into the killing ground either. Someone had thought of that. Someone wanted blood.

"We want to make a clean sweep of all insurgents, not let them scatter to regroup later."

The road was little more than a dirt track. Other units were tackling the main roads. We saw very little. The main attack force was staging to the north. From the city itself came sporadic gunfire – insurgents staging live-fire exercises.

Time ticked by, hot and slow beneath that burning sun.

Late afternoon.

"Heads up!" Chas Nixon shouted.

Men reached for their guns, stood ready. I held my SA80 at port-arms, ready to rock.

A group of people were coming down the desert road. Four women, two girls. Two men in their seventies. A man of about forty, holding the younger girl in his arms. A man in his twenties. Two boys in their teens.

I stepped forward, held up a hand. "Ads?"

Ads was our translator, a scared young local. We called him Ads because it was all we could pronounce of his name.

The group stopped.

The man holding the child spoke. He looked tired. Blood on his hands and face.

"He says they want no trouble. They just want to leave the city before the attack starts."

"Ask him where the blood came from." It was a delaying tactic.

I had my orders.

Ads spoke with the man. "It's from his brother. He was hit by sniper fire."

"Insurgent?" asked Chas.

"Ours."

"No. I mean, was his brother one of them?"

"He says no. They were trying to get out, that's all."

It didn't matter. "The women and girls can go through."

Ads translated. The father looked from his family to us. He spoke again. His voice had risen. Chas stepped back, lifting his rifle. The older girl – about fifteen – screamed. The father shouted over her. Ads was still trying to talk to him. One of the women moaned. Another seemed to be praying.

Ads turned to me. "He says they're not insurgents."

"We've got our orders. Turn them back. The women can go through. Not the men. That's final. No negotiation, alright? You want to debate it, talk to whoever the fuck's in charge."

Chas glanced at me.

The strain was showing. Who the fuck *was* in charge? What the fuck were we doing there? None of us seemed to know anymore. But here we were.

Ads stared back at me. What did he want me to do?

Of course, I knew. He wanted me to act like a man with a mind of my own. With some measure of fucking humanity in me. He wanted me to say, *fuck my orders*. He wanted me to say, *stand down, lads*. He wanted me to say, *let them through*.

But I didn't.

Big soldier-boy, with his big gun, and a fucking coward under it all. Not even the guts to stand up to something a blind man could see was wrong.

I was a coward; Ads and the civilians had exposed it. And I hated the whole fucking crew of them for doing it.

I shoved him back towards the roadblock. "*Tell him.*"

Ads started talking. The father shouted over him. The little girl he was holding began to wail.

Finally, he thrust the child into one of the women's arms and turned back to us. Pointed at me. Shouted something.

The men had their rifles shouldered. I waved them back, but kept my own gun ready. "What's he saying?"

"He says..."

"What?"

Ads looked back at me. "He says you're sentencing them to death."

I moved closer to the barricade.

"He says if you're going to kill them, do it yourself. Get it over with. It'll be quicker."

The man was shouting the same phrase over and over. He had a beard, dark hair to his shoulders. Western dress – white shirt, jacket, trousers. No tie. The children were all fucking wailing now.

Later, Ads told me the man had been shouting *Do it. Do it. Just do it.*

The man reached out and shoved me.

"Tell him to fucking cut that out."

The man shoved me again.

"Ads!"

I jabbed the rifle towards the man.

He tried to knock the barrel aside.

I pulled the trigger.

A high velocity rifle bullet, fired at that range, let me tell you:

Going in, it makes a small, very neat hole.

The hole it makes going out is a different story.

Blood hit my face and hands, sprinkled my uniform. Blowback from the entry wound in the man's chest.

Blood sprayed out of his back, splashed the women, the children, as he fell and lay still.

One of the old men, behind him, screamed and fell too. The bullet had shattered his upper right arm. Must've hit the brachial artery; blood hosed out across the dusty road.

Screaming.

So much fucking screaming.

The teenage girl, the little boy – they fell on the body. The girl screaming, over and over: *Baba, baba.*

Daddy. Daddy.

Rifles were up and pointed, a hairsbreadth from cutting loose.

One of the older women – the man's wife, I was guessing, the man's widow – she was screaming at us. Ads didn't need to translate. I could guess.

Bastards. Cowards. Murderers.

Nothing I wasn't already calling myself.

The old man went into convulsions. I shouted to the section medic who ran to him, fending off blows from the women and the younger men.

Some tiny piece of mercy. Too little, too late.

The old man died too. Shock and blood loss.

Desert spread out each side of the road. Scrub trying to hold the sand together. A crosswind blew plumes of sand across the road. It clung to the blood, soaked and blotted it. Crumbs of it clung to the dead faces of the men I'd killed. And to the blood on my face and hands.

The report said *suspected insurgents*. The report cleared me.

But I'd know. I'd always know.

How long listening to the women scream at me? How long wanting to shoot them, or myself?

But it ended.

They picked up their dead and walked back towards the city. All of them. A Muslim has to be buried within twenty-four hours.

They walked away down the road. None of them looked back. The sand plumes blew back and forth, obscuring them.

I was screaming after them, screaming at Ads that the women could go through. Ads did as he was told. He shouted after them. But if they heard, they gave no sign.

One turned back and looked. Just once.

It was the older girl. Her face was blanched and streaked with tears. Hatred I could have borne. But all I saw was grief, and mute incomprehension.

She turned away and followed her family.

When she was older, she would have been beautiful.

If she'd lived.

THE RUMOURS OF civilian massacres came out later, of course. And I saw with my own eyes the white phosphorous dropped on the town.

Estimated civilian casualties: 6,000.

Piss-pathetic by the standards of the flood and what's come after, I'm sure. But I'm guessing the population's much smaller by now. So it'll probably sound as bad as it deserves to.

I can't be sure they died. I only went into the city once, after the attack. I saw the shattered houses. The bodies piled up in the streets. The burned ones, bodies half-turned to ash, skin hanging off – the skin of the hands hanging down like gloves.

I couldn't speak of what I'd done. Not even to my wife. Especially not Jeannie. I couldn't bear to take comfort from her. I could *not*.

I had no right to it, not anymore.

She tried to stay the course. The drinking. The depression. The outbursts of violence and rage.

But one day I came home and found her gone.

No more than I deserved.

So now you know.

* * *

PRETTY MUCH DONE now.

Dawn is breaking. I'm inside the farmhouse at the foot of Pendle Hill, finishing off. Just a matter of time now befo

"SARGE! SARGE!"

Fuck, I think, and put down the pen. Parkes, bursting into the room. "What is it?"

"We've raised Windhoven on the radio, sarge."

"Fucking brilliant." I'm on my feet, energised. "Where?"

"Chinook, sarge."

"Let's go."

On board – Hendry, hunched over the comms.

A woman's voice crackling out of the speaker. "Windhoven to Osprey. Osprey, this is Windhoven."

Hendry leans forward. "Osprey here."

"Who am I speaking to?"

"Flying Officer Hendry, ma'am. Also Sergeant McTarn – he's the ground commander here –"

"I know who McTarn is." Christ, my reputation travelled.

"– and Private Parkes." Which sounded too much like a bad joke.

"This is Captain Bowman. Where's Squadron Leader Tidyman?"

Hendry looks at me. "Killed in action, ma'am."

"Christ. What's your status?"

"Still on the ground at Pendle, with the surviving ground force and about a hundred civilians. Been trying to contact you for a while now."

"I was wondering where you'd got to."

"The Squadron Leader hadn't briefed us on your location. The paperwork was lost with him. Captain, can you give us your co-ordinates? We're under siege and need an evac."

"Not much point, I'm afraid."

A cold finger up my arse. "Ma'am?"

"Started showing up about a fortnight ago. Didn't do anything at first. Just wandering around. We shot a few. But then more turned up. We've got virtually the entire former population of the Thames Valley here right now."

"What's your status, ma'am?"

"Not good, Hendry, not good at all. Attack began in earnest day before yesterday. They've managed to breach the underground base, overrun the aircraft bays so we can't get out. We've been holding them off, but..."

She doesn't say more; just lets the hiss of static do that for her. I can hear distant gunfire.

"Can you get to the surface, Captain? We could fly in, hit them on the ground. At least give some of you the chance to –"

"Negative. We can't hold them. We're running low on ammunition, and they just keep coming. Soon, we'll be fighting them hand to hand. We'd be long gone by the time you got here. Besides, sounds like you have problems of your own."

"You know what they say, Captain; it's grim up north."

Bowman laughs. There's an ugly, jagged edge to it. "Any luck raising your regional control centre?"

"None, ma'am."

"Us neither. My guess is they've either gone under already or are in the same boat as us. I'm afraid you're on your own, Hendry. Take what action you see fit."

"Copy, ma'am."

A pause; muffled voices in the background. "I'm afraid that'll have to be it. They're breaking through. Must dash."

"God be with you, ma'am." I never pegged Hendry as religious. Then again, I never asked.

"You too, Hendry. Windhoven out."

The line goes dead.

"Sarge? They're moving."

This is it. This is it. The fuck do I do now? Chas?

I've got your back, Robbie. You need help, you got me. Alright?

I need help, Chas. Need it fucking now. Where are you? Where?

"Sarge?"

"Move..." *Focus, Robbie, focus.* "Move 'em out, Parkes."

"Yes, sarge."

So, then. It's here. At last.

Outside, other survivors huddle under tarps. Those we've the space for – the women, the children – they're crammed into the farmhouse, or Stiles' caravan. The rest are out there, under whatever shelter we can improvise.

We won't need it much longer anyway.

The P226 at my hip. The SA80 at my side. Chambering a round as I go. The pages folded in a plastic bag, tucked under my arm.

Katja in the field, huddled under tarps with the rest. She'd given up her billet for someone she thought needed it more.

You should have been in charge. Not me.

I walk to her. She stands. I give her the papers. We don't speak. There is nothing to say.

Stiles appears at the caravan door. He's pale. He half-raises a hand to me, in some kind of salute. But I'm already running.

*   *   *

ON THE SIDE facing Barley, we found a couple of farmhouses – one a working farm, the other converted into a residence – bracketing a dirt road.

They stand just below a ridge of high ground with the footpath cutting down it. On the left side of it is a field ringed with a solid drystone wall, where we've taken up positions. We've got Gimpys, Minimis, rifles, Molotovs, a few grenades. On the right is a small, pointed plateau, where we've set up a Gimpy and a couple of riflemen.

The fields, meadows and other open ground below us are all as heavily mined as we were able to manage, enough that any of them advancing over the open terrain will be blown to fuck. Parkes is down there with Neil and Steve. The fougasses have to be detonated manually. That's their job. Their orders are to wait until the nightmares are in range, blow the charges and run.

If we can use the fougasses to force the nightmares onto the footpaths – like the one leading up to the farmhouses and the space between them – they'll pour out into what we'll be able to turn into a perfect killing zone.

In the farmhouses, there's Levene and a few of the better local rifle shots, to whittle the odds down as they come up the path.

It'll work as long as the fougasses keep them to the paths. Or until they realise there'll be no further explosions once the mines are blown; when that happens, they'll start using the open ground again, and our last advantage will be gone. All we can do then is hold position as long as we can.

I crouch behind the drystone wall. I can feel my hands shaking. *Fuck.* Chas, pal, I need you here now. Mleczko's good, but it just isn't the same. He isn't Chas.

Even if we *can* get the Chinook up again, what then? A stay of execution? In the long run, the result's the same. We all die. Nothing lasts. No-one gets away. One by one, we all fall down.

The nightmares move so slowly – except when they come at you in those short, deadly, bursts – it's easy to believe you can outwit them, outrun them. But they're untiring, relentless. And sooner or later, you have to stop.

For nearly a minute, I just crouch there, terrified someone'll ask me for an order. Hopelessness is a huge fucking weight, crushing me so flat I can hardly breathe.

Come off it, Jock. You've got a job to do. Deal with each problem as it comes. Worry about this attack, then worry about the next one. Worry about getting the chopper off the ground again, then worry about where you're gonna go. And for fuck sake, Jock, stop fucking snivelling.

"*Sergeant* Jock to you, grotbag."

"Sarge?" Mleczko, blinking.

"Noth –"

And that's when the fougasses go off like a fucking cannonade.

Yelps, a couple of whoops. I peer over the wall. Plumes of smoke rising. Flames crackling further down the slope.

Levene's voice, crackling out of the communicator. "It's hitting the bastards, sarge. Got to have taken out hundreds of them."

"Good. And the rest?"

"Hang on..." A tinge of excitement in the voice. For Levene, that's saying a lot. "Yes. They're taking the footpath. I can see them at it, sarge. They're heading our way."

"Okay." I raise my voice. "Everybody, weapons ready. Company's coming. Levene?"

"Sarge?"

"Hold fire. Let 'em get in close."

"How close do you want 'em?"

"Wait 'til they start entering the killing zone. Then hit the ones who're still coming in. Hit them too early, they might pull back. I want this to fucking *count*."

"Copy, sarge. Just keep them out of here, okay?"

"We'll cover you, Levene. Just make sure you do the same for us."

"Copy that, sarge."

We can hear them coming now. The tramping squish of feet in mud. The distant hissing sounds. I flex my hands on the SA80.

And the smell. The thick ripe stench of the dead. Like a finger touching the back of my throat. I gag, spit out bile. More coughing and retching further down the line.

"Our guests have arrived, sarge."

No shit. "Everyone stand ready, but hold fire until my command. I'll fucking feed you to the bastards myself if you fire early. Clear?"

"Sarge," comes the echo down the line, even from the civvies. There isn't really that much of a line between us and them now. We're all in the same boat. And it's sinking.

"Wait for it... wait for it..."

Sighting over the wall. The green-stained bodies shuffling forward. Yawning faces, blackened teeth. Eyes glowing with green torment, as they close in with outstretched, grasping hands...

Closer... closer...

"Fire!"

I shout orders, point. But everything seems too slow, not quite in step. It's not them. It's me. I'm out of sync. Not fast enough.

Not now. Stay together. Focus. *Focus!*

They go down quickly. They don't fall back. They keep coming. Until they're all cut down.

There'll be more of them soon.

"Sarge! Sarge!" Parkes.

"Parkes, go ahead."

"They're back on the open ground. There's something different... oh, shit."

"What?"

"Sarge, you're not gonna believe this."

"What is it, Parkes?"

"God almighty, there's gotta be thousands, but –"

"Spit it out!"

"They're spread out in groups of fifty or so. Big gaps between them. The fougasses'll hardly dent it."

"Looks like they mean business this time."

"'S what it looks like, sarge."

"Okay. Blow the remaining charges and get back here. Levene?"

"Sarge."

"Cover their retreat, then get back to the bastards on the footpaths. Fire at will. Let's see how far we can whittle them down." I raise my voice to the others. "All riflemen move forward. Get into a position where you can see the enemy. Take your time. Acquire your target. Be sure of your shot. And drop the fuckers. Make every bullet count. Every one we kill now is one less to deal with at close quarters."

"Like when they get here, you mean, Sarge?" Mleczko murmurs.

"Bang on, Mleczko."

The fougasses going off. Levene's rifles start firing seconds later. I move forward into the yard of the working farmhouse, sighting down on the nightmares entering the wide-open meadow below.

Parkes and the others are running. The nightmares are close behind though, closer than they should be. Some of them break into runs. One leaps on Neil's back and he goes down. Others falling on him. Neil screaming.

I aim, look through the sight. A face swims into focus. I centre the tip of the blade in the Trilux sight between its eyes. Squeeze the trigger. It drops.

Good shot. Now do it again. But even with that slow, shuffling pace, how long before they get here? And if they run...

Fire. Fire again.

Parkes and Neil scrambling up the meadow and into the farmyard.

And then –

"They're running!"

"Fuck!" Yelling into the communicator. "Levene, get out of there now! Fall back, we are falling back!"

I unpin the grenades I still hold – one white phosphorous, one frag

– and overarm them both into the advancing horde, then run as the explosions ring out behind.

Diving over the drystone wall. Aiming over as the nightmares come crawling up into the farmyard, onto the footpath – fucking everywhere –

Focus!

"Covering fire!"

The MGs chattering. Levene and the others pour out of the buildings. Two, from the farmhouse on the right, aren't fast enough. The nightmares pull them down. Mleczko running forward, firing from the hip, lobbing a grenade.

"Mleczko!"

An explosion. Mleczko ducking, the others running past him. Levene hanging back, firing at the nightmares, a rearguard –

Going after them. "Get back here, the fucking pair of you!"

Levene trips, falls. Half back on his feet when one hits him in a flying tackle. Two, three, four more hurl themselves onto him, grabbing, tearing. He screams.

"Levene!" Mleczko, turning back.

"You can't do anything! Get behind the wall! Hold the line!"

I cover him as he goes. Nightmares closing in. I shoot one in the forehead. Then another. And another.

I realise I'm laughing.

I realise I'm going to die. Here, today, now.

I realise it's what I've wanted for a long time.

The girl turning back, the last look on her face as she goes.

For a second I see her, and lower the gun.

For a second, it's her father, and I don't shoot. And it never happened. And I'm redeemed.

And then I realise it isn't her or him at all, it's a nightmare. It looks a little like the man I shot. Tubby, a beard, shoulder-length hair. What's left of it.

Its eyes, burning.

I point the gun.

I pull the trigger.

Click.

Fuck.

It jumps.

I'm drawing the P226, but it's on me, teeth going for my throat. I get my left hand under its chin as we hit the ground. Its jaws snap, its lips brush my cheek – but not its teeth. Pushing it away from me, pulling the Sig-Sauer free to kill it. Thinking: *Lucky bastard, McTarn* –

Still thinking how lucky when it twists its head and bites three fingers off my left hand.

* * *

DARK. THICK DULL throb of pain in my hand.

My hand.

"Fuck!"

"Easy, sarge." Hassan, pushing me back down on an improvised pallet bed. The ceiling above me. Spinning. I feel drunk.

"Alright. Alright. Get off." I put a hand to my forehead. It burns.

Gunfire. Close to.

"Where?" I bat his hand aside and sit up. My head and stomach roll.

"Sarge, take it easy."

"Bollocks." More gunshots. "Bastard things are right on top of us." I look at him. "Aren't they?"

He nods.

"What happened?"

He drops his gaze. "Mleczko killed your attacker, carried you back."

I remembered Levene. "I told the little bugger to leave the wounded. Still, if he knows when to disobey an order..."

Your attacker.

"Shit!"

"Take it easy, sarge."

"Stop fucking saying that! Fucker bit half my hand off." I swallow hard. Nothing seems quite real. "I'm gonna become one of them. Aren't I?"

"You might have a chance."

"What do you mea..." I close my eyes and raise my hands to my face, but only one set of fingers touches it.

There is a swaddled stump where my left hand was. I hold it up, to be sure he's not just bound the undamaged fingers and thumb in tight. No. It's gone.

I let out a laugh that sounds odd and weak and strange to my own ears.

"Sarge..." Hassan, reaching for a needle.

"No!" I fend him off. "No time." I get off the table. My legs wobble. No. *Stand straight.* I'm in my underwear. "Get my fucking combats."

"Sergeant, you've just had surgery."

"I was bitten, Hassan. I'm fucked."

"We may have cut the infected tissue away in time. You might have a chance."

"Get me whatever pills and shots you need to keep me on my feet. I'm no fucking good to anyone in here. So do as you told. I'm giving you a fucking order."

Christ. I sound like Tidyman.

* * *

IT HASN'T WORKED. I can feel it. A terrible burning pain, in the stump of my wrist. Nausea, a pounding headache. I walk on.

Behind me there's the Hill, the farmhouse, Stiles' meadow. In front of me, another meadow, leading down to drystone walls and a gate. The defenders spread out along the wall. Mleczko at the gate, shouting orders.

Beyond the gate, down the path, they're coming in small, scattered groups.

Their eyes are glowing green.

Green like the sea. Like the deep sea.

I can hear, from far off, over the shouts and gunfire, the lapping of sea on the shore.

I reach the gate. Slump against it. Mleczko jumps, stares at me. "Sarge!"

"Mleczko. What's the situation?"

He looks older than before. Command'll do that. "They marched more of the fuckers up slower, while we were still fighting that first lot, so then they could go flat out. Full speed, you know? They were coming in on all fronts. Had to fall back, but soon as we got one defensive line, they were on top of us again. In the end, we didn't have anywhere else to go. So here we are." He rubs his face. "Lost a lot of people. Lot of kit, too."

"What we got left?"

"Still okay for rifles. Few Minimis, couple of Gimpys... pretty much it."

"Then we make them count." I look down the lane. There don't seem to be many of them. A few dozen, hanging back. They drop one by one as the bullets whine and crack out. "Doesn't look like much of an army."

"Not compared to what they were hitting us with before."

Green eyes glow down the path. I stare into them; they expand and swallow me up.

The sound of a huge ocean. Waves. But there's something else. Listen. *Listen.* I can hear voices. Human voices.

The refugees, back in the meadow...

No. Not them. This is different. I'm not even hearing the gunshots anymore. I can only hear the sea. And the voices.

They're crying out. I hear men and women. Children too. Crying for mercy, for release. In rage, at lives cut short so soon.

The gnawing pain in the stump of my wrist, the thump of my heart squeezing new pain through my body. I can feel it spreading. They've slowed it down. But once it takes hold, there's no shifting it.

Mleczko's mouth moving. Saying something. But I can't hear. And now all I can really see, all that really matters, are those glowing green eyes.

And the light flickers and fades and contracts – shrinks from a glow filling the whole world to two dying bulbs, the eyes of a nightmare falling forward as it dies.

"Sarge? Sarge?"

I turn back to Mleczko. "Alright. Here's what you do. Hendry made any progress with the Chinook?"

"If he had, we'd be airborne by now, Sarge. And I don't reckon he's got long to pull one out of the hat."

"What d'you mean?"

"I think I know why they're holding off."

I picked the right man for the job, because I think I know too. "They're going to wait 'til dark."

"Yeah. In my eyes, that's what they're gonna do. Keep throwing cannon fodder at us, tire us out, use our ammo up. But once it's dark and we can't see the fuckers, they'll rush us. The lot of them. And they won't stop."

My forehead's burning. Rain hitting it. "Right. Here's what you do. Start picking people for evac. Find out what's the maximum the Chinook'll carry. You're gonna have to pick who goes and who stays. Tell Hendry if the fucking thing's not ready to fly by dark I'll feed him to the nightmares myself."

Mleczko glances down the footpath. "What about..."

"I'll handle it here." He opens his mouth. "None of your lip. I'm not dead yet. Get your arse in gear."

I draw the Sig-Sauer and look down the lane, thumb on the hammer.

DUSK. THE SKY growing dim. A dulled sunset seeping through the clouds. Blood soaking through a bandage.

No word on the chopper. It was always a long shot.

They're gathering down the road. Clusters of tiny lights.

I've a splitting headache. The stump of my wrist throbs. Not just the stump, in fact. My whole forearm, now. The bandages are wet. Something seeping through.

Hassan gave me pills. Morphine and codeine. I dry-swallow two, think *fuck it* and down a third. Probably not a good idea for a man with a gun, but fuck it all over again. We left proper procedure behind a long time ago.

The lights moving. Shuffling forward. I can hear the sea again. Growing louder. The voices. Screaming. Moaning. Sobbing. Wailing.

Footsteps, coming up behind me.

"Mleczko? Hendry got that fucking chopper fixed yet?"

"No."

And it's not Mleczko, either. It's Katja.

She comes to stand beside me, watches the gathering mass below us. "Are you alright?" She shakes her head. "Stupid question."

There's someone else with her. His silhouette looks strange. Fucking drugs. I'm dizzy, weak. When the nightmares come I won't stand a chance. How much of them lingers on? Some fragment, some flicker of consciousness? I remember the empty farmhouse, the father staring up at his old home. The thought of being aware as my body kills and eats people I know...

Kills and eats Katja.

But it's not the drugs. It's...

"Stiles?"

"Yes." He looks very calm. Katja isn't looking at him.

He's wearing a wetsuit. An aqualung. A diving mask pushed up on his forehead. Boots, but a pair of flippers hang from his belt.

"What the hell?"

"He's going to get himself killed."

Stiles reaches out and touches her arm; she pulls it away.

"Katja, we've talked about this. I have to try. It's the only chance."

"What is?" I demand.

"This."

He climbs over the gate before I can stop him, before I even realise what he's doing. "Stiles, for fuck sake –" I'm scrambling forward, to go after him. Down the road, the nightmares have started shambling forward.

But Katja stops me. She's crying. "No," she says. "Let him go."

I stop and stare. Confused? That's not the word for it. She turns and goes to the gate. He looks down the path at the nightmares.

"You're sure?" Her voice is tiny. Almost a child's.

"No," he says. "But I've got to try."

He turns back. They come together and kiss. I have to look away. Not out of jealousy. I'm past that now.

"I love you," I hear him whisper, and her whisper it back.

When I turn back, he's walking down the footpath. The nightmares have stopped their advance. They just stand and watch him, with their glowing eyes, in the deepening gloom.

Stiles reaches them and stops. For a frozen second, it's just them, contemplating each other.

The eyes of the nightmares in front of him begin to pulse, just like the ones back at the army base did. Stiles sways, nearly falls, but doesn't.

The pulsing stops, and –

The nightmares are parting. Stepping aside to leave a clear path. Stiles starts walking. They turn their heads and watch him go. Then they turn back to watch us.

It's like a ripple effect, extending as far down as I can see, as he goes. Until he's out of sight.

"What the fuck?" I say again. I tear my gaze from the nightmares and stare at Katja. "What the fuck is going on?"

"They want him," she says. "They always have."

"What?"

"His notes. Didn't you read them? It's all in there."

"What the fuck's he trying to do?"

"Save us all," she says.

"He's..." I remember the wetsuit, the equipment. "He's going diving?" She nods.

"But I thought he couldn't. I thought he'd die if..."

She nods again. Then she turns and walks back the way she came.

I turn and stare out at the nightmares. They stand and watch us. Eyes glowing. As the darkness deepens.

A COUPLE OF minutes pass. I lean on the gate, shivering in the chill of the rain even as I welcome it falling on my burning forehead. A footfall behind me.

"Ged."

"Lad." He leans on the gate too, on folded arms, a farmer surveying his land. The SPAS-12 is slung across his back. "How you doing, lad?"

"How do you fucking think?" He doesn't answer. "Sorry."

Smiling slightly, he waves it away.

"I'm dying," I say at last.

"Aren't we all?"

And I have to laugh.

Ged chuckles as well. "So, what you planning to do, lad?"

"I'll stop here," I say. "This is it for me. Even if we get the Chinook airborne again, I'm fucked." I hold up the bandaged stump. Another sick, fevery shudder passes through me. "So I might as well go out on my own two legs, eh?"

Ged nods. "Good enough. If you've no objection, I'll join you."

I turn and stare at him. "Are you mad?"

He just looks at me.

"Ged, I'm not gonna be falling back, did you hear me?"

"I know the score, lad. They'll not get that chopper airborne again. We both know it. This is it for us all now. Barring miracles."

"Believe in them?"

"Oh, miracles happen." A smile softens his face. "My missus saying 'yes' when I asked her to marry me, that were a miracle alright. And our Cla..." he trails off, the smile gone.

"I'm not holding my breath for any tonight."

"Nor I. If I've got to die, I'll do it here. This far and no farther, all of that. I've run enough, from them bastards killed my Clare."

There nothing to say to that. "Alright," I say. "I'd be honoured."

"I know, lad."

"Just one thing, Ged?"

"What's that?"

"Can you stop calling me 'lad'? My name's Robert."

"Alright then, lad. Robert it is."

THE SUN IS nearly gone.

And so am I.

I can barely stand. The pain and the sickness are almost too much to bear. The stump of my hand is like a second heart, pumping poison. With Mleczko's help and a roll of gaffa tape, I've strapped the hatchet to the stump of my wrist. Makes it hurt all the worse, but at least I can do some damage.

My hand shakes. I'm sweating like a pig. When I wipe it away, my forehead's burning like hot coals.

They're just shadows now. Shadows with eyes. Their outlines blur and break up as the light fails.

A full clip in the P226. No spares. How the fuck am I supposed to reload? I have an SA80 too, propped on the gate; I can fire one-handed.

Mleczko's on one side of me. Ged and Katja on the other. Others spread out behind the walls.

In the camp behind us, people are crying. Someone praying. A few ragged voices rise in a song. A hymn, a folk-song, or just something that was in the charts a few weeks ago. I can't make it out. But I can hear the sea. Louder and louder, trying to drown everything else out.

The sea, and the voices.

> *why me why me? i didn't want to die*

no no no my baby my baby

> *bastards you bastards*
> *for being alive*

dear father in heaven

> *pater noster pater noster*
> *hail mary full of grace,*

the lord is with thee, blessed art thou amongst women, blessed is the fruit of thy womb jesus christ, holy mary mother of god pray for us poor sinners now and at the hour of hour of our death

want to live want to live want to live

> *no not like this not to die like this not like*

this not like this

"Fuck," says Mleczko. "Here they come."

Down the road, the forest of glowing eyes is moving.

bastards bastards want to live why me and not you?

will live will live will live again kill you kill you KILL YOU

EAT EAT EAT EAT EAT

Like a wave, a tide of souls.

Rising. Gathering. And then the wave breaks.

"Open fire!"

The GPMGs and Minimis sweep the advancing ranks. But the next wave just scramble over the fallen bodies. And that means you've got to aim up to hit them in the head. And the twilight makes accurate firing harder and harder with an automatic weapon.

Aim and fire. Aim and fire. They keep falling. But they keep coming too.

This is it. No matter how hard we hit them, they won't fall back this time.

Then they burst into a jerky, scrambling run. They're not coming direct for me. They're focusing in, closing on specific points, choosing their targets.

They're going for the machine guns.

Faces leap out, rotten. Aim and fire. Aim and fire.

Not one of you yet, you bastards, not one of you yet.

The answer is a furious wave that crashes on a sea wall. Their voices are screaming in rage. All the different voices, blending in and out. Now and again one voice leaps out. But it's a whole. An organ note. Sounding together. One voice. I stop shooting as I realise that. One voice blended out of many –

"Sarge!"

And if I listen to it closely I can hear what it's trying to say.

"Sarge!"

What?

"Robert!"

Katja's voice. Maybe the only one that could snap me out of this. As the wave of the dead crashes against the gate.

Firing. Bodies dropping. A nightmare trying to climb over, then jerking, falling past me, its skull shattered. They stumble back, bracing against the tidal force of the multitudes behind them. Hurling themselves forward again.

Screaming from further down, on either side. They've reached the machine guns, grabbing the barrels and dragging them down, leaping over the walls to fall upon the gunners. The other defenders fire into them, but it's not enough, never enough.

"Robert!"

Firing out the SA80, letting it fall –

"Back!"

They crash against the gate. I can hear it cracking, buckling.

"Back!" Mleczko, running. They're all running.

Except me. Me and Ged. Back a few paces to stand our ground.

Katja wrenching at my arm. "Robert! Robert!"

"No." My voice sounds thick and slurred. "Go. Go." I don't look at her.

Can't. What must my face look like now? So sick, so sick. I'm full of it now, the sickness. The infection. All I can hear in my ears is the ocean's pounding roar. I can barely hear her voice.

holy mary mother of god, pray for us poor sinners now and at the hour of our death

Ha. Funny, an old bluenose coming out with that at the last.

"Go on, lass," I heard Ged say.

"Go," I tell her. "We'll cover you."

I can't hear her reply, if she has one. But I feel the touch of her lips, a last kiss, on my cheek.

And then me and Ged are alone and the gate's giving way. They burst through and I raise the gun and aim on the first one and I pull the trigger and its head snaps back. And I aim again and...

We back away as they swarm through and over the gate, Ged still thumbing the last few shells into the SPAS-12, then firing, firing, firing.

Raising the Sig-Sauer, shoot – a nightmare close in – I swing at it, smash its skull with the hatchet taped to my wrist, shoot again.

Shoot and strike, shoot and strike.

The axe gone, buried in another nightmare's head, the bone locking round the blade, pulling me off-balance, the haft breaking. A nightmare diving on me; I fire upwards, into its gaping mouth. Somehow I manage to stand.

The shotgun empty; Ged using it as a club, smashing skulls.

But there are so many of them. Too many. And then they're on him. He goes down, thrashing and fighting, and I hear a scream torn from his lips.

I aim and fire on him, hitting him in the head. He falls and I'm screaming now, firing into the face of another nightmare, and then another, and –

The P226's slide locks back. Empty.

Fuck.

They stop and stare, facing me.

I throw the gun aside. I can still fight. I grab at the ground. Fumble for a chunk of rock as they shamble towards me.

But my legs give way and I collapse as they gather round me with their burning eyes.

I grip the rock, somehow manage to lift it a few inches off the ground with an arm as weak as an old man's.

"Come on, then," I say, then shout up at them. "*Come on!*"

Ged rises, torn and ravaged, missing chunks of flesh and his eyes glowing, but still – just about – recognisable. And stumbles off after the rest.

A wave of sickness and shivering, a terrible weakness. I feel my bowels and bladder fail. A rush of shame, and then –

Screaming after them, but I can't even hear my own voice now it's so fucking loud, the sea, the voices
flesh and blood, flesh and bone –

make us whole

again

let us live don't want to die let us live

rage rage rage against the dying of the light, against those still drawing unearned breath on land

leaving us down here in the darkness
down here in the darkness cold and alone

alone

ALONE

– drowning me out, eclipsing me, eclipsing –
Who? What's my name?
WHAT'S MY FUCKING NAME?
I scream – soundlessly to my own ears ––and fall back to the earth. Too weak now. And they just keep coming on, stepping over or around me,

me,

me,

Me, Robbie McTarn
ROBBIE MCTARN MY NAME IS ROBBIE MCTARN
And I realise why as the sickness rises one last time like a wave and the pain washes through my body.
My heart is hammering hammering hammering, fastfastfaster, and I'm burning up, oh, god I'm burning up.
And then the thundering jackhammer rhythm of my heart is all I can hear, even the ocean is gone and I hear the rhythm thunder thunder thunder
   And skip,
falter,

Stutter erratically
and then,
finally,

   it stops.

And I can't move my eyes, can't look beyond what's in front of me as I lie dying, dying, DEAD upon the dull earth, as dead men and women stagger past me, mind screaming, beating the bone walls of its cage as it dies from lack of oxygen, the lights going out for good.
Things slipping away from me. My dad, something about my dad... did I love or hate him? Can't remember now.
I want to scream out in rage at it. Scream out in the fear I feel. But can't.
All I can hear are the screams I can't utter.
The screams others are uttering for me.
rage rage rage

oh god no not me not like this

And I'm falling, crashing down, plunging through a deep dark endless ocean, glowing green eyes and rotting hands and faces reaching out for me.

Screams and voices all around me. And they're all my own.

I can't remember my name anymore.

Vaguely I realise my limbs are moving but it's not me moving them, that this is the last awareness of my body I shall have. I can't remember can't remember anything I'm just the tiniest little spark of consciousness and all that is left is my rage and my terror to swell the waters of this ocean and I feel myself fading and when this is done I will not exist at all anym

PART THREE

Storm Surge – Fathom Five

how is it
That this lives in thy mind? What seest thou else
In the dark and backward abysm of time?

Shakespeare,
The Tempest, Act I, Scene ii

CHAPTER NINETEEN

Stiles

MY AIR HOSE. That was where it started. I was exploring a wreck off the north-west Scottish coast, and I snagged it on a sharp edge of some kind. I didn't see what.

The hose snapped.

Bubbles everywhere. Silt billowing in the water as I scrabbled for a way out of the wreck. Banging into walls, practically blinded.

My life didn't flash before my eyes. Instead I thought about the life I *wasn't* going to live. I was thirty-one, with a PhD, and I'd spent my life, one way or the other, immersed in the sea. Pun intended. But I had a shopping list of other plans: marriage, kids, a house –

All going now in this storm of bubbles and silt. This stupid death. Stupid accident. *Stupid.* A pratfall, almost.

Not like this. Not like this.

Trying to grab the air-hose, feeling it flail away, pushed out by the jet of air. Bruising and slashing my arms and legs on the rusted, barnacled hull...

And then I was in open water.

It's blurred here, but I remember:

Holding breath. Lungs bursting. The air-hose, couldn't find the air-hose, hands scrabbling at the water for the FUCKING AIR-HOSE –

Blue water

> *Rocks and sand, the sandy bottoms of the ocean*

Up above

above, light,

> *coming down through the water*
>> *Long away above.*

>>> *No time,*

>> *no time*

striking up for it.

> *too deep, too deep – must decompress, acclimatise*

But no time.

Swimming up towards the light.

And –

LOOK AT A bottle of Pepsi, Coke, Irn Bru if you like. Whatever you prefer. An unopened bottle. It's not fizzy, is it? Not until you break the seal and release the pressure. At high pressures, gas dissolves in liquid. When you dive, when you go deep and stay there, the nitrogen in the air you breathe dissolves in your blood.

Clear so far?

When you surface, you release that pressure. Remember the bottle of Pepsi? Imagine that happening in your blood, lungs, brain, eyes.

Divers working at depth are supposed to resurface slowly. That way the nitrogen is released gradually and without causing any harm. If you surface too fast, the bubbles of nitrogen form inside your body. They can form in the brain, in the jelly of the eye. Most commonly, they form in your bone joints.

Doctors call this condition decompression sickness or barotrauma, sometimes caisson sickness. Divers call it the bends.

But if you're forced to surface at speed, most ships equipped for diving carry a hyperbaric chamber. This is a sealed structure where gas can be pumped in or released to increase or reduce the pressure. Turn the pressure up, the nitrogen dissolves again. Then release it – *slowly* this time – and it's released gradually, like it should've been in the first place.

Do this, and all should be fine.

But this wasn't a diving ship, just a fishing boat I'd chartered for the day. I was on holiday. I hadn't dived in weeks, and I'd been impatient to get out there. I'd dived before, dozens of times.

Overconfidence. I forgot one tiny, massive detail. The sea is an alien world; we only exist in it on sufferance. One slip can be fatal. And almost was.

Sometimes, even now, I wish it had been.

THE PAIN BEGAN as I ascended, and the gas bubbles expanded in my joints. Imagine your wrist trying to push your hand off; imagine your elbow trying to push your forearm down and away. The skin and muscle stops that happening. But the pain...

Lying on the deck of the ship. The agony was beyond anything I'd ever known. The boat turning coastwards – the reek of petrol fumes, the deck vibrating. My nose and mouth full of blood. Frothing. A taste of bitter iron.

"HOW ARE YOU feeling?"

The doctor went by the rather wonderful name of Naomi Scrimgeour. The first sounded very pretty and very gentle – which she was – while the second brought to mind a Viking raider come to remove vital organs with an axe. *Are you on the NHS, sir, or would you like an anaesthetic?* Old joke. Less funny than ever now.

"Fucking awful," I said. She looked down. I felt like a prize arsehole. "Sorry."

But, in truth, the pain was constant. Which she should have known. She was the doctor, after all.

There'd been damage to the nervous system. A common side-effect. Intermittent numbness, shooting pains, weakness down the left side of my body.

"What's the prognosis?" I finally asked.

They'd moved me into a private room, thankfully. The hospital was near the coast. I was never sure where. Outside, I could hear the cry of gulls.

She still wasn't meeting my eyes; her face was flushed. She shuffled the papers in front of her. "Um – well –"

Bad news she wasn't sure how to break. I'd pretty much guessed it already.

"Doctor. I'm sorry. But please tell me." My voice was a gravelly croak. I wondered if that was permanent too. "I respect honesty and directness. I try to deal with others on that basis, and I like the same in return."

If I'd felt like an arsehole before, I felt a prize ponce after delivering *that* one, but she looked up and smiled. Not an entirely comfortable smile, but a smile nonetheless. "Alright, Dr Stiles –"

"Ben."

"Ben." I'd tried to get her to call me by my first name on the half-dozen times we'd previously spoken. Success at last.

Dr Naomi Scrimgeour's glasses were small and neat. So was she, generally. Five or six years younger than me. Minus the glasses, her eyes were blue and tilted up at the corners. Short brown hair with subtle blonde highlights. A face made up of small, neat angles. Tiny bones, a rosebud mouth, peaches and cream skin. A pimple just above her left eyebrow, a tiny mole above her right cheekbone; flaws that made the rest more real.

Her voice was soft, gentle and low, but the content, as she'd promised, was blunt and to the point. "You've some nerve damage which will impair your dexterity, and will cause random shooting pains. The gas bubbles are trapped in your joints, and there's nothing we can do about them. The pain from them will be constant."

"Permanent?"

She looked back down at the papers in her lap and gave them a meaningless shuffle. "Permanent. There's medication to help you manage the pain. We'll probably prescribe DHC – dihydrocodeine – but there are other options available, up to and including morphine."

"Life expectancy?"

"Reduced."

"By how much?"

"Dr Stiles –"

"Ben."

"It's hard to be exact."

"You must have some idea."

She touched her hair. "A lot depends on how closely you follow the prescribed regime."

"If I do?"

"You'll live longer than you would otherwise."

"How much longer?"

She looked up at me, took a deep breath. Never easy, a job like this. "With luck and good pain management, you could reasonably expect to reach your fifties. Possibly even your sixties."

"My sixties."

"Or longer. It's hard to be exact."

"Appreciated."

"You asked me to be honest."

"I know. And I'm glad you were." I made myself smile, to sweeten the pill. "Just wish the news were better."

"If it's any consolation, so do I."

She was the kind of lady I would have asked out in a moment – attractive, intelligent, not too much confidence. Which hardly paints me in a good light, but I'm afraid it's true. Sara, my last girlfriend, told me that despite the whole 'New Man' act, what I still wanted was a traditional WIFE – Wash, Iron, Fuck, Etcetera. That was why I never lasted with women – I was after someone I could talk with as an intellectual equal, but who'd still be happy to spend her life either in the kitchen or popping out babies. I'd begun thinking I needed to change my ways, if I was to settle down and start a family as I wanted to. But there was still time, another six months, just to sow some wild oats –

But tomorrow, as my old mother used to say, is too late.

"Of course," she said, "they're making new advances in medical technology all the time."

"When they tell you that," I said, "you know you're fucked."

"All I'm saying is, you don't know what might be around the corner in terms of new treatments."

"I know. Just trying to cope with it. Humour, you know?"

She puckered her mouth and pretended to glower. "Is that what you call it?"

She sounded like my dad talking about my taste in 'music' – always in inverted commas as far as he was concerned – so I chuckled. Then silence. She looked down at her notes again.

I glanced at the bedside mirror, as I kept doing out of morbid fascination. I'd been considered good-looking, before. There'd been no serious relationship since Sara left, but no lack of one-night stands or month-long flings.

But the face looking back at me now was lined and creased like an old handkerchief. Gaunt, as well. I'd lost nearly two stone. Sunken, bloodshot eyes. And my hair, once a proud glossy black, was a greasy, tangled mess, at least half of it gone grey or white.

The girls would not come running anymore.

And never mind the pain.

There was something else. I knew the answer, but needed to hear it. "Dr Scrimgeour?"

She smiled at me. "I think you can call me Naomi now, if you want to."

"Thanks. Will I... I mean, is there any prospect... any chance... could, maybe, in the future..." She nodded, eyebrows raised, egging me on. That small, sweet, bright smile in place. Her lips, so red. I was staving off the inevitable here. Just do it, Stiles. "Will I ever be able to dive again?"

Her smile faded. Again, she struggled to meet my eyes. If I hadn't known her answer already, that would've told me. "As a result of the accident, your blood's ability to dissolve nitrogen has been massively reduced. If you dive again, surfacing would kill you. So the answer is no, you won't. I'm sorry."

I felt my hands come up to cover my face. She spoke, but I didn't hear it. She must have realised that, because after a while, her hand touched my shoulder and squeezed lightly. Then she left.

A PIECE OF rusty iron. A moment's panic. And everything changes. Go into the water with one life, come out with another.

"I've loved the sea since I was a kid. Whenever we went to the beach, my parents could never get me out of the water. I might still be able to swim, at least. If I'm careful. There's that, at least."

"Well, that's good anyway."

Dr Whittaker shifted in his chair, an ageing teddy-bear in smart casuals. His office was like him – likeably cluttered, lived-in.

A clock ticked quietly on the wall. I lay back on the couch. Faint sounds of birdsong and distant traffic came from outside. It was early October, but the light filtering through the windows was still warm.

"Have you given any more thought to your future?"

What future? But that would be Negative. That would be A Bad Sign. He'd want more sessions. Fuck that. All I wanted now was just to get away. No more sympathy. No more understanding. Just leave me alone, *everybody*.

"Not as yet. It's hard to say."

"Well, no reason you can't continue your work as a lecturer, once you feel able. You said they were holding your post for you?"

My day job – lecturer in Marine Biology at Manchester University – was purely academic; I'd dived chiefly when I *wanted* to, in my own time. No. No reason I couldn't go back. Except the way the students would look at me, especially the pretty ones I would have flirted with before the summer break... a thousand years ago.

"Yes. Leave of absence. Get myself back in order."

"How long?"

"The next academic year, at least."

"Generous of them."

"Yes." I was reasonably popular, not bad going with half-a-dozen exes on the staff. But I was always good at staying friends. As a lover, I'd never been cruel. Just wanted more than they could give. Or they'd wanted more from me. Depends on who you asked.

"So, a year to recuperate and..." Whittaker spread his hands. "Chart some sort of course. Any ideas as yet?"

"Not for the long-term, not yet. But for now I've taken a lease on a place in Wales. Away from it all. The city's too..."

"Whereabouts in Wales?"

"Barmouth. Gwynedd coast. Nice place."

"The coast."

"Yes."

"Do you feel that's wise?"

"Yes. I do." I heard my voice rise. But I was tired of having my thoughts and motives picked over. Another reason I had to get away.

"Well, if you're sure..."

"I am."

"I'll give you my number, of course. Any time, night or day, if you have a problem."

"Thanks, doctor."

And I meant it, even though I had no intention of calling him.

"Ben?"

I stopped at the door.

"Is there anything else you want to discuss, before you go?"

I pretended to think it over, then shook my head. "No. Really. Thanks."

A lie, of course.

There were the dreams I kept having. I kept waking from them, sure I could still hear the sound of breaking waves. In the hospital I'd put them down to the sea's proximity, but they'd continued in Manchester.

So had the echo of voices, calling my name.

I told you my memories of the accident are blurred. In particular, what happened right after my hose broke. Bubbles and silt, blind panic, trying not to breathe in...

There were images in the dreams. Of the accident, except that I could see more clearly in the whirling dark. And there were faces in it, coming out of the darkness, out of the water itself.

Faces with eyes that glowed green.

I MOVED OUT of my flat in Didsbury village that weekend. Went round the place packing stuff. What to keep, what to throw away.

I took my old diving equipment. Wetsuit, aqualung, flippers and mask. I should have junked it. But somehow I couldn't. It was too final a goodbye.

One of my exes – a sweet, kind-hearted lady called Janet who I really should've appreciated more – drove me down one evening, saw me safely into my new home, pecked me on the cheek and drove home, gracefully turning down my offer of dinner.

Probably just as well.

I stood outside my front door gazing out towards the harbour. It was dark by now, but I could hear the break and hush of the waves. I stood listening to them for a while, savouring the wind's salt tang, then went inside.

CHAPTER TWENTY

I woke on a cold November morning. When I squinted at the red numerals on the bedside clock, they told me it was actually a cold November afternoon.

I tried turning onto my back, and immediately wished I hadn't. Debilitating pain burst from every joint in my body and washed through me in a sickening wave. My stomach rolled slowly. I moaned and clenched my teeth. It was hard to separate the dull throb and nausea of my hangover from the constant joint pain.

I lay for a while in that particular circle of Hell where the pain is prolonged because moving makes it worse. Finally, I grabbed the blister pack on the bedside table and fumbled for the water bottle beside the bed. Praise Jesus, it wasn't empty. I popped two of the waxy tablets into my mouth and washed them down.

I'd had trouble sleeping the night before, so I'd been up until the small hours watching DVDs, fortified with whisky. I hadn't made it to bed until 4.00am. At least I'd managed that. Falling asleep in a chair left me in worse agony still.

I thought of showering, but it seemed too much like hard work – undressing, staying upright in the cubicle. Sod that. Instead I clung onto the banister rail and limped downstairs for coffee.

By the second cup, the pain was subsiding. The fridge yielded two rashers of questionable-looking bacon and three eggs. I put the bacon under the grill, broke the eggs into the frying pan and hunted down the heel of a loaf. Pepper and brown sauce made the whole lot vaguely edible.

Get out and about, lad. Come on.

It was almost 3.00 PM now. Maybe two hours of daylight left.

Just another day in my new life.

THE PAIN WAS constant, as forecast, and as prescribed I'd 'managed' it with DHC. Although the lovely Dr Scrimgeour would've had a seizure if she'd known I was replacing it with gin and whisky of an evening. I had days where I'd skip the evening dose of DHC in favour of getting ratarsed instead. Unlike most opioids, alcohol didn't induce constipation.

A range of high, craggy hills called Dinas Oleu overlooked the town – in Welsh, 'the Fortress of Light' – but hill-walking was another pre-accident pleasure I could forget about now. The altitude change would expand the bubbles in my joints further, shifting the pain from 'medium, constant' to 'utter fucking agony.'

I walked every day, as much as possible. With the aid of a stick I got around reasonably well. There was still pain, but I blocked it out as best I could. I wasn't going to be robbed of any more pleasures than I had to be.

In short, I alternated healthy, outdoorsy stuff and exercise with getting thoroughly wrecked. I got by.

I still had those dreams. Virtually every night, unless I drank myself unconscious.

I went to a couple of shops, replenished vital supplies and dropped them back off at my digs, then wandered out again. I started at the harbour. Even at that time of year, it was picturesque. Fishing boats bobbing at anchor, Dinas Oleu and Cader Idris looming above, the iron bridge across the mouth of the estuary. After that I walked down the promenade that cut the harbour off the from the beach. I had to use the top of the seawall, because the footpath was long gone, vanished under the piled-up sand.

The prom led to a long, stepped concrete jetty extending halfway across the harbour mouth. Broken mussel shells littered the jetty, dropped or beaten by gulls to smash them open. They crunched underfoot.

I reached the end and limped down the steps. A warning beacon stood at the bottom. I turned my back on the town and harbour until I could only see the steel-grey ocean. The sun was dying behind thick banks of cloud, but a dull red glow burned through and made the waters blaze further out.

The waves were breaking in a soft, lulling rhythm. I closed my eyes and tilted back my chin; the wind rose, blowing my matted, greasy hair back and chilling my face.

Above the sounds of wind and sea, I heard somebody crying out.

I opened my eyes. No-one in sight. A car moving along the coast road, under the hills, away from the town. The sea was empty too. But I could hear a voice. Two voices. Male and female. But not the words. I couldn't tell if the tone was anger or fear.

The wind was moaning. I had to shout over it.

"Hello?" I called out. "*Hello?*"

The wind died, and the voices with it. Waves burst on the sand.

I looked around, still saw nothing.

Carry on.

I didn't feel comfortable on the jetty anymore. Too open, too exposed. Too easy to go in. I knew how the sea could be. A huge predator, waiting for one mistake. I'd forgotten that once; look at me now.

"Well chuck yourself in, then, you bastard. Finish the job. Why should you be alive when we're not?"

I started, almost overbalanced. The voice was right in my ear. But no-one was there when I spun around. And that last sentence – it *couldn't* be real. Maybe just my unconscious talking. Not necessarily a sign of madness.

Naomi had warned me that opioids like DHC occasionally caused hallucinations. But I'd been taking the stuff for months now; surely it would've happened sooner?

I walked back along the jetty and came down onto the beach. A ridge of dunes had built up between sea wall and shoreline in recent years, topped with coarse marram grass. I climbed them, as I did more or less daily, and walked towards the shore.

I felt the surf wash around my boots. Touched my fingers to the waters as they lapped round me, then to my lips to taste the salt. Felt the fresh briny smell blow in, the smell of rotten fish and seaweed too. But something rotten doesn't have to smell bad. The smell of autumn is of decay, of leaves rotting and mulching down, but you can't beat a walk in the woods. Not as far as I'm concerned, anyway.

I looked out towards the horizon. I don't know how to describe it. Perhaps... if I said it's like living across the street from someone you once passionately loved. Someone you shared everything with, every thought, every dream. You've slept together. You've seen them naked. You know their body, maybe better than they do. They know yours the same way. You know where and how to touch them, how they like to be kissed. And you'll never see them that way again, never sleep with them. You had that intimacy, but it's been withdrawn. Lost. Gone forever.

"Doesn't have to be," a voice said in my left ear.

No way could this be a hallucination. It was real. But something was wrong with it. Something missing. What?

"It doesn't have to be," the voice repeated. It was a man's. Scottish. "You can go back to her if you want."

I didn't turn around. Couldn't. I didn't understand why. It should've been simple. But I couldn't.

"It's *easy*," said a second voice. It was a woman's. An older woman, forties or fifties, husky and velvety. "It's where you're happiest, isn't it? So why don't you?"

I didn't answer her either. There was something *wrong* about her voice too. I still didn't know what, but it was there.

"Benjamin?" Jesus Christ, even my mother didn't call me that any longer. "It's very rude to ignore people when they're talking to you. Wasn't this always where you were happiest?"

"'Course it was," said the man. "We all know that."

"You loved her, didn't you?" The woman went on. Her voice was caressing and tender. "The ocean. She could take you deeper than any woman ever could. That's the real reason you've never married, isn't it? It's why Sara left."

I could feel them stood behind me. And I did *not* want to turn around, I did *not* want to see their faces. Mustn't. Because now I'd realised what was wrong with their voices. Their lips were so close they must be all but touching my ears, but when they spoke, I couldn't feel any breath.

"'Course it was," the woman said. "She knew she'd always be second best. Didn't she?"

"What do you bloody want, boy?" the man asked. "Hobble around like this for however fucking long you've got left, pissed out of your skull so you'll not have to think about it anymore? 'Cause you're not just drinking to numb the pain, are you? Not the one in your body. No. It's because you can't be in there, isn't it? Can't be inside her like you used to. So are you gonna moon around like a lovesick teenager? Or are you going to be a man and go to her?"

"I can't," I hissed at last.

"But you *can*." The woman's voice was soft as feathers. It went with touching, somehow. I should have been feeling her fingers brushing down my arm, but thank God, I wasn't. "Just put one foot in front of the other. Just walk out into the water, and keep going."

"What?"

"You heard. She'll take you into her. You'll be inside with her always. That's what you want, isn't it?" The woman was murmuring into my ear now. That velvet voice. Despite everything, I felt my cock stir. "Go to her, Benjamin. Go to her."

"No," I said.

"You know you want to."

"*No.*"

"You're just making it harder for yourself in the long run, laddie," said the man, but there was an edge to his voice.

"Leave me alone."

"Go into the water, Benjamin." The woman sounded as though she was speaking through her teeth.

"Why the fuck should you get away?" demanded the man. "How fucking dare you be alive when we're not?"

"Go into the water." The woman, all tenderness gone. Her voice was a cold command. "Go into the water and *drown*."

And at last whatever paralysis held me broke, and I could move. "Fuck off!" I shouted, and wheeled round, lashing out with my stick at –

Nothing.

Sweat clung to my forehead; my heart thudded against my ribs. The beach was empty.

I didn't look back at the sea, not then. I just stumbled up, back over the dunes in the gathering dusk, scrambling to the steps that led up to Marine Parade, firecrackers of pain going off in my shoulders, knees and arms. *That* was when I looked back.

A last gleam of dull red sunlight glanced off the water; then it dimmed and there was only the empty sea. But just for a moment, I'd seen something else. Only for a split-second, but just long enough to be sure it was there.

There'd been three, four, perhaps five of them, all standing in the shallows of the water. I couldn't see their faces, or even much detail about their bodies; that last dull blaze of sunlight had silhouetted them. But there had been something about them. Something... incomplete. But their hands had been outstretched. Beckoning me. And their eyes glowed green.

CHAPTER TWENTY-ONE

I DIDN'T VENTURE out the following day, or the one after. I could afford not to, as I now had all the relevant provisions – bacon, eggs, bread, milk – and most importantly a bottle or three of cheap Scotch.

By the second night, though, I was climbing the walls and decided to risk one of the local pubs, the Royal. I walked down Marine Road before going over the railway bridge. As I did, there was a brief, soundless flash. I thought it was lightning, but the brief report that followed wasn't thunder. A firework? But it hadn't had the loudness of a rocket bursting, and all I could see was a single pale spark, sinking and dying against a deep blue sky. Besides, I realised, Guy Fawkes had been and gone.

Signal rocket. I walked on because there was nothing I could do. The lifeboat would be going out if it was needed. Someone else would be fighting for his or her life. All I could do was silently (and drunkenly) wish them luck, whoever they were.

I only had a couple of pints in the Royal. It was more for the company, such as it was that time of year, than anything else.

The next day, for once, it wasn't an effort to get into the bathroom and shower. I even managed a shave beforehand. I'd been wearing the same clothes pretty much unchanged for the last two weeks; I threw them into the wash. I stripped the bed as well. This happened now and again; I'd experience a surge of revulsion at the state of myself, or the house, or both, and there'd be a burst of activity.

With that all done, I inspected myself in the mirror and pronounced myself almost presentable.

The mind, as somebody once said, is a monkey. I'd alleviated the boredom with imaginary conversations with people I knew – people like Dr Whittaker, Janet or even Naomi Scrimgeour, there was no-one I knew that well around here – about the incident on the beach:

"Ben, you know some opioids can cause hallucinations, DHC included. It's infrequent, but it can happen. If they come back, see a doctor."

"Naomi, I could *feel* them behind me."

"Did they actually *touch* you, Ben?"

"Well, no."

"There you go then."

"But I *saw* them, standing in the water."

"Only saw them for a moment, when the sunlight reflected off the surface. You said so yourself."

"...yes."

"Well, then. Look, Ben, you've been through a hell of a lot. And you've made a great deal of progress. But it won't all be plain sailing, and you won't get over it all overnight."

"Dr Whittaker is right, love. Give yourself some time. Get out a bit. Socialise. Last thing you want is to stay in and brood. Meet some people, make some friends."

"Janet, I'm fine."

"Then why are you sat around having imaginary conversations with us?"

I took my stick and went out.

ON THE BEACH, a bitter rain drove in from the sea like a cloud of nails. A tractor, its scoop raised high as if in triumph, trundled towards the water. It was towing a small, four-wheeled trailer. On it rested a bright orange inflatable dinghy with an outboard motor and RNLI on the bow, which pointed back towards the town. Four men, in the bright orange jackets and white headgear of lifeboatmen, sat aboard it.

At the water's edge, the tractor turned to face the sea. The lifeboatmen jumped out. A warning klaxon blared as the tractor reversed into the shallows, then the lifeboatmen lifted the dinghy into the water, then clambered back aboard. Within a few seconds, they were speeding out into Barmouth Bay.

I was in no rush – it wasn't really an option, in my state – and dawdled to study any random object that caught my attention or just admire the view; I reached the concrete jetty about twenty minutes later. As I clambered over the jetty and walked down the half-buried promenade to the quay, I saw the dinghy coming back in. They seemed to be empty-handed. A practice run, maybe, training.

Or perhaps they'd gone out to try and rescue somebody and failed, without even a body to bring back.

Not a pleasant thought.

It was 2:30. Still time, just, for lunch at Davy Jones' Locker.

The Locker is a small building, built from grey Welsh slate and dating back to medieval times. A small open deck out front overlooks the harbour. Inside, the rough, irregular stonework is whitewashed, except for the huge fireplace at the very back, which retains its natural grey. Sadly it's not a real fire, just red electric light seeping through the chopped logs in the grate. A huge stuffed fish (*an allis shad*, the old marine biologist in me noted, *a member of the herring family*) hangs over the front door. Seafaring paraphernalia adorns the nooks inside, or hangs from the black-painted ceiling beams – green-glass buoys in nets of knotted brown string, old fishing nets, a spider crab, ship's wheels, lengths of chain, winches, lobster pots, model ships, propeller blades, a sawfish's snout (*rostrum, to give its right name*), a basket of dried starfish, sea-urchin and empty conch shells, and a brass diving helmet with its single, Cyclopean window at the front. Lighting came from old ship's lanterns hung from the rafters and lit by electric bulbs within them.

They don't serve booze, but I could get by without for now. I was more hungry than anything else, so I took a table near the fire and ordered ham and duck eggs. I got a coffee as well, and drank it slowly. Outside, gulls wheeled low, letting out their mournful, repetitious cries.

Sally, one of the staff, came up. "Want another?"

She was about eighteen, with dark roots showing in her dyed-blonde hair. In my bad old days, I'd been known to sail close to the wind when it came to some of my students. Not anymore.

"Please."

"Same again?"

"Thanks."

She went back to the counter. It wasn't common practice – customers normally went and got their own refills – but she knew me and liked to save me the trouble. That day, I could've quite cheerfully gone to the counter under my own steam, but it was still nice to be waited on by a pretty girl. Even if it was more out of pity than anything else.

The café was quiet, but far from empty. As well as locals, people still came to the coast this time of year. Not the family holiday crowd, but it was a nice time of year for hill-climbing and watching the late autumn leaves fall. When the weather permitted, anyway.

I ate slowly. No rush. Besides, despite the booze and smoking, I still had a sense of taste. Might as well enjoy myself. I finished my meal, and lingered over the second cup of coffee. Sally collected my plate and offered another refill. I dug out the crumpled paperback I'd stuffed in my coat pocket before venturing out. Time passed.

"Mind if I join you?"

I looked up, but even before I saw her face I knew I was caught. A long black dress clung to a sleek, curved figure. Small, pale hands; pink nail varnish.

Her face was a pale oval, black hair piled on top. Large, dark eyes, a red rosebud of a mouth, pencilled eyebrows. A sharp nose, high cheekbones. A strong, handsome face overall. Not my usual type, but still...

She didn't look like a Goth. Maybe she'd just come from a funeral? But I didn't get that impression, either.

I didn't answer at first. I was – struck. Actually, *smitten* might be the proper term. She cocked her head slightly; raised her eyebrows, parted her lips.

"Sorry. Yes. Please do."

"Thanks." She sat. "I won't disturb your reading –"

"No, it's okay." I closed the book. "Nice to have a little company."

She smiled embarrassedly and looked down. Christ's sake, Stiles; a *little* less forward would be nice.

"Sorry – I just meant –"

"No, it's okay. Really. It's nice of you. I'm here with friends, but... they have different interests to me."

"Oh?"

"Well, they're off quad-biking today. And tonight... tonight they'll be roaring drunk and stoned."

"Not your thing?"

She twitched her nose and shook her head. "I'm a quiet kind of girl. Very boring, I know. Much rather go up in the hills or the woods and stand there looking out to sea."

"Yeah. I'm the same."

A pencilled eyebrow arched up. "Really? Somehow I picture you as quite the party beast." She smiled. It was mischievous, if not downright naughty, but most of all it was *real*. It also made the corners of her eyes crinkle in a very nice way.

I laughed. "Used to be."

"Not anymore?"

"I had an accident, few months ago. Have to take things easier than I did. But..." I smiled back at her. "...I'm starting to enjoy myself again."

"Glad to hear it."

"Need a refill, Ben?"

"Um no, thanks, Sally." I still had half a cup. Besides, any more and I'd be running back and forth to the toilet, which I didn't fancy. Unlike the lady in black. "Would you like –?"

"Oh, just a coffee, please. Black, no sugar."

Sally's mouth twitched at the corner, but she nodded, smiled and said: "Coming up."

"Something I said?" the woman asked, after Sally had gone.

I laughed. "No. She likes to save me the hassle because I'm not that mobile. But that's just for me, not every other punter in the place."

"Oh. I'm sorry."

"Don't be. My fault, not yours."

Sally brought the coffee over, gave me a mock glare and winked. *You're forgiven, but don't do it again.* I smiled and watched her go.

"I think she likes you."

"I'm old enough to be her dad."

"Funnily enough, I don't imagine that stopping you. For long."

"Ouch."

"Ben, did she say?"

"Yeah, that's right. You're –?"

"Ellen." She extended a hand.

"Pleasure to meet you."

"Likewise."

She sipped her coffee. I toyed with my cup. "Have you been up Panorama yet?"

"Where?"

"That's a no, then."

"I've only just got here." She took another sip, looked over the cup's rim. "But if you know of any good spots and don't mind showing me..."

Her eyes were very wide, very dark, and very inviting. A part of me wanted to make excuses. Run and hide. Too good to be true. Had to be some kind of a stitch-up. But I wanted to believe her.

"I'd love to," I said, and that sealed my fate. But of course it had been sealed long before then. "I can't take you there, though."

"Why not?"

And so I told her. Explained about the bends, how I couldn't travel to high altitudes.

She touched my hand. "Will you come some of the way with me? As far as you can? It would be nice to have the company."

What else could I say to that, but yes?

FROM THE TOP of Panorama, which lies at the edge of Dinas Oleu, right above the Mawddach Estuary, we could see the hills rolling inland to our left, the grey ribbon of the estuary winding through the sandbanks, wormed with narrow creeks, on each side. Turning right, beyond the railway bridge, the estuary opened out into Barmouth Bay and, beyond that, into the Cardigan Bay and Irish Sea. In the distance was the Lleyn Peninsula, the long arm of land reaching from the top of Wales, and the mist-shrouded contours of Anglesey.

We stood in silence. I'd seen the view before, but I was seeing it with Ellen now, through her first-timer's eyes. And of course, I'd never expected to see it again myself.

Teeth gritted, I'd started climbing the long, steep road up the side of Panorama with her, expecting the agony to explode in my arms and legs any second, doubling me up and humiliating me. And once it did stab me; I'd gasped, but she'd reached out a hand to steady me and... and the pain had ebbed away. She'd looked at me and smiled. "Okay?"

"Yeah." And I was.

"Want to go back?"

"No. Not yet."

We'd gone higher than I'd ever expected to, past streamlets trickling down rockfaces into little drainage ditches, coming off the mountain road and walking past the farmhouse that lay before the woodlands around the summit. Fallen leaves, rust-red, rustled in the light breeze. Stones thick with moss. All of this, and the landscape glimpsed in snatches through the trees, soon to be seen in full. The anticipation of seeing it again. Then out into the open air; restraining myself from looking around because I wanted to wait now until I reached the summit, determined to get there even if the pain, long deferred, exploded full-force. The last dozen yards were very steep, but I'd managed it, hardly even limping.

"It's so beautiful," she said at last; her voice hitched as she said it.

"Ellen?" A tear trickled down her left cheek, and another on the right. "Jesus, Ellen, are you alright?"

"Yes. Yes. I'm fine. No, really Ben. It's okay. It's okay. Really." She smiled, wiping her eyes. "It's just so beautiful."

"You've never been to Wales before?"

She shook her head and looked inland across the mountains. "I've never seen this land before."

A funny way of putting it, but I liked it. For a second I'd thought she'd said *I've never seen land before.* My imagination. It wasn't always reliable. I'd have to tell her that, if I saw her again. I knew I wanted to.

But not right now. Not just yet.

Ellen put her hand to her mouth and sniffed hard. Then again. And a long, sobbing breath out.

I put a hand on her arm, without thinking. She took her hand from her mouth, dabbed her eyes with a tissue. "Silly," she said, looking down, not meeting my gaze.

I touched her chin, tilting her face up. "It's okay," I said. "It's okay." My voice shook a little; I could've cried myself. Maybe out of gratitude. Maybe it was just her company, or maybe she had some kind of healing touch – the kind of crap claimed by the kind of people I'd avoided as peddlers of false hope, exploiters of the gullible, determined to try and accept my fate with some kind of dignity rather than chase pointlessly after non-existent miracle cures. I didn't know or care; something had happened I'd thought never would again. I'd climbed a mountain. And for whatever reason, it was because of her. For that alone, I could have loved her forever, right then.

That moment. When the eyes lock. When you know, you just know, it's just a kiss away. And the kiss is coming, due within heartbeats.

I touched my mouth to hers. Soft, yielding. Then the touch of her tongue in my mouth, her tongue on mine. That first kiss. Like so much else, it'd become so common I'd stopped appreciating it. And like so much else, I was finding it fresh and new, with her, with Ellen...

...what *was* her second name?

No matter. There was time for all that. However long she was staying for.

Where was she going back to? She hadn't said. It didn't matter. It could be the grimmest place on earth, and I knew if she wanted, if she'd let me, I'd follow her there.

Christ, Stiles, is this love at long last?

A faint taste of salt in my mouth, in hers. The tears, perhaps. Finally she broke free, a gasp of breath, her hands on my chest, pushing me back. "Enough."

"Shit – Ellen, I'm sorry."

"No. It's okay. I just..." She touched my cheek, eyes crinkling with that smile of hers again. "You're very sweet."

"Sweet?" Christ. Kiss of death, a woman calling you that.

"Sweet," she said, and kissed my lips again, the merest brush. "We have time, don't we? Ben?"

"Yeah." I was smiling too, the biggest and stupidest of my adult life. "Much as you need."

"Good." She still smiled; the most amazing smile in the world. I wanted to see it every day for the rest of my life.

Shit, Stiles, this is *love and all.*

"So," she said. "Where now?"

WE WANDERED SOME more over the hills, then down to the old slate quarry and the harbour, which nestles in the crook of the coast road. I kept expecting the pain to kick in, but it never did. Perhaps it was a once-only miracle, and if I tried this again I'd be in agony. Thinking that sharpened my senses; I don't think I'd ever been so aware of what's around me before. After a while I stopped worrying and lost myself in the moments.

We walked back to the Quay and up the High Street for a drink in the Tal-Y-Don. I don't remember what we talked about. Everything and nothing. All that young lover's stuff, except neither of us were that young anymore. Not old either, but I'd always thought myself long past being smitten like that, if I'd ever been capable of it to begin with.

We had dinner at the Last Inn, a restaurant just off the quay. I had baked seabass, Ellen steak and chips. Afterwards, as the night fell, I walked her home along the sea front, arm in arm.

"Won't your friends be worried about you?" I asked.

She shook her head. "They know I like to go off on my own."

The sky had cleared; there were few clouds and the full moon hung low over the sea, laying a silvery path from horizon to beach. A lover's moon, I thought, and said so.

"You old romantic."

We stood and looked out for a while. Then she turned to face me, taking a deep breath. Shit. Here it came. The bad news. She had a boyfriend, or a husband.

She looked up at me – those big dark eyes – and said: "Ben, I want to sleep with you."

The air left my lungs. Panic. What if she wanted to come back to mine? Despite my clear-out that morning, the place was still in no fit state to receive a guest.

"But not tonight."

I was half-relieved, half-disappointed. But, as she'd said, we had time.

"I don't want to move too fast," she said. "I want it to be right. Does that... make sense?"

"Yes." And it did.

"Good." She touched my face. "Ben..." She laughed. "I've just realised, I don't even know your surname."

"Stiles. What about you?"

The moon lit her face as she smiled. "Vannin."

"Unusual name. Beautiful, but unusual. Where's it from?"

Her eyes crinkled again. "That's for me to know..."

A last, deep kiss and she stepped away. "I'll say goodnight now. It's too perfect. Only be an anticlimax otherwise. Meet you tomorrow?"

"Sure. When? Where?" I was like a lovesick schoolboy all of a sudden. Addicted. I was addicted to her.

"The Locker? About eleven o'clock?"

"Sure."

"Goodnight, Ben Stiles."

"Goodnight, Ellen Vannin."

I watched her walking away. She looked back once, blew me a kiss, and then disappeared up one of the sidestreets. There were plenty of hotels along the seafront, but she wasn't at any of them. Another mystery to be solved. The click of her heels on the pavement faded.

Ellen Vannin. The name tripped off my tongue. It sounded familiar. From somewhere. God knew where. As long as she wasn't a convicted axe-murderer.

I laughed at myself and turned to go.

They stood in the surf.

There was a long line of them. A dozen, maybe twenty. As before they were silhouetted, but the light gleamed through them, in places. Through gaps that shouldn't have been in a living person's body.

Cold green light glittered where their eyes should have been.

The one in the centre extended a hand and beckoned. One by one, as I stumbled away, along the deserted seafront, the others beckoned too.

A cloud slid across the moon as I ran; the pavement darkened. When I looked back, it had passed, and the moon shone again on an empty sea.

CHAPTER TWENTY-TWO

THE NEXT FORTNIGHT was the happiest of my adult life. I dismissed the figures in the surf as another hallucination. I didn't dare tell Ellen. I trusted her – I thought I did. No, I *knew*. This was love. Total. All-consuming. I would die for her if I had to. I didn't think I could drive her away, but I didn't want to – *couldn't* – take that risk.

If you've ever been in love like that – and I pray you haven't, because it can only lead to pain – then you'll understand.

There were no further hallucinations, anyway; no voices in my ear or figures in the waves. And so the only shadow that'd lain on me lifted, and the days and nights passed with Ellen Vannin. We walked the hills together, ate and drank together. And, yes, we slept together.

The first time, I was afraid my body would disgust her. I was scrawny and pale, arms and legs like pipe-cleaners. Even on my good days, I moved stiffly, and had the face of a man twenty years older.

Well, she'd seen my face and she knew my story. But even so, I worried.

The first night we slept together, she insisted on undressing me, peeling off my shirt, pulling off my boots, stripping me naked. As she did, she kissed my body – my nipples and stomach, my knees and thighs, even the insteps of my feet – before pressing me back on the bed, bending over and pressing her lips down on mine.

"Beautiful," she whispered.

I reached up to touch her breasts, but she grinned and slapped my hands away, running her tongue over her top lip. "Naughty."

She kissed me deeply, and then worked her way down over my chest and stomach to my cock, kissing it gently, running her tongue up and around it. When she took me in her mouth, I cried out, grabbing fistfuls of bedclothes. "Stop. Stop." But it was too late. The orgasm was so intense it damn near hurt.

I sagged back with a moan. There was silence. Shit. I'd ruined it. Gone off like that. In her mouth as well; women didn't like that. I tried to mumble an apology, but she was laughing, wiping her lips.

"Well," she said. "I suppose I should take that as a compliment."

She stood up and released her long black hair, to fall around her shoulders. "Now," she said, "you've got no excuse. I expect you to last this time."

Her dress fell around her ankles, slithering down the pale slopes of her body smooth as water. She was naked, except for her black shoes. She kept them on throughout. "Touch me," she whispered, and guided my hand between her legs. She was already open and wet to the touch. With her free hand she drew my head to her breasts, and I took a nipple in my mouth as she stroked my hair.

My HEALTH, AS if in response, was the best it had been since the accident. I reduced my DHC dosage, even skipped it once and suffered no ill-effects. That *was* only a one-off, though; on the whole, I still needed to take the medication, but less than before. I had no doubt it was down to Ellen in some way. How or why, I didn't know and I didn't care. I just wanted it to last.

We didn't talk about her friends. Throughout that fortnight, I never met them, not until the very end. They were just a vague reason that Ellen was here in Barmouth. A plot device. Nothing more.

We didn't talk about the future. I was afraid of finding out that it was all just a fling for her, a holiday romance, to be consigned to a shoebox full of memories, of things that once were but no more. I didn't want to know I'd be just another faded snapshot – *do you remember that time in Barmouth, in the autumn of...*

I wanted this to be forever. I wasn't going to make the same mistakes I'd made with Sara, with all the others. I was ready to commit. I was ready to change, whatever was necessary. Whatever it took. And I knew that was reckless, and I didn't care.

For a few waking hours a day I was on my own. She had to spend some time with her friends. It was a teenage thing, to want to spend every second together... but still I begrudged every minute of the day that wasn't mine.

Still, there were things to do. My house was almost unrecognisable now, it was actually *clean*. Clothes were washed and put away (occasionally even ironed), the washing-up was done daily, the carpets hoovered and cleaned. Parts of the place actually *gleamed*. It looked like a place fit to receive visitors. When I wasn't busy with the flat there was still time for a walk along the beach.

Or to surf the internet.

I didn't have a home computer. I'd rarely worked on the things even at University, unless I had to. I much preferred to write longhand. It was more portable, less likely to go wrong, it could be done anywhere. After all, given the choice, where would you rather work? A grubby, ratty bedroom, or a beach or mountainside? The defence rests.

But there was a coffee shop at the far end of Church Street that doubled as an internet café. I used it to make my occasional contacts with the outside world via the web. Generally I used it to follow current affairs, music, literature, general stuff really. Today, though, I had something different in mind.

Today, the last day of that happiest fortnight – although I didn't know that then – I was doing a little detective work.

It was the her name; the nagging familiarity of her name. I *knew* I'd heard it before. I'd asked her, but she shrugged it off; she was no-one special, she said (I disagreed) and she'd never done anything to lift her into the public eye.

But it wasn't a common name. You wouldn't forget it once you'd heard it. And I was sure I had... but I didn't know where.

And so I sat in the café, cup of coffee at my elbow, and typed 'Ellen Vannin' into a search engine. And watched the parade of hits come up.

For a start, the correct spelling was Ellan Vannin. In the old Manx tongue, it referred to the Isle of Man.

But also, there were two songs. *Ellan Vannin*, a traditional Manx song, the island's unofficial 'national anthem.' And another, more recent, by a Liverpool folk band called The Spinners: *The Ellan Vannin Tragedy 1909*.

The SS *Ellan Vannin*. One of the Isle of Man Steam Packet Company's fourteen mailboats, all named after some feature of the island. Snaefell, Tynwald, Ben Machree... the actual ships had changed over the years, but the names had been passed down. All except one.

On December 3rd, 1909, the SS *Ellan Vannin* had sailed from Ramsey Bay for Liverpool, with twenty-one crewmen, fifteen passengers, and a cargo of sheep and turnips.

The weather had been temperate enough when she set out, but rapidly worsened to a Force 11 gale driving twenty-foot waves. Having been on the sea myself, I knew what that was like. The sad part was, she was close to port when it went wrong. She'd passed the Bar lightship and entered the Mersey Channel. Exactly what sent her down was never confirmed; most likely a massive wave had capsized her. There was no time to do anything. No-one made it out. All thirty-six people aboard her drowned.

It'd been the worst shipping disaster in Manx history. The name *Ellan Vannin* was never re-used by the company.

It was coming back to me now. The Irish Sea around the Isle of Man is notorious for its shipwrecks, and I'd gone wreck-diving off there a few years before. There'd been a few of us. One evening, we'd been in the pub. One of the party was a bloke called Hughie, a Liverpool man. He'd had a guitar, and he'd taken it out and played the Spinners song. Told us the story.

There was no woman called Ellen Vannin. But of course, it might be a family name... somewhere. Could just be a coincidence.

Coincidence? When you see dead things calling you from the sea, when their eyes glow green like the ones in your dreams and nightmares? Ever since you nearly died – in the sea, Ben. In the sea –

"Ben?"

I jerked round in the chair, fumbling for the mouse, as Ellen walked in.

"What you looking at, then?"

"Oh, nothing."

Her eyebrows went up. "Nothing?"

"Honestly."

"Nothing, tra-la-la?" She was looking at me the way she did sometimes, head half-turned to look at me sideways, a teasing, *I-don't-believe-you* smile on her lips.

Shit.

Then she grinned. "Hope you weren't looking at porn there." She leant forward and whispered. "You'll get in trouble if you do that here."

I leant over and whispered back. "Why would I need to look at porn, when I've got you?"

"You old smoothie," she said, and brushed her lips across mine.

The tension had passed. "Just checking my emails," I told her.

"Anything interesting?"

"Bugger all."

"Oh well. I'm bloody starving. Lunch?"

"Why not?"

*   *   *

WE ATE AT Davy Jones' Locker once more. It was a very mild day, so we chanced sitting out on the deck outside.

"Ben... I've got something to tell you."

My stomach lurched. Did she know I knew?

Know what? She's got a name that sounds like something else? Vannin's just her family name, Ben, that's all. It's coincidence.

But my eyes flickered out to look across the harbour where the tide had come in, sure I was going to see *them* rising up out of it.

Shit, she's pregnant, that's it, that's what she's going to tell you.

"I'm leaving tomorrow."

"Oh." A part of me was almost relieved for a second. Then it hit home. "Shit."

Her smile was crooked and her eyes glistened. "Yeah."

"When... when are you..."

"Don't know exactly. Probably early on."

We looked at each other, neither speaking.

"Do you work?" I asked at last. Weird. I realised it'd been another question I'd never got round to asking.

"Why?"

"I just thought..." – no, there was no other way, I had to ask her *now* – "...if you don't have a job to go back to, you could stay here a little longer. I mean, with me."

She stared at me.

"I'm sorry. I didn't mean to..."

"No. No, it's okay. You mean that?"

I nodded. Her laugh was half a sob. "I thought – I was afraid you just – that you didn't want... I mean, long-term..."

Her hand reached out across the table; I took it. "I was afraid that *you* didn't."

She laughed again, dabbed her eyes. "We're both bloody stupid, aren't we?"

"Yeah."

"But I can't stay here, Ben. I can't."

"Why not?"

"I just can't."

"A job?"

"Yes. No. Sort of. It's complicated. But... oh, God, I love it here. It's so beautiful. But I have to go back. At least for a while. But, would you consider..."

I wanted to hear her say it herself, but she left the sentence unfinished so long I had to do it for her. "Coming back with you?"

"Yes."

"Yes," I said. "I would."

"Yes? Really?"

"Yes."

"Ben, you don't know where I live. You don't know..."

"I don't care." I squeezed her hand. "Simple as. End of."

She wiped her eyes again with her free hand, and smiled. "You're sweet."

"Don't call a man sweet," I growled. "For God's sake."

"Oh for pity's sake," said Sally, collecting our glasses. "Get a room, you two."

THE SUN WAS going down; we walked along the sea-front, her hand in mine.

"Do you want to come back to mine tonight?" she said.

"Best had. My last chance, isn't it?"

"Mm?" She frowned for a second, then giggled. "Yes, of course. I was thinking you'll always be at mine after tonight." She looked ahead, and I glanced sideways at the sea; it was reassuringly empty. "Will you be okay?" she asked. "Just packing up and going like this?"

"Yeah. I'm used to travelling light." A thought occurred to me. "How are you getting back?"

"Mm?" For the second time she seemed distracted, thrown by what I'd said. Maybe the late nights were catching up with her. It wasn't as if we'd been drinking. We'd hardly touched a drop; my alcohol intake had fallen to almost nothing in the last two weeks. "Oh. Yeah. We'll be driving."

"I'll have to pack some stuff, that's all. Just wondering about room."

"There'll be plenty. Karl's got a van."

"Karl?"

"You'll meet him in a minute."

DINAS OLEU'S OUTLINES crumbling into the thickening dusk; a sharp tang of coal smoke in the air as we came down Marine Road.

The house stood near the railway bridge, one of a row of tall terraces, made up of bricks of grey Welsh slate. Ellen opened the front door.

"Hello?" she called. "We're back." She motioned me through, pushed it closed with her foot. Old newspapers were heaped up between the door and the wall.

The living room was on the left. The door was open. The light was off, and the only illumination was from the dim flicker of the TV. A woman with black, bedraggled hair slouched on the sofa.

"Carrie?" Ellen called. The woman didn't respond. "This is Ben."

The woman's head turned our way. The tangled mop of hair hid her face.

"He'll be coming back with us tomorrow."

Carrie nodded slowly. She half-raised a hand and made a faint noise that could have been, or meant, anything. Her skin looked very pale in the TV's flicker.

Down at the far end of the hallway, shoe leather scratched on linoleum. A tall, thin shape stood swaying in the kitchen doorway, backlit by the thin grey twilight. A second shape, smaller and plumper, shambled to stand alongside him with painful slowness. It wore an old print dress. The first figure put an arm around its shoulders.

"Ben, this is Donna and Charles."

Jesus, Ellen, who the hell are these friends of yours?

"And this is Karl."

She pointed up. The staircase to the right was very steep and vanished into darkness. Floorboards creaked. Another figure was coming down. He was very tall and very, very thin. He was barefooted, wearing jeans and a white sweater. His hair was longer than Ellen's or Carrie's, and hung lank and heavy.

I couldn't see any of their faces.

Ellen's hand gripped mine tightly. "Are you still sure, Ben?"

"What?"

"Sure you want to come with us?"

"Yes..." Why was her hand so cold, suddenly? And clammily damp? I forced a smile and waved generally at the group. Charles raised a hand silently in greeting. Karl kept coming downstairs, slow and purposeful.

"Why are all the lights are off?" I asked. "Forget to pay the bill?"

Charles and Donna rocked back and forth in silence. As Karl reached the bottom of the stairs, he shook his head slowly from side to side.

"They don't talk much," Ellen said. "They can't. It was enough of an effort, just for me to..."

"What?"

I was turning to look at her, but then I stopped. Something I'd seen from the corner of my eye, in the hallway's grey, crumbling, twilight dusk –

Charles and Donna were trying to get to us. The space between the staircase and wall was too narrow for them to walk abreast, but they squeezed close together and shuffled forward. It was like watching a grub squirming. Karl had stopped at the foot of the stairs, and had turned his head towards them.

"I brought them with me," Ellen said. "In case I needed help."

"Help?"

"With you, Ben." Her voice hitched. "With you."

The hallway wasn't quite as dark suddenly. I could see Charles and Donna a bit more clearly. The more I saw, the more I wished it was still dark. The flesh of their faces were hanging off the bones, barely attached. They faded back into the dark as Karl turned towards me, but by then I was looking right into the light source, into the discs of green light that should have been eyes, glaring through wet, tangled hair. His face looked grey. Something had eaten part of his nose. When his mouth opened, a hole gaped in his cheek.

Now Charles and Donna's eyes were glowing too, and their bustling down the hallway was like insects scuttling towards their prey. There was a thumping sound from the living room. I didn't look to see what Carrie was doing. Pain shot up my arm. Ellen's grip had tightened, and her hand was searing cold.

"I'm sorry, Ben."

"What?" I turned to look at her. Her profile was smooth, white, unmarked; eyes closed, a thin tear-track gleaming silver on her cheek. "What is this?"

"I'm sorry," she said again, as the green light began seeping through the join of her closed eyelids. Lighting up her face. The glow brightening as her eyes opened, as she turned to face me, the eyelids shrinking back and away like scorched polythene, the light blowing away softening shadows and comforting illusions and showing her face for what it really was, for what crabs and fishes and slow decay had left of it, the mouth snarling open into a scream full of blackened teeth as she lunged towards me.

CHAPTER TWENTY-THREE

I DIDN'T SCREAM as I staggered down Marine Road. I felt the pain exploding from my bone joints, but from a distance, like a report rather than the real thing. I vaguely realised I'd lost my stick and shouldn't really be able to move like this.

I didn't know, not then, that my jeans were sodden with my own piss.

I reached the intersection of Marine Road and Marine Parade, past the Sandancer nightclub and the amusement arcade. Beyond them were the seafront and the road to the quay. Waves were breaking; I heard them briefly over the roar of blood in my ears.

Not the sea. Not the fucking sea.

One lover betraying you is bad enough. But two is too much to bear. The sea always was my first love. Now that was gone too.

Barmouth was deserted. No sign of anybody. That wasn't right. It wasn't that late. There should be *somebody*. Somewhere.

Where now?

The police station. It wasn't far.

And tell them what?

The knowledge was in my head, never to be forgotten; it'd been branded into me in that endless moment before I'd – somehow – broken free of

Ellen and her 'friends'. I knew the truth now, but even through the terror and the chaos, I also knew it was madness and that to tell a police officer was a short cut to a night in the cells at best, being sectioned at worst.

Home.

The railway crossing was clear. I stumbled across it, past shops and cafes all closed up for the night, and right, down Church Street.

"Ben?" Ellen's voice, lilting coyly. A lover's coaxing, now obscene. "Be-en?"

They were coming round the corner, Ellen in the middle, hair wild in the wind and the long black dress flapping round her, eyes aglow. The others followed; Charles and Donna, still holding each other upright as they blundered like drunks over the pavement and the middle of the road; Karl's long gaunt frame, hair flapping loosely, arms stiff and swinging at his sides, hands hooked into claws, and Carrie, a thin, tiny shape, almost skeletal. Dear God, how old was she, how old had she *been*?

All their eyes glowing.

"Ben!"

I turned and ran. Pain stitched into my side, drove through my poor abused legs, but I had to keep going, had to keep going...

I didn't look back again. Didn't dare. God knew what I'd see. Karl, most likely. My one chance was the physical condition they were in, their shape. They weren't moving fast, not even Ellen. Maybe whatever had brought them back was weakening.

I reached my front door, shoved the key in the lock. My heart battered my chest; I thought for a second it'd burst. That would have been a bloody laugh, after everything else.

The shuffle and scrape of feet. *Don't look. Don't look.* The lock, not turning.

"Fucking twat!" I screamed at it, and the key revolved. The door gave and I shoved it wide. When I looked back, I saw they were closer than I thought, no more than ten feet off. Lamplight hit Karl's face, or what there was of it. His arms were outstretched, grasping.

I slammed the door shut, turned the key in the deadlock, put the security chain on.

The windows – I staggered to them one after the other. All locked. Hands thumped on the door.

Now I wasn't in flight, the pain hit me. The agony doubled me over. I climbed the stairs on hands and knees, every movement a wrench of pain, all the while promising myself just a little further, just a little further, just a little more.

"Ben?" Ellen was calling through the letterbox. "Ben?"

I collapsed at the top of the stairs, outside my bedroom door. I'd left the DHC in there, on the bedside table. I'd thought I didn't need it anymore. Maybe I hadn't, not then. I'd been drugged on something else. But that was gone now, along with all the other comforting illusions that had accompanied Ellen Vannin. Shoulders, elbows, wrists, hips, knees, ankles; they all grated and screeched like buggered hinges, every time I moved. Even if I didn't. But I had to move to reach the painkillers.

I lay there, sobbing through my teeth. Mostly from pure physical pain. Mostly.

"Ben?"

I closed my eyes. For a few precious but horrible seconds, the pain in my body faded away, as the other kind kicked in.

THREE-QUARTERS OF THE planet are ocean. At least, they were back then. God knows what the proportions are now.

We've used it since we first came down from the trees. It's fed us for thousands of years. We've learned to travel across, over, even below it.

But it can't be trusted; it isn't our home. You can drown in a few inches of water; it's home to creatures that kill with a bite or sting, or just plain devour you. And the sea itself. We can't even drink salt water. It's as difficult and dangerous to explore as outer space. You need breathing gear and protective suits just as you would in space, and even then, you're only one mistake away from death. Or worse. I'd forgotten that and look what it'd cost me. It had mauled me like a cat toying with a mouse, then left me for dead. Bored with the new toy. Forgotten me.

So I'd thought.

How many didn't get away? Shipwrecks, drownings, suicides? Storm surges, tsunamis? How many dead?

When I was at school, somebody told me that ghosts were formed like this:

Emotion is a form of energy. Brain activity is electrical; thoughts are like tiny lightning bolts jumping around your brain. Something bad happens – something violent or terrifying, something traumatic (oh yes, I knew long words like that when I was eleven, I thought I was clever and knew everything, but of course I knew fuck all) and there's a huge *storm* of that energy. You used to hear words like 'thought patterns' in science-fiction books. I'd always visualised bright imprints on the retina, afterimages left by intricate jumbles of electrical bolts, strange curlicues like Arabic writing or cuneiform.

Those patterns get thrown off, and they soak into the surroundings. An imprint. Like a snapshot of the soul. The same way sound, converted into electrical impulses, imprints a cassette tape. Waiting for something – the right kind of mind, a sensitive enough mind – to trigger it, connect. To complete the circuit. Heat energy is absorbed from the surroundings and converted, to make the recording run. This was why people who witnessed hauntings almost always reported a sudden drop in temperature.

A sort of tape recording, basically. But, possibly, with some rudimentary life, or consciousness of its own.

Later on I was told that, scientifically speaking, this is total bollocks.

But what if it's not?

And if – just *if* – it's not:

How many deaths in the sea? Over millions of years, how many lives ended there, in terror and agony – and rage, at the ending of your life – while others live?

Why me and not you? Why you and not them?

Millions? Billions?

How can every molecule of that vast, rolling deep not be tainted?

Water evaporates and is carried away. Haunted lakes, rivers, streams... but it all returns to the sea in the end.

Last thoughts, fears, suffering, all flying back and forth. Isn't that all a mind is?

The sea is vast, but not infinite. Sooner or later there had to be a tipping point. Perhaps it was the sheer volume of deaths. No one event, no bolt of lightning in a castletop laboratory, just... that.

The sea is alive. It wasn't before, but it is now. It's awake, and all it knows is wrath and terror, agony and rage.

When I nearly drowned, the sea reached out to claim me – the eyes, coming out of the darkness, the faces. Another mind, another soul. Because that was the worst of it. One mind – one single, planet-wide brain – and it was alone. Enough to drive anyone insane.

And Ellen... what was Ellen?

The Deep Brain – I had to call it something, and what better name than that? – was just becoming aware when it nearly took me. It had been... absorbing me. Taking me into itself. But awake now. Its mind had touched mine.

For the first time, it *knew* a living mind.

It knew something other than rage.

It was not alone.

But then I'd escaped, with my life if not much else. Back to dry land and stayed there for good. How could it reach me? The sea is governed by time and tide, the moon. It has no arms, no legs...

Only it does.

How many souls in the deep?

How many bodies drifting on the tides?

It had used them. Made them more fitting for its purposes – in Ellen's case, at least, it made her pass for a living woman. And sent her out.

But it was young and new, its strength limited. It had sent out a few emissaries, to look for me. It could sustain the deception, for a little time.

So many millions, billions of others in the world. So many others drowning every day, but they died and were taken and were lost. They just added to its strength, became part of it.

It had no-one. Nothing to make it complete. So out of all the billions, on the earth, the sea had come for me and me alone.

It had wanted to seduce me. But it couldn't sustain the deception. Maybe didn't want to. Wanted me to know where I was really going. And like any clumsy, untried, inexperienced suitor, it had revealed itself badly.

I began to laugh, rocking to and fro on the stairs as Ellen called my name.

I'd once heard a song called *Marry The Sea.*

I laughed all the louder.

"Ben? Ben?" Ellen's voice calling through the letterbox. Outside, I heard hands thumping on the windows. "Ben, let me in. You promised. You said you'd go with me. You said you loved me."

The oldest and most painful one of all: *you would if you really loved me.* Never promise you'll do anything for a loved one, because sooner or later they'll demand the one thing you just can't do.

"Ben, it won't be like the others." Her voice was hitching. There was a clotted noise in her throat. "You'd become part of me in full. We'd be one. Isn't that what love is?"

What could she know about love? She must know something, I supposed. She'd have to, to do this.

"Please. Don't leave me on my own."

Something thumped at the window at the end of the landing. I turned and looked. Karl. He'd climbed up, clung on. He had spread flat against the window. His eyes glowed through at me.

"Ben? Ben?"

I didn't answer.

"Alright, then!" Her voice had a dull, cold finality, worse than any scream. "We're going. We can't stay longer, and we can't take you by force. It has to be of your own accord. But if that's the way you want it, fine. I can live without you, and I won't always be weak. I'm growing stronger all the time." She paused. I wouldn't look at the window, but a dull green glow spilled from it across the landing.

"The icecaps are going, Ben," she whispered. "They'll melt, all of them, and they'll cover all the earth. And when they do, I'll take *everyone.* It'll be soon. Sooner than you think."

The green glow vanished. Downstairs, the letterbox banged.

And the house was silent.

* * *

I STAYED THERE all night and through into the morning. The agony got worse and worse. Finally, somehow, I made it to the bedside table and took the pills.

When I could walk again, I went downstairs. I opened the front door; the wood was scratched and scored.

It was early in the morning when I went back to Marine Road. The sun was rising over Dinas Oleu, which I knew now I would never be able to climb again. The sky was clear blue, soft pink near the horizon; the air was crisp and cold, the first snap of the incoming winter. The tang of coalsmoke hung in the air, and the long, mournful cries of gulls echoed in from the sea. They were the only sound.

There was a sign in the front window: AR WERTH. *For Sale*. The front door was slightly ajar. I nudged it open.

A thick, foetid smell washed out of the dim hallway to greet me; I pulled my sweater up to cover my mouth and nose. A thin buzzing sound. Flies.

I found a light switch and pressed it, but nothing happened.

The buzzing came from the front room. A small, thin figure slouched on the sofa, head hanging forward and down.

Carrie.

She was alone in the room. Flies crawled on one dangling hand; it was bloated and badly discoloured. The hair that hung and hid her face was matted and dry. The stench hit me even through the sweater. Gagging, I backed out of the room.

The kitchen door was open. Some light came through the window in the back. Flies were buzzing in there too.

A small dining room adjoined the kitchen. A chair lay on the floor. Charles and Donna lay beside it. I recognised the stained, faded print dress Donna wore. There wasn't much else to recognise. Charles was little more than bones and ragged clothes; Donna was badly bloated and in the throes of black decomposition. The carpet around them was badly stained.

The house was bitterly cold. I moved back. I needed to get out. Away from the house, before I was discovered here. Away from Barmouth. Away from the sea.

But I needed to know.

I went up the stairs. There was dust everywhere. A few footprints and marks, but otherwise no sign that anyone had been here in months, even years. In the empty bathroom, something dark and wet filled the toilet bowl, flies swirling above. I didn't inspect it any closer.

There were three upstairs bedrooms. I checked the one next to the bathroom first.

Karl lay sprawled on the bed. He looked quite recently dead. No bloating. His eye sockets were empty though. And there were the holes in his face. His nose half-gone. Eaten, I guessed, before he came back.

The other two bedrooms were empty.

I found no trace of the woman who had called herself Ellen Vannin.

I LEFT BARMOUTH that night, and booked into a B&B in Manchester. While I was there, I wrote down what had happened. I had to try to make sure of it. I knew I wouldn't be believed, that it was the end of my career. But what was I supposed to do?

Wrote it, typed it, emailed it out. To the University and to a friend who worked in a government ministry.

And then I looked for a new place to live, cheaply, out of sight and mind. A place to hide, far from the sea I'd used to love.

I CHOSE A village in north-east Lancashire, where there was no sea and hardly any people; I rented a static caravan and I drank and I drank. I wanted to kill myself, and put a knife to my wrist more than once, but I could never quite do it. So I drank instead, not caring about what it did with my medication. I was probably hoping the combination of the two would finish the job I couldn't. But my body seemed far more capable of absorbing the punishment I was doling out than I'd thought.

Through those years, whenever I was sober, I would hear the sound of the sea. And voices. Hundreds, thousands, millions of voices, calling my name. A murmur that rose and fell like the sound of the waves, until they couldn't be told apart, but growing steadily, relentlessly louder.

An incoming tide of souls.

There were rains, of course, and storms. Floods, too. At first, I'd been afraid, but after a while I dismissed them. False alarms.

But then the rains came and didn't stop. The floods got worse. The TV stations started going off the air, one by one, the remainder broadcasting old light comedy. When they're showing old episodes of *Morecambe and Wise* and it's not even Christmas, you know something's badly wrong.

And the sound of the sea grew louder.

When I heard shouts and screams in the distance, I ventured out into the rain and squinted down. Below, I could see where the waters had come in, and suddenly the sea, the voices, the souls, were louder than ever before.

I went back inside as the first shots rang out. The Deep Brain was testing its strength, and that of the defence. If the villagers put up a good enough fight, it would fall back, for a while. But sooner or later, it would come in force, and it wouldn't stop. And it would, most especially, want me.

Rain drummed on the caravan roof. In my head, the sea-sound was deafening. And the voices. All the screaming dead, all those last moments, caught like voices on tape.

It was when I heard a woman's voice say, loud and clear in my ear, as if it was next to me, "Ben?" – and visualised Ellen, Ellen naked with her arms outstretched, and remembered her face, that last time I'd really seen it – that I decided I could do it now, and better had, while there was still time.

I lay down on the divan with a bottle of whisky and drank most of it. It made the voices and the tide fade away, made sure I wouldn't hear Ellen's voice again. With the Dutch courage I could do it, and I wouldn't even feel what I was doing to myself, but I blacked out almost the second I cut into my left wrist. My next memory is of lying on the Chinook's deck, and Robbie McTarn standing over me.

CHAPTER TWENTY-FOUR

THE FOOTPATH IS steep, but that's not so bad, as I'm on the downslope. Trouble is, it's uneven, loose stones threatening to turn my feet as I go. Not easy with a limp.

Before the flood, the air was fresh up here. High above the world, far from the cities, *et cetera*. Oh, you'd catch a whiff of those nice agricultural smells, like silage and cowshit. But there'd be the smell of grass and fallen leaves too, wildflowers, new-mown hay, all depending on the time of year.

Not anymore. After the flood there was a constant stench of sewage and decay, from everything in the water. That began going in the last week; the air was fresh again, the wind with a hint of saltwater. Yes: the sea I fled from has truly come to find me.

The smell's changed again now. I breathe through my mouth as I wind my way down, between the ranks of the walking dead. For most of them, that green mould, or whatever it is, has arrested the decay. But not reversed it. Even a fresh corpse needs some time in the deep, being charged up with whatever powers the Deep Brain possesses, to develop that protective coat. So I get the smell of the dead, along with the stink of that green stuff. I don't know what the hell it is – maybe I would have once, back in my old life with more brain cells left to play with – but it smells like the bottom of a drained pond.

They turn and look at me as I pass. There is nothing on their faces. Slack and empty. I'm used to seeing that now. On the faces of the living and the dead.

Smoke still rising in the distance. Beyond that, far down, lies the open water. I keep walking. And no-one moves. There is only the silence. The cold hard wind blows keen across the fell. And I walk on.

I SPENT THE first night after the flood in an upstairs room at the farmhouse the soldiers commandeered. When I woke, I could still hear the sea-sounds. I went to the bar and got to work on the first available bottle. People glared at me at first; finally, they just ignored me as best they could.

Later on, there was shouting in the distance. Gunfire. A few minutes later, McTarn came in, and he brought a woman. She was in her late twenties and tallish, with chestnut hair. She was half-soaked and shivering, too, but you could tell she might be pretty, or more than that, under it all. Everyone was staring at her. McTarn reached out to steady her, but she pulled away.

"I'm fine. I'm fine. I don't need any help. Which way is the toilet, please?"

McTarn pointed. When she'd gone there were sniggers, a few laughs. Taking the piss. Uncomfortable.

Over the past few years there'd been plenty of time for brooding. And I'd done a lot of that, about Ellen Vannin. She had, literally, been made for me. Soft. Alluring. And in the end, *submissive*. A little coy and teasing, but... she'd asked for nothing. Just come along and given things to me, done things for me. Wanted nothing for herself. So what did that say about me?

The bed-hopping, the never settling down... I understood now, it was not because I had nothing to give, but because I *wouldn't* give. Oh, I told myself, and anyone who'd listen (less and less of them as time went by) I wanted to get married, settle down, but in the end all these women *wanted* things from me. Under the outdoorsy adventurer I played at, there was just a scared little boy who didn't want to get hurt again. That was who Ellen had been made for.

When I saw her – Katja – for the first time, I saw a woman who was the complete opposite of that.

When she came back from the toilet, a few minutes later, face scrubbed clean and hair scraped back, she didn't tell anyone anything. No effort to charm or flirt. I didn't understand why, not then.

I don't believe in love at first sight. It wasn't love. Not then. I just saw someone and realised I wanted something from her. Not sex. Just a pair of arms to hold me, to take the weight off my shoulders, soft hands to stroke and soothe the pain away.

I huddled down, away from the probing, demanding stares of all these people expecting me to pull some miraculous rabbit out of the hat. McTarn barking at me, spitting out his rage. I flinched from it; it added to the voices, calling.

And then I heard Katja saying "Please don't."

The sounds in my head subsided a little, as I heard her talking to McTarn in that low voice, that accent. So gentle and so soothing. The sea-sounds, the voices, were louder. I wanted to tell her. Warn her. I didn't know how. It hurt when I tried – the voices rose to a din.

Say something, Ben. You have to say something.

"They're calling me," I said to her.

She looked over at me, studying me. Those great dark eyes. "Who?"

"The voices. The souls. All the dead."

They roared. I gulped down whisky, refilled my glass. Pain stabbed behind my eyes. It faded when I drank.

"Go on," she said. It was a whisper. Soft as snow.

I shook my head.

"Please?"

"Can't."

"Why?"

"Hurts."

She sat there, waiting. I didn't want her to go. I started talking about the diving accident. And anything else I could think of. Maybe I could slip sideways onto the subject, tell her before the voices could realise.

She listened; of course she did. In case I said something useful. Because she needed to be useful, too. Be an asset, and not just a pretty face. There were too many men here, too much testosterone. Too much potential for things to turn ugly.

As it got dark, she walked me back to the caravan, up the dimming footpaths. I was very drunk. We didn't speak much.

I slumped on the divan. Katja sat on the one opposite. She smiled a little at me. Like at a pet, I thought.

"Will you..." I asked. "Will you do something for me?"

Her face lost expression. "What?"

"Just hold me." Her eyes narrowed. *Shit.* "I don't mean – not sex, I don't want sex." Although I wouldn't have said no. "I just want someone to..."

She pursed her lips. Thinking it over, calculating the odds. "All right." She knelt beside the divan, held out her arms. I rolled into them.

Drifting off to sleep; cool fingers stroked my brow.

* * *

THE TWO FARMHOUSES. The scene of the last attempt to hold them off. Bullets have chipped the walls and the windows are shattered. Scorch marks. Scattered remains of people. Ours, theirs, it doesn't matter now. Gnawed bones, torn fragments of clothing. A group of *them* crouch over four or five dead sheep. One tears at a severed leg. Another lifts a tangle of intestines, looped around its fingers like a bloated, slippery cat's-cradle and tries to bite through it.

SOME OF THE things are inside the nearest farmhouse. They're in the front room. I stop and look.

They're staring at the walls, looking around the way someone waking up after a long drunk might try to take stock, to understand where he is and what's happened. Take it from me on this one; I speak from long experience.

Another stands in front of the mantelpiece, staring at the pictures along it. It picks one up, holding it upside down, its head cocked to one side.

One of the sheep-eaters looks up from its feast. It's a fresh one, not covered in the mould yet. Blood smears its face. An eye has burst; the socket glows. The other eye burns dully, like a grimy light bulb. Its clothes are soiled with blood. So are its hands. Some of the blood might be its own; in places, the clothing is ripped open. Its stomach is an empty cavity. The meat it's been chewing drops out of it onto the ground.

The other sheep-eaters are staring at me too. Another stands in the farmhouse door, watching. The ones in the living room are staring out through the glass, even the one with the photograph. It falls from its hands and the glass shatters.

Stop dawdling. Stop mooning. Go. Go now.

Is that my own thought, or the message in their eyes? Or someone else, calling me? I start walking again. They part to let me through, dead flesh brushing mine. I pass without incident, but feel their eyes on my back as I walk on.

WHEN I WOKE next morning, I rolled over to see Katja with her foot braced on the opposite divan, lacing up a boot. It was one of mine.

"Where did you get those?"

She looked over at me. "We're the same size," she said. "I didn't think you'd mind. You've a few pairs. Is that okay?"

"Sure." Then I noticed something else. "Your hair..."

She half-smiled and ruffled it; she'd cropped it short. "I thought it was time for a change of image."

"Okay," I said, feeling stupid and slow.

Katja sat on the divan and faced me. "I want to know what you know, if I can. Not for McTarn or the others. For me. I need to make myself useful around here. Otherwise, all I'll be, sooner or later, is another hole to fuck." Her face went hard, her voice too. "And I will not go through that again." She took a deep breath and relaxed. "I'm going to McTarn now – see what else I can do to help. I can use a gun. I can fight. I think he might find that useful, don't you?"

"Yes," I mumbled. I felt betrayed. Weak. I couldn't look at her.

Then I felt her hand squeeze mine. Surprised, I looked up. "Last night," she said. "You liked that, didn't you?"

I nodded. I couldn't meet her eyes.

"I have no problem giving you what comfort I can. If that's what you want. In exchange, you tell me what you can."

"Difficult," I said. "Hurts when I try."

"Try," she said. "It's all I ask. Alright?"

"Alright," I said.

She stood, hands on hips. "How do I look?"

I almost said *beautiful*, then realised it was the last thing she'd want to hear. "Like someone you shouldn't mess with."

She smiled. The first real smile I'd seen her give, and it was all mine. It lit her face up, and I could see what she'd been trying to hide ever since arriving. "Good answer," she said. "See you later."

THE NARROW FOOTPATH leads along a twisting, sunken stream. From the banks, trees lean over the waters, branches splayed out like twisted hands, roots writhing free of the earth as if poised to strike. One has fallen in the stream. The chill waters wash and lap over it.

It's quite painful now. Every step brings fresh agony from my knees and hips.

I dig a quarter-bottle of Bell's from a pouch in the wetsuit, and take a deep swallow. The liquor burns its way down to my gut. The joint pain loses some of its edge.

Not far now.

Drinking alcohol before diving is a very stupid and dangerous thing to do. But in my case, so is diving, full stop.

But then, I'm not coming back from this one. I've always known that.

I haven't seen any of them since the farmhouse, except for a couple in the meadows below them, chasing sheep. They'll go after animals if humans aren't available. Hot blood and living flesh. Something that can sustain the existence the Brain's given them. All that energy's got to come from somewhere.

The path is clear. They must have congregated higher up. Ready for that last big push. Why are they waiting? Maybe because they know I'm coming to them. And maybe not. It'll be dark soon. That'll make it easier for them.

Katja...

I put one foot in front of the other.

Then I hear footsteps. Slow and dragging. They're coming up the path one by one. Single file. Slow, plodding steps; there's no hurry now, no sense expending energy. They're coming straight towards me.

No weapons. Except my knife. No diver leaves home without one. To cut whatever you might get fouled in. I could, maybe, get one of them with a lucky stab, in through the eye sockets, into the brain...

And the others would pull me down and tear me into pieces. Maybe better to use it on myself.

There's nowhere to go. No point, no sense in retreating. If I don't get where I'm going, it's all over.

It might be anyway. No guarantees this will work.

I grip the haft of the knife. I've run long enough. Not anymore. Not anymo –

The first has reached me. Literally inches away. It stops, staring into me with empty, glowing eye-sockets. And then it steps sideways off the path and crashes into the stream.

One by one, the others do the same. They clamber along the stream and then back up onto dry land as soon as they're past me.

My luck is holding. Or something is.

I press forward, starting to laugh as they drop out of my path. A couple step aside, up against the chicken wire fence hiving the path off from the field alongside.

I keep going, because I have to.

Katja...

QUID PRO QUO. That was what she was offering.

Katja would give me what I needed, in exchange for the one thing I couldn't bear to do.

I sat on the divan after she'd gone, and I thought it over long and hard.

What decided it for me, in the end, was the thought of the look she might give me if I said no. Or if I said yes and broke my promise.

Despite her hard-facedness, I had an odd feeling she liked me. I didn't want to lose that.

So, about an hour after she'd gone, I began whispering to myself. I imagined Katja sat there listening, and I started telling her about the Deep Brain.

The voices began rising almost at once, and eventually I had to give up. I flopped back across the divan, moaning. My head rang and throbbed.

I lay there and breathed deep. Then, after a few minutes, I sat up and began again.

By the time Katja came back, I was exhausted and running with sweat, but I was, at least, able to utter those few words when I limped down to the Inn. I was able, at last, to tell someone else about the Deep Brain.

Death is coming. Not the most cheerful way of putting it.

I slumped into my chair afterwards, barely noticing it when Katja came to sit beside me. "Are you alright?" she asked.

I shook my head. "Managed to talk about it. A bit. Difficult. Hurts." I told her about my day. "It hurt like hell, but I managed more than I had before." The pain was bearable now. I wasn't talking directly about the subject, so it dwelt in the background with a vague suggestion of menace.

"I'm proud of you," she said. When I looked, there was something in her face, something I hadn't seen before. Respect? Something like that, maybe. She had some idea, anyway, what it cost me to speak.

She touched my hand. "Why don't you tell me something else now?"

"Like what?"

"Not about these things. Not about this Deep Brain. Tell me something about you, instead."

"Really?"

"Yes. I would like to hear."

So I started talking. I was more than a little hammered by then, so I'm not sure of all of it. I'm pretty sure it was a fairly maudlin, rambling piece, most likely about my love life. I might have cried a little. I don't remember.

What I do remember is this: her taking my hand, stroking the back of it with her thumb. I didn't dare look up, to see her face, but I felt the warmth of her touch and thought that, perhaps, this was not an act.

I drank myself into a stupor that night, and so I didn't see much of her. Her and McTarn carried me back to the caravan. She came to see me the next morning, and held me a little while.

"Have you tried writing it down?" she asked.

"I did before," I told her. "When I sent in the report. But I destroyed my copies of it. There's nothing here." A pain unrelated to the hangover twinged at my temple.

"Perhaps you could try doing it again?"

"Perhaps."

Over the next fortnight, we spent more and more time together. After a few days, she began to volunteer information about herself. Where she'd come from, what had happened to her, the journey to Pendle. Her voice choked and halted at points; she didn't always meet my eyes, and I think once or twice she wept. Her hand was in mine throughout, and I no longer knew who was giving comfort and who was receiving it.

I MAKE MY way down the path where it rejoins the stream, and come out onto Pendle Row. The dead are shambling up; they bump and jostle me as I pass, but none of them offer any direct violence.

I step out into the road. There's more room now.

Smoke's still rising from the burned-out homes. I saw it from a long way off. The Inn is still standing, anyway.

Four of them are in the Pendle Tea Rooms as I pass, sitting at one of the tables. They look up and watch me as I pass, stepping over corpses and pieces of corpses.

The pain stabs at my joints. I sag against a wall, sinking down. The sun is sinking too. I must move on soon. And I will. But I have to rest. Just for a few minutes. I'm almost there.

KATJA AND I slept together for the first time about a week before she moved in with me.

I'd developed a schedule. After she'd gone for the day, I took pen and paper and wrote for as long as I could. Which usually wasn't very long. I'd have a drink, rest up, and then set to work where I left off. If I was lucky, I managed a third of a page a day.

Destroy it. Destroy it. Destroy it. I would hear a voice whispering that at least once a day, usually as the clamour of the voices rose to new, agonising heights, but always clear above them, and it was always the voice of Ellen Vannin.

But I didn't. I was, after all, used to living with pain.

I didn't talk to Katja about it. It took all my strength to focus on the subject long enough to write the day's quota down. The time I spent with her... that was for me.

"You're nearly done, aren't you?" she asked.

"About halfway," I told her. "But I'll get it finished."

She looked at me, stroked my face. I almost recoiled, it was totally unexpected. I was used to being held, to my brow being stroked as I drifted off. But this? "You are stronger than I thought," she said. "Ben..."

"Yes?"

"If you want to... you know... then we can."

I didn't know what to say. "But... but you said... I thought..."

"It would be..." she took a deep breath. "It would be because I wanted it too."

"Seriously?"

"Seriously."

"But... you were just... I mean, for the information, to be useful..."

"Things change."

It wasn't what you'd expect. You'd expect it to be pretty special, swinging from the chandeliers kind of stuff. I mean, despite my physical state, I knew what to do. Years of experience. And Katja – well, of course, she had a lot of experience too.

But it was different from that. More hesitant. This wasn't about her giving some punter his money's worth, or me showing what a stud I was. We undressed slowly and carefully. I folded back the sheets on the divan and climbed under them; Katja followed. We just lay there for a while, facing each other. I could feel the brush of her bare skin against mine.

"Kiss me."

I leant forward and put my lips to hers. I felt rusty, out of practice. Clumsy. Her too. Kissing was one thing she wasn't into. Each of us was afraid to make the first move, to start things, because we'd been something else before and that wasn't what we wanted to be now.

But once we started, we got there in the end. And, yes. It was good.

JESUS CHRIST.

It's almost dark. There should be lights coming on in the street. If this was the world we used to live in. But the only lights are from the figures walking up the road.

I stand. Joints scream in pain like rusty hinges. Start walking. Nearly there.

I reach the end of Pendle Row. Cross the bridge onto Barley Road. The road from the village descends and finally disappears, down into the water below. Dead men and women clamber out onto it and totter past me. Dead children. Further out, the converted mill sticks up; beyond it, the top of a drowned white house.

No dead animals, though. Odd. They'll kill and eat animals, and an infected bite'll kill a beast, but it won't come back. I don't know why.

This is it, then.

THE NIGHT BEFORE they destroyed Roughlee, the sea-sounds woke me. Katja was a soft, warm weight beside me on the divan, but I knew we weren't alone.

Above the bed, a dark shadow moving.

Above the bed, two dim green points of light.

Above the bed, the figure leaning down, the glow brightening, and Ellen's grey and rotting face coming down out of the dark, blackened lips peeled back for a snarling kiss.

"*Ben.*"

I screamed. Katja woke. The room was empty. But all I could do was babble it, over and over and over again.

"Ellen. Ellen Vannin. She's found me."

I PULL OFF the boots. Put on the flippers.

I walk down into the water. It laps coldly around my ankles. I can hear the sound of the sea breaking, hear voices moaning and crying. The water rises to my knees, to my thighs, my groin – *Fuck! My bollocks have just imploded* – then my waist, my chest.

I wet the diving mask and pull it over my eyes and nose, making sure the seal is watertight. Check my tanks.

"Ellen?" I shout it. "Ellen. I'm coming."

And I put the mouthpiece in and for the last time in my life, I dive.

CHAPTER TWENTY-FIVE

I UNCLIP THE diver's light from my belt and shine it ahead as I swim across the flooded road. The surface recedes, further and further above.

Eyes glow in the murk. Then the torch picks out their faces. They swim up, fast. One collides with me, sending me flying into the path of another, and for an instant I think they're turning on me. But they're not. They go past.

I'm feeling the pressure now. The pain begins. Up above me, dark bodies rise through the water, eyes green pinpricks, aiming for the dim, dying light above.

Ellen? Ellen? Where are you? I'm coming to you. This is what you wanted. Isn't it?

Ellen?

"BEN..."

Katja's eyes, bright with tears.

Outside, gunfire. McTarn and the others are further down, making a last attempt to hold the dead back. It's not going to work. We all know that. Why even try?

Because we have to. Because to give in goes against everything we are. But giving in is what I'm talking about doing.

"You can't," she says.

"I have to," I tell her.

"You don't even know it'll work."

"If it doesn't, we'll be no worse off."

She wipes her eyes. "We'd be together. Don't you want that, at least?" I take her hands. She pulls them out of my grip. "You know I do."

"Then –"

"I've got to try. It's what McTarn and the others came for."

"Fuck them."

"They came here because they thought I might have an answer. Well, I didn't. I don't now. Just an idea that might work."

"And it'll kill you."

"If it doesn't, those things will. If it does work, some of us might make it." I take her hands again. "You might."

Her eyes squeeze shut. Her lips peel back from her teeth and her head dips forward. "You bastard. God damn you, you bastard."

I grip her hands tightly. She grips back. There is nothing I can say that will stop it hurting. But that's the way of it.

"I'm tired of being a coward, Katja."

"You're not."

"Yes, I am. If I'd gone with Ellen, back at the start, none of this might have happened."

"That's stupid."

"If I'd gone with her, the floods might not have come. Or at least, not – what came with it. All I've done, all my fucking *life*, is run and hide. And I'm tired of it. Katja, I've got to try."

I hold my arms out to her.

And for the first time, it's me who comforts her.

ELLEN?

Is it too late? There's no answer.

From down in the depths comes the breaking of waves. And the voices. Screaming and crying out.

don't want to die

> *bastards up there in the*
> *air and the light still*
> *breathing*

> *mother*

father

> *brother*

sister

my daughter

my son

I strike out. Pressure. Pain. Deeper. Go deeper.

I don't have long. And I don't know what to do. I'm accepting an offer that might not even still be valid.

Ellen?

The valley floor lies open below. Up ahead is the white house.

"Ben?"

I know that voice.

"Ben."

She steps into view, outside the white house. An arm extends, beckons. And then she disappears inside.

I strike down and as I do –

THE VOICES EXPLODE into my skull like a grenade bursting, my barriers going down. I can't see straight – can't because I'm not seeing through my own eyes anymore.

It's dark. They move forward.

It's like a TV set picking up a thousand different channels. And someone's got the remote control, flicking from channel to channel to channel to channel to channel to –

The gate gives way. Ged goes down. McTarn – poor bastard, red and black rising across his face as the infection spreads – falls. They don't touch him, because he's one of them now. And even as he realises it, his heart stops. I feel his death. Because I know him, perhaps, the cameras zoom in, to get it from every angle – his mind dying, swallowed up in rage and terror that's sucked into the Deep Brain to make it stronger – strength then funnelled into McTarn's corpse to make it rise and walk. He leaves his gun behind. He doesn't need it anymore.

Guns firing, little spots and flickers of distant light. Now and again, a camera goes blank as a bullet hits home. But still they advance.

Jo, Katja and Mleczko taking charge, getting the remaining defenders to round the survivors up. There's only one place to go now.

Can't see. Have to aim down, hoping I'm still on course. Swim and swim. Ignore the pain. Please let me be right. Please.

Hendry refusing to leave the Chinook, standing guard, firing his last bullets into the attackers before they pull him down. They swarm over the Chinook until it rocks and falls, rotors breaking on the ground.

The survivors back up the hillside, firing. The steps that lead up Pendle. So steep. The dead are climbing too. Slow. But relentless. The dead don't get tired or out of breath. And so they steadily gain.

Parkes holding position, firing down the steps, buying time for other survivors to get past. But the dead get closer, closer – and suddenly leap in one of their terrible flurries of motion. Parkes has no chance; she has time for a single scream before they pull her down. Nearly a dozen of them fall upon her. In their hunger, they tear her apart.

People fall behind, collapsing – but no-one can go back for them, can't slow down the group to save one. So the too-old, the too-young, the weak, the sick – they're left where they've fallen, begging for help – until dead hands seize them and dead jaws tear the flesh from their bones.

The lucky ones, if there's time, might get a bullet in the head, to spare them.

My hands plough into something soft. My body is alive with pain, one long wire of it. I open my eyes and I can see properly. My fingers are buried in silt, lying thick over grass that comes loose in my hands, drowned and dead, the earth it's rooted in turning to slurry.

The house is in front of me. I swim for it.

I know I won't last much longer.

There's a door, and it's open. I swim down a flooded hallway, past a living room where a seat-cushion, bleached and bloated from its long immersion, drifts past.

"Down here, Ben. I'm here."

It's from the end of the hallway. Here's a door, ajar. I swim to it and push it wide.

The windows are shattered; drifts of silt and debris are piled everywhere. Cooker and microwave, washing machine and dishwasher, over there in the corner.

Ellen Vannin sits at a table in the centre of the room, in her long black dress. Her black hair drifts wild in the current. Her head rises. Her face is a grey, howling mask like perished rubber, fretted and holed, blackened teeth bared by fish-eaten lips.

I stop swimming and settle, let my feet touch the floor.

Her eye sockets blaze.

Her mouth tries to form a smile. "You came."

Yes. In the end.

"Thank you." She rises from the table. "You're sure about this?"

Yes.

She steps towards me. "The girl? Katja? You love her?"

I loved you too. And I can again.

She holds out her arms to me.

I unfasten the aqualung and let it fall, slipping the mouthpiece from my lips. A long stream of silver bubbles flies upward. I kick off the flippers and step into her embrace, lower my living mouth to her dead mouth, and breathe in.

*   *   *

AND ON TOP of Pendle Hill, Katja, Mleczko, Jo, Hassan and twenty or thirty other men and women can see out over half of what was Lancashire, for all the good it does as the dead swarm up it from all sides. Katja checks her pistol. Six rounds remain. She raises the gun and fires, hitting a dead thing between the eyes, thinking, four shots left. This time, she knows who the last one's for.

IT'S OVER QUITE quickly, without pain. I/we watch my body and the body I/we knew as Ellen Vannin topple and drift to the floor.

Then I/we turn our/my gaze outwards, out through the eyes of the myriad dead.

The survivors have huddled into a knot around the trig point on the summit. The dead are all around them.

In me/us there boils so much rage. The rage and the terror of all the dead. But now there is more. Now the Deep Brain is... a whole mind. At last. I am... not Ben Stiles anymore. But I am... was... him. Enough to know it is time to stop.

And so I reach out and I halt the dead in their tracks.

ON THE SUMMIT of Pendle Hill, a stillness falls.

Katja Wencewska, two bullets in her gun and only one for the dead things, freezes, looking sidelong at Jo, Mleczko, the others. Guns are held ready; axes, clubs, makeshift spears. All used and blooded. A steel baseball bat, buckled out of shape.

The dead surround them, unmoving.

All save one. One figure, shouldering through the ranks. At a first glance, you might almost think he was still alive. If his eyes didn't glow.

The body of Robert McTarn approaches; Katja aims at his face, finger tightening on the trigger.

The dead don't need to breathe anymore, but it's necessary for speech. I work McTarn's lungs to force out the words. Would he appreciate me using his corpse like this? Is anything of McTarn left, apart from the traces and echoes absorbed into the Deep Brain? Even I can't answer that.

"Katja, it's me. It's Ben."

It's not really, not anymore, but I have to put it into terms that can be understood.

I tell her that it worked. That now I am the Deep Brain. And it is me. That the dead are mine to command. That I will return them to the depths.

That the war is over.

But.

I warn her because I must. Because there are aeons worth of fury in the deep. I warn her because I cannot promise that I will remain in control forever. Because one day the rage might overwhelm me and the dead might walk again.

I will try to decommission my weapons. To let them die and decay. Most of them. But the Brain craves form, physicality, and I must give it that.

I tell her to be watchful, and to remember. I tell her to remember me.

And I cannot kiss her now, because the only lips I have the living would flinch from, but I kiss her in another way. Mind to mind.

Whispering, as I do: forgive me.

And then I turn the dead round and march them back, down the Hill. Back to the sea.

Until only the body of a man called Robert McTarn remains.

"I love you," I say through him, and then he too begins the long walk home.

And as he goes, I hear, above the keening of the wind and the wild laughter and rejoicing of those who have, at the last moment, been spared, the weeping of the woman I will always love.

PART FOUR

Storm Warning – Ocean Rising

Ancient ocean, your waters are bitter.

Lautremont, *Les Chants De Maldoror.*

EPILOGUE

Katja

MY NAME IS Katja Mleczko. Today I am forty-three, making me the oldest person in the Pendle Islands.

When I was born, most people lived to at least seventy. Even older. There were people more than one hundred years old. Impossible to imagine that now, after the Flood and the Rising. Even to the ones alive before them, like me, it seems unreal, a dream. Our children, with little or no memory of the world as it was – for them, I think, it's easier.

This life ages us fast. My generation took it all for granted; spoilt. Now we're where our ancestors were two, maybe three hundred years before. If that. Our only medicines are the ones we make ourselves. There are folk remedies – a piece of mouldy bread on a wound makes a crude antibiotic, they used it for centuries before penicillin – but still, illnesses that would have been nothing when I was a child claim more lives each year.

I've had nine children. The first came eighteen months after the dead things went back into the sea. The last, eight years ago, almost killed me. After that, I took precautions, although I was widowed soon after. I have had no lovers since; I'm past that now.

I married Danny Mleczko. He took charge after the dead things went away, and I soon saw he was interested in me. He was still a boy, in most respects, but he was sweet, beneath his brashness. We became lovers; when I fell pregnant, we married. It wasn't much of a ceremony – there was no priest – but Hassan did his best. He was the next most senior soldier present, so he officiated.

The Chinook never flew again. Any other survivors we met we reached by boat, or they found us. The strangest were a small group from Manchester, who drifted to us on makeshift rafts. They were workers from the CIS tower, led by a bright young woman called Vicky. They'd survived on the roof of the building. Somehow she'd kept them going, fighting off the attacks, downing passing birds with lumps of stone. She set them 'targets' for the day (she was in sales.) When the dead things stopped attacking and the food got scarce, she made them build rafts from flotsam and jetsam. She was a natural planner and organiser; I remember her fiancé had survived, too, and no sooner had they got to Pendle than she started organising her wedding. I was one of the bridesmaids. Vicky's still alive. She's the second oldest person round here now. We've become good friends.

There's nothing much left to scavenge from the old world. We have what survival skills we've learned the hard way, or from books we salvaged. A few generations ago, my family would've known all this. Now we're learning it all again.

We rear sheep, raise crops, and farm fish. The waters are full of them now. We collect driftwood, cut peat, fell trees for fuel and to build small boats to commute between islands.

We survive.

We tried to raise Windhoven afterwards, in the hope the miracle might have come in time for them too, but we heard nothing. We never heard from anyone else. Perhaps we're the last humans of all... but I can't believe that. Or simply don't wish to.

Danny became a fisherman. One day he went out in one of the boats and didn't come back. It happened; still does. I married him out of necessity – we had to survive, raise children, make homes and communities – but I loved him in the end. But never as I loved Ben Stiles. I wish I could've; he deserved it. But such things are not a matter of choice.

Three of my children were stillborn. A fourth died in infancy – pneumonia – and another died in a stupid accident, running on a fell. He broke his neck. He looked very like Danny. Bad luck in the Mleczko genes, perhaps. I don't know.

It hurts to remember these things, even now. But I must.

I have three sons still, and a daughter. Our population is growing slowly, but it grows, repopulating the islands.

We're nearly all gone now, the ones who were there at the start. Some have lasted longer than others. Jo died only a couple of years after that last battle; she never really recovered from losing Chas. Strange how, with so much changed, someone can still die of a broken heart.

Hassan died last winter. He was the last of the soldiers. He passed on all he could in the years before. The Islands have four healers now, carrying on what he taught them. My daughter is one of them.

She looks somewhat like my mother.

I called her Marta. The skies are always grey. I can't remember the last time we saw the sun, and it's almost always cold. The winters are bleak and killing, often claiming the old and very young. This winter may be my last.

But, little by little, the waters are relinquishing the ground they claimed, yielding new lands, thick with silt and richly fertile. Grass soon covers them.

I remember old nature documentaries from my childhood, of baby turtles hatching and scrambling down the beach to get to the sea. So few of them made it. Birds and crabs picked most of them off long before they reached the water. Darwinism in action. I am haunted, I suppose, by all the ones who never reached the sea. It's the price paid for having survived.

I suppose the regret will be bred out of us soon enough.

I wrote an account of the flood and my journey to Pendle shortly after arriving, in what little free time I had, so that at least other survivors would know what we'd gone through. It's the least you can do, for the dead.

Other than a bullet between the eyes, if that's what it takes to give them rest.

Not that we have any bullets left. Now it's back to bows and arrows, spears, crude swords and knives. With so much machinery obsolete from lack of fuel or ammunition, there's no shortage of metal...

Robert and Ben left their accounts too; I've put our stories together here. There are some parts of their stories I've written in myself.

When Ben died, he touched my mind, somehow. A last kiss, of sorts, I supposed at the time. But I saw – experienced – his death. And not just his: Robert's as well. Perhaps because Ben was speaking through the corpse, perhaps because Robert loved me. I'm not sure. I wrote down all that I could remember afterwards.

I thought long and hard about including them here, but in the end I decided to.

Writing materials are hard to come by, and we improvise. Parchment made from sheep's hide, ink from sloes gathered from blackthorn bushes. I've gathered the old, scribbled notes and transcribed them over the years. The ink is fading on them, the paper starting to crumble or become mildewed. It's important they be remembered, Robert and Ben. Between them, they helped save us all.

I played my part, of course; I saved lives and, without me, Ben wouldn't have found the strength to do what he did. But still, I've often felt like a witness rather than a participant.

Although that may be about to change.

There's a small island, one of the furthest out from us to be settled. One of our fishing boats made landfall there last week. There were half a dozen dwellings on the island, small stone and wood huts dotted round the slopes. All empty.

They found blood on the walls of one house. Most of the sheep were still there. A few had stampeded off one of the steep edges of the fell and had drowned, their bloated, bedraggled bodies floating in the shallows.

That last touch of Ben's mind when he died. *Forgive me.* At the time, I thought he meant for leaving me, for dying. But Ben knew that his remedy might not be permanent. Another reason for putting this record together.

If one day Ben started to lose control, if the Deep Brain's rage and fury began to surface again, the only chance to control it would be to take *another* mind into it as his had been taken. Strengthen the mix. The Deep Brain had forged a link with his mind. Ben would've had to do the same.

Forgive me.

I hope I am wrong.

Not just for my sake. If it's true, what happens when *my* control begins to slip? I'll have to forge the same link with someone else, to follow me when the time comes. Someone I loved. As Ben loved me. Someone with the strength to do what must be done.

And I think of my daughter, the healer, my best-loved child.

In ancient times, they made sacrifice to the sea gods. Is that our future? Have we come full circle?

I don't want to believe it. But sometimes, when I sleep, I think I can hear the sea. Even when I know it's calm and silent. I hear voices where there are none, *can* be none, because there's no-one there.

And... there is something else. That is why I am writing this last piece.

Last night, at dusk, I walked along the old Pendle Row, past the Inn's ruins to the bridge, overlooking the bay. It's receded in the last few years, but there's still deep waters out there. I saw movement down in the shallows, so I looked.

They were only there briefly, for a moment. Then the moon hid behind a cloud; when it came out again, they were gone.

There were three of them. One was small and lean, wiry and quick.

Another was tall and gangly. And the third seemed to have long, wild hair, and when it – he – moved, it was with a limp.

The men in my life, taken by the sea.

They beckoned me.

And their eyes glowed green.

THE END

ACKNOWLEDGEMENTS

'Lady' Andrea Power provided, in addition to her kindness, friendship and support, her extensive knowledge of narrowboats. Her extensive knowledge of real ale also came in useful, if not for the present novel.

To Simon C, former Army medic, I owe a debt of thanks beyond mere words; without his advice on barotrauma, military procedure and mindset, *Tide Of Souls* would be a far poorer piece of work. That he found the time to help me during what was a period of great personal difficulty for him only makes the debt greater. Cheers, Four-Eyes, from The Bearded Lunatic.

Anything I've got right about the relevant subjects is due in no small part to these two; any errors are entirely my own. Likewise, I'm responsible for any liberties taken with the geography of Lancashire. The flooding that occurs in the novel is a scenario entirely of my own invention, and is not based on any theoretical models that I'm aware of. Unless there's a global warning 'nightmare scenario' that also features zombies...

Jon Oliver, naturally, for ringing me up and asking "So, would you like to write a zombie novel for me then?" Also to publicity maestro Keith Richardson and all others sailing in the good ship Abaddon.

Lorelei Loveridge and Jaclyn Smith, for bigging me up.

Joel Lane's friendship, advice and support have been invaluable over the last ten years. Bernard and Clare Nugent, Mark Phillips, Jenny Bent, Clare Moss and Darren Bland, Matt and Kathryn Colledge, David and Jane Southall, Rob Krijnen-Kemp and my parents and grandparents are just some of the many who've provided faith and support – emotional or practical – over the years. A big thank you also goes out to Gary McMahon, along with my heartfelt apologies to anyone I've missed.

Indirect thanks are also due to: New Model Army, Justin Sullivan, The Jan Garbarek Group, Dark Sanctuary, The Cure and The Sisters of Mercy for providing a writing soundtrack.

SIMON BESTWICK was born in 1974. He writes horror fiction and the odd bit of crime, and wonders, in spare moments, if there's any connection to the fact that he lives in Lancashire. His short fiction has popped up all over the place, in the UK and the States, and is collected in *A Hazy Shade Of Winter* (Ash Tree Press, 2004, www.ash-tree.bc.ca) and *Pictures Of The Dark* (Gray Friar Press, 2009, www.grayfriarpress.com.) He's also written some decidedly off-the-wall stuff for radio, mostly comedy, which you can check out at www.darksmile.co.uk. He's worked as a fast food operative, drama teacher, typist, insurance salesman (which taught him a lot about the dark side of human nature) and a call centre operator. Ideally he'd like to con somebody into paying him to write for a living, as it's so much better than a proper job. Find out more about Simon at http://simon-bestwick.blogspot.com

HUNGRY HEARTS

BY GARY McMAHON

For John Worley
The best man in any company...

Thanks must go to the following good souls:

My wife for putting up with my insanity during
the writing of this book.
My mother-in-law for not getting angry when
I told her I'd killed her.
Stephen Bacon, Simon Bestwick and Gary Fry for help,
support, encouragement and invaluable friendship.

INTRODUCTION

WHEN I DECIDED that I'd like to write a zombie novel my first thought was: *you can't use the Z-word*. It's so lame, so familiar, that it's almost like a bad joke.

My second thought was: *I dare you to write a love story.*

So the whole thing started there, with a refusal to use the word 'zombie' in the novel and the desire to write a twisted romance that was also a metaphor for an extra-marital affair.

It was important to me to do something no one else (to my knowledge, at least) had done before, and to put my own stamp on the zombie sub-genre. The editor said that he'd commissioned me because he wanted to have a dark, gritty and bleak novel in the *Tomes of the Dead* line, and I like to think that I gave him those things. Indeed, *Hungry Hearts* might be just about the bleakest thing I've written to date. One scene in particular – you'll know it when you come to it – made me very uncomfortable as I wrote the words late one night in a dimly-lit room, with rain pattering against the windows. I laughed; I glanced over my shoulder; then I laughed again... nervously.

As well as these odd, personal touches, I also wanted to pay tribute to the films of George Romero. To be honest, I haven't read that much zombie fiction. But I think I've probably seen every zombie movie ever made, and let's face it, Romero is the man who invented the modern zombie film, with his astonishing *Dead* sequence of movies. And I love them all – even the later ones that nobody else seems to rate.

Before Romero ever brought us his original Vietnam-era ghouls, zombies were more like the one in Val Lewton and Jacques Tourneur's brilliant 1943 film *I Walked with a Zombie*: blank-eyed Haitian men and women who'd fallen foul of the local voodoo *Bokor*. They didn't eat flesh or brains, and they weren't dead – not really. But Romero brought the zombie out of the graveyard and right into our homes, our parks, our city streets – he made them our friends and neighbours, our mothers and fathers and children. He made them us.

Zombies in film and fiction haven't really come a long way since *Night of the Living Dead* in 1968, and the empty, profit-driven society they were created to represent has moved on even less. But zombies are hot property right now – they're the current horror fad, and have even leaked into the mainstream. Back when I was a goggle-eyed teenager, watching *Dawn of the Dead* on grainy third-or-fourth-generation VHS, if you'd have told me there'd be a hit American television show about a zombie apocalypse I would have laughed in your face and asked you to pass the popcorn.

But this, too, has come to pass. Zombies are the new vampires; eating flesh is the new bloodsucking. Zombies are a catch-all metaphor: they'll be whatever you want them to be. Rampant consumers, dead-eyed right-wing reactionaries, a mid-life crisis, the militarization of society... even a story about a love that won't die, can't die, will never die.

Personally, I'm still waiting for the Disney cartoon, the one where an anthropomorphised animal dies and comes back with an overwhelming hunger for brains; or the Pixar epic about a lonely wind-up toy looking for his key in a world that's been overrun by the living dead.

You laugh... but these films will appear, eventually. Mark my words, they will. Even if I have to write the fuckers myself.

Gary McMahon
March 2011

I will knock down the Gates of the Netherworld, I will smash the door posts, and leave the doors flat down, And will let the dead go up to eat the living! And the dead will outnumber the living!

-The Epic of Gilgamesh

PART ONE

The End Of It All

Truly, we are living in apocalyptic times.

Unnamed presidential advisor,
The Bush administration, 2008

CHAPTER ONE

RICK NUTMAN TRIED hard to breathe. It was something that should have been easy, a natural function of his body, yet he was currently unable to carry out the technique without feeling as if he were submerged in ten feet of dark water. The riot gear was heavy, constricting, and he was not used to being so trussed up.

Come on, he thought. *Get through this, get a grip. It's the real thing, not a training exercise, and if you don't act fast you might not see daylight. Or Sally... you might never see Sally again.*

The thought galvanised him and suddenly his lungs sucked in the cold air, filled up, and then pushed the whole lot out again. He saw pinpoint stars, but when he looked up into the sky, at the real stars suspended in the black night, his vision began to clear.

"You okay, mate?" Trevor Hutchinson, the man at his side, narrowed his blue eyes in concern. He cocked his head, adjusted the grip on his Glock 17, and smiled.

"Yeah," said Rick. "Just... had a moment – you know?"

Hutch nodded once and switched his gaze back to the stocky grey tower block they were supposed to be watching. Nothing moved in the darkness, but several lights were on inside the building, bleeding patches of sickly yellow onto the ruined lawn outside the main entrance. Rick thought they looked like pools of urine.

The air was charged with a strange combination of fear and excitement. Everyone was tense; they just wanted to get into it, to start the action. A lone aeroplane flew overhead, its wide contrail glowing white against the dark, star-flecked sky. Rick watched as it traced a line across the flat black heavens, wondering where it was headed. Then, abruptly, the plane began to descend. He knew there were no airports in the immediate area – Leeds/Bradford was a few miles away, and certainly too far for the plane to be dipping in so suddenly to land. Puzzled, he began to stand. Hutch placed a firm hand on his shoulder. His grip was like steel pincers.

Rick glanced at the other man. Hutch shook his head, eyes narrow slits in the dark smudge of his face. "Best sit tight. It's all going off very soon." He held Rick's gaze until Rick relaxed. They knew each other about as well as any two men could, had trained together, fought together and become disillusioned with army life together. It was Hutch who'd convinced him to try for the police after his medical discharge from the Parachute Regiment.

The plane's unusual descent forgotten, Rick stared at the building they were here to raid. It was a squat concrete structure; a block of forty-odd flats spread over three floors. Their targets were ensconced on the first floor – they knew that from intelligence reports gathered over the past few months – and the rest of the building was occupied by low-level drug dealers and long-term benefit claimants who did illegal black market work on the side. This was a rough area; no one who lived here was totally clean. That's what DI Harper always said: in places like this, even the innocent are guilty. It was a harsh doctrine, but one that had apparently saved the DI's skin on more than one occasion.

A radio belched static. Someone coughed softly. The sound of hardcore dance music drifted in from somewhere nearby. There must be a party going on somewhere in the neighbourhood.

Hutch's hand still clutched Rick's arm. His friend had forgotten to take it away. Rick felt comforted by the proximity. Tonight was not his first time in the thick of the action, but his first time out with the Armed Response Unit. In the army, he'd served in places like Afghanistan and Iraq, so knew a lot about the tension and pressure of warfare. But this was different: it was at home, in England, not some far-flung war zone where the enemy wore black turbans and spoke in another language. Home-grown enemies were much harder to identify.

Distant sirens wailed like neutered choirboys, emergency vehicles heading towards another fight in another part of Leeds. These were tough times: global economic slowdown, crime figures up through the roof, domestic violence on the increase, drugs and teen gangs ruling the streets. Rick was no mug; he knew what it was like out here, in the midst of it all, but to actually confront it was another matter entirely. He hoped he was up to the challenge.

He thought again of Sally, his wife of less than a year, and then pushed her pretty face as far as he could from his mind. She didn't belong here, with this shit. She represented what little good there was left in the world.

Someone whispered impatiently behind him, urging things to progress, and quickly. Rick knew how the man felt: the anticipation was almost unbearable. A woman's voice yelled through an open window, her words slurred and difficult to understand: something about spilling beer on the carpet. Someone sniggered. Hutch turned his head and glared at the offending officer.

They were crouched behind cars in the parking bays out front of the building. Another smaller team of men was hidden at the back of the block of flats. The plan was that their unit would storm the front of the building and enter through the main doors, then rush up to the second floor. The secondary unit would storm the rear and cordon off the ground floor, stopping anyone from exiting. It was a technique they'd carried out countless times in training, but only the superior officers had ever used it in the field. Both units were made up of a fair number of rookies, their first time out after months of training. Despite this being a suspected terrorist raid, intelligence led them to believe that there were only three suspects hiding out in the building.

In at the deep end, thought Rick, smiling despite the tension. It had been the same in the army. All the training in the world could not add up to the single thrilling-terrifying experience of a real-life operation. It set apart the men from the boys, the tough guys from the pretenders. Rick had proved himself several times in action, but he was still afraid. He'd learned to use that fear, to focus it and direct it inward, where it became a vital strength rather than a debilitating weakness.

"Just waiting for the order," muttered Hutch, almost to himself. He'd taken his hand away. Rick almost missed the human contact.

He took a deep breath, held it... held it... then finally let it out. Swallowing the fear felt good. His hands were no longer shaking. He was ready.

As he watched, a small, thin cat walked coolly across the grass verge a few yards in front of him. The cat paused, glanced over at the crouching men, and then moved away, unconcerned.

Off to Rick's left, he caught sight of movement. A lone constable ran, bent at the waist, from his hiding place to the corner of an adjacent building, where the command centre had been set up in an unmarked van. The van doors squealed open, the sound too loud in all that silence. Then, softer, they clunked shut.

Not long now. We're almost there.

A strange calmness descended upon him, coating him in a cool, dry layer. He was used to this from his time in the field. Once, during Operation Mountain Thrust, just before the convoy he was travelling in was bombed and came under fire from a small group of Afghan Taliban forces, he'd taken the weird sensation to be a warning, an indication that trouble was coming. The American forces leading them into the foothills to root out insurgents had sustained severe casualties, but because of Rick's sudden intuition his unit had come away relatively unscathed.

That moment of insight had saved his life. Now, in this grubby Yorkshire suburb, he took it to be a sense of calm before the storm.

When the order came he did not even hear it. Just a burst of rapid-fire static from his radio as everyone around him began to move in a rehearsed formation. Boots made little sound on the concrete footpath; voices were silent. Rick drew his Glock and remembered the choreography he'd been taught. He slipped into place alongside Hutch, who glanced at him and grinned.

The man at the head of the formation – Rick thought he might be called Tennant – ran silently towards at the unlocked double doors. He was a big bloke, and when he hit the glass barriers they flew open. Tennant was moving so fast that he almost fell, but managed to keep his footing. He ducked in under the stairs, pistol up, and scanned the perimeter. All clear. The men who'd followed him in fanned out from the doors and began to climb the stairs, moving from half landing to half landing and checking the area before overlapping each other in a quick ascent.

A door opened on the first floor. A black face peered out, eyes white as two dabs of flour, and then the door quickly closed. The sound of locks being shot echoed along the landing, louder than the silent assault. Pre-agreed hand signals were used to direct team members to their positions on the second floor. Rick, being the newest and least experienced member, hung back with Hutch at the head of the stairs. A door to his left opened and a small boy stood there in his pyjamas, clutching a grubby teddy bear by one ear. The boy's face was so dirty that Rick cold not even guess at his ethnicity. The interior of the flat behind him was dark. The hallway was clotted with what looked like building rubble – bricks and random lengths of timber.

Rick smiled.

The boy stared, his eyes wide but not afraid, barely even curious. He went to take a step forward but Rick shook his head and moved quickly towards the boy, pushing him back into the flat. The boy stuck out his tongue and slammed the door in Rick's face. Then, from the safety of the flat, he screamed a single word, louder than he looked able: "Pigs!" And he kept screaming it, over and over again.

That was the moment when everything began to go wrong.

Someone screamed "*Go-go-go!*" and a large man – not Tennant this time, but someone else, someone even bigger – ran at the door of number twenty-four with a battering ram. It took three hits close to the door handle for the door to buckle, and when it did the sound was like an explosive charge. The man stepped aside, allowing three officers armed with Heckler and Koch G3 machine guns to run into the flat past the flopping door, weapons held at chest height, faces white, mouths mere slits under the strengthened glass visors of their black riot helmets.

Suddenly, doors opened along the landing, and the space began to fill with smoke.

The other tenants, now aware of the police presence, were throwing burning rags and plastic bags soaked with petrol into the hallway in an attempt to confuse matters and allow their neighbours time to escape. Thick, acrid smoke rose, stole the oxygen and invaded the lungs. It was difficult to see. Shouting filled the air. The stench of burning petrol clogged Rick's throat. It was chaos, like a battlefield, and he felt his instincts kick in and take control. Keeping low, he moved along the landing, reaching up and dragging the doors shut to prevent any further missiles being thrown.

He was shocked to see that most of the perpetrators were kids, not much more than thirteen or fourteen years old. Behind one of them, standing in a darkened hallway, a fat woman with unruly hair laughed, holding her stomach and stamping her foot as if to the rhythm of madness.

The confined space of the landing was soon filled with the jagged, nerve-bashing sounds of coughing, slamming doors, running feet, and war-like screams. Rick's eyes were streaming. As he turned back to where Hutch was still waiting, he caught a stray kick to the head. Vision blurred, he reeled back onto his haunches; everything pushed in on him, pressing him down. He remembered the hot desert, a scouring diesel-tinged heat, the dull boom of explosions, and the cries of fallen comrades.

Then some damn fool started shooting.

CHAPTER TWO

DARYL WAS FASCINATED by the changes in Mother. In the space of three short months she'd gone from a spritely, if domineering, woman in her early sixties to a wasted, bed-ridden monster. Her body was rail-thin, the flesh hanging like wrapping paper from the gifts of her bones. Her small, nimble hands had lengthened into spiny claws. Her ribs protruded like the bars of a cage beneath the flattened expanse of her chest.

Mother's (never Mum or Mam or Mummy: such casual abuses of her title were simply not allowed) body was usually covered by sweaty sheets, so Daryl was spared the horror of looking at it every day, but her face remained above the covers, peeking out at him like a monstrous, wide-eyed baby.

Apart from these more apparent ravages, there had also been other, more subtle alterations to her physiognomy: the way her eyes looked glassy, like those of a doll; the waxen feel of her skin; the yellowish pallor of her sunken cheeks. Daryl stood over her now, staring into those black doll's eyes, wondering if she could still see him, or if she just sensed that he was there, as always, at her side.

"Mother."

The head stirred, twitching. The eyes widened impossibly – yellow gunk hung in strings from the thin lashes.

"I hate you, Mother." He smiled, rolling the words around on his tongue. Before her illness, Daryl would never have dared say such things. But now everything was different. Now, for once, he was in charge.

Mother let out a gurgling-rasping sound, as if she were trying to speak. She was in her last days now, which was why she'd been allowed home from hospital to die in her own home. Daryl had fought long and hard with the doctors to send her home, stating mock-sincere arguments for human rights, dignity; the fact that she should be given the choice where she would end her days. In reality, he just wanted her back so that he could torture her, just as she'd done to him his entire life.

Daryl knew that he was a pathetic specimen, a sad excuse for a man – Mother had told him this enough times that it had sunk in deep. But who was the more pathetic, the son or the mother who needed him?

"Sleep tight, Mother," he whispered, before turning away and leaving her alone, in the dark. She had always hated the dark, and insisted upon sleeping her entire life with a lamp by the bed. Upon her return from the cancer ward, Daryl had carefully, and in plain sight, removed the light bulbs from every light-fitting in her room. She winced as he smashed them on the floor, fearing both his wanton act of destruction and the darkness it promised. He had replaced the bulbs later, of course, but the act had been wonderfully symbolic.

He crossed the landing and entered his own room, glancing up at the print of one of John Wayne Gacy's prison paintings that hung on the wall by the door. He'd paid a small fortune for the framed print on eBay; it was one of his prized possessions.

His bookshelves bent under the weight of books on serial killers. The walls were plastered with newspaper cuttings, snips and snaps of unsolved murder cases and abductions. He was surrounded by his heroes, and each night before bed he would slowly leaf through the pages of one of his many scrapbooks, touching the glued-in faces of men like Ted Bundy, Fred West, Dennis Neilson and Albert Fish.

Daryl was intelligent and self-educated enough to realise that a lot of serial killers were mother-fixated and possessed limited social skills. He knew that most of them started when they were very young, torturing small animals. What he could not understand was the secret element these killers seemed to have, the factor that made them step forward and live out the fantasy. Although he had been planning his first murder for several years now, Daryl was yet to take that step, to thrust his head above the parapet of normality and seize the moment.

He ran a hand across the spines of his books, closing his eyes and sensing the company of murderers. He longed to join their ranks, to accept membership into an elite band of men (they were always men, at least the ones he admired) who had actually taken a human life – more than one; scores of victims. It was his dearest dream to be like them, his heroes, his fathers. His first experience was so close that he could almost feel it brushing against his skin. Someday soon he would act, and the line would finally be crossed.

His attention was drawn by a sound from Mother's room. He stood and listened, waiting for it to come again. A slow, lazy thumping, like someone banging on a distant door. He knew that she was trying to move, shifting her wireframe body in an attempt to sit up in bed. Maybe she was thirsty, or simply craving his company.

Daryl left his room and went downstairs, ignoring her feeble movements. Let the bitch suffer, just as he had suffered for so many years, unable to cut the leash and get a girlfriend, not allowed beyond the doors of the big old house he'd been born in.

His heroes had all tasted the fruits that he desired – sex, death, adventure. Daryl was yet to glimpse such fascinations: his scope was limited, the level of his life experience pitiful.

In the living room he turned on the television. A news broadcast flashed onto the screen, something about a series of unprovoked attacks in Leeds city centre. The newsreader was pretty, blonde, and aching to be slashed. He imagined cutting her, peeling off her insincere skin to reveal the truth of the musculature beneath.

"...police are advising Leeds residents to stay indoors and lock themselves in. Episodes of civil unrest are increasing throughout the night, and an official spokesman has said that these events seem entirely random and unorganised. When asked about the possibility of terrorist activity, he stated again that the events are not linked. In other news..."

Daryl muted the set and went to the stereo, glancing out of the window as he did so. The curtains were open; he could see the stretched sheet of the sky, a shooting star crossing it like an animated image. *Wow*, he thought, *that's the first time I've ever seen a comet.*

He watched the fiery nova until it flared briefly and then faded, feeling an obscure sense of loneliness deep within his core. Was this an echo of what everyone else experienced when they fell in love, had babies, made a home together? Had he just been offered a glimpse into the world they inhabited, like a shooting star himself, coming close enough to see but not quite touch?

He forced his attention back to the stereo, disturbed by such maudlin thoughts.

Mother hated any music other than old time jazz, the kind played by big bands with busty female singers, and her beloved hymns. Daryl had smashed all her jazz records in front of her the day after she'd come home from hospital, and urinated on the remains. They were collectors items, most of them, and it had felt good to rob the world of their worth.

Selecting a Madonna CD from the stack, he slid it into the player and cranked the volume up way beyond what Mother thought of as acceptable.

Madonna: there was another slut who wanted killing. He failed to understand why no one had ever tried.

Daryl danced around the large room, his movements almost comically uncoordinated. He would never dance in public; the shame would be too heavy to bear. Anyway, Mother had not once agreed to him going anywhere that he *could* dance, even at the age when all his schoolyard acquaintances (never friends; Daryl had no idea how to form and maintain conventional relationships) had gone to the pubs and clubs in town. But here, alone, he was happy to kick off his shoes and boogie on down to the murder bop.

He knew this was no way for a twenty-three year-old man to act, but he was celebrating his newfound sense of freedom. Before Mother had fallen ill, when she had ruled over his world with a sharp tongue and a hard fist, he would never have dreamed of doing anything to upset her. Now that she was unable to fight back, he was prepared to do whatever the hell he wanted. No: whatever the *fuck* he wanted.

Yes, that felt good. Profanity, even in the privacy of his mind, was forbidden. He never understood exactly how Mother knew when he was thinking bad words, but she always picked up on it.

"Fuck you, Mother." He giggled and spun, spun and giggled. Madonna sang about a holiday, and Daryl realised with no little irony that he was currently embarking on a permanent vacation from all that had gone before. A further irony was that he didn't even like Madonna's music.

When the song ended he sat down on the couch, sweating and panting for breath. He picked up the remote control and flicked off the stereo, preferring silence for a little while. Too much freedom was making him giddy. He needed to regain some composure.

He reached under the floral print cushion and brought out a small, worn hardback book, a volume of poetry he'd never read. Mother had given it to him as a gift when he was a boy, expecting him to respond to culture. Unfortunately, his idea of culture was something that grew in a Petri dish, and would ooze foul-smelling liquor if you stabbed it with the nib of a pen.

He opened the book to the middle pages and took out the single photograph which lay inside. He handled it carefully, like a religious artefact, touching it only with the tips of his fingers. He would never forgive himself if he smudged the image, defaced the immaculate face in the photograph.

There she was. His proposed first victim. The woman he'd been thinking about killing for six months. He'd first seen her at a petrol station forecourt on Kirkstall Road, filling up the tank of her green Mini Cooper. Something about her had attracted him, but not in a sexual way. Like most of the men he sought to emulate, Daryl did not have a conventional sexual drive. His needs were much more esoteric than those of the average citizen.

He remembered following her home that first day, trailing her to the nice city centre flat where she lived with her husband. They had not been married long, and still seemed flushed by the excitement of simply being together. Daryl could not understand such things. Emotions like love and compassion were off his radar.

He'd kept a close eye on her after that; then, coming to a decision, he'd upped the surveillance and begun to stalk her. For the past three months he had charted her every move, keeping a dossier on her. He knew her husband's shifts, her routines, her patterns. Monday, Tuesday and Friday mornings she went to the gym. Every week-day afternoon she worked part-time at an Accountants office, walking the short distance from the flat. Weekends were changeable, but still followed a basic routine: a brisk morning walk down by the canal, breakfast muffins bought at the Greggs bakery, then back to bed for a mid-morning nap – or, if her husband was not at work, a long work-out session between the sheets. Such creatures of habit, these people; they were so much more like him than they might like to think.

He'd taken the photograph early one morning when she was heading off for her usual visit to the gym. It was a full body shot, catching her just as she stepped out of the door, turning on her heel to close it behind her. Her almost shoulder-length blonde hair caught gems from the morning sun and her face glowed with what he could only describe as a supernatural radiance. There was magic in the picture. The sort of commonplace mysticism other people – normal people – might notice at sunset, or perhaps as twilight fell upon the land like a fine mist. Daryl loved the photo, and he loved the image it contained. As far as he was concerned, that also meant he loved the woman it represented. But it was not a natural kind of affection; no, it was something only he could understand, and to speak it out loud would end only in disaster.

Love, for Daryl, was a twisted thing, a malicious shadow tugging at his heels. Not for him the hearts and flowers of the rest of the world. He preferred knives and spleens, or skulls and hammers. Smiling, he brought the photograph up to his lips, kissed the air in front of it, and felt what passed for emotion in his dark world flood his senses like a short burst of bitter juice.

Daryl wanted to kill this woman so much it was an ache inside his gut, a low pulse that he could not deny. Lately the pulse had grown stronger, more difficult to ignore. The time was rapidly approaching

when he must either shit or get off the pot. It was a crude metaphor –
one he'd heard in a film – but a very apt one.

It was getting late. He knew he should be thinking about sleep, but
these days he felt energised at night, as if he drew inspiration from the
darkness. He thought he might torture Mother for a while before retiring
to bed. Perhaps the flame of a lit match applied to the soles of her feet,
or small slices from a razor blade directly under her armpits. There were
so many methods to cause another human being pain. He'd researched
them all, in books and on the Internet. The information was out there,
in a variety of forms, if you looked hard enough, and wanted to find it
badly enough.

He climbed the stairs and went to the bathroom, where he brushed
his teeth and washed his face in the sink. The bowl of the sink was
greasy with dirt; since Mother's illness took hold, he'd not bothered
to clean the house. He considered using the toilet, but did not need to.
He stared at his face in the mirror, reaching back behind him and to
the left to turn out the light. His round, bespectacled face darkened,
becoming something more sinister: a mask, with blackness peering out
from the eye, nose and mouth holes. It was a wonderful illusion, and
he marvelled at the fact that such hard truths nearly always presented
themselves when one was least expecting them.

The truth, Daryl knew, rarely ventured out of its hiding place. But
when it did... oh, when it did, huge changes were bound to follow.

CHAPTER THREE

RICK WAS SHOCKED into immobility for a half a second – certainly no more than that, but possibly even less – before his training kicked in. Hitting the floor, he rolled smoothly across the landing and kept close to the wall. If you stayed low you made a more difficult target, and moving in a straight line was out of the question. Confuse the enemy: do what is least expected.

Screaming and gunshots tore the air. Bodies tumbled by him, guns swinging up into active positions. Rick made his way back to the stairs, where Hutch was trying to aim at something through the dissipating smoke. "Good job," he yelled, his pistol twitching, shifting, eyes scanning the area for someone or something to target. He took off his helmet to scratch his head, sweat glistening in his hair and on his forehead.

Rick tucked himself in behind the thick concrete newel post, ensuring that he created as small a target as possible. He reached out to grab Hutch's arm, to tell his friend what he'd seen – the kids throwing smoking missiles, the laughing mad woman urging them on – but Hutch pulled sharply away, his movement violent and final. Rick felt a warm, moist sensation against the side of his face. His lips were pasted with hot fluid.

Hutch's body sagged. His gun fell to the floor; he began to inch backwards, down the stairs, his empty hands grasping at the air. When what remained of his face swung lazily into view, Rick saw that half the man's head had been obliterated. Bone was caught in a frozen spray; blood still spurted like strawberry syrup pumped through an air hose. Hutch's mouth was agape, but there wasn't enough of it left to describe a silent scream... his remaining eye had already rolled back into his shattered skull, and the other socket was filled with red.

Rick watched his friend fall, not even attempting to catch him. Hutch's slack body tumbled down the short flight, slamming into the wall on the half landing below, leaving bloody smears on the whitewashed plaster. Rick closed his eyes, pictured the scene, and started planning his next move.

Somehow finding a point of calm in the chaos around him, Rick rose and edged towards the mass of bodies around the door of the flat they were raiding – number twenty-four. Several police officers of various ranks formed a semi circle around the shattered entryway, most of them coughing; others ran along the landing, grabbing bystanders and pushing them back into their flats. Rick's emergency measures had not lasted: the doors inside certain buildings never remained closed for long.

"– fuck off me!" screamed a man who was backing out of number twenty-four. It was Tennant, the big man who'd been first inside the block. A woman hung from his chest by her hands; her feet dragged along behind her. She was spitting and snarling like a wild dog.

"Careful! HIV risk!" Rick did not recognise this second voice, but everyone seemed to take an unconscious step backwards, away from the woman who was trying her best to attack Tennant.

"Bitch!" said Tennant, swatting her away as if she were a small animal nagging him for food. The woman shot sideways, her head making contact with the door frame. Her eyes rolled back into her head and her tongue pushed between her swollen lips. She was tiny – almost a midget. Her hair was large and bushy, either completely unkempt or teased into some fashionable retro style.

Another officer emerged from the flat, his eyes streaming. Vomit speckled his lips and chin. "Oh, God," he said. "Oh, Jesus. Don't go in there."

The shooting had stopped. The hot stench of battle stung Rick's nostrils, but it was a smell he was used to, and even enjoyed in a twisted way. "What is it?" he said, stepping forward, taking the initiative.

The newcomer stared at him. His face was pale, bloodless, and his expression was one of utter despair. "I can't even tell you... it's a mess in there. A real fucking mess." The man stumbled off, heading for the stairs. Rick wondered if he'd puke again when he saw Hutch's body.

Hutch. The last of the guys he'd met all those years ago in basic training. They'd served their first tour of Iraq together, helping each other through, and left the forces at roughly the same time, if for different reasons.

How the hell was he going to break it to Hutch's wife, Jenny? It would have to be him; he'd known the woman for years, and liked her a lot. The baby was due in a month. The baby Hutch had left the army to be near.

Tensing his jaw, Rick moved into the doorway. No one else seemed willing to enter, and the superior officers were already inside. Without receiving further orders, Rick guessed that he was on his own. Maybe this was his chance to shine.

Someone pushed him forward, eager for another rookie to be thrust into the mix. Rick allowed his forward momentum to carry him across the threshold, and was immediately struck by the bloodstains on the floor and walls. So much blood. As if the short entrance hallway had been decorated with it. Smears and stripes and spatters – a Jackson Pollack configuration leading right up the wall to the tobacco-yellowed Artex ceiling.

The body of a man lay half in and half out of what he supposed must be the living room. He could only see the legs and buttocks. The upper half was inside the other room. The white slacks on the skinny legs were covered with blood. One shoe and its corresponding sock were missing (blown off in the fire-fight, or not put on in the first place?) The left buttock was a mess of raw meat where he'd taken a hit in the arse.

Glancing across the felled victim, Rick saw that the television was playing in the darkened room. It was tuned to a news station, and a series of images showing mobs attacking police vehicles filled the screen. Words scrolled beneath the footage: Live from Millennium Square, Leeds.

The volume was turned down low and some sort of dance music was playing on a sound system he could not locate. He resisted the urge to step over the corpse to closer investigate the news report.

Rick eased around the lower extremities of the corpse. He tried hard not to look, but when he drew level he was unable to keep his eyes from straying back into the room. Cheap wallpaper. Thrift shop furniture. Clothing scattered on the filthy wooden floor. The top half of the body had been almost severed at the hip. The man had taken several rounds before going down. A tiny bleb of creased intestine poked out from his side, just above the beltline. His dark shaven head was turned to one side, the cheek squashed against the laminated floor and one eye frozen open to stare into infinity.

Keep going. Let it all wash over you like a river over pebbles.

It was a mantra he'd heard during his final tour of Afghanistan, from a mate who'd been heavily into martial arts. The mate was dead now, like the rest of them, but his voice hung around like so many others inside Rick's head. Sometimes he thought those voices might never shut up; only fade into the background, a constant choral hum.

The voices of the dead; the voices of the dead men he had called friends; the voices of the dead friends whose lives had been wasted while his had been saved.

An open bedroom door further along and to the left offered him another glimpse of horror. Two members of his unit were kneeling beside the corpse of a young Asian man, this one with designer tram lines shaved into his close-cropped hair. Their victim was still twitching, gasping out his last breaths. The officers were silent, almost respectful, as they watched the man die. Blood on the floor; gasps in the air.

Moving on, he approached the kitchen. That was when things got bad.

"Nutman... that you, Nutman?"

"Yes, sir. It's Nutman, sir." Rick stopped outside the room, the familiar aroma of recent death in his nostrils. He removed his helmet and placed it on a shelf by the door, next to a long-dead prayer plant in a grubby plastic pot.

"Get in here, Nutman. You're not going to believe this, but try to keep your dinner down, yeah?" A large bulky frame hovered in the doorway. Behind him, a light began to flicker.

"Shit," said another voice. "All we need."

Rick stepped forward, his hands clenching into fists. His stomach was calm but his heart was beating double-time. He was sweating under the heavy riot gear; the stab vest stuck to his T-shirt; the T-shirt to his chest.

The first thing Rick saw was D.I. Harper's ashen face. The huge man was leaning against a kitchen work bench, his head down but turned towards Rick. His eyes were hollow, lifeless, and his mouth was a grim slit. "Fuckin' animals," he muttered, shaking his large head in disbelief.

There was a severed head in the stainless steel kitchen sink. What looked like viscera sat in a lumpy mess on the draining board – looking closely, Rick thought he could make out a lung, a heart, lengths of looped intestine. He tried to look away but was unable to unlock his gaze from the nightmare. He stared at the head. Its eyes were gone, the sockets smooth and empty. There were teeth marks in one cheek – they couldn't be anything else – and the nose was gone.

"Cannibals," said D.I. Harper, his voice thin and reedy. "*Cannibals.*" He began to repeat the word, not even aware that he was doing so. Two other officers stood against the wall. One of them was covering his mouth with his hand and staring down at his feet. His shoes were covered in vomit.

The fridge door hung open, its hinges broken. The shelves were sparsely stocked: a few pieces of cling-filmed meat, half a pineapple, an opened can of baked beans. At the bottom, where the salad shelves should be, there was an open space occupied by several human hands.

"Sir... this isn't terrorism. What's going on?" Rick felt like the floor was rushing up to meet him, but he composed himself by thinking of Hutch, of his wife, of their unborn baby. "What is this?"

D.I. Harper straightened, his head almost touching the low ceiling. The dim light flickered again, lending his features an unearthly tint. "I don't know, son. I really don't know. We have four suspects dead inside this place, and every room contains what seem to be partially consumed human remains. We've either stumbled on a gang of serial killers here, or some sort of weird cult. I've never seen anything like it..." he finished lamely, shaking his head and rubbing his neck with a big square hand.

Time stood still for Rick. He was trapped in someone else's nightmare. The blood hardly bothered him now; there was so much of it that he stopped noticing it. What hit him hardest was not the wet pile of guts on the draining board, nor was it the head in the sink that almost broke him... no, it was those hands. Clean, dainty human hands. Six of them: three pairs all lined up like crab claws in a neat row along the bottom of the fridge. What kind of insanity did it take to cut off those hands and then store them for later?

What stopped him vomiting was the piercing sound of screams erupting suddenly from the other room. At first he thought it was a woman, but then remembered that their unit was famously made up of all male officers. The only woman in the vicinity was the fuzzy-haired maniac he'd seen earlier, but Tennant had silenced her.

"What now?" D.I. Harper looked wasted, as if he could face no more of this night. The other two officers glanced at each other, then at Rick.

"I'll go," he said, turning away and walking back along the hallway. After three or four steps he saw where the screaming was coming from. Another rookie – someone whose name he had not been told – was shuffling backwards towards him, his backside scraping the floor and his hands clutching at the skirting boards. He was moving fast for a man on his arse, mainly due to what was pursuing him.

The designer-skinhead gunshot victim who'd been dying only moments earlier – the young man almost surely slain during the initial shoot-out – was slowly making his way along the hallway, lying on his belly and dragging himself forward with bloody hands, the bullet-addled lower half of his body spilling intestines onto the scuffed floor boards.

There was no way on earth the man could be doing this. He was dead, gunned down. But here he was, moving clumsily, inch by inch, and gaining ground on the screaming rookie.

"Shut up," said Rick, reaching down to grab the guy's shoulder. The rookie twitched, then managed to climb to his feet, using Rick's legs and torso as leverage.

The man – the dead man – moved relentlessly forward. His eyes were flat, dull, like old pennies, and his upturned face hung loose on his skull. He was grinding his teeth, just like Sally used to whenever she was nervous, before the dentist had fitted her with a gum shield to help her kick the habit.

But the dead man had no gum shield – he barely had any teeth. Those remaining in his head were shattered and projected from his lips like snapped pieces of wood.

"Shoot it!" Yelled the rookie. "For God's sake, just shoot it!"

Rick raised his pistol, aimed carefully, and put a shot in the dead man's shoulder. The dead man jerked like he was pulled by strings, but kept on coming. Rick put another round in his opposite shoulder. That didn't stop him either.

"*Oh-my-God-oh-my-God-oh-my-God-oh-my-God...*" The man at his side chanted like a Buddhist monk, fading from the scene, turning in on himself.

Rick aimed again, this time at the dead man's back, right above the heart. He pulled the trigger, feeling the gun buck in his hands. A chunk of flesh flew out of the dead man, blood tracing an arc in the air. He did not stop. His hands reached out; they were inches from Rick's boots. He shuffled backward, shoving the rookie out of the way. Then he aimed his Glock at the top of dead man's carefully crafted haircut, right between two of his carefully shaved tramlines.

Why doesn't he die? Rick thought, his mind focused, nerves strung as tightly as guitar strings.

The dead man looked up at him, nothing in his gaze.

This time, when Rick squeezed the trigger, blood and thick clotted matter sprayed in an elegant parabola, turning the wall and floor behind the dead man dark red. The dead man raised his eyes, and then lifted himself almost to his feet before toppling forward onto his face. The top of his skull was level with Rick's feet. He stared at the wound, at the grey-purple brains bulging out of the hole. They looked like those disgusting meat things Sally's granny used to eat – what where they called, faggots? Yeah, that was it: braised faggots.

The rookie started to cry. Rick turned just in time to see a dead woman emerge from the bedroom and grab the rookie's arm. She was Afro-Caribbean, with big eyes and thick lips, but her skin was curiously pale. Her teeth were shockingly white when she opened her mouth and bit down on the rookie's neck, scraping easily through the flesh to puncture his carotid artery. The spray of blood was majestic: a bright geyser. The rookie tried to slap her away but already his strength was failing; his arms flapped uselessly, his hands sliding off the dead woman's face.

Always a fast learner, Rick shot her through the right eye. This time the blood misted, forming an ethereal pattern in the musty air – crimson dust motes caught in the meagre illumination. Rick watched it, enraptured by its slow-moving dance, the way the flickering kitchen light caught like rubies in its diaphanous mass.

He stared at the Glock, hypnotised by the sluggish movement of smoke as it poured from the muzzle and traced a grey puzzle in the air directly ahead of him. Then he looked back at the woman, tilting his head to one side in an odd unconscious mannerism that, unbeknownst to him, he'd last done as an inquisitive child of seven. She was laying face-up on the ground, her eye socket enlarged and red matter hanging in strings from the damaged orbit. Blood pooled around her pasty features even as he watched, shining dully on the floor.

He shot her again, just to make sure she stayed down, and the top of her head was vaporised in a bright shock of blood, brain and bone. Rick felt something in his head click, as if a switch had been thrown – he was not sure what it was, but it felt like some old, long-neglected mechanism was once more becoming operational.

He thought of the desert. The screams. The friends he had lost. Somehow, the memories did not hurt half as much as they had even fifteen minutes before.

CHAPTER FOUR

SALLY HAD THE feeling that something was terribly wrong.

It wasn't the sirens, or the fact that the electricity kept threatening to cut out for minutes at a time, or even the intermittent shouting she kept hearing somewhere out in the city streets as the lights inside flickered nervously. No, some internal barometer was telling her that Rick was in some kind of trouble. Ever since they'd first met, Sally had felt some inner *tugging* whenever he was in jeopardy. During Rick's army days, she'd known about it when things got tough; when he was seriously injured during a Taliban attack in Afghanistan, she'd felt a terrible pain in her guts.

The television was on, but Sally was barely watching it. The show was sub prime-time filler: some kind of imported American talent contest between people whose only proximity to talent was by watching other performers on better TV shows. Sally wished that they'd all just demonstrate the good taste to take a running jump through the fuck-off door, but sadly that didn't seem like it would happen any time soon.

She grabbed the remote control and switched channels to an old film. Robert Mitchum. Gregory Peck. Good stuff, but she wasn't quite in the mood for film noir. Sighing, she took a sip of wine, closing her eyes as the wonderfully cool liquid traced a pathway down her throat.

She glanced around the small seventh floor flat, her gaze restless, moving from object to object like a butterfly in a garden. Despite all the familiar things around her, this place had never quite felt like home. A photograph on the mantle, showing Rick and several buddies just before the attack in Helmand Province. The heart-shaped stone he'd brought her back from the desert. The framed pictures hanging on the walls. The books and ornaments on the shelves. None of this stuff actually meant anything if Rick wasn't here with her, close enough to touch, to hold, to kiss...

The wine was making her maudlin, and the noise coming from outside was putting her on edge. She drained the glass but did not refill it.

When the telephone rang at first she thought it might be Rick, or worse still, someone calling on Rick's behalf to tell her that he'd been hurt, perhaps shot during whatever operation he was involved in. She rushed to the table by the door and picked up the receiver. "Hello."

"Oh, thank God. I've been trying to get you for ages. The lines have been busy."

"Mum? What's wrong, Mum?" Sally felt the tone of her own voice rise to match her mother's.

"Don't worry, I'm fine. Just a bit... well, to be honest I'm a bit unnerved." Her mother's voice sounded strange, strained.

"Tell me, Mum. What's up?" Sally's hand gripped the receiver, making her fingers ache.

"There's something going on. The lights keep flickering and going out; the TV won't come back on. The radio is reporting riots in London and Luton." Her mother was close to tears. Since Dad died, she'd been on her own and it didn't suit her.

"Calm down, Mum. I'm sure it's okay."

"I know, I'm probably being silly. But I'm sure someone was outside earlier, creeping around in the back garden."

Sally suddenly pictured her mother's house, located back from the road in a very quiet area just outside Bedford. The nearest main road was miles away; the surrounding countryside was beautiful during the day but at night could hide a hundred assailants. "Listen, Mum, please call the police and lock the doors and windows."

"I did all that ages ago. The police said they'd get here as soon as they could, but they're busy on other calls."

Sally held her breath, suddenly afraid. "Call Derek, then. Right now. He'll drive out to get you." Derek was the nearest neighbour, a widower who had a soft spot for Sally's mother that everyone but her could see.

"You know I don't like to be a bother... it's late; he's probably in bed."

"Call him, Mum. Promise me you will. You know he'll be happy to drop by and sit with you until the police arrive. I'll feel better if he does, too."

There was a silence, and then her mother reached a decision. "You're right, darling. I *will* call Derek. He'll know what to do. He always does."

Calmer now, Sally made her mother promise again that she would call her suitor, and then she reluctantly hung up. It was horrible being miles away from her family at times like these. On the rare occasions that her mother needed her, Sally was never close enough to do much about it. The best she could offer was a promise to visit the following weekend.

During the phone call the TV had gone off. The lights began to flicker again, but more slowly, dipping the room into darkness for brief periods that seemed longer each time it happened. Sally felt her chest tighten. She knew, just knew, that one of these times the lights would go out for good. She picked up the phone again and called Rick's mobile. As expected, a recorded voice told her that it was switched off.

"It's me. I'm scared. Mum just rang, and there's something going on outside. Come home soon?" She pressed the button to end her message, then returned to her chair.

Sally was used to fear. It was almost an old friend. When she had been younger, her life had been made a misery by local bullies – her weight and her unusual looks had led to her being called names like 'Fat Cat' and 'Slit-eyed Slut.' The name-calling had progressed to physical abuse, and she'd sported scrapes and bruises for most of her school years. As an adult, once she'd grown into her looks, things had changed and she became popular with the opposite sex. Those early days, however, left deep scars, and she found it difficult to form relationships, hard to trust anyone.

Rick had been different. They'd clicked immediately. But he had come with his own fears, and his tours of duty with the army had brought terrors like none she'd ever experienced.

She recalled vividly the call from a corporal to inform her that Rick had been shot in Helmand Province, in a region whose name she could not even pronounce. *He's alive*, they'd told her, *but more than that we cannot say*. It was a week before she knew for certain that he would survive, and by then she'd been allowed to visit him in the military hospital.

It all made her childhood fears seem so trite, so pathetic, but when she saw him lying in that hospital bed, his body thin and bandaged, it opened the old scars and made them into fresh wounds.

Rick's body had healed but his mind remained damaged, a flawed tool of his trade. There was the depression, of course – the constant night terrors and the way his eyes narrowed at the slightest sound outside – but worse than that, he could never settle. That was why he joined the police force – to focus all the nervous energy he gave off like a damaged battery. She also suspected that he missed the action.

Headlights splashed the walls, turning the net curtains white. She glanced over, caught off guard, and listened intently to the sound of squealing breaks. Whatever the vehicle was, its driver had lost control.

The brakes continued to scream and the sound was followed by a huge, rending crash of metal and a low, hollow explosion.

Sally ran to the window and peered through the partially opened blinds. Two hundred yards along the street, by the glow of firelight, she saw that a car had crashed into the concrete bollards along the side of the canal. Black water flared with reflected fire; yellow flames clawed at the dark sky. Someone was crawling from the wreckage. It was a woman, and she was moving slowly, clumsily, as she dragged herself through the shattered rear window. Another figure was slumped behind the wheel, but it was too obscured by smoke for Sally to make out if it was male or female.

The passenger squeezed out of the car and slumped heavily to the ground. She raised her head, staring at the night sky, and clutched at her cheeks, scraping them with her nails.

Sally stepped back, just half a step, and shot a glance at the phone. She knew that she ought to ring the police, an ambulance, but something about this scene struck her as all wrong. She looked back at the woman, and then it registered. Instead of screaming in pain, the woman was simply sitting there, on the ground by the canal, tearing at her own face. It was a weirdly compelling sight, and one that was unnatural in so many ways. After such an accident, the woman should surely be as dead as her driver – but there she was, out of the car and mutilating herself.

Sally held her breath, barely even realising that she was doing so.

The woman, as if sensing Sally's scrutiny, looked up and stared along the length of the canal, directly into the flat. Glimmers of firelight brightened her narrow face, and Sally could clearly see that the woman was smiling. But it was not a smile that held any trace of humour; it was the slack-jawed idiot grin of someone whose mind was simply no longer operating as it should. An alien smile: a smile that should never be seen by human eyes.

The woman then began to drag herself back towards the car. The flames were dying, burning themselves out. No fuel had ignited, just the paint on the bodywork. Small bright tongues licked at the smoke-blackened wings and wheel rims, the tyres were thick molten rubber bands. The woman slumped round to the driver's side, pulling her weight up by the door handle. Then, settling against the door, she reached in and pulled a fist-sized chunk of still smoking flesh from the side of the driver's neck. Her hand went to her mouth; the cooked meat slipped between her lips, her reddened teeth. The woman began to chew slowly, as if she were merely sampling a handful of *foie gras*.

Sally wished that she could look away, but her eyes were glued to the scene. There was still enough of the guttering fire left alive to allow her to witness exactly what was going on, but she could barely believe it.

"Oh, my God," she said, shocking herself by speaking out loud. "What the hell...?" She walked quickly to the phone, remembering Rick's oft repeated advice about keeping your head in a crisis. When she picked up the receiver, the line was dead. Not even the dull hiss of white noise on the line.

She fished her mobile out of her jeans pocket and pressed the button to, once again, call Rick – she had him on speed dial, in case of an emergency. If this wasn't an emergency, then she didn't know what possible situation might qualify for the title.

Now she did hear white noise, followed by a series of clicks and fractured bleeping sounds. Then a recorded message told her in a smooth female voice that the number was unavailable. Either Rick's mobile was still switched off or the networks were all busy.

"Shit. Shit." She crossed again to the window. The car was no longer alight; it was now a smoking shell. The body behind the wheel looked misshapen and... well, *incomplete*. Sally peered along the canal in both directions, trying to catch sight of the woman, but could see no one lurking in the vicinity. That was unusual in itself, as the canal at night was usually a regular hangout for drug dealers and homosexual pick-ups. She and Rick often stood at the window to watch the show, using it as a substitute for bad TV. Like most big cities, Leeds was packed with what Rick for some reason always called the 'Scum of the Hearth.' He always found that funny, but Sally had never really understood what it meant. Nor had she ever felt like asking. Sometimes Rick could be almost wilfully obscure and in a way that scared her, and she preferred to ignore those occasional glimpses of a somehow complex darkness making itself known to her.

Sirens wailed far off in the night, either approaching or moving away at speed – it was impossible to tell. As she watched, a fire started in the east of the city, its wan glow reflected in the cloudless sky, shimmering against the heavens like a misdirected spotlight. Shouts and blunt screams were carried to her on the light breeze, as if they'd been waiting for her to act as an audience to their grim proclamations.

Sally checked the window and shut the curtains. Then she went around the entire flat, ensuring that all the door and window locks were secure, wishing that there were sturdy shutters instead of thin curtains across the window glass.

When she was finished she sat on the floor in the middle of the living room. The TV was showing a pre-recorded interview with some MP she'd never heard of, and he was talking about riots across the city, lootings, rapes and murders. Sally had the telephone clasped between her knees. Intermittently, she checked it for a signal, but all she got was a dead line. She tried to ignore the sounds coming from outside, knowing that on the seventh floor she was too far up for any passing psycho to bother with, and the main doors to the apartment block were time-locked anyway.

The night stretched ahead of her, unfurling like a ribbon quilted with myriad atrocities. She wished that Rick was here, at her side, and wept because she could not reach out to him for comfort. Her old fears returned, mutated into something much worse: demons that leered from the corners of the room. She wondered, briefly, if she would ever see her husband again, and then hated herself for such a display of weakness. Rick would expect her to be strong, to hold things together until he got back.

And he *would* get back to her – of this single fact she was absolutely certain.

That was the last thought she had before the lights in the flat flickered a final time and then went out for good.

CHAPTER FIVE

RICK STOOD IN silence and surveyed the damage. There were bodies everywhere – the gunned-down remains of the people who'd been in the Dead Rooms (that was what everyone was now calling this place) and several of his fellow officers. It wasn't good. In fact, it was appalling. A deep, heavy silence had drifted in to replace the chaos of screams and gunshots; that silence was all wrong, as if he'd gone deaf after being caught in a bomb blast. Then, bit by bit, it was punctuated by the occasional stifled sob.

A grown man was crying. More than one, actually, but he couldn't see who or how many. Smoke hung in small drifting clouds, dissipating gradually. Voices became clearer; other tenants were being herded either back into their own domiciles or down the stairs into the parking area outside the block. Rick was clutching his gun so tightly that his fingers had begun to ache. It felt like he might be unable to break the grip when the time came to put the weapon down.

"Sally," he whispered, unsure why. Her name held an almost mythical resonance, a calming influence. He said it again: "Sally."

"You men," said D.I. Harper, his eyes still glazed, his face too pale beneath the dark riot helmet. He'd unbuttoned his stab vest, probably to help him breathe, to allow him to fill his lungs with the putrid air. "Start getting this place cleared up."

The remaining on-site Constables moved efficiently, considering the circumstances, checking bodies, searching the Dead Rooms, pulling plastic bags filled with drugs, body parts and all kinds of street weapons from various drawers and cupboards. Rick watched a young, fresh-faced lad heft a bread bag containing at least a hundred grams of cocaine from under the living room sofa. The body Rick had seen earlier – the first one he'd encountered, not the somehow reanimated madman – was still wedged in the doorway, its ruined buttocks standing proud.

Rick looked away. Blinked. The dead woman in the hallway – the one he'd shot through the eye – was being moved by two other officers who'd come in from outside. Their faces were grim; they worked in silence. Taking a leg each, they hauled her out through the front door and then disappeared into the smoke haze.

It was such a mess, the whole damn situation. Even D.I. Harper, a seasoned veteran of countless operations, looked haggard and ineffectual. All they could do was mop up the mess. The inquest would come later, when everyone was out of there and out of trouble. For now, the main objective was to control the situation, to resist any attempt by civilians to encroach on the crime scene, and to effectively calm everyone down.

He glanced back into the living room, wondering what the fresh-faced constable was doing now. Had he found something else in there?

The dead man was no longer in the doorway.

Somehow he'd managed to pull himself to his feet and stagger across the floor, where he was now closing in on the otherwise occupied officer.

Rick tried to remember where his gun was – in his hand? Yes, that was it. He raised the Glock, took aim, and shot the dead man in the back of the head, near the base of his skull. The air turned red. The dead man faltered, then froze. Finally, he dropped heavily, his face slamming bluntly into the floor.

The fresh-faced constable turned around, shock twisting his face into a weird white mask. "Thanks," he mouthed silently, unable to drag real words from his stunned mind.

The silence had lifted. Sound rushed back into Rick's ears, filling his head.

D.I. Harper had obviously regained some of his composure, but he still sounded like a bad impression of himself as he barked orders in the other rooms. "Come on, let's get this sorted. Fire and ambulance crews are on their way – we need to minimise any shock value here, troops."

Rick was still staring at the constable. The young man calmly lifted his hand and placed the barrel of his pistol between his teeth. He smiled around the dull metal, his eyes looking far beyond the scene, perhaps seeing some other landscape where he felt more at home: a land of the living and not the walking dead.

Rick turned his back on the officer just before the sound of detonation tore the air apart.

Things got a lot worse from that point on.

Out in the hallway a dead police officer was rising from the floor. It was the one who'd been attacked by the Afro-Caribbean woman, what seemed like hours ago but in reality had only been about thirty minutes before.

The dead officer moved in twitchy slow motion, like something from an old German vampire film Rick had once seen on TV – was it *Nosferatu*? He thought it might be, but he always got these things mixed up. Sally would know; she always remembered information about books and films. The accuracy of her memory was one of her many strengths.

Rick watched calmly as the dead man began to stand. His gun was ready; he had plenty of time to take a bead on the fucker and put him back down. So he watched with the casual interest of an impartial observer, not feeling part of the scene but nonetheless fascinated by what was happening.

The dead officer jerked once, an oval chunk of flesh flying out of his shoulder and hitting the wall, where it stuck like a thrown turd. Rick had not even heard the gunshot. He raised his eyes, peering over the dead officer's head, and saw Tennant standing there in the doorway, sweat on his broad face and killing in his eyes.

Tennant stared back at Rick. Nodded.

"The head," Rick heard himself say. "I think you need to shoot them in the head. Just like in the movies." *Dawn of the Dead, Zombie Creeping Flesh*. Rick had watched them all on video as a teenager, laughing and screaming in equal measures at the absurdly bloody onscreen spectacle. Not once had he ever entertained the thought that something similar might occur in real life. It was madness. The whole damn world had gone insane.

This time he heard the gunshot.

He closed his eyes and felt blood kiss his face, warm and wet and sticky. He heard the sound of a body slumping to the floor.

"Thanks," said Tennant, and when Rick opened his eyes again the other man was no longer there; the doorway was an empty frame with thin fingers of smoke billowing through it.

More acrid smoke drifted in through the doorway; people yelled out on the landing. Someone had set another fire in one of the flats, perhaps in an attempt to confuse them. It was working: officers ran like headless chickens across his line of view, guns cocked and ready, fingers like coiled springs on the triggers.

More gunshots. Someone screaming, their voice rising in pitch... going on and on and on, as if it might never end. It rung in his ears like the bells of Hell.

Smoke curled around his legs like oily grey serpents, and he backed away, as if recoiling from their touch.

The Dead Rooms. He didn't know who'd said it first – it might even have been Rick himself – but the name was perfect. These rooms, this building – they all contained the dead. The dead that refused to lie down.

Then, a voice: "This way, man. Get the fuck out of there." He stepped forward, towards the voice, and Tennant's meaty arm shot out of the flat slab of smoke-filled doorway to grab him. Rick let himself be hauled out of the flat and onto the smoky landing. Figures barged past, pushing him aside; screams filled the air. The stench was unfathomable: a combination of burning tyres and cooking flesh.

"There's more!" Tennant was screaming into his ear, trying to make himself heard above the cacophonous roar that now filled the upper storeys of the building. "In the other flats... rooms filled with dead bodies. Some of 'em are rotting, others are fresh... but they're all standing up and attacking people."

"What? Are you insane?" He felt his mouth moving, the shape of the words caressing his lips, but it didn't feel like he was speaking. Rick once again felt detached, apart from it all. There was an inner core of calmness, a small, bright place he'd always retreated to during battle. His own private Dead Room.

"The fuckers," said Tennant, his eyes wide, almost popping out of his large bull-like head. "They've been hiding their dead relatives, keeping them holed up in more Dead Rooms. Keeping them safe and sound and away from prying eyes." He began to laugh, but it was a hideous sound, even worse than the constant screaming Rick could still hear coming from somewhere off to their left.

Another gunshot. The screaming stopped.

Rick pulled away from Tennant and watched as the other man waded into the churning wall of smoke, aiming his gun at something Rick could not make out – just a bulky shape, crouching low to the ground. Tennant was still laughing; his massive shoulders were hitching and he even threw back his head like a bad actor in a shitty melodrama.

Rick picked his way slowly along the landing, remaining calm, cool and collected. He glanced through each of the open doorways he passed, looking into other rooms – other Dead Rooms. In one, a young woman was wrestling with a small child. The child was covered in blood that clearly wasn't his own. In another, a man he didn't recognise but who was wearing riot gear sat on an old man's chest, dipping his hands into his abdomen to scoop out what was inside.

Rick made it across the landing without further incident. He had a sudden mental flash of when he had been about twelve years old, a bad time in his youth. His best friend had lived in a block of grotty council flats a lot like this one. The boy, Murray Smith, had been a budding artist. He drew pictures that made Rick believe in something beyond the grimy streets, the rotten neighbourhood, and the borderline poverty.

Murray Smith had been killed by another local youth, a drug-dealing maggot aged thirteen; his throat had been slashed with a broken bottle on a narrow stairway just like this one. Murray had died slowly, and in agony. Not one of the neighbours had come out to investigate the sounds of his dying.

Rick failed to understand at first why he was recalling the awful memory. It was something he'd put behind him, a trauma he'd purposefully not thought of for years.

When he saw Trevor Hutchinson's body, he suddenly realised why Murray Smith had come lurching back into his mind.

Hutch had fallen face down, onto his front, but now he sat leaning against the concrete wall, blood down the front of his stab vest. The left half of Hutch's head was missing from the nose up. Rick could see Hutch's pulped brain through the gap in his skull.

"Oh, no," he said, pointlessly. "Oh, God, mate. No."

He'd served in the Paratroopers with this man, had even followed him out of the army and into the police. His friend; his comrade; his fucking *blood brother.*

Hutch moved slowly, awkwardly, like a man suffering from severe brain damage. He was pulling at the rim of his wound with a twitching hand, stringy matter stretching like pizza cheese between the long, white fingers. His one good eye blinked mechanically. He reminded Rick of one of those Disney World animals, the robot bears and raccoons playing banjos and pianos during matinee performances. It was creepy – even creepier than those terrible severed hands in the bottom of the fridge – and for a moment Rick could think of nothing to do but watch.

Then he knelt down by his friend. His dead-but-alive friend.

No, not his friend... something else. Something *unnatural.*

His friend had vacated this shell.

Reaching out with a tenderness that he felt was entirely appropriate to the moment, he slammed the dead man's head into the wall, mashing what was left of Hutch's brain. The body slipped down the wall, the limbs limp as spaghetti. Red pasta-sauce smears on the chipped plaster rendering. That single eye locked into a cold stare.

Unlike the things on the floor above, Hutch had not returned fully from his early death; like some idiot inbred offspring, he'd been only partially there, a fragment of a being. Rick was aware enough of his actions to consider this second death a mercy killing.

"Regroup! Retreat and regroup!" D.I. Harper's voice boomed down the stairwell, echoing like the voice of an angry god. He was back in control now, getting things sorted, just like he was paid to do. "Down to the ground floor, and then we fucking regroup outside the main doors! Now! Move! Move! *Move!*"

Rick did not need to hear the order again: he took the stairs two at a time. His boots thundered against the concrete but the sound they made was lost amid the deafening uproar of the approaching apocalypse.

CHAPTER SIX

THIS TIME DARYL knew he'd gone too far. He hadn't meant to cause that much damage, but there was something in the air tonight that made him feel reckless. He stared down at Mother, at her blank face and spit-frothed mouth, and felt a strange blooming sensation in his chest. If he had possessed any kind of normal human emotions, he supposed he might have recognised the complex reactions he was experiencing, but as it stood he was simply puzzled.

Mother's feet looked terrible.

Staring at the cigarette lighter in his hand, he wondered again how he'd managed to lose control so easily. Perhaps it was those earlier thoughts of Sally Nutman, or the fact that the city seemed to be exploding in waves of violence – the radio on Mother's bureau was reporting yet more riots breaking out to the south and west of the city.

Mother's feet were weeping blood and some sort of clear fluid that might easily become infected if he left them untended.

The voice on the radio said that police resources were at full stretch and the emergency services were unable to contain the outbreaks of civil unrest; that they were in danger of being overrun.

Those feet... the wounds were terrible, blackened around the outside and moist and meaty at the centre.

All other crimes, said the not-so-calm voice on the radio, were being left unattended. The violence and looting on the streets of Leeds were taking up all police time and effort. The fire service was struggling to cope with the blazes starting up across the skyline. The ambulance crews were at breaking point.

Daryl turned away from Mother's bed. He caught sight of fire in the sky outside; a pale yellow glimmer lightly painted the horizon. If he slowed his breathing and listened intently, he could just about make out the dull roar of an undisciplined crowd some miles away, like the sound of a football match being played at Elland Road Stadium.

Mother's room suddenly seemed so desperately small: the ugly patterned wallpaper pressed in on him, the badly plastered ceiling bowed towards his head, the hideous brown carpet bulged as if the floorboards beneath were buckling. The bibles and religious pamphlets on the shelves twitched forward, threatening to fall, and the posters of Catholic saints slipped from the walls, tumbling through the air like fragments of all the Christ-dreams Mother had ever forced upon him.

"Bitch," he said, enjoying the way the word filled the small space. "You. Bitch."

The world was changing. Not just *his* world, with Mother gradually but stubbornly leaving it. No: the whole world – the *real* world. His inner existence changed a little every day; the closer Mother edged towards death, the nearer he got to his dream of killing. He lacked the courage to take that final step, but Mother's eventual passing might see him transformed into another being, a man who could reach out and take what he wanted because the ties that bound him to banality were finally gone.

On the window sill there was an old framed photograph. It showed Mother with the man she had always told Daryl was his father. The couple stood smiling on a narrow promenade at some northern seaside resort, maybe Whitby. He reached out and picked up the photo, caressing it. As a child, he'd never been allowed to touch Mother's things – specifically her photographs – but when she started ailing, the first of his many tiny rebellions was to go through all of her stuff.

But he'd realised the lie years before, as soon as he was old enough to think for himself; and instead of making him angry it had made him laugh.

The photograph in the frame was a mock-up. Upon close inspection, it became obvious that the man had been cut out of a magazine and pasted next to Mother. She'd done a careful job that held up to distant inspection, but when you looked closer the colours didn't match; the man's image was slightly less faded than hers.

Daryl had seen the man on television when he was young, and at school, and then in newspapers, in retrospective documentaries and articles about

American politics. Yet somehow he had not made the connection until long after he should have done. The man's name was Richard Nixon; he had been the President of the United States before Daryl was even born.

Shaking his head, he smiled at the fact that he'd believed Mother's story for more years than he liked to admit. What else had she lied about? What other stories had she fabricated to cover up the signs of her own madness?

He put the photo frame back in its rightful place, adjusting it to the same angle it always occupied, with Nixon smiling towards Mother's bed, hands held up in his famous victory salute. When Daryl raised his eyes he saw movement outside, on next door's lawn. He moved closer to the window and craned his neck, staring down into the neighbour's garden.

Two figures were tussling on the lawn. Initially, Daryl suspected they were intruders, but soon realised that one of the figures was Mr. Willows. He'd never particularly liked the old man, but nor did he have any real reason to hate him. He was just some nosey old geezer who lived on the same street.

Daryl watched with interest. Mr. Willows was caught up in some kind of wrestling match with a woman dressed in a white smock. The woman was very thin, her arms and legs like tinder sticks. Her hair was patchy, showing pink flashes of scalp, and her mouth was open wide in a ferocious snarl.

The woman was Mrs. Willows.

She had been dead for eight weeks. Mother had been upset because she was too ill to make it to the funeral.

"Help!" Mr. Willows was shouting, straight-arming Mrs. Willows, one hand planted firmly on her flattened chest to keep her at bay. "Please... *help!*" he looked up, directly at Daryl, and when their eyes met Mr. Willows began to shake his head and shout even louder. "Daryl! For God's sake... help me... Daryl!"

Daryl cocked his head to one side. He was fascinated. Was this some sort of delirium vision, a hallucination brought on by excessive stress? It had happened before, on several occasions, and he knew enough about his mental condition to be certain that it was associated with his repressed urges to commit murder.

"Hello, Mr. Willows," he said softly, and smiled.

Mr. Willows' eyes widened when he realised that Daryl would offer no help. The strength seemed to go out of him then, and his face deflated like a popped balloon. His cheeks sunk, hugging bone, his eyes receded into his skull, and his arm slackened, bending at the elbow.

Mrs. Willows lunged forward, her teeth bared, and latched onto her husband's throat. Mr. Willows sunk to his knees, his legs buckling beneath the weight of his dead wife.

Daryl continued to watch with interest as Mrs. Willows tore out the old man's throat, greedily gulping down pieces of his wrinkled flesh. When she started on the wizened face, Daryl looked away.

Mother moaned. It was a small sound, tiny really, but enough to announce her returning consciousness. Daryl looked back to the window, at the scene outside, and saw Mrs. Willows shambling clumsily across the lawn towards her house. She was carrying Mr. Willows' severed right arm; it dangled from her hand like a toy. The old man's remains lay unmoving on the grass near a tall rose bush – the same rose bush Mrs. Willows had tended lovingly every day when she'd been alive.

"Is this it, Mother?"

Mother did not reply.

"Is this the End of Days you were always rattling on about? The Book of Revelations, the Great Beast, the Reckoning? Is this what your Bible warned you about, the hour when we will all be judged as unworthy?"

There was nothing – not even the slightest movement – from where Mother lay, dying and withering on her sick bed.

"Despite your lies and your myth-making, it looks like you were right all along. And the best thing is, you're too fucking ill to see it. Your beloved apocalypse, the time you've prayed for, begged for, believed in for so long."

Breaking glass. A distant explosion. Were those gunshots?

"It's here. It's happening. Your best, most hoped-for dream. This is the end of it all."

Mother did not say a word, but he imagined her cold, hard, brittle laughter, could almost hear it echoing through the empty rooms and hallways of the house. He was surprised and shaken to find that it comforted him.

He left Mother's room and went downstairs, shrugging on his coat at the front door. He opened the door a fraction, peering outside. Something was calling him, a sense of death, the essence of murder. He could smell, taste, hear it; death was so strong, so heavy, that it was like a giant striding through the night.

He could not possibly stay indoors when there was so much to be seen out there, so many fantasies to be acted out on the vast canvas of darkness.

He stepped outside into the chilly air, fastening his jacket. He'd neglected to bring a weapon – perhaps a knife for self-protection – but something told him that he would not need it... something old and weighty: a terrible presence long hidden beneath the weight of his life that was only now stirring, lifting its shaggy head up into the meagre light to taste the potential for mayhem.

He walked along the street, glancing at the houses on either side. Shadows danced beyond the windows, people embracing or rushing to shore up their homes against whatever was abroad in the night. Daryl did not fear this; he was rejoicing in the chaos he could sense around him.

A young woman in a nurse's uniform approached him at speed. She was running, one shoe missing and her stockings torn, her short chestnut hair in disarray. "Oh, thank God," she said, clutching at him. Her fingernails were painted bright red. Her hands were tiny, but the fingers were long. Daryl took in every detail, breathed in each vapour. She was wearing a fruity scent, something fresh and modern, not at all like the stale, cloying floral perfumes Mother always used to mask her unwholesome odour.

"They're chasing me. Three of them. In rags. Blood... covered in blood. Something going on. Riots. Killing." The girl was breathless, her words coming out like a garbled haiku. She had barely even noticed Daryl; he was just a body to cling to in her terror. "They came out of the hospital. The morgue."

Terror.

"I've been knocking on doors but no one would answer. Everybody ignored me..."

This was exactly what he sought: pure, undiluted terror. It tasted sweet, like honey, but possessed a wonderfully bitter aftertaste.

"Oh, yes," he muttered, reaching out a hand to stroke the girl's hair. Her boyish fringe had fallen across her lovely green eyes, obscuring them. Daryl thought of a quote often attributed to the famous American killer Ed Gein, something about whenever he saw a pretty girl part of him would imagine taking her out to dinner, sitting with her eating a nice meal. Another part of him always wondered what her head would look like mounted on a stick. "I see it," he said. "The fear. The potential."

For the first time since approaching Daryl, the young girl looked at him. She stared into his face, his eyes. Whatever she saw there, it scared her even more than her pursuers. She took a quick step back, almost turning the ankle of her shoed foot, and twisted into a shoulder-high privet hedge behind her.

Daryl stepped towards her, his skin tingling, fingertips on fire. Everything he'd planned and dreamed of was right here for the taking. The girl's features blurred, becoming indistinct, and another face overlaid hers like a fine line tracing. It was a familiar face, but one he'd only ever seen from a distance. A face he had coveted, along with the body it crowned, for too long.

The streetlights went out. An unholy roaring erupted from somewhere along the street. More gunshots.

The girl screamed, breaking the moment and bringing Daryl out of his trance. She turned and ran back in the direction she'd come from, kicking off her shoe. It seemed that she'd rather face whatever she'd been fleeing than remain with Daryl, the man she'd mistaken as a saviour.

Veering out into the road, the girl ran directly into the path of a speeding car. It took her down instantly, dragging her beneath the wheels and swerving, careering into a low stone wall at the street corner. The driver shot out through the windscreen, trailing a skirt of shattered glass. His body fell heavily, limbs loose and broken.

Daryl walked away, feeling more alive than he had in years. More alive than he had in his entire life until this moment, this glorious moment where he stood directly in the gaze of something majestic and so much larger than himself. His calling had come at last. After decades of dissecting stolen house pets, masturbating over pictures of corpses clipped from medical textbooks and pushing, pushing, towards some dimly realised goal, his time had come.

Daryl's head was filled with another image of Sally Nutman. He pictured her standing before him, unravelled, her skin punctured by his blades and the holes overflowing with his seed, babies of corruption being born through the wounds they had created together. She smiled; her teeth were eyes, her lips were the fingers of Mother's fist opening, parting, taking him in hand...

When he got back to the house he went to the kitchen and drank a glass of water. He put his head under the tap, washing away the stinking sweat of lust, the filth of transformation, and then climbed the stairs to his room.

He stared at the photograph of Sally Nutman, licked it, and pressed it against his face, his chest, his aching erection – the first one he'd had in months. Then he placed it on the bed and bowed down before it, paying homage to the woman who had stepped forward from the crowd to offer herself up as his first victim, taking his cherry and allowing him into a select brotherhood.

Faces stared down from his walls, their lips moving in silence: praying to a new young god in the making. Ed Gein. Jeffrey Dahmer. Dennis Nilsen. Peter Sutcliffe. Countless others; his chosen audience.

Daryl dragged an old, battered cardboard suitcase from under his bed, threw it down on the divan. Then, moving slowly and with much reverence, he popped the clasps and laid out the contents on the mattress. He looked at them with an almost religious awe, the same expression Mother had on her face whenever she saw the Pope on television.

Daryl had bought most of these things on the Internet. They'd been delivered right to his door. It was funny how the methods of murder were so easily obtainable, like an order of groceries or a print run of self-help books.

He giggled, and then stopped himself, aware of the stern and disapproving eyes that stared down from his walls. This, he knew, was serious business.

Twines of good grade fishing line. Two rolls of duct tape. Several short lengths of industrial strength bungee. A long hunting knife with a serrated blade, a tool generally used for gutting wildlife. A thin-bladed flensing knife.

These were Daryl's chosen tools of his wished-for trade, the artefacts of his dark religion. His ritual would be carried out using these perfect objects, each ideally suited to its particular task. He had practised often on Mother as she lay there dying, trussing her up and sealing her mouth, and only drawing back moments before the kill. Yes, a real victim would struggle more, but that would only add to the power of the moment, the intensity of the event.

Soon the act would be over; he could take off the mask and become his true self, the being which had been growing inside him for so long. The butterfly could emerge from the pupa. The hatchling would come scrabbling out to dine for the first time on the manna of the world.

No more pretending. No more faking it. Soon, and for the first time since childhood, Daryl would know what it was like to *feel*.

CHAPTER SEVEN

"WHAT THE HELL'S going on, sir?" Rick was standing on the grass verge, bathed in flashing blue light. The sirens were off but the warning lights pulsed, forcing an unwanted rhythm inside his brain. He stared at D.I. Harper, meeting the man's gaze, and refused to budge an inch.

"I dunno, son. This whole thing is a fucking mess." The big man shook his head, a sad look in his eyes. He was losing his grip, approaching an edge that he had previously skirted with ease.

"But... but what we saw in there, what we did. That wasn't normal. Any of it. There were people... *dead* people... fuck me, sir, you know what I'm talking about." Rick tensed his jaw, maintaining his gaze, flexing his fingers over the handle of the holstered Glock. It was a nervous habit, one he'd only just acquired. He wondered if it would be a keeper.

"Dead folk?" said D.I. Harper, his face a weird colour in the glow of the emergency lights. "Is that what you mean? Dead folk getting up and attacking us? Even our own men."

Men and women in uniform – police, ambulance, fire crew – were busying themselves at the scene, moving in well choreographed routines to secret music that Rick was unable to hear. His waltz was done, for now; but he was certain that it was too early to put away his dance shoes.

"Like I said, it's a mess." D.I. Harper had softened. His voice was low, slightly menacing, as if he were sharing a grim secret.

"What do you think caused all this?" Rick finally broke his gaze, glancing around at the activity. From the outside it no doubt looked frenetic, unfocused, but in reality everyone had a job to do and knew exactly what was expected of them.

D.I. Harper lit up a short fat cigar with a battered tin lighter. He rolled the lighter in his beefy hand, rubbing its well-worn surface with his fingers, as if it meant something to him – a gift, a memento. "My guess is that I have no guess. We could be looking at a new virus, or chemical warfare, even some sort of mass hallucination. But this is happening all over the city – all over the country. I suspect tonight is the culmination of events that have gone on for days, maybe even weeks."

Rick blinked, his eyes stinging from the smoke they'd run through inside the building. He was still focused, still in fighting mode, but some of his reflexes had slackened. "What are you saying, sir?"

D.I. Harper shook his massive head. His eyes were those of a wise old dog, one that's seen just about everything the world has to offer yet is still capable of registering surprise. "Call me a conspiracy freak if you like, but this is too damn strange for my liking. It could have been anything, really. Bugs. Space aliens. That experiment over in France, the one they rigged up to re-enact the Big Bang. Fucking hell, it could even be some kind of Internet super-virus aimed at Bill Gates for all we know!"

Rick knew that he should think his superior officer's wild theories funny, but he couldn't find it in himself to laugh. The things he'd seen, the bloodshed he'd been part of... none of it made sense, not in a sane world. Maybe this *was* the result of something being passed through the world's computers, or a mutated virus let loose during illegal genetic experimentation. Who knew? Not him; not them. Nor was it their job to know, or to even think. Their job was to clear up the mess. To always, always just keep the hell quiet and clear up other people's messes.

Dark clouds passed overhead, their shapes writhing in the sky like stricken behemoths. The air turned damp, edgy. It would rain soon, possibly even snow. Rick thought of Sally, sitting there at home worrying, watching the news reports of all this madness and checking all the doors and windows.

He excused himself and walked to the edge of the building. Two men were loading a body onto a gurney, strangely silent as they worked. The body was covered in a white sheet with red stains. Near the top of the body, the sheet was a lot flatter than it should be. Rick wondered if it was his friend Hutch.

He leaned against the wall and retrieved his mobile phone from a zippered pocket in his trouser leg. He took off his glove using his teeth, and then switched on the handset. The screen glowed, faintly at first but then brighter as the battery warmed up. When he was asked for his password he typed in the appropriate digits and waited for the handset to allow him to access the phone's memory.

The light grew brighter, stuttered, and then began to fade. He had two new messages, each of them from Sally. He listened to them both and smiled at the sound of her voice. She seemed wary but not terrified; worried but nowhere near to panic.

He dialled his home number.

A message appeared on the screen:

No network coverage.

He tried again and got the same result. Either everyone was clogging up the satellite relays and ringing their loved ones, or there was a problem with the signal. Of the two options, he preferred the former. It was easier to remain calm and focused if he thought that the reason he was unable to contact his wife was because the networks were busy – just like they got on the big holidays like New Year's Eve and Christmas Day – rather than imagining that the entire satellite grid had gone down.

Rick returned the handset to his pocket, forcing himself to remain in control. It was crucial that he was in charge of his emotions. He'd seen too many good men go down because they lost their heads in a crisis.

Like Hutch. He'd certainly lost *his* head in this crisis.

Not funny. Not fucking funny at all.

He stepped away from the building and joined a group of men he knew from his unit. They were jogging around the back, checking that the perimeter was still secure. This was what he needed: routine, training; the ability to focus on his job, no matter how insane the situation. It had kept him alive in Afghanistan, and saved his skin in Iraq. Now it would keep him going long enough to get to Sally, and he'd work the rest out then, once she was in his arms, the warmth of her breath against his neck.

D.I. Harper nodded at him as he passed by, speaking into a two-way radio. He sounded stressed again, like he was hanging on by his fingertips. They all were. There was no other way to hang, not here, not now, amid this insanity.

A crowd had gathered to watch the clean-up. Most of the onlookers were on edge too, just like D.I. Harper, but their edginess was different: it promised yet more violence. Faces peered at him, their eyes huge and bright and perched on the precipice of panic. Sirens wailed across the rooftops; the fires still burned in the sky; distant gunshots punctuated the music of the city, an off-tempo rhythm section.

"Get back! Just get back! We have this under control. Please return to your homes and go about your business." A suited man Rick did not recognise was screaming into a bullhorn, his cheeks puffing out like a crazed cartoon character. "Return to your homes. Clear the area!"

Nobody moved. They just stood and stared, violence brewing. This was their turf; these were their streets. Nothing was allowed to happen here without them knowing, or even granting permission.

"This is going to kick off. Big style." The man next to Rick had a high-pitched voice, but he was broad as an ox. "They're just about to blow."

Rick said nothing. He simply watched and waited.

More bodies were being brought out of the building. There were no survivors. The terrorists had all been killed – most of them twice – and those officers who'd fallen under fire had been taken care of. The other corpses were those which had been discovered in some of the other flats, the departed loved ones of drugged-up tenants who'd been confused by the sudden death and resurrection of their friends and family members.

It had become obvious almost immediately that anyone who died would rise again within minutes, and they would attack whoever was nearest. The only way to prevent this was a headshot.

Rick had witnessed D.I. Harper shooting an unmoving corpse through the temple. Just to be sure, to be safe.

"God," he muttered. "Holy God..."

"What's that?" said the man next to him, the one with the high voice. He had beautiful clear blue eyes – young eyes in a baby face.

Before Rick had the chance to answer, somebody started yelling.

The crowd began to surge, just a small movement but building slowly, a ripple from the back that became a wave when it reached the front row of the massed onlookers. A barrier fell forward. There was no one to pick it up; everyone's attention was focused back at the building, where the yelling was still going on. The crowd shifted forward, forcing their way close to the action.

"Oh, shit!" Babyface ran towards two more men and another sheet-covered gurney, his gun drawn in an instant. The man on the stretcher had pulled himself upright by clawing his way along the ambulance man's arm. The other ambulance man was backing away: it was him who was doing all that yelling. He was crying for his God, his wife, his mother. For anyone who might listen.

Babyface ran at the corpse on the gurney, clearly unaware of the information those inside the building had been party to – not knowing that you had to shoot them in the head.

The dead man was already biting into the ambulance man's arm. The victim pulled away, stumbled, and fell beneath the gurney, stopping it dead. The dead man rolled off onto the ground, hands clawing, his arms flapping. He was still trying to reach the felled ambulance man.

Babyface arrived at speed and kicked the dead man full in the face. Unfortunately, the dead man had his mouth open and Babyface's foot smashed into the top row of teeth as it entered the gaping maw. The dead man bit down, a quick reflexive action. Blood spurted from Babyface's boot, and then as the dead man jerked his head to the side, the end of the boot came away. Along with a few of Babyface's toes.

Rapid bursts of gunfire. The dead man was blown to pieces.

Babyface screamed. And screamed. And screamed.

Rick turned away, making a decision that would eventually dictate the course of the rest of his life. *Fuck this*, he thought. *I'm out of here.*

"Nutman!" It was D.I. Harper. "Don't even think about it."

Rick was too stunned to speak. How had the D.I. known what he was about to do?

He watched as the big man approached, striding towards him with a cigar clenched between his teeth. "I know that look. I saw what you were about to do. I need every good man to remain at his post – particularly men like you, men with combat experience."

"Sir." Rick was unsure how to react.

"This is turning into a war, Officer Nutman. A fucking war. I've just spoken to the boys at the station, and they're under attack. Running battles all over the fucking city. Reports of walking dead are coming in thick and fast. We have a combat situation on our hands here, and we don't even know who the enemy is." He grabbed Rick by the lapel, pulled him up onto his tiptoes. "So *you're* staying put. Just like everyone else." The benevolent father-figure had vanished; now, in his place, stood a warrior, a leader of men.

"Yes, sir." Rick gently took hold of D.I. Harper's big-knuckled hands, tried to prise them from his clothing, but the man's grip was like iron. "I'm with you, sir. I'm with you."

D.I. Harper relaxed then, as if realising that he was stepping over the line. He let go of Rick's collar, stood back, and glanced around at the mayhem. "This is all so strange. So very strange." He had a faraway look in his eye. "I've seen some awful things in my life, son, some truly awful things, but never anything like this." His shoulders slumped, the energy spent. Then he looked up, directly into Rick's eyes. "Just stay with me, son. We all need to stick together, to act as a team. If we're going to get through tonight, we need to stand together like brothers, all of us pulling in the same direction."

The man's platitudes sounded vaguely ridiculous, as if they'd been scripted, but Rick nodded in agreement. He felt obliged to obey his superior officer, no matter how much the man seemed to be losing his grip. Obeying orders – both those of his unit and his own body – had helped keep him alive. But he couldn't remain here for long, whatever he was told. Sally needed him. He'd give it another hour for things to settle down, then leave quietly, without causing a fuss.

Mere seconds after this decisive thought, Rick's attention was drawn by the sound of many running feet. The watching crowd had finally been stirred into motion, and even now they were pushing a line of uniforms out of the way to get at the building and see for themselves what was going on.

Officers moved in, weapons aloft, and Rick closed his eyes and took a long, deep breath before joining his colleagues in their positions at the front line.

Rick knew what was coming. He knew it intimately.

CHAPTER EIGHT

DARYL FELT ODDLY safe out on the streets. Despite the lawlessness, the fighting and looting and displays of aggression, he now possessed a self-assurance that had eluded him for most of his life. Were these simply more personality changes due to Mother's grip slackening, or had something occurred at a more fundamental level?

On his back was a new rucksack, the straps tight across his shoulders and digging into his armpits. Inside the bag were his tools, along with the photograph of Sally Nutman. She was his guiding light, his sole aim in all this wonderful chaos. With the city erupting around him, no one would even hear her death rattle; the extinction of her life-force would be lost amid the flowering brutality of this strange new world, a world he felt curiously at home in.

Mother's house was located in a suburb not far from the centre of Leeds. Daryl did not own a car, and he doubted that any taxis would be operating with so much going on, but it was a short walk, really. He'd traced the route many times in the past, and knew every shortcut along the way.

The best way was to follow the canal into the centre. It was usually a dangerous place to be after nightfall, but tonight *everywhere* was dangerous – indeed, the canal was probably safer than the streets and estates right now.

The moon was a faded orb, masked by heaving clouds. Starlight was negligible. The pathways were illuminated by the cold light of street lamps, and Daryl picked his way past wrecked cars, overturned bins and piles of shattered glass and rubble. The occasional scream leapt at him from the darkness, garbled words echoed along lightless ginnels and alleyways. Daryl kept moving, trying to blend into the night. He'd always been an unnoticeable figure, and tonight that anonymity was a weapon almost as potent as the ones in his rucksack.

He'd left Mother in her room, staring into the giddy blackness and fearing the sight of her own private Reaper. Perhaps it would have Richard Nixon's face, or maybe it would be dark and featureless, skulking in the shadows of her room. The latter thought pleased Daryl; because of Mother's fear of the dark, it suited that darkness would claim her.

The canal towpath crunched underfoot, pebbles and broken glass scattered across its narrow width. The black waters ran slow and sombre, with not even a duck or waterfowl about to mar its glassy surface. It *felt* like the end of the world.

Daryl hurried along the towpath, his thoughts filled with images of blood and the sound of muted screaming. He had another erection – this was a banner night for his libido. He wondered if Sally Nutman would recognise him, if she had noted his scrutiny at some point over the last few months. Part of him hoped that just before she died, her eyes would blaze with recognition. The other half of him prayed that she would die in utter confusion, not knowing who he was or why he'd decided to use her in such a way.

The waters shone blackly at his side, reflecting his desires. The canal was like a mirror; the images it contained matched those he'd carried around in his head since he was a child. It felt as if the landscape around him was shifting, altering to accommodate his new shape. The sky had lifted, allowing him to breathe; the trees and bushes bordering the path pulled back from his approach; the path itself twisted and undulated to meet his falling feet.

After years of feeling apart, isolated, he at last felt that he had a place in the world. A dark place, filled with demons.

It was only fitting that his first victim be as beautiful as Sally Nutman. He'd adored her features from afar, cementing that face in his mind. The slanted cat-like eyes, the firm jawline, the long, graceful neck. It would not suffice to kill an ugly woman first; a beautiful act must be carried out on a special victim. He began to regret that this long-awaited act might soon be over. He'd spent so long fantasising about it, building the whole thing up inside his head, that he feared the actual kill might be an anticlimax.

But, no. It was stupid to think that way. Here he was, on the cusp of *becoming*, and all he could do was whine! He sensed the disapproval of his heroes, his masters; their long shadows followed him along the towpath, maintaining their distance but never slackening their pace.

He heard a splash as he walked beneath a low concrete footbridge. Graffiti adorned the abutments, crude drawings and obscene slogans meant to express a rage that could never otherwise be demonstrated. The splash came again, softer, as if moving away.

Daryl stopped and looked out at the water, trying to make out what was causing the sounds. His eyes fell upon a discarded shopping trolley tethered to the opposite bank by the knotted fronds of some riverside weed. Nearby, a child's doll floated in a slow circle, pink and naked and deformed. Then, turning his head to face eastward, he finally saw what was making the noise.

A fat white corpse was struggling to climb out of the canal. Water-bloated and covered in black silt, the thing kept gaining a few inches before slipping back down the bank and into the water. Daryl could see it from behind, so was unobserved. He watched it for a while, enjoying its struggling motion. The body was naked, its flesh puffy and discoloured. The fat arms and stubby hands looked as if they were made of dough as they grasped at the mud on the sloped side of the canal.

Daryl edged along the path, watching. It was an amazing sight, when you thought about it, like something from a nightmare. He supposed that the corpse must belong to a drowning victim who'd suddenly risen from the murky depths, heading for shore to return home.

He paused, and wondered why he'd accepted all this so readily. Reanimated corpses. The living dead. Perhaps it took the truly insane to accept a truly insane situation?

The Michelin-man body rolled as it grabbed a handful off moss, its bulk turning in the water. The face was hideous: a mass of jellied flesh and fish bites. It had no eyes, which went some way to explaining why it found it so difficult to gain the canal bank. The nose was gone, too; all that remained was a ragged hole, through which Daryl glimpsed white bone.

The corpse opened its mouth as if trying to scream. Canal water slid from between its fattened lips, spilling down over its flabby breasts and corpulent belly. Its lower portion was obscured by the dark water, so Daryl could not make out if it was male or female. If he was honest, he'd rather not know anyway.

As he drew abreast of the corpse, a fortuitous accident occurred. Still caught in its slow roll, the body's momentum carrying it round in an agonising circle which pivoted at the thing's hand – which was still holding on to the side of the canal – the corpse began to slide towards a steel stanchion that stuck out from the bank.

Daryl watched in quiet awe as the stanchion pierced the side of the thing's head, just above the ear, driving slowly into the sodden skull as if it were paper. The head split, the length of steel tearing it so that the waterlogged contents of the brain pan spilled out into the canal.

The corpse hung there, twisting in the undertow. The split had stretched around the front of the head, connecting with the mouth, so that it resembled a smile. Or a salacious leer.

Daryl laughed, and then continued on his way. For some reason the whole episode felt like a prelude to something bigger. Knowing how silly it seemed, he felt that the drowned corpse had been sent to him as a sign to show him something he would only understand later, once he was indoctrinated into the league of killers he longed to join.

He passed a burned-out concrete structure, an old storage shed used now for drug taking. Dirty syringes littered the doorway, and something stirred within. Daryl glanced into the darkness and saw a thin figure sitting against the wall. Its white limbs were skinny as pipe-cleaners and pin-cushioned with needles as it searched for a vein.

He hurried on, processing the information in a rush.

Habit. It all boiled down to habit.

These dead things – these hideous revived remains – fell into the same habits they'd suffered in life. The drug addict returned to the needle; the mother came back for her babe; the victim of a drowning once more attempted to climb back on to dry land. Life, he mused, was full of such cycles. The living re-enacted their daily routines, their lives becoming like a film clip stuck on a loop. So when they came back from the dead, what else was there but to *resume* that loop, to climb back into the rut and carry on carrying on?

It made perfect sense to Daryl. The dead tried to copy the living. It was all they knew, all they had within them: primitive urges, tribal acts, a repetition of events tattooed onto their memories by social custom and workaday existence. Strip away the thought process and all we are is habit, routine, learned experience. Like a mouse stuck on an exercise wheel, the dead just kept on running, with no destination in sight.

He crossed the railway line and then doubled back in a loop, the city rising before him. He could see the lights – far fewer than usual at this time of night – and the rooftops of the higher buildings scraped the sky like glass and concrete fingers. He focused on his destination; one of the new docks along this side of the canal, where developers had built apartment blocks and fitness complexes.

Allinson Dock was less than a mile away. He knew the spot by heart, had traced the route both in life and in his dreams too many times to even count. Further along the river, at Clarence Dock, he could make out the blocky structure of the Royal Armouries Museum, with its hexagonal glass and steel tower set amid a clutter of oblongs. The windows reflected the canal water, glittering like huge insectoid eyes.

Daryl admired the illusion, enjoying the fantasy while it lasted.

He left the canal and cut across a short bushy verge, stepping over the town planners' idea of an urban green zone. Empty beer cans, bottles and used condoms were scattered between the shrubs.

Heading uphill, he reached a smooth, flat road surface. The road led into the apartment complex where Sally and her husband lived; it terminated in a few parking spaces that flanked the entrance to the underground car park.

Daryl squatted in the bushes and waited, scoping out the site. He watched a dark figure as it scuttled on all fours, heading for the canal. The figure – it looked like a woman crawling around in the mud – disappeared into the undergrowth, and there followed a single splash as she entered the water. Daryl held his breath; he heard nothing more of the curious figure.

Nearby, the burned remains of a car smouldered, the metal of the bodywork groaning and creaking as it cooled.

He stared at the apartment block, locating Sally's seventh-floor windows with ease. He knew exactly where they were. All the windows were dark, but that did not prevent him from identifying the ones Sally hid behind, thinking that she was safe and secure.

He smiled. The darkness nestled around him, wrapping him in a comforting cloak.

Minutes passed, but Daryl did not keep track of how many. Eventually his legs began to ache from sitting in the same position, his rear end held inches from the ground and all his weight taken on the annoyingly weak muscles of calves that simply would not develop no matter how hard he tried to train them. He stood, stretching, sucking in the night. Sally's windows remained black, silent, and blind to the terror he brought. The temperature dropped around him, the air becoming sharp.

After another few moments he moved on, cutting across the road and entering the landscaped area at the side of the building. A few night birds hopped between the branches of the low trees; something burrowed into the foliage at his feet. There might be rats this close to the canal, but it was probably something as harmless as a hedgehog.

"I'm coming," he whispered. "I'm coming, dollface." It was not the kind of casual language he ever used; the lines were taken from some film he'd seen. All of his best lines came from films, or books. Not that he ever spoke them to anyone other than his own face in the mirror, or perhaps Mother's closed bedroom door...

The main doors operated on an expensive security system, involving a pass code and a CCTV monitor, but there was a man who lived on the ground floor, in apartment Number 03, who habitually neglected certain essentials of home security. He always left his bathroom window ajar. The man worked nights. Daryl knew this from his surveillance exercises; either unaware or uncaring of the dangers inherent in city living, the man never bothered to close the window when he left for his job. Daryl stepped softly along the side of the building, ducking below the eye-line of the windows.

Soon he reached the open window.

He reached up, slid his arm inside, and popped the catch. It was that easy: the fine line between entry and exclusion, life and death, was a scant few inches of air between sill and frame. It was almost absurd, the risks some people took without ever acknowledging the possible consequences.

Daryl glanced along the length of the building, carefully inspecting the area for prying eyes. Then, satisfied that no one was around to witness him, he clambered up the wall, finding a foothold on the smart new cladding, and forced his thin body through the window.

Once inside the bathroom, he returned the window to its former position, being careful to ensure that it looked exactly as it had before. Once he was satisfied, he walked across to the door and stepped out into a long narrow hallway. The front door was located at one end of this hallway; the living room was at the other.

Daryl didn't bother to have a nose around the apartment. He simply walked to the front door, opened it, and let himself out. He moved swiftly to the fire stairs – the lift might not be working due to the power blackouts – and climbed to the seventh floor, where Sally was waiting for him.

He'd been inside before, sneaking in after another tenant before the main door could close. He'd received a funny look, but was not challenged, even though he had stayed there for two hours, exploring the interior of the building and waiting for Sally's husband to return home from a day shift so he could study any idiosyncratic lifestyle patterns the man exhibited. Even then he was aware that the slightest piece of behavioural data might help him in the future, when finally the time came to put his plan into action.

He was breathing heavily when he reached the seventh floor, and his lungs ached slightly. At home he lifted weights to add strength – but not bulk – to his wiry physique. He had the body of a distance runner: lean, powerful limbs, a hard, skinny torso, but his *lower* legs – specifically his ever-puny calf muscles – remained weak and his stamina was terrible. His upper body strength, however, belied the narrow build he hid beneath his baggy clothing.

He was certain that Sally would admire his physique. He would leave her no choice in the matter.

He approached the door to her apartment and stood outside, running his hands across the surprisingly lightweight wooden door. She sat behind an inch of hollow, low-grade timber, awaiting his ministrations.

"Oh, baby. Baby, baby, baby." He giggled, but made sure that he kept it low, under his breath.

Then, feeling an enormous surge of energy building from the soles of his feet and climbing the length of his body, flowering at the midriff, throat and face, he knocked six times in rapid succession upon the door – exactly the way he knew that Sally's husband, that idiot copper, always knocked.

He repeated the jokey secret knock – again, just like the husband always did – and then stepped back to wait for Sally to open the door and let him in; a shy suitor nervously awaiting his reluctant paramour.

CHAPTER NINE

The crowd's mood was turning nasty. Young men and women were pushing and shoving each other to get through the hastily assembled cordon of officers. Rick took his place in the line, using the riot shield he'd been given moments earlier by a stern-faced Sergeant by the name of Finch. A veteran of the miners' strikes back in the 1980s, Finch was a bull of a man with a broad build, a solid gut and a grey beard. His eyes were steely; they'd looked upon horrors normal men could barely even contemplate. His name was spoken in whispers along the station corridors, and his reputation was immense.

"Hold the line!" Finch's voice boomed above the noise, making himself heard despite the rising volume of other voices – shouts and threats and chants. "Make a wall. Be ready!"

Rick shifted backwards and tucked into the wall formed by his colleagues, holding up his reinforced plastic shield to link with those of the men on either side of him. The crowd surged again, forcing a way through. Finch barked more commands, but this time the sound of his voice was drowned out by the rising tumult of obscenities. The crowd would not be held. The mood was building, turning intense and somehow animalistic.

Rick raised his head from the line and looked up at the sky, taking a moment away from the melee. Tiny snowflakes had begun to fall, drifting like confetti thrown onto a wedding crowd. The noise receded; a silent weight flooded in to replace the jeers. He felt calm for a moment, above and apart from the commotion. Bodies slammed against him but he could not take his eyes from those wondrous white specks as they fell to earth in lazy, haphazard patterns. His breath misted before his eyes; he didn't know how long it had been so cold.

The snowflakes melted on impact with the ground, as if such a pitiless place could not hold on to their purity.

Suddenly the area was flooded with bright white light. The ground became a sort of screen; flat, blank and reflective. Two police helicopters swung low over the scene and hovered, the sound of their rotors deafening. The crowd seemed to pause *en masse* then, as if the mere presence of the 'copters had made each individual aware of what he or she was doing and re-evaluate their stance. Finch took the opportunity to strengthen the line, and the man with the bullhorn shouted instructions.

The crowd still seemed caught between two states of mind; they were all poised on the brink of something catastrophic, yet not one of them was willing to follow through. Then, just before a breaking point was reached, Finch fired his pistol into the air.

Five shots. Rick was so acutely attuned, so *hyper aware*, that he managed to count every one of them. The crowd seemed to take in a single breath, giving up an inch of ground, and at that point every officer present knew that the situation had been salvaged. This was northern England, not downtown LA; when someone started shooting, it was still an unusual enough event to shatter almost any moment of tension.

The life went out of the massed bystanders; they broke up into smaller groups, the mob physically losing its shape. The threat of violence was still there, but now it was subdued and had returned to skulk beneath the surface, peeking out like a naughty child caught in the act of an indiscretion.

"Let's get this shit cleared," said Finch, and Rick was unsure whether he meant the still-present crowd, the bodies, or the whole damn thing.

In Rick's experience, it often happened the same way in battle. One minute the dogs of war were straining at their leashes and the blood ran like lava in the veins of those tensing for war; the next minute, after the initiative had been taken and the pressure relieved, it was as if conflict had never been an option. He had struggled to acclimatise to the wild swings of emotion, the acute stresses, when he first joined the army, but after his initial tour of duty it became like second nature. First nature, if he was honest. Once a man has tasted the potential of battle, he never functions in quite the same way again.

A short time later it was like the standoff had never even happened. Clusters of bystanders still hung around on the fringes of the scene, smoking cigarettes, sipping cans of cheap supermarket beer, even eating burgers and kebabs – unbelievably, some opportunistic local vendor had set up his van a few yards away.

Rick stood watching the vicinity, awaiting further orders. During the lull, his mind returned to Babyface and the way the dead man had bitten clean through the end of the lad's tough leather boot. Surely that was not possible: no human being could bite through that kind of material.

But were these dead things actually human, or in the process of revival did all humanity simply fall away?

He recalled another episode from a few months before, when a training exercise had turned serious. He and a handful of fellow recruits had been practicing manoeuvres on a local football field after dark when a solitary figure had wandered over. The man was pumped full of illegal drugs – PCP, probably, judging by what happened next. The man had gone wild for no reason whatsoever, pulling out a kitchen knife from under his shirt. He stabbed one man and slashed two others, taking several truncheon blows to the head in the process, but kept on coming, swinging that lethal blade through the air.

Finally he'd been felled by a rubber bullet. None other than Finch, the principal officer in charge of the training exercise, had characteristically stepped up to sort things out. The man had gone down only because his body reacted to the shot; his mind was still on the attack, sending signals of aggression to his flailing limbs.

Maybe it was the same with these dead things? Because they were already dead, they felt no pain; their physical responses were not like those of the living. Maybe they would just keep on coming, brushing off all attacks, until somebody destroyed the brain – the engine that drove them.

"How are you holding up?" Finch stood at his side, appearing from nowhere. He was a legend among uniformed officers. He was always there, always watching and waiting for a problem to solve.

"Still here, sir."

Finch smiled. "Cigarette?"

Rick shook his head. "I don't, sir."

"I give you another three months before you do." Finch lit the cigarette, smiling around the brief flame. His heavy-browed face looked eerie in the flickering light, like a Japanese demon mask. His iron-grey hair was swept back from his hairline, and his eyes shone. "Listen up, Nutman. I know you have a new wife at home, so if you were to have vanished during that little skirmish back there I'd put in my report that the last time I saw you, you were holding the line with the rest of us." Finch raised his eyes, peering out from under his tough-looking forehead. Everyone knew he'd lost his wife to cancer. She had died slowly, and in great pain. After her funeral, the famously hardcore Finch had softened, but in a way that gained him even more respect. Almost overnight, as if it were the result of an epiphany, he'd turned from a hard-edged bastard into someone who genuinely cared about the men under his command.

"I'll hang around a while longer, sir. Just to make sure everything's okay. D.I. Harper's on the warpath. I wouldn't want to upset him again."

Finch smiled again, showing his shockingly white teeth; they looked nothing like the teeth of a heavy smoker. "Listen, your shift ended a couple of hours ago, everything's fine here. Go home, Nutman. Go to your wife. The shit has gone up all over this city – all across the country. Last thing I heard, London was going under. Liverpool is struggling. Fuck knows what's happening in Manchester. We're teetering on the edge here in Leeds. In another hour, you won't even be able to move across the city to get to your missus."

The gravity of what Finch was saying began to sink in. The man was right: if situations like this one were happening city-wide, the main roads would soon be blocked. Gangs and looters were already out in force and whatever units remained on the clock would be struggling to shut down the city, to keep it all under some semblance of control.

Things did not look good, whichever angle you viewed them from.

Finch finished his cigarette and threw the butt on the ground. He stamped on it more times and much harder than was strictly necessary, as if making a point. Giving one final glance at Rick, he winked. Then he was gone, gravitating towards some other part of the night, where men like him were needed, always needed.

The bloodstained desert of Afghanistan, many clicks south of Kabul, was never far from Rick's mind. Even now, back home, the sounds and sights and smells of the hot dunes remained with him, colouring his perception. Back in Helmand Province, when the gunfire had started and a concealed device had blown the tracks off the US military Humvee he and his two best friends were travelling in, he'd made a rushed promise to a God he did not believe in. He'd made a pact with whatever deity might be listening that if he survived this one, he would never abandon Sally again. Surely this was the time to make a return on that promise – if there was a test to be taken, what better time than now, when all the rules had changed and the world had become unbalanced?

Perhaps the God he'd never believed in *did* in fact exist, in such an altered world.

He glanced around, noting the positions of all nearby officers, then quietly turned and walked into the darkness towards a low brick wall, behind which lay a grotty urban park. He climbed the barrier in a second, hopping over it without making a sound. When he dropped down on the other side, he rolled and kept low as he moved towards the small stand of trees at the rear of the paltry half acre of faded greenery.

No one called his name. Nor did anyone come running to drag him back to his post. Acting on the decision had been easier than he'd imagined. Deserting his duty; it felt wrong, against his nature. But if he stayed put and hoped for the best, Sally would be forced to handle events on her own.

No way. That was out of the question.

If a trained killer could not protect his loved ones, then what good was that training? He'd done his duty, even in these extraordinary circumstances – no one could accuse him otherwise. Now it was time to let the populace take care of their own problems and hope that he did not have a serious one of his own.

He glanced back and saw a couple of dark, shadowy figures drifting away from the block of flats, heading off into the side streets and cul-de-sacs of the estate. Had Sergeant Finch whispered into more ears than his, or had those others reached the same decision as Rick on their own?

Good for them, he mused: strange times called for unusual measures, and in a world gone mad, the only thing stronger than death was love.

CHAPTER TEN

THE INTERNET SERVER was unstable but still Sally managed to establish a tenuous connection.

After the lights went out and the TV and radio died, she'd unpacked her laptop and set it up on the dining table in the open plan kitchen. She sat by the window, glancing occasionally over her shoulder to check on the situation outside. She'd seen no one else since the car crash, after which the hideously injured woman had crawled off into the darkness at the side of the canal.

The laptop battery had about an hour's worth of juice and she was linked up to a wireless hub. Scanning news sites and message forums, she'd already managed to establish the scale and immediate impact of events. It was massive: an international phenomenon, respecting no borders and tearing down all geographical and political demarcations.

London, the capital, was on its last legs. All the major cities were falling. The reason behind this madness was impossible to comprehend; even now, after reading so many first-hand accounts online, she refused to accept it as the truth.

The dead, those disembodied cyber personalities told her, had risen and begun to attack the living. Graveyards, morgues, the cold rooms in hospital basements: all were origins of the attacks. The buried dead, the recently deceased, the murdered, the accidents, the suicides... they were all climbing out of their coffins, off their slabs, up from their death scenes, and walking, attacking, killing. Eating.

It was insane.

Sally was monitoring a BBC message forum, a local chat group dedicated to the Leeds area. It was usually a place where people gathered online to discuss topics of concern or interest – crime rates, council taxes, wheely bins and forthcoming events in and around West Yorkshire. Tonight – or was it morning already; she'd lost track of time – the forum was buzzing with terrified people unable to sleep and sharing information about the situation outside.

MUM DIED HALF N HR AGO

It was an ongoing discussion in which Sally had been involved earlier: a thirteen year old girl whose mother had been attacked by a group of teenagers several hours ago as she went out to investigate a ruckus outside their home. The girl did not know how to drive and an ambulance had failed to arrive. The girl's mother had been stabbed. She'd died from her injuries.

STAY CALM, HONEY

Sally felt helpless. What else could she do but offer faceless support, floating around like an inarticulate god?

SHEZ MOVING. JUST SAT UP IN BED. LUKS FUNNY. LIKE SHEZ DRUNK OR SOMETHNG.

Sally's fingers hovered over the keyboard. What on earth was she meant to do? She didn't even know where the girl was located – just that she was somewhere in Leeds. Even if she did have an address, by the time she got there (*if* she even got there) it would be much too late to make a difference.

GET OUT. GET OUT OF THE ROOM. LOCK HER IN. LOCK YOURSELF IN A CUPBOARD.

Sally held her breath, waiting for the girl's response. She didn't even know her name.

NEEDZ ME. MAKNG THIZ LIKE CRYING NOIZ. MOANING.
THINK SHEZ THIRSTY. OR HUNGRY.

"No. Don't!" Sally typed quickly, trying to focus her energy through the keyboard, along the wireless connection, and out towards the girl. She needed help, but none was coming. None was ever coming.

DON'T GO TO HER. RUN AWAY. RUN RUN RUN RUN

The dialogue was over. The girl did not respond.

Sally waited, waited, her heart pressing hard against the bones of her chest, threatening to tear a hole in her breast. She could hardly breathe; this was all too much to handle. Just a girl – a young girl and her dead mother. It wasn't fair, wasn't right. None of this should be happening.

Tears came, with a force that actually stopped her breath, but they were not cathartic. They hurt, burning her cheeks. Sally's head dropped, her gaze at last leaving the laptop screen. She closed her eyes, wishing that it would all go away, that Rick would arrive and everything would return to normal.

When she looked again at the laptop, the resolution was fading, the screen light dimming. A message popped up in the bottom right hand corner.

Disconnected.

Then someone knocked on the door.

Sally turned to look through the kitchen archway, peering into the swirling darkness and wondering who it could be. Rick. Of course, it had to be Rick. He'd heard her messages and been allowed to return home. She suddenly felt lightheaded, like a love-struck teenager. It was an odd reaction under the circumstances, and the feeling took her by surprise. She'd expected relief, perhaps even a muted form of joy, but not this strange sense of wanton excitement.

Rick knocked again, six times; their secret code, instilled in her as a safety measure for when he was working the late shift. Even when he had his keys, he always knocked first just to let her know it was him.

"I'm coming," she called, struggling to her feet as she pushed the chair away from the dining table. The legs screeched on the hardwood floor. The laptop slid across the tabletop, forgotten for now. She could try to re-establish the connection later, once she and Rick had made the apartment secure.

Rushing along the hallway, she attempted to reign in her emotions. What if it wasn't Rick at the door? Surely he would have responded to her call, putting her at ease with soothing words or a snatch of gentle banter. She approached the door and pressed the palm of one hand against the grainy texture of its surface. The door felt cold to her touch.

"Hello?"

No answer. If it was Rick out there, he must be hurt; otherwise he would be calling her name, telling her to open up.

"Hello. Who's there?"

A short pause, followed by a low, smooth voice: "My name is Daryl. I live downstairs – the next floor down. My wife is hurt and no one else will answer their door. Please... please, I need help. The phone line is dead. I'm afraid."

She'd seen and heard nothing of the other neighbours, assuming they'd all simply gone to ground inside their own homes. This man sounded plausible; he needed help, and because Sally had been unable to rescue the girl she'd communicated with earlier, she felt the need to lend a hand here.

"Daryl? Are *you* hurt? Do you know what's going on?" She pressed her cheek against the door, listening intently to his voice, looking for a flaw in his story. Rick had always taught her to be careful, be sure of herself before trusting anyone.

"No, I'm fine. Just a little shaken. My wife collapsed. I don't know why. I called for an ambulance earlier, but the call was cut off. I'm not sure exactly what's going on out there... but it's bad. Really bad."

The final two words convinced her of his authenticity. His voice had cracked, as if the fear was overwhelming. It must have taken a lot of courage to even step outside of his apartment to go in search of aid. She wondered if she would be up to such a feat if the same thing had happened to her – if she needed to find help because Rick was ill or even (God forbid) dead.

"Okay, Daryl. Please step back from the door, and I'll open up. I want to see you first, in the security spy hole." She moved to the left and put her eye to the tiny glass peephole set in the middle of the door. A short, harried-looking figure stood on the other side, glancing nervously along the landing. He was shorter than Sally by what she guessed was at least a few inches, and his build was slight – even puny. As she studied his smooth bespectacled face, she realised that he did indeed look vaguely familiar. She must have seen him around the building, perhaps had even spoken to him in the lift on her way to work.

"That's fine, Daryl. I can see you. I've seen you before."

The man smiled.

"I'm going to open the door now. Get ready to step inside as quickly as possible. I don't want to take any unnecessary risks."

He smiled again. Sally realised that he must be experiencing intense relief that someone had responded to his plea for help. He must be terrified, and worried that his wife might die and... and become one of *them*: the things roaming around out there, in the night, grabbing hold of whatever warm flesh they could find.

Feeling slightly more in control now that she was doing something positive, Sally pulled opened the door and stepped to the side, allowing the man to squeeze past her and enter the apartment. He was a good two inches shorter than her – that must make him something like five foot five. His hair was uncombed and out of condition and he had a mild buzz of razor rash down one side of his throat. Her first impression had almost been correct: he was thin, but not scrawny.

"Thank you, Sally," he said, moving along the passageway and into the main living area. His feet trod softly.

"How do you know my name?" Sally did not follow him into the apartment. She stood by the door, one hand on her thigh and the other held loose, ready to open the door again if she needed to leave in a hurry.

Daryl grinned. "Sorry. I think one of the other tenants told me. I remember when you and your partner – is it Richard – were married. Saw the wedding cars parked outside."

"Rick," she said, shuffling forward, slightly more at ease. "His name's Rick. He's a policeman." She didn't really know why she'd added this information, but it made her feel better that Daryl knew what her husband did for a living. "Armed Response."

Daryl nodded. It was a slow, almost cautious movement. "Yes, I know. I've seen him around. Even spoke to him a few times, down in the lobby."

Sally entered the living room, keeping to the edges of the space. She was unsure of this man, but had no concrete reason to distrust his motives. He'd come here for help; surely that made him safe. "Where was it you said you lived? Which apartment?"

"Number three. Ground floor." He was examining a photo frame, holding a picture taken on their wedding day. A grey limo. Rick lounging on the bonnet in his rented suit and her clad in a second-hand wedding dress she'd bought from eBay. Trees stood in the background, soaked by the rain that had never stopped that day and went on well into the following week. A typical summer wedding.

"I thought you said you lived on the floor directly underneath. You did say that, didn't you?" She wracked her brain to remember, but couldn't quite grasp his words.

"No," he said, taking off his rucksack. It was new. He'd even left the price tag dangling from one of the zippers. "I just said that I lived downstairs. Didn't stipulate a floor."

Sally suddenly realised that Daryl had carefully worked his way around the room and now stood between her and the exit. He was taking off his coat. His glasses had steamed up, so he removed them and began to rub them on his sweater. The sweater was like something an unfashionable teenager might wear – some cheap knock-off from a shabby market stall.

"Well. Well, well, well." He laid the jacket across the back of a chair, stroked it with the flat of his hand. His rucksack was resting at his feet, a tame dog; it was still sealed but within reach. "I've waited a long time for this, Sally. You wouldn't even believe how long I've wanted to meet you." He put back on his glasses, smiling coyly.

Then she understood. This pathetic little man obviously had the hots for her. He'd spied on her from his apartment, wishing that he could orchestrate a meeting, and tonight had finally summoned the nerve to come calling. The opportunist little bastard. "What about your wife?" she said, glaring at him. "I thought she was hurt?"

"No. Not hurt."

She imagined Daryl's spouse sitting on her own downstairs, probably under the impression he'd gone to find out what was going on, when in reality he was stalking one of the neighbours.

"Not hurt. To be honest, she doesn't even exist. I made her up. I don't have a wife... just a... just a Mother." His empty smile was lopsided, like a morbid scar. It transformed him from a sad little wanker into something far more dangerous and worthy of a lot more caution.

"I... I don't understand. Which apartment do you live in?" The answer was already there, somewhere deep inside her brain, but still she felt that she must ask the question.

He took a step closer. Just the one: a short, nimble movement that surprised her with its elegance. "Don't be silly. I don't even live in this building. I've come quite a way to meet you, Sally Nutman. Further than you could ever imagine." He closed his eyes, inhaled deeply, and then opened his eyes again, staring right at her. Through the thick lenses of his glasses, those eyes looked huge and desolate, gaping holes in his skull.

Daryl moved forward again, exercising an impressive economy of movement. He was like a dancer, displacing the air before him rather than actually flexing his body through it. Shock waves shimmered across the room, unseen but felt by them both – a soft draft on the skin of the arms, a disturbance in the atmosphere.

"Don't come any closer..." Her words trailed off, useless.

"Do you even understand how redundant that plea is? Or was it meant as a threat? He bent from the waist and picked up his rucksack. Unzipping the main pocket, he took out a bundle of rags and discarded the bag. Unfolding the bundle, he first produced a knife. There where other things in there too, but Sally could not see beyond the long serrated blade, the blinking stainless steel smile.

"Oh, God."

"God?" Daryl slashed the blade through the air, practicing. "I don't believe in God. Certainly not Mother's God – and not after the things I've seen tonight. Do you even know what's going on out there, beyond the walls of your fucking ivory tower? The dead are walking about, refusing to lie down. They are no longer at rest."

Sally's gaze flicked around the room, looking for a weapon. Anything would do, but sadly there was nothing that she could use against him, not even a heavy ornament. She had never been a fan of having things cluttering up the surfaces; she preferred prints on the walls, books and photographs on the shelves. Under the current circumstances, she was beginning to regret her taste in furnishings.

Even the books she owned were lightweight; the thought of throwing a Ben Elton or a Jackie Collins paperback at his head provoked in her absurd, desperate laughter.

"Oh, *perfect.*" Daryl was grinning now, but still there was nothing beneath the expression – no depth, no real emotion: no humanity. "I've just thought of something. I can't believe that it's only just occurred to me. If the dead are getting up and walking, there's a fair chance that you might rise and attack whoever finds your body. When I'm done with you, of course. After I've finished."

He swayed like a cobra, music she could not hear ululating in his ears. His lips were open; there were twin white dabs of spit at the sides of his mouth. The skin of his cheeks flushed red, as if he was embarrassed. Or aroused.

Sally prayed for a miracle. She wished that Rick would arrive back home, tired and drained from the night's exertions, but still able to save her. Save her from the pain and degradation this abomination of a man must surely have been planning to put her through for such a long time.

As Daryl danced towards her, a silver flash in his hand and dark deeds in his heart, the last thing Sally thought of was her wedding day, and Rick's beautiful face dropping from the sky to engulf her own, lips parted, eyes on fire, teeth as white and as filled with promise as the years she'd always thought would stretch ahead of them.

The night opened before her like a series of gigantic black doorways; the apartment vanished, consumed by limitless darkness. A dull roaring sound filled the universe, and in every nook and cranny, every ditch and hidey-hole, each ancient, forgotten corner of the country, nameless and faceless creatures began to feed...

CHAPTER ELEVEN

...SUNDERLAND, A SMALL terraced cottage. A middle-aged woman named Beth Hardy readies herself for bed. Heavy winter nightdress, thick knee-length socks, a hot mug of cocoa. Climbing into bed, she hears a sound outside her bedroom window. It is late. She suffers from terrible insomnia. Who can be out and about at this hour?

Beth puts her cup down on the cluttered bedside cabinet, beside a James Patterson novel. She slips out from beneath the duvet and crosses the room to the window. Her late husband's watch, key ring and old-fashioned hairbrushes rest upon the top of the dresser, a small shrine to the only man she has ever loved.

Smiling sadly, an ache in her chest, she leans across the dresser and opens the curtains.

The face she sees looking in at her is at once familiar and totally alien. It *looks* like her late husband, has the same salt-and-pepper hair, squat American nose (he was born in Texas; his family crossed the pond to England when he was eleven), sad, almost mournful grey eyes, grizzled beard on his blunt chin, but surely it cannot be Norm? The man has been dead for nearly a year, after his heart failed during a midnight visit to the lavatory.

The Norm-thing shifts an inch to the left, the movement enough to break the spell and allow Beth to acknowledge the signs of decay. His cheeks have fallen into his face, those sombre eyes are dried out and sightless, the nose she once loved has been partially eaten away. The salt-and-pepper hair looks more like dust-and-cobwebs.

Beth knows that she should scream; can feel the response building in her throat, travelling up from her gut. But she does not make a sound. Instead she walks through into the living room, and stands before the front door. She listens, her ears alert to the shuffling sound as the Norm-thing traces a familiar route to the doorstep.

For years, her friends had warned her of his gallivanting ways, his dirty stop-out nature, but in the end, like clockwork, he always returned to her bed. No matter which whore he had on the go behind her back, she was always the one he came back to, cap in hand, dick in pants, an apology on his clever tongue.

Beth pauses before opening the door, and then flings it open to greet her dead husband. The Norm-thing, hung in rags and stinking of grave dirt, leans in for one last kiss...

...BIRMINGHAM, A RUN-DOWN sink estate. Danny Blake stands on a street corner, needing a fix. He doesn't care what he ends up with; he just wants something to ease the tension, remove the sights and sounds of the shit hitting the fan. He knows that it isn't exactly safe here, on this lonely corner, but none of his usual contacts can be reached.

He needs to find someone quickly; anyone with a deal to be made.

Becka moaned and griped when he took the food money, but the baby could always suck her tit if it got too hungry. Sure, it was a bit old for that, but when needs must...

A sound startles him. Shuffling footsteps. A can being kicked into the gutter. None of the lights in this grimy street are working; darkness sits heavy across his shoulders like a football scarf, his nerve endings are on fire. He wishes he had enough for crack, but Becka has already been to the shops this week and spent some of the cash. The fucking bitch: always squandering his dole money, using it for shite that means nothing to him. She doesn't even care about his habit. All she wants is his cock twice a week, his fist once a month, and his hard cash whenever he manages to grub enough together to buy the brat a new pair of shoes.

Fuck them. Fuck them both. Shit is going on that he doesn't understand. Back at the house, the baby hasn't moved for over an hour, and all Becka seems to want to do is cry. He heard gunshots earlier, and screams. The mates he rang on his mobile all told him to stay inside and wait for things to cool down.

Fuck them, too. He needs a fix, so a fix is what he is going to have.

Just then a figure weaves around the corner, clutching its head. It's Ally, the dickhead from Sully Street who always has something in his pocket.

He takes a step towards the dealer, raising a hand in greeting. The stumbling figure bounces off the wall, cracking his elbow against the brickwork but not even flinching.

Danny takes an involuntary step back, away from the stinking bastard – God, he smells like dogshit, like a fucking open sewer.

You got anything, like?

His words fall flat; the dealer isn't playing. He twirls in a slow circle, still grabbing at the side of his head. Danny sees that there's blood there, in his hair: it's all matted, like burned candy floss. There's something seriously wrong with the daft cunt.

Shit.

No fix, unless he can take it by force. The tosser must be legless, or stoned on his own gear. Maybe the goings-on tonight have been too much for him, too.

Danny moves in, as swift as he can but not swift enough – clumsy, strung out, reeking of the sweat of withdrawal.

The dealer becomes aware of Danny's presence. Looks up, his eyes black as liquorice coins, the kind Danny used to eat all the time as a young boy, running through these streets as if they were the whole wide world.

Got any gear?

The dealer pitches forward, towards Danny, his arms outstretched. Too late, Danny sees the knife handle sticking out of the dealer's chest, right where the heart is. Then he remembers the rumours he heard in the pub last night, the story about Ally getting on the wrong side of some twat from Acocks Green and getting himself done over. Danny hadn't believed it at the time; Ally was one of them lucky buggers, the type who never seem to come off too badly, who always seem to avoid disaster.

Danny barely feels it when the teeth sink into his cheek. Only when the hands come up to claw at his face, his throat, his chest, does he realise that this is not a bout of junkie delirium. Cunt! All he wanted was a fucking fix...

...BEDFORD, A SHELTERED refuge for homeless girls. Janice Smythe is sick of her job, sick of her life. These ungrateful young girls, the ones she works so hard to keep safe and secure and on the right side of the law, don't ever seem to realise how much she does for them.

Take tonight, for instance. Every twenty minutes or so someone bangs on the front door, making a racket. The police keep saying they are unable to attend because of civil unrest elsewhere in the town centre, but advise her to keep the doors locked, the windows shut. The girls are all in their rooms, listening to their ipods or chatting on their mobile phones, not even bothered that the neighbourhood has gone mad and the sirens outside always seem to be heading in the opposite direction.

So who's left to sort everything out, to ensure that things are kept under control? Muggins here, that's who! Bloody Muggins, the local doormat!

Entering the kitchen, she goes to check the basement door. One of the girls – she thinks it was Sophie – was down there earlier, storing some of her old belongings, and the girls never think to lock the door. The basement is a point of easy access; there's a row of small windows down there located at street level. Anyone could kick them in, bend down, and if they were small enough they might be able to squeeze through one of the gaps.

As expected, the door is wide open. A slight breeze wafts up the stairs, bringing with it the cloying aroma of mould. Janice hates the basement. It has always scared her. The earthy odour, the sense of being buried alive.

She closes the door, her hands shaking as she turns the key in the lock and then transfers the key to her pocket. Stupid girls: always thinking about themselves, or boys – never aware enough to consider the feelings of anyone else. She often wonders why she stays here, why she loves the girls so much.

Shrugging her narrow shoulders, Janice turns away from the basement door, a chill reaching up to caress her spine. She shivers.

The man who was standing behind her – who is now in fact standing right in front of her – doesn't move. He just stands there, expressionless, not even blinking.

Janice is suddenly cold.

She recalls:

The long days spent at Brighton Beach during her early childhood, growing up in Barnet, playing ball with the neighbour's kids; her mother's green housecoat, her dad's old Vespa moped, her sister's forearms, her first pet – a cat called Tony – and the way the wind sings in the eaves during a storm; the sound of rain on glass, a good tenor, cold dry cider, sausage and mash.

In an instantaneous flash of agonising insight, she knows that she will never experience these things, these blissful memories, again.

It has been a good life, of sorts, but also one stained with tragedy:

Her stillborn brother, dad's early death, her mother's stroke; the boyfriend who hung himself when he was eighteen, spoiling her for any other man; the bank robbery in Islington when she was punched in the face; the car crash the following summer, the rape, the abortion; the rotten flowers on her nightstand; the stinging nettles she fell into on holiday last year in Cornwall.

A good life, then – but also a bad one. A little bit of both, to balance things out, to make it like the lives of most other people.

She has nothing to regret; nothing to fear; nothing that important to leave behind. No impact on the world, and not much really to miss, apart from the girls.

The girls.

Who will take care of them after she is gone?

At least the man who will kill her has kind eyes, a nice white smile, nice cool hands...

PART TWO

The Heart Is A Hungry Hunter

I just can't get an angle
On this twisted love triangle

Human Remainders,
Nefandor

CHAPTER TWELVE

RICK STOOD IN the middle of the street and watched the flames as they reached towards the sky, his eyes dry from the heat and his face touched by a peculiar sensuous warmth. The kiddies' play park lay behind him, hidden by shadow; the light of the fire barely reached the footpath at the base of the high wall, the top of which he'd dropped down from as he left the park.

A small group of people stood watching the church burn. It was a new building, built to service one of the housing estates. Redbrick walls and geometric enclaves; a white plaster Saviour stuck to a black plastic cross; tasteful stained glass windows depicting not scenes from the Bible but simple pretty patterns.

Rick approached the conflagration, his hand straying to the holster on his belt. His boots crunched on broken glass. A few cars had been parked, crashed or abandoned at the roadside. The one closest to Rick contained a dead man who was slumped over the steering wheel, his hair a mess of coagulated blood and gore.

It had stopped snowing before it had even had a chance to begin in earnest. The air remained crisp and sharp but was not yet close to freezing.

A tall man in a shabby brown overcoat stood apart from the crowd, his hands in his pockets and a thin dog lead hanging from one wrist. He was about six feet tall but he stood with a slightly slumped posture, as if ashamed of his height. His brown hair was messy. Firelight shone on his intelligent face, creating dark hollows beneath his eyes.

"Quite a fire," said the man as Rick walked up to him. "It's the prettiest thing I've seen in days." His voice was on the verge of breaking.

"Why are they burning the church?" Rick glanced at the side of the man's sombre face, at his round cheeks and his unshaven neck. The man turned to face Rick, and for the first time he saw that there were tears in his eyes. Rick glanced at the dog lead, hanging as loose and pointless as a scarf from the man's clenched hand.

"These people no longer have need for churches. In case you haven't noticed, heaven is now full and closed for business until further notification." He flashed a grim half smile. "The dead are stranded here, with the rest of us." He blinked. His eyes shone with a terrible sick-house brightness.

"I see," said Rick, not really seeing at all. He was utterly unable to understand what was going on and why these things were happening. "So they've turned their back on God?"

The man shook his head, a rueful smile on his thin lips. "Oh, no. I think it's more a case of God turning his back on them. On *us*. All of us." He turned back to watch the capering yellow-gold fingers of the flames, his smile becoming a sad, strained expression, like a grimace of pain.

"What happened to your dog?" Rick wasn't sure why he asked the question. It was just something to say, a few empty words to fill the unearthly silence.

"My girlfriend ate him. She died earlier this evening, from a wound sustained when we were attacked by a dead man." Again that rueful, stillborn smile flashed across his weary features. "Then she came back and ate the dog. I had to kill her when she tried to eat me, too."

Once again, Rick was aware of the thin, wavering line between the absurd and the horrific. This entire situation was like a bad cosmic joke, a trick played by bored omnipotent entities making up some kind of awful game for their own eternal amusement.

Rick moved off as the man began to weep. He held the dog lead up to his face, his mouth, kissing it, smelling it. Then he dropped his head and let the battered leather lead fall to the ground, and walked away, shoulders slumped, feet dragging on the cracked asphalt. Rick wished him well, hoped that he found some kind of peace, that he survived.

He paused and watched the fire for a few more moments, and when the other onlookers began to drift away he headed back towards the car he'd seen earlier, the one with the dead man sprawled behind the wheel.

He surveyed the vehicle, noting that – as he'd first suspected – the keys were still lodged in the ignition. The windscreen was cracked, but hadn't shattered completely, and it would still be possible to see perfectly well through the glass. He only hoped that the engine wasn't damaged and there was still enough petrol in the tank to get him on his way.

Behind him, someone screamed. He took out his pistol and dropped into a crouch, scanning the streets and the shadowy, flame-licked houses. The scream did not come again. The people who'd been watching the fire had all gone elsewhere. He wondered if they had been the ones who'd set fire to the church, or if they'd simply turned up to watch it burn.

Holstering the Glock, he turned once more to the car. It was a small four-wheel drive, one of those nippy little Nissan jeeps favoured by hairdressers and young sporty types. He stepped over the rubble and grabbed the dead man by the shoulder, half expecting him to spring to life and attack. The dead man did not budge. As Rick pulled him into an upright position, he noticed the wounds in his skull. The entire top half of the dead man's head had been smashed in, the bone collapsing like egg shell to pierce the exposed brain matter.

He tilted the body and hefted it from the car. Straining, he then dragged the corpse a few feet away from the vehicle and shoved it into the gutter. He wiped his hands on his trouser legs, feeling that the blood of this night would never wash off. He was stained forever, destined to walk in a red shadow for the rest of his days – however long or short that might eventually prove to be.

Rick spotted a rag tucked into a map pocket in the driver's door. He took it out and cleaned most of the blood and matter off the steering wheel, dashboard and torn seat cover. Pausing for a moment to ensure that no one was sneaking up on him, perhaps a dead person drawn by the smell of blood, he then climbed into the car. He turned the key in the ignition and was almost overjoyed when it caught first time. The relief did not last long. He had other business to attend to.

The engine roared, healthy and eager to go. Looking at the dashboard, he saw that the tank was half full – more than enough to get him home and then a good way out of the city. All he need fear was the roads being blocked. He knew the area well enough to map out a route via the lesser known police rat-runs and backstreets, but when it came to leaving Leeds itself he expected to run into trouble on the motorway.

He pressed his foot down on the pedal, enjoying the sound of the engine as it soared. "Come on, my sweetie," he whispered, allowing a slight smile to twist his lips.

Then, not even bothering to indicate or check his mirrors, he screamed out into the road and set off for home, where he hoped that Sally was waiting for him, cowering behind locked doors and barred windows, or perhaps even hiding in a closet or the cramped section of storage space beneath the kitchen counter.

He knew that he'd taught her well. He had no doubt that Sally would do her best to maintain her own safety, and that she would have faith in him coming to get her as quickly as he could.

The roads were empty of traffic, but he passed the occasional figure as he sped towards the city centre. Some of those he saw were raging, waving their arms in the air in unfocused acts of aggression. Others were running, looking for hiding places. His sense of duty screamed at him to stop and help, to act like a police officer and do what he could. But then, with the unbidden intensity of a religious vision, he saw Sally's face: her open lips, her wide, fearful eyes.

Rick drove on, fighting against his training, following instead his instincts towards the one he loved – the one he had always loved, and who had saved him from himself when he'd returned from a war he had never truly understood or entirely believed in.

He passed the smoking, burned-out carcasses of cars and vans, the blackened spidery-shapes of wrecked motorcycles. Houses burned, too, along with shops and places of business. It seemed that these insane events had inspired within the populace a latent love of fire. Like firebugs, they'd moved across the landscape, lighting things and watching them burn. When the novelty wore off they moved on; or perhaps they fell foul of roaming bands of the hungry dead.

Occasionally he was forced to take a different route, to circumnavigate fiery ruins or impassable pile-ups in the road. Once, while skirting a famously rough estate, he encountered a gang of youths who were, for some reason, in the process of stripping a vehicle down to its chassis. The car's owners sat on the kerb. They were naked and shivering, too terrified to get up and flee as two boys casually urinated on them, laughing and chiding one another into further acts of depravity.

A weeping woman stared at Rick as he passed, her eyes pleading. Her male companion stared at his feet, piss running down his face and neck to pool in the gutter. Resisting the urge to lean out of the window and start shooting, Rick kept moving. The youths hurled bricks and pieces of wood at the speeding Nissan.

He regretted not stopping to help those people for the rest of his life.

Rick witnessed the dead, too, moving like ghosts – or demons – through the strange fire-lit darkness to scavenge scraps of burned meat, plunder abandoned corpses, and chase down ill-hidden victims. A few of them stumbled like drunkards, their movements clumsy and uncoordinated. Others ran at speed, nimble and graceful, and displaying great strength and agility. Most fell between the two extremes, walking stiffly yet unhindered and searching the night for food. He noted the differences in posture, movement and physicality for future study: when he had the chance, he'd try to work out why the dead did not stick to one set of physical characteristics.

The journey was tricky but not impossible. Vast tracts of the city lay in darkness, while other areas remained brightly lit, if only by flames. His speed ranged from a slow crawl through debris-lined avenues to a foot-down sprint along wide, empty boulevards. He kept away from the inner ring road, expecting it to be blocked. As long as he remained focused, and kept his mind alert, he would make it home before daylight.

Sally beckoned to him like a needy ghost. He saw her standing on every street corner and crouching in every shadow. Her presence was a constant; her need was like a drug. The only thing on his mind was her safety. If he failed to get to her before anything happened, before their home came under attack from either the living or the dead...

"I'm coming," he muttered under his breath, barely aware of doing so. "I'm coming for you. I'll get there. I promise."

The canal sparkled like a ribbon of diseased body fluid, tracing a putrid course from the morgue slab to the drain. He stared straight ahead, his eyes picking out the apartment block against a black slab of sky. The lights were out, like a lot of the lights around the city.

He swung the Nissan into the parking area under the apartments, jumping out and running across the cold concrete surface towards the locked doors. He searched his pocket for his swipe card, and then barged into the building, drawing his gun and heading for the stairs. The doors clicked gently shut behind him.

Something made a soft thudding sound behind a closed door; a voice called out from the floor above; gentle sobs echoed along the hallway to his left, then abruptly ceased.

Isolated by a mostly ornamental channel branching off the main canal, the apartment was a relatively safe base. Away from the rough areas, set back from the main roads, it had always been a quiet retreat from the chaos of the city; yet the city began in earnest just opposite, across the canal, where office blocks towered over the narrow stretch of water.

If the apartment block had been situated a mile or so to the east or west, it might have come under attack. As it stood, the place seemed intact. There were no tell-tale signs of forced entry, nor could Rick smell smoke or – worse still – blood.

Rick moved up the stairs, remembering Hutch's messy demise. The memory hurt, just like most of his memories, and he pushed it aside for later. Shadows stirred ahead of him, curling strands and shuddering bulges of blackness. He turned the corner at the top of the stairs and continued upwards, climbing through the heart of the building.

Finally he stood on his and Sally's floor. The landing was empty, its perspective seeming weirdly telescopic in the darkness, making it look like a constricting throat. Rick blinked, shook his head to dispel the illusion. Then he walked slowly forward, heading for his own door.

His heart dropped like a stone when he saw the open door. His hands began to shake as they clutched the gun. He was suddenly unable to move any farther along the landing; his legs seized, the muscles turning to hardening slabs of concrete. He heard Hutch's dying breath hissing through shattered lips; he felt the blast of an explosive charge in the dry desert heat; he heard the firewatcher's voice as he spoke of God abandoning his people; and once again he watched the twitching corpses in the Dead Rooms as they got up and walked, attacking his unit.

"*Please*," he said, not really knowing who he said it to, just repeating the words, like a mantra. "*Please*."

Finally he was able to move. He forced his feet onward, sliding them across the tiles. They made a horrible whispering-swishing sound, like a knife blade slicing through the air.

Gun held out, he kicked the door all the way open, watching as it slammed against the wall, the handle leaving a dent in the plaster. Darkness forced its way out of the apartment, enveloping him. He smelled the coppery aroma of freshly spilled blood.

A whining sound came to his ears, startling him as it rose in pitch, and it took him several seconds to realise that it was coming from his own lips, his dried-out throat. He swallowed; the spit hurt on its way down his oesophagus.

Let her be okay. Let her be alive and waiting for me.

Clomping along the hall, feeling heavy and lacking any kind of grace in his movements, he rounded the sharp corner at the end of the entry passage. The living room beckoned like an opening fist. Darkness squatted like beasts in the corners. Reflected fire limned the edges of the window frames, turning them a shade of umber. Shadows inched along the floor towards him.

Sally was stretched out on the floor, face-up, her arms flat and her hands lying limp at her sides, as if she'd been laid out to rest in a peaceful position prior to a dignified funeral. She was wearing a pair of old blue jeans, faded at the knees, one of his ripped gym sweatshirts, and her feet were bare. There was blood on the floor, near her head. It looked black in the dim light, like a puddle of tar, or crude oil.

Rick felt the room tilt and spin, like a fairground fun ride. Nausea built within him, filling his gut with heavy bile. It rose slowly up his throat and edged into his mouth, finally bursting, hot and bitter, between his clenched teeth. The hot puke spattered and rolled down his chin, staining his clothing, but he ignored it. His eyes burned, his hand shook. The gun went off, puncturing the silence. He stared at the gun, at his finger still pressing down on the trigger. It took a substantial amount of mental effort to take his finger away and lower the gun.

There was no one else here: he could see that. The apartment was empty.

But for him. But for Sally, sweet dead Sally. Whoever had done this – whatever kind of opportunistic murderer had broken in and destroyed his life – was no longer present; only his or her workmanship remained.

His hand dropped to his side, still hanging onto the weapon. He would not let it go; its work was not yet done.

Moving across the room, he went to her, kneeling at her feet and caressing the cold skin, rubbing the hard nub of her ankle, his hands travelling slowly upward, towards her thighs, her waist, and her flat belly. He paused there, palm open across her tiny taut stomach, trying to summon some remnants of warmth through the frayed material of the old sweatshirt.

None came. So he moved on, running his fingers along the nape of her neck, gently stroking her chin... then, at last seeing what was left of her face, he stopped, unable to go on any further.

As Rick suspected when he'd first seen her body, Sally's death was not the result of a clumsy attack by the reanimated dead. No, human hands had been at work here, and they had done their worst.

The skin of her face had been inexpertly peeled away from the bone, laying bare swathes of smooth red muscle. Her nose was gone completely, sawn off with careless hands wielding an unsuitable blade. Her hair was bloody, hanging around this horror-mask in tatty crimson ropes. Her skull was flattened into an oval, mashed and elongated by the force of whatever blows had fallen onto her unprotected head; the bones had un-knitted and returned to their separate shards, like the soft, unformed skull of a newborn baby.

No bite marks. These wounds were thought out, orchestrated, despite being messily executed.

"Oh, God. What have they done?" His breast felt like it was filled with a thousand tiny metal balls; he found it difficult to breathe as they rattled around in his chest cavity.

His reluctant hand hovered over Sally's ruined face, her tattered features, a mile of open space concentrated into an inch of air between his sweaty palm and her brutally ravaged flesh. He held it there, shaking, as if trying to counteract an unimaginable weight. Then, soon, he began to realise that the hand was caught fast and he could not shift it. He struggled against whatever held it there, but the dead weight of Sally's passing was simply too much to resist.

So he waited. And eventually the weight lifted, moved on, allowing him to release his hand from the tender trap.

He wailed like an animal, raising his head to the ceiling, reaching out beyond the structure of the building and into the sky and the stars and towards the cold dead light of the white-faced moon. He saw that the moon was death, too: a stark dead world where nothing stirred, no life existed. He felt like he was sitting deep inside a crater on that world, ensconced within a hollow formed by his own grief, and if he did not attempt to move he might remain there forever, trapped in this perfect moment of absolute loss.

Sobbing now, Rick dragged Sally's body up onto the sofa. One hand still held the gun, so it was difficult to manoeuvre her lifeless form. He struggled, pushing and tugging and finally shifting her, pulling her on top of him as he collapsed onto the cushions. He sat there with her poor flensed face in his lap, the stripped lips pressing against his crotch. He stroked her matted hair, singing to her in a language no other human lips had ever formed, not once in the entire history of mankind's grieving.

Rick was no longer aware of the passage of time. He had no idea how long he sat there, cradling his wife's torn head. He stared at her candyfloss hair, then at the shiny gun; long moments spent examining each, trying to come to a decision. He put the barrel of the gun in his mouth, feeling it click against his teeth and rest on his tongue. Then he took it out again, setting it down on the cushion but not quite yet ready to let it go.

He raised his hand and put the gun in his mouth again. Took it out. Repeat. Pause. Then repeat.

Again.

He thought of the song that had been playing the night they'd first met, pumping out of the jukebox of a boozy little joint up in Newcastle: *Solitary Man* by Neil Diamond.

Again.

A Solitary Man: that's what he was now, all right. Solitary. Alone. Left behind.

Again.

He tried to recall the words to the song, but all he could think of was the rhythm of the music, the way it had become the smooth, calming heartbeat of the whole wide world as they'd danced to the song in the middle of that half-empty bar, no one else on the dance floor that wasn't even a dance floor at all, just a wide empty space near the back of the room. Dancing, together, for the first time...

Then, achieving some kind of final insight on that ratty two-seater sofa, Sally's dead head resting in his unresponsive lap, he carefully placed the tip of the shaking barrel against his wife's smashed skull, his quivering, bloodless finger resting heavily on the trigger.

The lights came on, shocking him and bathing everything inside the room in an almost unreal level of illumination. The television hissed static. Over on the dining table, Sally's laptop clicked loudly and emitted a single loud bleeping noise before once again falling silent.

Rick stared at the gun.

CHAPTER THIRTEEN

THE BUZZ WAS fading already, so soon after the kill.

Daryl walked along the garden path, heading back indoors to come down from the emotional high he'd experienced when he'd murdered Sally Nutman. After so long planning the kill, dreaming and fantasising about it, he had finally stepped off the edge and done it.

It had felt good. It had felt strange. It felt... what exactly did he feel now, after the fact? Initially, immediately after the white-heat pleasure of the kill, he'd been energised beyond belief, but now all he felt was a quickly receding warmth and the distant memory of something good.

It was strange how soon the thrill wore off; he could barely remember what it felt like to have her fresh blood on his hands.

He went inside the house and locked the door. Outside, during his journey back, he'd been more afraid than he had been on the outward leg of his little jaunt. Hiding from the slightest sound, edging stealthily through back gardens and along lonely back alleys, he'd felt the tension in the air like an impending scream: yells, gunshots, roaring engines. Police helicopters whirring overhead. Mad – or dead, or both – men and women running through the streets, all baying for blood.

Now, once again behind closed doors, he took a moment to steady himself. His mind was racing; the thoughts inside were vague, blurred and blood-red. Before tonight he'd been a trainee, an *inchoate* murderer, but now he had developed and was almost fully formed. His bloodlust had risen to the surface and he had acted upon it, crossing a line that had vanished as he'd landed the first blow.

The first blow of many.

Thinking back, it had been a clumsy kill. He knew from his reading that most first kills were indeed awkward, graceless affairs. He recalled smashing his fists repeatedly against Sally's surprisingly brittle skull, smashing it against the floor; hitting her so many times that the bone cracked and he felt his knuckles pressing into the soft areas beneath, almost kneading the brain matter like bread dough.

Then, tiring of the effort involved, he'd started in with the knife.

Her face had not come off easily. In fact, it had only come away in pieces. Beforehand, he'd imagined skilfully removing that face like a mask and carrying it off as a ghoulish souvenir – all the best serial killers left the scene with a memento of their deeds; it was *de rigueur* in murderous circles.

But things had not worked out as he'd planned.

Instead of peeling away from the bone like some overdone mud-pack beauty treatment, the skin had sliced away in ragged sections. By the time he was finished she looked terrible, and all he was left with was a handful of bloody strips. Still, he'd wrapped them in a rag and put them in his bag, hoping that once he had the chance to examine them the face might look better than he'd first thought.

Entering the kitchen, he placed his bag on the table. He opened it and took out the bloody rag. Then he carefully unwrapped his keepsake and laid out the separate segments of Sally's face on the smooth tabletop. It looked like a badly constructed jigsaw: there was part of a cheek, a jagged flap of nasal cartilage, two thin slivers that could possibly be lips. It was pathetic – embarrassing, really. He'd hoped for so much more than a few bits of tattered meat.

Daryl swept his hand across the table, scattering the remains of Sally's face. The scraps hit the floor, along with a china cup, a crumb-covered plate, and a few pieces of Mother's best cutlery.

"No! Fuck! *Fuck!*"

Anger swallowed him, opening its whale-like maw and taking him down whole. His vision speckled with bright little pinpoints, his lungs inflated, and he could barely even summon a scream. It lasted only a few moments, but the intensity of the episode terrified him. Never in his life had Daryl vented his rage in such a manner; he'd always swallowed it down, just like Mother had taught him. Real men, Mother had always said, never showed their emotions.

He bent down and picked up the separate parts of Sally's face, arranging them on the draining board. He handled each one with care, fingering them, and washed them all with cold water in a plastic colander. Once the blood was cleared away, the pieces of flesh looked unreal, like joke shop artefacts: bits and pieces of a failed monster mask that had fallen away from the dirty mould.

Daryl walked away, promising himself that next time he would do better. His second kill would be more professional, better thought out.

Despite the lengthy planning stage, when he'd finally straddled Sally Nutman, feeling her panic, tasting her terror, he had been carried away by her wonderful reaction and everything had happened much too fast.

Next time, he swore, he would take more time and savour the moment.

In the living room, he tried the television. The TV came on, but there was nothing being broadcast. All the channels were dead, apart from scrolling text informing viewers to keep tuned for further news regarding the 'disaster'. That was what they were calling it, then: a disaster. How prosaic.

He turned on the stereo and tuned it to a local station. The hiss of static almost obscured what was being broadcast, but he managed to make out a few words from the pre-recorded interviews, looped tapes advising viewers to stay indoors and banal guidance on making oneself safe in an emergency.

No one, it seemed, was ready to admit the tough reality of what was actually happening – that the dead were rising to attack the living. They were still too busy rambling on about terrorism, a possible virus, suspected chemical warfare...

"Christ," he said, rising from his chair. "Do you think we're all stupid? Stick your head out of the window and take a look at what's going on! Hell is walking the streets." He ran his hands through his hair, trying to rub away the tension. Killing Sally had not provoked the required effect. He was still fraught, still frazzled and edgy.

The radio static suddenly cleared enough that he could hear the programme against only a slight background hiss. He sat back down, rocking gently back and forth, and tried to focus on the voices.

"...and some Government sources are reporting a possible terrorist attack. It has even been hinted that the local water supply has been contaminated by a poisonous substance, sending people amok. Other sources have told us that the origin of the violence is chemical. A leading scientist, who refused to be named, told us that a virus has almost definitely infected the populace."

Daryl listened, amazed by the steady, calm voice of the presenter, the way she had managed to detach herself from the story. He wondered if she was still alive, or if she had become food for the marauding dead.

Another voice, this one male, possibly belonging to a politician: part of an interview conducted earlier that evening, when everything had started going crazy.

"The fact remains that people all over the country are turning inexplicably violent, killing their friends, neighbours and loved ones. There have been tentative reports of victims of these attacks getting up to exhibit their own violent behaviour. We will report any new information as we receive it, but in the meantime the police are recommending that everyone stay indoors and take precautions to secure their premises. Do not go outside. Do not answer your door, even to those you believe you know. Repeat: do not go outside; do not answer your door..."

Daryl got up and turned off the radio, feeling like he was floating across the room, suspended mere inches off the carpet. He stared at his hands, at the light pink stains that remained stubbornly on his fingers like an obscure artistic representation of his actions; then he curled those fingers into a tight fist and examined the torn knuckles. Part of him was angry that because of the media breakdown there would be no one to report his antics. Another part – the darkest part of his character – knew that there would be survivors, and they would speak of him as a legend, passing along his story around campfires for decades.

After a short while he climbed the stairs to Mother's room.

The upper storey of the house was in darkness, leaving her drowning in the shadows she loathed – a sea of shadows, all whispering her name. This at least gave Daryl something to smile about.

"Mother?" he entered her room, clutching the door and easing it open.

She was sprawled across the mattress at an angle, having tried to move off the bed. Perhaps the dark had terrified her so much that she had attempted to get away, or had she simply been looking for Daryl to comfort her when she suddenly awoke?

"Come on, Mother. We can't be having you hurting yourself, can we?" he levered her back into position. "That's my job."

Her eyes skittered open, the lids flickering like hummingbird wings, and then she squeezed them shut. Her face was paler than he'd ever seen; its texture was greasy, like cold bacon rind. She was obviously on her way out – even Daryl could see that. He doubted that she would even see morning.

"That's better now. Nice and comfy." He nipped her upper arm, just to gauge the response. Nothing. She was beyond pain, her body no more than a shell for her fading consciousness.

"I finally did it, Mother. After all that planning and dreaming and wondering, I killed her. You would've liked her, too. Such a pretty girl. She was so very lovely, like an old-time film star."

Mother offered no response.

"It was glorious, Mother. *Glorious*. But only for a short time. The rapture soon faded."

Rapture. God, what a perfect word. It described the feeling perfectly: almost religious, verging on the sublime.

"They all say – all the convicted killers and sociopaths – they say that your first time is the best, and then you go on to spend the rest of your life trying to repeat that first-time experience. If only it had lasted longer. I've almost forgotten how good it was. How... *rapturous*."

A soft gurgling sound, like a plughole draining away a sink full of water, emitted from Mother's throat. It lasted a long time. Constant, never faltering, not even fading. Then, abruptly, the sound stopped.

"Oh, Mother. Can't you just listen for once? That was always your fucking problem. Fuck-fuck-fucking problem. You would never just *listen* to me." His heart rate became intense. It felt like tiny fingers drumming against his ribs. "Too busy with the shouting and the hatred and the hurting. Always the hurting. Never the *listening*. Never the affection I always craved, especially as a child."

Daryl leaned over Mother, sniffing her. She smelled of old shit. He reached down and grabbed the sallow skin of her cheeks, splitting it like paper. Then, his entire body tensing, hardening, he spat in her eyes. Just once; it was enough to vent the poison.

"I blame you for everything, Mother. Everything. The bullying at school, the ill-judged sexual experiences, the lack of any sort of cohesion in my life. The 'morbid interest in death' – isn't that what Mr. Rogers, my English teacher, called it?"

And still Mother said nothing. Did nothing. Was nothing.

"All of it. It's even your fault that I killed poor Sally Nutman. I mean, what had she ever done to me? Or to you? Nothing. She was just a beautiful woman who reminded me that there was no real beauty in my own life."

He stepped back from the bed, disgusted with her, and with himself for allowing her to affect him even as she lay dying. She couldn't even find it in herself to respond. He wished that she *were* dead; and that she was alive; and that she were both dead *and* alive. He didn't even know what he wished, but surely he must wish something. Wasn't it human to crave, to covet, to hope for things?

But Daryl wasn't human. He was a misfit, an aberration. He had nothing to wish for.

No, that wasn't quite correct; he wished that he could kill Sally Nutman all over again, but this time do it better. Do it *right*. This way didn't make him feel special; it had failed to separate him from the herd. All he had done was copy what others had done before him.

There was nothing unique about simply killing a woman, or a man – even a child. It had all been done before, and better: every depravity had been essayed by another, written in blood upon the pages of terrible history books by those who'd gone before him through this library of despair, treading a path through previously uncharted rows so that others, like him, might follow and read and learn.

Where was the import in being a simple copycat? What horrors remained to be claimed as his own, dragged screaming by his hands from the bloody womb of nightmare?

He thought about what he'd seen that night: the drowned corpse trying to claw its way out of the canal, the dead people hunting for live meat. When he'd watched that bloated river-bound corpse pierced through the head by a short steel bar, he had felt that he was being told something and its meaning would only come to him much later, when least expected.

That obscure message felt at once within touching distance. If he reached out far enough, he could grab it and pull it towards him.

Think, man, think!

Then, in an instant of clarity, it came to him.

Every serial killer in history had done the same thing: acted out subtle variations on the theme of murder. What was the one act none of them had ever carried out – the single trick that only Daryl might be able to pull off? The one that would guarantee his longevity, despite the fact that society was going to Hell?

He smiled, bathing in the lurid light of revelation.

CHAPTER FOURTEEN

DARK ECHOES RELEASE *falling stopping hungry quiet rising faster light up bright white feelings gone hungry pain gone life none sound fury hungry room motion smell hungry sorrow need memory rick husband meat hungry*

CHAPTER FIFTEEN

RICK STARED AT the gun.

It was beautiful, a marvel of engineering. The barrel was sleek and glossy, the handle a perfect fit in his hand. The trigger felt like a promise of salvation beneath the calloused skin of his finger.

He could barely believe how quickly everything had come apart; the sheer speed at which the world had unravelled like a ball of string toyed with by a giant cat. Rick had never put much stock in God or the Devil, in angels or demons, but current events were causing him to re-evaluate his entire belief system. If the dead could walk, if society could break apart so easily, then what did that say about the delicate balance of the universe?

Tears poured down his face. He had stopped sobbing, but the pain remained, a physical ache clenched deep inside him. His chest was tight, his arms and legs were growing numb, and there was a hollow inside his body where his heart had been torn out by invisible claws.

"Sally," he muttered, realising that even her name was dead. "Don't leave me."

Then, amazingly – like the greatest miracle on this wide, green earth – her head stirred in his lap. Holding his breath, he glanced down at the back of her head. The skull was cracked; sticky brain matter hung out in bloated grey clumps. He'd failed to notice before that one of her ears had been torn off – the left one. He wondered where it was, and had to resist the urge to go looking for it.

Sally's head moved, twitching to the side. Her hands clutched at his thighs, the fingers gripping and releasing the legs of his trousers. Her movements were slow, mechanical. She was like a ruined machine powering up from a major breakdown.

"Sally?"

She twisted her head so that her ruined face was pointing into the room, facing away from him. There was blood in his crotch; his trousers were wet with it. But he didn't care. All that mattered was that Sally was coming back to him, reaching out across a black void to return to his side.

"Oh, baby. I need you."

An awful wet rasping sound began in her throat, like a loud death rattle. He heard blood bubbling at her lips. Carefully, he reached down and began to turn her head towards him; slowly, and with great care he handled her damaged cranium. The flensed cheeks and torn forehead were horrific to see, especially now that her eyes were open. One eyelid was missing; the other hung loose, dangling across the eye like a broken fleshy blind over a tiny window.

"Oh, Sally. Oh, God. Poor, poor baby. Rick'll make it better. I'll protect you this time, and make sure nobody ever hurts you again."

Her mouth ratcheted open, the movement shockingly fast. Blood caught in thin red strings between her jaws. The sound she made was like a yawn, but deeper, more resonant. It was ironic, he thought, because she was in fact coming round from the deepest sleep of all. Her right eye quivered in its socket, the pupil so pale that it was almost white. There was a ragged hole in her skinned cheek and her teeth showed through the moist red tatters.

Rick took her into his arms, wrapping her up in his love.

Sally's head craned round on her neck, moving slightly swifter yet still lacking co-ordination. Her teeth snapped on empty air near his throat. Rick pulled away, pressing his hands into the mush of her face, pushing her teeth back whilst keeping her cold body close.

"No, baby. Don't do that." He felt something snap inside his head; just a fine white pain, like a needle sliding into a gum or a particularly deep paper cut. Lightning flared momentarily behind his eyes. When it cleared he felt changed, altered; the world seemed different, filled with fresh promise.

He held Sally's head away from his throat, watching her teeth continue to clamp down on nothing. She was trying to chew. Her movements were spastic, out of whack. He remembered Hutch, half his head blown away on the concrete staircase, and when he came back from the dead it was as if he'd suffered brain damage. Glancing at Sally's shattered skull, at the grey slugs hanging out of the red-rimmed rents, he realised that she had not returned whole. Pieces of her had been left behind, huge chunks of her consciousness. She was like a child, a damaged and hungry child, and he would have to care for her.

A noise not unlike wordless singing came from her mouth: a fractured tune, the song of the damned.

Rick closed his eyes and tried to clear his head. If he thought too hard about any of this, it would drive him insane. Or perhaps he had already lost his mind, back in the Dead Rooms. Maybe he was still there, lying on the floor with his blood draining out, and these were his final thoughts before death – a weird phantasmagoria of love and loss and longing...

Easing Sally's head onto a cushion, he got up from the sofa. He took the gun and placed it back in its holster, knowing that he no longer required its bleak promise. He'd turned his back on the offer of smoke and darkness.

Sally squirmed on the cushions, unable to stand. She had forgotten even the most basic elements of locomotion. This was good, it would make her easier to control. He could handle her, exercising authority over even her most fundamental functions. He watched her for a short while, wondering if she might fall onto the floor and hurt herself. Then he remembered that she was dead, and the dead can no longer be hurt. Pain was for the living, but even they must put such physical discomfort behind them in this weird new world, this hideous reversed Eden.

There was a new world order forming, and only the strong would survive.

Rick went to the window and looked out at the sky. The promise of dawn hovered at the edge of the horizon, a long, thin band of light shimmering like a mirage in the distance. There was still a long way until daylight, but it was making its presence known. He wished that time would freeze and nothing would ever change again. It was all too much, he needed time and space to sort things through, to get it all straight in his head.

He sat down at the dining table and pressed the power button on Sally's laptop. The screen hovered in darkness, and then reluctantly stuttered into operational mode. Rick connected to the Internet. It took a long time for the connection to be established, and when the window finally opened up a gateway to cyberspace, the graphics had broken up into a clumsy pixellated mess.

Rick attempted to access a few websites: BBC, CNN, Sky News. None of them had been updated for some time. The headlines still comprised of reports of civil unrest, terrorist attacks, rapes and murders and looting in all the major cities of the world. By now things would have moved on. The survivors of the initial outbreaks would be trying to form groups, arming themselves, searching for food and water. Whole streets would be occupied by a civilian militia, areas shut down by gangs. The police would be helpless. There was too much to cope with and their limited resources would be stretched beyond their capabilities. The combined threat of walking corpses and roaming mobs would be too much for the authorities to deal with all at once.

Maybe this uncontrollable free-for-all could work in his favour. If the security forces were busy fighting, then he could move freely. He had his police warrant card, his weapons and riot gear. He even had a sturdy vehicle with which he could tackle potential barriers.

Things were never as hopeless as they seemed. It was a lesson he'd learned in army training and had served him well in all other areas of his life. There is always another plan, an alternative option. Never give up, never surrender. Keep going, keep fighting. Don't stop moving unless you are backed into a corner, and even then make sure you come out shooting.

Sally had slipped half off the sofa. Her arms were trapped beneath her body and her legs were kicking wildly, drumming on the floor. Rick crossed the room and lifted her back onto the cushions, placing her gently across the sofa. She seemed to calm down when he was nearby, but he was unsure if that was simply because she saw him as meat or if there remained a vestige of affection in her vandalised brain.

He'd always been a bit of a romantic but sentiment was something he could ill afford. He decided that Sally was merely responding to the proximity of his flesh rather than demonstrating any tenderness of the heart. The promise of food settled her down, made her rest easy.

He left her there and went through the cupboards, the shelves, the fridge. There were steaks in the freezer and he took them to the sink and ran the hot tap, trying to defrost the meat.

Sally groaned, whined, made other less recognisable sounds.

Rick hammered the frozen steaks on the draining board; he punched them against the walls. The meat began to soften, but only slightly. He carried it over to Sally and sat her up against some cushions, which he laid over the arm of the sofa.

Her mouth opened, the jaw shifting sideways in blind chewing motions. She made nasal grunts, throaty belches, and strange drawn-out wheezing gasps. Rick pressed one of the steaks against her tattered lips. It was bloody, the meat growing softer in his hands. Sally bit down, tried to chew. Her teeth went right through the partially frozen meat, slicing into it with a power and strength that disturbed him. He remembered Babyface and the dead man who'd sheared off the rookie's boot end. Despite their apparent weaknesses, it seemed that these dead cannibals possessed an amazing strength in their jaws, as if all their remaining energy was focused there.

Keeping his fingers away from her mouth, Rick awkwardly pushed the food between her lips. Suddenly, as if realising the meat was no good,

Sally began to gag. She regurgitated the still-frozen flesh; shredded strips dropped from her mouth and stuck to her clothes.

"Eat it, Sally. Come on. Eat it up."

She spat out the meat, turning her head to one side. His fingers brushed against her wounds, and he drew his hand away, dropping the rest of the steak onto the floor. Apparently it was no substitute for warm flesh.

He returned to the kitchen and opened a drawer beneath the sink. Dragging things out and scattering them across the floor, he found the first aid box Sally always kept well stocked in case of emergencies. He opened the plastic box and took out all the bandages he could find, and then returned to his dead wife. She sat on sofa and swayed like a drunkard, her neck barely supporting the weight of her head. Her fingers flexed in her lap and her muscles were out of control, tensing and relaxing as if an electrical charge was being passed through her body.

Ensuring that he kept away from her slow-snapping jaws, Rick stuffed wads of cotton wool into Sally's mouth. He packed it tight, forcing her teeth apart and ramming it down her throat. When he was done, she was unable to close her mouth properly.

Then he began to wrap the bandages around her bloodied head. He smothered the damage, swaddling her head like that of an Egyptian mummy, ensuring that the bandages covered every inch of exposed, wounded flesh. The first layer absorbed the congealing blood quickly, red stains blooming and spreading and coming together to turn the wrappings into a patchy crimson mask.

Rick applied another layer, continuing to cover her head until the blood stopped appearing on the fresh white dressings. By the time he'd used up all the bandages, the bleeding seemed to have stopped. Sally's features were concealed; her head was a smooth white oval.

He returned to the kitchen and found some tea towels, which he tore into strips. These he wrapped tightly around her hands, giving the illusion that she might be a burns victim. It also served to protect him from her nails, which were long and sharp and could easily rend his skin if she became too excited.

He would need to procure more bandages, but that was something he could control, a normal problem well within his capabilities to solve. He wished for more banal tasks, rather than the outlandish chore of hiding his wife's condition from prying eyes.

This might just work, he thought. *If I'm careful. If I keep a cool head and stay away from trouble.*

Sally was now at rest. Her padded hands rested in her lap and her large white head nodded, as if she had a tune running through her mind. If indeed there was enough of a mind for a tune to pass through. Rick doubted there was; the truth of it was that she was an animal now, a simple thing of hunger and blind instinct. Yet still, despite all this, he loved her. He had always loved her; and he would continue to love her until his own life was over, and possibly even beyond.

Rick sat next to his dead wife, one arm hanging loosely around her shoulders. He stared at the side of her head, at the bandages wound tightly around her skull. There was a perverse beauty to this; she possessed a strange and almost erotic allure. His hand moved across the rough material of the dressings, his fingers tracing the smooth hollows of her eyes, the gentle outlines of her nose and lips. She did not breathe – she was dead, so why should she require oxygen? The chill of her skin made the bandages cold to the touch.

Rick leaned in and softly kissed her cheek. It felt odd, like a kind of blasphemy, but it also felt right. Love, he thought, illuminated even the darkest corners, picking out small pieces of hope amid the most devastating forms of destruction. If love did not exactly conquer all, then it was at least a damn good weapon to have on your side.

CHAPTER SIXTEEN

It is busy in the pub. No room to swing a twat, as Hutch might say. He's a charming man, that Hutch, always ready with a witty line to win over the ladies.

"My round, I think," Rick says, moving towards the bar. Bodies sway and press against him, their warmth passing through his shirt and into his already sweaty flesh. "I'll get them in – you lot stay where I can see you, so I don't have to come looking!" His words are drowned out in the clamour of music and voices.

Rick shoulders his way through the crowds, suddenly thirsty now that the bar is in sight. The black ribbon of the River Tyne twinkles through the huge picture windows, and Rick feels an odd mixture of extreme drunkenness and misty nostalgia. How can you be nostalgic about something you'd never even seen before now?

"Four cans of Red Stripe, please." He shouts the words at the barmaid, unable to take his eyes off her barely-clad torso. Another thing about Newcastle that has taken him aback: the barmaids all walk around with their flesh showing, without a care in the world.

The heavy-set girl turns to the chiller cabinet without saying a word. She hasn't even acknowledged his order, and Rick isn't completely sure if she is getting his drinks or serving someone else. She bends down, her short black skirt rising up to a level where he can clearly see her buttocks, then straightens up with four cans clasped between her forearms and that wonderful sweet-counter chest.

Rick pays the girl, takes the cans, and moves away from the rugby scrum at the bar area to find his friends.

They are standing by the door, enjoying the cool breeze that wafts off the narrow river. Hutch is chatting up some girl – a tiny blonde with big blue eyes. Micko and Jeffty are watching that afternoon's football highlights on a television screen high on the wall, beneath a gold-sprayed bicycle frame meant as some kind of post-modern decoration.

"Cheers, mate!" Hutch smiles as he snatches the drink from Rick's hand. He winks at Rick, then shuffles closer to him, the blonde girl in tow. "This is Kath. She's up from down south for a birthday bash. She seems to have lost her friends."

"Me and Sally," says the girl, swaying to whatever song is serving as background to the raised voices in the pub. Rick doesn't recognise the tune. He isn't very good with current chart music.

It is then that Rick notices the other girl, the one standing on the other side of the door. She is tall, athletic, and has the most amazing eyes he's ever seen. Cat eyes: long and narrow and slanted gently upwards.

He smiles. The girl – Sally, is that her name? – smiles coyly back.

Rick raises a hand; she raises hers in return, mirroring the gesture. Something passes between them, some unspoken truth, and his life is changed forever.

Rick and Hutch ditch the other two men, taking the girls to another, quieter pub. They walk along the bustling Quayside, laughing and joking and feeling like they have all the time in the world. Groups of revellers jostle past; football songs fill the air; women squeal their delight at simply being young and alive and in a place where they can follow their desires.

Rick likes the girl, Sally. They get along just fine. As they move along the bank of the river, they automatically hold hands. The four of them climb the stairs to a bar that overlooks the water. They drink cheap cocktails, sling foul-tasting shots down their necks, and touch each other in that tentative yet eager way potential lovers often do.

Hutch and Kath are soon ensconced in a corner, making a knot of their tongues. Rick shakes his head, knowing that Hutch has a girlfriend back at home and this can never be anything serious, anything that might possibly last longer than a single night and maybe the next morning. He glances at Sally, sensing something more between them than a potential one-night stand. He smells liquor and cigarettes, the heat in this bar presses in on him, making him stumble.

"Let's go outside for some fresh air," she says, taking his hand.

They walk for a while, then come to a pub doorway. She steps inside, beckons to him. He follows. The place is very small, a haunt for real ale drinkers and those who want a respite from the party-frenzy elsewhere along the Quayside. They drink beer that smells of stale farts and eat pretzels from a china bowl. Their hands touch often; Rick wishes it would go on forever.

"I love this song," she says, standing up from the stool at the bar and twirling in a slow circle. Her knee-length dress hovers around her thighs, a beautiful centrifuge. She skims across the bare wooden floor, shoulders shrugging in a comical dance move, mimes pulling him towards her with an invisible rope.

Rick is unable to resist. He likes the song, too, but he likes Sally even more. So they slow-dance to Solitary Man, *watched by drunken strangers. The pub empties before they even realise the evening is almost over. Still they dance, locked into an act that is so sexually charged the bouncer who comes in from outside is afraid to disturb them.*

"Please," whispers an anxious barman, standing at the edge of their passion, afraid to intrude upon such a rare moment. "I need to go home."

HE WOKE ON the floor, stretched out beneath the window. At first he could not remember where he was or what had happened, but the memories flooded back in as soon as he opened his eyes. Sally. Where was she?

He looked over at the sofa. She was still there, where he'd left her. The washing line he'd used to tie her arms and legs before he lay down to rest looked vaguely ridiculous; he could never understand why Sally had bought one coloured day-glo green. She'd grinned when she'd unpacked it from the shopping bag, holding it above her head and spinning around on her heels.

"Oh, very 'eighties!" She'd laughed, still spinning. "I couldn't resist."

She lay there now, her arms pinned to her sides and her legs laced together, unable to even move. Her head twitched occasionally, rising from the cushions as she attempted vainly to bite through the cotton wool and bandages. There was blood on the side of her head where it had seeped through the dressings. Not much, but enough to cause him concern. He would have to get more bandages before leaving the apartment.

Standing, he opened the blinds and peered out of the window. It was daylight, but drizzle hung in the air, darkening it to a subtle dusk. A burned-out car sat on the bank of the canal. Two young boys squatted on the ground. They were slowly tearing pieces off the remains that sat behind the wheel, stuffing the charred flesh into their mouths and chewing idly, staring across the canal like bored kids stuffing their faces in a McDonald's window seat.

Rick felt the proximity of madness. It leaned in towards him from all corners of the room, throwing its arms around him and sticking its tongue in his ear. His brain flexed, pulsing in response. He closed his eyes and turned away from the window, his hands fumbling with the blinds until they closed.

Bandages. He needed more bandages. Perhaps he'd find some elsewhere in the building, in a neighbour's place or cleaning cupboard along the landing. It was the first time he'd even considered the other people in the building. He wondered if they had all barricaded themselves inside their apartments, or if any of them had been foolish enough to venture outside.

"I need to get some stuff," he said, walking towards the sofa. "I won't be gone long. No one can get inside when I lock the door, and I'll have the key to let myself back in."

He was talking to a dead woman. The thought wasn't as crazy as it might seem. Yes, Sally was gone, deceased, but her body was still present, still capable of movement. He'd never believed in the soul anyway: that was so much religious bullshit. So what if she wasn't all there? He could pretend that she was simply damaged, a victim of a road accident or a sporting tragedy. If she'd been crippled or brain damaged, he'd still love her just as much and care for her as long as he was physically able. What was so different about this?

She was dead.

Yes, but she still moved and made sounds and tried to do things. Even if those things were frightening and... and *wrong*.

Dead. She's dead.

"Shut the fuck up," he told himself, leaning down to inspect the nylon washing line, checking that the knots would hold while he was away.

"Just a bit of light bondage," he said. Then he giggled. "We always did have an adventurous sex life, didn't we baby?" He giggled again, but this time it was shrill and difficult to control.

Sally wriggled under his hands, her cold limbs tensing. A muffled sound came from her throat; a low, soft gurgling that made him feel nauseous.

What if she's being sick? he thought. *What if she chokes?*

But she couldn't choke, not now. She was dead.

Dead but here, with him. Always.

"I won't be gone long." He caressed the bandaged side of her head with his open palm, feeling the chill through the bindings. "I promise."

Okay, sweetheart.

So now she was answering him. Great. Just another small step along the insanity highway, and another voice to add to the growing number already taking up residence inside his head.

I'll miss you.

He stood and went to the door, where he placed his forehead against the frame and tried to clear his mind of all thoughts but the immediate.

That was how it had to be now; he could focus only on what lay directly ahead. Everything else would have to be relegated to the back of his mind, where he could smother it in shadow.

If he accepted that his dead wife was sitting upright on the sofa, her head wrapped up in bandages, then he also had to embrace the fact that she was somehow speaking to him. Simple leaps of logic: but not any kind of logic that had even existed in the old world.

A strange ringing sound filled his ears, building from somewhere deep inside his skull. At first he thought it was a siren, perhaps an ambulance passing by out on the road, but after a few seconds he realised that it was simply the bright-breaking sound of insanity.

"Go away," he muttered. "Leave us in peace."

The sound intensified, building towards a crescendo, and then abruptly ceased. His ears felt numb, as if he'd taken a blow to the head. Was that it? Was he now officially mad?

He unlocked the door and peered around into the empty corridor. He craned his neck and looked both ways along the landing. There was blood on a closed door further along, on the opposite side of the corridor: a small red handprint near the tarnished brass handle. Rick paused and listened, but he could make out no sounds out there. Whoever had left that bloody print was either long gone or shut up inside the apartment.

His hand was moist as it gripped the door handle. His fingers ached. He pulled the door inwards and slipped out onto the landing. Nothing moved out there. One of the ceiling lights began to flicker, casting long shadows near the floor. He held his breath, straining to hear even the slightest sound, but none came to his ears.

Rick took out the Glock and held it with both hands wrapped around the butt. He licked his lips and stepped out into the corridor. Moving slowly, he began to head towards the stairs. He wasn't quite sure where to look for more bandages, but he figured he had to find them somewhere. In one of these rooms, on one of these floors, he was sure that there would be some sort of medical kit.

Just as he drew level with the door with the bloody handprint, he heard a slight sound, like the scuff of a heel or a gentle rapping of knuckles. He stopped, turned slowly, being careful not to make a sound himself. He backed up, the gun pointed at the door, until his back hit the wall behind him. Then he took a single step forward, away from the wall, just to create some space to manoeuvre.

The sound came again, louder this time. It was a footstep; it had to be.

There was someone on the other side of that door, and judging by the smudged blood they'd been injured – which meant that they were probably dead... or worse.

He raised the pistol, levelling it at where he guessed was around head height on an average male. He blew air out through his lips, deflating his lungs, and then held his breath. His finger tightened on the trigger, stroking rather than squeezing it at such close range... *Blam! Blam! Blam!* Three rapid shots, each one a killer.

He listened for the sound of a body slumping to the floor, but wasn't sure if the sound he did hear was anything of the sort. It could have been scuffling feet, or a heavy object being dropped onto the floor.

He put two more shots through the door, the second one blowing away the lock and handle. The door swung open a couple of inches. No light bled through the gap, only darkness, and the promise of horror.

Rick stepped forward, tensed and ready for either fight or flight. His training had kicked in: his senses opened up, taking in every tiny detail. He felt the slight breeze from an air vent above his head, heard the sighing of air through the grille; saw the shadow of a dead moth through the plastic light-fitting encasing the flickering bulb; tasted cordite from the gunshots; heard the hushed sound of someone's hand as it brushed against the inside of the door through which he'd just shot.

He was already letting off another round when the door swung open, but it was aimed too high. A small, thin child charged out of the apartment, his face twisted into a mask of rage and hunger and something so alien and ugly that it was completely unreadable.

The short body hit Rick at waist level, shoving him back against the wall. The kid was growling like a wildcat, white froth frosting his teeth and lips. Instinctively, Rick brought the gun down on the boy's head, delivering a glancing blow to the nape of the neck. The boy's feet slipped on the tiled floor and they both went down, with Rick on top. The boy's jaws snapped at Rick's face; cold spittle flecked his cheeks, getting in his eyes.

He groped for the boy's chin, grabbed it, and managed to push his head sideways, into the floor. The boy's flailing hand had grabbed the gun, and Rick wrestled with him to release it. He heard the kid's neck crack, felt his head swing loosely on the smashed vertebrae. The kid's jaws still clamped down, snatching at Rick's fingers as they slid from his chin.

"Fucker!" Rick brought up a knee and slammed it hard into the boy's chest. More bones fractured. There was a sickening crack as Rick's knee sunk down into the yielding torso, breaking right through the ribcage. He wrenched his gun hand free, dropped it and shoved the barrel of the Glock as hard as he could against the kid's eye. It sunk into the aqueous matter up to the trigger guard. Rick pulled the trigger without even pausing to think about what he was doing. The sound was deafening in the enclosed space, and left a ringing sound in his ears.

He was unable to look down at the boy as he climbed off the body. He could barely see through the tears as he turned away, rubbing his hands clean on his already-stained stab vest.

Stumbling, he moved to the apartment door and kicked it open. The hallway beyond was dark, with dust motes slow-dancing in the air. He moved along the hall with the gun held out, still focused despite the horror he'd just endured. He'd process all that later, when he could afford the luxury of trying to piece together what remained of his mind.

He found two bodies – or what was left of them – in the living room. Thankfully the curtains were closed, so he could see little of what had been done to them. A hand sat in a plant pot on an occasional table; the bloody wrist looked like it had been gnawed. The lower half of a leg was propped up against the television. The upper half of a face had been pressed against the wall, where it had adhered to the wallpaper like something dreamed up by a dead Damien Hirst.

Once again Rick felt laughter building up inside him. He bit down on it, aware that to release it would mark the start of something he did not have the strength to stop.

Rick went through the kitchen cupboards and found a large box filled with professional medical supplies. There were plenty of fresh, clean bandages, and even a couple of hypodermic syringes. He filled a pillow case from the bedroom with canned food and bottled water, and at the back of the fridge he found some glass vials marked as containing morphine. He knew a doctor lived on this floor, but had never been sure which apartment.

He kept his head turned away from what he guessed must be the nursery – the open door was decorated with childish stickers and a plaque bearing the words: *baby's room.* There was blood on the doorframe, and from the corner of his eye he could see a small red lump on the floor, its edges oddly flattened out across the laminated timber boards.

He put the morphine in his pocket and left the apartment. The kid's body was still there, where he'd left it. He put down the food and the bandages and grabbed hold of the kid's legs, dragging the corpse through the doorway and into the entrance passage. The head flopped freely, almost coming off altogether as he manhandled the body a few yards along the hallway, away from the door.

He gently closed the door, picked up his haul, and returned to his dead wife, blanking it all out, swallowing down the pain and the anguish and the hatred he felt for all of humanity.

FINALLY THEY MANAGE to *prise themselves apart, blinking like sleepers woken from a wonderful dream. Rick feels that something has been lost forever, but there is also the promise of so much more; a hopeful sense that the future has just opened up before him, and Sally is part of it, an essential element in all the days to come.*

Electricity sparks between them. The earth begins to alter its axis and slowly rotate around the point where they stand. The universe halts, making them its centre.

They are standing at the crux of something exquisite, an experience neither of them will ever recover from. The barman turns off the jukebox and they leave the pub, hand in hand, fused forever. That night is their first, and like all first nights it is imperfect – but it is at least the start of something perfect, and even then, at such an early stage, they both know it and cling to it and appreciate its worth.

CHAPTER SEVENTEEN

DARYL STOOD NAKED before the mirror, the washed and scrubbed pieces of Sally Nutman's face stuck with glue to his forehead and cheeks. He stared at the absurd partial mask, as yet unmoved. His penis was semi erect, twitching occasionally as he tried to focus his thoughts. He'd tried to masturbate, but could not sustain the energy required for completion. Sally's name was scrawled across his thin, hairless chest in thick black marker pen. His wiry arms were rigid – unlike his dick – and he was straining against something unseen.

It wasn't working. Nothing he tried made him feel any better, or any closer to the truth that he sought. This simply wasn't him, his identity. Perhaps if he tried something else, like a shopper trying on coats in a tailor's shop, he could pick the right direction for his desires.

He flicked and picked the meat from his face and turned away from the mirror, feeling foolish, as if he'd been observed in this undignified act. His skin was sticky with glue, the areas where he'd applied the solution beginning to itch.

The room was gloomy. Not much light could get through the narrow boards he'd hastily nailed across the windows. The back and front doors were protected, too. It had taken him ages to remove some internal doors to nail across the main ones. The back door was blocked permanently, but he'd managed to fashion something over the front door that acted like a medieval bar across a castle entrance. If he needed to get out of the house quickly, he could simply lift it and flee the premises.

Daryl went into the kitchen and glanced towards the cooker. Perhaps if he cooked the remains of Sally's face? Cannibalism might be his thing, if only he tried it. Would it be better pan fried or roasted in the oven like strips of chicken?

But no, the mere thought of such an act repulsed him. The idea of eating someone else's grubby flesh (however much he cleaned and prepared it beforehand) failed to appeal.

Just what kind of serial killer was he, if he lacked the stomach for the more extreme end of the spectrum? It was almost funny: a squeamish killer, put off by the thought of a little recreational anthropophagy...

Looking at the tiny exposed area of the kitchen window, he wondered what was going on out there. Clouds blocked the weak sun, light rain acting as a further filter to restrain the flimsy daylight. The electricity was still out, so he had been unable to receive any news from the outside world. Since last night's revelatory experience, he'd felt trapped inside Mother's house, like a zoo animal shut away from the public, a beast not fit to be seen. There were killers out there now, and they were just like him – or at least very similar. He should fit in perfectly well, if only he could break the final bonds that held him to Mother and step outside these ugly walls.

The long-held illusion that kept normal people from going crazy had been stripped back to reveal the bitter truth: that society was a sham and it was good to do what the fuck you wanted; take stuff, do things, hurt or even kill people. The ones who accepted this truth quickest would reign supreme. Everyone else was just cattle.

He looked up at the ceiling, trying to see beyond the cracked plaster. A spider web caught his eye, strung delicately between the light shade and its fitting. The web contained several dead flies, all balled up to be consumed at a later date. The powerful visual metaphor was not lost in him; he knew that he had to sit down to his own feast. But the Mother spider was holding him back; poised in her web, she still had influence over his behaviour.

"Bitch!" he slammed his hand down on the kitchen counter, ignoring the pain when he caught the edge of a knife left out God knew how many days before.

A dull thud came from upstairs, drawing his attention. He glanced once again upwards, narrowing his eyes, his skin tightening across his skinny muscles. A large black spider scuttled across the web, heading for an early dinner. Daryl smiled. "*Bon appetit.*"

The sound was repeated, louder this time, more insistent. Was Mother trying to climb out of bed again? He could not imagine where she might get the energy, or how she had summoned the strength to move even an inch across the sweaty mattress.

Anger flooded his senses, filling him up like steaming water poured into a bathtub. Everything he ever tried to do, every plan he made and each tiny step forward he took, she was there, preventing him from revealing his true self. Keeping him trapped.

He turned and left the room, heading for the stairs. Pausing at the foot of the stairs, he cocked his head and listened. It was now silent up there, as if she knew he was coming. Slowly, he placed his foot on the first stair, feeling yet again like a character in a film. All his life, at every important juncture, he'd felt exactly like a character following a script. The only time he'd felt real, less like a cipher, was when he'd murdered Sally Nutman.

The carpet was almost unbearably soft beneath his feet. He climbed, brushing his hands against the ugly wallpaper – he'd never liked Mother's taste; she made the entire house look like a funeral parlour. There had never been anything young or vital in this house. Even as a baby, she'd dressed him in Victorian style clothing and done his nursery out like a workhouse bunkroom, stifling him before he even developed into a person; cutting off his as yet unformed identity at source.

Shadows gathered at the top of the stairs, shifting across the landing. The curtains were all closed up there, keeping Mother in the dark – just as he'd been kept in the dark regarding his father's identity.

Up the stairs. Up, up, up we go; up the wooden hill to Bedfordshire. The silly children's rhyme repeated in his head, playing like a stuck record or a scratched CD. He could not stop it, and even that small fact began to annoy him.

"Mother," he whispered. "I'm coming, Mother."

He was reminded of times during his childhood when he'd been ill – or when she'd told him so many times he was ill that he began to exhibit symptoms. Stepping out onto the landing, crossing to the stairs, slowly moving down them: afraid of everything and of nothing that he could possibly name. Calling out for Mother, but she was praying in the kitchen, her bare knees on the cold floor, face raised to the ceiling, eyes awash with bitter tears.

She'd always ignored him on these occasions. Or been completely unaware that he was there, out of bed and desperate for contact. So he'd pour himself a glass of milk and return to bed, rejected and forlorn, listening to her fervent chanting as it rose up the stairwell and crawled into every corner of his small room.

"Oh, yes, I'm coming."

Suddenly he became aware of his erection, raising its engorged head when it was least welcome.

Where were you when I needed you?

At the top of the stairs, standing next to the huge vase packed with false flowers, he paused and took a breath. He slapped his disobedient penis, but this only served to make it harder, and sent shivers along its thickened length. The beginnings of an orgasm clutched at his lower abdomen, tightening around his balls like tiny fists.

He could no longer hear Mother. She had either given up or managed to make it out of bed. Either way, she would be exhausted. Outside, a distant siren wailed, rain began to stroke the windows, a dog barked three times before whining and falling abruptly silent. Another sound, like the roar of some injured animal, cut across all these other sounds, but he blocked it out, unwilling to even imagine its source.

Finally he walked towards the door to Mother's room, his hand reaching out to turn the handle. He pushed open the door, stepped inside, and closed it gently behind him.

"Mother. You've been a bad girl, and I must punish you." He tried to ignore the fluttering at his crotch; it felt like silken wings beating against his pubic bone.

A slow stirring; something hunched, something pained, something slouching out of the shadows at the far side of the room. It moved with a deliberation that at first kept him rooted to the spot, unable to look away.

"Mother?"

And then she was upon him, with no time for retreat and no room for error. Her hands clawed at his face, going for his eyes, and her jaws snap, snap, snapped like a mantrap. Her eyes were all white, no pupil; in death, they had turned back inside her skull. Blind, dead, hungry, she snorted like a pig in search of truffles, snuffling, sniffing for his blood, his fear, his meat.

Reflexively, Daryl threw up an arm and caught her in the face. Her grip relaxed for a moment, just enough for him to make some space for himself and ease backwards, evading her clutches. Her fingernails scraped along his upper arm, drawing white lines on the skin. He still sported an erection; it refused to dwindle, even under threat of being ravaged by a dead mouth.

He ran to the other side of the bed and faced her. She stood between him and the door, shoulders hunched, chest curved and unmoving, hands twisted into bestial talons. "Fuck, Mother." He was breathing heavily, unable to say much more.

His dead Mother began to ease around the bed, moving closer towards him, saliva dripping in a thick ribbon from her mouth. Her nightgown was torn; her withered left breast was showing through the rent in the heavy material. Her scrawny bird-like legs were bowed, incapable of adequately supporting even her slight weight.

The tumours that had grown inside her had wormed their way to the surface. They seemed the only living part of her, and they boiled and popped across the surface of her body, a mass of undead cells creating their own rules, exercising their individual hungers. One of them slid down her arm, across the back of her hand, and slopped onto the floor. It began to inch across the carpet like a fat red worm, still attached to her by thin thread-like veins.

"Oh, Jesus."

Mother seemed to react to the words. Always fanatically religious, the name of the Saviour triggered some kind of instinctive response in her back brain. Her head rolled on her neck; she opened her beak-like mouth and made a strange shrill hissing sound.

"*Jsssssssssssssssssssssssssssoo,*" she whined.

Daryl edged towards the foot of the bed, his foot coming down on the runaway tumour. It was hard and moist underfoot, and it popped like an egg when he brought all of his weight down upon it. Gagging, he forced himself to remain calm. In this grave new world, all the rules had changed: dead people were killers, cancers became sentient and serial killers were relegated to the bottom of the predatory pile.

"*Eeeh-eeh!*" said Mother, her jaws snapping on air. The sound they made – a hideous *click-snap* – was horrible in its intensity.

"Sweet Baby Jesus. Lord God Almighty. Hail Mary. The Holy Trinity." Daryl chanted the words, believing in them for the first time in his life – their power, the faith they represented, the undeniable beauty they conjured in that gloomy little room on a grubby little street in Leeds.

"*Eeeeeeeeeeeeeeeeeeeeeeeeeh!*" Mother bleated horribly, moving lightning-fast, click-snapping towards him just as he reached the window and halted. She hit him hard in the side, her sheer momentum carrying him and slamming him against the wall. His upraised arm smashed the window, letting in the cold, harsh night and the ice-cold rain to slap him across the face like an open palm.

"*Moth–*" Daryl scrabbled on the floor, trying to fend her off, but she somehow managed to remain on top, smothering him. Always smothering, even now, when she was dead.

Daryl struggled against her. She wasn't exactly strong, but certainly possessed more strength than when she'd been ill and bedridden, unable to even sit up without his help. Her legs kicked, finding no purchase against the floor, and her hands grasped at his face, his eyes. One of her fingers slipped between his lips and into his mouth. Daryl bit down; it was an instinctive reaction over which he had no real control. He felt his teeth sink into her thin flesh, grinding through the gristle and severing the bone. The finger came off in his mouth. He spat it out, vaguely disgusted.

And all the time, during this ridiculous attack, he was able to keep a part of himself at a distance from the action. He watched closely as he fought his dead Mother, noting how her flailing limbs moved without real purpose and her hideous jaws were the only part of her body to pose a genuine threat.

Still slightly detached, he managed to roll her off him, and he slid out from beneath her. He crawled quickly away on his knees, pulling himself to his feet using the bed frame for support. Then, turning, he looked for a weapon – anything would do, just to stop her.

Mother pulled herself across the floor, not even bothering to stand. Her jaws *click-snapped*; her eyes saw only food. Then, like some Chinese martial artist, she somehow flipped her body up so that she was resting on her haunches. She let out a strange strangled cry, like a dying bird, and then leapt towards him.

Daryl shifted to the side, throwing out an arm to grab something, anything, with which to hit her. His hand fell upon a familiar shape, an example of something Mother had kept at her side for most of her life.

Just as she fell upon him, Daryl's hand closed on the crucifix.

Mother's mouth clamped onto his arm, but for some reason – possibly the timing of her lunge – she gained no purchase and her teeth merely grazed the flesh, not even breaking it. Daryl brought the big metal cross between them, as if clutching it to his chest. Then, with a single sharp motion, he twisted his wrist and used the artefact to smash her in the face. Mother's teeth shattered, her body rocked backwards, and once again Daryl forced the crucifix into her face.

The sharp end of the vertical member went straight into her left eye, bursting the china-white eyeball and entering her brain. Mother froze instantly, as if someone had simply thrown a switch to cut off her power. Saliva dribbled from her mouth. Cloudy fluid oozed from the shattered eye socket and down her cheek.

Daryl stepped away from her corpse, fascinated as it toppled forward. Her cheek hit the wooden boards, the fragile bone breaking on impact. The crucifix remained where it was, sticking out of her face like a bad visual joke, an obscene pun he didn't quite get.

Daryl backed up until he hit the door to Mother's room. Then he slid down it, his legs giving way through sheer exhaustion rather than as the result of any recognisable emotion. He stared at Mother's corpse, entranced by the sight of her ruined features. Her clothes seemed to be moving on her body, rippling, as if they were alive. Then, horrified, Daryl realised what was causing the effect.

The tumours that had been growing inside her for so long were attempting to escape their cold host. They burst to the surface of her papery flesh, ripping it and bulging out of the wounds. They looked like raw meat: fist-sized pieces of cheap steak that had gone bad.

Daryl watched as the tumours dropped to the floor, already withering and dying, rolling around as if they were small animals in search of a private place to die. They did not survive long outside of Mother's corpse. Separated from her essence, they became pointless, their parasitic *raison d'etre* now gone.

Daryl, on the other hand, would thrive now that she was gone. The old Daryl did not exist: in the blink of an eye, and the flash of a crucifix, he had been replaced by someone else, a being who would rejoice in the chaos around him and make it his own.

And this brand new being had witnessed such *rapturous* sights, things that the old Daryl could not have imagined, even in his most intense moments of fantasy. Because the old Daryl was dead: he was dead and born again through the destruction of this woman, this monster... this twice-dead Mother.

CHAPTER EIGHTEEN

RICK FILLED THE hypodermic with the morphine he'd scavenged from the doctor's apartment. He wasn't quite sure of the correct technique involved, but was certain that it wouldn't matter if he got it wrong. Sally was dead, so he doubted that a mistake, or the wrong dosage, would cause her much pain.

She'd become restless since his return, as if something had disturbed her. *Hungry*, he thought. *She's probably hungry.* He tried not to think of the human remains he'd seen earlier, pretending that Sally wanted a burger, or a pizza from the local takeaway. He recalled the way she'd refused the frozen steaks...

It had taken him quite some time to remove the dirty dressings, clean up the congealing crimson mess of her skinned face, and then apply a layer of kitchen cellophane before putting on the new bandages. But he didn't mind. It was his job; the job of a husband and lover; the job of a true friend.

"This won't hurt," he told her, smiling. "Not really. Just a bit of discomfort, then you'll feel a bit sleepy." He hoped that was true. During his time in the Paras, and then again in police training, he'd seen the effects of morphine and other painkillers on human beings. But those subjects had been alive; this one was dead. What would the morphine do to dead tissue? Would it even work?

Sleepy? Can we make spoons?

"No. No, we can't." He flicked the syringe, looking for air bubbles. Not that it mattered. He jammed the plastic hypodermic between his teeth, nervous of accidentally pricking himself in the face. Then, slowly but firmly, he braced Sally's arm and rolled up her sleeve. The flesh was already turning pale blue, the tell-tale hue of oxygen starvation. Haematomas had erupted along the length of her arm, discolouring it even further. Under her clothing, she was cold to the touch; her veins stood proud, the blood frozen in her system because the heart had ceased to beat.

Rick took the syringe between finger and thumb, lined up a particularly large vein... and then stopped. If the blood was not being pumped around her circulatory system, then how was the morphine meant to do its job? He knew enough to be aware that it worked by affecting certain receptors, a few of which were distributed in parts of the spinal cord. Most of them, however, were located in the brain.

The brain. It was the only part of these dead things' anatomy that seemed to work, however weirdly. He stared hard at Sally's freshly bandaged head, at the shallow pits where her eyes would be.

"I'm sorry," he said, his voice dropping an octave.

Its okay, baby. I know you're just trying to protect me.

It was incredible how quickly he'd adjusted to her speaking to him in this way. He knew it wasn't real, that Sally could not really communicate and he was imagining her voice, but all the same... it helped, and made it easier to carry out the extreme acts necessary for survival.

I know you would never hurt me.

Without thinking, he diverted the needle to her right eye socket, slamming it in and depressing the plunger. With any luck, the massive dose of opiate would bypass the usual route and go straight to the brain, doing its job and sedating her while also shutting down whatever remained of her central nervous system.

For the first time he wondered why the young doctor across the way had kept morphine in his apartment, especially when he had kids on the premises. He was probably an addict; perhaps he got hooked on the stuff during his training, working impossible hours and surviving on hardly any sleep at all. Rick knew a lot of medics in the army who'd used drugs to get by, particularly when they were posted in high pressure locations – often it was a necessary evil, a way of being able to do your job in impossible situations.

Rick's drug of choice had always been alcohol. He craved a drink now, but forced himself to wait until this unpleasant task was done. Glancing over at the drinks cabinet, he fixated on the whisky bottle. Fifteen year-old Glenmorangie: a nice drop, bought for him as a gift by Sally.

The morphine seemed to be working. Sally was slumped sideways on the sofa, her body loose, and the tension had gone from her limbs.

Sleepy... so sleeeeeepy... time for beddy-bye.

She was docile, easily manoeuvred. Rick put away the drug kit and transferred it to his rucksack, which he'd taken out of the wardrobe earlier. Inside the bag were also the neighbour's medical kit (including the rest of the fresh bandages), toiletries, some ammo for the Glock, a map and compass, some Kendal mint cake and a few essential items from the cutlery drawer – a can opener, a spoon and a cork bottle-stopper he'd grabbed purely because it reminded him of their holiday in Greece the year before.

Rick left Sally on the sofa and retreated to the bedroom. He took off his clothes and laid them out on the bed, then went to the bathroom and took a shower. There was still enough hot water for him to remain under the jet until he felt at least partially cleansed.

After showering, he cleaned his teeth with Sally's toothbrush until his gums bled. The bristles were worn, but he imagined that they tasted of Sally. Tears ran down his cheeks. He refused to wipe them away. In the mirror, his face had become harder, leaner; the face of the killer he was trained to be. That face had always lurked beneath the face he wore every day, waiting for the slightest opportunity to surface and show itself to the world. It was a face that had felt the desert sun, the hot shower of blood, the grit of nearby explosions and gunshots. It was the ancient face of warfare, a dark countenance worn by so many before him and countless more warriors who would come marching after, battling their way through whatever kind of world was left behind.

In the bedroom, he opened the secret door at the back of the wardrobe. He was forced to remove all the clothes on hangers to gain access, but Sally would not need her blouses and dresses any more. He picked up a long overcoat she hardly ever wore and put it to one side. He would put it on her before they left the apartment.

Inside the hatch was an M16 assault rifle he'd managed to smuggle back from Afghanistan. There was also a second-hand gun, another Glock like the one he had in the holster on his belt. Boxes of ammunition for these two guns sat on a couple of shelves. Hanging on a hook was a large hunting knife, one edge serrated and the other smooth and scalpel-sharp. Fresh riot gear hung on a peg. He put on the clothing, enjoying the clean feel of it against his skin.

Rick took the guns, knife and ammo and returned to the living room. He wrapped the M16 in an old black dress Sally used as a dust sheet whenever she decorated, and put the other stuff in his rucksack. The bag was full now, but he still managed to squeeze in the whisky bottle and an old photograph of Sally, taken by a mutual friend, name now forgotten, when she and Rick had first become a couple.

Sitting on the floor, the rucksack between his knees, Rick sipped the whisky. It burned a path down his throat and heat bloomed in his stomach, making him feel that somewhere at the end of all this there was hope. He finished his drink and set the glass on the floor. Then, standing, he prepared to move Sally.

First he inspected the landing. It was clear; nothing had disturbed the silence since he'd shot the kid. He traced a route along the landing to the stairs, then descended the stairwell with his gun at the ready. He propped open the doors along his route, mindful that if he was carrying Sally's by now largely unresponsive body it might prove difficult to open them as he went.

Outside, he pulled the Nissan up to the front entrance, scanning the entire area for movement. He left the car doors open and made for the cover of the lobby. Pausing before re-entering the apartment block, he stared around him, taking in the seemingly tranquil atmosphere. Nothing moved, and there were no sounds other than that caused by the light sing-song motion of the canal. Even the birds had stopped singing.

Overhead, the sky was a vast dark canopy, covering the hell below. There were no planes up there, not even a light aircraft. The extent of the situation must be huge: it was impossible to prepare, to set out plans, for something as insane as this. He wondered again if, as had been suggested on the few news reports he'd managed to glimpse, terrorists were responsible, or if this was some kind of cosmic accident. Perhaps God had judged humanity as unfit to carry on, and instead of another cataclysmic rainfall he had simply decided to flood the earth with the dead.

It was clear now that anyone who died would return to attack the living, and that all they wanted was to eat. Humanity stripped down to an awful basic drive to consume. Take away the trappings and progress of evolution, the intellectual ground man has made up over the millennia, and all that remains is a brutish appetite. Beneath all that emotion, beyond love, hate and even fear, all you have left is hunger.

For years now, he thought, *we've been trained to become the ideal consumer. Now that's all we are. Mindless consumers, just not in the way they intended...*

Rick turned his back on the thought and entered the building. His finger was light on the trigger of the gun, but the triggers at his nerve-endings – the ones that really mattered – were all-too-ready to react and make him spring into action.

He made his way back up the gloomy, windowless stairwell, keeping an ear out for the telltale signs of anyone creeping around on any of the floors. All was silent; the other tenants were either dead, had hit the road in an attempt to escape the city, or were hiding indoors, afraid to even move.

Then: laughter. A soft, echoing chuckle that rose up the concrete throat of the stairwell. Rick stopped, turned around, and dropped to his knees, peering back down the way he'd come. The laughter did not come again, and after several agonising minutes he stood and climbed to his floor.

Sally looked as if she were asleep when he entered the apartment, her head on the cushions, arms lying straight down at her sides. Her white-covered hands were clenched, the fingers stiff as windblown twigs against her thighs.

Earlier, when he'd cleaned her up, he had slipped some running shoes on her feet and managed to get her to slide her arms into a heavy woollen cardigan. Now, he eased her upright so that her back was against the rear of the sofa, and clumsily manhandled her into the long overcoat he'd retrieved from the wardrobe along with his portable arsenal.

Sally moaned once, almost a word... a real word, not one that existed only inside his mind. Then, like a blissed-out crack-head, she lapsed into a deep silence. He slung her up and over his shoulder, into a fireman's lift. She was heartbreakingly light, not much more than a bag of bones. Her muscles were already beginning to waste away, hanging slack on the bone beneath. Rigor mortis would set in soon – maybe that was why some of the dead things moved so stiffly, their limbs seizing up hours after death. The state, he knew did not last long; and after it wore off, the arms and legs would move easier, but still they lacked co-ordination. Sally, her brain only partially functioning, would probably be incapable of independent movement: even without the morphine, her body would be as floppy and unresponsive as a rag doll. The drug was more for his peace of mind, a safety precaution in case the hunger that drove these things broke through and gave her away.

Rick could barely believe that he was about to try and pass off his dead wife as the victim of an accident. She certainly looked the part – no problem there; the disguise was realistic to a fault. But the psychological ramification of his idea, the damage already being done to his sanity, was surely immeasurable.

He carried Sally downstairs without incident. By the time he'd buckled her into the passenger seat of the little four-wheel-drive vehicle, the washed-out sun was already on the wane. Night was dominant in these dark days, as if what was happening to people was somehow reflected in the very cycle of the earth as it shuddered through a mockery of its usual routines.

Rick started the engine but did not drive away from the apartment block. He stared through the windscreen, at the sketchy twilight, and wondered if his slowly emerging plan could ever work. He had a vague idea that rural areas might be the safest places to hide, and he and Sally had rented a cottage up in North Yorkshire two summers before. He still knew the way, and they had always planned to return to the cottage. They had spent a two-week period there which had, in retrospect, been one of the happiest times of their lives.

The cottage was miles away from the nearest town, and hidden from the road by acres of fields and woodlands. It had taken them hours to find it, that first time. Every trip out to the shop, or to some local point of interest, held the fear that they'd get lost upon their return to the small stone cottage.

It was the best he could do, the only option he could think of. He hoped that no one else had gone there, and that the roads were passable. If they couldn't make it there, to that isolated potential refuge, then he was fresh out of ideas.

He glanced at Sally. She was still out cold, her head tilted against the headrest. A scrap of hair had crept through a fold in the bandages, and the sight of it almost killed him. Even now, like this, he loved her – but was it really her that he felt compassion towards, or some other woman who had taken her place? His wife was dead, and this slow-witted impostor was all he had.

Rick closed his eyes and turned away. He could not let himself dwell too long on such thoughts: that way lay madness, and probable destruction. He let his foot fall onto the accelerator and pulled away, the rear wheels skidding on a patch of gravel. Their old home shrank in the rearview mirror, turning into a small-scale replica of the place where they had lived. Like the rest of the world, it was becoming even smaller, dissolving into nothing more than a wan memory of what had once been and could never be again.

"I know exactly where we're going," he said, still not looking directly at Sally, "but I'm not sure if we'll ever get there." He watched her reflection in the darkening glass of the windscreen. She did not stir.

CHAPTER NINETEEN

Two-Time Killer.

No, too cheap and pulpy, like an old 1950s film noir.

The Man Who Killed Her Twice.

Ditto.

Daryl smiled as he packed his bag, amusing himself by imagining alternative titles for the TV-Movie-of-the-week that would never be made about his exploits. He knew that he should be shaken by what had happened with Mother; but, as usual, human emotions were beyond him, as if separated from his body by a plate glass window. He could see them capering around in the outside world, and even believe that others experienced them, but to him they belonged to an unknown culture he did not understand.

Instead, all he felt was... well, a bit *tired.*

He finished packing and went to the bedroom window, looking down into the drizzle-damp street. Only a few people had passed by since he'd despatched Mother, and they were either racing along in bashed-up vehicles or running on foot. Most of these latter were carrying weapons – garden tools, table legs, cricket or baseballs bats: anything they could get their hands on.

For now, the street was once again quiet and empty. The embers of dying fires were reflected in the sky, but there were no more sirens tearing through the evening air. Daryl remembered reading somewhere that society was always no more than four days away from absolute chaos. This was at least the second day; perhaps that estimate had been off by about forty-eight hours.

Daryl passed Mother's room on his way to the stairs. He paused outside the door, trying to feel something. His body felt like an empty canister; nothing stirred in there but the blood pumping through his veins. His mind, however, was a nest of vipers, a coiling mass of madness.

"Goodbye, Mother." He continued to the stairs and descended to the ground floor, where he headed straight for the front door. There was nothing left here – not a single thing to keep him or even to delay his journey. The only thing that mattered lay somewhere out there, in the gathering darkness: Sally, his first, his one true victim.

The absolute love of his life.

He had a rough plan to retrace his steps along the canal and see if the Nutmans were still at their apartment. He imagined that the husband might have committed suicide when he came home to find his new wife slain. That would make things so much easier. If, when he got back there, she had risen and was occupied feasting upon her husband's corpse, he could move in for a swift second kill. Or, better still, he could somehow incapacitate her and enjoy himself, making the second time last longer than his first stab at killing.

First stab. That was almost funny. And the perfect title for his imaginary biopic!

He reached the garden gate without incident, then heard a strange sound. He paused, listened, and identified it as the sound of eating. Standing beside the high line of privet bushes that separated Mother's property from next door, he remembered the neighbours and their earlier battle. They must have ordered out for food, and were now enjoying an open-air meal.

He smiled. Then crept softly to the end of the garden and turned right out of the gate, heading for the end of the street where he could access the canal.

At first he thought that someone was coughing, or more likely struggling to breathe. Then, as the sound became louder, whatever was making it drawing closer, he realised what it was. The noise was too muted and belching to be coming from a motorcycle, so he suspected that there was a moped heading his way, like the ones used by pizza delivery men.

Daryl ducked into some bushes and waited as the vehicle sputtered towards him, its rider bent over the handlebars and not wearing a helmet. Comically, there was a large white plastic container attached to the front of the moped, the words PIZZA YOU, PIZZA ME stencilled across it in bright red letters.

"You've got to be kidding. End of the world take-out food?" This whole situation just got funnier and funnier, as if the movie of Daryl's life were morphing from a low-budget horror movie into a knock-about farce.

He took a short crowbar from his bag and waited until the farting, belching machine drew level with him. Then he threw the crowbar as hard as he could, aiming for the front wheel. The projectile fell short of its target, hitting the asphalt road. But, absurdly, the ten-inch long piece of machined metal bounced when it made contact, flipped up and caught the rider on his knee. The bike swerved, the rider shocked and hurting, and then it went down, skidding into the gutter a few yards along the road.

Daryl ran out and reclaimed the crowbar. Then he jogged to where the young man was sprawled in the road, clutching his knee and trying not to scream yet still making an awful din. Glancing around, Daryl was all too aware that dead things might arrive at any moment. Bushes rustled. Someone – or some *thing* – began to wail. A metal gate screeched not far from where he was standing.

Acting quickly, Daryl headed immediately for the moped. He righted the small, unwieldy machine and climbed on. The engine was still running, so he simply slipped the clutch, revved it, and set off in the direction of the canal. He glanced once in the rearview mirror and saw the dazed young man sitting in the street, still holding onto his knee. Behind him, advancing at varying speeds, approached three dead people. One of them was a small child; the lower part of its face was crimson with whatever it had been feeding on prior to the idiot moped rider announcing himself with his pitiful cries.

"Pizza you, pizza me," said Daryl, unable to resist. It was a shame that such high humour was wasted without an audience.

When the man finally began to scream Daryl could not help but stop the moped. He kept the engine running and climbed off, turning to watch. The three dead people had already set upon the young man. He was flailing beneath their combined attentions. Two women – one fat, the other slender as a rake with either clothing or flesh hanging from her in strips – were busy disembowelling him, while the small child buried its face in his crotch.

Daryl watched for as long as he felt safe, then climbed back on the moped and set off. The last thing he'd seen was the dead child playing with the young man's head and the two women fighting lazily over a length of grey intestine. The fat one was winning by weight advantage alone.

This was going to be easy. Things had reached such a stage that Daryl could move unnoticed through the world, killing whoever he pleased. Like a virus moving through the bloodstream of a butchered body, the greater damage would mask his presence. It was every killer's dream come true: an avenue of hurt opening up before him, stretching ahead towards a distant blood-red horizon.

He pushed the little moped as hard as it would go, passing the occasional mutilated corpse in the road. Often he encountered the dead, reaching out for him as he passed them by, but no contact was ever made. Daryl was now untouchable. He had travelled so far away from humanity, and had become such a different beast, that he moved among them like a chill wind, slipping through their fingers and barely even registering in their vision.

A police car was parked on the corner of Whittington Road and Commonwealth Avenue, its doors flung open. The body of one officer hung out of the driver's side, his belly opened, ribs sticking out like accusatory fingers. He was stirring, trying to move, but the lower half of his body had been so ravaged that it would no longer respond to whatever was driving his brain. His mouth gaped, the jaws clicking from side to side like a feeding cow. His eyes were white, turned back in his head, and his useless hands grabbed at his ruptured abdomen, dragging out chunks of bloody meat and stuffing them between his teeth in a horrific act of auto-cannibalism.

The other officer was on the ground, not much left of him but bones. The flesh had been chewed away, and the ruin that was now trying to crawl across the road and join his partner in the nightmarish feast could barely move without more of it falling away.

Daryl rode on, feeling like he was journeying through a Hieronymus Bosch painting: scenarios of damnation plucked directly from Mother's Old Testament picture books unfolded around him. But whatever god walked here was one of blood and brimstone, a vengeful maniac, a self-unaware psychotic.

"You would have loved all this, Mother." Daryl threw back his head, the wind in his hair; the stench of death was in his nostrils. "It's all your warnings come true, your dreams become reality."

He dropped down onto the familiar canal towpath, guiding the moped along the rutted route much used by weekend walkers and mountain bikers. He heard splashing sounds in the water but did not glance away from the track. He had to be careful. If he fell and was injured, he might die alone here... and to die meant that he would rise again, hungry for human flesh and with no memories of how to do anything but search for food.

When he reached the apartment block he had a gut feeling that he'd already missed them. His initial thought was that Sally had killed her husband, but then another idea struck him. What if the man had not even found her, and she was roaming the area for prey?

He parked the moped and ran into the building through the unlocked main entrance, ready to bolt if anyone approached from behind the closed apartment doors. He heard somebody weeping, saw a discarded child's doll in a corner, smelled the bland aroma of gas – the result of some poor bastard putting their head in the oven or gassing their children as they slept. He wondered, if he kicked down a few of these doors, would he find behind one of them a family curled up together like sleeping animals, their faces blue and elongated, their knuckles white as they'd clutched each other in their death throes?

To Daryl, the whole idea of suicide had always seemed like an easy way out, an escape route that offered nothing but brief pain followed by infinite darkness. *And besides*, he thought, *if you topped yourself you might miss all the fun when all the idiots who claimed to care but never really did found you dead.*

The door to Sally's apartment was open. He knew the place was empty even before he stepped inside. The floor beside the sofa was littered with bloody bandages: they lay in a coiled heap, like the shed skin of an ugly snake. A lot of the kitchen drawers and cupboards were open, their contents spilled out onto the floor. Someone had packed in a hurry.

In the bedroom, behind the main door, a wardrobe hung open. The back wall of the wardrobe contained a wooden hatch, which was also ajar. Daryl reached out and pulled it fully open. He saw a couple of leather gun holsters and some empty ammunition boxes on a shelf, but nothing more.

"So," he said, impressed. "You think you can save her?" Shaking his head in the mirror on the dresser. "And I thought I was fucked up."

Daryl went through a chest of drawers, upending each drawer until he came to one containing women's undergarments. He ran his hands through her underwear, bringing up to his face sports briefs, thongs, lacy dress-up panties with see-through gussets: a cornucopia of knickers that sent him reeling back on his heels.

Raking with his fingers to the back of the drawer, he discovered an old threadbare pair of granny knickers with a stained crotch. *These*, he thought, *must be the pair she wears when she's on her period. Oh, God...* he held them up to his nose, inhaled, and took in the coppery scent that still clung stubbornly to the worn material.

Grabbing a second pair – blue, frilly, scanty – he retreated to the bed, where he lay down on his back and loosened his trousers. He was already hard, so began to stroke himself, wrapping the blue panties around his fist. The other pair – the stained, dark-gusseted period pants – he pressed against his nose, pushing his finger against them and into one nostril.

He tried hard enough, but was unable to climax. Even the scent of her blood didn't do it. He came close when he recalled cutting off her face, but the memory remained at a distance, too far away to engage with.

Disgusted with himself, Daryl stood and pulled up his trousers. He tossed the underwear into a corner, pretending that it did not exist.

He heard Mother's voice in his ear, her awful brittle laughter; then he felt her warm breath on his neck as she whispered to him that she was the only girl he would ever need and hers was the only true love he could know...

"No!" His voice hung in the air, a mockery of negation, a sad, wasted energy that even now seemed weak and inconsequential.

Blocking out the ancient memory, he left the room and surveyed the living area. The laptop was dead, the TV lifeless. The lights were out. The local electricity supply must have been interrupted, either by the dead or by vandals. If he was honest, the only difference between these two groups was the hunger... they were identical in every other way: mindless, moronic creatures with no real purpose to their existence. Only the *form* of their hunger differed.

He spotted on the coffee table, by the window, a pair of leather gloves. Slim, brown, obviously belonging to a woman: Sally's gloves. He strode over and picked them up, forced them onto his small hands. The fit was tight, but they were not uncomfortable. He stroked his cheek with her fingers, licked the end of her thumb. The old, faded leather smelled wonderful.

Daryl left the apartment and descended the hollow staircase. Outside, he climbed back on the moped and thought about where they might be heading. He glanced away from the city, along the new blacktop road that led towards the motorway. Lights flickered in the distance, beyond the trees. He glanced at his hands, wrapped up tight in Sally's gloves. He imagined that they were still warm from her flesh.

Revving the small engine, he set off, certain that he had not seen Sally Nutman for the last time, and that their paths would eventually cross again. He did not know where this certainty originated, but he trusted it implicitly. If he was honest, there was little else to do now but follow his hunches. Who knew where they might lead, and what blood-filled adventures he might experience?

Once again, just to occupy his racing mind, he imagined the titles of the popular paperback volumes that would never be written about him: *Kill Me Again, Death in Double Doses, Murderer of the Living Dead...*

If anyone living had been around to hear it, the high, whooping sound of his laughter would certainly have chilled them to the core. This thought, when it came to him, just made him laugh all the more.

CHAPTER TWENTY

MOTION EMPTY DULL voice engine what how hunger hunger taste dry empty live not dead not something sweet dark inside forever hungry forever hungry pain release rage hunger hungry

CHAPTER TWENTY-ONE

"I'LL FIND A way to get you to safety." Rick barely believed his own words, and wondered if he was speaking them to soothe his fears or those he imagined for Sally. She sat beside him, her hands limp, the seatbelt forming a tight diagonal band across her stomach and chest, saying nothing.

"I promise you, honey. We'll get to safety somehow."

Darkness fell from the dusky sky, wide drapes lowering over the top of an open coffin, hiding from sight what had been laid to rest inside.

I know. I know you will.

He screwed shut his eyes, fighting against a force he didn't want to confront, and when he opened them again he saw lights in the distance. About a mile along the road, off the main route, tall lampposts were still shining. When he passed the signpost he realised what the lights represented: a service station. He glanced at the petrol indicator on the dashboard: still almost half full. *Or half empty*, he thought, *depending on your point of view.*

These days Rick was definitely a half empty kind of guy.

His hands gripped the steering wheel, his knuckles white, and he kept his eyes locked dead ahead. He'd seen no sign of life (or death, or any other state of existence) since leaving the apartment block behind, but he couldn't be sure that there wasn't some danger lurking at the side of the road, just waiting to pounce.

Anything that strayed into the road – be it human or otherwise – he was simply planning to mow down. There was a specialised impact bumper on the front end of the Nissan, and he fully intended to test it.

The clouds smothered the sky, breaking apart into rough-edged stains. The stars were nowhere to be seen, as if even they had given up the hope of illuminating mankind. Everything felt fragile, temporary, as if something was rapidly approaching an end.

Rick tensed when he heard gunshots. They didn't sound too close, but if he could hear them it was close enough to cause concern. Considering his passenger, he needed to be wary of everyone – especially some gun-toting broth-head who thought the best way to sort out this situation was by shooting anything and everything in sight.

The stark service station lights loomed closer. One of them flickered, but the rest remained constant, bathing the concrete forecourt in a harsh white glow that hurt Rick's eyes when he looked directly at it. He eased the Nissan off the main road and guided it onto the forecourt, checking the immediate area for signs of potential danger.

He drew level with the first petrol pump and switched off the engine. As he listened to the mechanism cooling, he strained to hear anything beyond the faint clicking. There was nothing, not even the song of night birds or the thrum of an overhead police helicopter. The world felt empty, a huge open space waiting to be filled with death.

"I won't be long," he said, opening the car door.

I won't go far.

He smiled, but the expression felt horrible as it spread across his face, like a badly healed scar opening up to infection.

Rick unlocked the petrol cap and slipped the nozzle into the slot. He pressed the lever, hoping for the best, and felt like cheering when he felt the hose tug against his grip as fuel poured into the tank. He remained stationary, scared to move his hand even a millimetre in case it stifled the flow of fuel – a silly, superstitious action, but nonetheless one to which he clung until the tank was full.

He gazed at the back of Sally's head through the window, inspecting the wrappings for signs of leakage. They looked fine, and when he pulled the fuel hose out of the tank he managed to drag his eyes away from her.

He was just about to climb back into the car when he was halted by the sight of the small shop attached to the service station. It was the kind of thing he saw every day, a small grocery store stocked with everyday provisions, ready-made sandwiches, vehicle maintenance accessories, and hot and cold drinks.

Rick shut the door and walked across the forecourt, Glock in hand, eyes skinned and expecting an assault. He reached the main entrance unmolested, and gently pushed open the glass door. A buzzer sounded somewhere deep inside the bright one-storey building, and he clenched his teeth in anticipation of sound and fury and bloodlust. None came. So he stepped into the shop.

Overhead fluorescent lights droned like insects; his feet slapped on the smooth tiled floor; the door whispered shut behind him, once again setting off that damned buzzer.

Rick paused, dropped below eye level, and waited.

Be ready for anything, he thought. *Any-fucking-thing.* It was something Hutch had often said during their army training; a lesson they'd both learned together but that only Rick was still alive to follow.

He could hear the low, maudlin murmuring of a refrigerator unit, and moved slowly towards it. He could do with stocking up on bottled water. In a few days the stuff would be worth more than gold. Unless someone had been here first and cleared the shelves, he could fill up any large bag he found with bottles and then get the hell out of there and back on the road. A few sandwiches would be good, too; maybe some chocolate bars.

Rick's mouth began to moisten at the thought. When had he last eaten?

The shelves around him were fully stocked: bread, a few canned goods, biscuits and family-packs of kettle chips. It looked like this place was so out of the way that it had been missed, or perhaps there were simply no looters in the area. At least not yet.

Places like this held a strange atmosphere when they were emptied of people. It was like the entire building was holding its breath, waiting for something to happen or someone to arrive. The effect was unnerving; it made Rick feel a strange mix of paranoia and vertigo, as if he were falling through miles of empty sky into a giant, silently waiting mouth.

Rick tried to recall if he'd noticed the service station before, but had no memory of it. He'd lived here for two years, so must have passed the station countless times without ever really noticing it. Like most of the trappings of modern life, he'd simply taken it for granted, not seeing it until he actually needed it, as if his desire had summoned it from the greyness of non-being and brought it forward to supply him with whatever he required. And wasn't that just the purest metaphor for a consumer society? The common magic of need.

Rick didn't even realise he'd heard the tiny sound until his gun hand twitched, drawn in its direction as if magnetised. It was followed by a low whisper, hushed words of warning to whoever had made the initial sound.

He moved along the narrow aisle, crouching, with both hands on the handle of the Glock.

The shuffling of feet on the polished floor; followed by a small voice, almost a stifled cry. Then silence, but not enough of it, and what little there was seemed haunted by the words already spoken, however quietly.

He saw them before he even reached the end of the aisle, folded into a corner next to the coffee machine. An old man and a young girl, reflected in the convex security mirror on the wall next to the lavatory door. Rick relaxed when he saw them, allowing the tension to leave his arm and the gun to drop a fraction.

"Listen to me," he said, trying to infuse his voice with authority. "I'm a police officer. I mean you no harm, but I *am* armed, so I'd strongly advise against any sudden or threatening moves."

In the mirror, the stunted image of the man wrapped his arms around the girl, who looked up into his face, her eyes wide and wet. Small freckled face; a question mark-shaped cluster of those freckles on her right cheek.

"I promise you that I do not want to hurt you. I repeat: I mean you no harm." He paused, allowing them time for the information to sink in.

"Okay. We're coming out. We're unarmed, and I have a little girl here – my granddaughter. She's... she's very scared."

Rick felt his body relax; he let out the breath he'd been holding. "I assure you, sir, I don't want to hurt anyone. Just step out where I can see you and we can talk."

The reflection nodded, and then stood awkwardly, as if the man's aging limbs were stiff. The two of them walked out from the end of the aisle, hand in hand. Their steps were small, tentative, and Rick lowered the gun to assure them once again that he was not an enemy.

The man raised a hand, a nervous half-smile on his lips.

"Hi," said Rick, standing and returning the Glock to its holster. "My name's Rick Nutman, and I'm just here to get some supplies."

The man shuffled forward, keeping himself between Rick and the girl. Rick admired that. It was a simple gesture, but one that told him a lot about the man's character.

"Is there anyone else here?" Rick nodded towards the back of the shop.

"No," said the old man. "I suspect the cashier legged it when things started to get weird. We found the door unlocked, so we came in for a while. Just getting supplies, the same as you."

His grin was a desperate lunge for approval.

"I'm Stan Rohmer, and this is my granddaughter Tabitha... Tabby." He walked forward, his hand now outstretched in an awkward greeting.

"Good to meet you," said Rick shaking the hand and smiling at the girl. She peered out from behind her grandfather's leg, yet to be convinced that it was safe to come out.

"We've been hiding out from... well; I assume you've seen them for yourself." Rohmer was a tall man. His limbs were rangy, almost gangly, and his back was bowed, giving him the appearance of being much shorter than he actually was.

"The dead people," said the girl, stepping out from behind Rohmer. "We're hiding from the dead folks."

"I've seen them," said Rick, once more crouching down, this time to meet the girl at her own level. "Hello, Tabby. I'm glad you found somewhere safe to hide."

"Oh, it was Granddad's idea. He's very clever."

Rick smiled. Rohmer laughed, ruffling the girl's reddish-brown hair with the palm of a long-fingered hand. His face was small, and he wore large black-framed glasses. He blinked as he spoke again: "I'm not that clever. If I was, we'd be far away from here."

"Where are you headed?" Rick moved to the drinks cabinet as he spoke, filling a sports bag he casually picked up from a display with bottles of water.

Rohmer began to fill a second bag without being asked. "Down to the canal. We... I have a boat."

Rick paused, turned to stare at the old man. His long grey hair was pulled back into a ponytail, and strands had come loose from the rubber band he'd used. Those huge eyes blinked. "Why are you telling me this? You don't even know me. I could be lying about not wanting to hurt anybody."

Rohmer placed a hand on Rick's arm. He did not pull away. His long fingers twitched like pale stick insects. "Listen," said the old man. "You have a car and I have a boat. We could help each other. You're armed, and presumably know how to look after yourself. I'm an old fuck trying to look after the only thing of worth left in his life." His eyes became larger, more desperate behind the comically thick lenses of his spectacles. He licked his lips.

Rick nodded. He glanced at the girl and nodded again. He and Sally had often discussed having children, and although neither of them had ever voiced an opinion, he knew for a fact that they both wanted a girl. "I'll help you," he said. "You and the child."

Tabby looked at him, her gaze bold and unflinching. "Thank you, mister."

They filled their bags and set them down by the door. Then they filled two more, and scoured the place for weapons. Rohmer found a baseball bat under the counter, and hefted it as he walked down the aisle towards the doors.

"Why can't anyone have a cricket bat these days? Have we all become so Americanised that the good old willow is no longer the home security implement of choice?"

Rick grinned. He was beginning to like the old man.

They stood at the entrance and stared out at the forecourt, checking the shadows for movement. The long grass at the side of the service station undulated in a breeze, the trees shivered, the overhead telephone wires seemed to spin.

"Who's that in the car?" Tabby tugged at his sleeve, her mouth dark with chocolate from the bar she'd opened as the two men filled the bags.

Shit. He'd neglected to tell them about Sally. "That's my wife." He spoke steadily, keeping his nerves under wraps. "She was injured earlier this evening – had her face burned in a fire when everything started going crazy. I'm trying to get her to safety."

Rohmer put down the bag he'd been holding and turned to face Rick. His face was solemn, unreadable. Did he know that Rick was lying? Had he seen through the deceit? "I'm sorry to ask you this, but... well, was she bitten?"

Rick frowned. "What do you mean, bitten?"

"By one of those things. The dead people." Tabby took a step back, moving away from him.

"No. No, she wasn't bitten."

"You sure?" Rohmer's grip tightened around the bat's handle. His arms were rigid.

"I'm absolutely positive." Rick's hand rested on the butt of the Glock.

"I'm sorry. I really am, but I've seen a grown man get bitten on the hand and die within half an hour. Then he came back... came back and killed his wife. Killed my daughter." His comedy eyes swelled, almost pressing against the thick lenses of his spectacles.

Suddenly Rick understood the depth of what these people had been through, and felt sorry for their loss, for everyone's loss.

"Anyone who dies comes back. If you're bitten you die – why wouldn't you? They're dead, and dead things carry infections. So, you get bitten, you die, you come back. Everybody comes back."

"Unless you chop off their head," said Tabby, at his side, once more feeling safe enough to stand close to him. Her hand slipped gently into his. Her mouth worked on another chocolate bar.

Rick nodded. "I know. I'm sorry. I..." he didn't know what else to say.

"I've seen so much over the last couple of days... so much horror. Dead bodies dragging themselves out of graves, murdered neighbours in turn murdering their own children, men and women I have known and loved eating the ones they knew and loved. We've entered dark times, son. Dark and insane times. Those of us left, the ones who survive... we're gonna have to rebuild it all, from the bottom up."

Rick reached out and laid a hand on Rohmer's shoulder. The old man looked at it as if it were something he no longer recognised. Then, slowly, with great affection and dignity, he placed his own hand over the top of it and nodded.

"My wife's hurt very badly. I'm keeping her on morphine, just to ease her pain. She isn't dying, but the burns were bad. I have them under control, but eventually she'll need proper medical care."

Rohmer squeezed Rick's hand. "Don't worry, son. I know of a place, somewhere we can get all the help we need. It's where we're heading."

Tabby wandered to the rear of the shop, picking sweets off the shelves. She was singing a simple tune, something Rick remembered from school but couldn't name.

"There's an island," said Rohmer, his eyes staring beyond Rick. "I know someone who works there. It's a mile or two off the northeast coast, not too far from the Scottish border – Northumberland. You know: Hadrian's Wall and all that? Off the coast between two little villages called Bamburgh and Seahouses, a place called the Farne Islands. The whole mass of islands is a bird sanctuary, with the inner islands and a few smaller islands scattered around them."

He paused, swallowed, and then continued.

"They're doing all kinds of experiments there. The last I heard from my friend was to warn me that something was happening, and if I could make my way to the island he'd take good care of me. Told me to bring along my family, my friends... the next day, all this happened. I realise now that he was warning me, but I was too slow to act."

Rick stared at the old man, hypnotised by his words.

"There's help there. I know there is. He even told me to try and bring along the bodies of anyone who died. I thought that was a crazy thing to say... at the time. But now I know better. Now I realise that they must be working on a cure, that they probably need test subjects to develop an antidote or something."

Rick could barely believe what he was being told. If this old man's friend had known about all this before it even happened, and then contacted Rohmer to warn him, what did that really mean? That this whole thing was man-made, or at least someone had prior knowledge?

"What are you saying? What exactly are you telling me here?"

Rohmer's head swayed, as if he were about to faint, but he managed to pull it together. "I'm saying that I think my friend knew that this was about to happen, and that he tried to warn me. I even suspect that he and his colleagues might be responsible for at least part of it. Maybe they were working on some kind of chemical weapon – that happened during the war, you know: scientists working in isolation to produce new weapons. Nerve gas. Poisons. Weird neurotoxins and compounds. It wasn't just the Germans who carried out unethical tests. I know because my friend was part of it."

Rick grabbed Rohmer's shoulders, shaking him. "How do you know? Who are you?"

Rohmer's trapped eyes glazed over; they shrunk behind the chunky lenses. "Me, I'm nobody. But my friend – he and I were lovers once, a long time ago. He worked for the government, on all kinds of things.

It's why I left him and married my wife, trying to lead a 'normal' life. I couldn't live with some of the things he told me he'd done in the name of progress. But we always kept in touch, all through these years, and finally he came through for me, only I was too fucking stupid to listen." Then he fell silent, his head drooping, hair coming loose from the ponytail.

"Granddad?" Tabby was back at their side, her face pale and terrified.

"It's okay, baby." Rick leaned down and picked her up, hugging her to his chest, stealing her warmth. "He'll be fine. We'll all be fine, when we get to this island of yours."

Tabby wrapped her arms around his neck, almost choking him. It was the closest thing to affection he'd experienced in days, and the shock of it sent him reeling.

Seahouses. The Farne Islands. He'd never heard of these places, but by God he'd find them. Even if it was the last thing he did. Even the slightest hope of a cure was enough to make him change his plans. He'd keep these people safe so that they could all travel there together, and when they reached Rohmer's unnamed island, everything would be better. It would be fine.

It was all going to work out okay.

Rick dropped Tabby to the floor, where she stood between him and Rohmer, holding one of their hands in each of hers. And as they watched, something truly magical happened: flowers of colour lit up the heavens, exploding in the darkness like a thousand tiny sparks of crystallised hope. Distant detonations peppered the night; the sky bled spots of fire.

Yes, thought Rick, *it really is going to work out okay.*

CHAPTER TWENTY-TWO

EYES OPEN SEE *nothing dark smell not hope food hunger promise stirring bang pretty sky bang imagine flowers loud colour memory opening heart soon gone bad head bang live smell hunger moving past present gone now end hunger*

PART THREE

True Love Ways

But I do love thee! And when I love thee not,
Chaos is come again

William Shakespeare,
Othello. Act iii. Sc. 3

CHAPTER TWENTY-THREE

DARYL FELT THEIR gaze upon him as soon as he entered the bar, crawling across his face and body like swarms of insects, picking at his clothing and trying to get underneath, under his skin.

"This is Daryl," said the girl... what was her name again?

"Who is he, Claire?"

Ah, yes, that was it: the lovely Claire.

"I just told you, he's called Daryl."

"I don't care about his name, I just wanna know who the fuck he is." An old woman stepped forward, away from the wall, where she'd been sitting on a pile of blankets.

"I'm no one," he said, at last. "Just another survivor, like you people."

A low murmur passed through the group of nine or ten people; most of them were nodding, and Daryl knew he'd said the right thing. After a lifetime of being verbally challenged, at last he seemed capable of saying the right thing, and at the right time.

"I said we'd help him, Rose," said Claire. She looked a lot like Sally, which was why Daryl had stopped to help her when he'd spotted her running along the road in her bare feet. She'd been trying to escape a group of youths, who'd decided it would be fun to rape her, and when she clambered onto the back of the moped Daryl had enjoyed the way her arms went around his waist and her chin pressed into his back.

"If you vouch for him, then I suppose I can't argue with that," said the old woman, retreating to her nest of blankets. "Just keep out of my way – both of ye!"

Claire grabbed his hand, her grip warm and tight. She possessed Sally's build, and had similar cat-like eyes. But her hair was short, and the wrong colour. Instead of Sally's ash-blonde bobbed style, this girl had a dull brown mop-top cut far too close to her skull and above her small ears. She wore clothes that Sally would never buy, too. Trendy rags Daryl wasn't taken with.

But she would do for now, until he could have the real thing. Then he would dispose of her, and enjoy doing so, but right now she was an adequate substitute.

"This way," said Claire, pulling him away from the others. They turned away, he had ceased to be of interest. "My stuff's over here." There were no lights on in the pub, but he could still see well enough to make his way behind her.

Just as they approached a booth near the back of the bar, there was the sound of gunfire outside, distant yet close enough to be heard clearly.

"Somebody's shooting," said a male voice. "Is it the police?"

"Will you look at this?" This was spoken by a woman, her voice rising with excitement. "Come here, Penny. Come and look at the loud colours in the sky."

A short, stocky Downs girl with her hair tied in bunches moved forward and approached the window. Her face reflected the fireworks outside and her eyes were filled with tears. "Beautiful," she said. "The loud colours are beautiful."

That phrase... it triggered something in Daryl's memory. When he was ten years old, Mother had taken him to the dentist to have a tooth removed. He'd been eating too many sweets, drinking too much fizzy pop. This was back in the days when dentists still used gas to knock out their patients, and Daryl recalled the stale rubbery smell of the mask as it was lowered onto his face, the way it had smothered the world with its cruel odour. Then, the gas: it smelled of rubber too, because, of course, it was odourless.

While he was under Daryl had a vivid dream, really a hallucination. He'd been sitting in a small wooden rowing boat, looking up at a bearded man dressed in a long white robe. The robed man was using a long paddle to push the boat through what looked like quite shallow water. But the water was black, and it was impossible to see what lay beneath it.

The man, Daryl had known instinctively, was Christ. But he was the Christ as pictured in Mother's picture books: tall, robust, serene, and very white. A picture-perfect Anglo-Saxon messiah, with clear blue eyes and a big white smile.

Daryl had looked around him, peering into the darkness that surrounded the boat. He noticed that they were sailing through an arched chamber, and before long he realised that the low, vaulted roof and ribbed walls were in fact the ribcage and vertebrae of a huge fish, or possibly a whale.

This strong caucasian Christ was steering them through the belly of a whale.

"Why am I here?" The question had seemed perfectly natural at the time; the right thing to ask.

Christ looked down at him, smiling that toothpaste ad smile, and spoke softly: "The loud colours will smell of the universe."

The phrase troubled him, and just as he was about to ask for clarification, he'd woken up in the dentist's chair, minus one back tooth. Daryl had experienced nightmares about the dream for weeks, and had wept in confusion, wondering what Christ had meant. He had not thought about it for years, but now he felt as if one of life's mysteries had been answered.

He moved to the window, with Claire at his side, and watched the impromptu firework display. At the edges of the city, in all the estates and suburban communities, people were letting off fireworks. They appeared in small pockets, ripping up the sky. Other areas answered with their own brief displays, like small signs of life amid all this marching death. Who knew where it had started, but it continued for quite some time, mystical and magnificent, a crude form of magic.

"Oh, God. Do you realise what day it is tomorrow?" Claire held his hand; her fingers were warm.

Everyone gathered around the windows, opening the shutters and staring out at the display.

"No," he said. "What day is it tomorrow?"

"It's November fifth: Bonfire Night."

Daryl smiled. "And that, of course, makes this Mischief Night." The irony was almost painful, and he saw it as yet another example of how comedy and tragedy were intrinsically linked, like two chords tied into an impossible knot.

Mischief Night.

Twenty-four hours before bonfire night, or Guy Fawkes, as it was more commonly known when Daryl was a boy; the evening when the youth of Yorkshire were expected to play pranks in the streets, egging cars and houses, letting down tyres, playing all manner of practical jokes and causing low-grade problems for their neighbours. It was a tradition, something he'd even feared as a boy.

"Oh," he said. "How fucking perfect."

All too soon the fireworks ended. People shuttered the windows, pulled the heavy drapes, and drifted back to their positions, none of them willing to speak and break the momentary spell.

A man was drinking at the bar; he was the only member of the group who had not watched the fireworks. His face was set into an expression of determination, as if he were insistent upon getting drunk. His hand rose and fell like a metronome, its rhythm compelling. Daryl watched the man for a while as Claire made up a bed on the long velvet-lined seat. The man's chin was covered in a thick layer of dark stubble and his eyes were darker still. He narrowed those eyes and glared at Daryl, then nodded once. Daryl nodded back before turning away.

"We can rest here," said Claire, settling down onto the cushions she'd piled up on the seat. She had on a short skirt which showed off her bare legs. Her feet were bare, too, and dirty from the road.

"Thanks," Daryl lay down next to her, unsure of how to act. He'd never had a girlfriend, had never even had a girl as a platonic friend. Females were strange to him; all he knew was Mother, and he knew just enough to gather that she was not typical of her gender.

Claire cuddled up close, her arm going around his waist; the other hand crept into his lap, where it rested like a contented house pet. "Where were you going when you saved me?"

Her use of the word 'saved' was weighted with significance, but he failed to understand what that meant. He was wary, yet at the same time her body was warm and soft, and he felt a new sensation stirring within him, a sense of closeness; a sort of heat that he had never before experienced.

"Mmm..." she murmured, burying her face in his side.

"I was just driving, looking for somewhere safe." He could barely form the words; his lips felt like rolls of rubber and his teeth had grown suddenly too big for his mouth. "What about you? How long have you been here, in this place?"

"We all sort of gathered here last night, when everything went wild. Tonight, I got caught out looking for supplies – we're running low on food – and I got separated from the others." Her hand spread out across his lap, teasing him erect.

Daryl shifted his body, trying to protect himself from her touch. This was all too much; it was way beyond his narrow understanding of human relationships. He felt more comfortable thinking about murder than he did sex. "I need to pee," he said, getting up and crossing the room, eyes searching for the bathroom.

"Over there," said the man at the bar, the heavy drinker, as Daryl passed his position.

Daryl headed for the bathroom, barged through the door, and leaned his back against it. He closed his eyes and counted to ten, willing his erection to go away. He thought about Sally's battered body, but that only aroused him more, so instead he thought about Mother and the prayers she had muttered every day of his life. The darkness in the bathroom pressed in on him, faces lunging out of its depths: Mother, Sally, Richard Nixon (of all people!)... Daryl gritted his teeth and wished them all away.

When he re-entered the main room, the drinker at the bar motioned him over. "Drink?" he raised a spare shot glass.

Daryl approached him, not yet willing to return to Claire. "Thanks," he said, reaching for the glass. The man grinned. His eyes shone, spit glistened on his brown-stained teeth. He was pissed.

Daryl sipped the clear fluid – was it vodka? The taste was awful, like strong medicine, but he enjoyed the way it burned his throat, cleansing it. "Cheers," he croaked.

"She's had them all," said the drinker, motioning his head towards Claire. "All the young blokes. She used to be a regular in here. I'd watch her chat 'em up, take 'em home, and then ignore 'em the next night in favour of some other stud." His eyes rolled in their sockets, dull and unfocused. "She'll show you a good time, mate. Give her one for me." He raised his glass, belched.

Daryl staggered away, back to the girl, her flat, lifeless eyes, her base lust, her small soft, breasts and the unknown wetness between her legs. She reached for him, her fingers like claws, and he could do nothing but succumb to her hunger. Her lips, when she pressed them against his mouth, were bland and moist and puffy; her hand grabbed at his cock, pawing him like a piece of meat. He thought of the dead things out there, the way they pulled bodies apart, and only then did his erection return.

She fucked him right there, under the thick blankets, with everyone ignoring the sounds they made in the musty darkness. Daryl allowed her to control it all, watching from afar, inspecting how she pushed him inside and rode him, her mouth open, eyes closed; the way she no doubt imagined that he was someone else – someone better – as she bucked against him and brought herself to a shuddering climax. Daryl had little to do with the act. It was all about Claire, *her* need, *her* desperation. He could have been a tree stump, or a fence post.

He rolled away from her, his cock still sticky. He wiped himself on the blanket and stared up at the ceiling. Someone laughed nearby, and when he glanced over at the bar, the drinker was watching, always watching, and he raised his glass in another of his mysterious silent toasts.

Give her one for me.

Daryl did not even know what that meant.

If this was what it took to be a man, to be human, then he did not want to know. He was better off remaining free of emotions, staying away from social and sexual intercourse, and killing those he felt drawn to. This girl, this cheap barroom slut, was nothing compared to Sally. She might possess a slight passing resemblance, but that was where it ended. Sally would never act this way. She was pure and graceful; even dead, she was better than this filth he'd rutted with on a low bench among strangers.

His mission was firm in his mind now; at least he could thank Claire for that. The initial repulsion he'd felt gave way to something akin to pity. He felt sorry that she was forced to live this way, and that she had never been given a direction in life. Bar to bar, stranger to stranger, she had been passed along like a shared cigarette. She had no idea what she was worth, yet in his eyes she was truly worthless.

Daryl watched her as she snored beside him. He snaked his arm around her neck, feeling her warmth. She snuggled up against him, turning her body slightly and raising one leg to slide it across his belly. He lay on his back and thanked her for showing him the true face of human relations, the grubby reality that skulked beneath the surface glitter he'd seen in films and on television.

Better to be a killer than a lover, he thought. *At least killers wake up alone in the morning.*

A solitary firework detonated far away, on the other side of the city, as if punctuating the thought.

CHAPTER TWENTY-FOUR

THEY STOOD LOOKING at the Nissan, each waiting for one of the others to speak. Tabby still held the two men's hands; she was the glue between them. Rick watched the dead man stumble out of the bushes, amazed that such a decayed corpse was still capable of motion. Bones showed through rents in clothing and flesh, and the hairless skull moved jerkily on the wasted muscles of the withered neck, as if it were a shoddy computer animation.

"It's a shambler," said Rohmer, taking a step towards the doors.

"What's that?" Rick stared at the man, thinking he'd probably lost his mind.

"Haven't you noticed there are different types? This one's a shambler. It's probably been dead for ages, and clawed its way out of the grave."

The barely mobile corpse continued its slow advance, shuffling in jittery half-steps towards the petrol pumps, and the jeep where Sally was still knocked out on morphine. She would be due another dose very soon, and Rick would rather not leave it until she began to stir.

"There are also two other main groups, or types." Rohmer was warming to his theme. "Runners are the freshly dead. They can move fast, almost as fast as us, but they are uncoordinated and easily confused."

Rick was impressed with the man's powers of observation. He'd noticed these things too, but had not given much thought to what they actually signified.

"Then," continued Rohmer, "we have the partials. These are the ones who return with some kind of brain damage. Either they've taken a knock to the skull, and the brain matter has suffered serious trauma, or they have actually had part of their brain destroyed. They move slowly, if at all, and act like severely retarded mental patients, the kind you see in old stills and movie reels from Victorian asylums. They remind me of lobotomy victims, all weak and clumsy and incapable of autonomous motion."

Rick glanced at Tabby, but the girl was occupied tying her shoelace. She'd apparently heard her granddad's theories before. "You've put a lot of thought into this, haven't you?"

Rohmer turned and looked into his eyes, not smiling; not now. "It wasn't by choice. I've see a lot of these things over the last twenty-four hours, and if you watch closely enough, certain patterns become apparent."

Rick swallowed; his throat was dry. He uncapped a bottle of water and took a sip. "What are you... what *were* you, before all this happened? You know, back in the real world." And wasn't that exactly how it felt? Like they'd left their own world behind and entered another realm, one filled with the dead?

"Oh, I used to be a lab technician, but I've always had an interest in anthropology. I read a lot, you know. Well, I used to read a lot. Hopefully I can do so again."

Rick didn't have an adequate response, so he left it at that. He glanced back over at the shambler, which had not got far. Its left leg was twisted around so that the foot faced almost backwards, and its right arm was not much more than bare bone.

Slowly, he opened the left hand door with his foot. Then he raised the Glock and waited until the thing gained a few more feet. The shot took off the top of its head, sending up a cloud of dried-out, decayed matter. The shambler began to weave on the spot, like a comedy drunk in an old film, and then simply tipped backwards, hitting the floor with a barely audible *whump*.

"Shall we?" Rick used his body to open the other door, and stepped aside for the others to follow him out of the building. The fireworks had stopped a little while ago and the sky was dark and silent. A few birds had returned to the trees, but their song was cautious, as if they were testing the air before committing fully to the nightly chorus. "The Farne Islands, you say?"

Rohmer smiled uneasily, as if he still wasn't quite sure he should be doing so. "Yes. It's a bird sanctuary. The island we need is more of an islet. It doesn't even have a name."

"Okay," said Rick, leading the way back to the jeep. "Let's get going." Tabby once again took his hand. For a moment, he felt like crying. Reality quivered at the edges, threatening to tear away and give him a glimpse of things as they really were, but then his gaze fell upon Sally, propped up in the front seat, and those edges repaired, the illusion holding. He squeezed the girl's hand, and they all made for the jeep.

Rick opened the back door and helped the girl inside, nodding at Rohmer, who glanced at Sally. "My wife," he said. "I'll have to give her more painkiller soon."

He eased behind the wheel and started the engine. He gave one last look around the service station, and then pulled away, the rear wheels spitting up loose stones in a tiny round of applause.

"Which way?" He kept his eyes on the road, conscious that if there was one dead person wandering around there could easily be more. From what he'd seen, they tended not to act in groups, yet seemed to mass together out of some vestige of racial instinct.

"Down to the canal," said Rohmer, from the back. His voice had changed, becoming slightly anxious. "I'll direct you, but we're going to a little place called Crow's Beak Corner. That's where my barge is tethered."

They continued for a while in silence, then Rohmer began to call out "left" or "right here." Rick concentrated on the road, his attention occasionally drawn by Sally, who stirred very little in the seat next to him. Once she moaned softly, but she didn't call out again.

"Here. Take this gravel road. It's a bit bumpy, but the vehicle should be able to handle it." Rohmer's hand rested on Rick's shoulder, and gave it a little squeeze.

Rick took the vehicle off the road, under some straggly trees, and followed the path the old man had indicated. The road itself was an unmade track, covered with loose gravel that became dirt after a few hundred yards. It led downwards, to the canal, and when they emerged from the undergrowth Rick's breath was taken away by the sight of the moonlight on black water.

He pulled up beside a short concrete jetty. The edges had long ago crumbled into the canal, exposing rusted steel reinforcement bars, but Rohmer's barge was exactly where he'd promised it would be.

"There she is. The *Queen Anne*. Named after my wife, God rest her soul." Rohmer's voice cracked on the last few words, as if it still caused him pain to speak of her. "It looks quiet. No one ever uses this place – they go to the better sites further along the water. But we always liked it here, under the trees, in the shade..."

"Okay," said Rick, trying to bring the man out of the past and into the potentially dangerous present. "You go and sort out the barge, and I'll dose up Sally with some more morphine."

"Is she all right? Your wife. She seems bad." Tabby's concern touched him more than he thought possible. He turned and faced the girl in the darkness of the car, hoping that she could at least see his smile.

"She'll be fine, thank you. Just needs some medicine. She's not quite given up yet." He blinked back tears, his eyes burning. His hand rested on the seat back. He wished someone – anyone – would hold it.

"Are you sure about this?" Rohmer leaned forward out of the shadows now gathered on the back seat like uninvited passengers. His face was rigid, his bug-eyes hard. "She doesn't seem too well."

Rick sighed. Everything felt so heavy – the weight of his responsibility to Sally, the expectations of these people, the night itself. "I promise you," he said. "If it comes to that, I'll do her myself. I have plenty of ammunition, and I'm not about to allow anything to put you and Tabby in danger." The lies tripped off his tongue, smooth as honey, cold as ice. He felt nothing but justified in his actions. She was his wife, and he loved her. Everything else was just dressing; ultimately pointless.

"Here," he said, handing Rohmer the second Glock, the one he'd picked up back at the apartment. "Just in case."

The old man stared at the gun before taking it.

"Just point it and squeeze the trigger." Rick nodded.

The old man held the gun away from his body, as if he were afraid of everything it represented. Then, glancing at Tabby, he slipped his fingers around the butt of the gun and swallowed hard.

Rick watched the old man and his granddaughter as they climbed slowly out of the car. He kept his window down, the barrel of his pistol pointed out into the darkness. The moon had emerged from behind the wispy clouds, and it lit their way, but anything could be hiding in the trees and the shadows.

Once the two of them were untying the boat from its moorings, and when he was sure that Rohmer was ready with the gun, he took the morphine from a pocket in his rucksack. He administered the dose once again through her eyeball. Even if he ruined her eyes, she would have no further use for them. What did it matter if she were blind and dead or just dead? As far as he was concerned, it mattered not one bit.

Sally's hands flapped in her lap, bandaged birds shifting in their uneasy dreams. He held them, clasping both, and waited for her to quieten down. "It's okay, baby. I've found somewhere to take you – a place where we might be able to make you better."

I know.

He stared at her covered face, imaging how it had looked before any of this happened. The more time moved on the less he could remember the finer details.

Just promise that you'll always love me.

He shut his eyes, lowered his head. For the briefest moment, there in the darkness of the car, he felt that he would never be able to raise it again. The weight of the world was pressing down on the back of his skull, threatening to break it.

Then, after what seemed like a thousand years contained within the blink of an eye, he opened his eyes and looked up and out of the open side window. The old man and the girl were standing there, watching him. Rohmer's hand was resting on Tabby's head, his fingers curled over her scalp. They both looked sad, tired, and afraid. Rohmer held the gun loosely in his free hand. He kept his fingers well away from the trigger.

"Tabby, come and help me unload the stuff. Your granddad can keep watch while we load the boat." He widened his eyes, asking a question.

Rohmer nodded and took his hand away from the child's tousle-haired head.

The water chortled as they worked, amused in its own mysterious way. Birds moved in the trees, but remained relatively silent: just the occasional chirp of song, the sudden flapping of wings. The canal was wide where Rohmer kept his barge, and the water was deep. Rick saw the black glint of a fish turning in the water, but only heard the splash it made a split-second later.

Nature, it seemed, went on, even when the men who had tried to master it were suffering. The world kept turning, the tides came and went, all the creatures of the night continued their usual rituals, if a little more subdued than usual.

Only man was changed; the rest of the animals simply watched on, possibly even amused by the failings of the bipeds who had always sought to master them.

Once the guns, ammunition and other supplies were firmly tied into the barge and covered by tarpaulins, Rohmer climbed aboard and started the small engine. It was initially too loud for such a low-key craft, but Rick soon became accustomed to its throaty growls.

"All aboard who's coming aboard," said Rohmer, a feeble attempt at a joke that nonetheless had Rick laughing.

Rick returned to the car and picked up Sally's unresponsive body, hauling her across his shoulder. He carried her back to the jetty and placed her gently into the craft, wedging her in so that she would not slip or fall overboard.

Tabby watched in silence, her tiny pale face a bright spot in the darkness, the question mark on her cheek seeming to demand an answer to all the questions in the world. Rohmer stared at the canal, his focus on the dark waters that might just lead them out of this, keeping them safe from the madness occurring along the shore.

The engine guttered; thick, acrid smoke poured from somewhere at the back of the craft. Rick held on to the sides of the barge, feeling as if he was sitting too high above the surface of the water. When the barge began to move, slowly, with no sense of panic or haste, he felt a little calmer. The more distance he put between Sally and dry land, the better he felt. The little Nissan moved away from them, twisting slowly on an unseen axis as they made for the middle of the river.

"She may be slow," said Rohmer from his perch at the head of the barge. "But she's reliable. Never let me down yet!" He almost sounded happy. If it were not for the knowledge of his wife's cold, dead hand resting not far from his own, Rick might have closed his eyes and pretended that they were on a relaxing boating holiday, and Rohmer was the captain of the craft. But the illusion would not hold: bloody reality crept in from the edges, turning everything red.

Have some rest. We'll be safe out on the water.

He turned to face her. She sat near him, her head turned as if she were looking out at the canal. The bandages looked too bright under the eager moon, and he wished that none of this had ever happened – then he wished that this moment would never end.

"We need to head for the Selby area," said Rohmer, raising his voice to compete with the sound of the engine. "We can hole up for a while in a cottage I have there before setting off again on the roads to Northumberland. I have transport there, and plenty of supplies. It's been my little bolthole for years now."

When Rick turned back to face the front of the barge, Tabby was watching him. Her face was unreadable, and the smile she finally offered was stunted, a thing not quite fully formed.

Rick wasn't sure how long he could keep up this charade, but when the truth broke he hoped that he would not have to hurt these people. Especially the girl. Maybe he could make her see that this wasn't wrong, that he was acting out of love. He thought that she might be young enough and innocent enough to appreciate the sentiment.

The water rolled out beneath them, a black carpet leading to the promise of salvation... or a rippling, blackened tongue leading down into an infernal throat. Either way, they were safe for the time being.

Something flopped heavily in the water. Rick couldn't bring himself to look and identify what it was.

CHAPTER TWENTY-FIVE

DARYL DIDN'T TRUST the lone drinker.

The man was still awake while everyone else slept – or tried to grab some sleep – and had, by now, consumed so much alcohol that his head was tipping slowly forward towards the damp length of wooden bar top. He kept mumbling: incoherent words, snappy little phrases that meant nothing to anyone but him. They could have been the words to his favourite song, the names of his wife and dog: anything.

Claire was snoring lightly at Daryl's side, lying flat on her back with her mouth open wide. Her breath smelled of slightly degraded eggs.

"In the boxes," she muttered, tossing her head on the cushion. "I put 'em in the boxes."

Daryl had no idea what she was babbling about. He leaned in close so that his face was directly over hers, blocking his nasal passages so that he didn't catch a whiff of her breath, and carefully dribbled a long line of saliva out of his mouth. The thick string of spit dropped slowly, stretching, and finally broke, hitting her cheek just below the left eye before it oozed down and across her temple.

"*Bull's-eye*," he whispered, grinning. A child's game, but it was something to do. He remembered being pinned down years before in the school toilets at break time and having the same thing done to him...

and with worse substances than spit. Much worse.

The thick drapes and wooden shutters at the windows kept the interior of the pub dark. Sleeping people were simply twisted shapes scattered in all that blackness, some grouped together and others yet further apart.

The drinker sat alone, twitching, still muttering darkly.

Daryl wasn't sure how long these people had been here, but it seemed that the beer was yet to run out. There were still plenty of bar snacks on hand – crisps, pork scratchings, salted peanuts – and the water supply had not yet been cut off. If they were careful, this lot might just be able to ride out the worst of it in here, rationing their supplies and going out on missions like the one Claire had been running when he encountered her. If they were organised, and did not make any silly mistakes, they were onto a good thing here.

He inspected the bar, taking note of the solid oak doors, the old-fashioned leaded windows, most of them with wire mesh security barriers attached to the outside, set a few inches in front of the glass. Yes, he could see the appeal of staying here... but it was not for him. The old Daryl would have been happy to cower in the shadows, finding protection in numbers and allowing himself to be one of the sheep. But the new Daryl... oh, he was a lone wolf, a man on a mission. The new Daryl would hear nothing of crouching in the darkness, waiting for the storm to pass. The new Daryl *was* the storm – at least part of it, a significant element within the overall terror.

Daryl eased himself from beneath the thin blankets Claire had provided and slowly picked his way across the room. He was not quite sure why, but he felt drawn to the solitary drinker at the bar. The man had a presence about him; he stood out from the crowd, and not just because of his actions (or lack of them). He possessed the air of a minor celebrity now gone to seed, someone who might once have been important but was now just another nobody in a grimy parade of nobodies.

Daryl slid sideways onto a worn barstool beside the man, watching him as his head dipped forward once again, and then jerked abruptly upwards. "I think you might have had enough." He reached out to take the glass from the man's hand.

"Fuck off," said the man, surprisingly lucid for his apparent state. "I'll have had enough when all this *shit* goes away." He made an expansive gesture with his free hand, and then gulped at the glass, emptying it completely, before pouring himself another. It looked like whisky, but the label was peeled off the bottle, so Daryl could not be sure. The result of idle hands; a nervous drinking habit, like the way some people tore up beer mats.

"Sorry. I thought you were about to black out." He kept his voice low, unwilling to disturb anyone else in the large room, but the acoustics made the words seem louder than they actually were.

"That's what I'm aiming for: total fucking oblivion. Unfortunately, the void is yet to swallow me up."

Daryl examined the man properly for the first time. He had shoulder-length brown hair, which had turned greasy. His dark eyes were intelligent, but dulled by alcohol. His narrow face was shadowed by stubble and there was a faint air of nobility to his features. The dark shirt he wore was stained with dried blood and one of the sleeves was torn. Visible on the wedding finger of his drinking hand was a pale, untanned band of skin.

"Cheers," said the man, sipping slower this time, savouring the drink.

"What you said earlier. About Claire. What did you mean by that?" Daryl felt at once defensive, slightly on edge, but could not understand why. She was nothing to him, this girl, just something to cling to for a while. Yet still, he felt the need to stick up for her, to protect her honour – if indeed she had any, which seemed doubtful.

The man smiled. His teeth were coated brown; his tongue resembled a slug coiling in the wet cave of his mouth. "She was a regular here, came in all the time. In the few years I've been coming here, I must've seen her dance with every man in the place." He raised his eyebrows: fat slow-worms wriggling across his brow.

"Dancing?" Daryl felt dumb, as if he were a child struggling to decipher the codes and ambiguities of an adult's conversation.

"Come on, you know what I mean. The dance. The horizontal mambo. She fucked them all, sometimes more than one at a time." He swayed on his seat but managed to correct his balance by grabbing the edge of the bar. The ends of his fingers were yellowed with nicotine, but Daryl had not yet seen him smoke. "She's nothing but a filthy whore."

"She fucked everyone," said Daryl. "But she didn't fuck you." Finally, understanding dawned upon him. He had cut to the quick of the man's hurt. He smiled, pleased at gaining the upper hand. "You sad old bastard. You've been letching after her forever, just wishing she would look your way, give you more than a drunken smile. But she never did. She took on all comers... *apart from you*." He laughed softly, enjoying the man's silent rage and the way he was now asserting his will upon the sorry old sop.

"That's where you're wrong," said the man, his voice dropping. "I did have her *once*. Just once."

He stared at Daryl, his red-rimmed eyes moist.

"Outside in the alley, up against the wall. She kept calling me by another name, but I didn't care. Not while I was inside her." He paused, regaled by the power of the memory. Then his face took on a pained expression, as if the recollection was not in fact everything that he had wished. "She called me all kinds of names, before, during and afterwards. But she never called me by the right name. The one that would hurt the most." He winced, clutched at his side with a beefy hand. "She never called me *Daddy*."

Daryl at first thought he'd misheard the man, but there could be no mistake. He stood up and backed away, terrible memories of his own threatening to burst through the mental dam he had spent so many years constructing. Mother's bare thigh, the feel of her hands on the bones of his hips, the slow journey her tongue had made over his face, down across his chest and lower, lower, until she had him right where she wanted...

"No!" he lashed out and grabbed the bottle with the peeled label, striking instinctively. The bottle caught the man on the backswing, making contact with the side of his head and knocking him sideways off the stool. The sound it made was almost surreally loud.

The man hit the floor heavily, a sack of meat; as if there was already no life left in his body.

Then Daryl was upon him, gloved hands going for his soft, exposed throat, fingers closing around the frail trachea and crushing it as easily as he might bend a plastic pipe, feeling little resistance to his grip.

"Not again. Never again, Mother!" He squeezed as tightly as he could, a sense of power surging through him. Mother's face overlaid that of the man, her mouth open, a thin white trail of fluid snaking from between her lips to stain her chin. Blood flowed from the wounded temple, pouring onto the grubby boards. The man made an odd croaking sound; it seemed to go on forever.

At last the man's hands came up in weak defence, but it was much too late to matter. They batted lamely at Daryl's forearms, bouncing off like small birds flying into a brick wall. His face was already swelling, the skin turning a bright shade of crimson, and his blue-black tongue pushed between his ugly teeth to loll horribly across his lower lip, like a sodden flap of untreated leather.

Hands grabbed at him, clutching his shoulders and tugging uselessly; pointless voices screamed in his ears. But Daryl would not, *could* not release the man until he was dead. It really was that simple.

Finally, the body beneath him went limp, and the stench of fresh shit drifted into his nostrils. The yelling continued around him, and when he blinked his eyes and turned around everyone had taken a single, almost choreographed, step back, as if put off by the terrible faecal odour.

"It wasn't me," said Daryl, needlessly. "He crapped himself. They sometimes do that as they die." Again he felt on the verge of hysteria, as if crazed laughter was building up inside him and demanding release. He was giving these people data from the books he had read, offering up snippets of information like an eager student.

"What have you done? He wasn't doing anything." The old woman from earlier had once again assumed the role of mouthpiece for the small band of survivors. "He was just drunk. Not causing any harm." She made the sign of the cross, her eyes flashing wide. "You're evil. A *devil*. No better than those things outside."

Feet shuffled on the boards. Someone shoved Daryl back onto his knees.

Sighing theatrically, Daryl righted himself and got slowly to his feet, well aware that these people were frightened of him. The reality of the situation flared before him, bright lights at the frayed edges of his vision. This was the power he had always felt that he deserved, the awe to which he was surely entitled.

"Oh, I'm a lot worse than them." He chuckled, adding to the effect, bringing yet another dimension to the character he was still in the process of creating.

"Please." Claire approached him. "Leave him alone," she said to the onlookers, her hands held out before her, palms open. "I know why he did this. He did it for me." She eased to Daryl's side, one arm snaking around his waist and the other held outwards as if she were stopping traffic. "That rotten bastard had it coming."

This turn of events confused Daryl even more. He would never get the hang of human emotions. Every time he felt that he'd made up some ground, grasped something of vital importance, the rug was deftly pulled from under him by someone acting completely the opposite to the way he'd come to expect. It was fascinating, really; a profound learning process.

He stared at Claire, saw something cold and terrible flick like a snake's tail behind her eyes, and was suddenly drawn to it.

"Get out," said a man Daryl could not identify in the gloom. "Get out now."

"Leave," said the old woman, moving sideways and setting off a chain reaction so that the others followed suit and an opening appeared in the small, agitated group. "Make your own way. You're more suited to this world than us."

"Go."

"Get out!"

"Fuck off!"

The chorus was raised; they sung their little hearts out. Even those not part of this immediate group joined in, shouting from their cosy hidey-holes.

Claire gripped Daryl's leather-clad hand as he began to walk towards the main door, trudging like an ancient warrior leaving the battlefield. He paused so that Claire could grab her things, and then turned to face his audience. "Don't think you've seen the last of us," he said, making it up as he went along. "It's a small world and it's about to get even smaller." Then, with Claire at his side, he concluded his dramatic exit, silently congratulating himself on improvising such a good last line.

A short man with muscular arms unlocked the main door, and the two of them strode out of the building, arm in arm, like a nice modern young couple.

The street was empty, but that state of affairs might not last for long. Daryl went to the alley where he'd hidden the moped when they'd arrived, kick-started the machine, and waited for Claire to hop on behind him.

He thought that he might keep her for a while; at least until she got boring. He'd originally intended to either leave her in the morning or kill her when he got the chance, but her strong performance in the pub had changed his mind. There was more to this girl than met the eye, and the more she appealed to him the more her resemblance to Sally Nutman grew.

Every star needs a leading lady, even if she is the understudy.

Then, feeling like he'd just given a triumphant performance, Daryl resumed his epic journey to nowhere.

CHAPTER TWENTY-SIX

THE *QUEEN ANNE* moved at a sedate pace, but sitting on its cramped deck Rick felt safer than he had for some time. He'd moved Sally down into the rear cabin, out of sight of the shore, but could still hear her occasional soothing communications.

I love you.

We'll be safe.

He hoped that she was right about the latter, and that it wasn't just wishful thinking – *dead* wishful thinking.

Can you still hear me, lover?

Hear? Was that the right term to describe how he picked up her thoughts? He didn't really *hear* her voice, just caught an echo of it in his mind, like a series of vibrations on the surface of his brain. Yet as their journey continued, that voice became increasingly real – more solid and meaningful than anything else going on around him.

"Do you believe in God?"

Rohmer's question pulled him out of himself, dragging him back into the immediacy of their situation. "Sorry?"

"God," said the old man, still facing forward, his eyes on the water. "Are you a believer?"

Tabby was in the main front galley, trying to find a broadcast on the portable television or the old transistor radio Rohmer kept onboard, so the two men were alone up there on deck. The sound of the diesel engine was now a gentle rumble, and the sound of the water lapping at the sides of the vessel was strangely soothing. Rick had never been on a canal barge until now, but he could certainly see the appeal. There was a strange beauty here, a sense of being apart from the crowd.

"I never used to believe in God," he said, flexing his hand, trying to relax his fingers where they were stiff from clutching the gun for so long. "But now I'm not so sure."

"I've been a believer for ten years, since my Anne died." Rohmer still stared ahead. The darkness before them was lifting, making way for faint glimmers of early daylight. "Faith helped me through some dark times after her death. It got me off alcohol and made me start to engage with people again."

There was a pause then, during which both men simply listened to the throbbing of the engine and watched the black and undulating surface of the canal.

"It's like this whole thing has changed me in ways I never thought possible," said Rick, glancing at the wooden floor and imagining Sally down there on a bunk, her bandaged head resting on a soft white cushion. "My wife and I drifted apart, but this thing brought us together. It's made me realise that my entire worldview was naïve. I've come to appreciate that there *must* be something else to the world than what we can see and feel."

Rohmer grunted and nodded his head. His ponytail swung like a pendulum.

Rick continued: "When I was in the army I saw a lot of men die. Some of them were my friends and the others were enemies that I killed."

The lapping of the water against the boat. The soft fuzz of pre-dawn light spreading like a film across the canal.

"The first man I shot was a Taliban soldier in Afghanistan. I was in the Parachute Regiment, third battalion. It was during Operation Mountain Thrust, July 2006. I can remember it like it was yesterday. The Yanks were leading us into the hills to oust Taliban insurgents. We were ambushed. Snipers pinned us down. Eventually we got the upper hand, and I shot a man in the head. I cradled him in my arms as he died, and as I watched him something went out of his eyes – a light dimming, going out. Call it what you will: his soul, his life-force, his essence. I just call it his presence in the world. Once it had gone, there was nothing left of him. Just meat."

Rohmer turned around then, and there were tears in his eyes. "What about these things? The dead. Are they just motorised meat, or is there something – the presence you describe – trapped inside them? Are they more like walking ghosts, with a sliver of their soul stuck inside their bodies, or is it a case of the soul being partially reactivated like a damaged computer hard drive?"

Rick glanced behind and over to his left, out over the water. Two people stood on the canal bank, waving and shouting as they jogged along the towpath, but they were too far away to hear. He raised his hand; shards of brightness were visible through the gaps between his fingers, but when he let the hand fall the light had all but vanished.

"There has to be something human left inside them, powering them." Rohmer's attention was focused elsewhere. He did not even notice the couple on the bank. "I mean, they look like us, move like us, were once exactly like us. Just because they're dead it doesn't mean they're monsters.

The couple continued to wave, their movements frantic. They were running now, clearly in distress, trying to catch up with the barge.

"Why are there no dead animals running around attacking us?" said Rohmer. "It's only humans who are coming back. That *must* mean something."

Rick stared at the couple. The woman was still waving, but the man was now bent over and rummaging inside a bag. Was she trying to summon help? Did she want them to guide the barge ashore so that they could come aboard? There wasn't enough room on the boat for passengers, and Rick wasn't sure if he liked the idea of exposing Sally to the scrutiny of yet more strangers.

"I think God is responsible. Perhaps he's had enough of what we've become – violent, warlike, empty of everything but the hunger to accrue and amass more and more money and useless items. Maybe He wants to punish us, make us pay for forgetting about Him."

The man on the canal bank stood upright and brought up his arms in a rigid yet amateurish shooting posture. Before Rick could move, the man had opened fire.

"Get down!" he yelled. "Shooter! Get down in the boat!"

But the sound of gunfire was distant and the handgun was too small a calibre for the bullets to reach them. Rick peered up from behind the faded wooden rail that ran around the craft, then when he was certain that he was in no danger, he raised his head into the open. The woman looked like she might be weeping; the man kept firing the empty gun, long after the ammunition was used up.

Rohmer resumed his station at the wheel. The couple retreated into the tree line, moving away from the canal and out of sight. The man had his arms around the woman, comforting her.

The barge kept moving, sticking to its own steady pace. Tabby popped up her head from below deck and asked if anyone else was hungry.

Both men shook their heads, and she went back down into the galley to prepare herself something to sustain her until the next meal time.

Dawn broke slowly, as if the day were reluctant to emerge. Once again the sun was weak and the clouds were heavy. It grew colder as the light bled across the land and the water. Rick thought it might try again to snow, and the thought depressed him more than he could express.

Rohmer remained stoically behind the wheel of his vessel. He had not said much since mentioning God, and Rick thought that the man was sinking into his own inner landscape, searching for a sign. Perhaps he was even thinking about his wife, or his former lover – the man on the island. Now there, thought Rick, was a strange and tangled situation...

Then, as they approached a lock, Rohmer broke the silence: "I'm starting to think that it might not be such a bad thing to die. I mean, to die properly, not come back as one of those things. The world is dying, and what's left behind will be unbearable." He slowed the boat to a crawl, and then turned to face Rick. "You know what I'm saying, don't you, son? What I'm asking."

Rick swallowed. His throat felt constricted. "Don't worry. If it comes to that, I have more than enough ammo to make sure the three of us don't come back."

Satisfied, Rohmer nodded once, and then returned his attention to the looming lock. "You stay on board and I'll see to getting us through. You're better with the gun, and I can turn one of these things quicker than you ever could." He grinned, winked, and eased the boat towards the waiting gate, his hands firm on the wheel.

"Come on, grab the wheel."

Rick went to the front and took up his position, one hand steering the barge and the other releasing the Glock from its holster. The gun felt more natural than the wheel.

Rohmer leaped from the barge and opened the lock gates, then walked quickly up the incline to the lock gear. Rick watched him closely, ready to start shooting at the slightest provocation.

The two stone walls encompassed the craft as it entered the tunnel, and Rick began to feel on edge. It was fine when they were in motion, but this close to dry land they could be asking for trouble.

Rohmer worked the rack and pinion and released the gears, allowing water into the lock. The vessel rose slowly, buoyed on the surging waters. It took five long minutes for the lock to be filled, and finally Rohmer released the top gate so that Rick could guide the barge to the upper level of the canal.

It all went smoothly until Rick saw the pike.

The fish was trapped in the lock, and had risen to the surface. It nudged the side of the barge, blindly looking for a way around the vessel. Rick watched it, slightly puzzled. He was anxious, but had nothing upon which to focus his bad feelings.

"Nearly done," Rohmer shouted from above. The water level was almost right; Rick's hands tensed on the wheel.

As if in a dream, a fat white hand broke the surface and grabbed the angry pike from below, pulling its long sleek form swiftly beneath the restless waters of the lock.

Rick aimed the pistol at the spot where the fish had been, trying to keep his breathing shallow. Concentric circles painted the surface. His hands shook with tension. Something clattered gently, gently, three times so gently, on the underside of the hull.

Rick tensed, watching and listening. The sound was not repeated.

"Guide her through!" Rohmer was oblivious to what had just happened.

Slowly, Rick returned his attention to the lock and eased the boat through the gate. The balance beam across the top of the metal gate clanked loudly, the sound dull and somehow even more frightening than what he'd just glimpsed in the water.

Rick watched closely as Rohmer closed the gates and made his way back to the barge. He saw nothing this time – certainly nothing that resembled white, pulpy flesh – emerging from the water inside the lock. Whatever was resting there, rested for now still and easy. But the incident had changed the entire complexion of the journey for Rick. Now he realised that he'd been foolish to drop his guard and relax, even for a moment.

Even when danger was out of sight, it remained a constant reminder of the fragility of human existence. One false move, a single moment of distraction from any one of them, might cost them all their lives.

He stepped back and allowed Rohmer to take control of the *Queen Anne*. Only when it was back in the middle of the canal did he begin to feel less anxious. The memory of the white hand claiming the pike felt like a brief warning of worse things to come.

CHAPTER TWENTY-SEVEN

SLOW RHYTHM SOUNDS motion hungry dark throb muted pain lurch
hungry voice language girl child smell food hungry lapping
swell hungry hungry hungry hungry hungry girl hungry hungry
hungry hungry child hungry hungry hungry hungry hungry
hungryhungryhungryhungryhungryhungryhungryhungry

CHAPTER TWENTY-EIGHT

DARYL HAD NO idea what they were doing down by the canal. After leaving the temporary shelter provided by the public house, he'd simply allowed the moped to carry him wherever it may. Rattling along empty streets, turning a corner at any junction where he suspected that trouble might lurk up ahead, he had enjoyed the sensation of the vehicle under his body. Claire's arms around his waist had been a novelty, and for a wonderful moment he felt halfway normal. Whatever 'normal' actually meant.

He heard the gunshots first: short barks from what sounded like a toy gun. They went on for a little while, and then stopped abruptly.

"What is it?" Claire rested her chin on his shoulder, her cheek pressed against the side of his neck.

"What does it sound like?" He was rapidly losing patience with her idiot questions.

"Gun."

"Clever girl. Now let's see if you can spell that."

"Fuck off." She pulled back from him, her arms unloosening the knot they'd made around his middle. A sigh escaped her lips; the air against his face felt stale and odorous. He held his breath.

"I vote that we head away from the gunshots. We don't want to run into any of those things."

He sensed rather than saw her nod in agreement. Her hands returned – lightly – to his waist, the touch almost cautious. Daryl released the throttle quickly, causing the moped to jerk forward slightly. Claire's grip tightened abruptly, and he grinned, feeling the liquor of his power over her as it coursed through his system.

He guided the moped along the track through the trees, keeping his speed down so as not to upend them and damage the machine. The last thing he needed now was damage that he did not possess the knowledge to repair.

The sun was rising slowly; its light was feeble, a flicker of brightness against the charcoal sky. Again he felt like he was stuck in a monochrome movie, and as usual the thought pleased him.

"Look." Claire pressed against him, drawing close in a sudden burst of terror.

He slowed the moped, placing one foot down on the stony track and dragging it along to cut a swathe through the dusty, uneven surface.

Two figures ran out of the trees a few hundred yards up ahead. They did not look Daryl's way, failed to even notice the moped and its gawping riders. The couple ran, hand in hand, into the bushes on the other side of the track. The woman was repeating something over and over, but Daryl could not quite hear what it was. A word? A name? Perhaps it was even a number. Just one more thing he would never know...

Turning his head to the left, Daryl caught sight of the canal glinting darkly through the trees. He stared, trying to make out what he thought he saw... an object on the water, heading along on the tide. A long barge, with a couple of figures standing on deck, both of them staring in the direction of the bank, probably at the retreating figures who'd passed only moments before.

Daryl experienced a temporal shift: reality seemed to bend, curling in on itself and meeting at both ends like a Möbius strip. He had the sensation of watching himself watch himself, as if he stood in an endless hall of mirrors. Then, just as quickly as it had occurred, the weird sensation passed, leaving his head spinning with a combination of vertigo and a strange giddy nostalgia for something he could not name.

"Are you okay?"

God, he wished that stupid bitch would just shut the fuck up and allow him to enjoy his little epiphany, whatever the hell it meant. The closeness he'd felt towards her back at the bar, when he had been afforded a glimpse into the darkness at her core, was now forgotten. He could barely believe that he'd felt anything other than disdain for this ridiculous puppet.

"No." He eased the moped forward, sending it rolling onto the rough ground at the side of the track. Then, parking it up, he climbed off and began to walk down the embankment towards the towpath that ran below.

"Wait. Daryl, wait for me!"

He kept on going, hoping that she'd trip and fall, maybe break her leg so that he could leave her there to become food for passing dead folk.

The thought made him smile, easing the frustration.

"Wait. I'm coming, too." She sent loose stones tumbling down the incline as she came. It was lucky for her that the barge was too far away for the crew to hear the commotion; otherwise he might be forced to silence her.

A distant gunshot, or perhaps the sound of a car backfiring, drew his attention away from the canal. He stared back, over Claire's shoulder, but could see no one in the vicinity. Listening intently, he picked up no incongruous sounds other than the ones made by the silly girl as she clumsily descended the embankment. A dog began to bark and howl, but it was not close by; after a few seconds the anxious baying ceased.

Daryl turned back towards the canal, his attention drawn to the boat like iron filings to a magnet. He was not sure what the pull was, but he was unable to ignore it. Something about the figures on deck – at least one of them – seemed familiar and important. The way he stood, moved; the shape of his body. Like an echo from a dream he'd once had.

He trod carefully the rest of the way down the cluttered embankment, his feet sinking into the debris, dead leaves and fallen branches at the base of the incline. Litter was everywhere; a tawdry second skin over the earth.

He stopped behind the last line of trees, their November branches already shedding to adopt winter's skeletal nudity. Pressing himself against one of the wider trunks, he watched as the barge chuntered lazily towards a distant stone footbridge.

Finally he realised why he'd been so drawn to the vessel. The old man piloting the craft he did not recognise, but there was no doubt in Daryl's mind that other man – the younger of the two – was the policeman: Sally Nutman's husband. Daryl watched as the man stood and stretched, scanning the towpath with a pistol in his hand.

"Well, well, well..."

Claire finally reached his side. She was panting, struggling for breath, and Daryl manhandled her as he grabbed the torn pink rucksack she wore on her back. He pulled the flap open and removed the binoculars from inside. Putting them to his eyes, he focused on the policeman. Oh, it was him all right; there could be no mistake. He zoomed in on the man's face. His mouth was a tight line; his eyes were narrowed; his cheeks were dark and sunken, shaded by thick stubble. He looked... *hard*. Hard as nails.

Daryl would have to be careful with this one.

He watched the barge until the policeman's face was out of eyesight. Then he took away the binoculars and watched it still, hoping that Sally, sweet dead Sally, would emerge from the space below deck – what was it called, the galley, the hold? Something like that.

She did not appear.

The two men chatted while Rick checked his pistol, running his hands over the weapon in a way that seemed almost loving. Then, eventually, Daryl decided that he had seen enough.

Was this luck or fate? He had known all along that he would run into Sally again; it was a certainty. He had not once questioned this eventuality, simply accepted it as a fact of this strange new life. But for it to happen so soon, and when he least expected it, was wonderful; a gift, a favour. It was almost enough to make him believe in Mother's God. Almost.

"I need to go," said Claire, shuffling her feet in the loamy earth.

"Go where?"

"*Go.* You know. The toilet." She rolled her eyes, and he imagined popping them out of their sockets and rolling them across a flat surface – a tabletop, or perhaps a smooth stretch of footpath.

"Oh. Yes. I suppose you'd better go over there, in the bushes. I'll make sure no one sees." He smiled.

"Very funny," she said, drifting off toward a dense stand of trees surrounded by waist-high foliage.

Daryl watched as she pulled down her jeans and knickers in a single swift movement (oh, she was used to that manoeuvre, if her father was to be believed), and squatted, her pale backside swamped by the almost leafless yet still thick undergrowth. She stared at him, and when he did not look away she averted her gaze, cheeks and throat flushing red.

Daryl watched her straining to urinate. It was the first time he'd ever seen anyone but Mother do their toilet, and he was fascinated at the way her thighs tensed and her hands gripped the belt-band of her trousers.

"Holy fuck!" She tried to run while still in a crouch, her legs tangled with her clothing. Her feet slipped on the knotty ground, and she went tumbling forward, rolling a little way down the incline. Her buttocks were dirty and as she rolled he saw that her pubic hair glistened, like the pelt of an unwashed dog. He felt suddenly nauseous.

"Get the fuck away. Fuck, fuck!" She struggled to get to her feet, tugging up her clothes. Daryl stepped towards the spot where she'd been urinating.

"What is it?" he said, gaze fixed on the ground, then flicking upward and taking in the damp, dense foliage.

"In there," she said, breathless, pointing directly into the undergrowth, right behind where she had been squatting. "It's in there..."

Daryl inched forward, his hand straying to the kitchen knife he now kept tucked into the back of his pants, wrapped in a ragged square of chamois leather to prevent the blade from slicing his flesh. Then, when he saw what Claire was making so much fuss about, he had to restrain himself from laughing out loud. He doubted that she – or anyone else for that matter – would see the humour in such a gruesome sight.

The remains – for that was surely what they were – consisted of male body parts. The torso had been pummelled and stripped clean, the offal removed. Ribs were broken, sticking out of the compressed mass like white spiderlegs from a mutated arachnid. Various innards had been left behind, but Daryl was unable to identify them: a gristly chunk of what might have once been part of a heart; bloodless strings of arteries; a few sausage-like sections of intestine attached to a rubberised section of bowel. The rest was just so much red gunge.

He stared at the thing, truly amazed at the baffling sight.

Its head was relatively intact; the throat had been peeled back, exposing its inner workings, cheeks stripped away like wads of paper, half a nose with one wide nostril left to gape.

But the eyes... they were a lovely shade of cornflower blue, heavy-lidded, and blinking.

Blinking.

Somehow, against nature, what was left of the corpse had returned to a travesty of life, and even now its shattered jaw snapped shut on a flap of its own shredded flesh. The limbs were bent and folded; the whole stunted cadaver was collapsed in on itself, forming a tight knot of living-dead matter. And it was steadily eating what little meat remained on its own bones.

Daryl watched in silence as the jagged teeth tore free a large slab of flesh, chewing it; as the meat was swallowed; as it journeyed down into the exposed stomach cavity to plop onto the long grass, completely undigested.

The thing did not even know what it was doing. Brute instinct had taken over, the desire to feed... no, not feed: the desire to *eat*. There was no sustenance being gained here. This was simply eating for the sake of it, like a morbidly obese patient hiding cold burgers under his hospital bed, or a greedy child forcing down sugared donuts even as he vomits them back up.

"Fascinating," he said, unmoved yet interested on an academic level. Even if there was nothing left in which to store food, these things ate. If you dissected one of them, vivisecting it to the bone, reducing it to nothing but a mouth attached to a brain, would it still try to consume?

It was an interesting theory, and one that he would love to test if ever he had the necessary time and privacy.

Maybe it was even something he could try out on Sally, a way of discovering exactly how much he loved her.

Instead of putting an end to her living death (or should that be her dead life?), perhaps he could kidnap her and use her as a test subject. If the policeman had her with him, on the boat with others, she was obviously under some kind of strict control – he must have used medication, rendering her placid.

The possibilities of love, he was beginning to realise, were endless.

CHAPTER TWENTY-NINE

IT SEEMED LIKE months had passed since they'd been on the canal, and yet Rick didn't want the journey to end.

"It's just over here," said Rohmer, easing the barge towards a short bank overgrown with ferns and hanging flora. Their leaves kissed the water, causing tiny ripples to disturb the stillness beneath the gravel towpath.

Rotting timber boards made up most of the old jetty. It looked unsafe, but Rohmer promised them that it was fit to walk on. "It never gets used," he'd said. "Except by me. There's nothing near here but my cottage."

The barge drifted inward, cutting a calm line through the water. Rick had brought up the M16 from below. Rohmer kept the second Glock pistol close to hand.

The heavily thatched roof of a thick-walled stone cottage rose suddenly into his eye line. It sat on a rise, which made it easier to defend if it came to that, and Rick guessed that the cottage probably lay a few hundred yards from the bank.

"I think your wife is trying to get up." Tabby's head popped up from below. Her eyes were startled, too wide, like those of a shocked cartoon character.

"Thanks," he said, ducking down and passing her on the tiny set of wooden steps. He headed towards the rear of the barge, noting a nasty smell that hadn't been there before. Was Sally the source? He thought of her decaying flesh, the hideous dry wounds beneath the dressings.

He approached the bunk and lowered the rifle. She was sitting up, her hands twitching on the thin mattress. She was making a low sighing sound, air escaping through dead lungs, slashed lips.

"Hush, baby. It's me. It's Rick." He sat on the edge of the bed, no longer quite knowing how to touch her. She was like a stranger, another woman whose quirks and habits he was forced to learn.

Are we there yet?

"No. Not yet. But almost." He already had the syringe in his hand. He introduced the morphine by the other eye, taking turns so that he didn't ruin whatever matter was left in the sockets. He knew he'd have to change her dressings again before long, and his mind withdrew from the thought of what she might now look like under there.

That's better.

Her body slumped; the tension went out of her limbs. Could a dead person even become tense? Did their bodies react in the same way, even though there was no blood being pumped, no oxygen fuelling them? Perhaps they could explain everything on Rohmer's island. When they got there it would all be put in some kind of order.

But did he really believe that, or was he simply clinging to an old man's second-hand hope of salvation?

It'll be all right. We can be together like we used to be. Once we get there, you can undress me and love me again.

Undress... did she mean the bandages, or was there something sexual to the invitation? He felt like an adulterer: his wife was dead, and this was his lover, his easy, queasy lover.

He giggled, and then quickly cut off the reaction. A shudder passed through his body, not of fear but of loneliness; a deep, almost supernatural loneliness which knew no bounds, not even death.

Sleepy. So sleepy.

He watched as her body slumped even further down onto the bunk. Her hands relaxed; her skin was white as new, unmarked paper. He bent down and hoisted her across his shoulder. Her body was as light as a sack of bones dumped in a bin outside a fried chicken joint. It scared him to feel her fragile body under his fingers, her delicate skin against his shoulder.

Back on deck, Rohmer was slowly pulling in towards the jetty. Rick's breath misted white in front of his face. In a few days, if the temperature drop continued, the water at the sides of the canal would begin to ice over. He picked up his bag, held the M16 at the ready. Sally was still draped around his shoulders like a human stole. He could barely even feel her weight.

The barge nudged the bank, scraping against the loose dirt and stones.

"Keep an eye out." Rohmer gritted his teeth as he brought the *Queen Anne* around to berth, her nose pushing into the long grass that grew in the shallows. Then, nimble as a man half his age, he leaped ashore and tethered the barge to the moorings – a series of short wooden uprights, each lopsided and not looking even capable of the task for which they'd been driven into the ground.

"Come on, now. Let's be quick."

The cottage was no longer visible from the jetty, but Rick was heartened that they didn't have far to run. Despite Sally's negligible weight on his back, he didn't feel safe enough to make a long trek inland.

"We ready for this?" he glanced at Rohmer, then into Tabby's wide eyes. They both nodded, silent and watchful.

Rohmer looked back at the *Queen Anne*, his right hand drifting unconsciously to rest above his heart, and closed his eyes briefly. When he opened them again there was steel in his gaze. "Let's go."

Rick took the lead, tapping like he was back in basic training. His legs adjusted quickly to the familiar pace, the muscles flexing as if in recognition of the labour ahead. He climbed the slight incline and stood on the gravel path. Now the cottage was visible again: its rough-crafted roof poked up teasingly above a thin line of trees.

Rohmer and Tabby came up behind; they were both breathing heavily. Rick made a mental note to remember that his travelling companions were an old man and a small child. He would have to restrict his pace if he wanted to keep them with him. And he did, he admitted to himself at last, want them with him. He wanted that more than anything else.

This was his family now: a ragtag pair of strangers and a dead wife hanging like a hideous neck scarf across his battle-broad shoulders. A family unit forged in the fires of hell.

Rohmer held the gun like a pro. The man obviously adapted quickly, and this trait made Rick respect him even more. Tabby was in good hands here; even if Rick hadn't stumbled across them, he suspected that her beloved grandfather would be doing a sterling job of keeping her alive.

"Okay," he told them, ducking down out of sight. "This is how we do it. I'll run ahead and check the area for strays. You two stay here and watch my back. Let's not mess this up."

"I hear you loud and clear, son." Rohmer tensed his jaw. He was serious, ready to do what was necessary. If anyone else had called Rick *son* in the easy manner of this old codger, he'd have put them on their arse. But it felt natural coming from Rohmer; he was the father Rick had never known.

The realisation shocked him. Was it really this easy to accept someone?

"Be careful," said Tabby. "All of us, just be careful."

Rick straightened with tears in his eyes. Pretending to adjust Sally's position on his back, he winced to clear his vision. "She keeps wriggling." The lie burned his tongue. He wished that he could be honest with these people, above all others, yet knew that it simply wasn't possible.

He turned and jogged along the towpath, gravel crunching underfoot. The rifle kept him company, and he knew it would never fail him. This rifle had blown the heads off enemies, punctured holes through doors behind which dwelled those who meant him harm. It was a good friend, a valued servant.

Don't drop me.

"I won't. I'll carry you forever." He knew it was true. This burden would remain his and his alone until their journey was done, wherever the darkened road might lead.

There was a dark blue Volvo estate parked beside a small outbuilding near the cottage. The car's headlights had been left on, but the light was weak, the battery running low but not quite dead.

He recalled that Rohmer had mentioned a family who sometimes rented out the cottage. They must have come here seeking refuge.

Shit. He didn't think he could carry any more baggage. He gripped the rifle, wondering...

When the gun went off he knew exactly what had happened, and his heart sank through his body and deep into the earth. *Nothing lasts*, he thought. *It all goes away in the end.* Then he dropped Sally onto the ground and ran back along the towpath, not even pausing to assess the situation.

Don't leave me.

He took it all in as he ran, looking for a shot.

Unfortunately, there was no shot available.

Tabby was moving in a low crouch, trying to gain her feet as she hurried away from what was happening immediately behind her. Because of Rick's position in relation to her and Rohmer, she was blocking his direct line of vision, making it impossible to squeeze off a few rounds while he was running.

So he dropped to his knees, the gravel grazing his kneecaps, and carefully took aim along the length of the assault rifle.

Rohmer was panicking and grabbing at the gun; because of his unfamiliarity with firearms, he was unable to act quickly in a crisis. Rick suspected that the gun had jammed – something he'd be able to resolve in an instant but a novice would struggle to deal with. Again, the shot was blocked because of the old man's position.

It was another of Rohmer's shamblers. In all honesty, it wasn't fit to be much else: there wasn't enough left of it to do anything *but* shamble. And eat.

The thing moving slowly towards the old man had at one time been human, but now it looked to Rick bizarrely like a tree. That was the image his racing mind grabbed onto: a fucked-up mobile sapling; bonsai of the living dead.

Below the beltline, the thing was intact, with thick legs clad in bloodstained jeans. It tottered on those sturdy legs, understandably unable to find a centre of balance.

Above the waist was the spine, a long, white segmented tube that had been picked clean of flesh. The naked spinal column moved like a serpent, swaying from side to side in a hypnotic fashion. The splintered ribcage retained a covering of meat, but it had been shredded and mostly flayed. The odd red mass looked like the branches of a tree, spindly appendages stuck out at odd angles and festooned with dangling leaves of shredded skin.

The neck, like the lower torso, had been stripped of flesh; the shocking white bone glinted in the weak daylight. The bottom jaw was missing completely – perhaps torn off when the thing had been created. A top row of teeth lined the area above this, and the tongue lolled insanely long from the crimson cavity.

The top of the head, from a line level with the eyebrows, had been scalped. Runnels and tears in the pate; vague tufts of fuzzy hair left to cover the area like random bristles.

It was the most bizarre sight Rick had yet seen, and again the image of a tree snagged in his mind. That burst ribcage was the foliage, balanced atop a skinny trunk of spinal chord.

"Move!" he yelled, trying to get the thing in his sights. "Get out of the way!"

Tabby finally got to her feet, but instead of running towards Rick she turned to help her grandfather.

Rick jumped to his feet and thundered towards them, screaming sounds no one would have recognised as words.

The tree-thing reached Rohmer in what seemed like slow-motion. It reached out its grasping hands, took hold of his shoulders, and drew him into a weird embrace, that juddering upper mandible gearing up to scoop out his throat.

Rick, acting on instinct, shot the old man through the meat of his upper shoulder, hoping that the exit wound would be in the right place. The dead thing twitched backwards, and thankfully Rohmer stepped back, giving Rick a single clear shot at the gaping jaw.

He took off its head whilst running at speed. It was the best shot he had ever pulled off, and there was nobody there to admire his skill.

"I'm okay," Rohmer was saying, trying to calm down Tabby, who was almost strangling him as she wrapped her arms around his neck.

"Did it bite you?" There was no time for niceties. Rick still held the M16 at waist level, not yet ready to lower it fully.

"No bite. It was a close thing, though." Rohmer's face was drained of blood; it was a paper mask, a child's sketch of an incredibly ancient man.

"You sure?" Rick lowered the rifle.

"That was good shooting, son. A one in a million shot. Gave me a nice flesh wound."

"What happened?" Rick nodded at the gun, still gripped in Rohmer's hand. His other hand clutched at his wounded shoulder.

"I dunno. It just seized up in my hand."

He stepped inside, reaching past the still sobbing Tabby, and took the pistol. Aiming it up, he pulled the trigger, letting off two shots. "It's fine now." He handed Rohmer the gun.

Rohmer's face was whiter still; as if he'd only just realised how close to death, or something worse, he'd been.

"If it happens again," said Rick, "remain calm. Here." He took the hunting knife from his belt and handed it to Rohmer, who took it gratefully. "A back-up plan."

Rick turned away and headed back along the towpath, towards Sally. His hands were shaking, but he didn't want anyone to see. "Follow me," he ordered. "And for Christ's sake, keep close. We don't want any more accidents."

They reached Sally together, and Rick picked her up like she was a bundle of dirty rags. "Who are they?" he said, motioning towards the Volvo.

"The Kendalls," said Rohmer, one hand resting on top of Tabby's head. She seemed unwilling to let him go. "The family who come here when I'm not. They must've fled town and thought they could hide out here, until all this is over."

Rick resisted the urge to comment on that final remark. "We tread carefully." He glanced at Rohmer, saw the new fear in the man's old, old eyes. "I don't want to lose either of you, not when we've only just become friends." He smiled.

Rohmer nodded, unable to speak. He gripped his wound, blood squeezing through his fingers.

"I'll sort that out once we're safe," said Rick.

Rohmer nodded. His lips were tight and bloodless.

Rick walked towards the cottage, making sure that they stayed close. He didn't know what he was going to find in there, but for the first time in over a day the terrible Dead Rooms of Leeds crossed his mind, and he prayed that after his scare Rohmer would be quicker to react.

What remained of their future might depend on it.

CHAPTER THIRTY

DARYL HAD FINALLY grown tired of the stupid bitch.

"Will you please just shut up for a moment? I'm trying to think."

Claire sat on the moped, her bare feet dragging in the grass. She was pouting, putting on a ridiculous show to stir his emotions. If only she knew that Daryl did not possess emotions; that would be a laugh. Oh, how he'd laugh... right before he cut off her head and used it as a hat.

"I just want a little attention," she said, folding her arms across her perky breasts. She pouted again, a pathetic council-estate Monroe. It probably worked on most of the men she'd been with – but Daryl was not like most men.

Daryl tried his best to ignore her and watched the cottage through the binoculars. It was located on the other side of the canal, and the old barge was moored at a shitty little jetty right near it. They must be inside the cottage, hiding out for a while, taking a breath. All of them. The policeman, the old man, the little girl. And Sally, his one true love.

He looked again at Claire, and wondered why he'd thought she even slightly resembled Sally. She didn't. She was crude and cheap... and stupid. That last was the most unforgivable thing of all. It made her just like everyone else, one of the mindless swarm of humanity Daryl had always felt separate from.

At first he'd thought that her hurt had singled her out and formed a connection between them. Now he realised that it made her the same as the rest of them – everyone has their own private parlour of pain, the place into which they like to retreat and act like a martyr.

"Silly bitch," he said, almost snarling the words.

"What was that?" She stood, hands on hips, and tried to act like she was strong. Her legs were shaking and her face was pallid. She looked about as strong as a child's doll.

"I said," he advanced towards her. "Silly. Fucking. Bitch." He slapped her across the face before she could respond, taking her by surprise. Her feet went out from under her, and she fell on her scrawny arse, a look of pure shock on her face.

Daryl's hand stung from the contact, even inside Sally's increasingly tattered gloves. He began to laugh, flexing his fingers and staring at them as if they'd suddenly taken on a life of their own.

The look of shock on Claire's face turned quickly to one of fear, and she tried to shuffle backwards, retreating from him. "What's wrong? Why are you doing this? I thought we were... friends. You know – a couple."

"A couple of cunts," Daryl snapped, between bouts of girlish giggling. His mind was strung between high wires, stretched so thin that it just might snap. He could picture it spread out above his head like a fleshy sheet.

Once the bout of uncontrollable hilarity had passed, he grabbed Claire by the hair and dragged her to her feet, gritting his teeth against the death lust that rose up his throat and into his mouth like bile. He could almost taste her extinction, and it was wonderful, growing within him like the shivery stirrings of an orgasm.

"Get on the bike," he said, pushing her towards the machine. "We're going."

"Where?" she whined.

"Just going." He nipped her arm, prodded her left breast, kicked her up the backside.

"Ow," she said, rubbing at the spots he was casually abusing. "That hurts."

"Good. It's meant to. Much more of this nonsense and it'll hurt a lot more than that."

Their relationship had entered a new phase. Now that the thrill of sexual conquest was over and done with, Daryl felt nothing but disdain for this snivelling little bint. She was an annoyance; a mere sub-plot in the ongoing script of his life. The sooner he wrote her out of the story the better he would feel about the whole thing.

Carefully he steered the bike along the track, dodging large stones and heading for the footbridge he had spotted some time ago. He didn't want to enter the cottage and spook them. All he required was a safe vantage point, a place from which he could continue to watch the show. They were doing fine, this shabby band of survivors, and watching them was like viewing a film running in conjunction with his own wonderful cinematic adventures.

Daryl was not yet ready to switch the channel.

The gunshot was close. He heard it as he pulled up the moped at a fallen tree trunk, bringing the rear end around in a looping skid in the loose earth. It sounded to his untrained ears like an old blunderbuss, or something; someone's inherited shotgun? He'd never been educated in firearms, and all big guns sounded the same.

He sat on the bike and listened, waiting for the sound to come again. Claire's hands pressed into his sides, unnecessarily tightly. He shifted on the seat; her grip tightened. The sound of laughter was carried on the breeze, putting him on edge.

"Bloody hell," he said.

"What is it? Are we in danger?" Her voice was quiet, fear-soft. He liked it that way.

"I don't know. It could be the police or maybe some yokels messing about with a gun. We need to be careful."

She whimpered like a hurt dog. Daryl was not even sure that she was aware of making the sound. It made him dislike her even more. Jesus, what had he ever been attracted to? Ah, yes... he remembered now: her *ease*, the way she had given herself up to him in a flash.

He got off the moped and pushed it over to the grounded tree trunk. Claire got her leg stuck as she swung it over the seat, but managed to dismount before he forced her off the vehicle. She scowled at him, arms crossed and feet splayed outward. Her forearms were folded across her chest, as if barring the way.

"I'll check this out," he said, not even looking at her. What on earth had possessed him to let her tag along with him in the first place? Could the unaccustomed attention of a female have given him such a buzz that he was blinded to her obvious flaws?

Yes, he admitted to himself. *That's exactly what it was.*

"Don't leave me here..." She took a few steps towards him and then stopped, torn between maintaining her pained demeanour and following him into the trees. The undergrowth rustled, and somewhere above them a bird took to the air, rattling the dry branches like castanets.

"I won't be long. Just hang around here, and yell if anyone comes along. Yell and I'll come for you." He pushed through the undergrowth and headed towards the area where he thought the gunshots had originated. There was no more commotion, but the air felt pressurised, as if a thunderstorm were approaching. There was a sense of unresolved anxiety, of violence waiting to happen.

Small animals scurried before him, following unseen trails and fleeing from his approach. Daryl enjoyed the sense of power. It was an echo of how he felt when he ordered Claire about, and he realised that this was also part of the reason he had allowed her to hang around for so long. But the novelty was wearing off; her questionable allure had become stale. She did not have long left as his side-kick: it had always been a temporary position, a mere cameo role in the film he was creating.

Up ahead appeared, out of the limp greenery, the grey bulk of a single-storey structure. It looked like a disused power station, an old reinforced concrete shell once used to contain electrical apparatus that had long ago been abandoned and left to rot. Parts of the structure were missing – rusted steel rods stuck out of the crumbling concrete like lethal booby traps. Daryl recalled the public information films he'd seen in school, vicious shorts made in the 1970s and featuring bowl-cut teenagers coming to dire ends in such derelict properties. There was a famous one about the 'spirit of lonely water' that had fuelled his fantasies for years... a hooded figure that hung around isolated ponds and lured kids to a death by drowning.

The young Daryl had masturbated over that commercial, filling his mind with images of dead boys and girls floating face-down in shallow water.

He smiled at the memories. This type of recollection was rare from his school days – most of the time he'd been bullied and pestered – so when good thoughts came to mind he felt that he should always take the time to enjoy them.

"Fuckin' hell!" The voice came from just up ahead. It was dull, uneducated, lacking any favourable qualities as far as Daryl was concerned. It reminded him of the voices of kids he'd attended school with and the moronic adults they had developed into. Ugly boys usually brought up in single parent families, who would rather hit someone than discuss any potential differences in a calm, sensible manner.

"Took its bastard leg right off!"

Daryl crouched down and moved slowly, not wishing to be seen by the owner of the voice. He suspected that despite the changes currently reshaping the world, his presence was still something a certain kind of person might not exactly cherish. It had always been this way, and Daryl never expected it to change. Some things would remain the same forever; some people were incapable of transforming themselves into different personalities.

Thankfully Daryl was not one of these people. He was changing all the time, with a regularity that made him feel frightened and thrilled in equal measures. A few days ago he would never have treated a woman how he was treating Claire; today he could just as easily slit her throat as offer her a kiss. Tomorrow... well, who knew? Daryl the ever-changing was an unreadable entity, and he was quickly learning to live life day by day instead of the long, unbearable sequence it had been with Mother.

He watched the two men as they drank beer from cans and giggled. They were wearing winter clothes, some of which still had the price tags attached – gear they had obviously looted from a store. Their faces were ruddy from drink and their postures were loose and unpredictable. They laughed like madmen, slapping each other on the back and dancing in little circles, shuffling their booted feet on the hard dirt.

Daryl was more afraid of these men than he was of the walking dead.

There was a doorway in the side of the concrete power station: a rectangular opening made irregular by vandalism. The door itself was long gone, leaving just a dark hole. The concrete slab floor at the centre of the doorway had been broken away by the ravages of time and the elements to reveal a shallow basement, and suspended above this dark space, tied into a makeshift harness, was a severely mutilated body.

Daryl realised immediately what was going on here and the knowledge sickened him, despite his own recent activities.

The two men were using the woman's reanimated corpse as a target for shooting practice. Both of her legs had been blown off, leaving rough-edged stumps, one of her arms was missing below the elbow, and there were several huge wounds in her naked torso. Her head remained intact, but her face had been slashed to ribbons.

The dead woman made tiny moaning noises as she swayed on the harness. Loops of rope had been wrapped around her shoulders and under her armpits, the other end looped over the steel lintel above the broken door opening. Some of the rope coils were red, and it took Daryl a little while to realise that her stomach had been opened and her intestines looped around her body along with the hemp.

"Get her in the head," said the smaller of the two men, lighting up a hand-rolled cigarette. "Get the bitch in the fuckin' mush! She's asking for it."

His friend laughed, and then tried to aim, but his hands were unsteady – probably due to his alcohol intake. Cans and bottles littered the ground at the men's feet, and there were a couple of crates of beer leaning against a rotten tree stump. "Can barely see the twat," he said, swaying slightly from side to side.

The small man laughed, a manic chuckle that chilled Daryl more than the cold and the sight of the guns.

A selection of weapons were laid out a few short yards away from Daryl – guns, knives, a machete, even a bow and arrows.

He eased forward, keeping his eyes on the two men. They were too drunk to even notice as he inched through the undergrowth, heading towards the makeshift armoury.

"Your turn... I can't even see, I'm so pissed." More laughter.

Daryl reached out carefully. His fingers grasped the handle of an old-fashioned shotgun and he lifted it, glancing at it briefly to register that the barrel had been sawn off half way down its length. He knew enough from movies to realise how much damage such a weapon was capable of doing to the human form at close range.

He brought the shotgun into his hiding place, cocked the hammers, and then stepped into the open, hoping that he'd done enough to arm the thing – and that it was loaded.

It took several seconds for the men to notice him, and Daryl waited until they had turned to face him before opening fire. He wanted to see their faces as their bodies were torn to shreds by the wide spray of pellets.

After he had let rip with both barrels, Daryl stood shrouded in smoke, the stench of cordite burning his nostrils, and the two men lay on the ground. One of them was still twitching; his torn clothes were bright red with blood and as he raised his head, his eyes rolled in their sockets. His screaming was loud and wordless, like a siren. Daryl listened to it for a while, amazed that the throat could contort enough to make such inhuman sounds.

Then he stepped over to the man and brought the stock of the shotgun down on his skull with all the force he could muster, the bone cracking in a straight line down the centre of his brow. He repeated the process until the man was still and his head was reduced to a red mush, and then moved on to the second motionless moron: he did not want these two to come back. Even the dead had standards, and these two scumbags would bring down the entire group.

Daryl was sweating, his arms ached. He had an erection.

"Fuckers," he whispered, all too aware that by killing them he had been venting his hatred of the people who had made his life so empty. For all his days he had been harassed by men like these; his every move mocked, each word he'd spoken turned into a joke. Manual workers, office drones, every so-called 'real man' he had ever encountered: stupid muscle-headed fuckwits with more machismo than common sense.

But now it was Daryl's turn to assume the role of the alpha male, and if he could reduce a few of these idiots to shredded meat along the way, then that was fine by him.

"*Gnnnnnnn...*" The dead woman moaned again, her bloodless torso thrashing. Daryl had forgotten that she was even there, and her movements dragged him back to reality. She was twisting on the rope, her shattered body moving like a bizarre mobile or weather vane.

Daryl bent down, retrieved a small handgun from one of the men's cold hands, and shot the rope that held her. She fell into the hole that led to the basement, cracking her head on the rim as she vanished into the darkness. The accuracy of the shot had been a result of pure luck, but it made him feel once again that certain scenes had already been written for him to enact.

Daryl heard shuffling sounds, and then other moans emerged from down there in the black basement. He realised that there must be more dead people beneath the ground, perhaps deliberately trapped by these two men to provide more savage sport to amuse them. He actually appreciated their methods, and thought that if they had not been such arseholes he might even have joined in their fun. Unfortunately, men like these were not worth the trouble. They were better off out of the picture.

Daryl walked over to the hole and leaned over it, staring down into the basement. The floor was formed of compacted earth and there was just enough light to see the space was sealed. It was more like a pit than an actual room, and as far as he could see there were at least three or four other dead people in there beside the twisting torso he had released from the harness. He caught a glimpse of pale limbs, dirty clothing, and thin, shadowy faces with gaping mouths.

Daryl smiled. An idea had begun to form, and it seemed to him that he could have a little fun while ridding himself of a problem.

"Claire!" He doubled back and pushed his way into the bushes. "Claire, get over here."

He glanced at the men's bags and his eyes widened when they fell upon a small digital video camera. He picked it up and located the power button. The compact hand-held machine whined and then the lens cap slid back and the tiny screen flared into life.

Daryl pointed the camera at the power station and watched it on the screen, one remove from reality. It was the way he had always felt before these events: separated from everything by a camera lens, as if his life were being projected onto a vast screen for the amusement of others. Only this time *he* was the one being amused; the film was turning into something of his own devising, and whoever had scripted the first act was long gone.

He listened, heard the clatter of Claire's clumsy approach through the undergrowth, and stepped back, smiling.

"What is it?" She was breathless when she broke through the trees.

"It's okay. I've taken care of these jokers, so we can have a look around and see if they had any supplies." He watched her through the camera, sizing her up for the next scene.

Claire was already rooting through their bags, her face lighting up at the sight of the beer. "Well, they have this." She lifted a whisky bottle from the pack, grinning and smacking her lips.

The little camera whirred. There must be something broken inside, but it still worked well enough to allow Daryl to view the events around him. Even if the playback function had been disabled, it was enough that he could experience this all through a viewfinder. It felt more real this way.

Claire was standing so close to the pit that Daryl was amazed she did not hear the sounds coming from down below. It just went to show how unobservant she was, how up herself. If it wasn't directly beneath her nose, then the bitch remained unaware, utterly absorbed in her own activity.

Daryl raised the pistol he had taken from the dead men's stash.

"Claire?"

She looked up, her eyes shining, cheeks full of rose petals as she drank deeply from the whisky bottle.

Daryl shot her once in the left leg, knocking her sufficiently off balance that she fell right into the pit. For the second time that day he was pleased with his aim, considering that he was a total novice, and was holding the camera to one eye as he pulled the trigger. A second shot went astray, missing her completely. Claire screamed his name, her hands grasping at the uneven edge of the pit as her body weight pulled her down. She stared right at Daryl, a look of dawning horror on her face, and then she slipped beneath the surface of the earth. Screaming.

"I'm so sorry, dear," said Daryl, walking softly towards the pit, filming it all. "But you were getting right on my fucking nerves." The sounds of her screaming were already dying out; they were soon replaced by those of feasting.

Daryl peered into the pit but could only make out a large shape being torn apart by other shapes. Even the camera's screen showed only a hazy image. The best was kept from him by darkness: he barely even caught sight of the blood as Claire was stripped to the bone. However long the dead people had been down there, it was long enough to make their hunger insatiable. The sound of their feeding frenzy was repellent, and Daryl had soon heard enough. He turned off the camera, the scene at its end.

Slowly, he walked back to the moped. There was a tin of corned beef in Claire's rucksack. He fished it out, opened it, and began to eat. By the time he had finished the meat, Claire was a distant memory. Her name, her face, the echo of her words no longer made an impact on the surface of his life; not even the slightest ripple.

He packed up his stuff, slid the camera into his bag, climbed onto the moped, and set off towards whatever future he chose to create.

CHAPTER THIRTY-ONE

THE FRONT DOOR of the cottage was locked but Rohmer already had his key out as they approached, clutching it like a talisman in shaking hands.

Rick quickly scanned the area, seeing nothing to be afraid of, while the old man unlocked the heavy wooden door. It swung open soundlessly, with not even the hint of creaking hinges. Rick was almost disappointed; his senses were unnaturally keen at this point, and a jokey horror movie sound effect might have served to break the tension and relax them all.

"Wait," he said, moving inside the building and pressing his back against the wall. He moved along the short hallway and entered the first door on his right, adjacent to the stairs.

The room he surveyed was long, with a low ceiling, and not an item seemed out of place. The neat furniture was clean and undamaged, the shelves and writing desk had not been interfered with, the floor held no bloodstains. Rick's keen battle senses did not even detect the telltale atmosphere of recent violence.

Judging by the presence of the car parked outside, the visitors – the Kendall family – must still be somewhere on the premises. Rohmer had said that the family consisted of a middle aged couple and a thirteen year-old boy. They'd probably fled here when the city erupted in violence, and had no doubt been planning to hole up for as long they could, existing on whatever supplies they'd managed to bring along and those already in the place. According to Rohmer the cottage was well stocked, with a large fruit and wine cellar, and even had its own independent source of power – a small emergency generator located in one of the outbuildings at the rear of the property.

"Hello!"

Rick waited for a response, but none came. The place *felt* empty... it was a sensation he had encountered before, during training missions. When a building is occupied it holds a sense of life between its walls, a certain tautness in the air, but when there is no one living in the vicinity, that too becomes obvious, by the same invisible vibrations.

He moved back out of the room and into the hall, where he dropped to his knees and aimed the M16 up the narrow staircase. Nothing moved, but the darkness seemed to swirl before his eyes: a slow snake-curling motion that unnerved him.

Then Rick heard a single sound: a soft knocking, as of a fist rapping lightly on a door, or the tip of a boot making brief contact with the base of a skirting board. It wasn't much, but it was enough to set his well-honed instincts popping, especially after what had happened outside, when Rohmer had almost been killed by what amounted to a walking skeleton.

He waited. And, as expected, the sound came again. It continued, building a rhythm and gaining in volume, like someone slamming their hand against a wall up there.

Thud... thud... thud...

Slowly, cautiously, Rick began to ascend the stairs, keeping his feet light by taking up as much of the tension as possible in his calves as he gently lowered the soles of his boots onto the timber treads. His nerves tensed with each footfall, expecting the squeal of old boards and the creak of support timbers.

The thumping noise continued. It was a regular beat, with a few seconds of silence separating each strike of whatever it was that was making the sound.

Thud... thud... thud...

Like a drumbeat, the sound continued, guiding him up the stairs towards the landing.

The stairs began to creak slightly as Rick climbed them, but he managed to adjust his centre of balance just enough to minimise the noise. He glanced back, over his shoulder, but could no longer see the front door. He hoped that Rohmer and Tabby were okay standing out there on the doorstep. The old man had proved more of a hindrance than a help during their last encounter with the dead, and he hoped that a lesson had been learned. Rick hated the thought of anything happening to his recently adopted family.

The thought disturbed him, yet he was overwhelmed by the fondness he felt towards these people after such a relatively short amount of time in their company. He had allowed himself to grow close to the man and the girl, and keeping them alive came second in importance only to the safety of Sally.

He dropped to his knees when he reached the upper landing, keeping the rifle at the ready. He wished he'd swapped it for the pistol, in such a confined space, but it was too late now to regret thoughtless decisions. The secret of success was to work with what you had, to focus on the moment and nothing more.

The thumping sound continued.

Thud... thud... thud...

It was coming from behind the closed door that lay directly at the top of the stairs.

Rick peered along the landing in both directions, noting that all the other doors were also closed. If anyone was hiding up there, he would be signalled of their intention to attack by the door opening. It might just give him enough time to gain the upper hand: the difference between life and death, survival and extinction, often hung on such minor details.

Thud... thud... thud...

He shuffled forward in a low crouch, keeping his head below the level of a stray gunshot. The rug shifted beneath him, inching across varnished boards, but he had faith in his sense of balance.

When he reached the door he stood and quickly slipped to one side, taking a deep breath. He waited. Listened. The timbre of the sound had not altered, nor had its rhythm changed in any way. Either whoever was making the sound was locked into some Zen-like state, or it was simply the sound of a loose pipe knocking against the wall or a faulty window latch shifting in the breeze.

Thud... thud... thud...

Rick moved smoothly and quickly. He faced the door and kicked it open, ready to fire.

The room beyond was small – more of a storeroom than a bed chamber – and sparsely furnished. There was a single bed pushed against the rear wall, a low cabinet piled with papers and magazines to his left, a narrow wardrobe to his right... and at the centre of the room the reanimated body of a young boy hung from his neck by a noose.

Thud... thud... thud...

It was the sound of one of the body's feet clattering against the back of the wooden chair which he had clearly used to climb up to the noose. He must have kicked the chair away as he stepped off it, his body plummeting, and the chair had fallen not quite far enough away from the body to leave the floor beneath clear. Then he'd come back and found himself still hanging there.

So as he swung in place, clawing at his throat and trying to escape the noose, his foot came into regular contact with the chair back.

Thud... thud... thud...

Rick's vision blurred, and only when he blinked to clear it did he realise that he was crying. He adjusted his aim and fired a single round, taking one side of the boy's head off and sending part of the skull spinning across the room. It came to rest like a little bowl near the wardrobe.

The thumping sound came no more and Rick had never been happier to hear the end of something. He knew that he would hear that sound in his dreams, probably for the rest of his life. It would sound behind the voices he carried within him, a low-tempo backbeat to their unending screams.

"Rick?" Tabby's voice drifted up the stairs, soft and tentative, yet with an edge he could not identify. Was it terror? He realised that so far he'd not seen the girl truly afraid. It was as if she had the utmost faith in her grandfather, and now in Rick. As long as they were by her side, she would never be completely afraid.

But now she sounded lost and alone in the dark, just like everyone else.

"I'm coming." He ran down the stairs, making sure that the door to the small bedroom was closed firmly behind him. "What is it?"

Her face was wet; fine red veins stood out in her eyes, a tracery of pain. "It's Granddad."

"Where is he? I told him to stay outside with you and keep watch." Rick moved to the door, the hot barrel of the M16 nosing before him, sniffing out danger. The front door was closed.

"There were sounds... something was moving out there. He pushed me inside and said that he'd get them away from here."

"Where's Sally?"

The girl shook her head, her eyes growing even wider. "With Granddad. She sort of stumbled off... and he followed her. He told me to come and get you."

The old fool. He was planning to take on the dead in numbers in order to keep them away from his granddaughter... and from Rick.

"Stay with me. Don't leave my side." He grabbed the girl roughly by the shoulder and opened the door. "I don't know if it's safe in here, so we need to stay together."

Tabby nodded just as the gunshots began.

Rick headed for the back of the cottage, the girl keeping pace. He could hear her breathing, sense her panic as it rose within her tiny frame, but she moved with the speed and grace of a gazelle. He wanted to cry; he refused to let the tears come but they came anyway, washing down his cheeks like warm rain.

"Where's Sally?" Panic was rising in him, too. It made his limbs shudder and his resolve harden. Like always, he drew strength from it, using it as raw fuel.

I'm here, darling. Don't worry.

Sally was wandering around in the open, a few yards away from a low barn. She looked like a lost sheep, turning in slow circles, unable to locate herself and pick a direction. The morphine must still be working.

"Stupid old man! I told him to stay put. I *told* him..."

When he reached Sally he gently guided her away from the barn and sat her down on a tuft of grass at the base of a slight rise. He kept one eye on the open barn doorway, and both ears open for anything that might signify trouble. Rohmer must be in there: it was the only logical place he could have gone. Perhaps he'd chased one of his runners in there, and that was the source of the gunshots.

"Rohmer! I'm coming, mate. Just keep cool!"

Sally flopped onto her back, the morphine still doing its job and dulling her senses. Her hunger.

I'm okay. I just went for a little walk. Tired now...

Rick stroked her bandaged head, feeling the rough contours of whatever was left of her face. The wrappings were grubby, but he had not been able to bring himself to remove them again, not yet. Maybe later, when all this was over and done with and they could rest for a while.

Standing, he walked straight towards the barn, not even pausing on his way through the doorway. Whatever was in there, it was going down.

Tabby was behind him, her view blocked by his body, so thankfully she did not see what had happened to the old man.

Rick turned, angling his torso so that she would not catch sight of what now lay behind him, almost unseen in the dim interior. "Go and stand outside. I need you to do this – you have to do what I say. Stand over there and look the other way. Keep an eye on Sally and scream like fuck if you see anything."

Tabby's eyes widened... then she knew; she was not a stupid girl, and she knew immediately that something had gone badly wrong. She pressed her lips together, being a brave little girl, and Rick's heart tensed as she took a few steps away from the barn's entrance.

Rick made sure that she was still in plain sight yet unable to see deep inside the barn. Then he turned his attention back to Rohmer, poor, poor Rohmer.

The old man was on his back and holding his throat. Blood had sprayed the front of his jacket and even now continued to seep out of the ruptured artery in his neck. His eyes were almost fully closed, but he nodded once, signalling his approval at Rick's actions regarding the girl.

Two bodies lay nearby, each of them sporting gunshot wounds to the head. A woman in a long skirt and a short coat was missing the front of her face; a man was sprawled face down, the back of his head splayed outward in a white flower of bone.

The pistol was still in Rohmer's hand. He lifted it and pulled the trigger. The hammer clicked onto an empty chamber. His eyes were wide and tearful. If a man could apologise without words, then this was it.

Rohmer closed his eyes and removed his hand from the side of his throat. Blood gushed at an alarming rate, there was so much of it that it looked black in the dimness.

"Oh, fuck." Rick shot Rohmer in the face and turned quickly away. He did not want to see this man die. He could not bring himself to witness what he had been forced to do. As he stepped outside he heard the distant groaning of a small engine – perhaps a little motorcycle hammering away in the distance. He went to Tabby, fell to his knees, and held her. Her grip was slack at first, but soon she clung to him with a force and an immediacy that was terrifying in its intensity. Rick waited for her sobs, but they did not come, and when finally he pulled away her face was vacant, her eyes staring into the middle distance.

It was a look he'd seen before in the desert: the face of clinical shock.

When he turned back to look at Sally, the place where she had been was empty. His gaze returned to the barn doors, and what lay beyond.

Rick stood and walked back inside the barn, gun loose at his side.

She must have crawled in there on all fours, like an animal, perhaps smelling Rohmer's blood through the bandages. She was kneeling before him, both hands on his leg, and attempting to take a bite out of his thigh. Because of the double layer of bindings, and the cotton wool in her throat, she was unable to do much else than scrape her mouth against his trousers. Rick could see her jaw muscles working; the motion beneath the bandages was strong and deliberate, despite the fact that her body was still floppy from the drugs.

Even doped up to high heaven, his wife was trying to eat.

Rick walked towards her, grabbed her by the neck, and dragged her away. There were no tears now, nor was there any room for rage. He felt numb, empty, bereft of human feelings. Even the love he felt towards Sally was mutated, a shapeless thing twisting away into an inner darkness.

Tabby had not moved, so he grabbed her with his other hand and guided both his girls back to the cottage, his face slack, eyes seeing nothing but what was directly ahead of him. He felt like he was crossing some imaginary border and entering a place where few men had ever been: a blasted zone where the dead walked and he loved a hungry corpse with all the compassion that remained in his withered heart.

Back at the cottage he barricaded them in. Sally was on the sofa, dosed up with yet more morphine; Tabby stood in a corner, refusing to sit, just staring at the wall.

Thank you, darling. That feels good... safe.

He tried to ignore Sally's voice, but was unable to shut it out. Each time she spoke in his head, he felt that dark love pulsing like a cancer.

He checked every inch of the house and proved to himself there were no other bodies present. He cut down the boy and disposed of him in a ditch out the back, where he found the tattered remains of three more cadavers. There was not enough left of these to get up and walk, but he stamped on their skulls anyway, reducing them to flattened pulp. As little as a few hours ago his actions might still have disgusted him, but now he saw these remains only as meat.

He surmised that the boy's parents must have died and come back for their son, and that they had perhaps fed on a couple of passing strangers – maybe people hiking to safety, or a wounded man and wife who had stopped by for help. The boy had probably hidden from his dead parents, and taken the only way out he could think of when he realised that no one was coming to his aid and his mother and father wanted to devour him.

Rick admired the boy's single-mindedness. It took a lot of courage to leave behind all that you loved, however much they had changed.

What a fucking mess. And not just this situation: the whole world was a calamity, an ongoing mindfuck.

He found a bottle of wine in a kitchen cupboard, then some medical supplies in another. There were plenty of bandages.

It took him quite some time to coerce Tabby up the stairs and into the bed in the main bedroom. She was stiff and unresponsive; her eyes remained open but she was asleep on her feet. He left her clothes on and covered her with fresh blankets from a drawer. He stroked her forehead and sang to her – not a real song, just a strange tune that occurred to him, possibly a jingle from some advert he'd seen back when the world was still in one piece.

Once he was sure that she was finally resting, he left the room and went back downstairs.

He positioned Sally at the dining table, propping her up in a high-backed chair. Then, acting out of impulse, he loosely tied her legs and arms to the chair. Her head rolled on her neck and she was making tiny grunting noises.

Hungry.

Rick closed his eyes, resisting the urge to answer.

He cut off the bandages with a pair of medical scissors he had found in the kitchen, being careful not to cause any more damage to Sally's face. The cellophane-wrapped wounds were completely bloodless by now. With her heart no longer pumping, any blood remaining in her system would probably have pooled in the lower cavities, forming bruises on the dead flesh.

He averted his gaze as he applied the fresh dressings, preferring not to examine too closely what her features had become. He was reminded of the aftermath of atrocities he'd seen during his tours of duty in war-torn trouble spots: the shredded corpses of bomb blast victims; dry dead flaps of skin; slashes of yellowing bone.

As he was working, the neck of Sally's top slipped sideways and down, baring the upper part of one still-perfect breast. He wasn't disturbed to find that he had an erection, merely surprised that he still had the energy to be aroused.

"There, there... soon be safe. Once we get to Rohmer's island everything will be different." He no longer even believed it; for all he knew, the island itself was little more than an urban myth, a hopeful dream concocted by a desperate old man to calm his terrified daughter and provide meaning in the madness the world had become.

I know, baby. I trust you. Always have, always will.

He finished up with the dressings and emptied the wine bottle. Standing, he crossed the room and grabbed another from a shelf just inside the kitchen doorway. He downed half the second bottle in a single mouthful, and only when he closed his eyes did he feel the buzz of the alcohol.

Not too much, baby. You never could stomach a lot of red wine.

It was dark now, so he secured the shutters and closed the curtains across the small cottage windows. Nothing moved outside; even the air was calm and still.

He inspected the bookcase along one wall, finding mostly text books, and then stumbled upon a record collection. No CDs here: just an array of old vinyl albums. It felt like fate when the third one he slid off the shelf was a double-album collection of Neil Diamond's greatest hits... and, yes, *Solitary Man* was on there. Side one, track four.

Perfect. What could be better on a night like this? The kid's in bed and we have the whole night ahead of us...

Rick felt the magnet-pull of attraction, and with it came a strange guilt. This was his wife, the woman he loved, yet she was also *another* woman, someone with which he was having some twisted kind of affair. Was it even possible to be unfaithful to the dead?

He'd noticed some candles in a kitchen drawer, tea lights. He fetched them and brought them into the main living room, then dotted them around the vicinity, lighting each one with matches from a box he found in the same drawer.

On one level he knew exactly what he was doing, but on another he watched the whole thing play out like a stage performance, a sad, melancholy drama.

Romantic light caressed Sally's white-masked features, soft shadows creating new dips and hollows across the clean padded surface of her face. It was like seeing another woman – or seeing Sally for the first time, stripped of all artifice and illusion. She had become the meat behind the mask, the reality beneath the torn veil.

He approached the table and poured her some wine. She was still tied into the chair, and he decided to leave her that way. Back in the day, they'd both enjoyed a little light S&M as foreplay.

"Merlot... it's your favourite." He smiled, touched her cold arm. There was nothing inside him but a screaming wind, and at the heart of the storm rested a kernel of desire.

Thank you, baby. You always knew how to take care of me.

He put on the record, and the sound of Neil Diamond's husky voice sent shivers across the exposed flesh of his arms and neck, making the small hairs there stand to attention in the same way as his dick now stood proud.

Our song.

"It always will be. No matter what happens, we'll always have that night... and I'll never stop loving you. I love you more every second of each day we're together. I know things are different now, and you're a different person..." – the wind within howled and dipped, leaving behind a void – "a different... being. But still I love you."

I love you more.

He sensed her smile beneath the bandages, even imagined that he saw the faint twitch of movement.

Slowly, he moved towards her, the world dimming and the edges of the room fading to a soft-focus blur. He felt exactly like he had on that first night, when they'd entered the bar and danced like no one else was there. He and Sally became the focal point of the universe, the pivot on which the heavens tilted.

"I never stopped loving you and I never will. Nothing can separate us... *nothing*. Not even this."

His hand gently traced the line of her shoulder, feeling the still ice of her skin. The flesh rippled, slipped, folded... lacking its former elasticity, it remained that way, curled up like crepe paper. It was new and interesting; he thought he might even like it.

Leaning in close, he placed his lips against the spot where he knew her mouth would be. She had no breath. Coldness seeped through the wrappings; it made his lips harden and his cheeks prickle. He kissed her softly, carefully, not wanting to cause further damage to her frame. His tongue lapped at the dim curve of her bandaged mouth.

The fact that she did not respond to his advances seemed like a come-on; she was simply playing hard-to-get.

He caressed her cold, hard breasts, the nipples like tiny stones beneath her clothes. Running one hand down her body and across her thigh, he eased in towards her, bending her back on the dining chair. The legs creaked under their combined weight, but he slid into her lap and wrapped his legs around her waist, straddling her like he used to do. It was all so natural, like things had never changed between them.

His hand found the place between her legs that represented a kind of heaven, but it was cold, desolate... a barren region that now shunned life. He ploughed on, refusing to accept that this wasn't working, that it was impossible to make love to the dead. His hips bucking wildly against her lower abdomen, he attempted to transfer the heat of his erection into her stalled system, as if the very energy of his passion might rouse her enough to couple with him.

Darling... it feels so good.

He lifted his feet off the floor and pushed his chest against her, feeling her eager stiffness and trying to break through the barrier death had placed in his way. He felt her striving towards him, straining to make contact...

When the chair leg broke, tipping them both onto the floor, he continued his seduction as if nothing had happened, fumbling at the buttons on her pants and pulling them down to her ankles. He forced her unresisting legs apart with one knee; while at the same time he dragged his own trousers down to release his throbbing erection.

Don't, baby. Not here. Not now. It isn't right.

He wept into her throat, thrusting his dwindling cock against her. Its softening tip entered her ice-cold navel, and then slid down against the roughened skin to probe her knotted pubic thatch. He reached down to guide himself inside, almost snapping her spine with his ardour. Rubbing at her to sustain the moment, he suddenly felt something writhe wetly against his fingers... he pulled them away and lifted his hand to his face, amazed that he'd encountered moisture.

Maggots curled around his fingers, fattened on the corruption at his wife's core, their lazy white bodies falling from his knuckles and landing on her chest, where they coiled sleepily.

Sally's covered mouth nuzzled at his chest, her ineffectual jaws trying to clamp down on his flesh.

"Nooooo!" he lurched to his feet, pulling up his trousers, and lashed out at the table behind him. The wine bottle shattered, slashing the skin of the world, and suddenly he became aware of what he had been in the process of becoming – a rapist of the dead.

"Aaaaargh!" The sounds he made were barely even human, just empty noises.

He fell to his knees, pounding his fists on the floor, and heard sharply and clearly the final strand of his sanity as it snapped with a loud thunderclap. That internal wind returned, this time haunted by the moans of the deceased.

Then he was still. The earth spun beneath him, continuing its rapid journey towards oblivion, but Rick was a statue, a man frozen in one moment forever – however long that might be.

Sally was motionless, her bare legs bruised and blackened, the skin ruptured in several places and white maggots boiling forth. Her white-wrapped head seemed incongruous, like some kind of allegory for a reality that was now far beyond Rick's grasping hands.

Her head moved from side to side. He could see the shape of her mouth under the wrappings, and yet again she was attempting to clamp them down onto something... to feed.

Hungry.

He stood, stared at her damaged body. "You want something to eat?" He was snarling now, leaving his old self far behind at the side of a road, a track which could only lead deep inside the darkness that sat at his centre. "You want some fucking *food*?"

He shrugged on his jacket and stalked outside, heading towards the barn. The moon hung suspended, like a cheap prop in a bad movie, and beneath its chill light he passed into the dense shadow cast by the barn.

Rohmer would have wanted to be of use; he would have hated his body to have gone to waste, rotting in a quiet corner of an empty barn.

Rick crossed the space and grabbed an axe from its place near a pile of chopped timbers. Its weight was a comfort in his hands, promising the nullifying emptiness of manual labour. He turned, walked towards Rohmer's cooling corpse.

The body was already stiff, but there was plenty of meat on it.

CHAPTER THIRTY-TWO

HUNGRYHUNGRYHUNGRYhungryhungryhungryhungryhungry hungryhungryhungryhungryhungryhungryhungryhungryhungry hungryhungryhungryhungryhungryhungryhungryhungryhungry hungryhungryhungryhungryhungryhungryhungryhungryhungry hungryhungryhungryhungryhungryhungryhungryhungryhungry hungryhungryhungryhungryhungryhungryhungryhungryhungry hungryhungry

CHAPTER THIRTY-THREE

AFTER WHAT SEEMED like hours, Rick left the barn and returned to the dismal moonlight.

He felt exposed.

His hands were bloody and he was carrying an old sack he had found hanging from a nail on the wall. The sack had originally contained a few pieces of rusted engine – random machine parts perhaps meant for the scrap yard – which he'd emptied out onto the ground. Now it contained only meat.

Faceless, nameless meat.

Back in the cottage he sat Sally on the sofa and once again removed the bandages from her tattered head, then placed the resultant white snake on the floor at her feet.

So much had changed between them but he and Sally had never been closer. He recalled the man he used to be with fondness, and truly waved goodbye to the past. Those were different people, the ones who had lived in a nice apartment and went to normal jobs. The people they were now would not even recognise themselves in the shabby meat puppets who had gone before.

The ghost of himself passed quietly from view, head down, hands open... he stared at Sally with fondness: her slashed features, the maggots that writhed in her bloodless wounds, the alien hunger that drove her.

Things were different. *They* were different. He loved his new wife in a way that he would not have been able to imagine as little as a few days before.

Very carefully he took the wadded cotton wool from her mouth, pulling it out of her throat like some huge mutated eel or giant maggot – the larger brother or sister of the ones he'd found between her thighs.

The cotton wool was now densely compacted, and it had absorbed whatever moisture had remained in Sally's throat after her death. When it was removed, the throat closed up over the absence; it made a faint sucking sound, like a vacuum.

Rick got a knife from the kitchen – the sharpest he could find – and cut Rohmer's meat into strips. He also found a tool box in there, so he brought it through, a rough plan forming in the fractured landscape of his mind.

Then, carefully, and without tears, he dropped the strips into Sally's open mouth, forcing it down the unnaturally tightened cavity of her throat with the handle of the knife. After a few scraps had passed along her throat and the swollen, dead muscles relaxed a little, he was able to simply scoop the meat into her mouth.

It reminded him of a nature programme he'd once seen, where a mother bird dropped bits of food into the upturned beaks of her brood.

Despite the morphine, Sally's jaws worked well enough to snatch at the slivers of flesh.

Rick kept his hands well out of the way, mindful that she did not snap off the end of a finger or thumb. Hideously, her yellow teeth began to crack when they came together, the force of her jaws too strong for the thin pieces of meat to fully absorb, and the jagged shards which remained looked lethal as tiny daggers.

After Sally had taken her fill he smashed out the rest of her teeth with a hammer.

CHAPTER THIRTY-FOUR

HEAT MEAT HURTS *good light dawn sparkling full ease good good mine good god good red wet meat god content*

PART FOUR

And All Is Meat

Is not the life more than meat, and the body than raiment?

Luke 12:23

CHAPTER THIRTY-FIVE

IT WAS THE fire that woke Daryl, or at least the reflection of it behind his closed eyelids. He stirred, bringing up his arms and feeling like he was restrained somehow, as if someone had tied him up while he dozed.

His limbs ached. The air was freezing; the chill had slipped between his layers of clothing to caress his skin and cool his blood. It was dark, daylight was still a couple of hours away.

He was sitting within the desiccated branches of a stout bush, half-hidden by the grasping twigs and the thickened roots showing above the soil. For some reason he'd felt the spot was a good vantage point – like a hide used by birdwatchers – and had positioned himself there hours ago.

The fire flickered in the distance, catching his attention from behind the trees on the other size of the canal. Because of his elevated position, he could clearly see the cottage and the two vehicles parked outside. He'd watched Nutman drive the ex-army jeep into the open during the night, scrutinising him through the binoculars. The man had looked intense as he worked; his face a mask of concentration, his hands steady as he manoeuvred the jeep across the uneven ground and parked it next to the Volvo estate.

Nutman had spent a few moments looking up at the dark sky before returning inside, and the look on his face had been unreadable. Daryl had been unable to work out if it was fear or longing or both...

Not long after that, Daryl must have fallen asleep.

He watched the flames as they licked at the side of the barn, clasping the structure from beneath like a giant demonic hand. Nutman stood nearby, staring at the conflagration. Daryl raised the binoculars and examined him close-up; his eyes were like stones in his unmoving face.

Daryl wondered if the man had finally lost his mind.

"Join the fucking club," he said, easing his arse off a particularly tough root.

He used the binoculars to glance along the edge of the canal, a few miles east of where Nutman was setting fire to the outbuildings. Off in the distance, a group of dead people wandered in a field. He watched, fascinated, as they pulled apart an old scarecrow, as if thinking it might contain some meat. One of the group was not much more than a skeleton with drapes of flesh hanging from its bones; the rest were in good condition, apart from the usual bloodless bite marks, death-wounds and missing bits and pieces. One of them sported gunshots; large holes peppered its torso and half the biceps on its right arm had been vaporised.

It was fascinating. No matter how they died, except for destruction of the brain, they came back. They returned, picking themselves up and running, shambling, even crawling across the landscape in search of prey. Daryl mused about their hunger for human flesh. Just why did they need to consume human meat? Was there something in the warm flesh, or maybe in the fresh blood, that eased the pain of being dead – or was it simply a natural desire, repressed by eons of evolution, which awoke after these things were revived?

So many questions... and Daryl doubted that anyone had an answer. Not the absent media, the surviving dregs of the government, or whatever doctors and scientists had managed to escape to secret think-tanks.

All we have is faith. That was something Mother had always believed in, even near the end. She swore that society was constantly on the brink of coming apart, and rather than rely upon politicians or scientists we should all be putting our faith in God.

Daryl thought she might have had a point. Not about God – no, he could never believe in that bullshit. But perhaps her ideas regarding faith were pretty much correct. When everything else slips away, and the world becomes a battleground of the dead, faith is all that remains: faith in oneself, faith that good will triumph, and faith that before your end arrives you'll have one bullet left to put in your brain.

Faith.

The fire had almost consumed the barn when he swung the binoculars back in the direction of the cottage. Nutman was nowhere in sight.

Daryl struggled to his feet and crossed the dirt to the moped. He could barely believe that such a ridiculous vehicle had served him so well. He'd had ample opportunities to trade it for something bigger and better – a real motorcycle, or a fast car – but for some reason he'd kept the moped. It seemed fitting somehow that the world's greatest serial killer, the only man ever to kill the same woman twice, should possess such an idiosyncratic chariot.

"Hello?"

Daryl tensed at the sound of the voice behind him. Then, taking a breath, he continued fastening his bag to the moped.

"Oh, God. I'm so glad to see you..."

He slowly turned, pasting a smile onto his face, and confronted the owner of the voice.

A tall man stood there, framed by the distant flames and the black smoke. He was slim, narrow of build, and was leaning on a thick branch to support his weight. Daryl glanced at the man's leg and saw that it was strapped up with rags; broken, by the look if it.

"I never thought I'd see another... well, living person again. Everyone's gone, out of the city and into the countryside. I haven't seen a live one for at least two days." The man was smiling. He seemed on the verge of genuine joy.

"Where have you come from?" Daryl took a step forward, keeping his hands behind his back.

"Leeds," said the man, stumbling forward a few steps. "The whole place has crumbled. Buildings on fire, looters running wild, what few police left on the streets killing people on sight. By the time I got out of there, there was hardly anyone normal left. Just dead people and crazy coppers. It's carnage." His eyes were wide and wild; his teeth were black and his lips split and swollen.

"I'm Daryl."

"Alan. Alan Harley. It really is good to meet you, Daryl. I had some trouble about a mile back, came off my bike when I ran into some of those dead bastards in the road. They nearly got me..." He glanced at his leg. "It smashed when I hit the deck. Hurt like hell, but still I managed to get up and run."

Daryl nodded, pretending that he was interested. Then, swiftly, he brought out the camera from behind his back.

"I'm making a sort of documentary, Alan. Filming people I meet; capturing their stories in digital media. It might be useful once everything goes back to normal. A kind of document of events from ground level."

"Uh-huh." Alan did not look convinced. He was too tired to even attempt to hide his frown.

"Care to participate?" Daryl switched on the camera and began to circle Alan, viewing him through the lens. Everything looked different through the lens: it looked better than reality.

"I... I'm not sure, Daryl. I mean, isn't this a little crazy? I kind of need some help here, you know."

"Oh," said Daryl, lowering the camera. "I see. You don't want to play."

Alan's confused smile hung on his lips; his eyes were wet.

Daryl took the gun from the waistband of his trousers, bringing it around to point the barrel at Alan. The other man did not at first register the weapon, and then when he finally saw it he sighed heavily. That was all: just a sigh.

"Goodbye, Alan." Daryl pulled the trigger. The first shot missed its target, pinging off into the air somewhere to Alan's left. Alan stupidly turned his head to follow the round, as if trying to catch sight of it in mid flight.

Daryl pulled the trigger again.

This time blood spattered from Alan's left arm, high up near the shoulder. The man pitched backwards, his balance lost.

The third shot caught him in the face, smashing his nose and cheekbones and turning the grey air around his head a bright powdery red.

Daryl did not even watch him fall.

He returned his attention to the burning barn, filming it with the camera. Soon Nutman came out of the cottage, carrying the young girl in his arms. He held her close to his chest, like a baby, and stared into her upturned face. It took him several minutes to lay her down in the rear of the jeep and cover her with blankets. Then, after reaching down to muss her hair, he turned back and once again entered the cottage.

This time he was carrying Sally. Her bandaged head looked bright white in the darkness and her limbs hung stiffly as he carried her to the vehicle. He placed her in the passenger seat, pressing her legs into the foot well.

Daryl alternated between camera and binoculars, caught between viewing and filming.

Nutman watched the blaze for a little while longer and then climbed into the jeep. The rear tyres spat up dust as he drove away.

Daryl turned around to climb aboard the moped, and was mildly shocked to see Alan standing behind him, his shattered nose not much more than a hole in the centre of his face.

"Oh, my," he said, aware how stupid that sounded. "My, oh my. What do we have here, then?"

Alan opened his mouth and bared his blackened teeth. He hissed like a cat; spittle erupted into the air. His eyeballs were red, filled with blood from the damage, and Daryl was fascinated by the aura of menace the corpse wore.

"Come on, then. Let's be having you." He felt no fear. All that was well behind him now, back in his old life; fear had died with Mother, and any lingering traces which may have been left behind had gone with Claire into that pit under the dilapidated power station.

Daryl was now a man without fear, a breed apart from other men.

Alan sidestepped, then lumbered forward. If it were not for the broken leg, he would have moved a lot faster: freshly dead, with no damage to his brain, he should have been quick and nimble. The shattered limb meant that Daryl had time to watch.

He lifted the camera to his eye and did just that, grinning at the silly dead bastard. "Action!" he said, trying not to laugh.

Alan pushed off his back leg, lurching towards Daryl. His hands were quick, and his jaws snapped at the air. Daryl jumped to the side and jogged around his attacker, entertained by the developing scenario.

He continued this mad dance for a few minutes, but soon grew bored. Alan slashed at the air with his hands, moaned and made inhuman sounds, and continued to fail at every attempt to capture Daryl.

The dead man was teaching Daryl nothing; all he demonstrated was that once a human being was dead whatever intelligence he or she had possessed simply left the scene. These things were like idiot animals, absurd creatures existing only to feed. They had no reasoning, no sense of the world around them. They were simply eating machines.

"God, you dead people are dumb. It's all very disappointing." He pointed the gun and pulled the trigger. There was no boom or recoil; either the gun was jammed or it had run out of ammunition. Daryl knew absolutely nothing about firearms, so made no attempt to examine the weapon. He threw it to the ground, annoyed and impatient.

"Fucking hell! You are bothersome, aren't you, Alan?"

He moved in close, dodging Alan's clutching hands, and kicked the broken leg out from under the corpse. Alan fell to the ground, his red eyes wide and panicked. He clawed at the earth, grabbed at bushes and the bases of trees.

Daryl looked around, and when his gaze fell upon a long stick with a pointed end, he smiled.

"This shouldn't take long," he said, and moved in for the kill.

He stabbed Alan through the right eye and twisted the branch as it went in, grinding it thorough the gristle and deep into the brain. Alan's hands stopped clutching, his jaw dropped open and his eyes sunk into their sockets. The pointed end of the stick penetrated Alan's skull, emerging out of the back to sink into the soil. Daryl leaned on it, pressing it down until he was bent over at the waist. Alan's mouth snapped open and closed like the beak of a demented turtle.

Daryl left the corpse and climbed onto the moped, lamenting the loss of the handgun. He had not had anywhere near enough fun with it. Perhaps he'd get lucky and come across another; next time he might even stumble across something bigger. If he'd been thinking straight back at the power station, he could have taken the rest of the guns. But it was too late now to regret the omission. He could never go back, only keep moving forward and into the third act of the motion picture of his life.

He patted the bag, feeling the bulge of the camera through a side pocket.

Then he started the moped and headed east, towards the coast. He had worked out by now that must be where Nutman was heading. It was a good idea: most other people seemed to be going in-country, trying for the woods and the open fields. The coast was a sensible option; it presented opportunities for crossing the ocean, if suitable passage could be found.

He thought of Alan as he rode towards the rising sun. What a pathetic excuse for a being. Even the dead, it seemed, were useless. Daryl had briefly hoped for more – that they might exhibit more potential than the living. But that was not to be. Meat was meat and dead was dead boring.

His story was the only interesting one left; all it lacked was an appreciative audience.

He hit the road and kept an eye out for danger, expecting attackers from all sides. Empty cars littered the roads, bodies were scattered here and there, a lot of them partially eaten. Smears of red marked the blacktop.

Daryl stopped at a petrol station and filled the moped's tank to the brim. He also filled two plastic containers and strapped them to the side of the vehicle. This was one reason he should have upgraded to a bigger machine: the moped hardly held much fuel, and if he failed to keep an eye on the level he risked being stranded.

He passed a family laid out neatly in the road – mother, father, son, daughter, their bellies opened and cleaned out, their faces gnawed off, their limbs stripped clean. It struck him as odd that their positioning was so tidy. Rather than sprawling like broken dolls, their corpses were set in a row, each facing the same way.

Beyond the disturbing familial frieze, a small roadside house was in flames. Daryl stopped the moped to watch it burn, and he was perversely pleased to hear the windows shatter and pop from the intensity of the heat. The fire must not have been going for long.

A naked woman ran out of the front door, her hair aflame. Her hands were raised above her kindling head, clutching at the heavens, and as she ran by him she did not even notice Daryl. She passed by so close that he could feel the heat of the flames and smell her burning hair. Her screams were thrilling, a polymorphous perversion.

The woman made it a few hundred yards along the road before she went down, thrashing at the asphalt with her fists. Eventually she grew still. Then, after something like five minutes, she calmly stood up and kept walking in the same direction, hair smouldering, the skin of her neck and back blackened from the flames.

The time between life and death was but a fraction, a sliver; a journey so brief that it was barely consequential. Daryl wondered if she had remained sentient as she had passed between states, or if the transformation had been like a switch first flicking off and then turning on again, but with something missing.

"What are you?" he whispered, awed by the sight. He watched the woman as she padded into the distance, vanishing over the brow of a hill. The molten flesh on her shoulders had looked like a shawl.

Was she still alive in some way or truly dead? What powered these corpses when they returned? He refused to believe in the fairytale of the soul, but could think of no alternative theory.

Mind. Body. Soul. Surely they were all the same thing; and the living brain was a filter for the body's interaction with the world in which it existed. The human machine, as Daryl had come to understand it, was a combination of all these elements, and they were merely a function of the body reacting in and to the world.

But what did that theory mean when you applied it to the walking dead?

"What are we?"

Nothing answered. So he rode on, perplexed by his own inadequacies and his inability to understand the subtleties of this damned entertaining apocalypse.

DARYL JOURNEYED THROUGH a landscape that Mother might have referred to as Hell: small villages and towns either taken over completely by the dead or populated by only a handful of survivors, the rest having fled to the imagined safety of the countryside. He passed wan faces at boarded windows, peering out through narrow gaps and pleading for aid.

If this *were* a movie, he thought, these images might be part of some lengthy slow-motion montage. Classical music playing on the soundtrack. The dead plodding through empty streets, looking up as he motored by, reaching out for him...

He saw the occasional police or army vehicle, usually parked at the kerb or pulled up on the verge. None of the officials he caught sight of looked sane; each of them had a look of madness in their eyes. He passed through unmolested. The atrocities being committed – people dragged out of burning houses, the dead used as target practice, women and children raped on the front lawns of country houses – were enough to keep these bastions of a dying civilisation busy for now.

Daryl knew that if he ever stopped at one of these places he would become a victim, just like all those others he saw kneeling before uniformed madmen, screaming at the sky, or staring blankly at the moped as he roared through the epicentre of their agony.

Often he raised the camera to one eye as he rode, logging countless images of bloodshed: a pack of dead men and women bringing down and tearing apart a small boy; two men in uniform raping a teenage girl while a uniformed woman leaned across the bonnet of a police car smoking a joint; a dead schoolgirl, still dressed in her pleated skirt and blazer, walking along the footpath holding onto a severed head by its hair.

None of this stirred him; it did not move him at all. Daryl remained intrigued yet distant. It was all background to his story, secondary characters crossing the scene. He was the focus.

Then, after what seemed like years of travel, he began to near the coast. Seagulls flew overhead, the salty air stung his nostrils, the horizon flattened out and turned a shade of grey which held a sullen dash of blue.

Figures moved in the fields to his left and right, their ragged silhouettes giving away nothing about their state. Alive or dead, it didn't really matter, not to Daryl. He had begun to realise that everyone was dead; it was simply a question of how far along the process each individual was. A line from an old song crossed his mind: born to die. Yes, that was exactly the truth of the human condition.

Humanity was a dead species, a race born into instant obsolescence. Only those who stepped to one side and abandoned the herd were ever truly alive. Men like the killers Daryl had once idolised and now only looked with pity, as even they had not completely realised the essence of what it is to live, to be alive, to exist.

Daryl was the first of a new breed. Once he had killed Sally Nutman for the second time, he could accept his crown and rule as king of the dead. His entire life had been but a preamble to that moment, every step along the way bringing him closer to what he had always been meant to do.

The sun glimmered behind a sheet of grey. The flat fields stretched into forever. Daryl roared ahead into a world he was busy recreating with every mile he travelled, every piece of black road that unfurled before him.

It was a world of infinite possibilities.

CHAPTER THIRTY-SIX

RICK NO LONGER felt like himself. It was a strange sensation, but not an unpleasant one. People spent small fortunes on drugs, alcohol and new-age religions to achieve the same thing. All it had cost him was the world.

He'd driven all day, across and up, always parallel with the sea, keeping a few miles away from the coast as they headed towards Northumberland.

Rohmer's directions, given during the trip along the canal, had proven sound. Rick had kept away from the larger towns and cities, hugging the jagged coastline as they skirted places he'd never before heard of, and soon began to notice road signs for Sea Houses, the place Rohmer had told him to head for.

A lot of the small towns and villages they passed through were deserted. Burning buildings, broken windows, abandoned dreams. Relics of a dead age littered the streets and footpaths: images like snapshots; of a child's bike, a school blackboard, scrawled with obscenities, a burned and blackened sofa, a row of stuffed toys lined up outside a house with shattered windows.

The dead roamed in the ashes of this dying way of life, feeding off scraps and hunting down stragglers. Rick had not stopped to help anyone; his focus remained on the road ahead, and the promise of a perhaps fictitious sanctuary.

Now it was dark again, and Rick was exhausted. He had not slept well last night. After the failed seduction, he had lain awake staring at the ceiling, listening to Sally's subtle movements in the dark. He had not dared sleep next to her and had instead lain on the floor beside the sofa. She was always within touching distance; he had reached out several times in the dark just to feel her cold skin against the back of his hand.

Rick couldn't remember the last time he'd eaten. He was surviving on a combination of whisky and adrenalin.

Not long now, he thought. *Then I can finally rest.*

He was surprised at how easy it was to continue the myth, to keep believing that Rohmer's island was the answer to everything. He supposed that when the alternatives are unthinkable, any scrap of faith is worth clinging to. He had never believed it in the past, but now he was certain that faith was the only thing that could save whatever was left of humanity.

He prodded the camp fire with a stick, turning the embers and sparking fresh flames. It was a smaller version of the blaze he'd started back at the cottage, the one which had served as Rohmer's funeral pyre. He was sure the old man would have appreciated it.

The camp was in the middle of a small grassed roundabout. Rick had lain out blankets and built the fire. He was more comfortable out here in the open, where he could see anyone who wandered by, living or dead. After the cottage and what had happened there, he wasn't quite ready to be crowded in, blocked on all sides. Open air was better, it felt freer, less restrictive.

Tabby sat at his side, unmoving, and stared at a point beyond the fire. She had said nothing since her grandfather's death; nor had she moved very much, apart from when Rick had coerced her into some kind of action. She was limp and unresponsive: it was a classic symptom of shock fatigue. Rick had seen this all before, out in the field, but still it unnerved him.

They weren't very different right now, his dead wife and his surrogate daughter. Neither of them spoke, and each had their own strange hunger.

The sky was black and starless, with thin clouds hovering overhead. The transition between day and night had been almost seamless. The only significant alteration was that the shadows had become longer before vanishing, and the moon was a segment of the pale circle the sun had been.

We'll be fine when we get there.

Rick smiled. "I know we will. It will all be different then."

They'll cure me. We can start again.

They. It was always *They*. Whenever things went wrong, or when people needed someone to blame, they called out to the mythical They:

They put a hole in the ozone layer; *They* started the War on Terror; *They* put the chemicals in our food; *They* destroyed the environment; *They* brought the dead back to kill us.

"We did it," he whispered, once more stoking the fire. "*We* fucking did it all."

He looked up at the sky, peering into the blackness. He couldn't remember the last time he'd seen a plane, or a police helicopter. Back on the road he'd passed various groups of refugees, both large and small, and none of them seemed to have any idea what the powers-that-be were doing to solve things. For all anyone knew, there were no powers left; the government were all dead and roaming around Westminster looking for people to devour. Just as they'd done all along, but in a more literal manner.

Among the people he had seen on the road, one or two of them had even mentioned the island. He hadn't stopped to talk to anyone for long, but had felt compelled to pass a few words with the occasional stranger, if only to pretend he still had a link to the remains of a crumbling society.

One man had spoken of a small island in the Outer Hebrides.

An old woman had told him of a land mass located off the coast of Ireland.

Two children – a boy and a girl – had passed on the story of a supposed sanctuary on the Isle of Dogs, in London.

It was like the old game, Chinese Whispers, where the truth was mauled in the passing of information. Each time the tale was told, it was altered: parts were added or taken away, even changed completely to fit the world view of the teller.

The island was an urban legend, a story that might be told forever, by dirty survivors huddled around dwindling campfires; a modern myth sent down the generations to comfort those as yet unborn. Santa Claus. Jesus Christ. Rohmer's Island.

Rick smiled, and the expression felt funny, like it didn't belong. He was no longer used to smiling...

"I know she's dead."

Rick twitched in shock when the girl spoke. It had been so long since he'd heard her voice that he had almost forgotten what it sounded like.

"What do you mean, love?" He was afraid to turn and look at her in case it made her lapse back into silence, so he stared ahead at the flames, making mental pictures in their midst.

"Your wife. She's dead. I've known all along."

Rick closed his eyes. When he opened them again his vision was blurred, as if he was crying... but there were no more tears left in his body. "Why didn't you say?"

"Because I liked you. We liked you, Granddad and me. We both knew that she was dead, but we just let you get on with it. We had no right to judge you."

"Well, I'll be damned." His amazement was not directed at what the girl had said, but at the tears now rolling down his cheeks. It seemed that there were some left after all, and they had arrived in abundance.

"I'm sorry." Only now did he turn to face her.

The side of her face was bathed in firelight; her eyes were wide, expressive, but he could not decipher what secrets they held. "It's okay."

"No it isn't. I should never have lied to you. Not to you..."

But she said no more, and it was dark and it was cold and the heavens were empty of everything but the suggestion of a deeper darkness, an empty void that even now was curling around the edges of the sky, threatening to swallow it all.

She's lovely. Our daughter. The one we can never have. I'm glad I haven't been able to get to her. To eat her.

Rick felt like screaming, but he bit down on his tongue, keeping it all inside. The darkness hovered, poised on the brink of complete destruction, and then slowly receded, going away for now, yet more than capable of returning at any time. His illusion was so fragile; none of this was ever meant to last.

He stood and crossed the roundabout, the M16 in his hand. The roundabout was located at the top of a rise, which was why he'd chosen it. An elevated position was always easier to defend: you could see whoever was approaching a long time before they announced themselves, and taking the high ground was difficult when it was already occupied.

He thought again of missions in Iraq and Afghanistan. Old friends screamed inside his head, their long-dead voices struggling to be heard amid the uproar. No words made it through, it was just so much mental white noise.

"I'm going to secure the perimeter." He marched across the road and into the trees, heading towards the open land beyond. Sounds were muted; the air was thick and pregnant with expectation. Rick's senses became attuned and he heard the struggling of night creatures through the landscape: their constant endeavours for survival never ceased, despite the fate of the humans who thought that they ruled over the earth.

But that imagined rule was about to end.

Beyond the grove of trees he came to a clearing overlooking a valley. There was a shopping centre located at the base of the valley – large prefabricated sheds containing rows and aisles of foodstuffs and clothing and every other kind of knick-knack everyone had thought they'd needed; the separate components that together were meant to construct a happy life.

The mall was surrounded by scores of the dead. They stood in unmoving rows, circling the buildings, following some instinct that had brought them here to the places they once haunted when they were alive. The place was far enough away that Rick had no fear he would be seen, yet still he stayed back in the shadows, cupping his hands to his eyes to examine the pathetic scene.

The dead had returned to their old stomping grounds: shops, supermarkets, city centres. That explained why huge swathes of the countryside remained clear of their presence. They had begun to mass in the only places they could remember, the churches of capitalism, the prayer grounds of a lost world.

He heard the sound of distant gunshots. Someone must be hiding out in the shopping centre, thinking it a good place to sit out a siege. There would be plenty of food there, and all the things they had ever wanted before the world went tits-up. It was what Rick's generation had been taught all along: there is comfort in stuff, safety in the pursuit of objects. This was the living end of that empty philosophy, and Rick pitied the fools who had believed it right up until the last cash register had rung up its final sale.

He watched the dead as they swayed in place, moving to some unheard rhythm. They stood facing the shopping centre, most of them simply standing and staring. When Rick concentrated, he could hear the sound of their moaning: it was a sad song, a lament for everything that had been lost.

He turned away, feeling emptier than before.

Trudging back to the camp, he wrestled with the thoughts he had experienced when he'd watched them, grouping together for the World's-End Sale, the Last Great Shopping Spree of the Century.

Sally had not moved when he got back to the camp, but Tabby was now lying down, perhaps even sleeping. He hoped that she was at least getting some rest. All of this had been so hard on the girl – first she had lost her parents, and then the old man. Rick was all she had left, and even he was uncertain how much he could do for her or how long he might be around.

He heard the sound through his babble of thoughts: a low stuttering roar, like bees swarming around a hive.

Rick turned quickly and dropped to his knees, shouldering the rifle and looking along its sight.

A small moped struggled up the hill, heading towards the roundabout. A scrawny man sat astride the machine, leaning into the climb. The bike was festooned with bags and plastic containers, which probably contained food and fuel. Rick could make out no heavy artillery either on the bike's frame or strapped to the man.

He stood, but did not lower the rifle.

The moped halted a hundred yards away. The rider sat staring at Rick, and at this distance he could not make out the stranger's face. The man raised a hand in greeting, then he turned off the little engine. The silence filled the space between them, pouring in like flood water into an open grave.

Rick kept his sights on the man.

The figure climbed off the bike and started to walk towards the roundabout, his hands held out from his body. He had a rather feminine-looking bag on his back, the straps hanging loose at his shoulders, and unless he was mistaken the kid was wearing an ill-fitting pair of women's leather gloves. As the visitor drew closer, Rick could see that he was smiling, but the expression didn't seem to fit his face. It was sickly, like something painted on in haste.

"Hello. I'm unarmed." His voice was slightly high; he sounded like a small boy rather than a fully-grown man.

Rick kept the rifle on him, not ready to trust anyone, even a seemingly harmless young man with a girl's rucksack on his back.

"I'm alive... not one of those dead things. I've travelled a long way. I could do with some company, if that's okay by you."

There was something *off* about the kid, a certain insincerity that niggled at Rick's keen combat senses. None the less, he lowered the rifle slightly, nodded.

"Thank you. I'm saddle-sore from that thing. If I could just rest for a while by your fire, I'd be grateful."

"Come on up," said Rick, finally dropping the gun. He took his finger off the trigger and let the weapon hang at his side. "I have some hot tea if you'd like. A few biscuits."

The kid clambered up the side of the raised roundabout, his thin arms and legs scrambling for purchase on the soft ground. "Thanks. That would be wonderful."

They stood not quite face-to-face; Rick was at least three or four inches taller than the younger man and much broader at the shoulders. If the little fucker meant trouble, he figured that he could overcome him in seconds.

"My name's Daryl," said the kid, sticking out a small hand.

Rick shook the hand, feeling briefly like he was missing something, some vital element that he needed to complete the picture. "Rick. You're welcome here, in our camp."

"What happened to them?" Daryl tiled his head towards Sally and Tabby. His eyes shone, but Rick thought it was just the reflection of the camp fire flames.

"My wife was badly burned. Our daughter is in shock. We were attacked yesterday and her grandfather was killed. I had to deal with him; make sure he didn't come back." Rick walked towards the fire and made sure that he positioned himself between Daryl and the girls.

Daryl nodded. He obviously had his own story, and Rick thought that everyone's tale would be much the same: dead friends and relatives, lost loves, abandoned homes and lives.

"You look like you've been through some stuff yourself, Daryl." He lifted the tin pot from the fire and poured some tea into battered mugs.

"Yes. I used to live with someone. She died and came back. Just like you, I was forced to deal with her." He stared into the flames, his eyes empty and reflecting only the brightness from the fire.

Rick felt that the kid was leaving something out of his brief account. It wasn't a problem, but the whole thing rung false somehow. He was sure that he was being told the truth, but with certain elements excised, or perhaps altered for public consumption. There was something about this Daryl... something unpleasant. He didn't come across as a complete person; for some reason, the kid seemed more like an actor playing a part. He said all the right things, paused in all the right places, but it was all too studied, as if he were striving for an effect rather than being open and natural.

They sipped their tea in silence. It was too hot and too weak; there was no milk or sugar. The sky felt like a vast canyon yawning above them, as if everything had been turned on its head and somewhere up there was the earth. The effect was disorientating, and Rick tried not to dwell on it.

A breeze moved through the foliage at the side of the road, ruffling the tops of trees and disturbing the night birds. Something cried, far off and moving away from them; from somewhere inland came the muted sound of a single scream. Rick looked in the direction of the sound, but he knew that the awful cry was being carried on the wind, and whoever had made it was perhaps miles away.

Daryl did not even glance away from the fire.

Send him away, baby. I don't like him. He isn't right.

Rick tried to ignore Sally, but as usual her voice cut right through his brain and into his very core.

He wants to hurt us.

How could she know that? On the surface, the kid was harmless: a skinny little runt in search of some company. But underneath the performance, at the heart of the matter, he might be very dangerous indeed. Long ago Rick had learned never to trust the image a person was attempting to portray. Initial instincts were usually correct; whatever you felt about a person within the first five minutes of meeting them was all too often close to the mark. In the field you learned to read people fast or you died. It really was that simple.

What he read in Daryl was an empty page, a space waiting to be filled. There was no real person here, just the reflection of how he thought a real person should act. In the silence that hung between them there was an absence; rather than a companionable lull, this was a shocking emptiness, a lack of contact at a fundamental level.

"I think you should go now." Rick grasped the rifle. He did not raise it, but he did enough to inform Daryl that he was ready to use it if necessary.

"But why? What have I done? Or failed to do?" The kid's eyes were stones, pieces of mineral stuck into a hunk of flesh. There was nothing behind them; no personality to tie everything together into a whole human being.

"Cut the fucking act and leave. Move or I'll take off your head." Rick stood, slipping his finger beneath the trigger guard.

Daryl finished his tea. It was still hot, but he took it in one large swallow. Then he stood and turned away without speaking, heading back towards his silly little moped. He climbed onto the bike, scratched the side of his face, and cocked his head like a dog. "I'll be seeing you," he said, and then before Rick could answer he fired up the engine and *put-putted* away, his back held straight this time and presenting the perfect target.

Rick raised the rifle and took a bead on that slim back. His finger tensed on the trigger.

Do it.

One round. That was all he needed. It was an easy shot.

Kill him, baby.

He blinked hard, aware of that white noise behind his eyes again. Then he lowered the rifle and went back to the fire, where he took some more of the weak tea and wondered what had held him in check. It would have meant nothing to have killed the kid; just another dead man among the many who now inhabited the world. Maybe that was why he hadn't done it. Perhaps the lack of meaning in the act had stayed his hand.

CHAPTER THIRTY-SEVEN

DARYL WAS EXPERIENCING a rush like a sky diver must feel. Adrenalin powered through his body, making his extremities tingle. His vision possessed a clarity which he could not quite believe and the moped bucked beneath him like a stallion as he roared towards the coast.

After returning down the hill he had doubled back, just to ensure that Nutman didn't realise he was being followed. But Daryl was no follower now; he was the leader.

He still could not believe that the policeman had left the maps in full view. Granted, that wasn't the reason why Daryl had approached him – it had been more of a personal dare, a test to see exactly how far he had come on his journey and how much he had changed from the fearful runt he had been before Mother's death had freed him.

No, the maps were an added bonus. All laid out at the fireside, with red pen marking the route. He'd probably seemed rather suspicious as he pretended to stare into the fire, all the while trying to peer at the maps, but that did not concern him. He did not plan to be face-to-face with Nutman again – not until he killed him, of course, prior to reclaiming the lovely Sally.

Sally. She had been so close – near enough to touch. To cut. To bludgeon.

God, how his mind raced. He went through a hundred different methods of killing her, each one more extreme than the last. He could kill her again and again, as long as he protected her brain.

He could even have killed her then, in front of the bastard she had married, his love rival.

But then had not been the right time. He must wait until he could take her with the minimum resistance from her dangerous husband; perhaps their destination would offer up the perfect opportunity.

The Farne Islands.

Daryl had even been there before, on a school trip years ago. As far he could recall the place was a bird sanctuary; the only people who stayed there were ornithologists. He remembered a lot of terns, guillemots and puffins. Back then, the puffins had made him laugh, even when the school bullies had forced him out onto a rock ledge and left him stranded there.

He wondered what was there, why Nutman was heading for the sanctuary. Was it something to do with the old man – the girl's grandfather? It amused him that Nutman had referred to the girl as his daughter: he was either delusional or spinning a yarn to cover his tracks. But why would he even need to fabricate a cover story? He had no idea that he – or, more precisely, his wife – was being stalked.

The salt air grazed his nostrils as he approached the coast. The stench of rotting fish and seaweed accosted him as he swung into a tight curve and the sea finally lurched into view. The sky was huge and wide above the flat line of the sea; sea birds hovered far out, dipping towards the waves to pick at whatever scraps they could find floating on the surface.

Daryl grinned. He actually hated the sea, but it was worth putting up with if it meant that he could spend time with Sally. If he could get to the island first and identify where they were going, he could prepare an ambush. Then it would be – heh – plain sailing.

The air was harsh; the temperature was even lower here than it had been inland. There were no vessels out to sea; the expanse of faded blue water was empty, bereft of the boats or yachts or working ships which usually cluttered the horizon.

A few dead people roamed on the dull yellow sand, stumbling around like wind-up toys. One of them had wandered into the surf and fallen to his knees; the waves kept tugging him off balance as he attempted to right himself.

"Stupid," said Daryl, appalled at the sight. "Fucking stupid corpse."

He pushed the moped along the empty coast road, heading towards what appeared to be some kind of small private dock. There were boats anchored at a jetty – expensive looking crafts and smaller, cheaper working boats. He did not have the first idea how to sail, but it would come to him. He was capable of anything lately, even things he'd been afraid of in the past.

He stopped at a huge weather-worn National Trust sign that offered local information, climbing off the moped to inspect it close up. The sign gave brief details of all twenty-three separate Farne Islands, and listed all the endangered species – sea birds and seals – which made their homes there.

Daryl remembered walking across guano-spattered rocks as a child, afraid of the birds yet fascinated by their natural beauty. When he returned home and told Mother all about the trip, she'd claimed that God was present in places like these – His work evident in the birds and animals, even the tiny rocky islands themselves.

She had never missed an excuse to invoke the name of her Lord. It was habitual, her way of coping with the world and of codifying everything within it.

According to Mother, everything was God's will, even the bad stuff. *Especially* the bad stuff. It was meant to test us, or so she said.

"God moves in mysterious ways, all right." He smiled, placed a hand on the large wooden sign, feeling a thrum of latent energy. Or did he just imagine that? He could no longer be sure.

Birds called out far above, their screeching voices a constant backdrop to the sound of the surf. White bird shit covered everything like spilled correction fluid: evidence of God's typist correcting the errors in the ongoing script of creation.

Daryl brandished the digital camera, taking a shot of the information sign, the unruly sea, the ugly beach... the scattered dead who walked there, unable to leave the sand, like machines stuck in grooves. Maybe they'd keep going until they ran out of steam, and then simply keel over and stop. Didn't sharks do that? Just keep on going until they stopped swimming, and when they did cease moving through the deeps, they just died on the spot.

Or was that another myth, a piece of misinformation?

Nothing was certain these days. Everything was in flux.

The idea of sharks seemed somehow fitting. The dead were like land sharks: eating machines, roaming across the earth and consuming anyone they encountered.

He got back on the moped and headed towards the jetty. There were a lot of spaces between vessels, probably caused by people frantically taking to the sea to find somewhere to wait out the apocalypse. Daryl imagined hundreds of them, sitting on small land masses, running out of supplies, trying to summon a voice on a failing radio set.

The damn fools. Did they not realise that it was all here for the taking?

Daryl strode along the timber boards, looking down past his feet at the gaps and the water beneath. The sound of water lapping at the rotting timber pilings was hypnotic. He glimpsed movement down there: darting shapes, sharp little waves caused by something shifting in the water...

So caught up was he in the water's weird movement that he failed to see the dead woman as she lunged at him from behind a boat. Daryl glanced up at the last minute and sidestepped, so that she caught hold of his jacket rather than his skin. She was quick, strong. Her face hung in tattered strips from her skull and her tongue lolled snake-like from the black cavern of her mouth.

The woman's skin was waterlogged; it sagged on her bones. Her eyes had been mostly eaten by fish or seagulls and her reaching fingers flashed bone-white as they tightened around his collar. Her clothes were sodden, hanging heavily around her.

Daryl lashed out and caught her on the side of the head. She barely moved, just tightened her grip and shuffled towards him. He kept backing away, trying to keep his balance so that they did not pitch over into the water.

The dead woman made a hideous gurgling sound deep in her throat. That tongue flapped at her chin, far too long, the colour of raw liver.

"Get off!" He back-peddled furiously, terrified of losing his footing, yet desperate to be away from this ravenous creature. Her jaws snapped shut like steel pincers, severing the tongue. It slid down the woman's flattened chest and dropped to the timbers, where it slid off the edge and into the restless water like an eel returning to its natural habitat.

Then Daryl slipped. His feet got tangled up in a thick rope line, and he teetered backwards, grabbing the dead woman's forearms. He dragged her down with him, trying to turn so that she did not fall on top of him and pin him down. Timbers creaked; water lapped; the woman hissed again.

He saw the anchor as he fell, and acting quickly he somehow managed to twist so that the woman fell towards it. He pushed out, forcing her to the side, and was relieved when he felt her body shudder as it made contact with the metal anchor.

The top of the anchor pushed out of the centre of her chest, forcing apart ribs and sending a rush of stagnant water gurgling out of the wound. The stink was horrendous: dead fish, decayed matter.

The woman was pinned like a butterfly in an exhibit. She struggled madly, arms and legs pounding against the wooden jetty, but was held fast by the anchor.

Daryl got to his feet and shambled over to her, keeping his distance. Her blind eyes turned upon him, and for a moment he was convinced that she could smell him – live meat.

He grabbed a boathook from a stand and held it poised above her. Then he brought the end of the hook down and drove it through her skull, just above the brow. The top of her head peeled back like an opened can, the skull cap splashing into the water below. Small crustaceans and silvery fish wriggled out of her head, the drowned remains of her brain following them down into the grubby waves lapping at the jetty supports.

He heard running footsteps, and when he glanced behind him he saw more dead people moving towards him. There were four of them, with a further group running up the beach to join the fun. Those closing in on him were in better condition that the woman he had dispatched, but still they were repulsive. Missing limbs. Black, rotten flesh. Holes where faces should be.

Daryl turned away and jogged towards the nearest boat.

He moderated his breathing and controlled his heart rate; he felt like an athlete, in supreme control of his body and able to bend his physicality to his will. In the past a manoeuvre like the one he'd used on the dead woman – twisting and turning to slam her onto the anchor – would have been utterly beyond him, but now it was like second nature. A paradigm shift had occurred; Daryl had finally *become*. But what was it he had turned into? What exactly had hatched from the shell of his old life?

Finding out would be such fun...

THE OLD DARYL would never have dreamed of even attempting to sail a craft, but the new Daryl carried it off with ease. Granted, it was a basic vessel, with only a small outboard motor to power it, but his body adjusted to the demands of the boat with an alarming speed. Daryl had the feel of the craft, became attuned to its gait in the water, within the first few moments of it cutting through the waves.

The dead stood at the edge of the jetty, bellowing as he left them behind. One of them dived into the water but did not resurface. He remembered a probably spurious statement he'd once read that stated dead things would not immediately float when dropped into fluid; instead they sank, their trapped internal gases dragging them to the bottom until they rose only much later.

He headed for the islands, which he could just about see in the rising gloom. They stood proud against the sky – dark silhouettes, their angles and edges sharp and inhospitable. They seemed huge.

Daylight was now shuffling onto the scene, and within thirty minutes he expected to be able to see the ring of islands in all their glory. He could already make out the slashes of dark birds as they flew around the rocks, and the sound of their cries was carried to him across the surface of the water. Watching them, he could almost believe that nothing but him had changed, that the rest of the world carried on as usual.

He guided the craft towards the group of islands, being careful not to fall foul of hidden rocks beneath the choppy waters. Soon he could make out the white shit-coated outcroppings, the many tiny hides dotted along the humped backs of the islands, and the occasional stone ruin, wooden shack or simple dwelling. He knew from the school trip that scientists conducted studies of the indigenous flora and fauna, and kept records of the birds, but was unsure if they actually stayed overnight on the islands or lived on shore and travelled out on the morning tide.

The sign back at the jetty had said something about Inner Farne – the central island of the group – having a lighthouse, a historic ruined chapel and some kind of visitor centre. There had been no mention of proper accommodation, but he would have bet that there was some kind of National Trust presence based on at least one of the more hospitable islands – a couple of wardens who passed their time diving and fishing.

Some of the islets apparently hid underwater at high tide; others were simply inaccessible, or so it looked. A red and white candy striped lighthouse caught his eye; stone dwellings perched on precarious ledges; the islands seemed to shift as he approached them, as if moving away from his gaze.

Daryl was just beginning to worry which island Nutman might be headed for when he saw the sign. Splashed across a thrusting pinnacle of rock face in bright red paint was a single word:

SANCTUARY.

It meant more than the birds and the rare grey seals; this was an invitation, a message to inform all-comers that here was safety, and perhaps even answers to all the questions of the past few days. There were people here and they were trying to put things right, perhaps even seeking a cure to whatever had caused the mass reanimation of the dead. Maybe they had already found it.

Daryl would take great pleasure in destroying it all, burning it to the ground and pissing on the smouldering ashes.

He slowly turned the boat – amazed at himself – and brought the craft into a natural bay carved out of the bald rock face. The boat drifted in when he cut the engine, aiming straight for the area where the land fell to provide a low platform ideal for disembarking from a small craft.

A small flag fluttered in the breeze. It was attached to a pole wedged into the rock face.

The faded words printed on the tattered flag proclaimed: *Staple Island, Outer Farne. Population: Zero.*

If it was some kind of joke, the humour was lost on Daryl.

Far above him, perched on the topmost edge of one of the frightening stacks of rock, he could see a ramshackle single-storey prefabricated hut. Its windows were boarded, but there were lights fixed under the eaves. Some of the lights – those which had not been shattered – were on; they bled sickly illumination across the crap-stained crags to light his way to the heights.

The words on the flag must be lies.

It was almost as if he were expected.

"Somebody up there likes me," said Daryl, staring up at the sky, at the struggling sun and the threatening clouds. He imaged that he saw faces up there: long, gaunt, undead faces; leering grins and laughing mouths. They spoke to him, those hungry mouths, but he was unable to hear what they were saying... or perhaps they were simply chewing, consuming the lost souls from the sky, the ones that never quite made it to Mother's picture-book heaven.

The boat edged into shore and Daryl threw a line at the platform. He climbed from the boat and tied it up, making sure that it was unable to drift away, even if the wind got up and stormy weather tugged at it. He thought that he might stay here for a while, but he also wanted the option of escape. The new Daryl always had a back-up, a Plan B to utilise if everything else went wrong.

He trudged across the rocky ground, moving ever upwards, dodging wide slits and gullies as he climbed towards the bare, grassy plateau above.

Birds wheeled overhead but kept their distance. Even they knew not to annoy him. In his new incarnation, Daryl felt sure that if he wished he could simply pluck them from the sky and break them like so many miniature Icaruses having flown too close to his blazing radiance.

CHAPTER THIRTY-EIGHT

RICK WATCHED THE dead as they moved through the town, brushing up against the quaint stone buildings and bumping into each other as they paraded along the narrow cobbled streets. Sea Houses was the type of place tourists loved, sitting in a pretty bay and packed with B&B establishments and bric-a-brac shops. The dead looked incongruous against its quaint backdrop, like a turd in a flower bed.

Rick stared along the sight of the M16, wondering how the hell he was going to get a shell-shocked young girl and his dead morphine-addled wife to the sea front and into a boat without being brought down and torn apart. It was a conundrum he didn't really want to think about.

He let off a shot and a head exploded; another shot and a thin, pale face turned into a large red flower, blossoming quickly over a bone-white skull.

Picking off a number of walking corpses, he weighed up the odds.

The only plan that seemed like it might work was the most direct: he would simply drive through the bastards, mowing down however many stepped into his path. The jeep was long and low and compact, but it was a heavy vehicle with a big engine. As long as he kept his nerve, he could carve a path through the dead and make it to the bay ahead of them. They were like cows; not very bright, and one tended to blindly follow the other.

He was currently lying on the roof of the jeep, and when he stood he felt faint for a moment. The roof creaked beneath him, his boots dimpling the thin steel capsule. His head swam, the visions barely kept within it.

He leapt down and opened the passenger door. Sally was sitting in the seat, a seatbelt wrapped around her torso and her hands tied in front of her with a length of rope. The morphine had run out and he was afraid that she might get frisky, so had taken the extra precaution to ensure that if she broke free of the grip of the drug she couldn't get to him without first warning him of her intentions.

I promise I'll be good.

He shook his head. "I'm sorry, Sally. I can't take that chance. If it was just you and me, things would be different. But we have Tabby to think about now. We have responsibilities as adoptive parents."

She said nothing more.

Rick glanced at Tabby, who was lying on her side across the back seat. Her face was blank, devoid of anything approaching a readable expression; her wide eyes stared at nothing. There was no way he could manhandle these two down to a boat; his initial plan would have to suffice.

He stowed the rifle on the back seat, next to Tabby, and grabbed the Glock from the glove compartment, where he'd stashed it earlier. It was fully loaded. He was expecting a lot of resistance.

"Here we go." He climbed behind the wheel and gunned the engine. It sounded healthy, as if Rohmer had maintained it regularly. Every car Rick had ever owned had been falling to pieces, so it was nice to drive something someone had taken real care of – their pride and joy, something they appreciated. It was also a pity that he would have to wreck it by driving into dead people.

He pressed the accelerator, and then let out the clutch. The jeep darted forward, and Rick steered it along the picture-postcard streets of the small town, feeling not for the first time like this was all some weird dream, a surreal sleep episode from which he would soon awake.

He hit the first column sooner than he'd expected: a small group of them came stumbling around a corner and headed directly into the road.

The loose-limbed bodies made loud noises of impact; their dead weight slamming against the front bumper and bonnet caused shock waves to course along the length of the vehicle.

A woman stood and watched his approach, her mouth hanging open in a perfect circle, eyes peering, hands grasping at empty air... her head left a red smudge as it slammed into the windscreen and her body skidded cleanly across the bonnet and into the gutter. He felt the bumpy motion of the rear wheels rolling over her flailing limbs.

Rick began to pretend that it was all an elaborate video game, a major new prototype he'd been asked to test. If he thought of it this way, he could almost have fun. He was steadily losing his grip on reality. His mind had broken long ago, and the remnants of his sanity were now being blown away like dust in the wind.

"Fuckers." He spoke harshly, through gritted teeth. Another body rolled beneath the jeep, causing him to tighten his grip on the steering wheel as the vehicle lurched sideways.

Calm down, honey. Nearly there.

He resisted the urge to turn and gaze at Sally. She did not look at her best: the bandages had come loose near the bottom of her face, exposing a part of her chin. He caught movement out of his peripheral vision, and swallowed hard. The drug was wearing off now; she was flexing her dead muscles and limbering up to attack him as he steered the jeep.

He had to get her on a boat quickly, if only to ensure that he could properly restrain her.

Tabby stirred on the back seat, mumbling something under her breath. It sounded like she said the word "love," but he couldn't be sure.

The rear wheels slid away from him as he turned sharply, the jeep drifting round to face the dead. More of them had now emerged from shop doorways, the broken windows of terraced houses, overgrown gardens and upturned trash containers outside deserted fish and chip shops. Some of them ran, others shuffled, and yet more half-jogged-half-fell in a pathetic facsimile of movement as they chased the car towards the sea.

He felt like a sardine in a can.

Rick pressed his foot down on the brake and fought to control the skid. Finally the vehicle stopped, and he wasted no time in jumping out, opening all the doors, and grabbing his bag and the M16 from the back seat. He already had his eye on a boat, and prayed to the God he now seemingly believed in that it was fuelled and ready to go. He ran towards the small vessel, bent down and untied it from its moorings. It was a white schooner – tiny but with plenty of room on deck and a small hold – and Rick believed that he knew enough to at least sail it out to sea. After that, he would simply put his trust in God... and in love, true love, which had already guided him here.

He ran back to the jeep and lifted Tabby from the back seat. She was limp and unresisting, almost like a corpse herself. He slung her over a shoulder, alarmed by how light she was, and then released the seatbelt from around Sally. He grabbed hold of her arm and dragged her unceremoniously from the seat, not caring when she fell to the ground. She was dead anyway; further injury mattered not one bit.

He made his way to the boat, a young girl over one shoulder and hauling his dead wife along the ground like a caveman with his mate.

He threw Sally onto the deck of the boat, wincing only slightly at the loud, loose sound she made as she fell. Tabby he lowered gently, taking care not to hurt her.

He took one final glance at the pursuing dead, and then leapt aboard, pushing the boat away from the side with his feet. He was a car's length away from the concrete moorings before the first of the dead halted at the edge, roaring and waving their arms.

He turned away, no longer interested in them.

Sally was crumpled like an abused shop window mannequin. Tabby lay curled in a foetal position near his feet. His heart broke, just as his mind had, and he wished that there were tears left to shed. The poor girl... his surrogate daughter... she should not have to suffer this. It wasn't fair; none of it was fair at all.

He looked around for God, and then looked within, finding the holy spirit cowering in a dark part of himself that he'd left on a distant battlefield. It was now time to let that part out of the darkness and force it into the grey light, where it could take over for a while and allow him to rest.

Rick sat at the bow and stared at the islands, frightened by their appearance: splinters of rock which had shattered and thrust out of the sea, grasping at the sky. Hundreds of sea birds circled these jagged pinnacles, soaring and landing, then taking flight again. The birds acted as if nothing was unusual. It was nature's cycle continuing even as the earth's dominant species surrendered to nightmare.

Rick sailed by instinct, feeling as if he were channelling Rohmer, and the old man's restless ghost guided his hand. He threw a blanket over Tabby but let her rest. For the first time since the cottage, her eyes were closed and he thought that she might even be sleeping.

You'd have made a great dad. The best.

He closed his eyes and wished that Sally wouldn't talk like that. It reminded him of all the things they would never do, never have. The empty years that now stretched ahead.

"I love you. But I also hate you."

She went quiet, pondering that one. He felt bad for saying it, but he could no longer understand his emotions. It felt like his sense of humanity was dripping away, leaking from the wounds in his psyche, and the closer they got to Rohmer's island the less human he felt.

Fingers of rock stretched upwards, piercing the grey gloom and striving toward something better. Rick guided the boat around the island, and saw the red-painted sign. "You'll know it when you see it," Rohmer had said, not even certain himself how they would identify the island his ex-lover had summoned him to.

But here it was: the island. Sanctuary. The old man had been right; it wasn't a lie or a myth. It was real, and they were here, at last.

A small wooden boat was already tied up at the makeshift landing station, a large rent in its hull where it had either hit the rocks or someone had deliberately sabotaged it. Rick pulled up alongside the boat, fighting the currents to keep the boat safe. Something told him he might still need it, and that the island might not represent the sanctuary Rohmer had claimed it to be. It was too quiet. There was no welcoming party or waiting committee. The whole place felt as dead as the cold, lifeless husks of people he'd left on the shore, raging for his flesh.

Sally was moving. Her legs twitched, the soles of her feet drumming on the deck, and she was writhing against her bonds. The bandages had unravelled and he could now see most of her butchered features. As he watched, she somehow managed to get one hand free. She began to claw at her face, pulling away the bandages, and then tugged at the wadded remains of the cotton wool he had forced back into her throat.

She was awake.

And she was hungry. Oh, so very hungry.

He moved over to where she flailed on the deck and grabbed a long rope. He lassoed her, and then carefully wrapped the rope around her body, working it like the coils of a spring and lashing her arms to her sides.

Sally seemed to realise, dimly, what he was doing, and she began to fight against him. But it was too late: she could barely move her arms. The bandages had fallen off completely, and lay at her feet like party favours. Her face was puckered, unrecognisable, and the deep cuts opened and closed, sending him gruesome air kisses. Her mouth, now bereft of teeth, gaped like a landed fish. The gums were raw, and snapped together like a beak.

Once he was satisfied that she was properly restrained, Rick tugged the rope and encouraged her to walk ashore. She stumbled, her co-ordination long gone, and he had to be patient as she limped after him. It would make a comical sight, he thought, if anyone were to see: a man walking his dead wife like an oversized and disobedient dog.

He tied the rope to a sturdy rock and went back for Tabby, lifting her gently and carrying her off the craft. She stirred, her eyes flickering open. "Granddad..." Her eyes held a panicked look, and it took the girl a few moments to get her bearings and recognise Rick. She said nothing more, but at least she was awake and partially focused.

Rick set her down on the ground and grabbed his bag and the rifle from the boat. When he returned ashore, Tabby had moved away from Sally, who was walking in small circles around the rock to which he had tethered her like an unruly beast.

"I'm sorry," he said, not knowing what else to say, or how to say it.

It's okay. We'll be home soon. A new home, where we can be happy. The three of us.

He had finally emerged from the grand illusion that Sally was communicating with him, and realised (or admitted) now that he was putting the words in her torn and twisted mouth. But just because the words were his, and he was making her say what he wanted to hear, didn't mean that they were untrue.

If Sally was in fact capable of speech she *would* be saying all this, and all he was doing was providing her with a voice.

"Are you okay to walk? It's bit of a hike." He stared at Tabby, thinking for a second that she might answer. The girl said nothing, but she did glance up at the craggy rocks they were about to climb.

Rick untied the end of the rope from the boulder and took the lead, heading up. "Stay close to me, but I'll go up first. If there's any trouble, I want to be the one to tackle it." He held the Glock in one hand and the loose end of the rope in the other. Tabby followed in silence, her feet firm on the uneven rock.

A group of small boats had been dumped behind a large granite shelf, their hulls punctured. Whoever had been staying on this island had not intended to leave. Now he knew what had happened to the other boat, the one they'd passed earlier.

He peered over his shoulder at Tabby. The girl was doing okay, keeping up the pace.

If he and Sally had at any point been blessed with a daughter, he would have wished that she were exactly like this girl. Tough, resilient, and filled with so much love that she almost glowed.

It was a steep climb but not a long one. Rick managed it without letting go of the pistol or the rope, but Tabby often had to bend over and drag herself along with her hands, grabbing onto small, dry shrubs and spiky boulders.

Along the way Rick saw several instances of a shape carved into the rock. It was clearly not a natural occurrence; the carvings where too regular, too deliberate. Soon he recognised it as the Egyptian ankh; the symbol of eternal life.

He smiled at the irony.

At the top of the crag sat two small prefabricated sheds, one on the edge and the other set slightly back. A hillock linked the two structures, suggesting some sort of underground compound beneath the sheds. It reminded him of the places they'd used during army training: temporary barracks hastily assembled in far-flung locations. For more than one reason, the end of this journey felt increasingly like he was coming home.

A few signs were attached the sides of the sheds, and there were yet more ankh symbols embossed onto the external walls. One of the signs read *Hummingbird Inc*. Another was a hazard warning announcement detailing what looked like a list of emergency procedures, but it was so weather-beaten that Rick could hardly make out any of the text. Words like 'danger' and the phrase 'ultimate precautions' stood out, but the rest was a faded blur across a disfigured grey board.

The doors of both of the sheds stood open. The far one was charred, as if a fire had been set inside. There was no smoke, no heat, so Rick assumed that the blaze had gone out days ago. The closer shed, the one he now stood beside, showed no signs of destruction, but there was a lot of litter in the entrance. Boxes and cans of food, torn textbooks, broken medical equipment and computer terminals... someone had really gone to town here and smashed the place up.

Rick at first thought that a dead body was lying half concealed inside the shed. It had no head. The body was badly mutilated, as if it had been flattened somehow; the hands and feet were missing. Rick could not even tell if it were a man or a woman: a body, just another body.

As his eyes became accustomed to the murk inside the shed, he realised that the body was in fact a pile of clothing – a uniform of sorts, consisting of a rumpled grey boiler suit. Other clothing was piled next to it, overflowing from several receptacles and spilling onto the wooden floor. He could now see that the breast pocket had been torn from each suit, where someone had removed the name tags of the missing workers.

"Wherever we go, we see death. We can't escape it. It's everywhere, in every little thing, at every junction. I can even taste death."

At the sound of her voice, Rick turned towards Tabby, but her face was once again blank, as if she had not uttered a word. Was he simply imagining that she was speaking now, just as he'd been doing all along with Sally?

Madness was now a comfort, a warm bed, a perfect home. He never wanted to be sane again.

The wind was wonderful up here; a sharp, cool phantom that coiled around his head, clearing his mind of the clutter it had accumulated over the past few days – the past few years, if he was honest. He imagined that wind entering his ears, nose, mouth, and cutting through the matter of his brain, scouring his soul.

"Come on," he said, squeezing the Glock. "We have to get to the end of this, if only for your grandfather's sake."

Then he stepped across the threshold and moved inside the shed, and was swallowed by an unearthly darkness.

"Welcome to Sanctuary," said a voice.

CHAPTER THIRTY-NINE

THE CELL WAS six by ten paces; Daryl had walked it repeatedly to measure the dimensions of the room. The man who had brought him here seemed reasonable enough, but there was the whiff of madness and neglect about him. He wore a dirty grey boiler suit with the name 'Tim' stitched onto the breast and his beard was long and straggly.

Tim had been waiting for Daryl at the top of the bleak rock finger he had climbed, sitting on the stubbly grass and drinking water from a plastic bottle. He'd guided Daryl into the shed and then down into the low tunnels beneath, saying little. Daryl had followed because he could not think what else to do.

They had eventually come out into a wide passage with a series of doors on either side. Each of the doors had windows set into them at head height, but Tim had prevented Daryl from looking inside.

He'd been brought to this cell to 'wash and brush up' in the tiny bathroom, and Tim had quietly disappeared, mumbling something about food.

This was some kind of military or government compound, but it was all so basic that it felt like a forgotten relic from the Cold War. With its low ceilings, steel doors, stone walls and floors, there was very little that was even remotely high-tech about the whole set up, and Daryl was even more confused as to what Nutman actually wanted here.

He walked to the door and tried the handle. It was unlocked, which startled him; he'd expected to be locked inside like a criminal.

He opened the door.

The corridor outside was cold and bare, and curved away at each end so that he could not see where it led. He went back into the room and picked up the digital camera from the bed. The red warning light was flashing to inform him that the battery was just about flat. He felt sad that the movie was almost over... but perhaps there would be a sequel.

He returned to the door, examined the corridor through the camera lens, and picked a direction. Left: the way of all things evil.

A corridor curved around the perimeter of the compound. He guessed that Tim had brought him right through the middle, and then led him part of the way around the outer ring.

Soon enough he came to the junction with the tunnel he'd walked down earlier, straight and lined with doors. Now he would get his chance to see what was inside those rooms.

He heard the sound of water dripping, the groaning of hidden pipes, and the fractured wheezing of a cheap air conditioning unit. Behind all these were voices; soft, flat, monotonous, they seemed to be chanting. Was this, in fact, the home of some kind of religious cult, hermetic monks hiding out from the end of the world?

Like Mother, clinging to some stupid religion.

Cool air buzzed through poorly installed vents, in a chorus of whispers.

The chanting remained constant, the volume neither increasing nor decreasing; it was eerie, particularly in this banal setting. If he closed his eyes, Daryl could imagine that he was deep within the catacombs of some Italian church vault and not crawling around inside a hollowed out, bird-shit-covered rock.

He came to the first door.

Slowly he approached it, reaching out to touch it with the palm of one hand. The steel was cold, impersonal, a barricade meant to keep something in as much as to deny prying eyes. He had to stand on tiptoe to see through the glass; the weirdoes who made their home here must all be taller than him. Everyone was taller than him, it had always bothered him.

The glass was grubby but he was able to see into the room. It was sparsely furnished, with a bank of old-fashioned computers, the free-standing kind like those in early James Bond films. They looked ridiculous: ceiling-height towers of flashing lights and tape decks, with tickertape print-outs piled in wire-mesh baskets on the floor.

Against the far wall there was a gurney, and on it was a painfully thin, naked woman. She lay flat on her back. There was a sheet draped across her lower torso, but her bony upper body was bare. The low temperature had made her nipples hard; gooseflesh striated her pale skin. Daryl gaped at the woman, unsure what to think of the scene. There were wires taped to her temples and between her breasts; they trailed back to the absurd computers, where they were connected to black plastic terminals.

Daryl moved on without trying the door. He did not like the look of the woman, and was damned if he wanted to be on the other side of the door if she woke up.

The next door was more promising. Through the small glass window he viewed more modern equipment: desks and chairs, laptop computers, flat screen monitors, slim-line terminals. The walls were covered with computer printouts – graphs and bar charts; 3D graphic models and photographs – and religious iconography. There were wooden crucifixes, paintings of the Madonna and child, even a Day-Glo Jesus standing on a crowded bookshelf, arms held aloft to welcome the righteous.

Daryl pushed open the door.

He liked unlocked doors; they were welcoming.

The room was very cold; the air conditioning was obviously set at a level to cool the computer apparatus. He walked around, examining the posters and pictures and cheesy religious artefacts. Mother's room had contained similar items, and over the years he had grown to loathe them. His vision shimmered, blurring, so he raised the camera and took it all in through the lens. That was better: things were clearer when viewed as isolated images.

A central desk was flanked by two large filing cabinets, and on the shelves were hundreds of box files marked with dates. From the files he examined, the contents went back to the mid nineteen-sixties, and those were just the ones left out in the open.

He picked a file at random. It was dated a few years before.

Opening the file, Daryl saw that it was filled with reports and memos. They outlined some kind of medical tests, pertaining to a major breakthrough. Something called 'The Ankh Derivative' was referenced throughout. From what he could make out, the experiments involved some kind of toxic plant from the Amazon, something discovered in the late '50s by a German anthropologist named Hoffman. The plant had been synthesised and a drug produced.

He went through more files. One of them outlined US army test subjects in Vietnam: they had been given the drug and went on a killing spree, mutilating the bodies of VC collaborators in a small village called Tai-Mah.

There was a memo from an American government official, which essentially presented the plan for covering up the massacre.

Daryl put down the file and picked up another. Here he read about a political uprising in Italy. 1976. Bodies from a morgue in central Rome that got up and walked, attacking the general public, causing a minor riot. Another major cover-up was orchestrated, blaming the Cosa Nostra for everything.

There were too many to count. The governments of the world had been hiding this information for decades, conducting their immoral tests and burning the evidence of their failures.

Daryl was impressed by the ruthlessness of what had been going on.

"It all started so well."

Daryl spun around, dropping the file on the floor, where it clattered like a gunshot. Another man – not Tim, but someone equally as spaced-out – stood in the open doorway. His face was etched with black cruciform tattoos; holy wounds that ironically contorted his features into something devilish.

"We meant well at the start... at the beginning of all this.

"Hoffman's plant was first used by a lost tribe to make their enemies into *zombis*: not the type you see in films, but shuffling, somnambulistic echoes of people who were used as slaves.

"When we first brought the plant into the civilised world, it was meant to be used to synthesise a new drug, an anaesthetic inherent in its sap. It took patients so far under during surgery that they were almost dead. They became very cooperative, and open to suggestion. Life signs were minimal. The heart rate dropped alarmingly. By the end of the '60s the drug was almost ready – we called it 'The Ankh Derivative' because it represented a step towards extended life. If we could put people that far under, then who knew what medical miracles could be performed..."

The man's eyes were blazing above his inked cheeks.

Daryl backed up, his hands scrabbling across the desk at his side. He fingered a staple gun, pens, pencils, a pencil sharpener, Post-it notes.

A letter opener.

"Like all things that start off being about the greater good, it was hijacked by those seeking power. There was an accident... a mistake. A team working with the plant somehow managed to extract a further toxin from the root. This one was much more powerful. They were all deeply religious, this team, and they worked in an atmosphere more like a cathedral than a lab. They brought in members of the clergy at gunpoint and had enforced prayer breaks, they read their bibles... and *something* happened. It was like a synthesis of science and the supernatural, and what they created was a fusion of the two ideals. All kinds of holy relics were ground down to powder and synthesised – the finger bones of Saints and martyrs, a supposed drop of Christ's blood from a church shrine in Bruges, even what was meant to be a cutting from the Turin Shroud. It was crazy."

Daryl clutched the sharp little blade, wrapping his fingers around the cold shaft.

The man lowered his head. "They blurred the limits between life and death and tore a hole into the eternal. What leaked out of that hole then combined with the Ankh Derivative to produce something – well, something *terrible.*"

Daryl took a step forward. He noticed then that the man was weeping: a holy fool shedding tears for what he had done – what they had *all* done.

"I'm sorry. We've brought many people here and used them. Used them as guinea pigs, test subjects to help us go further; deeper, darker. Then we used them as meat for the ones we keep in the corral. The dead ones we examine, chart, and vivisect, trying to find some kind of meaning in their condition."

Just as Daryl raised the blade, the man looked up. His eyes were beatific, as if he had seen the face of something wonderful; the face of God or the Devil or something between the two.

"Why are you telling me this?" said Daryl, ready to strike the man down.

"Because there's nobody else *to* tell. We're finished here. A joke. A handful of broken men looking to God for an answer... but we don't even know what the question is." He paused, catching his breath before the big finish.

"Two weeks ago the transformed and mutated Ankh Derivative was released into the atmosphere. I thought it was another accident, but it wasn't. There are no accidents. They did it on purpose, as part of some larger, top secret test. Once it was let out, there was no turning back." He fell to his knees and exposed his throat. "There can never be a way back, not now. This is just the beginning, the curtain raiser: what follows will be so much worse."

Daryl stepped forward and slashed at the man's throat. Blood spattered in a thin arc, spotting the desks and the computer screens and the filing cabinets.

With his other hand Daryl raised the camera and watched the man die.

Then he stabbed the man through the eye and into the brain, just to make sure that he could not come back for revenge.

Moving away from the bloody corpse, he swung the camera in an arc around the cramped room, taking in the shelves and the drawers and the crazy décor.

What follows will be so much worse.

The man's words echoed around Daryl's skull, like the backing track to his movie-in-the-mind. He remembered the faces he thought he'd seen forming in the clouds, the sense that something greater than himself was peering down from far above.

Then he pointed the camera at the motionless corpse, following a trail of blood as it snaked from the sliced neck and across the uneven stone floor.

"Fucking maniac," he muttered.

CHAPTER FORTY

"WE USED TO have funding. This was once a major site dedicated to medical advancement."

Rick kept the Glock pointed at the bearded man as he spoke, but he did not seem to notice. He just kept talking as he led them down a narrow staircase, along a low hallway, and into a wider area filled with medical supplies and boxes of canned foods.

"We were working on something big, a project that would change everything about the way we live... and the way we die."

Rick was barely listening.

Tabby gripped his hand and stared into space; Sally followed close behind, her mutilated head twitching. She was still attached to the rope. The man had not even mentioned her condition, just thanked Rick for bringing her. "We need fresh subjects," he said. "To find a cure." The last few words had seemed like an afterthought, something tacked on to garner his trust.

Rick didn't trust the man as far as he could spit – which wasn't very far as his throat had dried up hours ago.

"This is all we have left, now." The man kept walking, his long strides putting distance between him and his guests. "The rest of the world is tearing itself apart at the seams, so we simply continue our work. It's all we know. We run the tests and tabulate the results, then we run them all again and look for discrepancies. God is in the minutiae, the tiny, seemingly inconsequential details. But they *are* of consequence, believe me. That's how this all started: with someone forgetting to monitor the minor details."

He quickly genuflected, making the sign of the cross.

"Where is everyone? Your bosses? The military?" Rick felt like shooting the man just to shut him up, but he needed answers more than silence.

"There's no one else left. Just me and a handful of lab technicians. Even the project supervisors are gone. We used them as subjects for a while. Some of them are still in the corral, waiting to be fed."

If Rick was crazy, then he also recognised the madness in this man. He was long gone, his mind was blown. There was nothing here that Rohmer had promised: not sanctuary or salvation, not friends and saviours. Nothing. Just like out there, back in the world.

"So you can't help us? You can do nothing for my wife?" He already knew the answer, but needed to hear it spoken aloud, as if that would make it real and give him the encouragement he needed to put his final plan into action.

"I'm sorry," said the man, without even breaking his stride.

Rick's body clicked into combat mode, the remnants of his mind flapped like a sheet in the wind.

"Where's this corral you mentioned?"

The man stumbled once, and then resumed his regular rhythm. "It's at the end of this tunnel. A doorway marked with a red symbol. You'll know it when you see it."

"Thank you."

Rick shot him once in the back of the head. The sound of the gunshot echoed loudly, reverberating through the stone rooms and hallways before finally giving up the ghost.

No one came to investigate.

Rick was alone, with his dead wife and his comatose daughter. *The family that slays together stays together*, he thought, recalling the tagline from some old horror movie. He pulled Sally's rope; Tabby simply followed, a lame dog trailing behind its master.

He kept going, glancing into the rooms along the tunnel. Behind one door was another man in a grey boiler suit. He was staring at a TV screen, watching a video recording of some old game show. Rick kicked open the door and shot him in the face, not even pausing for breath. He shot the television, too, not really understanding why but feeling better for the act of destruction. Television and the media were part of the old ways, the time before.

When he arrived at the door that was marked with the bright red ankh, he stopped and stared at it, his thoughts empty.

Sally moaned.

Don't do this. I love you.

"I have to." He opened the door next to the one which led to the corral, and stepped into the room. One wall was covered with TV screens, each one displaying a different series of images. There were news clips, clearly filmed before and during the madness outside; amateur footage filmed on mobile phones and handheld cameras played on a continuous loop; the panicked faces of officials and world leaders filled the room, their dead eyes and slack mouths reciting the prayers of a lost world.

The sound was muted on all these televisions, and in its place was religious chanting: low, reverberant male voices repeating a Latin lament over and over, their separate voices blending into a single dirge. If this was a prayer, it was a dirty one, something about the underlying cadence made him feel unclean.

The sound was maddening. Rick began to fire the pistol blindly, hoping to hit the hidden speakers and silence those terrible tones forever. The other voices – his voices; the ones he carried within him – joined in the chant, taking up the refrain and filling his head with the profound sadness of its litany.

"Shut up!"

He let off round after round, reloaded with his last clip, and then kept firing until finally he hit the target and the chanting ceased. Tears painted his cheeks; his eyes were burning. A static hiss filled the room, coming from a speaker he still could not see.

"*Nnnnnngeeeee!*"

It was Sally, but this time her voice was not trapped inside his head. This time it was out in the world, straining at the tawdry remains of reality.

"*Nngyeee!*"

He dropped the pistol, fell to his knees, and raised his head to the low ceiling, and cried out her name, again and again and again...

And someone stepped through the open doorway, entering the room with slow, deliberate steps.

CHAPTER FORTY-ONE

HUNGRY

CHAPTER FORTY-TWO

"AND SO WE meet again." Daryl stepped forward, his eyes focused on Sally's beautiful torn face. Had he really done that? Was such gorgeous carnage the result of his own fair hand?

If time did not heal, then it certainly made the wounds prettier.

"I'm glad you managed to turn off that racket. Fucking awful, wasn't it?" He took in the sight of Nutman on his knees, unarmed and begging for destruction. It was a fitting final image, really, and he slowly raised the camera to record it for posterity.

The battery light flashed madly, and then went out. The automatic lens cap closed over the aperture, prematurely ending the film.

"Shit. I was hoping that wouldn't happen." He shoved the tiny camera into his jacket pocket and adjusted his grip on the letter opener. He had already proved that it was a thoroughly lethal weapon, and Nutman seemed too far gone to fight back.

He stared at Sally: her artistically starved carcass, the way the already decaying skin clung taut across the cheekbones like plastic sheeting. The wounds were wonderful; extra little mouths ready to swallow his seed.

He ignored the little girl. She was not important; a mere bit player, a non-speaking extra. When the audience departed, they would forget she had even been involved.

Sally turned her attention on him, her lower jaw hinging open. She had no teeth, just swollen, blackening gums. Her lips were torn, frayed, and the skin around her mouth was paper-thin. He imagined that he could see her tongue through the almost translucent sheet of her cheek, wriggling like a fat black snake in its den.

He giggled, and then fought to regain control.

Control was important now. He had come too far to give himself over to hysteria.

"I'm afraid this is the final scene, the one where the anti-hero kills the protagonist and gets the girl. It was always going to end this way. The best films always do." He smiled, enjoying the direction the scene was taking.

Nutman did not respond; instead he stared at the floor, his eyes narrowed, his hands folded loosely in his lap. He was a wasted man, a shadow, a wisp. There was barely anything of him left to kill. Daryl almost felt sorry for him – at least he might have done if he were still human.

He circled the policeman, examining his torn uniform, his loose arms, the lack of expression on his defeated face. He had come so far, gone through so many horrors, only to end his time on his knees. It was almost poetic, in a twisted kind of way. Daryl savoured the moment, tasting it, touching it, experiencing an almost sexual satisfaction from prolonging it. Time stretched, broke, and then reformed again, lifting him up, spinning him around, and then setting him down in the exact same place where he'd started.

"Oh, my." His words were not enough, but they pleased him. "My, my, my. What to say? What to do? Isn't this almost an anticlimax? I've rehearsed the moment so many times in my head, but it never played out like this. Usually we fought. You were stronger, of course, but I was always your intellectual superior. Eventually my brains always outdid your brawn, and I waltzed off into the sunset with Sally, my Sally, where I could enjoy killing her for all eternity."

Nutman shuffled on his knees. He placed the palms of his hands flat on the ground. He then began to make a low whining noise at the back of his throat, which increased steadily in pitch and volume. It was slightly irritating, and Daryl raised the blade, ready to silence him with a delicate flick of the wrist.

"Please," he said. "Let's not be undignified about this. Leave that to me, later, when I'm alone with your wife."

He was giggling uncontrollably now, unable to stop. But it did not matter; why not have a little fun now the game was just about over?

The television sets around the room were smashed, apart from a single screen in the corner. Religious imagery played out silently on the screen: static images of the crucifixion, crowd scenes featuring men and women in white robes, shots of Roman soldiers constructing huge wooden crosses. Then there came a scene portraying a white, bearded Christ on the cross, his hands and feet nailed to the timber axis. It was the same figure from Daryl's childhood vision in the dentist's chair – the one who had passed on the cryptic message about the smell of colours. Christ hung there, in that famous pose, and watched as people gathered beneath him. One by one these followers looked up, and each of them was a rotting corpse, a reanimated cadaver.

Christ wrenched one hand from the crossbeam, the thick iron nail tearing his palm. Then he reached down into his loincloth, took out his holy penis, and began to urinate on the watching masses, anointing them. Daryl saw that Mother was part of the crowd. She stood there with a look of adoration on her shrivelled face as blessed piss poured down into her open mouth...

Daryl blinked and the images scattered like insects. The screen was blank, a large crack bisecting it from top to bottom.

He knelt beside Nutman, placing an arm around the man's shoulders. He ran the blade across his cheek, down along the side of his neck, and finally across his throat. Nutman tilted his head, looking up and exposing the underside of his chin, baring the soft, yielding meat.

He wanted to die.

"*Ungyee!*"

Daryl looked up, startled. His grip slackened.

Sally was swaying on the balls of her feet. She had gathered up the end of the rope that was bound around her and was toying with it in her small hands. She stared at Daryl, nothing but a depthless hunger in her ruined eyes. Then, slowly, she began to stagger towards him, dropping the end of the rope and taking awkward steps across the cold stone floor. Her feet made a scraping sound; her jaw clicked as she opened and closed her mouth lightning fast, the speed of her response belying her slow approach.

Daryl was hypnotised. The woman he loved was finally coming for him, ready to fall into his arms and be swept away into a brand new form of horror.

"I love you," he whispered, his arm slipping from around Nutman's neck.

"*Ungyee!*"

"I know you are. I know you're hungry. So am I, but I think we both hunger for different things. Maybe when I'm done with you, we can get you some food. I could keep you fed as long as you keep dying for me. It's a deal, yes?"

He stood, feeling all-powerful, like a god. Indeed, he was about to commence upon a godly act, to carry out godly things: life and death, love and hate, beginnings and endings. A heady cocktail of creation, all mixed up and with a cherry on top...

Everything after that moment happened far too quickly for Daryl to properly assimilate.

The policeman suddenly grabbed him by the arm, pulling him round and hitting him in the face with a clenched fist that felt like solid rock. Sally toppled forward, uncertain on her feet and falling face-down on the floor. The little girl (who he'd already forgotten) appeared in the doorway. She was grinning. Freckles formed a question mark on her pale cheek. Her dark red hair was lank and greasy.

"I've let them out," she said, her face calm, white and shining, like an angel. "I've let them out of the corral." A *vengeful* angel.

Then the girl was gone, as if she had never really been there and was just a mad vision, an angelic avatar summoned by his freewheeling imagination. He glanced again at the television screen; the girl was there, too, and he watched as she ran along the tunnel and out into the main area. Then she went through the outer door and was gone, lost to his dimming sight.

When he looked back at the doorway where the girl had stood, he saw a nude man with deep diagonal gashes across his belly and chest, hands grasping the door frame, bald head pivoting like that of a strange giant bird as he heaved himself into the room.

"Fuck off!" Daryl snarled and grabbed the policeman's gun. He went down on his side, turned, and aimed the gun at Nutman's wide face.

Nutman seemed to stir again from his stupor. Before Daryl had the chance to pull the trigger, he siezed the gun and tried to wrestle it from Daryl's grip. The two men rolled on the floor, kicking and punching and biting. Daryl thought for a moment that he might even gain the upper hand, but then he was flat on his back and Nutman was straddling him, beating him around the face and neck with his fists.

This scene was so very different to the one he'd imagined.

The gun was lost, perhaps dropped in the confusion.

Daryl closed his eyes, barely even feeling the pain.

Behind the closed lids he met Sally, who was there waiting for him. She opened her arms and he fell into them, his cheek on her soft breast, her blood warming his face.

When he heard something crack he did not even realise that it was his cheekbone. The sensation of his neck breaking was nothing, a mere trifle. He was at last with his love, his one and only love, and they were floating above it all, bathed in a deep red glow that could only be blood

blood

red light

dark echoes release falling stopping hungry quiet rising faster light up bright white feelings gone hungry pain gone life none sound fury hungry room motion smell hungry sorrow need memory sally love meat hungry

*   *   *

RICK HAD BROKEN the bastard's neck with his bare hands, twisting, twisting, until the bones ground together with a sound like boots crunching on gravel.

The kid had gone still; all his struggles had ceased. He was dead.

He was dead for a moment.

And then he came back.

Rick scrabbled on all fours for the Glock, scurrying across the floor to locate the weapon, wherever it had fallen during the scuffle. Finally his hand fell upon it, and he almost raised it to lips and kissed it. Instead he turned, aimed, and fired, all in one quick, fluid motion.

The kid's forehead creased, and then broke apart, a huge flap of bone unhinging and hanging by a thread of skin. Blood poured down over his battered face and his body crumpled, deflating, dying again.

Dead. Really dead.

Sally was rolling on the floor, trapped by the rope he'd used to restrain her. Behind her, a horde of the dead were stumbling through the open doorway and into the room. They were in different stages of decay, and all of them were naked. He remembered the discarded grey boiler suits with the name tags removed, the untidy stacks of clothing left upstairs in the dark of the empty shed.

He scuttled over to Sally, held her, fought to calm her.

"I'm here, baby. I'm here."

She made baby-sounds: small moans and groans and belching noises. Ever since she had attempted to speak, to form words in her dead throat, the voice he'd supplied her with had faded. He doubted that he would ever hear that voice again.

"Come on, Sally. That's it, my love."

He dragged her backwards, moving across the stone floor on his backside. The dead people were crowding the doorway, jamming themselves into the narrow gap. They could not make headway into the room. It was a slight delay, but all he really needed.

He knew what he was going to do, and he required very little time to finalise things.

His madness had come full circle and become instead a new form of sanity: for the first time in his life he saw things clearly, as they really were, and he was almost happy.

"I hope you're okay, Tabby. My daughter. I hope you got out alive."

He backed up against the far wall, expertly untying the rope from around Sally's waist and midriff. He released her with ease, and then pushed away from her, taking a deep breath to prepare himself for what came next.

The corpses in the doorway were struggling free, as if fighting against their own decay. Eventually one of them collapsed inside the room. He stood and stared, inspecting his new surroundings. A woman joined him, one arm missing, half her face a crimson ruin. Together they began to advance upon Rick, smelling the meat of him, dancing the dead dance and eager to sate their hunger.

"Sally. I love you, and I have always loved you. I give you everything. I offer you my heart and my soul... and my flesh."

He tore off his stab vest and the shirt beneath, baring his heaving chest, exposing the wounded heart that beat beneath his aching ribs.

"*I give you my heart.*"

Sally struggled to her knees, suddenly keen and alert.

The dead moved ever closer, groaning and hissing.

Sally leaned in close, her jaw dropping, the tortured gums bared. Her dead breath chilled him, penetrating the muscle and going in deep, straight for the innards.

"Eat me," said Rick, closing his eyes and giving himself over to true love. "Eat. Me."

As long as she left enough of him to return afterward, they could still be together again, undead and happy and existing on this rugged island, hungry for all eternity.

She fell upon him, her gums barely penetrating the flesh despite the strength of her jaws as they worked at his chest. He felt them nipping at his arm, his shoulder, his throat. He threw back his head to aid her, opened his arms in a wide embrace. Sally's hands raked at the soft flesh of his throat, finally breaking the skin. She tore at the flesh, tugging the slit wider, pushing deeper, and then she hauled her arms down, ripping off his skin like a thin layer of clothing.

Rick ignored the agony and felt the love... so much aching love.

Surely it was meant to hurt this way; the blood-bright agony was the price you paid for feeling so deeply, loving so truly.

He bled for her, for his darling wife, and thought that he could not imagine a more fitting end, a better way to die; and when at last she tore the fluttering heart from his shattered chest, he opened his eyes and stared into her lovely wreck of a face, watching her consume the very best part of him – the part which had belonged to her all along.

CHAPTER FORTY-THREE

DARK ECHOES RELEASE falling stopping hungry quiet rising faster light up bright white feelings gone hungry pain gone life none sound fury hungry room motion smell hungry meat husband rick

rick?

EPILOGUE

THE YOUNG GIRL lay on her back in the wooden boat and looked up at the sky. It was pale blue, almost grey. Wispy white clouds hung motionless, strung across the faded expanse like fine cobwebs in an attic.

Enormous faces seemed to form above that cosmic ceiling, peering down at her with vague interest. A group of birds wheeled overhead – seagulls foraging for carrion – but they remained at a height, afraid to fly any lower. Their cries were muted by the distance, the tiny screams of lost souls.

The sun was weak and insubstantial; a light slowly going out in that huge attic, perhaps forever.

The faces receded, disinterested for now in her lowly existence.

The girl could not remember her name.

She had no memory of how she had got here, in the little rowboat.

Her arms and legs were aching and there were cuts on her knees and shins. The skin of her hands was lacerated. Fresh blood stained her clothing.

She sat up and stared at the distant shoreline, blinking as she examined the lines of the dead who stood calmly looking out to sea, as if waiting for something. They stood in neat rows, stiff and unmoving; their white faces were a series of smudges atop their ragged shoulders. One or two of them raised their arms and pointed out to sea, towards her; others followed suit, setting off a chain reaction. Before she turned away, most of them were pointing at her, singling her out. For an instant the girl thought that she recognised one of them, but could not be certain.

The girl's boat was moving away from the dead, drifting gradually out to sea, buoyed on the strong current. She was glad: they looked scary and threatening.

They seemed ravenous.

The girl hoped that she would be lucky enough to run into a ship and be rescued. Otherwise she might simply drift until she starved to death. And then she would return, weighed down with a hungry heart that could never be satisfied.

THE END

GARY MCMAHON'S fiction has appeared in magazines and anthologies in the UK and US and has been reprinted in both *The Mammoth Book of Best New Horror* and *The Year's Best Fantasy and Horror*. He is the British-Fantasy-Award-nominated author of *Rough Cut*, *All Your Gods Are Dead*, *Dirty Prayers*, *How to Make Monsters*, *Rain Dogs*, and has edited an anthology of original novellas titled *We Fade to Grey*.

Forthcoming are the collections *Different Skins*, *Pieces of Midnight* and *To Usher, the Dead*. You can visit Gary's website at www.garymcmahon.com

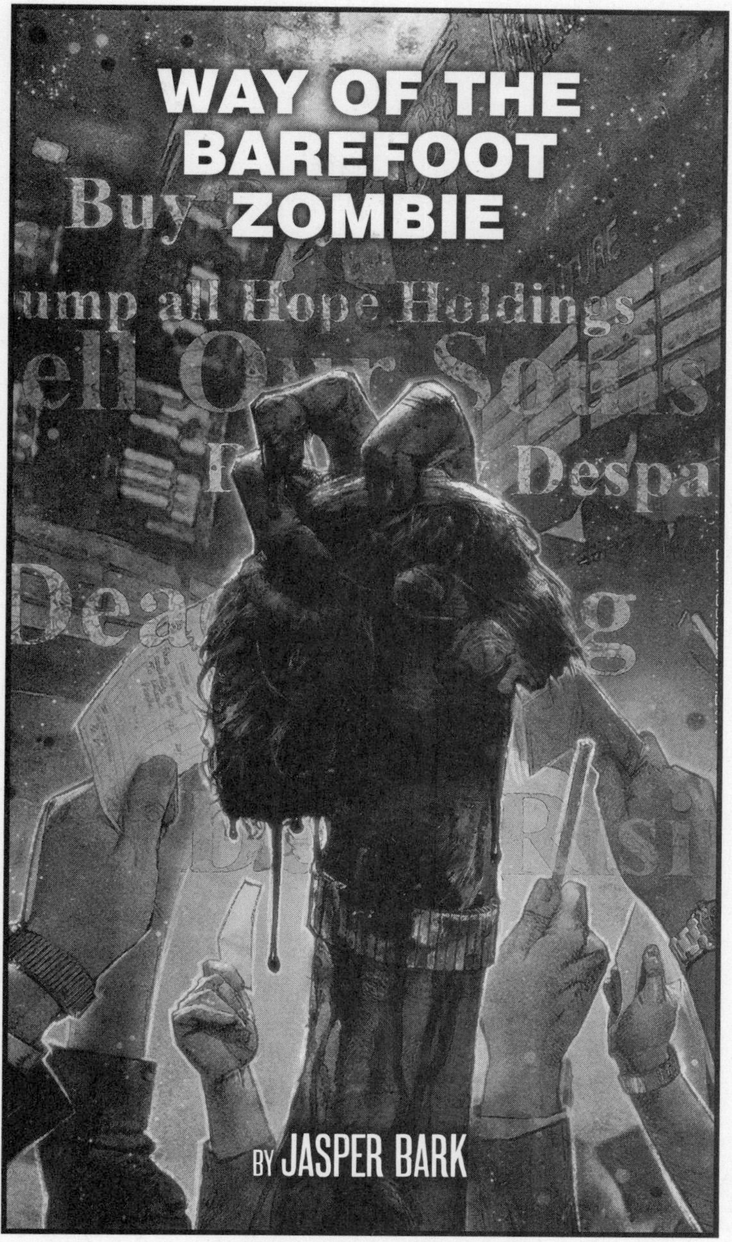
WAY OF THE BAREFOOT ZOMBIE
BY JASPER BARK

INTRODUCTION

THIS BOOK WILL change your life. No, really.

You see, we all have an inner zombie. A snarling, conscienceless brute with an insatiable appetite that sits at the very core of our being. A driving, unstoppable force that objectifies anything that gets in the way of whatever we hunger for.

This little monster is the key to gaining more wealth than you can spend in ten lifetimes. All you have to do is set it free. Let it slip out from under all those shackles that hold it back, like your conscience, your respect for other people and their right to life.

That private island you always wanted, the yacht staffed with a personal harem of hotties, the sports team you've been meaning to buy. All of it could be yours. All you have to do is free that inner zombie and it's all yours for the taking.

What you hold here in your hands, gentle reader, is more than just a cautionary tale. It's a step by step guide to freeing your inner zombie and coping with everything that comes after.

You've been warned. Read it at your peril.

Jasper Bark
April 2011

To find out more about
The Way of the Barefoot Zombie,
please visit:

HTTP://WWW.YOUTUBE.COM/
USER/JASPERBARK

CHAPTER ONE

Is this where the adventure begins? thought Benjamin. *In the john on a private jet?*

His Uncle Brian once said there were no beginnings or endings in real life. Just a sequence of events from which we draw our own significance.

Brian, who was actually his step uncle, had been killed by a frozen turd. Benjamin wondered what significance Brian would have drawn from that. Personally, Benjamin couldn't take a dump on a long haul flight without thinking about it.

The homicidal turd had fallen off some budget airline with a cracked sewage tank. The plane was so high up that the turd had frozen solid. It remained intact and rock hard as it plummeted the whole 35,000 feet.

It fell vertically and the wind resistance honed the end to a fine point. It had picked up quite a bit of speed by the time it hit Brian. It bored right through his skull and embedded itself in his brain; he died instantly.

This probably came as quite a relief to the Peruvian tour guides with Brian. He was lecturing them on why sanitation was so important to modern society and how this made New York far superior to anything the ancient Incas built.

He was on vacation in Peru at the time. Or rather he was indulging in a 'unique recreation experience' that his 'lifestyle-management expert' had organised for him. Brian indulged in these several times a year, just like all his super-rich buddies.

For seventy thousand bucks they'd do things like fly to South Africa and take pot shots at some endangered species the natives had tied down for them. Then over dinner, in a Michelin starred restaurant, some local celeb like Nelson Mandela would pretend their coked-up rant about the importance of an unregulated market was full of profound insight.

This time around it was a guided tour of the ruined city of Gran Saposoa in the middle of the jungle. Brian's body had to be airlifted out and shipped home. The turd had thawed by the time the astonished medical examiner dug it out of his brain. There was a lawsuit of course, but it didn't go anywhere.

The most ironic thing for Benjamin was not how Brian died, but where the turd had come from. Brian was an insufferable snob. If there was one thing he hated worse than taxes and Democrats, it was the poor.

For Brian they were another species. They shared certain physical similarities with real humans but they were quite mentally inferior. That's why he crapped on them every opportunity he got. Waiters, parking attendants, hotel porters, all of them had to be put in their place.

It amused Benjamin no end to think that some immigrant flying coach had dropped his pants and done to Brian what Brian had been doing to the poor his whole life. That the frozen aftermath of one cheap airline meal had totalled the one thing Brian was most proud of – his cultivated brain.

That's where Brian's adventure ended. Benjamin's began here as he took the zombie stud out of his ear. He'd kept it in as a final act of defiance, but that was stupid. He was trying to blend in, to look as though he was born to this, and the earring didn't help that a bit. As he took it out, shedding the last trapping of his old self, the transformation was complete.

Benjamin checked his reflection in the mirror to see how well he looked the part. His chestnut hair was cut short. The jet-black dye had grown out. As had the ragged and uneven clumps into which his hair had previously been cut.

His intense blue eyes were no longer obscured by opalescent contacts and red eyeliner that made them look like a dead man's.

He even noticed, with amusement, that he was getting a tan. It was strange how healthy his skin looked when it wasn't made up to look like a corpse. He wasn't used to seeing himself in an Oswald Boateng suit either, but it fitted his tall, thin frame alarmingly well.

One of the other passengers shot him a supercilious look as he headed back to his seat. A platinum blonde in an Armani suit. She probably wasn't used to flying on a jet she didn't own.

Most of the passengers had arrived at the offshore meeting point in their own private jets, or docked their two-hundred-and-fifty-foot yachts in the adjacent marina. Some landed in their helicopters so as not to appear too ostentatious.

The meeting point was a remote spot on the south coast of Texas. When Benjamin arrived some of the other guests were kicking up a fuss. There was a lot of discontent about the travel arrangements. People were incensed that after staking five million dollars worth of assets on the course they were expected to fly together on a single luxury jet.

"Why not bump us down to coach with a bunch of peasants and be done with it?" said one man with a red neck and an English accent.

The staff handled the outrage professionally. They were courteous, but insisted that the guests were contractually bound to abide by all the course rules. No privately owned jets could enter or leave the island's airspace. Failure to abide by any of the rules would result in a total loss of the attendants' stake.

The stake was what got the attendants a place on the course. It guaranteed that only the right kind of people would attend. If they didn't have access to five million dollars worth of assets then they weren't rich enough to be considered. And if they weren't prepared to stake that much then they didn't have enough conviction to study the Way of the Barefoot Zombie.

Richard's lawyer explained all this to Benjamin when his family agreed to make the stake in lieu of his inheritance. Upon completing the course the assets could be bought back at less than cost over a period of years, providing the attendant didn't break any conditions in the contract. This was all part of the 'incentive to succeed' that the course offered. It was also an effective way of maintaining control over people who were not used to being controlled.

Within only an hour or so of meeting, the guests were already jockeying for position. Some applied their charm and charisma, others flaunted their wealth and influence. All of them were trying to establish their supremacy. They sickened Benjamin, but this time his disgust was tinged with panic. He was used to setting himself apart from such behaviour, but now he had to blend in with it.

He was gripped with self doubt. Would he really be able to pull this off? There was so much more at stake than money.

They were already singling him out as someone who didn't belong. The platinum blonde wasn't the only one to look down at him. How long before they found out why he was really here? What would they do to him when they did?

Benjamin could sense the undercurrent of animosity towards him. Beneath the civilised veneer of their thousand-dollar hair cuts and their designer suits he was aware of the guests' true nature and their vicious intolerance of outsiders.

It's okay, he told himself, taking deep breaths. *You can do this. They're not on to you. You know these people. You were born for this.*

He calmed his breathing and his heart stopped pounding. He glanced around him to make certain no-one had seen his moment of weakness, then he joined Tatyana and slid back into his seat.

Tatyana had transformed herself too. Her long blonde hair fell off her shoulders like she'd just stepped out of a salon. All the plastic bugs and stuffed rodents she'd once sewn into it had gone.

While her dark brown eyes and Slavic good looks stopped her looking like a typical WASP, when her face wasn't made up to resemble a decaying cadaver, she glowed with good health and affluence. Benjamin put his arm around her slender shoulders.

No-one would have picked them out as Deathwalkers now. There was nothing about their appearance that suggested they belonged to a cult that idolised the living dead.

"You okay?" said Tatyana, sensing he was on edge.

"Yeah," he lied. "What you doing?"

"Trying to find St Ignatius on Google Earth," she said, playing with her iPhone. "It just goes all blurry every time I go north of Haiti though."

"That's because they'll have blocked it. That's the kind of power they have. It's a totally private island. It's not on any maps or in any guidebooks."

"So how do we know that's where the plane's going?"

Benjamin pointed out the window at the small island below. "See for yourself. We're coming in to land."

Tatyana leaned into him "Nervous?"

"Nah. I'm pumped. Just think, in a few days we're going to see our first real live zombie."

"Shouldn't that be real *dead* zombie?"

"You know what I mean smart ass," he said and kissed her to hide his nerves.

CHAPTER TWO

"Are sir and madam travelling together?" the guy with the parasol asked them. All the passengers were met by a member of staff as soon as they stepped off the plane. "There is another vehicle allocated if you want to ride separately," he said, adjusting the parasol to make certain they were both sheltered.

"That's okay," said Tatyana. "We're fine together."

"This way then ma'am," the man indicated a fleet of Mercedes Maybachs. He escorted them to their car where a chauffeur stood ready with the door open. Benjamin followed Tatyana onto the huge leather backseat. More than twenty feet long and looking like something out of *The Great Gatsby*, the Maybach was Mercedes' answer to Rolls Royce's Silver Phantom and a seriously impressive vehicle.

Benjamin's step cousin Brad had been showing his Maybach off at the Town and Country club a few months back. Brad had flaunted the fact that he'd paid way over the three hundred and eight-five thousand dollar price mark in order to jump the two-year queue to buy one.

Benjamin was astonished that they had a fleet of them here on St Ignatius. Just another sign of how powerful they were. Of why he had to be so cautious.

"Is the temperature okay sir, ma'am?" the chauffeur asked. "I could cool the seats if you like, or even heat 'em. If you want to let go of any tension from the flight you can put the leg rests out and I can put the massage setting on."

"Everything's fine, thanks," Tatyana said.

"There's Champagne, water and other refreshments in the refrigerator," said the chauffeur. "And there's glasses on the Champagne holder."

"Water's great," Tatyana said, grabbing two bottles from the refrigerator and handing one to Benjamin.

"So," said the chauffeur as he pulled away. "Which way would you folks like to go? There's the main highway, the scenic route through the jungle or I can take this baby up to one-fifty-five along the coast road."

"Just take us where the fewest people are going to be," said Benjamin. The chauffeur smiled. "Scenic route it is then."

Benjamin stared at the back of the chauffeur's head and tried to make out whether he was smiling to himself. Benjamin had been waited on his whole life, and knew that the people who worked in service industries were often more judgemental than the people they served. Their deference was simply a way of hiding this.

The unspoken judgement, implied in a glance or a tone of voice, always stung Benjamin more than his peers' outspoken judgement. He didn't want to be held to their standards. He hated it when people who weren't a part of that world tried to put him in it, then secretly looked down on him because he didn't fit.

He should probably cut the guy some slack. He was only trying to do his job the best he could. Benjamin had to watch he didn't get paranoid. Even so, he knew that if he was going to pass for one of these people, convincing the service staff he belonged was a crucial part.

"Have you worked on the island long?" Tatyana said to the chauffeur. It was one of her endearing little habits. She always spoke to cab drivers, receptionists and store clerks. Benjamin worried for a moment that the chauffeur would think it unusual or inappropriate behaviour. That Tatyana was about to blow their cover. But the guy seemed quite cool about it.

"About a year," he said. "I started on short term contracts and spent the rainy seasons driving limos in Florida."

"They have rainy seasons here?" said Tatyana.

"Sure. There's two, just like in Haiti. It's what keeps the weather so humid. Seeing as it's the end of October though, you got nothing to worry about."

"Is that why you've got so much jungle here?" Tatyana asked, looking out the window at the dense foliage that surrounded the road. The fierce afternoon sun struggled to break through a canopy of palm leaves and only just dappled the narrow road they drove along.

"I don't know if it's 'cause of the weather," said the chauffeur. "'Course, this was all sugar cane fields a hundred years ago, before they let it grow wild."

"Really?"

"Yeah, that was back when Mary Papamal owned it."

"Who?"

"Are you guys serious? You never heard of the Scarlet Witch of Mangrove Hall?"

"No," said Benjamin. "Should we have?"

"Well, no, I guess I was just surprised. She's the most famous person to have lived on St Ignatius, being a serial killer and all."

"A serial killer, for real?" said Tatyana. "And she came from St Ignatius?"

"Well, she was born in France. Her parents moved to Haiti when she was four years old. They both died of typhoid when she was fourteen. She was raised by her Haitian maid, who took her to Voodoo ceremonies and taught her magic. When she was eighteen she found her trust fund had been spent by the relatives put in charge of it and her only hope was to marry some rich dude. So she seduced Jean Papamal, the guy who owned Mangrove Hall. He was forty at the time and she was nineteen."

"Aw, man, that's gross," said Benjamin. "Imagine doing someone twice your age."

"Maybe he was cute," said Tatyana. "Besides, it wasn't like she had much choice. She'd lost both her parents and all her inheritance was stolen. I feel kind of sorry for her."

"Don't feel sorry for her," said the chauffeur. "She more than made up for the bad start she got in life. She murdered her first husband within a year of coming here and had his body bricked up in the wall of their bedroom. Then, when she discovered he was so in debt he was going to lose the whole plantation, she married a rich Admiral to save it."

"Did he last any longer than her first husband?" said Benjamin.

"Nope. By this point Mary had started to take lovers from the plantation slaves. So, one night she sneaks three of them into their bedroom and waits until the Admiral comes to bed. Then she has two of them hold him down and strangle the Admiral while she does the third slave and makes him watch. The last thing the guy sees before he dies is one of his slaves humping his wife. Then apparently she had a foursome with all three slaves while her husband's corpse was lying in the bed next to them."

"Whoa," said Benjamin. "She sounds like quite a chick."

"Oh yeah," said Tatyana. "*Now* you like her, soon as you find out she's into kinky stuff."

"She did a lot worse than that, " said the chauffeur, settling into his story. "Afterwards she had the three slaves stripped naked and tied them to the back of her carriage. Then she rode all over the island until the slaves were just bloody lumps of meat.

"Eew," said Tatyana. "And she got away with all this?"

"She ruled the whole plantation like a tyrant. Who was going to stop her? She used to take male and female slaves to her bed then have them killed the next morning. She would have other slaves whipped to death just for looking at her the wrong way. Everyone was terrified of her. Eventually she overstepped herself though."

"What happened?"

"There was a small colony of natives on the north side of the island who all practised Voodoo like she did. Mary took up with their Houngan, that's what they call a Voodoo high priest. They all have these rattles that hang round their necks that are called assons. No-one else is allowed to wear one, 'cause they're like a badge of office or something. This priest was a guy by the name of Toussaint. This was all fine until Mary gets the hots for the guy who was betrothed to Toussaint's daughter. When the guy turned her down, she kidnapped Toussaint's daughter and planned to sacrifice her in some evil ceremony. So Toussaint led a revolt of the slaves. They stormed Mangrove Hall, murdered Mary and set light to the building. The whole plantation was in ruins for nearly a century until Doc Papa, the guy who runs this place, restored it two years ago."

"So what happened to all the slaves and their descendants?" said Tatyana. "Did they stay on the island?"

"Erm, I dunno. I guess they all went to Haiti or something."

The Chauffeur lapsed into silence, looking uncomfortable. He probably didn't know as much as he made out. Tatyana changed the subject.

"So are you still on short term contracts, or do you work here full time?"

"Full time now. Pay's phenomenal and so are the incentives."

"Incentives?"

"Let's just say I found a way to put all of my soul into my work."

"Ooh, sounds intriguing."

The chauffeur didn't elaborate, and there was an uncomfortable pause. "Hey do you guys want to listen to some music?" he said, eventually. "I got digital. You can get almost any station."

"That's okay man," said Benjamin. "Silence is good."

"Okay," said the chauffeur and put the visor up between them.

Tatyana looked at Benjamin as if to say *what the fuck?* Benjamin shrugged. They guy seemed to clam up pretty quickly. Had he rumbled them? Did he think Tatyana was coming on to him? She was pretty friendly. Some guys misread that.

Benjamin didn't think so. The chauffeur looked tense, a little nervous even. Like he'd let something slip. Said something he shouldn't have.

But what? Was it all that stuff about Mary Papamal? If she was so well known, why wouldn't he be allowed to tell them?

THEY WERE THE last to arrive at Mangrove Hall, a beautiful three-story stone and timber-framed mansion built in the eighteenth century. It sat at the top of a hill, surrounded by beautifully kept terrace lawns with lush tropical plants in the borders.

To the left of the mansion the five-star apartments of the guests' accommodation. To the right was a building that looked like something out of Silicon Valley. God knows what went on in there.

From the moment they stepped through the doors of the restored mansion, a hundred sets of eyes were on Benjamin and Tatyana, all of them silently assessing how much they were worth.

Clothes, hair and jewellery, shoes, watches and handbags, all of it was given the once over by the staff and guests alike. The price of every item was mentally calculated; brand labels spotted and judgements made. The scrutiny was that much more intense for how casually and thoroughly everyone indulged in it.

Benjamin acted as though he was slumming it just to be seen in the place. Tatyana tried her best to follow suit. Inwardly he recoiled from identifying with these people. Secretly he suspected this had as much to do with wanting their acceptance as it did with despising them.

They checked in at the main desk and were shown through to a hospitality suite where a light buffet and drinks were laid on. The suite was in the mansion's old ballroom, which looked like something straight out of *Gone With the Wind*. Benjamin wondered what sort of infernal gatherings Mary Papamal had presided over here.

Waiting staff circulated with bottles of vintage wine as the other guests picked over the exotic buffet like carrion birds. Pecking orders were already being established as they sized each other up.

A grey-haired man with rattlesnake skin boots and a Texas drawl was holding court.

"So I get into the lift with this lawyer and she says to me: 'Mr McKane, can I give you a blow job?' And I say: 'Okay, but what's in it for me?'"

"Oh Sam, you're too much," said the platinum blonde from the plane.

"Yeah. Too much for *your* price bracket."

Benjamin and Tatyana helped themselves to braised Guinea Hen with truffles and sipped glasses of Dom Perignon. They acted as though no-one dared talk to them to hide the fact that no-one could be bothered to talk to them. Most likely because no-one knew who they were.

Benjamin was just wondering if this could be used to their advantage when the room fell silent. Samuel Palmer, the CEO of St Ignatius, had stepped up to the small podium in the centre of the room. He was a tall man in his early forties with a long face and a completely bald head, penetrating brown eyes and a predatory smile. You couldn't miss his natural presence and the commanding aura of power he gave off.

"Esteemed guests," he said. "I am delighted to welcome you to St Ignatius. I can promise you this, the next few days will be the single most important time of your lives. You are on your way to joining the world's one true elite. Sure you're rich. Some of you even have a little influence. You wouldn't be here otherwise. But you're looking for something more, something bigger and something better. And why not? You deserve it. You've all proven that.

"You've come here to find that extra something. And you won't be disappointed. You know there's more to be had, and you're people with a lot of initiative. If there was another way to get hold of it, you would have found out about it. But there isn't. Only we hold the key to success beyond success. Only we can point you down the path to wealth beyond reason and power beyond excess.

"What we're offering is more than any human can take. So we're going to make you more than human. Then you can take more than anyone's fair share. You will walk where most others fear to go. Your feet will tread the Way of the Barefoot Zombie."

There was huge applause and whoops of excitement from the guests. They devoured his words like cash-starved banks in a government bail out.

"Tomorrow we begin the work in earnest. Tonight I suggest you take advantage of our hospitality and unwind a little." Palmer raised his wine glass to the guests and they returned the gesture.

A palpable thrill ran round the room. There was intense expectation, a sense that everyone was about to be let in on one of the most powerful secrets in existence. That there was no other place in world to be at that moment. That all the right people, and only the right people, were there.

A waitress moved past Benjamin, swerved to avoid another guest and bumped into Tatyana. She dropped the tray of half empty glasses she was carrying and they soaked Tatyana's shoes.

"I'm terribly sorry, ma'am," the waitress said, kneeling to clear up the broken glass.

"That's quite alright. Here, let me help you."

The room went quiet. Everyone turned to look at Benjamin and Tatyana. She'd broken a fundamental rule of conduct: you don't offer to help people who are paid to wait on you.

Benjamin felt them circling, as though a room full of wolves had just discovered two sheep with the temerity to dress in their clothing.

He went cold, and sweat broke out on the back of his neck. Panic threatened to overwhelm him. They were going to be revealed. They'd only just got here and everything was falling apart. He had to do something. He had to do something right now.

Uncle Brian came to his rescue.

Benjamin emptied his glass over the waitress's head. "Yeah, let me help you, bitch," he said, throwing the glass on the floor next to her. The waitress gasped. "Let me help you clean this up properly."

He put his foot on the back of the waitress's neck and forced her face down into the broken glass and spilled alcohol. "You lick this shit up. Lick it up, because you're dumb and worthless and mopping the floor is the only thing your ugly face is good for."

He was channelling Brian now. Spitting out all the rage and disgust he'd seen his uncle heap on those beneath him. Had Brian been this frightened when he did it? Had he enjoyed it this much? Benjamin was disgusted with himself. Disgusted that it felt so good.

He looked up to see the other guests smiling with approval. A couple of them even applauded. He relaxed. Their cover wasn't blown. He'd passed the first test and they'd accepted him.

He belonged. They knew that now. But worst of all, so did he.

CHAPTER THREE

TATYANA WAS FIXING her make up in the bathroom mirror. Applying another mask, creating another identity to hide behind.

Ironically it took her a lot longer to apply a little foundation, some mascara and lipstick than it did to apply all the make up she'd used as a Deathwalker. Then she'd been trying to make herself look like a walking corpse. Now she was trying to pass herself off as something even more hideous.

Benjamin came up behind her as she reached for some lip gloss. He put his hands on her hips and pulled her to him; she could feel his hard-on in the small of her back. He slid his hands around front and cupped her breasts.

"How about a little make-up sex?"

She shrugged him off. "We don't have much time. We've got to be there at eight and I'm trying to fix my make up."

"That's what I'm trying to do. Fix us and make up. Shit, you're not still pissed about last night are you?"

"I'm not pissed, I'm just... I hated seeing you like that. I feel weird. Being around you right now brings up all kinds of memories."

"I'm not your father, Tatyana."

"I know you're not."

She turned to face him. He was slumped against the polished marble wall. She thought about reaching out to him, of maybe even dragging him onto the huge bed next door to make up. Then, before she could stop herself, she said: "But you did a pretty good impression of him last night."

Benjamin lost it. "Well I had to do something. They were on to us, you saw them. If I hadn't acted as quickly as I did we might have blown the whole thing. It's not my fault that you..."

"That I what?'

"Nothing."

"Go on say it. It's not your fault that I fucked up. That's what you think isn't it?"

Benjamin looked away. He stared at the floor and shrugged.

"Well, you did go to help that waitress. I mean, what were you thinking? You know what these people are like. How they think and the way they treat staff. We're trying to blend in. To act and think like them, so they accept us as one of their own. I did what I did to look like one of them. To fit in. We've come too far to blow it all now."

Tatyana turned back to the mirror. She didn't want to look at herself, so she gazed at the sink. "You're right," she said after a long pause. "It's just, well that wasn't *you* last night. And it scared me. It's a side of you I would never have guessed existed. And it did... well, it did bring back memories."

"I'm not your father."

"I know you're not, okay? You don't have to keep saying that. But that is just the sort of thing he would have done. And even now..."

"Even now what?"

"Look, I'm not accusing you, I'm not blaming you, but you sound just like him."

"Oh come on Tatyana!"

He was about to blow up again. She reached out and took hold of his hands. "Please, I'm trying to reach out here. I'm trying to explain how I feel."

"But saying that I sound just like him..."

"I'm not trying to pick a fight, but you *do*. That's exactly the sort of thing he used to say. 'You don't know the sort of people I have to mix with. I only do what I do to fit in with them.'" Her light Russian accent became thicker as she impersonated her father. "That was always his excuse."

Benjamin let go of her hands and went to leave. She caught hold of his arm. "Wait. Look, we're both on edge. It's this place. It's doing things to us. But you're right; we have come too far to blow it all now. There's too much at stake. We need each other. Please, let's not fight. You did what you had to do and I can't help feeling the way I do about it. But I love you and I need you now more than ever."

Benjamin stood with his shoulders slumped, staring at the floor. He sighed. "Okay."

"Love me?"

"Always."

Tatyana smiled and kissed him on the cheek. "We've only got a few minutes before we're due in the lecture theatre. Can we take a rain-check on that make-up sex?"

"You bet."

CHAPTER FOUR

THE LECTURE THEATRE was in the high-tech annex on the other side of the mansion. Like everything else on St Ignatius, it reeked of quality and taste. From the plush leather seating to the fully articulated screens around the stage, the attention to detail was flawless.

Tatyana wasn't the only one to be impressed. For all their sophistication, many of the other guests shot admiring glances at the facilities. Some caught each other's gaze and exchanged guilty smiles, as though caught out for not being jaded enough.

One guest stood out from the others the minute she walked into the room. She was a tall, elegant African-American wearing a traditional African dress. She appeared to glide rather than walk, and there was something almost noble in the way she carried herself.

Two course officials pursued her into the theatre.

"Excuse me, Ms Chevalier," said one, he was out of breath.

"Call me Miriam,"

"I'm terribly sorry. But there's a strict dress code for these lectures."

"There's nothing wrong with what I'm wearing."

"You have to wear a suit," said the other official. "Or some type of formal business wear. It is course policy, I'm afraid."

Miriam straightened her back and pushed her shoulders back. Her voice took on a strange, hollow quality. Like it came from somewhere far away. "I said there's nothing wrong with what I'm wearing, it's perfectly suitable for the occasion."

The body language of the two officials completely changed. Their faces relaxed and they seemed to be looking far into the distance, paying no attention to what was going on around them.

"There's nothing wrong with what you're wearing," said the first official, in a deadpan tone.

"It's perfectly fitting," said the other.

"Thank you," said Miriam and the two officials drifted away in a trance.

Miriam became aware that Tatyana was watching her and looked her right in the eye; she seemed quite shocked that anyone had seen what had just taken place.

Tatyana smiled in a nervous but friendly way. Miriam did not return the smile. She appeared cross. Tatyana's head started to spin and her vision blurred, and she slumped against Benjamin, who helped her sit down.

"You okay?" he said. "What happened?"

"I'm not sure. I... I can't seem to remember."

"Look," said Benjamin, helping her back to her feet. "We'll go sit at the back, okay? So we don't draw any attention."

"Okay,"

He guided her into a seat. For a moment or two she couldn't remember where she was, or what she was doing here. Then it all came back in a sudden jolt that made her gasp.

Several guests turned to look at her.

"She's okay," said Benjamin, with his best winning smile. "Too much celebrating last night."

The lights dimmed then, drawing attention away from her.

Tatyana knew where she was now and why she was here. But for the life of her she couldn't remember getting to the lecture theatre. The last thing she remembered was the fight she had with Benjamin that morning. Everything after that was a blank.

A single spotlight picked out a glass podium that rose out of the stage floor. Samuel Palmer stepped up to it.

"Good morning," Palmer said. "I trust you enjoyed our hospitality last night? I know some of you made very good use of it." Palmer leered frighteningly, and the low chuckle that came from the audience was even more unsettling. Tatyana was thankful she'd gone to bed early.

"But that isn't what we're here to talk about. You're eager to meet the man behind this whole operation. How do I introduce a man like Doc Papa? I should probably turn to Shakespeare, because only the greatest writer in our language could do him justice. Shakespeare said: 'Some are born great, some achieve greatness and some have greatness thrust upon them'. There aren't many people for whom all three of those are true. But Doc Papa is that rare exception. A man who has gained power and knowledge beyond human reckoning."

A low rumble of drums started in the background, pounding out Voodoo rhythms that built to a crescendo as Palmer said: "Ladies and Gentlemen, I give you Doc Papa."

The sound of the drums filled the hall. Tatyana felt them reverberate deep within her, drawing her pulse into the beat, and felt something ancient and primal awaken inside her. Like a distant memory from a time beyond recollection. It was as though there was another presence in her mind, whispering to her in a language she could neither hear nor understand. It felt alien from anything she'd encountered, but at the same time friendly and pure.

And then it was gone, like a lover withdrawing on the point of orgasm. She hadn't realised how intimate it was until it was over. The lost memories of the last half hour flowed back into her mind in its place.

Before she had a chance to process the memories, two Haitian dancers entered the stage, a man and a woman, both dressed in traditional garb. The man carried a large boa constrictor on his shoulders. The woman had a long necklace of beads with seven rows in the colours of the rainbow. They each held a lit torch in one hand, and a bottle of rum in the other. The six screens came together and began to show intricate symbols drawn on bare ground in white dust.

The drums got faster and the dancers became wilder and more frenetic. As the drums reached a rhythmic peak the dancers took a deep swig from the rum and then blew it in a fine spray at the torches.

The stage was shrouded by a curtain of flames. When they cleared, there stood Doc Papa. And as quickly and mysteriously as he seemed to have appeared, the dancers were gone.

Tatyana started when she saw him, as did everyone else. His mere presence seemed to have a physical impact on all of them, as though he had reached out and slapped them.

Tatyana could not take her eyes off him. She had never seen anyone with so much charisma. It emanated from him with all the force of an ocean breaking against the shore.

"*Honneur la maison!*" said Doc Papa in a rich deep voice that filled the hall. "*Messieurs et Dames, bonswa.*" He held his arms open and smiled so broadly that everyone felt honoured to be greeted by him. He was a tall, imposing man with the light brown complexion of a Creole. Though he carried a lot of weight he moved with such an assured grace that you hardly noticed it.

He wore a dark blue suit and a white silk shirt that probably cost more than an average person made in a year. Around his neck, on a golden chain, hung a rattle covered with a network of what looked snake vertebrae. That must be the *asson* that the chauffeur had told them about, Tatyana realised.

"Congratulations on becoming one of the true elite," Doc Papa said. "As a breed apart, you are used to making good decisions. This is your best one yet. To walk with me along the Way of the Barefoot Zombie is to transcend your humanity. To become one of the masters, not one of the prey.

"Under my tutelage you will learn to use great powers. You may not realise it but you have already learned to use one of the prime magical systems of our age. I am talking about money.

"We in the Western world are not conditioned to think of money as magic. But that is what it is. I amassed a fortune in hedge funds before I realised this, before I saw money for what it is. A spirit that mediates in the affairs of men. One that assures people reach agreement when buying and selling. One that decides who profits and who loses. A spirit that establishes the natural order of society, raising up some to great heights of power and laying others low.

"'Ah yes,' you might say to me. 'But that is not the way that money works. Money is not an immaterial spirit. It sits here in my wallet, it lies in my bank account and it pays for my homes.'" He took a hundred dollar bill from his pocket. "What is this note though? It is not the things you can buy with it. It is a promise to pay the bearer on demand an agreed sum. But what is the bearer being paid on demand? Where does this sum come from?

"Anyone with even a pedestrian knowledge of banking will tell you that money is created with a push of a button every time some poor slob takes out a loan. That loan itself becomes an asset to be sold on by the bank.

"The price of the asset is based on the amount of interest the moron will be paying for the rest of his life. Yet any economist will tell you that this system of monetary creation is incapable of generating enough capital to repay any of this interest.

"Yet if the pathetic slob fails to repay the interest that our economy is incapable of generating, we come and take his car, his house and all of his dignity while we're at it. Because he failed to give back to us something that never existed in the first place. By taking the guy's house in lieu of the loan, which never existed in the first place, the bank literally gets something for nothing.

"Smoke and mirrors, it's the ultimate conjuring trick, creating something out of nothing. Magic, my friends. Magic, pure and simple.

"Still don't believe me? Then let us look at what magic is. Consider Voodoo and the service of the Loa. What is the magical system that a

Houngan uses? It is simply a means to impose his will upon the world, using symbols imbued with power through ritual and ceremony.

"A Houngan draws symbols called Vévés on the ground to conjure up the Loa, the spirits that will do his bidding. He then bargains with the Loa to impart power to the symbols he makes or draws on paper. How does he bargain? Through ritual and ceremony. A group of believers come together at a preordained place to act in a preordained manner in order to bring power to their symbols so that they can invisibly affect the world to their benefit.

"Now let us look at the stock market. Consider what happens when some klepto-communist gets elected leader of a third world country and starts to threaten land reform and nationalisation. The first thing we do on the stock market is speculate against their currency to drive down its value. Then when the country is on its knees with hyper-inflation and spiralling unemployment, where does it turn but the IMF, desperate for a loan?

"The IMF agrees the loan on the condition that the country implements stringent economic measures. These of course will include abolishing minimum wage and mass privatisations, allowing Western companies to move in and snap up local resources at bargain prices.

"This has been accomplished many times, from Latin America to South Africa, without any show of force. How is this done? Quite simply, a group of people known as traders come together at a preordained place – the stock market – and act in a preordained manner. They do this to bring power to a group of symbols known as the currency index so that they can invisibly affect another nation's economy to their benefit.

"A hand is raised on a stock market floor. A series of symbols appear on a screen and a whole nation is placed in complete thrall to another. Magic, plain and simple."

Doc Papa spread his arms wide and smiled. The audience were transfixed by his words.

"Like all magic, however, money is purely a means to an ends and not, as many peasants believe, an end in itself. Like all magic, it also takes a little while to master, but with the right teacher you can use it to accomplish anything. To change the world in any way you want"

A thrill ran through the audience at the prospect of attaining such knowledge. They were sitting up in their seats, rapt with attention.

"Before you can change the world," said Doc Papa. "You have to change yourself. You have to shed the last vestiges of that enfeebling impediment we like to call our humanity. You must be reborn as something more than human. Something shorn of all the frailties and defects that confine the others to the common herd. Something a little like this..."

Doc Papa bent down and picked up a large metal ring, attached to two heavy chains, running to trapdoors in the stage. They were attached to the metal collars around the necks of two figures that rose up from inside the trapdoors.

Tatyana felt a jolt of anticipation when she realised what they were, and turned to Benjamin. He grinned back with excitement and grabbed her hand. This was the reason they came to St Ignatius. For the first time they got to see the noble monsters they had travelled so far to save.

The figures were motionless. Their bodies were limp and their eyes lifeless; their skin had the pallid texture of a corpse. Doc Papa clicked his fingers. With a shudder that ran the length of their bodies, the figures started to move.

Their nostrils started working first. They flared them like animals scenting the breeze. They bared their teeth and started to gnash them. Mouths that didn't look capable of eating showed a grim parody of hunger.

Their muscles began to twitch and twist their bodies into clumsy postures of menace. Both figures crouched low and, with an unexpected burst of speed, sprang at the audience.

Doc Papa yanked on the chains and they stopped just short of the front row. Their heads jerked about as they caught the scent of flesh. Like wild animals, they snapped at the prey just out of reach.

Their decaying bodies could not accommodate the ferocity of their appetites. The violence of their actions strained the tendons and ligatures of their arms as they flailed and clawed at the living.

The skin across the cheek of one began to tear as the jaws worked ferociously. A loose tooth flew out of the ragged hole as its jaws clamped down on empty air.

The people in the front row scrambled out of their seats, while those in the back rows craned forward to get a better look. There was an intense excitement in the room, a grim fascination that came from witnessing a very real threat to their lives.

"Magnificent, aren't they?" Doc Papa said as he tugged the chains they were straining at. "Look at how they thirst for your blood. How can you not admire that single minded sense of purpose? That hunger so great they would destroy their bodies just to feed it. Is there anyone here who thinks they would survive an encounter with them? Anyone care to brave it if I let one off the leash? No? I thought as much.

"What it is that makes them dangerous? Unlike them, your bodies work and your brains function, so why could they physically overcome any of you?

"Because they want it more. They are not confused by the things that inhibit you, like a conscience or social custom. Their hunger is raw and real and quite, quite prefect."

"*Rete!*" Doc Papa commanded. "*Dans le nom des Gédés, Rete!*" The figures dropped their arms to their sides and became perfectly still.

"*Isit.*" The figures turned their backs on the audience and walked towards him. At his signal they turned to face the audience once more, placid and still.

"If there are any among you who still doubt the existence of magic, look now upon the proof. I instilled that terrifying drive in them and I alone control it. You can instil it in yourselves without having to give up your lives as they have. That is what you came here to learn.

"It is this drive that I am referring to when I speak of your 'Inner Zombie.' It is the first of many powerful secrets you will discover when you walk in the footsteps of the Barefoot Zombie.

"This is how you dominate the market and impose your will upon it. This is how you become its master, not one of the timid quislings who are prey to its fluctuations.

"Any decent economist will tell you that the market works best when it's free of government intervention or regulation. This is the nature of the beast you must tame. To take hold of it and make it submit to your bidding, you must let go of anything that confines you. Any cloying weakness with which society has tied your hands. Once you have released your Inner Zombie you have the power to enslave the wildest of free markets.

"Before you can release your Inner Zombie and instil your own terrifying drive you have to encounter it. You have to meet it head on and find out what it is. You must discover what you are truly capable of being.

"These will be the first steps you take along the Way of the Barefoot Zombie. They will be the most terrifying and the most empowering thing you have ever done with your lives. You have spoken many times about 'making a killing on the markets' without once getting blood on your hands. It is time to learn what killing is really about.

"These two zombies are far from the only two specimens here on the island. Any cheap necromancer can raise a couple of corpses and command them. I have created the world's first and only captive colony of zombies.

"There has never been a better opportunity for studying the zombie. For living with them, acting like them and learning to become one of them. That is what you are going to do over the coming weeks."

CHAPTER FIVE

ONCE DOC PAPA'S lecture was over, the head Group Encounter leader came on and told them what to expect over the next few days. Tatyana's mind drifted off. She was far more interested in the half-hour of memory she had suddenly lost and just as suddenly regained.

That woman Miriam Chevalier was responsible. She'd done something to her mind. Tatyana was sure of it.

Tatyana looked over to where Miriam was seated. There was a strange, hazy field all around her. It was hard to look at Miriam, and Tatyana's eyes kept wanting to slide away and look elsewhere. This only intrigued Tatyana more, and she concentrated harder on looking at Miriam, on fighting the impulse to look away and forget all about her.

Why had this woman reached into Tatyana's mind and taken away her memory? More importantly, how?

Tatyana watched as Miriam stood and left her seat. Partly because of the field around her, and partly because everyone was paying attention to the stage, Miriam was able to slip away without anyone noticing.

Tatyana knew she had to follow. She slipped out of her seat and headed to the back of the theatre.

Unlike Miriam, she didn't have any field around her to deflect scrutiny. Several heads turned as she sneaked away. Tatyana tried her best not to catch anyone's eye. Benjamin had gone on for ages about how important it was not to draw attention to themselves. She knew he was right, but she also knew this was more important.

Miriam turned her head, and Tatyana bent down behind a row of chairs and pretended to adjust the Jimmy Choo shoes Benjamin had insisted she buy.

When she looked back up Miriam didn't seem to have spotted her. Tatyana had spotted something of interest, though. Miriam's field left a ghost trail behind her. If she was careful, Tatyana could just catch sight of it out of the corner of her eye.

She slipped off the shoes so her heels didn't clatter on the floor and, acting on an instinct that surprised her, she chased after Miriam, stepping inside the ghost trail.

She had no idea why, but the trail lent her the same ability to deflect attention as Miriam's field. Not even Miriam noticed her so long as she stayed within it. This wasn't always easy though. The trail had a tendency to waft in an out of Miriam's footsteps as if an invisible breeze was blowing it. Tatyana had to side-step quite a bit to stay inside it.

She followed Miriam out of the lecture theatre and around a corner into a corridor she hadn't seen before. Miriam raced along at a pace Tatyana found hard to match. Even at speed, she moved with effortless grace.

Miriam opened a service door at the end of the long corridor and snuck through it, and Tatyana ran to catch the door before it swung shut. The narrow passageway beyond wasn't as opulent as the rest of the annex; bare pipes and electric wires ran along the unpainted concrete walls.

At the end of the passageway a metal staircase descended into a large service bay. Food goods and domestic products were stacked against concrete pillars in large polythene-wrapped palettes.

Miriam moved through the bay onto a large walkway. At the end of this was a hi-tech security door with long corridors running off to the left and right. Miriam stopped at the door, took out a piece of red chalk, and drew several symbols on the wall around a card-swipe mechanism. The symbols looked similar to those she'd seen on the screens drawn in white powder.

Tatyana stood in the shadows and watched as Miriam prayed under her breath. She seemed to be in a trance. Miriam took out a card and ran it through the swipe on the wall.

The lights went out. Tatyana couldn't see a thing. She wedged herself into a corner as the sound of running feet hurtled towards them.

"This is a restricted area, ma'am," said a man's voice. "You just tripped the alarm. I'm going to have to ask you to stand still with your hands on your head."

Two torch beams clicked on, directed at Miriam. Tatyana could see the torches were mounted on the automatic weapons of two guards.

She was very nervous. She'd seen the guards all over the island; they tried to maintain a discreet presence in front of the guests, but now they were pointing guns at a guest Tatyana had followed into a restricted area.

Way to go not calling attention to yourself, she thought.

The guards clicked off their night-vision goggles.

"You're not supposed to be down here, ma'am. You're life is in danger. Not just from us. There's an army of the undead on the other side of that door. I'm going to have to ask you to lie face down with your hands behind your back."

Instead of doing what the guards told her, Miriam looked up at the ceiling and began to mutter something in a whispered voice.

"Ma'am, get on the floor please," said the guard, more urgently.

"On the floor, bitch! Now!" shouted the other guard, taking a step closer to her.

Tatyana's heart was pounding in her chest. She hardly dared breathe and one of her legs shook so hard she couldn't stop it. They were going to shoot her, and Miriam wasn't doing a thing about it.

Tatyana closed her eyes and waited for the shot. She wished she wasn't an atheist, that she believed in anything enough to pray to it right now. She pictured a stained-glass window of the Virgin Mary she'd once seen that had changed the way she felt about religion. It was the closest she'd ever come to having faith in something. She held the image in her mind like an invisible guardian and begged it to stop the guards finding her.

Instead of hearing a shot Tatyana felt a calm and loving presence all around her. Was this the Virgin Mary?

Don't worry, I won't let any harm befall those who love me.

Tatyana was confused. *But I'm an atheist,* she thought. The tone of the presence changed at this. It was still warm and loving but she could swear it was laughing. The same way her mother would laugh when, as a little girl, Tatyana had said something cute without realising it. Then the presence faded.

Tatyana looked around the corner and saw something even weirder. The guards weren't moving. They stood staring straight ahead without any expression.

Miriam was reaching her fingers out to the air either side of the guards' temples and coaxing what looked like a fine black mist out of their heads. Tatyana blinked and looked again, sure that she hadn't seen what she thought she was seeing.

But there it was. The black mist and Miriam's fingers. What was she doing to them? Why weren't they moving? Was that their memories Miriam was taking? Was that what Miriam had done to her earlier?

Before Tatyana could come to any conclusions, Miriam shook her hands and seemed to banish the mist. The guards didn't move as she walked past Tatyana and back down the walkway.

Tatyana watched her disappear into the darkness and then glanced back at the guards. They weren't even blinking.

She had no idea what had just happened, but she knew she had to get out of there quick.

It was already beginning to seem like a dream as she stumbled back down the walkway. She kept hoping she was going to wake up as she felt her way along the wall and tried to remember the way back in the pitch dark.

She couldn't repress the feeling that she'd just had an entirely different sort of awakening, though.

CHAPTER SIX

"So, where did you go?"

"Oh, you know, just around." She was being evasive, and setting off all his old paranoia.

Benjamin had been trying to get Tatyana to talk about where she went since he found her up in their room hours later. She seemed shaken and said she was tired, so he'd let her get some sleep without bothering her.

Now she'd had a good night's sleep, he tried again, rolling over to hold her.

"No, I don't know," he said. "That's why I'm asking."

"Why is it so important to you?"

"Well for one thing you might have seen something that could be vital to our mission. Even the tiniest detail might have a significance you haven't realised yet. I can't understand why you don't want to tell me about it."

"Look, I'm still processing it all, okay. I'm not even sure what happened myself. I just need a bit of time."

"Won't it help to talk about it?"

"Can we just drop it, please?" She reached under the covers and took him in her hand. "Maybe we could have that make-up sex you've been promising me?"

He grew hard the minute she touched him but he couldn't keep the nagging suspicions out of his mind. "Is it because you were with someone you don't want me to know about? Did you sneak off with someone?"

"One of the guests, you mean? Come on, give me some credit."

"I did give you credit before, remember? Look what happened then."

"Do you have to keep bringing that up? Can't you cut me a little slack and maybe just trust me for once?"

"How can I trust you when you won't talk to me?" He pushed her hand away and slid out of bed. "I'm going for a shower."

Tatyana rolled over and stared up at the ceiling with an angry sigh.

Benjamin punched the shower control and hurt his hand. The hot water relaxed him as he rubbed his sore fingers. He was more angry at himself than Tatyana. Partly because he'd just turned down the opportunity to have sex, and partly because he hadn't gotten over that business with her old boyfriend.

It was stupid, really. It had happened six months ago. They'd been going steady for a while when Tatyana told him she was going to see an old boyfriend who happened to be in town. He'd been perfectly cool with it at first. But there was something about the way she'd said the guy's name that kept eating away at him.

On the day in question he took Richard's Bentley and followed her. He knew it was stupid but he couldn't stop himself. He pulled up next to the park where she met the guy and kept tabs on them through field binoculars. He felt kind of creepy doing it and he had no idea what he'd say if a cop saw him.

Nothing happened for ages. They wandered about, chatted and ate ice cream. Then, just when Benjamin was feeling like a total putz and was about to slope off, they kissed. He nearly dropped his binoculars.

The guy moved in on her. They were laughing and she gave him a look that Benjamin knew all too well. The guy leaned in and she turned her head. He took her face in his hands, turned it to him and kissed her. They really went for it, tongues and everything.

Benjamin couldn't believe it. He was so mad he was shaking. He threw the binoculars on the floor and battered the dashboard with his fists. He should have left right there and then but he wasn't thinking rationally anymore. He waited until they parted and confronted Tatyana.

She couldn't believe he'd followed her. She was incensed at the way he'd behaved. Imagine the gall; after what she'd just done she had the nerve to get mad with *him*. They had a blazing row right there in the park and she stormed off.

It was two weeks before he heard from her again. She sent him a couple of texts which he ignored. Then a week or so later he finally gave in to his Mom's nagging and tidied his room.

At the bottom of a pile of dirty briefs and magazines he came across the DVD of *Zombie Flesh Eaters* that she'd bought him for his birthday. Inside the case was the note she'd written him:

> Yours are the hands that pulled my eye onto the splinter of love and embedded it in my brain. Yours are the teeth that gnaw on my guts every time I think about life without you. You are the zombie that wrestles with the sharks of my fear and shines the sunlight of love on my despairing sea.

He broke down and bawled like a kid when he read it.

Their first date had been a midnight screening of *Zombie Flesh Eaters*. The scene where the zombie fights the shark. That was their scene. They had their first kiss during it. Then, during the infamous scene where the splinter is driven into the Doctor's wife's eyeball, she gave him the best hand job he'd ever had.

Holding the note, he knew right there and then, that he would never find anyone to write him a more tender and touching love letter.

They got back together the next day. He forgave her, of course, but he could never bring himself to forget.

He kept playing the image of her kissing the other guy over and over in his mind. It was like a scab that he couldn't help picking. It wasn't just his jealousy and insecurity that drove him to keep going over it; if he was honest, he realised that it turned him on.

Every time he thought about their kiss he took it that little bit further. He imagined the other guy's hands roaming over Tatyana's body. Taking her dress off. Pinning her down to the park bench...

Even now, just thinking about it in the shower made him harder than when she'd held his penis. He poured the shower gel onto his palm and took hold of himself.

"Enjoying yourself?" said Tatyana. He dropped the shower gel and spun round to see her standing by the door in her robe. "It's okay. I only came to say sorry. You're right, I should have opened up to you. I've remembered something I saw. Something that could be really useful to our plans. I know a way to get into the compound where the zombies are."

CHAPTER SEVEN

THE DRESS CODE for the first encounter session was smart casual. Benjamin wore his Yves Saint Laurent shirt with a pair of Ralph Lauren jeans and his limited-edition Nike trainers. He helped Tatyana pick out a long sleeved Gucci top with slacks and pair of Manolo Blahnik slingbacks.

He still felt sore at her even though she'd told him about the basement and the hidden door to the compound. She hadn't told him what she was doing down there. Still, they were making an effort to get along and be civil, for the sake of the mission if nothing else.

Coffee and *petit fours* were being served in a room just off the mansion's entrance hall. They were among the last to arrive. The platinum blonde sashayed up to Benjamin the minute she saw him.

"If it isn't the handsome young man who knows how to treat a lady," she said. "So long as she's staff that is. I'm Lavinia Ponsonby, I don't think we've been introduced." She flashed him her teeth, her cleavage and her jewellery as she offered him her hand. They all cost a fortune, Benjamin was sure.

"I'm Benjamin Hollinger. This is..."

"Your charming young friend," Lavinia said to Tatyana. "Love the slacks, dearie. How brave of you to wear them."

Tatyana bristled at this. Benjamin had never seen her do that before.

"There's some people here I really must introduce you to," Lavinia said, taking Benjamin's arm and leading him off. "Hope you don't mind me stealing your man away," she said to Tatyana over her shoulder.

Tatyana shot Benjamin an angry look that said *don't leave me alone here*. He shrugged and shot one back to say *sorry, got to fit in, you know that*. Out of the corner of his eye he saw Lavinia flash Tatyana the sort smile a lioness would give a young cub whose prey she'd just stolen.

They were totally fighting over him. He couldn't believe how much that turned him on. Seems Tatyana wasn't the only one with options.

Lavinia steered him over to a group of three men and a woman. "This is Benjamin Hollinger," she said, displaying him on her arm like she'd just landed him. "I simply had to bring him over. This is Sam McKane." Lavinia pushed him towards the grey-haired Texan he'd spotted on the first night.

"Good to meet you," said Sam, crushing Benjamin's hand in his huge mitt.

"Is that a Frank Muller Aeternitas?" said Benjamin, pointing at Sam's watch.

"Why, yes it is, young man," said Sam, pulling back his sleeve to show it off. "Accurate to within one hundredth of a second. Tells the day, date, months and moon phases for the next thousand years, even takes leap years into account. You wear a Frank Muller yourself?"

"Got one for my Dad's last birthday," said Benjamin, not mentioning that it was lost at a crap table in Vegas the next month. "People with a Frank Muller on their wrist, they're an elite. Like an exclusive club, you see someone wearing one, you know they've got class."

Sam McKane threw his arm around Benjamin's shoulders and punched him affectionately in the chest. "I like this kid! He's got taste and character. C'mere, you gotta meet these yahoos. This here's Arthur Sonnenfeldt. He owns a lot of real estate." A short, plump man shook Benjamin's hand. "George Griffin here founded a few investment groups," Benjamin shook hands with a tall, thin man who wore glasses and an air of smug superiority. "And Bessie here runs a shop or two."

"Oh don't listen to him," said Bessie rolling her eyes in mock outrage. "I own several chains of exclusive boutiques." She was a redhead in a power suit who looked around thirty, but that was probably because she had a good surgeon. Bessie air-kissed him and squeezed his biceps. "Someone works out," she said with a wink.

"Hands off," said Lavinia. "I saw him first." She snaked her arm around Benjamin's waist and pulled him to her. It felt good. A few weeks ago these people wouldn't have given him the steam off their lattés, now they were slapping him on the back and praising his opinions. He was alarmed by how much he liked this.

"Ladies and Gentlemen, my name is Dr Susan Chen," said an Asian woman mounting a dais at the far end of the room. She was wearing a white coat and a headset mic. "I'm going to be leading your first encounter session. If you'd all kindly follow me, we can begin."

Tatyana tapped him on the shoulder. "Can I have a word?" she said, glowering.

"Sorry sweetie," said Lavinia, with a menacing smile. "But he's promised he'll walk *me* to the compound and I won't hear of letting him go."

"I should probably meet you in there," said Benjamin, in an attempt to relieve the tension. Lavinia whisked him away, leaving Tatyana looking far from happy.

"You're all mine today," said Lavinia in a voice that made him nervous and excited. "One thing you'll learn about Lavinia Ponsonby, she never lets go of what's hers."

Dr Chen led them all the way through the annex and up several flights of stairs to a state-of-the-art observation corridor. It was constructed entirely from glass and gave an incredible aerial view of the zombie enclosures. Immediately below them Benjamin could see at least eight zombies milling around the grass huts and crumbling concrete walls of their specially constructed environment.

There was a cold knot of anticipation in his stomach as it dawned on him. This was for real. He'd pictured this encounter so many times and here he was. About to get up close and personal with the noble monster for the first time. Un-freaking believable.

"There's a few things I need to take you through before we can expose you to the undead," said Dr Chen as the guests gathered round her. "I'm a scientist, not a magician. I can't tell you anything about how these corpses came to life, but I've been studying the undead on St Ignatius for over a year now. That's why, after a careful series of observations, I'm authorised to advise the following precautionary measures. We are not legally responsible for your safety in any way. If you want to stay alive it is essential that you bear them in mind at all times.

"The golden rule in any encounter with the undead is to remain calm at all times. Just like dogs, they can smell when you're afraid. Most of their other senses are as good as dead. But the lack of them seems to have sharpened their sense of smell.

"They can scent blood and adrenalin from up to ten feet away. If your heart is pumping and your adrenalin is high they will be driven to attack." Dr Chen tapped the glass behind her and a screen appeared showing a CGI model of a zombie.

"The zombie's bloodlust comes from a very basic survival instinct. It would appear that an infusion of human flesh and blood can slow down their body's decay." Dr Chen tapped the stomach of the zombie image and the screen zoomed in on a shot of its insides. "The undead don't feed like normal living creatures. However, just as their muscles can replicate basic motor functions, it would appear that their guts can also perform a type of basic digestion. They can't ingest normal food but they can break down living human blood and tissue to replenish themselves."

She changed the screen again. It split in two and showed accelerated footage of two different zombies strapped to operating tables. One decayed rapidly as the other remained unchanged. "The undead that we starved decayed at the normal rate of an unpreserved corpse. While those that received a regular diet of blood remain unchanged for an indefinite period."

It was worse than Benjamin thought. Here they were openly flaunting the fact they were starving these proud monsters to death.

"Is that where their hunger comes from?" said George Griffin.

"Yes, it is," said Dr Chen. "What makes it so pure is that it's the only basic drive the undead have. It's what sets them apart from any other predator. They have no fear of death or injury and no biological imperatives, such as the need to procreate and protect their young. They've nothing to lose and everything to gain. Hunger is what they're all about."

The screen changed again. This time it showed footage of a zombie in a cage. Benjamin hid his fists in his pockets.

"Never show any emotion or make any sudden movements in the presence of the undead. These are the things that identify you as prey. When people are first exposed to the undead they tend to exhibit hysteria or try and run. This is why they are attacked. As the following footage shows."

The screen showed a clip of a woman in a white coat sobbing as another researcher shouted: "You're an idiot, an idiot!" at her. The caged zombie flew at the bars.

Next it cut to a young researcher with a pony tail. He was dancing to his ipod. The zombie's arm reached through the bars and grabbed the researcher's hair. Another arm came into shot wielding a machete. It hacked off several of the zombie's fingers and the researcher's pony tail setting him free.

Incredibly, the final clip showed a guy on a surf simulator next to the cage. Surf music played as the guy wobbled about on the board. He turned and screamed as the zombie smashed into the bars and grabbed the board. The zombie pulled the board and the guy fell off. He ran as the zombie cracked the board and threw it aside, grasping after him through the bars.

It would have been comical if it wasn't so wrong. They were taunting the zombies, torturing them and pretending it was science. Benjamin felt his excitement sour. Several of the guest laughed and many smiled.

He remembered why he hated them. Fuck their attention and approval. They didn't understand. They weren't capable of understanding anything he held dear.

He wasn't a part of their world. He couldn't be part of any world that treated the noble monster in this way. He looked for Tatyana. She caught his eye and nodded to show she shared his sadness and anger.

He realised what a jerk he was being. Lavinia had let go off his arm and was staring avidly at the window. He sidled away from her and over to Tatyana. The look on her face reflected her relief and anger at him.

"Whenever you are exposed to the undead you need to keep in mind five basic rules," said Dr Chen. "These are the 'Five Rules of Interaction.'" The screen flashed up these rules as she spoke.

"Number One: Show no signs of life. Take small shallow breaths, try not to twitch or scratch yourself and keep your expression blank.

"Number Two: Move in slow motion. Keep every movement extremely slow and deliberate. The longer it takes for you to do something, the less likely the undead are to notice you. Only sudden movements draw their attention.

"Number Three: It doesn't matter and you don't care. Nothing here is personal, the less you care about the zombies and what's happening around you the less likely you are to show an emotion. The less emotion you show the less likely you are to be attacked.

"Number Four: Follow the herd but think ahead of it. In the case of the undead two heads really are better than one. They tend to form packs quite quickly. The more undead there are, the closer they come to exhibiting something approaching thought. Whatever tiny brain functions they have seem to increase *en masse*. Always act how the majority of the undead are acting, but concentrate on their reasons for acting the way they do so you can pre-empt them if you need to. When you are more advanced, this technique can be developed to control or shepherd them.

"And, finally, Number Five: Master yourself and nothing can threaten you. Self awareness and self control will allow you to interact with the undead in perfect safety.

"If you keep these rules in mind at all times, you will be able to observe the undead from an unprecedented perspective. You will be able to study them and become like them. You will face certain death every day and become stronger for surviving it."

Dr Chen switched off the screen and led the group down the observation corridor. "Now if you'll follow me I'll show you to the changing rooms where you'll be fitted with the appropriate garments."

CHAPTER EIGHT

"Ugh, why'd they give me this shirt?" said Tatyana. "It stinks like a corpse."

"That's the whole point," Benjamin said. "They're clothes people died or were buried in. It makes us smell like the zombies."

They were standing outside the security doors to the compound. They'd been through the changing area where they were measured and fitted with damp, encrusted clothes.

They'd been split into two parties of ten. Benjamin and Tatyana were thrilled to be in the first group chosen for an encounter. Dr Chen entered with four others all dressed and made up to resemble zombies. Benjamin was instantly jealous. He'd never been able to get the look down as well as they had. He took mental notes for future use.

"These are your encounter group leaders," said Dr Chen. "They're going to spend a bit of time teaching you to move properly, then they'll take you in. This is a controlled environment and these are entry-level undead. They've been chosen for their docility and their familiarity with the living. So long as you stick to the Five Rules of Interaction you'll be perfectly safe your first time out."

Dr Chen stepped back and the four guides moved in on them. A Latino guy came over to Benjamin and Tatyana. He was tall and good looking and moved like a dancer. His manner was camp, but relaxed and commanding.

"Okay guys, my name's Raoul," he said. "I'm going to be taking you through a few moves. Let's start with your posture. I want you to stand with your feet apart like this. Now, relax your shoulders and let your arms hang down by your sides. Okay, that's good, now I want you to let your head roll forward onto your chest."

Raoul checked they were doing it properly and adjusted Benjamin's posture, pulling his shoulders down to relax them more. "Good. Now, when you move, you have to use as few muscles as possible. So shift the weight from foot to foot like this, using only your leg muscles, and let the rest of your body move by itself."

Raoul lurched forward, looking exactly like the zombies Benjamin had seen. His legs moved spasmodically and his feet shuffled side to side while the rest of his body hung limp and swayed.

Tatyana had a go and Benjamin followed. Neither of them were any good. Raoul had made it look so easy and they were messing up.

I should be better at this, Benjamin thought. *How many zombie flicks have I watched? I should nail this first time.*

They tried a couple more times. Raoul gave them a few pointers and then they were good to go.

"Okay everyone," Raoul said to the whole party. "This is what we're going to do. As a group we're going to move slowly into the centre of the space. We're going to stay there, standing very still until I give you the signal it's safe to move. I'll roll my head side to side like this. At that point you're free to walk off and explore. Take a look at the zombies and try and copy them. Don't go close until you're absolutely sure you're safe. If any of you get nervous move slowly back to join the four of us in the centre. You're safer in a group and we'll protect you. When I do this," Raoul shuffled back and forth in a particular manner. "I want you all to come back and join me. That's when we'll leave at a slow and measured pace. Has everyone got that?" Everyone nodded, doing their best zombie impression. "Okay. Time to dance."

The automatic locks on the security doors clicked open and slid apart. The group moved out onto the sandy ground and into the blazing heat.

Benjamin's whole life had been leading up to this moment. There were real zombies all around them. He stole glances around him as they shuffled into the centre of the space with the rest of the party.

They were as magnificent as he'd imagined they would be. Shambling about in the noonday sun just as he'd pictured them a thousand times in his mind.

Noble Monsters, Death Defiers, Graveyard Rebels, none of the names he and his fellow Deathwalkers used to describe them did the awesome creatures justice. They were the ultimate passive-aggressive subversives.

They'd given death the middle finger and refused to lie down just because they weren't alive anymore. It was defiance that kept them up and running. Not hunger, like the idiots all around him thought. The pure defiance of anyone who tells them how to act or what to do. Defiance of the ridiculous hypocrisy of Western consumer culture and everyone who tries to uphold it.

Rule Number Three: It doesn't matter and you don't care.

That had been his daily mantra for the last ten years. Ever since his Mom left his Dad for a blue-blood banker and thrust him into a world of false appearances and phoney standards. He'd stumbled through each day wanting to eat the brains and tear the guts out of everyone he met. That was why he understood the zombie better than anyone on this island.

Here he was face to face with his idols. And suddenly it did matter, and he couldn't help but care. He cared about what they were doing to these proud monsters. It mattered that they were being locked up and exploited like this.

That's why he was here, pretending to be like these despicable cretins.

Rule Number Four: Follow the herd but think ahead of it.

That was exactly what he was doing. He was biding his time until the right moment came to strike. When it did, he'd make them all pay.

They stood in the centre of the space for what seemed like ages. Hardly anyone dared move. They were huddled together in a group, with four guides circling them for protection.

Finally Raoul gave the signal for them to move off and start exploring.

Benjamin headed very slowly over to a group of four zombies crouched over a carcass. They were gnawing the last of the meat off its bones as the flies buzzed around them.

Benjamin wasn't sure where the corpse had come from. He rather hoped it had been donated to the island, in the same way that some people leave their bodies to medical science.

Lavinia sidled over and circled the group of zombies. She winked suggestively at him. He should've snubbed her. Instead he smiled sheepishly. God, he was shallow. But she gave him a hard on. What could he do?

They were supposed to be copying the zombies' actions. Benjamin just stood very still and watched them. He was fighting to keep his excitement under control. And, although he didn't want to admit it, his fear too.

Lavinia was a lot bolder than he. She knelt ever so carefully down next to the feeding zombies and stuck her head into the carcass. Benjamin was impressed. She had guts. With great care and patience Lavinia reached into the carcass and took out a thigh bone.

She brought the bone up to her lips and began to nibble at it. She was slow to begin with, running her teeth and her tongue along it. Then she attacked it with more relish, mimicking the zombies' mindless gnawing.

Benjamin couldn't take his eyes off her. He really was getting a boner at the sight of her with the bone. Christ, he was a sick puppy.

A female zombie looked up and put her hand on the bone Lavinia was gnawing. Lavinia snarled at the zombie but it only tightened its grip on the bone.

Lavinia wouldn't let go. The zombie put its other hand on the bone and began to pull harder. Lavinia tugged right back and bared her teeth.

"Mine, bitch, it's mine," she shouted and yanked the bone out of the zombie's hands. Benjamin winced as he heard one of its fingers break.

There was an ominous moment of silence as everyone turned to look at her, including the other zombies. From the look on her face Lavinia knew that she'd just fucked up.

The female zombie started to make a weird noise in the back of its throat, gradually increasing in volume, and then sprang at Lavinia.

Lavinia was just as quick to her feet and brought the thigh bone down on its head. Benjamin heard bone fracture but the zombie was undeterred and kept coming for her.

Lavinia swung twice more, beating the zombie back a few steps. The bone splintered against the zombie's skull.

The zombie lurched at her and grabbed her shoulders. Lavinia put her hand on its forehead to hold it back and stabbed at its face with the splintered end of the bone.

She rammed the bone into the zombie's eye socket, causing its other eyeball to pop out of its head and slither down its cheek. Blood and brain tissue bubbled out of the zombie's empty eye socket and nasal cavities.

"Die, you fucking whore!" Lavinia shrieked.

Without thinking Benjamin stepped forward to protect the zombie and tripped over the carcass. Too late, he realised his mistake.

The other three zombies got to their feet and started to make the same guttural noise the female zombie had. All the zombies in the compound were making it.

Lavinia pushed the motionless female zombie away and bolted for the exit. Most of the other guests were running too. The zombies charged after them.

Benjamin stood absolutely still as alarms started to blare. A zombie hobbled right up to him. He tried not to breath or shake as it stared him directly in the face. The front of his pants became warm and damp.

Oh, God, I'm going to die, he thought. His heart was battering at the inside of his chest. *I don't want to die. Not here, like this.*

For some reason he thought of his mother. More than anything, he wanted her to hold him and make everything better.

Time stopped altogether. He waited for the zombie to strike. To tear open his throat with its teeth. He wondered if it would hurt as much as he feared.

The killing blow never came. The zombie simply turned away and shambled off.

Benjamin was elated. It knew. It could sense there was something different about him. That he had a rapport with them. That he understood. It could tell he had a special connection to the undead.

Several secret doors opened and guards ran in with flame throwers. They fired controlled bursts, to drive the zombies back without harming them.

They corralled the zombies as the security doors slid open and the guest were ushered through. Benjamin sauntered up to the doors without any sign of panic. He had nothing to fear from the undead.

He walked up to the other guests with a cool air of superiority. They were all staring at him. Was that awe in their eyes or admiration? Then he realised his pants were wet; they could all see that he'd pissed himself.

"ONE THING I learned about Lavinia Ponsonby," said Benjamin. "She never lets go of what's hers."

They were standing in one of the reception rooms off the lobby.

"You meant no more to her than that bone, you know," Tatyana said.

"And what were you?" he said. "Another zombie?"

"I was just in her way. You're lucky she didn't try and break you over my head."

"You're right. I was a jerk."

"*Jerk* doesn't begin to cover it."

The other guests were cackling and gossiping. Schadenfreude was the order of the day.

"That five mil she put down," Benjamin heard Arthur Sonnenfeldt say. "That was more than she had. She was maxed out on credit just to get that."

"Never venture what you can't afford to lose," said George Griffin. "It's a basic law of finance. Risk doesn't drive your bottom line. It merely adds to it."

"She's lost it all now," Bessie chimed in. "Some people never learn. You never touch your reserve. You only spend the interest."

They'd been called down as soon as they'd showered and changed. Samuel Palmer made a brief address, claiming no responsibility for the incident. Instead, he chided them like school kids. "The lesson to be learned from this is that when you're dealing with zombies, don't make it personal. With the undead, just as in business, nothing is personal."

Lavinia was being sent home, under guard, and she'd lost her deposit. Not only had she disobeyed the rules and broken the terms of her contract, according to Palmer she had also destroyed valuable property.

The nerve of the guy, referring to the noble monster as a piece of property.

A door opened on the other side of the room and Lavinia strode in with her luggage. She held her head high. The armed guards at her side completely failed to intimidate her.

Benjamin realised she'd purposefully chosen to walk through the room where all the guest were gathered. No sneaking shamefully out the back entrance for her. You had to admire her spirit. She was a formidable woman and she was going to let everyone know it.

Some of the guests turned away as she walked the length of the room. Others nodded in respect. Sam McKane stepped up to take her hand. "Lavinia," he said, with affection.

"Sam."

"These galoots treating you right?" he said pointing to the guards.

"I've got them under control."

"You need anything?"

"I'm a big girl, Sam. I can look after myself. But thanks for asking."

They smiled and she walked on. As she was about to leave, Benjamin stopped her. "Listen, Lavinia," he said. "I just wanted to say how sorry I am about the way everything turned out. And if things had been different then, y'know, maybe..."

Lavinia looked at him with ice cold contempt. "Maybe what? We'd ride off into the sunset together, hand in hand? Do me a favour. Get over yourself and grow up." With that she swept out of his life forever.

Benjamin glanced over at Tatyana. She wasn't impressed. She raised an eyebrow as if to say 'what did you expect?'

"You're right. *Jerk* doesn't begin to cover it."

CHAPTER NINE

Three Months Ago

A MESSAGE POPPED up on Benjamin's screen.

> 2:03PM
> LUCIO
> DUDE, YOU DOIN ZOMBIE CRAWL THIS WKND? SHD BE A BLAST. LOL.
> 2:03PM
> BEN
> SORRY, GOT BIGGER FISH TO FRY. ;-)
> 2:04PM
> LUCIO
> KLKL, IT'S GONNA BE A GD 1 THO.

Yeah right. Zombie Crawl was okay for bored teenagers who enjoyed parading through town with a bunch of friends dressed as zombies. But it was no place for a serious Deathwalker. He was about to take things to a whole new level.

"Benjamin, have you tidied your room like you promised?" his Mom shouted.

"Yes, Mom," he lied. He'd stuff everything into a bag and jam it under his bed later.

His Mom always went into meltdown whenever she was throwing some lame social event for Richard. A whole army of cleaners and gardeners descended on the house. His room was on the third floor anyway. It's not like any guests were going to see it. Even those that were sneaking off to schtupp someone else's wife.

He signed out and closed his laptop. He had guests of his own coming. Better get the basement ready for them.

He spotted Richard as he stepped out onto the landing, and automatically put his head down and tried to walk past without being seen.

"I thought we weren't doing this anymore," whined Richard.

"Uh, yeah, hi," Benjamin grunted, still looking at the floor.

"Are you helping your mother get ready for the party?"

"Uh, yeah," said Benjamin. Then added, "Just going to tidy the basement."

"That's right, you've got your own... friends coming. They do know to use the side entrance don't they?"

"Uh, think so."

"Think so?"

"They do."

"Good."

There was an uncomfortable silence, then Richard said. "Is that a scar on your cheek?"

"It's an open pus wound. I just made it."

"An open pus wound," Richard shook his head and sighed. The dickwad. Why'd he have to act like that? Always putting Benjamin down. Never coming right out and saying it, but acting like Benjamin was this weight around his neck that he had to drag around everywhere.

It wasn't like *he* was perfect, with his goofy Hawaian shirts and sandals. *And his golfing sweaters*, thought Benjamin. *Don't get me started on those.*

Richard looked like he wanted to say something, thought better of it and walked off. Lucky escape, then.

An hour or so later Benjamin left the basement and headed to his room. The guests were starting to arrive. A few minutes' tidying would keep his Mom off his back. He was just making his way across the hall to the stairs when he heard a familiar voice.

"Hey, sports fans!"

Oh shit.

"Hi, Mr Petersen," Benjamin turned to see a fat guy with a ginger buzz-cut bearing down on him.

"Benjamin, I got three words for ya," said Petersen clapping him on the back. "Sub Prime Mortgage! It's the future of finance, my boy. Now a bright boy like you is bound to want to follow his old man into the profession."

"What, Richard?" said Benjamin, unable to hide his contempt.

"Hey, don't knock 'im, guy's a shark. Mind like a bear trap. You wanna take on your old man though, ya gotta know where the action is. See, the way this thing works, it's beautiful. Now ya can't have a growth economy without debt, but sooner or later every schmuck who can afford it is gonna be maxed out. Ya gotta have new frontiers, see? That's where the CDO comes in. That's a collateralised debt obligation, work of genius. Ya take a bunch a debts from a bunch of schlubbs that no bank's ever gonna subsidise and you mix 'em up with a bunch of legit credit, takes all the risk out of the deal. The toxic debt gets a triple A rating and the profits are through the roof. Through the roof, ya follow me?"

"I think so."

"Good man! See, ya get rid of the toxic debt same way ya get rid of toxic waste: ya dump it into a fresh reservoir and all the risk gets flushed downstream and disperses naturally. Genius! Remember ya heard it here first."

"Okay, thanks Mr Petersen, I'll bear that in mind."

"Where'd ya get the scar? That a sports injury?"

"Something like that."

Benjamin wrestled himself free and made a bolt for the stairs.

"Sub Prime Mortgage!" Petersen called after him. "It's a source of profit that ain't ever gonna dry up."

Benjamin smiled and ran. Sheesh, had the guy never heard of Listerine? Toxic debt? More like toxic breath.

"Just a minute, young man." Benjamin was on the second floor when a hand grabbed him and dragged him into one of the guest rooms.

"Mom," said Benjamin, with more than a hint of complaint in his voice.

"Don't you 'Mom' me," she said. She was holding a large vodka Martini. "You promised me you'd tidy your room. I've just been in your room and if that's your idea of tidy you might as well live on the street."

"You're soused."

"I'm nothing of the sort. And this isn't about me, it's about you. I thought things were going to change. I thought you promised to start making an effort from now on."

"Could we do this later? I've got people coming."

"And I've got people here already. Your room is a pig sty and I've just laid out five million dollars so you can run off and play at being a vampire. Is it too much to ask that you uphold your side of the bargain?"

"It's zombies, Mom; not vampires, zombies. And you didn't lay out five million. Richard agreed to put it up to prove to you what a fuck up I am, because he expects me to fail."

"Don't you go disparaging Richard."

"Why not? That's all he does to *me*."

"He's been very generous to the both of us. He's opened his heart and his home to us and we owe him for that."

"That's bullshit, Mom! Richard bought you to have something beautiful to show off on his arm. Just like those Picassos and the Matisse he has downstairs. He's not an art lover, he just wants to show people what he can afford to buy."

His Mom went really quiet. She was real mad. No, she was beyond mad. He'd said too much, way too much. Suddenly he was a little boy again, caught playing with matches and the world was about to fall on his head. Shit, was he going to cry?

No, his Mom beat him to it. One huge tear ran down her cheek, taking a gob of mascara with it. She knocked back the Martini and sat on the bed.

"Look Mom, I'm sorry, I shouldn't have..."

"No, no, you're right," she said, opening a draw in the bedside table and pulling out a pack of Winstons.

"I didn't know you smoked," he said as she lit one.

"I could fill a book with what you don't know," she said, blowing out smoke. "I know this hasn't been easy on you. I know you miss your father. Hell, there are times when I miss him, even after everything he put me through. He was so handsome. You look so much like him too, even with all your Frankenstein make up."

"It's zombie, Mom."

"He was great in the sack too. Probably the best I ever had."

"Mom, too much information."

"What? You think because you're young you've got the market on sex cornered? Why do you think Richard took us in? Do you think anyone's ever done him better than I have?"

"Eew, gross Mom, that's an image I don't want."

"It might surprise you to find that quite a few men still find me attractive," she paused and gave him a serious look. "When did I lose you, Benjamin? We used to be so close. We used to tell each other everything. Do you have any idea how much I miss that?"

Benjamin didn't say anything. He felt embarrassed and uncomfortable. Why was she suddenly getting all *Melrose Place* on him?

"There was this one time, you were only seven years old, but you were so wise and brave you nearly broke my heart. I'd just found out that your father had pawned all my jewellery. Everything that my mother had left to me. It was all I had to remember her by; there was stuff in there that went back to my great, great grandmother. Things she'd had made personally, unique and irreplaceable. He pawned them and blew everything in a crap game. I wasn't ever going to see any of it again.

"I was kneeling on the kitchen floor and I was sobbing my heart out. For the jewellery that I'd lost, for the mother that I'd lost and for the whole marriage your father had thrown away on cards and horses. Then I hear your little feet come up behind me. You put your hands on my shoulders and you lead me to the table. Then you fished your Mickey Mouse handkerchief out your pocket and you handed it to me and do you remember what you said? You said... you said: 'Dry your eyes, Princess. 'Cause I'm here now and I won't let anything bad happen to you.'

"And I flung my arms around you and I cried even more. But not for what I'd lost. For what I'd found. I realised that what I had in my arms was a million times more precious than any stupid jewellery. *And he'll never take this away from me*, I thought. *He'll never take this away.* But I was wrong.

"It was the vase, wasn't it? That damned Lalique that Richard was so proud of." She stopped and dabbed her eyes with a tissue. Benjamin hung his head with a shame that was eight years old and still powerful.

He hadn't known his Dad like he did now. He used to save up the weekly allowance Richard gave him for his Dad's monthly visits. That way they'd have money for all the things his father would take him out to, funfairs, meals out, ice cream parlours. He even paid for the gas to drive them there.

His Dad would always go on about how much money Richard had. And how he'd have that much money one day, Benjamin would see. All it took was one winning streak. Then he'd buy the hot dogs. You could be sure he would.

He started to ask Benjamin about all the nice things Richard had about the house. Asked him if there were any items that Richard wouldn't miss. Expensive things that his Dad could loan to his friends for safe keeping. Only there was this horse and it couldn't miss and when it came in the two of them could go on holiday together. All he needed was to raise enough cash.

Benjamin took the vase and gave it to his Dad. He knew it was precious because Richard had said so. His Dad said he'd give it back to him before anyone even noticed. That was the last he saw of the vase, and his Dad, for a long while.

"I told Richard I'd broken it while dusting, you know," his Mom said. "He was furious. He wanted to know what I was doing, demeaning myself, when he paid a staff of cleaners to do the dusting. He actually sold some of the jewellery he bought me to recoup the loss of the vase. Can you believe that? What is it about men and my jewellery?

"I confronted your father, of course. Told him if he ever did that again I'd have him thrown in jail and he'd never see you again. He got so mad at me he refused to see you for years. And who did you hold responsible? After I'd lied to protect you.

"You stopped speaking to me. You were the only man I ever loved who didn't shit all over me. My father did, he was a bastard, and both my husbands have had their moments. There was only you. And yet we drift further and further apart every day. Why am I always in the wrong? Why don't you ever cut me some slack? What's so bad about the life I've given you? What do you want that you don't have?"

"A life that I actually like, for a start." He shouldn't have said that. "Look, Mom, I don't want to fight. I still love you, but you know I'm not seven now. I'm sorry if I don't give you my Mickey Mouse handkerchief anymore, but I've got my own things going on."

"Just tell me what I need to say, Benjamin. Tell me what I need to do to make it all better. Mommy always used to make it all better, remember? Once upon a time there wasn't anything I couldn't fix."

He could feel his eyes filling up with tears. She had a way of doing that to him. No matter how old or independent he got there were buttons only she could push.

"Mom. Can we please not do this now? I've got people on the way and you've..."

There was a knock at the door. "Who is it?" said his Mom.

"Sorry to disturb you, Ma'am," said one of the staff. "But there's been a disturbance downstairs with one of Master Benjamin's guests."

"I'll be right there."

"No Mom, it's okay, I'll go. It's my friend. You fix your make-up and go look after your guests."

A COUPLE OF hours later Tatyana arrived. She was the last to get there. She phoned Benjamin on his mobile and he went to meet her at the side entrance.

She looked fabulous. Everyone had pushed the boat out with their zombie make up, but he'd never seen her go to such trouble. She could have been the real thing.

She winced as he kissed her. "Wait a minute. That split lip and those bruises are real aren't they?"

"Some of them," she admitted.

"It's your father, isn't it?" He could feel his rage rising like mercury in a thermometer. "Motherfucker!" He punched the security pad by the side gate and felt a stabbing pain shoot up his arm. Tatyana led him towards the house.

"He's not himself lately," she said. She was always making excuses for her father, in spite of what a bastard he was. "He's being threatened with extradition. President Putin wants to prosecute him for tax evasion. He could go to prison. He's worried about becoming another Khodorovsky."

"Who?"

"You're so American sometimes. If it doesn't happen in your backyard then you don't want to know about it. Don't you ever watch CNN?"

"Richard does, I prefer to be out the room when he's around."

"Mikhail Khodorovsky used to be the wealthiest man in my country. He was an oil tycoon who was charged with fraud by the Prosecutor General's office and sent to prison for nine years. Things are not good in my country and Putin likes to throw the masses an oligarch's head now and again to keep them quiet. Now he's got my father in his sights."

"Well if you ask me, your father deserves to go to prison."

"Thanks, and where does that leave me and my mother? We'll have to go back to Russia with him. He'll lose most of his money and that means I won't be able to come on the mission with you."

"Oh."

"Oh indeed."

"That still doesn't give him the right to knock you around."

"Okay, can we drop it now. Are the others here?"

"They're in the den. Klaus got here first. He parked his old truck on Richard's ornamental lawn. When I got there he was calling the staff fascists and pawns of capitalist exploitation."

"Hah! That sounds like Klaus. Doesn't stop him enjoying the benefits of your stepdad's capitalist exploitation."

"First thing he did when he got in was grab a bottle of Dom Perignon and a jar of Beluga."

They headed down the basement stairs and into the den. *"White Zombie?"* he heard Dan say. "I don't get it?"

"Ja," said Klaus. "If you're wanting a black and white movie why aren't you picking *I Walked with a Zombie*?"

"No. You're not getting it," said Andy. "It's the birth of the genre. The first zombie film ever made. What better film to have playing as your child comes into the world?"

"Nein," said Klaus. "I am still casting my vote for *Braindead*. It has the first scene of zombies giving birth."

"In a zombie's case," said Andy, "I think technically it's called 'giving death.'"

Tatyana didn't tend to join in with the guys' debates. She went and gave Tweakie a hug.

"I love your new hair," she said running her fingers through Tweakie's bright red locks.

"Thanks," said Tweakie. " I was going for a Linnea Quigley in *Return of the Living Dead* look. Hey check it out, have you seen my new eye?"

"Oh my God that's so cool," said Tatyana, touching the prosthetic eyeball that dangled out of Tweakie's socket. "Did you make it yourself?"

"Yeah, I did it at work. Told them I was trying out some new effects. We're waiting to see if we get this gig with HBO."

"Doing make-up or effects?" said Benjamin.

"Both," Tweakie said. "Should be a blast. *Six Feet Under* but with zombies. That's the pitch."

"Awesome," said Benjamin.

"What are the boys arguing about?" said Tatyana.

"Dan wants to know what film he should have playing as his kid is born," said Tweakie.

"How long to go now?" Tatyana asked Dan.

"Six weeks. Hey, check it out, I've got this birthing pool for Sarah right, she's gonna have a home birth. We're gonna spray it black and have eyeballs and severed arms floating in the water when Sarah gets in. Man, the midwife's gonna shit! Loving your make-up incidentally, how'd you get that grey mottled skin?"

"That's an air brush job, right?" said Tweakie.

"Right," said Tatyana. "Is that, like, a shroud you're wearing?"

"It's a smock," said Dan. "I'm going for a classic *Living Dead at the Manchester Morgue* look. I've been watching it a lot recently. They have it playing on a loop at Romero's when I'm behind the bar."

"Ja," said Klaus. "That's why you never get any work done."

"Least I don't clean the toilet with my head. When you gonna get a proper haircut?"

"The Mohican is a classic look," said Klaus running his hand over the stiff purple hair. He was a tiny guy with a big beak of a nose and small round glasses. "Zombies are the ultimate punks. The two looks go perfectly. The zombie rebels against the graveyard. The punk rebels against society. I am being the ultimate rebel against the living death of capitalism. Hey that reminds me, Benjamin, did you find that old Rolex you were going to be lending me?"

"No I gave it to Andy. He's using it to house some of the radio equipment we'll need."

"What, we're gonna have wristwatch radios?" said Dan. "Just like Dick Tracy?"

"Err, no," said Andy. "That's science-fiction. This is the real world, where the dead walk."

Benjamin loved Andy. A lot of people found him hard to take because of his Asperger's Syndrome, but once you got past his odd manner and his freakish intelligence he was one of the sweetest guys you could meet.

Andy dropped his knapsack on the card table and pulled out Benjamin's Rolex, a pair of limited edition Reeboks and an aerosol.

"This is what I wanted to show you two," he said to Benjamin and Tatyana. "This is how we're going to stay in touch."

"Why can't we just text?" said Tweakie.

"There's no mobile reception or internet access," said Benjamin. "They block it all to keep you isolated."

"Which is why we're going to communicate with miniaturised long-wave radios," said Andy. "I've disguised it so you can carry it in without being detected." He folded an aerial out of the aerosol, took the soles off the shoes to reveal the receivers and showed them how to assemble the disguised equipment.

"Whoa, that is totally old school James Bond," said Dan. "You're like the undead Q, Andy."

"Yes I am. Licensed to chill. And there's more." Andy held up the Rolex. "I've replaced the workings of the watch with a device capable of releasing an electro magnetic pulse. This will overload the circuits of most security locks. There won't be anywhere you won't be able to enter."

"That is so cool, Andy," said Benjamin.

He put his arm around Andy's shoulder to congratulate him. Andy stiffened and put his hands up. "No touching!"

Benjamin backed away. "Sorry bro, I forgot."

"That's perfectly alright. Worse things happen at sea."

"Yeah, speaking of which," said Tweakie, wearing a bemused expression. "What's the latest on your Dad's yacht?"

"Richard's yacht," Benjamin corrected her. "I've had keys copied without Richard knowing. I'll give them to you before you head off to the marina. Remember to board when it's dark and to sail at first light."

"Yeah, yeah, okay dog, we know the plan," said Dan. "What's with all this 'sail at first light' shit? What are you, the Ancient Mariner?"

"It's the safest time to leave the marina without being seen," said Benjamin. "Andy, do you think you can handle the satnav?"

"If I can handle advanced calculus with a migraine and severe allergies, I don't think a little thing like a satnav is going to phase me."

"Probably not," said Benjamin. "Follow the coast down to Florida but stay in open water. You don't want the coast guard coming down on your ass. Then it's straight across the Gulf of Mexico."

"I am loving this," said Klaus. "We are using the trappings of Western consumerism as a weapon to undo it. Hey, we can still get cable while we're out in open water, can't we? I will be dying if I miss *Wheel of Fortune*."

"I dunno, Klaus," said Benjamin. "I'll get it taped for you if you can't. Now, you'll be okay to locate the island, won't you? 'Cause you know it's not on any maps."

"We'll be okay, Ben," said Tweakie, putting her hands on his shoulders. She turned to Tatyana. "Does he always fuss like an old woman?"

"He hasn't even started yet," said Tatyana with a smile.

"So it's for real, then?" said Dan. "We're actually doing this. We're going to put the Zombie Liberation Front on the map and wake up all the Deathwalkers."

"Hey, ja," said Klaus. "You know what we should do? When we free all the zombies we should be taking one to Romero's. Give him a plate of brains and leave him at the bar."

"That'd put the shits up all those teeny Deathwalkers who hang out there" said Dan. "They think they're so radical 'cause they go on Zombie Crawl once a month."

"No I'm having it even better," said Klaus. "We take a bunch of them to Zombiestock. Not even Burning Man has a pack of real zombies. We'll become the top festival."

"You could get some to perform onstage with your band," Dan said to Tweakie. "That'll get you on the main stage."

"Are you dumbasses for real?" said Tweakie, shaking her head. "Have you forgotten why we're doing this? If we try and turn these noble monsters into some sideshow attraction we're no better than the rich bastards who are exploiting them."

"We're going to release them into a safe jungle environment," said Tatyana. "Somewhere where they're beyond the reach of civilised man and his exploitative ways."

"Like the Bronx, you mean?" said Dan.

"Not the Bronx, wiseass," Tweakie smacked the back of his head then turned to Benjamin. "Where *are* we taking them exactly?"

That was the tiny flaw in his plan. "I'm still working on that," he admitted. "Don't worry, I'll find somewhere before we leave though."

"You better," Tweakie warned him. "'Cause it's your butt it's gonna come out of if you don't."

"We're going to be out in open water with a hold full of noble monsters," said Tatyana. "I don't think it's just Benjamin's pert little butt that it's gonna come out of."

"Listen, guys," said Benjamin. "I don't want to get all sentimental on you or nothing. But I just want to say thanks. For ages I've been looking for a group of committed individuals to take Deathwalking to the next level. Now that I've found you, well, I couldn't be happier."

"Hey, don't sweat it, dog," said Dan. "We got your back. We're family."

"Here's to the ZLF," said Andy raising his soda in a toast.

Everyone raised their drinks. "To the ZLF."

"Ja," said Klaus raising the half empty champagne bottle. "We are tearing down the beliefs of the Bourgeoisie and trampling the opiate of the masses. Hey, do you think anyone upstairs can get me some coke?"

CHAPTER TEN

"WHAT ARE YOU doing?"

Benjamin was bugging her again. He was like a little kid sometimes. Always wanting her attention. If he wasn't so cute she'd have given up ages ago.

It's like her aunt said. though. You don't meet the perfect man – you make him. You start with the best raw material you can get and you sculpt it into something worth having.

Not that it had worked too well for her aunt. She was constantly improving men only to have them stolen away by younger, slimmer women.

"Are you okay? C'mon, speak to me."

"I was practising my zombie breathing, dumb ass," Tatyana said, sitting up in bed. It was the first time she'd moved in thirty minutes. "You know, like they told us to do – at least three times a day."

"Oh yeah, guess I should probably be joining in. You're getting rather good, though. Had me worried for a second. You had almost no vital signs. For a moment, I thought you'd actually died."

"I find it weirdly relaxing, actually. Just letting go of everything and resting, taking a break from actually living. It's like a drug, you know, sort of addictive."

Benjamin got excited at this. He jumped off the bed and started gesticulating. "I know exactly what you mean. I'm in the zone out there. I'm at one with the noble monster and they can sense it. I've definitely got the most developed Inner Zombie on the island."

"Steady on, genius. We've only been at it a week. Don't get ahead of yourself."

"I'm not getting ahead of myself. I'm good at this. Things are starting to make sense for the first time. Even you and me are getting along better."

"Now there's no women flirting with you."

"Aw c'mon, cheap shot."

"Okay, you're right. I am happier, about us, about everything. It is beneficial. I guess that's why they charge so much for the course."

"They said they've got something special planned for us today. Time to take the next big step. I am *so* ready for it."

"Well you better get showered and changed, then. We're supposed to be down there in ten."

"Oh shit!"

TODAY'S ENCOUNTER WAS in a different part of the compound. They assembled in an observation room overlooking a large enclosed arena. Tatyana shared the anticipation she could see on the faces of the guests. They could all tell that something different and special was going to happen.

Raoul, their movement coach and encounter leader, came in to address them. "As promised, today we're going to move you on to the next stage of your training. As this is a moment of significance, someone of great consequence is going to address you."

Tatyana felt an immense presence behind her. Everyone in the group turned at the same time, to face Doc Papa. He smiled with satisfaction at their shock and awe.

"Good morning," he said. "A pleasure to see you all again. I understand from my staff that you've been doing rather well. Now it's time to do rather better. So far we have shown you the Way of the Barefoot Zombie. But there is a difference between knowing the Way and *walking* the Way.

"Tomorrow night I am hosting a dinner for some special guests. We are going to be joined by St Ignatius's Board of Directors and the previous graduates of my course. It's fair to say that between them they control most of the wealth on the planet." Tatyana saw the excitement and anticipation on the faces of the guests at the mention of this. They were like a bunch of groupies who've just been told their favourite band were oiled, naked and waiting in the next room.

"Whether or not you join us will depend on how well you perform today. If you fail, you are going home. To survive in the company of merciless killers is not enough. You must learn to become like them in order to dominate them. To become like them you must kill as they kill – without thought or compunction. Observe."

Doc Papa pointed to the window and they all turned at the same time to look out of it. They were like living puppets. He just had to pull their strings and they did whatever he wanted.

A cage descended into the centre of the arena. It was held by a heavy chain and stopped about twelve feet above the ground. Inside was a man with a thick black moustache, wearing a Hawaiian shirt. He looked Latin American. He was frightened and disoriented, moving about the cage, testing the bars and trying to see what was going on in the arena below.

"This pathetic specimen is a militant trade unionist from Venezuela," said Doc Papa.

A set of gates opened onto the arena and two women, Latinas, stumbled in, blinking and shading their eyes from the sunlight. The man in the cage called out to them and they went to stand beneath him.

"His wife and sister are also in the same union," said Doc Papa. "They've been causing a lot of problems for Western clothing companies. Instead of being thankful for the work their benefactors provide, they've been spreading scurrilous lies about the state of their factories, calling them sweatshops and trying to bully the companies into paying higher wages. They've even gone as far as trying to hamstring legitimate operations by demanding an end to child labour."

Tatyana saw many of the guests sneer, shake their heads and make disparaging noises.

"Instead we called an end to their activities. Observe how to deal with labour relations the Barefoot Zombie way."

Two more gates opened on to the arena. Speakers clicked on in the observation room so they could hear what was happening in the arena.

"Madre de Dios," said one of the women, clinging to the other. The man in the cage started shouting to the women and pointing at the gates.

Around twenty zombies shambled into the arena. One of the women started crying and wailing at the sight of them. The zombies scented the air and began to lurch towards them.

The man in the cage reached down through the bars, and the slimmer of the two women tried to jump up and catch hold of his hands. The other woman ran back towards the gates they'd come through.

Four zombies gave chase as the woman hit the gates, which proved to be locked. She battered on them as the zombies bore down on her.

A scrawny female zombie got to her first. She tried to push the zombie away, but it caught hold of her hair. She put her hand against its face to hold it off.

The zombie opened its mouth wide and bit down on the woman's hand. The woman shrieked in pain and yanked herself away, leaving the zombie with great clumps of hair in its hands.

Two of the woman's fingers were missing. Blood poured out of the stumps, covering her hand and the sleeve of her blouse. The woman gasped in shock, staring in disbelief at her hand.

She backed into a fat zombie coming up behind her. The zombie caught her by the shoulders and lunged for her neck, but she managed to twist free from its grip and it fastened its teeth on her shoulder instead.

The woman screamed and punched the zombie in the head with her uninjured hand; the zombie bit harder but she managed to tear herself away. It chewed on scraps of skin and fabric from her blouse as it lumbered after her.

Three more zombies loomed up in front of the woman as she fled her attackers, maddened by the smell of the blood gushing from her wounded shoulder and finger stumps.

They encircled her and dragged her to the ground. Tatyana could see the woman's legs kicking as the three zombies began to feed. She was still sobbing with pain as the other two joined them and yet more scrambled over for a taste of flesh.

The slimmer woman had managed to catch hold of the hands of the man in the cage. He was trying to pull her to safety as the zombies circled below.

The woman's legs flailed as she tried to pull herself up onto the cage. A tall male zombie caught hold of her foot, and she kicked at it, her shoe coming off.

The zombie chewed on the shoe for a few seconds then threw it away and stretched up to grab her naked foot. The woman cried out in terror as the zombie tried to drag her back down, and the man in the cage tried to pull her up, but he wasn't strong enough.

The zombie bit into her foot, tearing off skin and cartilage. The woman howled in pain and let go of the cage, hanging from the man's grip.

The woman thrashed, sending droplets of blood raining down on the zombies that were gathering beneath her. They looked up towards the source of the blood, their jaws working hungrily.

The tall zombie got hold of her foot again and yanked, and a tug of war ensued between the zombie and the man in the cage. The woman's screams of panic became shriller and shriller until the man lost his grip.

She hit the floor and the zombies pounced. The man in the cage let out a howl of dismay, beating his fists against the bars and spitting angry curses at the zombies, and then curled up into a ball and sobbed his heart out as he watched what they were doing to the woman he obviously loved.

Tatyana buried her face in Benjamin's chest and tried to block out the woman's screams. Everyone else leaned forward to get a better view of the feeding. Benjamin was torn between comforting her and watching himself.

She'd seen thousands of zombie movies before. Seen them pull people apart and cheered with her friends. This was different. This was really happening. These were real zombies and real people, not bad Italian actors and cheap special effects.

These women had been sacrificed for trying to help children. She couldn't bear to listen to their screams of torment. She felt physically sick as the other guests cheered their slow agonising deaths.

Benjamin pushed her gently away and turned her head to the observation window. His eyes implored her not to lose it. She knew what he was doing. This was all part of the test Doc Papa had mentioned; if they didn't play along, if they showed any signs of weakness, they'd be sent home. The mission would be aborted and it would all have been for nothing.

She looked out over the carnage, the zombies feeding and the caged man's tears. She looked, but she tried not to see or hear. She remembered the last time she'd felt like this. She'd been ten years old and having dinner with her parents.

Her mother had over-cooked the roast. Her father was angry about his job and was looking for someone to take it out on. He picked her mother as usual. He'd thrown the gravy at her and then punched her to the ground.

Tatyana had dropped her cutlery and moved to help her mother but, terrified for her welfare, Tatyana's mother had told her to sit and to keep on eating, to mind her manners or her father would become even more angry.

She had to sit at the table and carry on as if nothing was happening. As if they were a normal family having a normal lunch. As if she couldn't hear her mother's cries and the sound of her father beating her until his arms ached.

Tatyana slowed her breathing to almost nothing. She let her limbs relax until all the energy drained out of them. Let her heart rate drop until it was hardly beating at all. She was tired of living right now. Tired of all the pain it brought.

She wanted a break. They'd told her to practise her zombie breathing. Well, now she was.

CHAPTER ELEVEN

"Now it is your turn," Doc Papa said. The zombies had picked the corpses clean and had shuffled off to find other distractions. "Now you must hunt in a pack. You must kill as they kill, with bare hands and teeth. You must gorge yourselves on raw human flesh."

There was a collective intake of breath among the guests. Tatyana could see their looks of apprehension and anticipation.

"You have a small window of opportunity in which to attack. It is imperative that you strike swiftly and decisively. The victim is traumatised and disoriented. He does not understand what is happening to him. Nothing in his life so far has prepared him for this.

"He is like a faltering national economy in the aftermath of a calamity. A struggling country hit by hyperinflation, natural disaster or years of war. Ripe for exploitation!

"It is in these times that multibillionaires are made. When, disguised as foreign aid, the IMF is able to demand economic shock therapy. Privatising public industries, slashing public services, raising taxes on the poor while systematically cutting their wages. Because the populace is too shocked to even realise what is happening to them, let alone resist or fight back.

"You must be like a multi-national descending on a weak nation. Just as they strip the country of its public coffers and natural resources, you must strip him of everything. Tear out his guts, gorge yourself on his life blood and suck the marrow from his bones. Squeeze the life out of him like it was the last penny of an impoverished people.

"Because he is in a position of weakness and you are in a position of strength. Because you are clever enough to have seen the opportunity and to have found the means to exploit it. That is what creating wealth is all about. That is the Way of the Barefoot Zombie. The lessons you learn in the arena today will determine if you are fit to be among the world's most rich and powerful."

Doc Papa's words charged the guests. Tatyana could feel the hunger growing in them, a deep-seated hunger for blood, and for the wealth and influence they saw within reach. She felt like she was standing in a pack of starving jackals.

Raoul and the other encounter leaders took them down as the zombies were cleared from the arena. They were told to strip to their underwear and then led to a set of gates.

As the gates opened, they spilled out into the arena. Most of the guests were pumped, filled with excitement and bloodlust. Others were apprehensive but, from the looks on their faces, ready to kill.

The bottom of the cage opened and the man tumbled onto the arena floor. Five of them were on top of him before he even had time to stand. They tore off his shirt and sunk their teeth into his neck and arms, but found it difficult to even break his skin, let alone tear it.

"*¡No, no, parada! ¿Qué usted está haciendo? ¡Párela, en nombre de Dios parada!*" the man called out.

An Asian woman tugged the man's hair to keep his head still and bit his cheek. The man screamed in pain as she managed to draw blood and peel off a chunk of his face.

At the sight of blood, the other guests went wild. Four of them lunged at his face with open mouths. Tatyana heard the man's nose break. Someone else tore off part of his bottom lip, exposing his teeth.

The man kicked his legs violently and thrashed around. He almost succeeded in getting away from them. His foot connected with one guy's mouth, who reeled back and spat blood.

"Oh, my God, he just broke my crown!" the guy said. "Do you have any idea how much that dental work cost, you little shit?" He went to kick the man, missed and hit one of the guests. He lifted his foot to try and stomp on the man but Raoul and another encounter leader stopped him and led him out of the arena. Someone wasn't going to make the dinner tomorrow night.

Benjamin was kneeling next to the man's midriff. He grabbed Tatyana and pulled her down next to him. The man was naked now, still writhing and screaming, but that only seemed to get the guests more excited.

All of them were chewing on parts of his body, trying to shred his flesh. Bessie, the ageing redhead, was trying to tear his penis off with her teeth. Tatyana could see the years of bitterness and broken marriages coming out in the vicious way she gnawed on his flaccid member.

Using their teeth and fingernails, someone managed to part the man's stomach wall. Benjamin saw his chance and stuck his hand in. He pulled out a section of the man's intestinal tract.

He turned and offered a section to Tatyana. He seemed almost pleased with himself. He waved the intestines under her nose but they were too gross to even touch. He implored her with his eyes, saying 'please don't fuck this up.'

He was right. She took the pink, bloody tube in her hands. It was hot and heavier than she thought it would be. She put it slowly to her lips and gagged at the smell. Benjamin bit into his section and Tatyana tried to do the same.

The wall of the intestine was thick and rubbery and slick with blood. Her teeth just slipped off. Benjamin had more success than her. The intestines tore and a thick liquid poured out. Benjamin retched as it spilled into his mouth, and tried not to vomit.

Tatyana could hear the man moan in pain. He was still alive and she was trying to eat his innards. Tears ran down her cheeks and mingled with the human blood dripping from her chin.

Make this end, Tatyana thought. *Oh, God, please, please make this end.*

She looked up and, out of the corner of her eye, she suddenly became aware of Miriam. She had that hazy field around her again. Maybe it was only because Tatyana's eyes were full of tears that she could see her.

Miriam was moving her hands about in a series of precise movements and muttering what looked like some sort of incantation. She was doing it so she didn't have to join in with the carnage, Tatyana realised.

Tatyana reached out a hand to her. She wanted nothing more than to disappear into that hazy field. To find the blind spot and just fade from view.

Her hand was slick with blood, though. Miriam and her field disappeared the moment she reached out for her.

What was she reaching out for?

She'd been thinking about something... fading from... what was it?

No, it was gone.

She looked down at herself. Her face and chest were smeared with blood.

The stains would never come out.

CHAPTER TWELVE

Sʜɪᴛ, ᴡᴏᴜʟᴅ ᴛʜᴇ taste never come out? Tatyana had brushed her teeth, like, twenty times now. Her gums were bleeding and her mouth was raw. She couldn't tell if she was tasting her own blood or the man's.

The man. That's all she could think of him as: 'the man.' That's all he was. She didn't know his name or anything about him other than he was once in a union. That's how they wanted it. The less she knew about him the easier he was to kill.

That was the whole point of it, she supposed. The zombies who tore those women apart didn't know anything about them and weren't capable of caring if they did. That was how she was supposed to be, uncaring and insensible. But there was a point that she couldn't go beyond. And she couldn't help but care.

She scrubbed the back of her tongue. Maybe that's where the taste was. The toothbrush hit the back of her throat and she retched. Thank goodness she wasn't going to be... *Oh no, here it comes.*

She bent forward and threw up into the sink. Her vomit was pink and speckled with shreds of undigested flesh. She hoped to God it was her own guts she'd just puked up.

Guts. Oh, God.

She threw up again. And again. And again, until her stomach was empty and even then she kept retching. Bile burned the back of her throat and the inside of her mouth. She let go of the sink, slid to the floor and started to cry.

"Shit, are you alright?" Benjamin said. He was standing in the bathroom doorway.

"No I'm not alright. I've just puked someone else's guts into the sink. What the fuck makes you think I'm alright?"

"Alright, calm down. Don't take it out on me. What did I do?"

"What did you do? What did you do? You took me to this island. You fed me human flesh and tried to turn me into a fucking zombie. And that's just for starters!"

"So you just want to give it all up and go home, is that? You just want to turn your back on these noble monsters after everything you've seen? You know what they're doing to them here. Can you just turn your back on that?"

"Right now, Benjamin, I don't give a shit about some murderous corpses."

"I don't believe I'm hearing this. How could you say that? How could you?"

"How could you feed me some guy's guts as he lay there on the ground, screaming in pain? Answer me that, huh?"

"You know why I had to do that. Do you think I liked doing it any more than you?"

"I don't know Benjamin, I don't know. And right now I don't fucking care. I'm sorry, but that's just the way I feel. No, fuck that. I'm not sorry. I'm sick of saying that." She put on a ditzy voice, parodying herself. "'I'm sorry, it's just this place. C'mon, let's have sex and make up.' Fuck that. Fuck the zombies and fuck you!"

There was an ominous silence. Benjamin just stood there looking stunned. Tatyana felt sick. Not from what she'd eaten, but from what she felt. These emotions didn't agree with her.

There was laughter in the corridor outside their room.

"What's going on?" Tatyana said.

"There's a party going on downstairs. They want to celebrate... y'know."

"They would, wouldn't they?" Tatyana said. "Do you want to use the bathroom? Is that why you came in?"

"Erm, no, I was going to use the radio to contact the guys. They should have reached the Gulf of Mexico by now. That's if they haven't killed each other yet."

"Yeah," Tatyana tried to smile, but failed.

"Don't s'pose you want to come and help me?"

"No, don't s'pose I do."

"Okay. Only I found somewhere for them to dock. It's on the south side of the island, so they can probably get there without being detected."

"Oh," she said, trying to sound interested.

"I found it on the map of the island in the lobby and I think I've worked out the exact co-ordinates."

"Good for you."

Benjamin left and returned with a blanket. "Thought you might need this," he said putting it around her shoulders. "You were shivering."

She felt tears in her eyes as she looked up at him. He was trying. He had no idea how to handle her like this, but he was trying, bless his heart.

"Thanks," she said.

He nodded and pulled his cute little half smile. She almost forgave him.

"I love you," he said.

"I know."

He stood in the doorway without moving. She looked up and caught his gaze. There didn't seem to be any words to bridge the gap between them. Or if there were, neither of them were clever enough to find them.

CHAPTER THIRTEEN

NEWBIES WERE SO dull once they'd popped their murder cherry. You'd think they were the first people to ever tear someone apart with their bare hands and teeth.

Samuel Palmer raised a glass to a group by the bar who caught his eye. They were flexing their muscles and pulling their guts in to impress some Swedish escorts.

He was obligated to attend these functions as part of his job. Another fifteen minutes and he'd have done his time. Then he could slip away for a little celebrating of his own.

The strangest thing about killing someone is the huge appetites it awakes in you. To begin with a lot of people throw up. But when the nausea wears off the hunger kicks in. You want to eat and fuck like they were Olympic events.

It was probably something primal, Palmer had decided; some throwback to Cro-Magnon times when killing your opponent meant you got to fuck his women and steal his food. It meant you were a victor and not a victim.

Whatever the reason, St Ignatius made certain to cater to those appetites. It was all part of the process and it made what came later that much more effective.

So they laid on a buffet of the rarest delicacies, prepared by chefs so talented they wouldn't demean themselves by appearing in a Michelin guide. For desert they flew in an army of high-class escorts trained to cater to every taste and persuasion.

There was even a dispensary providing designer drugs, from the finest Colombian coke to Viagra, E and narcotics that weren't available on any open market. All washed down with vintage Champagne.

God, he found these events tedious.

Bessie Smetherington, the boutique queen, sauntered past him and winked. The dyed red hair and the expensive boob job weren't fooling the Brazilian hunks she had on either arm. Palmer saw her stop and chat to an Amalgamated Plastics heiress – what was her name again? Moira Jacobs, that was it.

"Fabulous arm candy, darling," said Moira. "Where did you pick up such exquisite ornaments?"

"Aren't they great? I think they'll look fabulous in my room. I'm surprised you haven't picked out a bargain for yourself yet."

"Well the night is young and I'm feeling a little curious this evening. Think I might choose myself a his and hers set, if you catch my drift."

"Taking the rough with the smooth, are you?"

"Darling, I'm taking more than my fair share, like I always do," Moira said and went to ogle some Thai women. Bessie left with her hands on two perfect Brazilian butts.

Palmer did one more circuit of the room. He slapped backs, kissed cheeks and generally pressed the flesh. The party was beginning to move upstairs. He wouldn't be missed when he left.

He went through the kitchen and out into a service corridor. At the end was a goods elevator. He rode down to a sub-basement.

No-one else came down this far. He was the only one on the island with the access codes. He punched them into the keypad and the reinforced steel door slid open.

The room beyond was lined with huge metal draws like the ones found in a morgue. He breathed in the sweet mortuary smell – disinfectant and dead flesh.

It always triggered the same memory in him. The first time he'd ever smelled it. His third year at Harvard. He'd been drinking with one of the med students, James something-or-other.

When they were good and tight James revealed he had the key to the place where they stored the cadavers for the students' exams. He invited Palmer to come take a look, just for kicks. It sounded fun, so Palmer agreed.

It was the second time he'd ever seen a corpse. James pulled out several for him to see. One of them was hot. A girl in her twenties who'd choked on a doughnut when her boyfriend did the Heimlich manoeuvre wrong.

"Hey, you wanna see something cool?" said James. He picked up a large hollow needle. "This is a trocar, they use it to get fluid out of the corpses." He slipped it down the end of one corpse's penis, making it stand up. "Look. He has a boner."

"Hey, you know what we oughta do?" said Palmer. "We should get the hot chick out of her draw and make him bone her."

"Man, that would be awesome. Wait, wait we're gonna need this." James opened a draw and took out a tube. "It's lube."

Palmer didn't ask what it was doing in the morgue.

He got incredibly excited as they lifted the hot chick's corpse out of her drawer. The smell of her dead flesh, the pliant way her body moved in his arms, it turned him on.

A tiny sliver of blood escaped from her mouth as they slid her onto the dead guy. Palmer had never seen anything so beautiful in his life. The sagging flesh of the dead guy just sank beneath her weight.

Look at the useless prick just lying there, not even knowing how lucky he is, thought Palmer. He realised he was eaten up with jealousy.

James was giggling fit to bust. Palmer was pissed at him. He was having an erotic revelation and James was killing the romance. He was about to pop him one right in the mouth when they heard footsteps.

"Shit, it's the guard," said James. "We gotta get outta here."

"Wait, shouldn't we put the corpses back?"

"There isn't time. C'mon, man, we gotta leave *now*!"

Palmer took one last look at the hot chick's corpse. He was filled with longing as James grabbed him by the collar and dragged him out of the room. They got out of the building without being caught and went back to their frat house.

There was a minor scandal on campus when the bodies were found, but it was soon put down to a student prank and the faculty preferred to brush the matter aside to avoid bad publicity.

Palmer always avoided James after that. James didn't make any effort to see him either. They shared a guilty secret that they'd both as soon forget.

What Palmer couldn't forget was the hot chick's corpse. The way it felt in his arms. The odours it gave off. How cold it felt against his skin.

He'd lie in bed at night and fantasise about breaking into the morgue on a white charger and rescuing the corpse from its slab. He'd picture himself riding off into the sunset with the corpse in his arms, her mouldering head resting gently on his shoulder, his nostrils filled with the sweet scent of her decay.

He even found out where they'd buried her remains, after she'd been dissected by some student. He used to visit the grave and dream about digging her up. Stitching her body parts back together. The ultimate act of love and devotion to the object of his desire.

After a while he realised his obsession was never going to come to anything. So he put it out of his mind and shifted his desires elsewhere. But the fantasy never went away. Like a tap that drips just as you're about to sleep, it would wake him up in the middle of the night. It was getting so he couldn't ignore his desire for the dead any longer.

Leaving college, he found he had a talent for playing the market. It was like a beautiful and harmonious machine to him. It operated according to perfect laws that carried people and nations along in its wake. Its workings beguiled and enchanted him. Everything was ordered according to bottom lines and balance sheets.

His star rose on Wall Street and so did his portfolio of holdings. As a treat on his thirtieth birthday, when he'd amassed more wealth than he could ever spend, he bought himself a chain of morticians.

He took to making surprise inspections of these establishments. Late at night, when the staff had gone home. That was when his second life began. When he found the space to be the person he truly was. Where he could indulge all those fantasies he hadn't dared admit before.

As befitted someone with his wealth and ability, Palmer did everything with class. He chose his lovers very carefully. He didn't want just any old cadaver. He went for a certain type. She had to have a hot body. He preferred blondes, but he could always have the hair dyed or buy a wig. And she had to be under thirty, preferably twenty five or younger.

This made his quest for love a little more tricky, but he was a resourceful man. He expanded the chain of morticians into twelve more states and instigated an aggressive campaign for new business. As a result his investment thrived. And so did his opportunities for romance.

He scoured the obituaries for new conquests. When he found one he would take personal charge of the burial. He even liaised with the family and helped them through their time of grief. He would comfort a mother at a graveside while he was secretly preparing her daughter for a passionate encounter.

He would start by buying her gifts. A Prada evening dress, with matching heels or a set of diamond earrings. She had to be properly kitted out before she could be wooed.

He had a private room built into each of his mortuaries. Each was unique and done out with perfect taste.

He would have a meal sent over from the area's finest restaurant and set a table for himself and his date. Only when the correct rituals of courtship had been observed would he think of touching her.

It made the whole experience that much more exquisite. He would luxuriate in his new love for days on end. Hardly leaving her, except to deal with pressing business. But eventually the blossom of his passion would fade as her flesh began to decompose.

By their very nature, his romances were fleeting. At times his heart would be broken. But there was always the obituary page. Another sad loss would catch his eye and the thrill of the chase would begin again.

As his mortician empire grew, so did the occasional problem with staff. It seemed men and women of his persuasion were often drawn to the profession, in much greater numbers than most people suspected. Palmer would be especially vigilant for the tell tale signs. No-one knew them better than he.

He couldn't be everywhere though, and he couldn't check every person who worked for him. It never crossed his mind that they would be just as wise to him. He had been so careful for so many years that he was surprised when he received the first e-mails.

They were from an online group called the American Necromantic Adventurer's League. They had set up a forum and were campaigning to rehabilitate necrophilia. They aimed to change its public image from a sociopathic act to a lifestyle choice. They claimed necromantics were using their sexuality to come to an emotional and spiritual understanding with death.

The e-mails revealed that certain anonymous employees had highlighted him as a possible patron for their activities. They suggested that he shared certain values with the group and that sponsoring them would be the best way to maintain the secrecy surrounding his own love life.

Palmer was not intimidated by their veiled threats. He defended himself by going on the attack. He led a prominent campaign against League members within the industry as a way of deflecting attention from himself. He paid private investigators to hunt them all down and had them arrested. His wealth and influence guaranteed stiff sentences for them all. Then he sold his holdings in the mortuary business.

Palmer was in his forties by this point and had begun to tire of the bachelor life. He started to long for a more permanent relationship. His dilemma was that he didn't feel any attraction towards living women and he didn't want to give up the variety of bodies and experiences he was used to.

That's when he was approached by Doc Papa. It seemed another group of people, with whom he shared common interests, had been watching him – the super rich. They were head hunting a CEO for a private enterprise in the Caribbean. One that would cater exclusively to the monetary elite.

When they described the proposition to him in full, he was struck by two things. It had a sound business model and it would transport his love life to a whole new level.

*   *   *

PALMER SAVOURED THE mortuary aroma for a few seconds longer. Then he opened the door of a large refrigerator and took out a bucket of fresh human brains.

He pulled open a drawer from the middle row. Inside, his current favourite concubine strained against her straps and snapped her teeth at him in greeting.

"Hello, my sweet," Palmer said, stroking her bleached, straightened hair. "I know, I know, I've missed you too, but Daddy has to work, yes he does."

Palmer reached into the bucket and chose a ripe brain. The concubine's nose twitched as she smelled it. She rolled her milky white eyes in their encrusted sockets. She was coming on to him. She was such a minx.

"Patience, my sweet," Palmer said, dangling the brain over her mouth like a bunch of grapes. "Eat your brain first. They're good for you. The doctor told me so. They're the best thing to slow your decomposition, yes they are."

The concubine tore the spongy, pink tissue of the brain with her dead teeth, swallowing each mouthful as quickly as she could. Palmer dabbed the blood and brain tissue away from her mouth with his handkerchief.

"There, that's better, isn't it? You're all hot for Daddy now, aren't you? I can tell you are."

Palmer unbuckled his belt. The other concubines caught the scent of the brains. They got excited inside their drawers. They writhed and kicked in excitement.

"Wait my angels, wait. I don't have anywhere to be until five am. I will see to all of you soon enough."

CHAPTER FOURTEEN

"Ow! WHAT ARE you, some kind of fascist?" Klaus winced from the slap she gave him upside the head and sloped off, rubbing his scalp. "Are you having your period or something?"

Tweakie raised her hand again and he cowered. "I told you to put the champagne and caviar on ice. Since when did 'on ice' mean pour it down your scrawny gullet? We were saving that to celebrate once we make off with the zombies."

"It was an act of love," said Klaus, he tried to look wounded and indignant. "A supreme sacrifice. I was saving Ben and Tatyana from the trap of their pampered upbringing. Too much decadence can sap the revolutionary spirit. I was keeping them pure for the cause by taking all temptation out of their way."

"Say what?"

"You don't think I am enjoying stuffing myself with expensive delicacies, do you? Of course not. But I'm prepared to be doing anything to further the cause."

"Un-fucking-believable!"

Tweakie turned away from him, for fear of what she might do if he got too close. They'd been out on the open sea for two weeks now and she was beginning to wish Benjamin's folks had bought a bigger yacht. Two hundred feet seemed tiny when she had to share it with these three guys.

It had been fun for the first few days. Stealing the yacht had given her a rush, like jacking cars back in middle school. Only this thrill was a hundred times bigger. The yacht was awesome and took off at an incredible rate of knots.

For a few hours, she felt thirteen again, drinking cheap wine in the back of an old convertible they'd lifted from the front of the trailer park. Those were some of her happiest memories. Driving around all day, getting bombed. Forgetting all about school or having to go back to her Mom's trailer and the wandering hands of whatever drunken dumbass she'd dragged home.

"Now don't yuh say nuthin' to yore Momma little gurl, it'll only go worse on yuh."

Course the yacht was a serious step up from a broken down old Dodge. It had a king-sized jacuzzi, seven cabins, retractable plasma TV screen, twin jet skis and its own helicopter pad. And that was just the upper deck. The lower deck had a fully equipped gym, a swimming pool and a dance floor with a well-stocked bar.

From what she'd seen of Benjamin's folks, she couldn't imagine them busting any moves though. Or using what she swore was a stripper pole in the middle of the dance floor. Still, there was no telling what some people got up to in the privacy of the Mid-Atlantic.

The trip started out with calm waters, blue skies and glorious sunshine. By the second day, thanks to her boat-mates, it turned into a perfect storm of hissy fits and fall-outs.

Straight after breakfast, Klaus annexed the lounge bar with almost military precision. That was where the plasma TV was. He seized control of the remote on behalf of the people.

They weighed anchor after lunch and Dan and Andy stormed the gates of the lounge bar. They demanded a vote on which channel to watch and overruled Klaus on the viewing schedule.

Klaus called them all fascists for bringing democracy into the lounge bar 'against the will of the people.' He became as welcome in the lounge then as a hurricane in Haiti, and stormed out.

The next morning Dan had finally charged the batteries on his camcorder, something he'd forgotten to do before they left. Just in time to film Klaus as he seized control of the means of producing breakfast.

A heated debate ensued over whether the worker's council they'd formed to run the kitchen should get an equal say in the food they prepared and who washed the dishes.

Klaus argued that he should lead the kitchen on behalf of the masses because only he was qualified to say what a real revolutionary menu looked like. Besides, he had a skin complaint that made him allergic to detergents and he was requisitioning the maple syrup because he was diabetic and if his insulin levels dropped he could die.

Tweakie stayed mostly in her cabin after that. Klaus and Andy debated whether she was more like Trotsky for deserting the revolution or Che Guevara for taking the struggle on to new territories. It was no skin off her butt, so long as she didn't have to listen to them argue.

She only came out to take her turn at the wheel or to help Andy navigate. So long as she made allowances for his weird behaviour, he was easier to get along with than the others. Andy seemed quite glad of her company too. He called her 'quite useful to have about.' Like the servobot he'd always wanted, 'only with slightly smaller breasts.' She guessed that was a compliment, in his bizarre world.

Dan did try and get her to talk to camera as part of the documentary he was making of their 'ground breaking voyage.' She wasn't into it but she agreed to keep a video diary just to get him off her back. He lent her his spare camera, but she never got round to recording anything.

She was just on her way to return it when she'd run into Klaus finishing the last of the caviar. She headed up a flight of stairs to the control deck. Dan had the camera on. He was interviewing Andy at the wheel.

"Do think we'll pick up the techniques pretty quickly?" said Dan. "Or do you think we'll have to hang back for the first few days?"

"Well that all depends on how good Benjamin and Tatyana prove to be as teachers," said Andy. "I imagine we'll get better at interacting with the undead once they pass on what they've learned, and we've had a chance to try it out. I don't think we'll have much of a choice about learning quickly when the whole boat's stuffed full of noble monsters though."

"Yeah I don't s'pose we will. Do you think you'll be able to build a rapport with the noble monsters?"

"I think I'll build a better rapport with them than I have with most humans."

"Why's that?"

"Well, for a start," said Andy, pushing his glasses back and nodding at Tweakie in the doorway. "They're not encumbered with emotions like humans are."

"Encumbered with emotions?" said Tweakie. "You going all Mr Spock on us, Andy?" She handed Dan the spare camera. "Here, this is yours."

"Did you shoot anything?"

Tweakie shrugged. "I'll get around to it later."

"Well I don't see any practical purpose to most peoples' emotions," said Andy. "Except to confuse people. There's no problem trying to read zombies like there is with people. You don't have to decipher their emotions by the weird faces they pull or the inexplicable way they suddenly start to act. Like if their faces gets red and they start shouting loudly then they're probably angry. Or if their mouths turn down and their eyes get watery then you know they're sad. But even then that could also mean they're happy and proud, like when you graduate MIT with the highest grade in your class at only fifteen. Then they want to tell you how proud they are, when you still think you've upset them in some way and they try and hug and kiss you. Zombies don't kiss. That's the best bit about them. You don't have to worry about smelling their spit on your cheek."

"So you understand them better," said Dan. "Is that it?"

"Yes, I would say it is. You know where you are with a zombie. The way they act makes sense. That's why they're so noble."

"How about you, Tweakie?" Dan turned the camera on her. "Zombies and their lack of emotion, is that what does it for you?"

Tweakie considered giving him the finger but thought better of it. "It's not the fact that they don't feel emotions. They don't feel anything, period. That's the attraction. Nothing hurts them. They're invulnerable."

"And that's a good thing?" said Andy.

"Growing up how I did, it's a godsend," said Tweakie, chewing on a fingernail. "I had to learn that. Took me years to get to there and I'm still not always safe. Nothing touches them. That's what I admire. What I long for myself."

"Yeah, they're bad asses," said Dan. "Like me."

"Oh, and you're a bad ass all of a sudden?" said Andy with a smirk. "Because you got kicked out of UCLA for dealing drugs?"

"Better believe it," said Dan taking the camera from his eye and flexing his biceps. "Bad to the bone. You wanna try me?"

"Your make-up's smudged," said Andy.

"Is it?" Dan turned to Tweakie. "I've been meaning to ask you about that. Am I using the right foundation? Only all the sun and sea air is playing havoc with my pallor. I keep sweating and then it streaks and I swear I start looking like Alice frigging Cooper."

"You want something with a powder base that absorbs moisture."

Everyone jumped when the radio crackled to life. "This is Agent Z to Deathship One. Are you receiving me?"

"Shit, that's Benjamin," said Dan. "He got through. Your freaking contraption worked."

"Of course it did," said Andy, looking affronted.

"I repeat, Deathship One, are you receiving me?"

"What's happening? Are you having secret meetings without me?" Klaus appeared in the doorway.

"It's Benjamin," said Andy. "He's just made radio contact."

"Reading you loud and clear, good buddy," said Dan. "You nailed any noble monsters yet?"

"Only your momma," said Benjamin. "Betcha didn't know she was here, did you?"

"Was *your* momma who invited her, if I recall."

"Listen, we're days away from liberating the noble monsters. And I've found somewhere on the island you can dock without being seen. Was used by smugglers back in the day."

"Sounds awesome."

"It's perfect," said Benjamin.

CHAPTER FIFTEEN

"So does every temple..."

"Ounfó."

"Sorry Ounfó, have one of those poles in the centre?"

"Yes it does," Doc Papa said. He put down the knife and wiped his fingers. The blood was making them slippery. The three drummers increased the tempo. "That's a Poteau Mitan. It's a link between the worlds below and the worlds above. Like a great tree of life with its branches in the heavens and its roots in the waters below the Earth. It represents the royal path taken by the Loa to meet with humanity. "

"And these Loa are like spirits, right?"

"They are the intermediaries between God and His creation. They are present in all realms of nature and create the structure of time and space. They preside over all areas of human activity from agriculture to war. They also guide those who serve them, sometimes they intervene in our lives. We summon them in our ceremonies and they take possession of their servants when they have important news to impart."

"I see, and the colours and marking on this Pot... erm..."

"Poteau Mitan."

"Yes, Poteau Mitan, sorry. Do they have a special significance?"

"They represent the Serpent and Rainbow. The sacred symbols of the Loa Dambala and his consort Ayida Wédo. They symbolise the essence of creation and the sacred link between land, sea and sky."

"Fascinating, fascinating, I heard a lot about Voodoo last year when I shot a film in Haiti about the aftermath of the hurricanes. You might have seen it."

"I'm afraid I don't care much for your work."

"No, no, I don't suppose you do, given your... err, political leanings. It was about the ecological disaster in Haiti that's killed thousands of people and left millions homeless. The US and the World Bank pressured Haiti into opening its markets to US imports, which ruined local agriculture. The unemployed peasant farmers were driven into city slums with no food or fuel. That's what drove the deforestation. Haiti has less than two per cent of forest cover. When the hurricanes hit last year they destroyed most of the country's harvest and left all but a few areas uninhabitable. If Haiti had had more forests the damage wouldn't have been so great and fewer people would have died as a direct result of US intervention."

"Well that's one opinion," said Doc Papa, slicing through a layer of subcutaneous fat.

"Sorry I was getting on my soap box a bit there. I tend to do that when I'm nervous. What I meant to say was I heard a lot about Voodoo while I was out there, but this is the first actual rite I've seen. What is that pattern you made on the floor with the white powder?"

"It's a Vèvè," said Doc Papa. "A mystic symbol intended to invoke the presence of a Loa. Like a sacred access code to call them down."

"Okay, and which Loa is this for?"

"We're conducting a Petro rite to invoke Erzulie Zantor."

"Petro, now forgive me if I'm wrong, but isn't that like the dark side of Voodoo? And Rada I think it's called, is like the light side?"

"That's a rather simplified western view," Doc Papa said and began to remove the first of the vital organs. "The original rites that evolved into Voodoo come from several different parts of Africa. They were brought over to Haiti by the tribes that were conquered and sold into slavery. Petro, Rada, Kongo, Nago: these are names of *nanchons* or nations. They refer to the rites used to invoke certain Loa. It so happens that if you use certain rites the Loa you call upon may come in their vengeful form. This rite, for instance, is outlawed among most practitioners and conducted only by those of the red sect."

"Why is that?"

"All Loa demand a sacrifice. They must be fed before they manifest themselves and enter the bodies of their followers. This rite demands a *Cochon sans poils*."

"And what's that?"

"A human sacrifice.

"Is that my liver?"

"Yes it is. It's actually very healthy for a man of your age."

"Oh God, I'm going to die, aren't I?"

"I would say that's inevitable."

Doc Papa stepped back and looked over his handiwork. The sacrifice was staked out on the ground. His middle was split from stomach to sternum like the subject of an autopsy. All of his vital organs had been removed with great precision and laid out on the ground around him according to tradition. They glistened in the light of the ritual fires, throbbing with an unnatural life.

"Look, Mr Papa, or whatever your name is, if you put me back together again and let me go I swear I won't tell a soul about the island. I could even be useful to you. I've got contacts. I could get you some really good publicity."

"You have nothing I want. Don't try and bargain."

"I've got money, if that's what you want. I have independent means. It's how I fund all my films. It's yours, all of it. All you have to do is stitch me up and send me home."

"You're being kept alive through magical labours because it is necessary to the ceremony. To resurrect you, though, that is beyond even my powers."

"I'll be missed, you know. I'm a public figure. Questions will be asked. You'll be called to answer for what you're doing."

"Your body has already been found and your obituaries written. No-one will question a thing."

"Why? Why are you doing this to me? Why me? What have I ever done to you?"

"You produce irresponsible films that interfere with my business and that of my colleagues. Your so-called 'exposés' of human rights infractions cost us money. You are an overhead we cannot afford, and so you have been silenced."

"You can't do this. You can't. It's not fair. It's not humane. Please, I beg of you, please..."

"Hush, now, can't you hear she comes? And she is so very, very hungry."

Doc Papa reached into the sacrifice's chest and pulled out his heart. He kissed it and held it aloft. Vincenzo, his *Commandant Général de la Place*, gave the signal and the flag bearers began to parade around the Peristyle, the area of the Ounfó prescribed for dancing. They were followed by the Ounsi, his female followers. Clad not in the traditional white, but red as befitted the rite. The drummers changed the beat to a call and response between the Manman, the largest drum, and the two smaller drums, the Grondez and the Ka Tha Bou.

The sacrifice began to scream as Doc Papa chanted over his heart.

"*Ahi coeur de Cochon gris!*

"*Tambour moin rélé.*

"*Jou-t' allongé... Ahi!*

"*Ahi! Erzulie Zandor... Ahi!*"

The heart in Doc Papa's hands stopped beating. The sacrifice was accepted and his spirit consumed.

The Loa Erzulie Zandor gripped Vincenzo and shook him violently. Vincenzo's body convulsed and he threw himself to the ground before leaping into the air and then hitting the ground again. He looked like a rag doll in the hands of a malevolent child.

Doc Papa allowed himself, for just the briefest of moments, to see into the world of spirits and view Erzulie Zandor in her actual form. She was a being of impossible angles spilling into dimensions he couldn't comprehend, surrounded by an aura full of colours no human eye can see or brain process. It hurt him to his very core to even try and behold her.

For the sake of his sanity he shifted his konesans into a different conception of her. She was the very essence of every mother who had ever killed to protect her young or murdered a rival in a fit of jealousy. She was the ultimate female of her species and more deadly than any male. Her beauty was terrible to behold.

Erzulie Zandor had taken full possession of Vincenzo now. She grabbed one of the female followers and beat her viciously until she bled, then flung the woman to one side. She knocked a flag bearer to the floor, sat astride him and rode the man like a bitch in heat. She spat on him as she did and cursed him for the miserable piece of filth he was.

Then she turned her attention to Doc Papa and stalked towards him. He held up his asson as a sign of his authority.

She sneered at him. "Do you think that pathetic child's toy can protect you from me?"

He ignored her taunt. "I have need of your wisdom and your special knowledge. Grant me your insight, Erzulie Zandor, most deadly and magnificent of all the Loa."

"And why would I speak with a speck of shit like you?"

"I have fed you, great Loa, and I have called you here into my Ounfó when few others would dare. I have given you flesh to wear and blood to drink. I ask only that you confer on me that which costs you nothing to share. There is an artefact in the invisible world that I need to locate, will you help me?"

"Mmm. That costs me nothing, does it, little piss-pot? How poorly you value my blessings."

"They are of inestimable value to me, great Loa. That is why I have gone to such pains to prepare an audience with you. Have my labours fallen short of your expectations? Is my hospitality lacking? Just tell me, and I will rectify it."

"You've gone to great pains to use me for your own ends, you little shit-bag. And don't think I don't know it."

"And you have only come because it suits *your* purpose, great Loa."

"Don't think to second guess me, you little piss-stain. I've come because it amuses me to watch you grovel. All tall and proud like a blood-stiffened cock you are. And how you wilt before me. How you crawl back into your scrotum. What would you have of me, man child?"

"As I said before, I need your assistance locating an artefact. It's known as the Gateway of the Souls, it is crucial to my plans."

"And you can't find it anywhere, can you?"

"No, Erzulie Zandor."

"And without it, all these webs you've been weaving will come unstuck. Can't have that, can we? Can't lose all those fat juicy flies you've captured."

"No."

"No indeed. And what prizes these flies are, how fat and juicy. And yet your plans are so much more than any of them suspect. So audacious, so bold, no-one has ever aimed for such power and control."

"Will it work? Will I gain what I seek? Will you help me find the Gateway of the Souls?"

"So many questions, like an eager hatchling you are, grabbing for worms at his mother's beak."

Erzulie Zandor eyed him for a long while without talking. She was weighing something up. Doc Papa felt the sweat trickle down the back of his neck. Finally she spoke. "Will I help you find it? Will I? Will I? Will I? Why, yes, I think I will. It amuses me greatly. I think there is a beautiful irony about it. So many souls harnessed to the tyranny of one mind. No-one has achieved that before. It will be a lesson to many. I will lead you to the Gateway of the Souls, but it won't be where you expect. This is your very last chance to step away from this path. If you have any doubts, heed them now."

"I have no doubts. I am committed to this."

"Good. That's what I was hoping you would say."

This was more than he could have hoped. He maintained his calm demeanour, but inside, his spirit leapt with elation. He was quite sure Erzulie Zandor could see this. She cackled indulgently.

"This is not a simple matter, though," she said. "The Gateway is tied up in a blood feud. And a curse that, after all these centuries, remains unresolved. It emanates from the same source as the Gateway."

"I have dealt with that already."

"Have you? Have you really? There are ancestors present who say otherwise. Dead who are unfed and hungry for revenge, who cry out for retribution to any Loa who will listen."

"They petition against a crime I had no part in," said Doc Papa.

Erzulie Zandor threw back Vincenzo's head and laughed from inside him. "That is not the way it works, little shit smear. You have inherited this blood debt and the dead say it is due for payment."

"I thank you for the warning, then. I will take steps to ensure it's dealt with."

"Be sure that you do, little man. Be sure that you do."

Erzulie Zandor threw Vincenzo back and left his body before it hit the ground. From the vicious thump it made, Doc Papa imagined Vincenzo would be lucky to escape with just heavy bruising.

The female followers ran to help Vincenzo and their sister who had been had beaten. Doc Papa turned away as they bent and attended to the two of them on the ground.

He was on the verge of controlling more wealth and power than any human being had ever had. Of fashioning a future for humanity like nothing it had ever seen.

Yet deeds from the past had been put around his neck like millstones. Events that took place centuries before he was born threatened to jeopardise it all.

There was nothing he wouldn't do to prevent that from happening.

CHAPTER SIXTEEN

Nine Months Ago

TATYANA WAS PETRIFIED.

The day had started out so well. Everything had been so perfect. It could only go hideously wrong from now on.

She was riding with her mother in the back of the Rolls. Her mother had promised to let her ride back alone, but she wanted to savour this moment with her daughter. Tatyana could hardly begrudge her that.

When she was Tatyana's age, her mother could only dream about going to a ball thrown by the Daughters of the American Revolution. Nothing like it ever took place in Stalingrad. She would read about these events in the glossy magazines she found at her uncle's dacha. He was a diplomat, and the Party gave him a nice house in the country for his services to the Soviet state.

He brought the magazines back for his wife, but Tatyana's mother was allowed to flick through them when her family came to visit. She was studying English at school and it was thought to be good practice for her to read them. What she recalled most when she told Tatyana about it were the pictures.

They were so full of colour and excitement. The men looked so dashing in their tuxedos, and the women so glamorous and fashionable in their gowns. The colour and the opulence of the society events in the magazines seemed so thrilling and forbidden compared to Stalingrad with its drab clothes and Soviet architecture.

Tatyana's mother would fantasise about attending one of the balls she'd read about as she stood in line for hours to buy bread or potatoes. Now here she was, riding through Manhattan with her only daughter in the back of a Rolls Royce, on the way to the Waldorf-Astoria.

Her mother had chosen the Vera Wang gown she was wearing; Tatyana had to admit she looked good in it. Much better than she ever thought she would. She'd been surprised when she saw herself in her bedroom mirror.

Her mother had cried when she saw Tatyana. Her father came in to see what all the fuss was about and even he smiled when he laid eyes on her. He put his hands on her shoulders, kissed her and told her she looked beautiful.

Getting an invitation to the DAR Debutantes' Ball for his daughter was a big deal for him too. It meant that all the money he was spreading about to gain acceptance in the Fortune 500 circles was working. Tatyana was going to be presented to the cream of New York society.

For that moment, at least, things felt right for them. Her father wasn't brooding or flying into dark rages. He was proud of his wife and daughter. They didn't have to tiptoe round him for fear of his temper. He loved them both and wanted to let them know it. He even waved goodbye to them as they drove off.

That's why Tatyana was so terrified now. Surely things couldn't remain this good for long?

They didn't. Cross town traffic was appalling and they arrived late. Tatyana was met by Ingrid Hedberg, the chair of the ball committee, as she arrived in the lobby and was whisked away to take her place by the stage.

Tatyana had to run the gauntlet of the whole committee on her way. Elderly women with expensive jewellery and puckered up faces who tutted their disapproval as she walked past.

As her father wasn't permitted to present her, a special chaperone had been found for just that purpose.

"This is Frank Tufts," said Ingrid, introducing Tatyana to a tall, portly guy in his late fifties. "He's a stockbroker now, but he used to play baseball for the San Francisco Giants."

"Well, now, that was a good few years ago," said Frank, with a genial smile. "It's a pleasure to meet you, young lady."

"Thanks. You too."

The formal presentation had already begun by the time she was positioned at the end of the receiving line on the main stage in the ballroom. She was hidden in the wings for most of the ceremony, which suited her fine.

Frank took her arm when it came time for her to be presented. The announcer mispronounced her name, calling her Tatania Bulgakov.

Frank walked her around the stage and stopped in the centre. "This is the part where you curtsey, dear," he whispered.

Tatyana hadn't curtsied since her childhood ballet class. She could just about remember how to do it. She put one foot behind the other and bent her knees. The heel on her left shoe skidded out from under her as she did and she nearly fell.

"That's okay, I've got you," said Frank helping her back up.

A bunch of the other debs giggled, until Ingrid silenced them with a stern stare. Tatyana was blushing so much she could have heated the whole ballroom. Her escort joined them on stage. He was a short frat boy who was rather full of himself called Thomas Miller the Third. He escorted her off the stage, tried to feel her up as they approached the dance floor, then promptly dumped her to join his friends at the bar.

Tatyana wandered around, feeling a little aimless. She didn't know a soul there and wasn't a part of any of the cliques. She spotted the girl she'd stood next to in the receiving line. She was over by the punch bowl.

Tatyana walked over to join her.

"Hi," she said.

"Hi," said the girl, then turned back to the two girls she'd been chatting to.

"We're like best friends at the ball," said one of the other girls.

"Yeah," said the other. "We, like, met at Bergdorf Goodman's. I was, like, about to buy this one dress and I looked over and saw Patricia."

"And I was, like, trying on exactly the same dress as Abigail."

"And we were both, like, 'Oh My God!'"

"So neither of us, like, bought it."

"But then the weird thing is, when we arrived we saw this other girl wearing the same dress."

"And she looked, like, really fat in it."

"Yeah, and we were, like, 'hasn't she ever heard of the South Beach Diet?'"

"So you had a lucky escape then," said Tatyana. The three girls turned to look at her. Their expressions weren't friendly. "I mean, not buying the dress."

"I'm sorry," said Patricia. "Did you, like, want something?"

"Yeah," said Abigail. "'Cause you're, like, blocking the punch bowl."

"Oh, I'm sorry," said Tatyana and sloped away.

She didn't feel much like dancing, and no-one had asked her anyway, so she snuck outside and stood on the balcony. She was gazing out at the Manhattan skyline, wondering if she could spend the whole ball out there and not supposing she'd be missed, when a young man joined her.

"Nice to see someone else who loves these events as much as I do," he said.

"I'm sorry. It's just rather hot in there and..."

"Stuffy?"

"Stuffy doesn't begin to cover it."

He smiled at her remark. He had a really cute smile. She felt a little nervous flutter in her stomach. He looked kind of out of place though. He was wearing an expensive tuxedo, but it was covered in soil and the sleeves were torn. His face was white with make-up and he had lots of fake blood on him.

"Are you a goth or something?"

"A goth?" he snorted with derision. "A goth, gimme a break, that's so like last millennium. I'm a Deathwalker."

"A Deathwalker, is that some sort of emo thing?"

"An emo thing," he said with a look of amused horror. "You really don't get out much, do you?"

"Probably more than you do. You look like you've just dug your way out of a grave."

"Exactly. That's totally what I want to look like. Deathwalking, it's not a goth or an emo thing, it's way more punk than that. Deathwalkers revere the living dead, corpses who've risen from the grave."

"You mean like zombies?"

"Yeah, only we like to call them the Noble Monster or the Graveyard Rebel. They're the ultimate passive aggressive icon of rebellion against society. There's no hypocrisy or phoniness with a noble monster, like there is with all those jerk-offs in there."

"I'd certainly love to see a load of zombies go apeshit on them."

"Now you're talking. Wouldn't that be awesome? I'm Benjamin, by the way."

"Tatyana. Did they let you on stage like that?"

"No, and the girl I was supposed to escort was pissed, I can tell you."

"I bet she was. I'm surprised they even let you in the building."

"Oh they didn't want to, believe me, but my stepdad made the second highest contribution to the ball, so they had to."

"Second highest?"

"Yeah it would have been the highest but, at the last minute, some Russian gangster spunked like half a mil so his little daughter could play at being a debutante."

"That would be my father."

"Oops," he said and smiled bashfully. "I'm sorry, I thought you were French or something."

"French?" Now she pretended to be outraged.

"Well I heard your accent was European and I knew it wasn't English so I just assumed you were French or something."

"That's so typically American."

"You must think I'm such a dick."

She didn't, actually. She thought he was rather cute. She was also fairly sure he was checking her out. She didn't really get checked out by many cute guys, except for those who came on to her just to see if she would put out on the first night. When they found out she didn't, they lost interest.

It wasn't that she was bad looking. She didn't have the classical waspish good looks, but she wasn't unattractive, at least she didn't think so. It was more that she was a bit socially awkward. They could tell she didn't fit in easily. They usually wanted some cheerleader type so they could show their friends they were 'The Man' when it came to macking and all that.

"Hey," Benjamin said. "Do you wanna get out of here and go somewhere really cool?"

"Okay."

"Great, let's bounce."

"THIS IS SOMEWHERE really cool, is it?" she said as they got out of the taxi at Church Street between Fulton and Vesey.

"What do you mean? This is awesome."

Benjamin jumped the rails and helped her over. Tatyana looked around at the sycamore trees and the ancient marble tombstones.

"This your home away from home, is it?" she said.

"This is the oldest graveyard in Manhattan," he said and pointed at the chapel up ahead. "Do you know how many Presidents have worshipped at that chapel?"

"Do you?"

"Erm, it's four or five I think. I wasn't paying that much attention. But I know George Washington did something here on Inauguration Day and even ol' Dubya's shown his face."

"Should I be impressed?"

"By Bush or my knowledge?"

"By your idea of how to show a gal a good time."

"Hey, you ain't seen nothing yet. Come with me."

He took her hand and led her over to the chapel. She got another flutter of excitement as his fingers closed about hers. They stopped at a back door.

"Wait here," he said.

He disappeared and left Tatyana standing in the cold air, wondering why she'd left the ball with a complete stranger. Was she really that reckless? After about five minutes there was a faint click and the door opened.

"How did you get in?" she said.

"You don't want to know."

They walked through a porch in total darkness. Then they passed through a storage room and into a larger room.

"This is the vestry," Benjamin said. He lit a zippo and held it up to get a better look at the place. There was a coffin over in the corner, propped up on a table. He went and took a look inside.

"Is it?" Tatyana said.

Benjamin shook his head. "There's no-one in there."

They left the vestry and went through what looked like a hand-carved door into the main building. It was a bit too gloomy to see the interior of the church properly. The streetlights spilled in through the stained glass windows and lit up different details of the brownstone architecture and the woodwork.

"Shouldn't there be benches or something for people to sit on?" she asked.

"You mean pews? They had them all taken out a little while ago. To cope with all the visitors. This place has been kind of popular recently."

She couldn't believe she was standing here with some guy she'd only just met. Being here gave her a double kick; not only was she breaking and entering, she was inside a religious building.

As a former officer of the KGB, Tatyana's father was a devout atheist. He had always taken a Marxist approach to the evils of religion, even after he became a capitalist. He swapped 'scientific rationalism' for 'dialectical materialism,' but his basic opinion remained the same. It was a "superstitious throwback to a less enlightened time."

Now they lived in the West, he claimed to see "that it had certain uses for controlling the stupider sections of society," but it wasn't for him and his family.

Churches were forbidden, even exotic, spaces to Tatyana. Somewhere that people from different countries and cultures went. She'd never been to a wedding or a funeral in a church. That was something other people did on the TV and in the movies. Her grandfather had been buried in a municipal cemetery and her cousins had been married in state offices.

For as long as Tatyana could remember, she'd had a strange fascination with religion. It was like her mother's fascination with western high society, or the fascination she, and the other girls at her private school, used to have with sex.

It was the pomp and ceremony of it. All those rituals churchgoers use to mark the different stages of their lives. The way it brought families together to celebrate the most diverse things, like rejoicing in marriages and mourning the death of those they loved.

She still wondered what it felt like to believe in something that sounded so impossible, and to be filled by so much hope because it *was* impossible yet you knew it was true. She couldn't think of a single thing she believed in that much. She wasn't sure she even wanted to.

"So, what do you think?" asked Benjamin.

"Actually, you're right," Tatyana said. "This *is* really cool."

"Come with me," he took her hand again, much to her delight. He guided her over to a window by a street lamp. The light struck the stained glass and hit the floor in a mosaic of colours.

Benjamin stepped into the multi coloured rays and his white, pallid face became a harlequin's mask. Tatyana did the same and the colours lit up her perfect white ball gown like it was a patchwork quilt. She laughed and twirled round, sending her dress spinning out to catch the different colours.

Tatyana stopped and looked up at the window. It showed the Virgin Mary in a classic pose with the young Christ Child on her lap. She was surrounded by angels singing her praises. The light coming from the halo around her head was the brightest. Its rays fell on Tatyana and seemed to fill her with the same light.

Is this what it feels like to believe?

"Who's there?" demanded a voice from the nave. "Don't move, I've got a gun."

"Shit," said Benjamin. "It must be a security guard. Come with me."

He grabbed her arm and dragged her towards the vestry. They ran past the pulpit on the way. He charged up to the altar and lifted a bottle of wine. "What are you doing, wasting time?" she hissed.

"It's okay. I've got a plan."

They stumbled into the vestry but couldn't see a thing. Their eyes hadn't adjusted to the dark. They ran to where they thought the door was and hit the coffin. The footsteps behind them sounded like they were catching up.

"Quick, hide in there," Benjamin said, directing her into a broom closet as he clambered into the coffin.

Tatyana watched through a crack in the door as the security guard burst into the vestry and shone his torch around the room. He was a large guy, who could stand to lose a few pounds, not to mention the ridiculous walrus moustache on his top lip.

She really *was* petrified now. Getting caught or arrested didn't worry her. She was terrified of what she was going to say to her father when she arrived back home in a police car with a criminal record for breaking and entering. How was she going to explain to him why she'd left a ball he had paid a small fortune for her to attend, to break into a church with a guy she'd never met before who was dressed like a zombie?

"You punks are in trouble now," the guard said. "I'm warning you, come on out and don't try anything funny." His torch beam stopped on the coffin.

Benjamin's fingers appeared on the side of the coffin. He let out a deep groan and sat up, really slowly, like he was in some corny old horror movie. His skin looked extra white in the torch beam. The bloody wounds stood out on his face, as did the soil on his tuxedo.

He turned to the guard and opened his mouth. A gout of wine spilled out like blood. "I... want... to... eat... your... brains!" he croaked, like he was coughing up loose earth.

The security guard let out a high pitched scream. He sounded like a scared little girl. Tatyana had never heard a grown man make a noise like it. He threw his torch at the coffin and ran, full pelt, out of the vestry.

Tatyana waited until the sound of his footsteps faded before stepping out of the closet. She was so relieved she was shaking. She started to laugh hysterically as Benjamin grinned at her out of the coffin.

"That is the coolest fucking thing I have ever seen," she said.

Benjamin winked and she almost jumped on him right there. "Do I know how to show a gal a good time, or do I know how to show a gal a good time?" Benjamin climbed out of the coffin and found the guard's torch. "Now we can see to get out of here."

PEOPLE WERE STARTING to head home when they got back to the ball. Gregor, her father's chauffeur, was waiting behind the wheel of the Rolls. He didn't take too kindly to Benjamin when he saw him.

"We better say goodnight here," Tatyana said at the top of the hotel steps.

"Okay," said Benjamin and took both her hands in his.

Shit, he wasn't going to try and kiss her, was he? Actually, she rather hoped he was.

"Listen," he said. "I had a really good time tonight."

"So did I." She licked her lips to make sure they weren't dry.

"I thought this whole ball was going to be one long drag, but you made it really special."

"Thanks, you kinda picked things up for me too." She looked at his lips. They were red with wine and fake blood. She wondered what they'd feel like pressed against hers.

"I'd really like to see you again," he said.

She put her head to one side and moved a little closer.

Come on, what was stopping him? Couldn't he see she wanted to?

"I'd like that too," she said.

Benjamin glanced past her. "I think your driver's coming over."

"Oh yeah, sorry about that," she glanced behind her to see Gregor advancing on them. "He's kind of protective. It's my father's orders."

"He's a lot bigger than me. I better go. Can I get your number?"

"Sure," she fumbled in her purse and dropped it on the steps. Its contents rolled out at her feet. "Shit, sorry," she said as she stuffed them back in. Damn, she felt stupid and clumsy. She found a card and gave it him. "My mobile number. Call me."

"Will do," Benjamin said. He smiled at Gregor and disappeared into the lobby.

"Everything alright, Miss Bulgakov?" Gregor asked. She was annoyed by him being there and embarrassed by his heavy Russian accent.

"Yes, yes. I'm fine, just take me home."

WHY DIDN'T HE *kiss me?* she thought as she lay back against the hand-stitched leather upholstery of the Rolls. Did her breath smell? Did she do something wrong? Maybe she should change her deodorant. She sniffed discreetly at her pits.

Maybe he was just a gentleman. A walking dead gentleman, now that was a turn up for the books. He had asked for her number though, *and* he'd said he wanted to see her again. She better charge the battery on her mobile.

What if he didn't call? She knew what she was like. She was going to be checking her phone every five minutes now until he did.

What a night, though. Who would have thought? The only way it could have been any more perfect was if they *had* kissed. Still, that was something to look forward to.

She wondered what she'd tell her mother in the morning.

So dear, did you have a good time last night?

Yes, Mother. I met a charming young zombie. He had the cutest smile and a butt you could eat your breakfast off. That reminds me, we must have him over for morning coffee. Oh, you'll laugh when you hear this, we broke into a graveyard together and terrified a security guard. You must be so glad you paid for all that private education.

She hoped he did call. He was cute and dangerous and he had this lost, sensitive look in his eyes that made her ache when she thought about it.

If they did get it together, he was a keeper. She knew that already. Once they were together she couldn't imagine anything that could come between them.

CHAPTER SEVENTEEN

PALMER HAD SHOWERED, changed and shaved by five am. The guests would all be sleeping off the effects of the night's celebrations.

In a few hours, when they woke, he would have the staff round up all the escorts. Then he'd have them ferried to a sound proof room where Doc Papa would put them into a trance and remove all memory of the last twenty-four hours, as a precaution against careless guests who let too much slip during pillow talk.

There was nothing like a good orgasm to stir up a loose tongue or prick a conscience. Many high class hookers were as much confessors as they were bed partners. He couldn't have them leaving the island with tales of murder and mutilation playing on their minds.

Doc Papa was already at the runway when Palmer got there. He cursed himself that he'd been beaten on punctuality, and the Houngan looked at him and grinned. That was the unnerving thing about him; he seemed to see the thoughts as they formed right there in your mind.

He took his place at Doc Papa's side as the island's private jet came in to land. The steps were wheeled into place by the ground crew, and a hand woven red carpet, trimmed with ermine, was rolled out to meet it.

A meat truck pulled up. The driver opened the doors and a group of miserable specimens trudged out, wearing dreadlocks, nose rings and sou'westers. They had badges pinned to their waterproofs and slogans painted on them. All in all there was about thirty of them.

At a signal from Doc Papa they lined up either side of the carpet and took carving knives out of their pockets. He had them in a trance, completely prey to his will.

The sheer power Doc Papa wielded over other humans never failed to excite Palmer. Just being in his company made the most audacious and remarkable things seem possible. Nothing and nobody was an obstacle to him. Everything he said and did was all about enforcing that.

The pathetic bleeding hearts lining the carpet called themselves environmental activists. They'd been taken in Japanese waters, aboard a boat with the cringe-worthy title of *Sunshine Superman*. They were interfering with international trade by sabotaging whaling ships.

Just because the idiots at the UN had decided to place an international ban on those waters, these contemptible meddlers thought it gave them the right to intervene in the whaler's activities. Hundreds of thousands of dollars worth of trade was being wasted through their actions, all to save some species that was near extinction anyway.

So they had been rounded up and taken to St Ignatius; Palmer himself had overseen the operation. Doc Papa was very pleased with the result. He hadn't said what the purpose of extraditing them was, but Palmer knew he had something spectacular in mind to greet the shareholders.

The door of the jet opened and the shareholders stepped out. Doc Papa shook his asson twice and the activists fell to their knees, raised their knives with both hands and held them over their faces. The shareholders didn't descend, but looked on with wry fascination to see what Doc Papa would have them do next.

At another shake of the asson the activists plunged the knives into their left eye sockets. With precision, they twisted the knives, slicing through the cornea and severing the muscles holding the eye in place.

Using their left hands, each activist then reached into their sockets and pulled their eyeball out of its orbit. Blood trickled from the sockets as the activists took the carving knives and sliced through the thin red optic nerves at the back of the eyeball that connected it to the brain.

The activists tossed their severed eyeballs onto the red carpet and repeated the process with their right eye. The shareholders responded with sardonic smiles and a smatter of applause. Doc Papa had rolled out a carpet of human eyeballs to welcome them.

As the shareholders descended the steps Doc Papa shook his asson one last time. The eyeballs started to squirm about of their own accord and arrange themselves into their original pairs.

The activists dropped their knives and started groaning and waving their hands in front of them as though they were trying to ward something off. They were still frozen to the spot, but Doc Papa had returned the power of speech and limited movement. Why were they responding like this, though?

Then Palmer realised. They could still see out of the severed eyes squirming on the carpet.

The shareholders realised it too as they began to walk over the carpet of eyes. The eyeballs popped with satisfying wet squelches when they trod on them, grinding the vitreous humour into the carpet with their hand-stitched leather shoes.

The activists screamed with pain and fear as their eyeballs were trampled. They implored the shareholders to stop. Calling out for mercy.

"No, don't, please, no..."

"Stop, don't, stop, please, I'm begging you..."

"Oh God, why are you doing this? Dear Lord, why?"

It amused Palmer that self-professed atheists and pagans always invoked God when they were about to die. They didn't call on the Great Mother or logical reason. Oh no, they all shouted for God without fail. And they all asked *why*.

If they couldn't see the point Doc Papa was making here, then they were beyond tedious explanations. It was simple. They had to be reminded of how powerless they were.

The world was run a certain way by a certain breed of men and there was nothing they could do about it. Palmer and his kind would do whatever they pleased, whenever it pleased them, and nothing would stand in their way. All these bleeding hearts could do was sit at the sidelines and look on as the ruling elite trampled over them.

In his novel *1984*, George Orwell had said 'if you want a vision of the future, imagine a boot stamping on a human face - forever.' He was partly right. Except it wasn't a boot, it was a $4,000 shoe, and it wasn't a face, it was an eyeball. A powerless eyeball that could only look up as the shoe came down and ground it into lifeless jelly.

Of course, that wasn't the only point that Doc Papa was making. He was also displaying the full extent of his power to the shareholders. He was letting them know who was fully in charge.

The men trampling the eyes into the ground were the richest and most ruthless operators in the world. They were without mercy or compunction. You never underestimated or turned your back on them, and you showed them no weakness at any time.

This was also what Doc Papa was testing with his welcoming stunt: the limits of their cruelty and viciousness. He was probing them to see how far they would go, whether any of them would show a sign of squeamishness or compassion. Not one of them did.

As the shareholders reached the end of the carpet, Doc Papa clapped his hands and the activist keeled over. Having broken their hearts, he now stopped them.

"Impressive," said Walden Truffét, the majority shareholder. "What do you do for an encore?"

"Bring them back to life," said Doc Papa shaking Truffét's hand. Truffét was a portly man with silver hair and large, horn-rimmed glasses.

"So you got the new recruits primed?" said Frank Evans, a short, stocky man with died black hair and a craggy face.

"Oh, yes," said Doc Papa. "All it will take is one little push and they will be right where we want them."

"Well," said O'Shaugnessy, a tall, freckled Irish man. "That's what *we're* here for."

CHAPTER EIGHTEEN

THERE WAS A new mood among the guests in the morning. Benjamin could see it in their eyes. The way they moved, the way they greeted one another; all of it was downbeat.

There was something muted in the way they filed into the lecture hall. An air of gloom hung over everyone. The triumph of the night before had been replaced by something a lot like regret. It felt like the bill for the orgy had just come and it looked to bankrupt them all.

No-one made small talk. Everyone avoided eye contact. It wasn't just that they were hung over or tired from their late nights. It seemed like it had suddenly dawned on them, in the unforgiving light of morning, just what they had done the previous day. And, in spite of everything they had been taught, they couldn't shake off the guilt it caused them.

Benjamin felt it too. He couldn't quite face up to what they had done yet. He didn't want to admit to himself that he'd played a part in it. That *he* was the sort of person who could commit such acts. Or force others, like Tatyana, to commit them.

She still wasn't talking to him, not properly. They had conversations and stuff, like what to order for breakfast and which draw she put his spare socks in, but she hadn't opened up to him about what she was feeling.

They were drifting away from each other and there was nothing he could do to stop it. It was like watching some dreadful accident in slow motion. He could see everything that was going to happen, but he just couldn't move fast enough to avoid it.

He didn't want to lose her, but he couldn't do anything until she told him what was going on inside her. He was numb from all the fear he ought to be feeling. Fear of losing Tatyana, fear of being revealed as an outsider, fear of what he was becoming and having to admit what he'd always been. No wonder he could identify with the gloom that had soured everyone's mood.

You wouldn't know it to look at the guests, but today was supposed to be special. The beginning of the pay-off for all their training. There were guest lecturers for the morning and hints of some special ceremony that night. If it was anything like the 'special' surprise they had yesterday, then Benjamin wasn't looking forward to it.

Palmer announced the first lecturer, Eamonn O'Shaugnessy. Benjamin was surprised to find even he knew who that was. He was a hero of Richard's and a cult figure on Wall Street. He commanded seven-figure sums for public speaking and those appearances that he made were always sold out.

He was tall, with sandy brown hair that was greying at the temples. He looked like the sort of guy you'd see hosting an infomercial for the Irish Tourist Board. Benjamin half expected him to raise a pint of Guinness and start singing the praises of the Emerald Isle.

Instead, the man shot them a smile that was half lovable patriarch and half man-eating shark.

"Good morning," he said as he took to the podium. "How are you all? I hear there was a good craic last night. Anyone nursing a hangover?" There was no response and he smiled a knowing smile. "No? No-one who cares to admit it anyway. And who could blame you? You're not going to admit a weakness, sitting here surrounded by your peers. I can tell by the bloodshot eyes I'm seeing round the room that more than a few you are feeling rough, though. And that's not all you're feeling.

"You know what got me ahead in business? Not my ability to read the market, though that's netted me a billion or more, to be sure. What's really clinched it for me is my ability to read people. To look into the other feller's eyes and see what he's thinking and feeling before even he realises it. That's what's been invaluable to me. That's why I'm standing here now worth more than the lot of you put together.

"Do you want to know what I see when I'm looking at all of you? I see guilt, and I see doubt."

There was a murmur of dissent from the guests. Eamonn raised his hand to still it. "No, no, I do. I know you're less likely to admit to that than being hung over, but it's written on every one of your faces. Once you know what the signs are you can spot it a mile off. Do you know how I know what the signs are? 'Cause I've been there myself.

"You've just signed over a fortune to be here. And for what? To murder some poor guy? To act like a vicious animal? No – worse, to act like an undead monster. Is that what you came here for? And what if someone finds out? What if word is leaked to the press or the authorities? What will you do then?

"What you're feeling is only natural. You wouldn't be human if you didn't feel a tiny bit of remorse. After what you've just done, anyone would. You're only human. And that's the problem. That's what we're here to rectify.

"You see, the regret you're feeling now can make you prone to the terrible allure of altruism. But you have to watch out for that, because it's a trap. You know the first thing you find when you make more money than you can ever spend? It doesn't make you happy. In fact, I'll go farther than that. You find you start to despise money. Because it's worthless. You went to so much time and trouble to make it and then you find it doesn't do a thing for you. And you're right to despise it. It's only when you hate it and you spit on it that it clings to you like a dog that's been kicked and is desperate for your affection. It's why poor people love money so much. 'Cause you have to hate money if you want to make a serious amount of it.

"But don't mistake this hatred for the source of your unhappiness. Just because it feels good to give your money away doesn't mean you're doing the right thing. And yes, I will admit that building a few schools in some African backwater feels better than building a new wing on your mansion. But doing your secretary over her desk also feels good, and that can get you into a whole heap of trouble with alimony, I can tell you."

O'Shaugnessy acknowledged the smattering of laughter with a nod of the head and then assumed a serious expression. "Don't let your ego get ahead of you. Just because you control more wealth than most first-world countries doesn't mean you need to start running them. You might be more competent than the people they voted in, but it's not your affair. If you start handing out cash to people who haven't got the sense or guts to make their own, they won't thank you for it.

"At best, they'll see you as a big tit that they can suck on any time they need it. At worst, they'll start thinking the reason they haven't got any money is not because they're stupid and lazy, but because you stole it all from them in the first place.

"Build them a welfare state and what happens? They stop working. It's the same with philanthropy. It takes away incentive and it turns grown men and women into little children waiting for Daddy to give them a hand out. And all because you were feeling a bit blue and wanted to stroke your own ego.

"Remorse, guilt, regret, it's a slippery road. And it leads to ruin. There is a way to avoid all this, though. As I said, it's a natural human failing. The way to get around that is to become more than human.

"'Now how do I do that?' you might be asking yourself. Well now, I'm not the feller to be telling you. So let me give the stage over to our host here on St Ignatius. My esteemed colleague, Doc Papa!"

There was a huge round of applause from the guests. There was something almost obscene about the way O'Shaugnessy had worked the audience, playing on their doubts and their prejudices to work them into a frenzy. It had worked, though. Boy, had it worked. The mood in the room had gone from despondency to eager anticipation.

Doc Papa shook O'Shaugnessy's hand and took the podium. "Thank you, Eamonn, for those insightful words. You are perfectly right, of course, in everything you said. Indeed, it does fall to me to reveal one of the most powerful secrets that we guard here on St Ignatius. I am talking about the process of transcending your humanity.

"Before you can achieve that, however, you have to consider what it is that makes you truly human. What is it that hangs a conscience around your neck to keep you down and hold you back from all you could be? I will tell you. It is that most misunderstood of all human commodities – your soul.

"It is your soul that now torments you. That plagues you with remorse even as you take the first steps towards greatness. No matter how hard you try to evade it, your soul will find a way to retard your development. Do not underestimate its strength or tenacity. It is the one part of you that is immortal and it knows more about you than you yourself know.

"Why do you think there are so many tales of men and women who sell their souls for success? Because that is what it takes to truly succeed.

"Let me draw you an analogy. Consider the gold standard. Until very recently the limits of a country's currency were dictated by the amount of gold in its coffers. The worth of every note its economy issued was controlled by the amount of interest it could raise on its gold reserves. Imagine: the summit of man's imagination, the peak of his potential to shape the world in his image, all of it was tied to how much yellow metal he could scratch out of the ground.

"When we abandoned the gold standard we created an unlimited expansion of credit. There was no horizon beyond which we couldn't sail. No end to the territory we could conquer and call our own. The potential for our endeavours was ours to create, and ours alone.

"Western alchemists were the earliest of what I call 'Economystics.' They searched for the philosopher's stone that would turn base metal into gold, that would breathe life into dead matter. And what was this gold they sought to wring from the meanest substance?

"Why, it was the human soul. The soul is the gold standard by which all human endeavour and achievement is measured.

"Once you have abandoned it, there is no end to what you can achieve. But that doesn't mean your soul has no value. It is worth more than your success, believe me. As a great philosopher once said, 'What does it profit a man to gain the world if he lose his soul?'

"Gold did not lose its value when we suspended the gold standard. Neither will your soul. Countries did not sell off their gold reserves. And you no longer have to sell your soul in order to succeed. You can simply lease it.

"Voodoo teaches that there are two component parts to the soul, the Gros Bon Ange and the Ti Bon Ange. It is the Gros Bon Ange that keeps track of every misdemeanour you commit. When you go to meet your maker and you're judged on whether you can enter paradise, it is your Gros Bon Ange who will argue on your behalf.

"When a person dies, the Gros Bon Ange does not move far from the body. There is a rite that captures the Gros Bon Ange and contains it in a vessel called a Pot-tet. This is essential for passage into the afterlife.

"And now I have perfected a means of removing the Gros Bon Ange from a person's body before they are even dead. In a unique marriage of science and Voodoo, I can lift the main portion of the living soul out of a person's body and maintain it in a state of suspended animation until it is ready to be returned to its owner.

"Think of us as a bank where you can safely store what is at once your most valuable possession and your biggest impediment. A bank that allows you to achieve huge success by removing the biggest obstacle from your path.

"Like all banks, you can make withdrawals as well as deposits. Once you've made your billions, your soul can be returned to you, completely unsullied by everything you've done. Not one of your sins will have touched it. Your Gros Bon Ange will have no knowledge of your crimes and will be as pristine as the day you banked it. All you need do is pay the release fee plus compound interest.

"This is a one-time offer. Tomorrow we begin the Festival of the Gédé, the only time of year when this rite can be performed. Any guests not wishing to participate are free to leave the island now, but your deposit will be forfeit. Are there any questions?"

George Griffin raised his hand. "You mentioned there were two parts to the soul. What happens to the other part, this Ti Bon something?"

"Ti Bon Ange," said Doc Papa. "That's a very good question, thank you. The Ti Bon Ange governs your higher faculties and your capacity to reason. It looks after the mind, in other words. It is not bothered by your conscience. This will remain with your body. In fact when it is freed from the shackles of the Gros Bon Ange you will find that the Ti Bon Ange actually sharpens your mental faculties.

"Now, if you're all satisfied, we can move on to the paperwork. There are legal disclaimers, NDAs and contracts to be drawn up, which will all have to be signed in blood. Please let the administrators know if that is going to be a problem. There are no more seminars for the day. We'll see you this evening at the celebratory dinner where you'll get a chance to meet the shareholders and previous course graduates."

Doc Papa left the stage and the guests rushed to sign up. The only people who lagged behind were Benjamin, Tatyana and the African American woman Tatyana was fascinated with, Miriam. Tatyana hadn't said anything specific about her, but Benjamin kept catching her glancing over at the woman. She had something to do with Tatyana's mysterious disappearance a few days ago, Benjamin knew she did.

He was having a hard time working out what was going on with Tatyana. Maybe she had the hots for this Miriam. There would have been a time when that thought would have excited him. Now he just wanted to get a handle on what she was thinking or feeling.

He stood up and turned to Tatyana. "Are you coming?

"Don't hate me, but I don't think I can do this."

"What? But..."

"Please don't, Benjamin. I know what you're going to say, okay? We go through this every time; I get worried, and you bully me into it so I don't let the cause down. This is different, though. This is some seriously heavy shit going down. They're talking about taking our souls away. How scary is that? I mean, how much further do we have to go?"

He felt a cold knot of fear in his gut. "Do you want to go home?" he said, praying she would say *no*.

"I don't know."

"Maybe we could do something. Y'know, like switch bloods when we sign. Or write our names wrong, so the documents don't mean anything."

"How would that help?"

"It might. I don't know. Help me out here. At least I'm trying."

Tatyana looked him straight in the eyes. "You are trying, aren't you? Bless you for that, at least."

"Tatyana, I... I don't..."

"I know. Okay, I'll stay. But it has to be tomorrow night. When all the guests are going to the rite, we'll sneak away and do it. I don't want any part of losing my soul."

"Sheesh, I thought you were an atheist."

"Well, maybe you thought wrong. Tomorrow night or I'm gone."

"Okay, tomorrow night it is, then. I'll radio the guys to make sure they're ready."

CHAPTER NINETEEN

"ARE YOU SURE this is the right corridor?"

"Look you asked me that the last two times and I already told you, I'm not sure." Tatyana was about to blow. "It's got to be one of these three."

"Well it wasn't the last two."

"So it's probably this one. Will you just give it a rest?"

"They've bound to have noticed we've gone by now. They could come looking at any minute."

Tatyana found the service door she was looking for. They headed through into the bare passageway and Benjamin finally shut up. He had no idea how close he'd come to a fist in the face. She shouldn't think like that, but he could be really annoying at times.

She was sweating from all the running. It made her scalp itch. She scratched her freshly cropped hair. She was going to miss her old locks.

They'd lined up all the guests first thing in the morning and cut their hair. Women's down to two inches, men's to an inch. The hair was collected and stuck inside the earthenware containers called Pot-tets where their souls would be kept.

It was really gross and eerie. The guests had to put their toenails and fingernails into the pots too. They even made everyone spit in the Pot-tet and pee in a jar so they could add that to the mix.

But that wasn't as bad as the poultice they made them wear. They slapped cornmeal, goat dung, chicken blood, feathers, herbs and raw eggs on to their foreheads and wrapped a big white linen bandage round it to hold it in place. They were supposed to leave it on until the ceremony.

Apparently each of these ingredients would feed their Gros Bon Ange and prepare it to leave their bodies through their foreheads. Tatyana didn't know about her soul, but last night's dinner wanted to leave her guts every time she caught a whiff of the stuff.

After that they'd been taken outside in the blazing heat and made to lie down on the floor of a mud hut. They were packed in together and told to lie on their sides, pressed up against each other as though they were spooning.

A creepy-looking guy called Vincenzo, who was some sort of assistant priest, came in. He told them to practise their zombie breathing and still their vital signs. Tatyana was quite glad of this. The heat, the smell and the physical discomfort were unbearable. Zombie breathing was her way of escaping.

As they lay on the floor barely breathing, women who were all dressed in white entered the hut. A single drum beat out a rhythm as the women sang high wailing songs in what they called Langay. This was some secret African language that the spirits they called the Loa spoke.

Vincenzo shook his rattle in time to the drum and every three hours he clapped his hands. This was a sign that everyone should turn on to their other side.

The purpose of this ceremony, it was explained to them, was to fool their Gros Bon Anges into thinking that they were dying. The songs were from the underworld of the Gédé, the Loa of the dead whose festival it was. They called to the Gros Bon Anges to leave their bodies and return to the afterlife.

It was dark by the time the ceremony finished. Tatyana ached all over, but she hardly noticed. She was totally out of it. The breathing, the drumming and the songs had put her into some sort of trance.

They left the hut and went on a procession into the jungle. Tatyana floated along the small dirt track with the other guests. She barely registered the tall trees and the dense undergrowth all around her.

A group of men she hadn't seen before led the procession, blowing strange multi-coloured bamboo trumpets. A group of drummers marched in back of them.

They were quite far in when Benjamin grabbed her arm and pulled her into some prickly bushes. She tripped on a vine and tore her skin, and Benjamin put his hand over her mouth to stop her crying out.

Tatyana tried to wriggle free of him but Benjamin held her tight. She wanted to carry on with the other guests, to follow them into the dark heart of the lush, tropical landscape. To give over her soul for the secrets the ceremony promised.

As the procession moved on, its hold on Tatyana faded, as the thick ferns and creepers of the jungle swallowed it up. Luckily, Benjamin hadn't been so caught up as her; he'd seen a chance to get them out and jumped at it. They traced their steps back through the dense jungle and returned to the mansion.

They had to be careful getting back in. The apartment complex was crawling with the new arrivals, the previous course graduates who had bored everyone rigid with how rich and successful they now were at the dinner the previous night. Keeping out of their way hadn't been easy.

Once they'd got back to their room they'd both showered and changed into some corpse clothes they'd stolen, and made their way to the annex on the other side of the mansion, where Tatyana had tried to retrace the route she'd taken when she'd followed Miriam.

At the bottom of the metal steps Tatyana tried to remember which way they'd gone through the service bay.

Benjamin lit his zippo. "Does this help?"

"Thanks. I think it's over this way."

She was surprised to find that she had less problem finding the compound than she thought. They got to the hi-tech security doors without being seen and Benjamin pulled out the Rolex Andy had fixed up for them.

"Do you think it'll work?" she said as Benjamin hooked it up like Andy had shown him.

"We're fucked if it doesn't. 'Sides, you gotta have faith in the Andy-droid. He's never let us down before."

There was a high-pitched whine, followed by a low hum, and the doors opened with a click.

"We're in," Benjamin said.

They stepped through the doors and dropped into their best zombie shuffles.

This was the first time they'd ever encountered the noble monsters unsupervised. Tatyana was struggling to keep her heartbeat down and her breathing shallow. She was excited and nervous. This was what all the months of planning had been about. This was the ultimate test of everything she stood for. There was no room for fuck-ups.

It took a little while for their eyes to adjust to the darkness; there was no lighting and they couldn't carry a torch or use a naked flame. Vague shapes loomed out of the darkness, making Tatyana's heart race. Most of them turned out to be inanimate objects. All the same, it was dangerous to have a high pulse rate.

The plan was to round up the biggest group of zombies, then head around the compound picking up any stragglers. Once they'd gotten all the noble monsters together, they were going to head out to the harbour on the south side of the island, where Benjamin had instructed the guys to wait.

The Fourth Rule of Interaction was *Follow the herd but think ahead of it.* Apparently this would eventually allow them to take control of large groups of zombies. Sort of like undead sheepdogs, was how Tatyana pictured it.

Dr Chen had said that it was only in large groups that zombies started to exhibit any sort of intelligence. Almost as if they developed a group mind that got cleverer the more of them there were. She and Benjamin figured the bigger the group got, the more conscious they'd be. The more conscious they became, the easier it would be for them to understand that Benjamin and Tatyana were there to help them.

"It's like any revolutionary activity, when you think about it," Benjamin said. "The more you raise the consciousness of the masses, who are like the noble monsters, the easier it is to get them together in greater numbers so they can, like, throw off the shackles of their oppressors."

Tatyana nodded, because she didn't want another argument. She agreed with the aims and principals of the ZLF, but it always worried her when they started talking about being revolutionary.

Her father had used the 'cause of the glorious revolution' to justify all the things he did for the KGB. She also knew that, deep in his heart, he regretted every one of those things, and took that regret out on Tatyana and her mother. She didn't want Benjamin to end up regretting what he did in the name of being 'revolutionary.' She wasn't going to bear the brunt of that as well.

They lumbered into the main area of the compound at a snail's pace.

Rule Number Two: *Move in Slow Motion. Keep every movement extremely slow and deliberate.* This gave Tatyana time to scope out the layout.

The compound was mainly scrub land with patches of grass and stretches of sand. Ruined stone buildings, with crumbling walls and no roofs, dotted the area. For the most part, the noble monsters just shambled aimlessly around.

It was the middle of the night, but there didn't seem to be any change in the noble monsters' behaviour. Tatyana wondered if zombies ever slept. What would a zombie dream of if it did?

Over towards one of the electrified fences was a building that looked newly built. It was different from every other structure in the compound, with a steel roof and reinforced doors and windows. Tatyana was quite sure there was something important inside.

Benjamin ambled over to a set of stone steps. They led up to a raised concrete floor that might have been part of a building once. At the top of the steps Benjamin turned and struck a pose like he was Lenin addressing the masses. None of the noble monsters paid him any attention.

So Benjamin raised his fist in a 'Black Power' salute and let out a long, low groan. A few zombies turned to look at him. Benjamin pointed towards the exit and then raised his fist again. What was he playing at? Did he honestly think he was going to get them to revolt? Who did he think he was, some sort of undead Che Guevara?

Most of the zombies ignored him. A small number stood and watched him for a moment. They sniffed the air for blood. When they realised there was nothing to feed on, they, too, turned away.

Time to give Benjamin a reality check. Tatyana signalled that she was going to check out the new building and that he ought to follow her. He tried a few more grunts and poses and then admitted defeat. Sadly, the oppressed zombies just weren't swayed by his revolutionary stance.

Tatyana remembered that one of Benjamin's favourite 'really bad zombie movies' was *Revolt of the Zombies*. It was a shame for him that he didn't get to play it out in real life, but someone had to get on with the serious business of freeing the noble monsters.

Besides, he'd get over it so long as he remembered Rule Number Three: *It doesn't matter and you don't care.*

The door to the building was locked. Luckily the lock was electronic. The Rolex Andy had fixed up did the business and got them in.

CHAPTER TWENTY

It DIDN'T SMELL right.

They'd never been far from the smell of death, from the moment they had arrived on the island. Not surprising when you spend all day with walking corpses. But the smell inside the building wasn't like the mortuary smell of the noble monsters; it was much worse. It was like rotting meat mixed with chronic BO.

They walked through into a room that looked like an abattoir. There was a large stone block in the centre that was covered in congealed blood. Two metal drains ran along the floor either side of the block, both caked with dried blood.

Along the wall was a long row of knives and saws, many of which were covered in gore. In the far corner of the room was a pile of sou'westers next to another pile of dungarees and other clothes, a lot of which had badges and slogans painted on them.

"This doesn't feel right," said Benjamin. "We don't have time to go exploring. We need to round up the noble monsters before they come looking for us."

"Wait," Tatyana said. "This is important. There's something here that can help us. I know there is."

They moved into an adjacent room.

"Oh shit," said Benjamin and threw up.

Hanging from two rows of meat hooks in the ceiling were around twenty headless bodies with their hands and feet removed. To one side was a huge plastic container filled with human heads. All of them were missing their brains and the tops of their skulls.

Lined up against the far wall were three meat racks that looked like cages with wheels attached to their bases.

"You okay?" Tatyana asked, putting a hand on Benjamin's shoulder.

"Yeah, yeah, fine. I think it's the smell. Caught me by surprise."

"After everything you've seen and done, *this* makes you puke?"

"Okay, don't go on about it."

"This must be how they feed the zombies. I don't even want to think about where they get these bodies from."

Tatyana went to examine the cages against the wall. She reached through the bars experimentally.

"Okay, we've seen what's inside here," said Benjamin. "Can we get back to rounding up the zombies? That is what we're here for, in case you'd forgotten."

"This is how we're going to round them up," Tatyana said grabbing a large pole with a hook on the end. "Here, give me a hand getting one of these stiffs down."

The bodies hanging from the ceiling were heavier than they looked. Even with both of them holding the pole it took them four attempts to get one down.

Benjamin staggered backwards and the headless corpse landed on his foot. He yelped and fell on his butt. Tatyana put her hand over her mouth to stop from laughing.

"I'm glad you find this funny," he said.

"I'm sorry," she said, trying to look sympathetic. "Here, we've got to get this body into one of those cages."

They lugged the headless corpse over to the cage. With a little effort and a lot of cussing they hung it from the middle bar. Tatyana shut and bolted the cage.

"Try reaching the corpse through the bars," she said. Benjamin stuck his arm through the bars. "You can't, can you?"

"So?"

"So we can use it as bait to lure the zombies. As soon as they smell the body they'll come running. But they won't be able to get at it."

"How's that gonna help us?"

"This cage thing is on wheels. If we keep pushing it round the compound they'll keep chasing it and we can round them all up. It's like the old carrot on a piece of string trick. Except this time it's a rotting corpse."

Benjamin shrugged. "It might work"

"If your Jedi mind powers fail, you mean?"

"There's no need to get snippy."

"You're right. Let's get this out of here. Don't know about you, but I'll be glad to get away from this smell."

They pushed the cage with the body in it out of the building and into the compound. The rattling of the bars and the squeak of the wheels caused a few noble monsters to prick up their undead ears.

The stench of the rotting corpse soon began to waft out on the humid night air. Tatyana watched as the noble monsters caught its scent. It was like a transformation. Suddenly they had a purpose.

They stopped ambling and made straight for the corpse. Some of them began to chew in anticipation, grinding their dead teeth together. Others raised their arms and began grasping for the flesh they could smell.

The noble monsters got to the cage and pressed themselves up against the bars. The corpse was out of their reach. They groaned in frustration, pushing stale air up through dead throats.

Benjamin and Tatyana started to move the rack forward as more and more of the living dead joined them. They had to keep turning it to make certain the zombies didn't crowd round all four sides and stop it moving.

As more zombies joined the throng Tatyana found herself crushed up against the bars. All around her the walking dead were straining for the corpse that was just out of reach. They jostled her, groaning, flailing and gnashing their rotten teeth.

It took a lot of self control to keep from freaking out. One wrong move from her or Benjamin and the zombies pressed up against them would realise they were right next to two living bodies and would forget the dead one in the cage.

Rule Number Five: *Master yourself and nothing can threaten you.*

Tatyana kept up her zombie breathing. Rule Number One: *Show no signs of life.* In this situation, playing dead was the best way to stay alive.

As more and more zombies joined the throng, something weird started to happen. Tatyana was sure she could sense them all thinking. Not proper thoughts, but they seemed to arrive at some sort of instinctive consensus that got stronger as more of them joined the throng.

The more Tatyana acted like one of them the more she was aware of the group mind at the fringes of her own. If she thought as slowly and deliberately as she was moving, she found she could nudge the group mind in the direction she wanted.

She and Benjamin no longer had to steer the cage around the compound, the whole group just did it by instinct. Noble monsters started joining the group because it was a group, not just because they could smell the corpse.

The more they started acting in unison, the less frantic and purposeless the zombies seemed. Benjamin and Tatyana were directing them. This was what Rule Number Four meant. They were following the herd but thinking ahead of it. They'd developed to such a degree they could take control of the noble monsters.

Eventually they reached the main gates to the compound. The group stopped. Tatyana willed them to step aside and let Benjamin get to the lock.

There was a slight pause, then the zombies started to move out of his way, shuffling a few steps at a time and making just enough room for Benjamin to squeeze past them. He got away from the group and used the Rolex to unlock the huge security doors.

The gates slid back to reveal a dirt track, winding off into the scrubland surrounding the compound. This was it. The plan was working. They were practically out of there.

"What the fuck? Jesus Christ, there's hundreds of them!"

Tatyana glanced up and saw two armed guards standing in front of the open gates. One of them spoke into his radio. "Central, this is Operative One-Five-Four. Come in, Central. We have a Code Red security breach in Sector One. I repeat, we have a Code Red security breach in Sector One. There's hundreds of the fuckers. Send back up immediately!"

One of the guards raised his weapon and let off a few rounds. His fellow guard stopped the man.

"Are you fucking crazy?" he said. "Do you know what they'd do to us if we harmed one of those things?" He turned and spotted Benjamin over by the gate. "Hey, you! What the fuck are you playing at?"

"It's just one of the monsters," said the other guard. "What you talking to it for?"

"No it's not. I recognise that kid. He's one of the guests." The guard pointed his weapon at Benjamin. "Hey, you! Yes, you! What the fuck are you playing at? Shut that fucking gate now. I said shut it!"

Benjamin froze. He looked over at Tatyana for help. She had no idea what to do either. The noble monsters were starting to get agitated. Tatyana could feel their group mind starting to fracture and come apart. The guard dropped a bullet into his barrel and aimed at Benjamin. "If you don't shut that gate I will shoot you. Now, do it!"

Tatyana reacted without thinking. The sight of someone threatening Benjamin's life enraged her. She pushed the cage and sent it careening into the guard.

The cage crashed into the man and sent him sprawling. He let off a shot as he fell. Benjamin screamed with pain and held his shoulder.

Tatyana felt a huge pang of grief. This wasn't happening. Benjamin couldn't be hurt. He couldn't. She ran to him without any thought for her own safety.

As she did, she felt the zombies' group mind shatter. The noble monsters fell on the guards like a tidal wave.

Tatyana was oblivious to the guards' screams of pain and terror as she reached Benjamin. He was lying on the ground holding his bloody shoulder and whimpering.

Tatyana helped him to his feet.

"He shot me," Benjamin said.

Tatyana removed his hand from his shoulder and inspected the damage. "He just grazed the skin. I think you'll live." Then she threw her arms around him. "Thank God you're alright. Thank God, thank God, thank..." Did she really just thank God?

Benjamin stiffened. Tatyana let go of him. He was shaking. She turned to see what had scared him. Thirty or more of the zombies were bearing down on them.

They could smell the blood. Tatyana stepped in front of Benjamin to protect him. She tried to do her zombie breathing. Her heart was beating too fast. She was afraid for their safety. It wasn't working.

She grabbed Benjamin's hand and tried to run for it, but they were surrounded. There were too many of them. There was no way through. They were seconds away from being torn apart.

Tatyana gripped Benjamin's hand. "I love you. You're a dickhead, but I love you."

She closed her eyes, but she couldn't hold back the tears. She didn't want to die. *Oh, God, please don't make it hurt.* She was sorry for everything. She was so fucking sorry.

She felt a dead hand grip her arm. *Will I come back as one of them?* she thought. She pulled herself loose and buried her face in Benjamin's chest.

This was it. This was the end. This was...

"*Rete*," someone shouted. "*Dans le nom de Baron Samedi, rete!*"

Tatyana clung to Benjamin. She waited for the teeth and the clawing fingers and the dead bodies to overwhelm her. But they never came.

She opened her eyes. The zombies weren't moving. They were standing dead still.

"What's going on?" Tatyana said.

"I don't know," said Benjamin. "They just kinda stopped after that woman shouted something."

"What woman?"

The zombies began to shuffle. Some to the left, others to the right until they formed a small path down the middle.

Walking towards them along the path, Tatyana was astonished to see Miriam Chevalier.

CHAPTER TWENTY-ONE

"Just what do you think you're doing?" Miriam said.

"We were... err, trying to free the noble monsters," Benjamin said.

Miriam looked puzzled. "You were trying to free what?"

"He means the zombies." Tatyana said.

Miriam threw back her head and laughed. "Noble monsters, is that what you call these poor creatures? After all the time you've spent with them, seeing what they've become, do you honestly think they're noble?"

"Well no, not when you put it like that," said Benjamin. "But you don't understand. It's not what they've become; it's what they represent, they..."

"Be quiet," said Miriam. She turned to Tatyana. "You haven't answered my question. What do you think you're doing?"

"We were trying to free them. Like Benjamin said."

"Free them? You mean you were just going to let them loose on this island? Do you have any idea how stupid that is?"

"No. We have a plan. We were going to guide them to the other side of the island. We've got a boat, a yacht, waiting off-shore. A big one, it's a hundred foot."

"Two hundred foot," said Benjamin.

"And what were you going to do with them once you got them aboard this boat?"

"We were, erm, going to set them free in the wild, I think," said Tatyana. "Somewhere where they couldn't do any harm."

Miriam shook her head in disbelief. "You mean you were going to let most of them rot away to nothing. And those that did survive would have attacked innocent people."

"Look, we weren't trying to do anything bad," Benjamin said. "You don't mean to tell me you think they should be locked up like this and exploited by these people? And what are you doing here anyway? Aren't you supposed to be at that ceremony with the rest of them?"

"That ceremony is a blasphemy and a perversion of Voodoo. I wouldn't have anything to do with it. And to answer your other question, no, I don't think these victims should be locked up and exploited like this."

"Whoa, victims, that's a pretty harsh word," said Tatyana staring at the motionless zombies. "What did you do to them? Those words that you shouted, that was some kind of spell, right?"

"That's one way of describing it. I have stilled what Doc Papa calls their 'perfect hunger.' You are safe around them for the time being, but it is only temporary. You mentioned you have a yacht. Does it have a crew?"

"Yes. I've told them to meet us at the little harbour on the other side of the island. It's about five miles south west of here."

"I know where it is," said Miriam. "Ultimately, these victims cannot leave the island, and I won't allow you to release them elsewhere. In the short term, however, I think it would be useful to remove them from harm's way. I'll let you take them on board the yacht for a brief period."

"Wait a minute," said Benjamin. "We don't even know who you are and suddenly you turn up, start giving orders and try to take over our mission. Why the hell should we listen to you?"

"Do you want me to leave and let these poor wretches tear you apart?"

"No," said Tatyana. "We don't want that. I'm sorry, we seem to have gotten off on the wrong foot. We're very grateful that you saved us and I think we want the same things. Maybe we can work together on this?"

"I'm prepared to let you come along on a temporary basis. So long as you do exactly as I tell you."

"Well that's mighty big of you," said Benjamin.

"Shut up," said Tatyana. "What he means is, just let us know how we can help."

Miriam nodded and turned away from them. She clicked her fingers and the zombies began to follow her down the dirt track.

"What are you taking her side for?" said Benjamin. "And why did you tell me to shut up?"

"Because you were being a dick," Tatyana said. "C'mon, they're going to leave us behind."

"You mean you're just going to follow her?"

"Well, duh."

"How do we know she's not in league with Doc Papa? What if she's leading us straight into a trap?"

"Benjamin, she's not leading us into a trap. She saved our lives. You heard how she speaks about the people that run this place. She doesn't like them anymore than we do and she cares about these zombies."

"So she says. But she called them victims. They're not victims."

"They're being exploited and locked up. How are they not victims?"

"Well okay, they're victims of exploitation. But she's making out like it's a bad thing that they're noble monsters. You heard how she spoke about them. I just don't trust her."

"You know, I can hear every word you're saying," said Miriam. "For your own safety you should stay with me here at the front."

Tatyana started walking to catch her up. Benjamin stayed where he was. She turned and gave him a look. He stuck his hands in his pockets and skulked after them.

"Wait, you're going the wrong way," said Benjamin, after five minutes of silence. "This isn't the road. I memorised the map."

"The one in the foyer?" said Miriam. "That's not a map. That's a pretty picture for tourists."

"So I suppose you know better?"

"I ought to. I've lived here most of my life."

Tatyana was stunned. "I thought this was a private island. I didn't know anyone still lived here."

"St Ignatius has been inhabited for as long as Haiti. Where do you think all these zombies came from? How do you think they got here?"

Tatyana was stunned. "You mean all these zombies..."

"Are my brothers and sisters, aunts and uncles, friends and lovers. They're the people I grew up with. The people I have sworn, as a holy duty, to protect."

CHAPTER TWENTY-TWO

THE GUESTS WERE right where Doc Papa wanted them. They lay prone on the floor of the Peristyle, the holy space where the ceremony was conducted. Their souls were banked in the Pot-tets. The drummers beat on the stretched skins of their Asòtòs, keeping the guests in their deep trance. They also kept his acolytes in a heightened state of consciousness.

They mirrored the pulse of the ancient energy lines that flowed down the Poteau Mitan in the centre of the temple. Drawn from the invisible world, these lines spread out across the Ounfó like a snare, a net to capture the souls of the world's richest people. With the blessing of the Loa, his Ounfó would become a temple to the economic dominance of the world.

The ceremony was past its peak. All that remained was to seal the Pot-tets with their Bakas. The sacred talisman trapped the Gross Bon Anges in the Pot-tets and stopped them from returning to the invisible world where the Loa dwelt, where the Gros Bon Anges had come from and wanted to return.

The symbols of the Baka were carved onto pieces of ivory and stained with guests' blood. They were magically designed to hold each guest's Gros Bon Ange captive and to stop them leaving the earthly plane.

Once they were on the containers, the deal was ratified and they belonged to Doc Papa. The guests didn't realise that yet, but they would soon enough.

There was a cryogenics centre built out back of the temple. With the Gros Bon Anges imprisoned, the Pot-tets would be taken there and deep frozen. They were the only truly recession-proof assets Doc Papa had ever encountered, because they were the true source of value in the world.

As the beat of the drums reached the right pitch, Doc Papa raised the sacred rattle of his office. Dark energies crackled down the Poteau Mitan and moved through his body, filling the rattle like a malevolent beacon.

Doc Papa's body shook as though hit by lightning; he could feel the awe he inspired in his acolytes every time he performed the act. Then he shook the Asson over the Bakas and let the energy leap out of it and infuse them all, empowering each one with the dark blessing of the Loa.

Something was wrong.

As the last of the dark energy moved from him into the Bakas, Doc Papa felt a presence at the outskirts of the Peristyle, a presence that shouldn't be there.

He looked across the space and saw Tomlinson, the Commander of the Armed Guards. What was he doing here? Doc Papa didn't bother hiding his fury. He turned to Vincenzo, and signalled for him to gather up the Bakas and place them on the Pot-tets arranged on the stone altar.

Tomlinson was a big man and heavily armed, but Doc Papa could see him shaking as he approached. He pointed to the door to the courtyard and Tomlinson followed him. As soon as they were through, Tomlinson knelt.

"Sir. I apologise for the interruption. I know it's unwarranted, but we've had a Code Red security breach."

"What?"

"The zombies. They've escaped, and killed two of my men."

"How did this happen?"

"I don't know yet, sir." Tomlinson un-holstered his pistol and offered it to Doc Papa. "I take full responsibility."

"Put that away, you idiot. If I wanted to kill you I have far better means. And don't think you'll get off that lightly if I do. Where are they now?"

"They're heading south, towards the coast. We've got a chopper following them. We also have reports of a vessel off the southern coast."

"Do not move from this spot until I tell you," said Doc Papa. Tomlinson saluted and bowed. Doc Papa left him and returned to the Peristyle.

He took Vincenzo to one side. "There are matters that need my attention. You will have to finish conducting the ceremony. If anything goes wrong, I will hold you entirely responsible. Do you understand?" Vincenzo nodded, fearful and surprised.

Doc Papa didn't bother to explain. He left Vincenzo and had Felippe, the largest of his acolytes, accompany him and Tomlinson to his jeep.

* * *

THE JEEP PULLED up at the edge of a rise overlooking the harbour and Doc Papa and Felippe got out. He told the guards with them to lift down the two sheep he'd brought, and he and Felippe led the animals away.

The chopper following the group of zombies had given them continual updates on the group's position as they'd driven over, Doc Papa didn't need to be told where they were going. He gave the guards precise orders where to head. There was only one natural harbour on the island. A vessel had been spotted; the zombies were heading for it. Someone must be guiding them.

Someone was trying to steal his second biggest asset. Three of the guests were missing. He'd despatched guards to find them as soon as their absence was spotted, and now he knew where they'd gone.

He didn't know whose pay they were in, but they would suffer as they told him. No-one tried to take what was his. He was going to send a message, written in blood on their broken bodies.

There was a tiny beach below, hidden from the harbour. They took the sheep down the steep path. This was the very beach where Doc Papa's body had washed up several years ago. It had significance for him, and therefore it had power.

He tethered the sheep to a tree at the edge of the beach. Their eyes tinged with green, they were the perfect offering.

Doc Papa removed the knife from his belt, took hold of the first sheep by its horns and said a prayer to Saint Ulrich, known as Agwe in Voodoo, sovereign Loa of the sea.

When the prayer was done, he slit the sheep's throats and caught the blood in two white cups, Agwe's favourite colour. He then slit the sheep's stomachs, cracked open their chests and removed their hearts.

Felippe placed a miniature flat-bottomed boat on the ground and Doc Papa placed both the hearts in it. Felippe added gunpowder, dried fish, white chocolate, a bottle of champagne and one cup of sheep's blood.

Doc Papa drank the other cup, then took a handful of corn flour and, letting it trickle through his fingers in a steady stream, drew Agwe's Vévé around the boat. When this was done, he lit an oil lamp in a white cup and placed it on the boat as Felippe started to beat on a drum.

Doc Papa spoke an invocation to Agwe, then raised a conch shell to his lips and blew. He placed the boat on his head and waded, with great care, into the sea.

He drew a breath and let the sea cover his head. The boat floated away. Doc Papa watched it from below as the waves carried it. It sailed some distance and then sank. It had been accepted; the ceremony was a success.

He felt something grip his legs and begin to shake him. It enclosed his body and squeezed the air out of his lungs. His body sank to the floor like a discarded skin as he was lifted out of it.

It was Agwe. The Loa had come in his most vengeful form. He was the crushing bleakness of the ocean floor, where no light ever shines. He was the boiling anger of the storm that capsizes stricken ships. He was the decimating force of the tidal wave, destroying coastal dwellings.

Although Doc Papa left his body, Agwe didn't take it over and ride him. Instead, Doc Papa mounted Agwe and rode him like the foam on the crest of a wave. Doc Papa's spirit skimmed along the surface with Agwe, as Felippe waded into the sea and pulled his body back to the shore.

Agwe took him to the yacht pulling into the harbour. There were four people aboard, a woman and three men, all in their early twenties. Borrowing the energy of the Loa, Doc Papa explored the yacht in his incorporeal form. He also explored the occupants.

One in particular caught his attention. He was a little younger than the others, but his mental faculties were far more developed. That was his weakness.

There was a huge imbalance in his psychic energy. A disproportionate amount was invested in certain cognitive functions, at the expense of the emotional and spiritual aspects of his consciousness.

As his reasoning and intelligence had grown and blossomed, the rest of his spirit had withered on the vine. This was like an open door to Doc Papa; he had none of the usual defences an average person has.

Andy was his name. Doc Papa began to pick over his memories as he seeped into the young man's mind and took control. Andy was so lacking in self awareness that he didn't notice he was being possessed. Way past the point when a normal individual would have noticed something was amiss and tried to fight it, he was still unaware. It was a *fait accompli*.

His memories were not like other people's. Anything to do with feelings or empathy was repressed or discarded due to his inability to process it. Instead, there was an endless array of facts and raw data, more than the average mind could hold.

Doc Papa found it overwhelming at first. With a little methodical sifting however, he found what he needed. It surprised him.

His estimation of the situation was wrong. These four were not in the employ of any rival. They, and two of the missing guests, were part of some guerrilla organisation. They viewed the theft of his property as some sort of political act.

How truly pathetic. They seriously thought the corpses he had animated were some sort of noble creature. Never in his life had Doc Papa seen a more miserable and ridiculous attempt at subversion.

They were about to see the error of their ways. They wouldn't enjoy it, but he would.

CHAPTER TWENTY-THREE

"Andy, have you seen Klaus anywhere?" It was the one called Dan, clattering down the stairs to the engine room. "That engine is sounding seriously unhealthy, do you know what's up with it?"

Doc Papa met him at the bottom of the stairs. "Oh yes," he said through Andy's mouth. "I know exactly why it's making that noise. Come and see."

Dan followed him without a second thought. He was looking at the camcorder he carried everywhere.

None of the others aboard the boat suspected a thing. They were used to Andy acting in a weird manner. They didn't notice any of the tell-tale signs of possession. The vacant stare, the hollow voice, the weird movements, that was just business as usual for Andy as far as they were concerned. It was too perfect.

"We're supposed to be docking now," said Dan. "They're gonna be waiting for us. It won't be cool if we just leave them hanging. Was Klaus any use to you or did he just get in the way?"

Doc Papa led him round the corner and showed him Klaus. "Actually," he said. "Klaus proved to be very useful. I learned a lot."

Dan reacted exactly as Doc Papa hoped he would, appalled and nearly hysterical with grief. It was good to have his work appreciated.

Dan dropped the camcorder, fell to his knees and vomited. Doc Papa was very pleased. He couldn't help but admire his handiwork. It hadn't been easy with Andy's puny frame, even though Klaus wasn't very big himself.

Klaus was stretched out like a dissected frog. His feet had been nailed to the floor and his hands were nailed to a low ceiling beam above the engine. There was a bloody hole in his throat where Doc Papa had removed his vocal chords; he hadn't wanted Klaus's screams to alert the others.

He'd needed information from Klaus, but it wasn't necessary for him to talk. Doc Papa had found other ways to interrogate him. Ways he was rather proud of, even though he'd had to improvise.

Klaus's stomach was slit wide open. Doc Papa had removed his intestinal tract and tied it to the propeller shaft. As the propeller spun, it had tugged Klaus's innards from his body.

While Klaus twitched and writhed in pain and tried to scream out of the red, bubbling hole in his throat, his life had flashed before his eyes. Doc Papa had watched with him, lifting the succession of memories, like a thin film, from Klaus's mind.

It was surprising how total someone's recall was at the point of death. The whole of Klaus's pointless little life was laid bare. Doc Papa saw his lawyer parents neglect him in favour of their careers, packing him off to boarding school at the first opportunity. He witnessed the older boys punch and taunt him relentlessly for being scrawny and big-nosed. He watched what the games master did in the showers when he kept Klaus behind after the lesson.

Doc Papa sneered as Klaus built the brittle facade of his character to protect himself from the betrayals and injustice he'd suffered. He sighed with boredom as the anger Klaus felt at his school and his parents became a general anger at authority and the state. He saw how this anger was really fear: the fear of a little boy, who never got over being bullied, dressed up in left-wing rhetoric.

Doc Papa brought this fear to perfect fruition in the last moments of Klaus's life. As the last memory faded and the breath slipped from Klaus's body, Doc Papa let him know that all his fears had come true. He was dying at the hands of everything he hated most. The corrupt capitalist system had finally come and tortured him to death, just as he always feared it would.

Doc Papa had also learned everything he needed to know about the ZLF and their pitiable attempt at direct action. Benjamin and Tatyana were the ringleaders. He had been wary of them, for reasons he couldn't explain, since the first background check; now he knew why.

Miriam Chevalier was still a mystery to him. Why was she helping them? Did they have something over her? There was nothing in her background to explain it.

Doc Papa would find out soon enough, just as soon as he had destroyed this yacht and killed its occupants. He flooded the fuel tanks and reached for a lighter.

Dan was still crawling around on all fours in front of Klaus, vomiting and weeping.

"Jesus Christ, Andy," he said. "Why? I mean, Klaus was a pain in the ass, but he didn't deserve this. No-one deserves this."

Doc Papa picked up a shovel with Andy's hands.

"Wait Andy, wait," said Dan. "I don't want to die. I want to see my child grow up. What the fuck are you playing at?"

"Call it a counter-revolution," said Doc Papa as he split Dan's head open.

CHAPTER TWENTY-FOUR

WHAT THE FUCK was happening?

Benjamin had been standing on the shore for nearly two hours now. There was a big black stealth chopper circling overhead and an army of guards likely to turn up any minute.

The yacht was only a small distance from the shore. They could see it clearly, but it hadn't moved an inch since they got to the harbour.

"Can zombies swim?" he asked Miriam.

She sighed and rolled her eyes. What the fuck was her problem? She said she wanted to help the noble monsters. Well, who rescued them from the compound? He did. So why was she giving him such a hard time?

"Could we send out a flare?" said Tatyana. "Or light a fire?"

"Have you got a flare?" said Benjamin. "'Cause I haven't. Or any wood for that matter and, in case you've forgotten, zombies are afraid of fire."

"I'm only trying to help. I don't see you coming up with any ideas. We need to find some way to talk with the guys on the yacht. Why didn't you think to bring the radio Andy made?"

"Where was I supposed to carry it? Up my ass?"

A couple of the zombies near them started to get restless.

"Stop arguing," said Miriam. "It makes them harder to control. You must remain calm at all times."

"Oh yeah," said Benjamin. "Like the First Rule of Interaction. *Show no signs of life.*"

"If you want to put it that way," said Miriam, turning away from him. What, was it her time of the month or something?

"Seriously, though," said Tatyana, taking shallow breaths and hardly moving. "We need to get in contact with them. Do you think they can see we're here from the deck?"

"I don't know," said Benjamin, trying to sound as emotionless as possible. He had a sudden flash of Richard and his Mom when they were really pissed at each other but were trying not to argue in front of him. This must be what they felt like. "Maybe they can't see us 'cause it's dark. I can't understand why they've just stopped."

Benjamin stared at the yacht. It was Richard's pride and joy. When Benjamin was younger, Richard had dragged him and his Mom away on trips several times a year.

Benjamin could remember standing in the marina with his Mom watching the yacht come in, willing it not to arrive. Trying to put off the moment when he'd have to get on board and watch Richard strut about and play captain. Benjamin was expected to act as an unpaid crew member, which meant Richard got to order him around the whole time.

Now, in a complete reversal, he was standing on the shore willing the yacht to come in. Willing it to move, or at least do something other than sit there dead in the water.

Then it exploded.

A giant ball of fire burst out of the stern of the yacht, tearing it into a thousand flaming fragments. Benjamin could feel the heat of the explosion from the shore. The noise was deafening. He felt a stabbing pain in his inner ear.

The front of the yacht keeled over into the water and started to sink. Burning debris rained down, sending the zombies into a panic.

Oh shit! What was Richard going to say? Benjamin was a dead man if he ever got out of this alive.

Miriam chanted in a weird voice to subdue the zombies. She was having a hard time of it, with flaming chunks of yacht falling all around them.

Benjamin felt numb with shock. Then he saw something moving across the water away from the yacht. Tweakie had gotten away on one of the jet skis. Thank God she was alright. Maybe the others had got out too. She was charging across the water at full throttle. As she came into view, Benjamin could see she was terrified; he'd never seen her so scared before.

He waded into the water to get her attention, but before he could shout to her, Tweakie hit a wave and took off into the air. She lost control of the jet ski and it flipped right over, smashing into her in mid air.

It hit the water upside down and sank. So did Tweakie.

This wasn't happening. They couldn't be dead. They just couldn't.

Benjamin started wading into the sea. He was going to swim out and pull them free. All four of them. They weren't going to die on his watch. No, sir.

Tatyana grabbed him and tried to pull him back to the shore, but he shrugged her off and kept going. But she wouldn't let up.

"Let me go," he said. "I've got to go save them. Let me go."

"You're not thinking straight. You're not going to save them. You're going to kill yourself."

"Get off me. I can save them. I can!"

"They're dead, Benjamin, dead. You can't save them!"

She was crying, and Benjamin realised he was, too. Great heaving sobs of grief broke out of him and he hugged Tatyana tight. They were quite far out and the waves were knocking them back and forth, so they turned and struggled back to the shore.

"Stay in the sea," Miriam shouted. "You're safer there. They won't follow you in."

The zombies still weren't under control. They were highly agitated. Some looked seriously dangerous, like cornered beasts, ready to spring.

The sea was cold and Benjamin was only wearing a dead man's shirt and slacks. The salt water stung the wound on his shoulder. His feet were numb and so were his nuts; he and Tatyana started to shiver. Even so, there was no way either of them were going to leave the water and face the zombies right now.

The chopper moved out over the water to where the yacht had sunk and then headed inland. This almost seemed like a signal. All the debris had stopped burning and Miriam's incantation began to work. The zombies became quiet and subdued again.

Benjamin's teeth were chattering as he waded back to the shore. There was a real chill in the night wind. He and Tatyana clung on to each other, not just for warmth, but also out of fear and grief, the two things that united them most at that moment.

There was a sudden burst of gunfire followed by controlled jets of flame from two flame throwers. A squadron of armed guards came into view. They were surrounded. The zombies started flailing and groaning again.

"Do not attempt to move," a voice called out through a megaphone. "We're authorised to use extreme force. We know there's three of you trying to steal the zombies. Lie face down on the ground and do not move until we've rounded them all up."

"Steal the zombies?" said Benjamin. "Do you believe these guys?"

"Be quiet and do as they say," said Miriam.

Benjamin turned to argue with her but he couldn't find her. He kept looking at where she ought to be but he couldn't see her. It felt as though his sight kept being pushed to one side.

Tatyana grabbed him and pulled him to the ground.

"Hey," he complained, but she pushed his head down. Miriam started chanting something in the strange language of the spirits.

"Hey, they're all moving," said a voice.

"Hold your fire," said another. "They're coming peacefully."

"What is this?" said someone else. "They ain't attacking or nothing? Look at them, they're just walking."

"Is it a trap?"

"Nah, it's gotta be somethin' the boss-man's done. That's Voodoo, that is. He's hexed 'em or somethin'."

"Well I ain't gonna complain. Last thing I want is to tussle with a flesh eater."

Benjamin glanced around him. The zombies weren't moving. They were all standing still or rocking from side to side.

"I don't see anyone in among the zombies either."

"They must've run off and ditched them. Thought I heard something in the water."

"Or maybe the zombies got out by themselves."

"Could be."

Benjamin listened as the footsteps of the guards receded. He got to his feet and helped Tatyana up.

"Was that you?" Tatyana said to Miriam. "Did you do that?"

"It was a simple illusion to get them out the way," Miriam said. "It won't hold for long, though. And if they run into anyone else it will be broken. We need to get out of here."

"Where are we going to go?" said Tatyana. "We can't get off the island now."

"Do you know where this Voodoo temple is?" said Benjamin. "The one where they're doing the ceremony?"

"The *Ounfó*," said Miriam. "Of course I do. But we can't go there."

"Why not? It's the last place they'll expect us to go. Which means we'll have the element of surprise."

"Yeah," said Tatyana. "But aren't we trying to escape them? I mean, why would we want to go to the one place where the most people are gathered?"

"'Cause it'll scare the shit out of them," said Benjamin. "Think about it, most of them are in a big daze from the ceremony. Now imagine a great horde of blood-thirsty zombies suddenly appearing out of nowhere, with no cages to hold them in and no encounter leaders to help them out. Everyone's going to freak out. There'll be panic and confusion. No-one will know what's going on."

"Okay," said Tatyana. "I guess that'll give a temporary advantage. But what about afterwards? What happens then?"

"Well no-one's going to hang around in the temple, are they? Not with an army of zombies milling around. So we'll have it to ourselves. It's right in the middle of the island, right, surrounded by jungle so it's going to be really hard to get troops in to attack the place. They won't be able to track us in the chopper 'cause the vegetation's too dense. And... wait, I've just realised, that's where all the souls are kept right?"

"Right."

"So, aren't they like the most valuable things on the island? If we're occupying the Ounfó, we can hold them to ransom. We'll have something to bargain with. Maybe enough to get us off the island."

"Do you know," said Miriam. "That is the first and only intelligent thing I've heard you say. Come, let's go."

With that she turned and led the zombies away from the shore. Benjamin wasn't certain whether she was being complimentary or if she'd just insulted him again.

Tatyana held his hand. "Well done," she said. "You're not such a dickhead after all."

"What the fuck is her problem?"

"I don't know," said Tatyana, smiling at him. "It's dark, y'know. Maybe she hasn't seen how cute you are yet."

Now it was his turn to smile. "Thanks. We better catch her up. We've still got a ways to go."

CHAPTER TWENTY-FIVE

Doc Papa had swallowed a lot of salt water. He coughed and retched it up onto the sand while Felippe stood guard to make sure no-one saw.

He was pleased with his work on the yacht, although he was aware that he now owed Agwe a great favour. He owed many of the Loa. Notching up debts as he built his empire, Doc Papa had promised much to the whole pantheon of Loa, more than any Houngan could ever pay back in a normal lifetime. When his plans came to fruition, however, he would more than wipe the slate clean.

Felippe handed him a bottle of water, and he rinsed his mouth and spat. He composed himself and returned to the jeep. Tomlinson looked worried. "I'm afraid there's another problem, sir," he said.

"I've just finished sorting out your last problem. What's happened now?"

"It's the zombies, sir. They've... well, they've disappeared."

"Disappeared! What do you mean?"

"The men rounded them up from the harbour as you ordered. But as they were escorting them back to base, they vanished. One minute they could see them all. The next minute they couldn't. I don't understand it myself."

"That's because you're an idiot. What about the three rogue guests? Do you have them in custody?"

"No, sir."

Tomlinson fought to keep his composure in front of his men as Doc Papa bristled. "The men never apprehended the guests. They weren't there when they recaptured the zombies. They reported some commotion in the water as they arrived, and assumed the guests had deserted the zombies and tried to swim for the yacht. I imagine they were killed when it exploded."

"You don't have any imagination. And your assumption is almost as stupid as your men's. Has the chopper been able to locate them?"

"No, sir. I've had it circling the area, but I haven't heard anything yet."

Doc Papa turned away from the idiot. He let his mind roam out into the invisible world, tracing the paths of the spirits and the demons.

"Sir, if I could just..." Tomlinson said behind him.

Doc Papa raised his hand to silence the man.

"But, sir..." Tomlinson persisted.

Doc Papa brought his thumb and middle finger together and Tomlinson's wind pipe constricted. As Tomlinson choked, his hands at his throat, Doc Papa let his mind roam once again.

Out in the jungles, where the spirits of the trees and the demons of the hunt roamed free, he found a collective zombie mind. It was a strong one. He had never encountered one so united. There were almost traces of innate intelligence in it. No wait, there was more. There was a human mind guiding them, one that knew Voodoo.

So that's why they hadn't been spotted. They were hiding in the jungle. But who was controlling them? Doc Papa edged closer to the zombies' group mind, homing in on their guide, but before he could get any closer he was out. The mind he had been looking for had detected him and pushed him away.

He tried to find them again but he couldn't get anywhere near. Whoever was controlling them was obviously skilled and powerful. But who were they? It couldn't be either of the trust fund babies. They were too young and feckless and there was nothing in their backgrounds to suggest they'd had any exposure to Voodoo.

It had to be the Chevalier woman. Her husband's family originally came from St Ignatius, but he was in real estate and her family were Catholics. Could she have been secretly trained? Surely he would have detected it if she had. Why had she come here? What was she doing with the undead?

Doc Papa slipped out of the invisible world and released Tomlinson from the choking spell. He waited while the man gasped for air and regained his composure.

"The zombies are in the jungle," Doc Papa said. "They're staying away from the paths and are hidden by the undergrowth. That's why the chopper didn't spot them. Your men never captured them. They were most likely taken in by an illusion."

"But who's doing this sir? My men said the three guests weren't with them. You're not suggesting they're acting by themselves?"

"Don't embarrass yourself more than you already have. Of course one of the guests is controlling them. Your men didn't see them because that was all part of the illusion. One of the guests is skilled in the service of the Loa."

"I'm sorry, sir?"

"They know Voodoo, you fool, and somehow they managed to evade my detection."

"I'll send every available guard into the jungle to round the zombies up, sir."

"To be honest, I'm more worried about the guests. I need them under strict control. Send a squadron of your men into the jungle to track down the zombies. I'll aid them through invisible means a little later. In the meantime, I want all available men posted to the harbour, the air field and the guest's quarters. I don't want anyone getting off this island. The whole of St Ignatius is on lockdown. Do you understand?"

"Perfectly, sir."

"Do not let me down again, Tomlinson. This is your very last opportunity to get off this island alive. Am I making myself clear?"

"Crystal, sir."

"Good."

CHAPTER TWENTY-SIX

BENJAMIN HAD A fucking hard on. This was the ultimate. This was what it was all about. He had never been so pumped in his life.

This was everything he'd been fantasising about since he first saw *Dawn of the Dead*. He was turning up with a whole posse of noble monsters to crash a party stuffed full of the type of dead-eyed phonies and snobs his step father hung out with. He was about to tear down the whole stifling world he'd grown up in.

Every fantasy he'd ever had about letting a horde of zombies loose among the privileged elite was about to come true. Let's see who didn't fit in now. He couldn't believe his luck. This was real payback.

The Ounfó, as Miriam called the temple, was in sight. The sound of the drums was furious, covering the noise of their approach.

"What are we waiting for?" Benjamin said. "Let's charge the place."

"Wait," said Miriam. "We have to do this carefully. I don't want anyone to get hurt."

"Why'd you care about not hurting these people? You've seen what they're capable of."

"And I've also seen what you're capable of, in their company."

"Oh, come on, that's totally different. That's not me. I only did those things to infiltrate them. I'm not part of their world."

"How can you afford to come here if you're not part of their world?" said Miriam. She really knew how to kill his buzz.

He turned to Tatyana. "Tell her. Tell her I'm not like them."

"It's 'cause you're *not* like them that you *won't* want anyone to get hurt," said Tatyana. "It's only when you try and fit in with them that you're not yourself. When you're not with them you puke at the sight of corpses, you don't try and make more."

The two of them were determined to bring him down. His stomach turned over at the thought of the corpses hanging in the compound. He thought about the things he'd done to blend in with the guests and he felt a stab of anger and hatred.

He wanted to punish them for what they'd made him become. His whole life they'd been trying to turn him into someone he wasn't. On this island they'd finally succeeded.

He imagined charging into the place with the zombies, locking the doors and letting them feed. He remembered all the horrific things he'd seen the zombies do while on the island. Then he pictured the guests suffering at their undead hands.

He saw Richard in the midst of his fantasy, trapped with all the other guests. He lingered on Richard's face as the zombies struck and wiped the smugness and superiority off it for good.

Then he imagined his mother next to Richard. He thought of the terror and pain that would be on her face. He felt a pang of raw emotion at the thought of his mother in peril. He wanted to protect her at all costs. He wanted to kill anything that came near her. He hated anything that would hurt her. He hated... he...

Surely not, he didn't... he couldn't hate... For a minute there he had though. He had *hated* the zombies. When he thought of what they might do to someone he loved, he saw them as monsters, as pure killing machines with nothing noble about them.

Miriam turned and looked him straight in the eyes. "You are carrying too much pain and hatred inside you," she said. "The weight of it is bruising your soul; you are close to realising this. Let the pain go."

That pain had defined him. His hatred and his anger had fed him, given him strength. If he let them go then he wouldn't be himself. Who would he be?

"Look, there isn't time for this," he said. "We've got to get these nobl... I mean these undead to safety."

"It is not for you or I to decide the appropriate time," she said. "That is God's prerogative. He has instructed His Loa and they move through me. Give me your hands."

He held out his hands and Miriam took them in her own. Her hands were warm and soft and pulsed with energy.

"It's okay," she said, smiling.

God, she had a beautiful smile. He could forgive her anything when she smiled like that. All the put-downs and the ball busting, everything.

She chanted soft words in Creole that sounded like music being poured out of a crystal container. He heard a name repeated over and over – Erzulie Dantò. He focused on the name and it seemed to resonate within him. As though someone had struck a tuning fork and his soul was vibrating in sympathy.

He was aware of a huge painful weight on his chest, stopping him breathing. He felt like he was going to fall backwards, it was so heavy. Then invisible arms caught him, encircled him and lifted him back up.

They were like the arms of his mother, of everyone's mother. There was peace, serenity and most of all love in them. A love that gave and accepted without measure or compunction.

As Miriam held his hands and continued to chant, the arms moved through him and took hold of the weight on his chest. Then slowly, as though they were removing a foreign object embedded in his flesh, the hands began to remove the weight.

As it was lifted from him, Benjamin felt the memories flood back in and he saw where the pain and the anger came from. Benjamin hated Richard because he blamed him for everything his Dad had done to hurt his Mom. He couldn't blame his Dad because he loved him, so he blamed Richard. He feared Richard would hurt his Mom.

He hated Richard's world because he couldn't live up to what it expected of him. He had failed. No, there was more to it than that. He *had* failed, but *what* had he failed?

As the weight on his chest got less and less, he found himself back in the kitchen with his mother sobbing on the floor. He realised then it was his mother he had failed. He hadn't protected her as he promised he would.

He really meant it when he handed her his handkerchief. He'd wanted to look after her. To rescue her. But he hadn't. He'd let Richard take her and make her unhappy. He'd never forgiven himself and he'd blamed her for that.

That was what had driven a wedge between them. That was where his pain came from and why he was so angry.

Then he felt a presence in his mind. It was foreign but totally familiar, wise but innocent and ancient but fresh. It was the mother, the sister and the lover he had always yearned for. It was a Loa, he realised. The one Miriam had named: Erzulie Dantò.

She spoke to him without using words. She told him the pain was no longer his and he was to let it go. Then she passed through him, took the pain, and was gone.

He felt so much loss when she left. Suddenly, more than anything in the world, he wanted his mother.

He broke down and cried like a little boy. Like his mother that day on the kitchen floor. Like a young man confronting himself for the first time.

Two sets of arms encircled him, real arms, Miriam's and Tatyana's. He rested his head on their shoulders and sobbed.

All around them the zombies rocked from foot to foot and began a low moan, like the wind keening around the corner of a building. Benjamin couldn't be certain, but it felt like they were sympathising.

The drums ceased as he stopped crying.

"It's time," Miriam said. "Are you okay to do this?"

He nodded and wiped his eyes on his sleeve. "Let's go."

CHAPTER TWENTY-SEVEN

It was pandemonium, as Tatyana thought it would be. Zombies jostled her on all sides. She was practising zombie breathing and moving with care; she was under Miriam's protection, but she wasn't going to take risks.

The zombies were excited. They could smell fresh blood and fear. The instinct to feed was beginning to override their behaviour. Tatyana could sense their group mind splintering. Only Miriam was holding it together. Her mind straddled the group mind, guiding it like a rider steers a horse.

Miriam was conducting the whole operation from outside the Ounfó. Before she sent in the zombies, they had cased the place, finding a yard out front full of trees, some of which were painted bright colours. Miriam explained that they were sanctuaries for the Loas.

Beyond the yard was a walled courtyard with a high roof and a bare earth floor. This was the Peristyle, where all the major ceremonies took place. To the rear of that was a small square building, the Holy of Holies, where only the Houngan or Mambo – the high priest or priestess – and his or her close circle of acolytes could enter.

Tatyana was enthralled. She felt something deep inside herself open up as Miriam spoke about Voodoo and serving the Loa, something she hadn't thought existed. Like a hunger for something she'd never tasted.

It seemed more than just a fascination with the forbidden topic of religion. She was genuinely excited about seeing everything inside the Ounfó. Miriam's descriptions and explanations left her exhilarated and confused. Was it Miriam? Did she just have a crush on her, or was there more to it?

Tacked on the back of the Holy of Holies was a building Miriam knew nothing about, all hi-tech chrome and glass. It looked totally out of place and gave them all a bad feeling.

Miriam went back round to the yard out front. She tapped the lower branches of a tree and a snake appeared, curling around her arm.

Miriam whispered to the snake; Tatyana heard her say the words "Dambala Wédo Yé-H-we" several times.

The snake seemed hypnotised by Miriam's words. She placed it on the ground and it slithered rapidly towards the side entrance of the Peristyle. The zombies followed it.

Miriam told Tatyana to go in with them and not be afraid, she would be protected. Her job was to make sure that the guests all got out unharmed. Miriam would remain outside with Benjamin until the Ounfó was cleared.

Tatyana was surprised that Benjamin didn't make any objections to this. He still seemed spaced out after the healing Miriam had performed on him. He was definitely changed, sweeter and less likely to fly into a rage.

The guests were still groggy from the ceremony as Tatyana and the zombies entered, but the sight of so many unsupervised zombies pouring into the place soon woke them up.

They couldn't have looked more horrified if their whole stock portfolio had just been wiped out.

"Jesus fucking Christ!" Sam McKane, the grey haired Texan, said, jumping to his feet. "It's an invasion. We're being invaded."

"Where the hell did they come from?" Arthur Sonnenfeldt said, trying to dive behind Sam. "There's so many of them. How'd they get out of the compound?"

More and more zombies filled the Peristyle, which was still littered with the remnants of the ceremony. Zombies skidded in the animal blood on the earthen floor. Their feet trampled the intricate patterns drawn in powder on the ground. The clouds of white dust they kicked up added to the confusion.

Tatyana saw Bessie, the red-headed woman she last saw trying to gnaw some guy's penis off, go into hysterics. She screamed, an honest to goodness scream of terror just like in the movies.

This was the cue for the rest of the guests to bolt for the entrance. Too many people hit the doorway at once. There was a jam and they began to push and shove each other.

One young guy punched an elderly male zombie in the face. Tatyana heard bones crack and saw dead skin tear, but the zombie hardly moved. It just bit at his fist when it smelled the fresh blood on his scraped knuckles and reached for him.

He kicked the zombie in the midriff to keep it away and fell over on his back. When he saw how ravenous the zombie had become, the man scrambled to his feet and scampered away.

A stocky man with sandy brown hair picked up a censer full of flaming oil and tried to ward them off, spilling onto his own shirt and setting it alight. He panicked and ran for the door, colliding with the tall guy, George Griffin. George pushed him away and he and two others got the man down and rolled him on the ground as he howled in pain.

Tatyana wended her way through the zombies as the last of the guests spilled into the yard outside. She watched from the doorway as they spread out and ran between the trees.

Snakes dropped out of the lower branches, dangling by their tails and hissing with menace or landing on the ground in front of the fleeing guests; the guests changed direction and ran through the middle of the yard. Miriam was shepherding the guests, making certain they went where she wanted.

Tatyana heard a scuffle over at the other end of the Peristyle. The creepy priest Vincenzo, and some other men dressed in white, came out of the Holy of Holies.

One of the acolytes raced through the zombies, waving a ceremonial flag and chanting as he ran to the multi coloured pole in the centre of the Peristyle. What had Miriam called it? The Poteau Mitain.

There was a coiled leather whip hanging from the side of the Poteau Mitain. The acolyte climbed on the pedestal at the base of the Poteau Mitain, took the whip down and began to crack it over the heads of the zombies.

The zombies all stopped and turned to look at him. He waved his flag back and forth and used the whip to corral the zombies.

"*Rete. Dans le nom des Gédé – Rete!*"

He was calling the zombies to heel and it was working.

Shit, what was going to happen if they lost control of the zombies? Tatyana started to edge towards the entrance so she could slip out unseen. As she did, she looked up and saw a giant constrictor curling its way down the Poteau Mitain.

The acolyte with the whip hadn't seen it. As he barked orders at the zombies in Creole it wound its way closer to him. He didn't see the snake until it slipped round his neck. His hands went up to it, but its coils were too strong. It pulled tight around his neck, crushing his windpipe.

The acolyte's face turned purple. He dropped the flag and the whip and clawed at the constrictor as his eyes bulged. Tatyana heard the crack of his neck breaking and the man fell to the floor.

The zombies nearest him smelled the fresh corpse and closed in on the dead body. Their jaws working in anticipation, they knelt and began to tear strips off him. Vincenzo and the other acolytes turned and ran back into the Holy of Holies. Tatyana heard their footsteps race through the Ounfó and into the hi-tech building behind it.

"Let them go," said Miriam. "The Ounfó is ours."

She looked around at the Peristyle. Some of the zombies were fighting over the corpse, scrabbling for the last few shreds. Others were milling around inspecting the space, staring at it as though they were trying to recapture some distant memory of their former life.

"I grew up attending this Ounfó," Miriam said. "I was initiated here, I became its Mambo and led the congregation for years. Yet now it seems as foreign to me as it must to you."

CHAPTER TWENTY-EIGHT

THEY LEFT THE zombies in the Peristyle and went into the Holy of Holies. Tatyana felt honoured. She could see Benjamin was curious and excited to be allowed into the inner-sanctum too.

The entrance chamber was lit by candles and had crude paintings of Catholic icons on the walls. Miriam explained that these were representations of the Loa that blessed the temple. On one wall was a picture of a dark-skinned St Patrick chasing the snakes out of Ireland. This represented Dambala the snake Loa of the heavens. On the opposite wall was a painting of Our Lady of the Immaculate Conception, who was the Catholic equivalent of Ayida Wédo, the rainbow Loa married to Dambala.

"Wait. I don't understand," said Tatyana. "How can you be a Catholic when you practice magic?"

"Voodoo is not magic," Miriam said. "It is a religion. One that embraces Catholicism."

"So you believe in God, but you worship spirits? How can that be?"

"God is in all things, all places and all times. People often ask how He can allow a thing to happen. They do not understand that He allows all things to happen out of His love for us. However, because He knows we look for divine guidance and intervention in our lives at a level He is too great to provide, he created the Loa to be his intermediaries. We serve the Loa because they fulfil the greater will of God."

Tatyana nodded thoughtfully as they passed through a coloured hanging into the main chamber. "Makes a lot of sense."

At the far end of the chamber was a stone altar, carrying a huge assortment of objects. There were dolls in ceremonial dress, Catholic icons, ritual rattles, jars and pots of strange herbs, flags, amulets and charms and several representations of serpents, including a large stuffed snake.

"That is the Pé," said Miriam. "This one is sanctified to the Loa Dambala. The other two chambers through there have their own Pés blessed by Ayida Wédo and Erzulie Dantò."

They didn't go through these other chambers. Miriam took them, instead, into another room. "This is the *Djévo* where the initiations take place. Normally you would never be allowed in here, but these are exceptional times. The Ounfó has been desecrated and I believe the Loas have brought you into their service." Miriam peered through the gloom. "That door should not be there."

On the other side of the room, standing open, was a solid steel security door. It had a huge circular handle in the middle, like the door of a bank vault.

Tatyana walked over and peered through it. "This must lead to that hi-tech building we saw."

Benjamin put his hand on her shoulder. "Careful. They could still be in there."

"I'm pretty sure I heard them running out," said Tatyana. They heard the engine of a jeep start up outside. "I think that means they're going."

They walked through an empty entrance chamber into a room that was filled with banks of computer screens.

"This doesn't look like Voodoo to me," said Benjamin.

"No," said Miriam. "This is anything but Voodoo."

On the other side of the room, the walls were lined with row after row of sealed glass compartments, holding the earthenware containers Doc Papa had called Pot-tets. A fine white mist swirled around each container and frost ferns were forming on the inside of many of the compartments. A gauge on the front showed the temperature inside the compartments was way below freezing.

At the opposite end of the long room were several huge tanks of liquid nitrogen. A network of tubes ran along the walls from the tanks to the compartments.

"Cryogenics," said Benjamin. "This is a cryogenics facility. They're freezing all the souls once they capture them, but why?"

"To numb them," said Miriam. "To put them to sleep and tie them to the earthly plane."

"So, does Voodoo include science as well as Christianity?" said Tatyana.

"Not this type of science," said Miriam. "Doc Papa has displaced the Loa of this Ounfó and made bargains with many other Loa who do not look kindly on St Ignatius or its people. Dambala and Ayida Wedo are not pleased with him or what he has done to their Ounfó."

"Like building this soul bank," said Benjamin. "And using it to freeze people's souls and stuff?"

"Precisely. He has desecrated this Ounfó and he has perverted our most sacred ceremonies."

"You mean that ceremony we took part in, to remove our souls?" said Tatyana. "That wasn't proper Voodoo?"

"There is no right or wrong Voodoo. But there is Voodoo that harms and Voodoo that heals and strengthens. The ceremony that you took part in was a twisted version of a ceremony that has been central to our worship for years."

"But you don't want to remove people's souls and capture them, right?" said Tatyana.

"No. The ceremony is called the Lave Tet; it means the 'washing of the head.' It is a ceremony in which the initiate is married to their patron Loa. The Pot-tet is prepared as a place for their Gros Bon Ange to reside while their Met Tet, or patron Loa, is inside them. When they die, their soul will also return to the Pot-tet on the way to the afterlife. This is meant to strengthen the soul and allow it to grow. Not to imprison it and hold it to ransom."

"No wonder the Loa are pissed off with him then."

"Indeed."

"There's loads of souls, though," said Benjamin. "Just about everyone on the island must have banked their soul here."

"It looks that way, doesn't it?" said Miriam.

A sudden burst of gunfire made them all jump.

"We know you're in there," said a voice from outside. "We have you surrounded. There's no use trying to run. Come out of the building and leave the zombies behind."

"What are we going to do?" said Tatyana.

"They won't try and storm the place," said Benjamin. "They can't risk damaging the soul bank or harming the zombies."

"Yeah, but we can't get out of here either," said Tatyana. "They've got us trapped."

"Their presence here is completely immaterial," said Miriam. "The Loa wish us to leave, but before we do we must perform a service for them."

"How can we leave when the place is surrounded?" said Tatyana.

"I thought we were going to use the souls to bargain our way out," said Benjamin.

"All will become clear in a little while," said Miriam. "First, we need to shut down the power to this building."

"I can do that," said Benjamin. "There's got to be fuse box, or a breaker board around here. I'm sure I can find it."

"Good. Please do that quickly."

Benjamin scampered off while Miriam took Tatyana back through to the Holy of Holies. She picked up a pole and used it to open a trapdoor in the ceiling of one of the chambers. Then she stood on a box and pulled herself up through the trapdoor. She reached out a hand for Tatyana. "Here, come on up."

Tatyana climbed into a narrow crawl space. Miriam led her to a tiny room just large enough for the two of them to sit up in. It had six large windows with no glass in them, only angled wooden slats.

"This is an old observatory," whispered Miriam. "It was built in the days when we had foreign missionaries and soldiers on St Ignatius. They feared our religion and tried to suppress it. At times the congregation had to keep watch for them. You can see the surrounding jungle from here without being seen."

Tatyana peered through the slats. She could see about ten men stationed around the Ounfó. Most were hiding behind trees and palms, looking hot and scared.

"I thought you said that Voodoo accepted Christianity," said Tatyana in a low whisper. "How come the missionaries wanted to persecute you?"

"Sadly they still see our religion as superstition and devil worship, no matter what we believe. Voodoo has also played a big part in the struggle against foreign oppression. So whether the occupiers are French or American, they have always tried to suppress us."

Tatyana jumped as the slats in the window she was leaning against started to rattle as though a fierce wind was blowing them. Three other sets of slats did the same, even though there wasn't the slightest breeze.

"Get down!" said Miriam. She pulled Tatyana to the floor as the slats splintered.

Gunfire raked the small observation room as Tatyana and Miriam pressed themselves to the floor with their hands over their heads. Tatyana could hear the bullets whistle and crack as they hit the wood inches above her head. They began to wriggle down the crawlspace as the whole observatory fell apart and blew away in a bodiless wind.

"What's happening?" said Tatyana as they dropped back into the chamber.

"I believe it's Doc Papa," Miriam said. "He's attacking us through the invisible world." A commotion broke out in the Peristyle. Tatyana could hear the zombies bellow and moan as she and Miriam ran to see what it was.

Tatyana watched as Miriam strode into the Peristyle and began chanting something. Some of the zombies became quiet and placid straight away, but many raged and fought among themselves.

Miriam's voice grew weaker and she put her hands to her head as though in great pain. She stumbled and fell to her knees. Tatyana went to help her, but Miriam waved her away. She was holding her throat and coughing. The zombies nearest Tatyana turned towards her, scenting her blood, and began to advance. With great care Tatyana stepped back inside the Holy of Holies. She was in danger, but she couldn't leave Miriam.

Miriam rallied, stopped coughing and seemed to gather herself. She got to her feet and sang out her incantation in a voice so clear and loud it seemed to still every other sound in the jungle.

The zombies fell silent. There was no sound for a moment and not even the air moved. Miriam strode back inside the Holy of Holies with her head high.

"We do not have much time."

The lights went out as soon as they stepped into the hi-tech building. The computers died and, with a click and a hiss, the cryogenic units stopped humming.

Benjamin appeared, carrying a lit candle. "Told you it wouldn't be a problem. I found these in a cupboard." He handed candles to Tatyana and Miriam and lit them from his. "What was happening outside?"

"We were under magical attack," said Miriam. "Doc Papa was trying to neutralise us so his men could move in and round up the zombies. We're safe for the time being, but we need to work fast. We have to get all the Pot-tets out of their compartments and arrange them on the floor."

"We'll have break the glass to get them out," said Benjamin. "But we can't touch them. They'll take the skin off our hands, they're so cold."

They hunted around the room in the candlelight. Benjamin found a couple of pairs of large steel tongs that must have been used to lift the Pot-tets into the compartments. He handed one to Tatyana then swung his into the door of a compartment. The glass shattered.

"Come on," said Benjamin. "There's loads, and we don't have long."

When they were done Miriam returned, holding a large flask of oil and a broom. She told Benjamin to clear away all the glass while she and Tatyana arranged the Pot-tets in a particular formation on the floor.

Once the floor was clear and the containers were in place, Miriam uncorked the flask and poured out the oil, drawing an intricate pattern around the Pot-tets.

"You're drawing one of those patterns I keep seeing everywhere," said Tatyana. "What are they called?"

"Vèvès," said Miriam. "They're used in most ceremonies. They represent a sacred geometry that creates a space for heavenly bodies to dwell. They reproduce the astral forces of the Loa and act as a beacon that calls them to our world."

"Do you have like, different Vèvès for every Loa then?"

"And every ceremony, yes. This is the Vèvè for the ritual of the Boulez-Zain-Les-Mort."

"I'm sorry to keep coming out with questions, but do you mind if ask what that is?" Tatyana said.

"No, I don't mind. There are forces at work here that compel you to ask those questions, and oblige me to answer them. You remember I told you that for a while the souls of the dead initiates return to their Pot-tets? They do this to shelter from the immense cold they feel after their earthly body has died. The Pot-tets is filled with remnants of their earthly form so they feel safe there.

"We must feed and nurture the deceased souls so they're strong enough to walk the roads of the dead and join the Loas in heaven. The Boulez-Zain-Les-Mort is a fire rite to warm the dead souls and set them on their way to heaven. Because the souls in these Pot-tets are not initiates and aren't dead it won't have that effect on them. It *will* break the spell they are under, though, and that will sabotage this whole soul bank."

"What will happen to all the souls?"

"Unless they return to their living bodies they'll be trapped on the earthly plane, unable to leave the Pot-tets. Without any strength or sustenance they'll begin to wither and slowly fade, denying their owners any chance of immortality in the afterlife."

"Whoa, that's harsh."

"Not as harsh as the fate to which these people condemned my fellow islanders," said Miriam, finishing off the Vèvè. "And it doesn't deny them the possibility of redemption."

She bent and set a candle to the oil. The flames raced round the Vèvè and crackled around the Pot-tets.

Miriam raised her arms in a gesture of great reverence and began to chant. "*O vèvè Voudoun vè, Bon Dié O! O vélà Kounn tié. Vélà Kounn tié! Dambala Wédo Kounn tié!*"

The flames leapt higher. The heat was immense. Tatyana and Benjamin had to retreat. Miriam seemed unaffected. The seals on the Pot-tets began to melt with the heat.

Tatyana heard a scream that seemed to come from as far away in time as it did in space. As it got closer, she felt it not just with her ears but with her whole mind and body. As the scream got louder, it drowned out every other sensation until it was too painful to bear. For the sake of her mind and her sanity, she let go of her consciousness.

CHAPTER TWENTY-NINE

COLD. SOMETHING WAS cold. His cheek. The side of his face. Benjamin's mind drifted back to his body. The cold sensation was like an anchor dragging him back to the present.

He became aware of his body. His shoulder hurt; he was lying on his side on a hard floor. He opened his eyes and sat up. Where was he? He didn't recognise the room. It was dark and shadows flickered warily across the broken glass boxes on the walls, as though afraid of cutting themselves.

A woman was standing in front of him holding a candle. Tatyana moved next to him. Tatyana! He recognised her, his first concrete memory. It stirred up others.

He was on an island – St Ignatius – in a cryogenics lab. There were souls in those pots. The spell that held them had been broken.

There was more. His Mom – he'd let go of the pain. He felt a sense of loss at this memory. No, not loss, lightness. The loss was for his Mom – the closeness they no longer felt. He missed that. He missed his Mom.

The woman offered him her hand. Miriam, that was her name. It didn't suit her. It was wrong somehow. He stood with her help.

"Miriam," he said. "That's not your real name, is it?"

"It's the name I wear with this body."

She was being mysterious again. She was like that. She'd trust them with a little bit of information then she'd pull back. He bent down and helped Tatyana to her feet. Miriam gave them candles.

"That was intense," Tatyana said. "Was I out for long?"

"Only a matter of minutes," said Miriam. "It was only because you were so close to the point of release that you passed out at all. The others will be unconscious for a long time."

"The others?" said Benjamin. "You mean the people whose souls were banked?"

"Yes, the ritual set off a... shockwave. It will have hit them hardest. I think it's time for us to leave."

"Where are we going to go?" said Tatyana.

"We need somewhere more fortified. I can't keep us all safe in the Ounfó. There's an abandoned copper mine about twenty minutes from here. We can hide out there until the time is right."

"Right for what?"

"To bring my people back."

"And how long will that be?" said Benjamin.

"Less than a day now. But come, we need to get going before the guards come around."

She left the cryogenics room and Tatyana went with her. Benjamin took one last look at the rows of shattered glass compartments and the blistered Pot-tets.

The seals on the charred earthenware containers were broken. In the wavering candlelight, Benjamin was sure the Pot-tets were making a noise. Not one he could hear directly; If he listened for it, it wasn't there. It was like those things that you only saw out of the corner of your eye, except you could only hear this out of the corner of your ear, if there was such a thing.

It wasn't a good noise. It was mournful and full of regret, like a wail of loss or a scream of self-hatred. He suddenly felt extremely unnerved and realised that he didn't want to be in this room anymore. In fact he never wanted to be in there again.

Benjamin joined Miriam and Tatyana in the main chamber of the Holy of Holies. They were watching an elderly female zombie standing in front of the Pé. The zombie was trying to pick up some of the pots on the stone altar and open them, but her dead fingers fumbled with the lids.

The zombie was transfixed by the stuffed snake on the altar. She put out her hand and her fingers brushed against the scales of the serpent. Benjamin had never seen a zombie do anything with such gentleness.

Her hand fell on a bowl full of white powder. She lifted it to her face and sniffed. Some of the powder stuck to the dry wrinkled skin of her face, giving it an almost comical look.

With even more care than before, she put her hand into the bowl. Benjamin could see her hands twitch as the wasted and rotting muscles of her arm fought to fulfil a simple task. Even so, she was able to lift some of the powder between her fingers and shake it onto the floor.

"She remembers," said Tatyana. "It's like she's drawing one of those things, a Vèvè. "

"In her day she was one of the most skilled and proficient of the Ounsi," said Miriam. "Her work was spectacular. No Ounfó was ever blessed with a better artist."

"So you know her then?"

"I ought to, she gave birth to and raised me."

"That's your mother?" said Benjamin.

He was suddenly moved by what Miriam must be going through. She was surrounded by the walking corpses of all the people she cared most for. He couldn't imagine how she felt. He remembered how he felt watching his Mom change when she married Richard. She'd been so full of fun when it was just the two of them. She was as much his best buddy as his Mom.

Then Richard came along and she totally altered to fit in with what he expected from a wife. As she became more formal and joyless each day, it was like something inside her died. But that was nothing like what Miriam was facing.

If anything, it was similar to what his great aunt had gone through when her second husband lost his mind. She had to watch him become a shell of his former self. There was nothing left of him at the end.

That was only *one* loved one. Miriam had to cope with her whole community becoming less than human. Benjamin began to feel ashamed that he'd actually referred to them as noble monsters. He had no idea at the time, but even still, no wonder she was such a bitch to him.

Miriam led her mother out into the Peristyle where they collected the other zombies and left the Ounfó. As they walked past the unconscious soldiers slumped over their weapons among the foliage the sky began to lighten. It would be morning soon.

"Were you close to your mother?" Benjamin asked.

Miriam shook her head. "We fought constantly. We were too alike, both headstrong. The last time we spoke I told her I never wanted to see her again. I wish I could take those words back."

"What did you fight about?" said Tatyana.

"A man. She never approved of my lovers. And it pains me to say it, but this time she was right."

"Was it one of the men here?" said Tatyana. "I mean, you know..."

"Yes, I know what you mean. And no, he isn't undead, but he is here on the island. In fact he now runs it."

"What?" said Benjamin. "You mean Doc Papa was your lover? I don't believe it."

"I'm afraid it's true."

"But that can't be. I don't understand. How come he didn't recognise you the minute he saw you? Why didn't he guess what you were going to do?"

"For a start, he thinks I'm dead and that he was the one who killed me. Secondly, as you quite rightly guessed back there in the Ounfó, Miriam isn't my real name, and this isn't the body I was born with."

"Now you've really lost me."

"What is your real name then?" said Tatyana.

"It's Brigitte. Brigitte Laveau."

CHAPTER THIRTY

A Year Ago

"BEHOLD, I TELL you a mystery. We shall all indeed rise again: but we shall not all be changed. In a moment, in the twinkling of an eye, at the last trumpet: for the trumpet shall sound and the dead shall rise again incorruptible. And we shall be changed..."

Oliver gripped Brigitte's hand as the priest droned on. It was the first sign that he was letting go of his emotions, like a sudden drop in temperature signals a coming storm. His shoulders started to shake. She put her arm around his waist. He dropped his head on her shoulder and began to sob. "Oh, Miriam, Miriam, Miriam," was all he could say.

"*Anima ejus, et ánimæ ómnium fidélium defunctórum, per misericórdiam Dei requiéscant in pace. Amen,*" the priest intoned as the coffin was lowered into the grave.

The air was still and the sun shone bright. It was unseasonably warm even for New Orleans, as though the weather was trying to make reparations for the fury it had unleashed so recently.

The familiarity her new body felt with Oliver's touch only distanced her from it. Though he had come to loom so large in her life, he was still a relative stranger. The handful of mourners who stood by the graveside and placed consoling hands on Oliver's shoulder were friends of his and Miriam's. Brigitte had never met any of them. From the grief Oliver showed, they all supposed that it was a close family friend he was grieving. None of them guessed it was really his wife.

It was a strange thing to attend your own funeral in a foreign land. Brigitte had to keep the mix of emotions she felt at bay, so she could be strong for Oliver. Seeing the coffin in the ground was not as unnerving as seeing her corpse in an open casket at the vigil the night before.

Her old body had seemed so alien to her as it lay in a coffin surrounded by candles. There was the old scar on her hand. There was the face she had seen in the mirror, whose changes she had tracked since childhood. Yet it no longer belonged to her. It was separate from her and she felt disdain for it.

"Take us home," Oliver told the driver as they climbed into the limo. "I want to be alone with my..." he hesitated to say the word 'wife,' settling on, "...we want to be alone with each other."

"What about your guests?" said Brigitte.

"They'll understand. Why, did you want to spend time with them?"

"No, it's alright. I'm happy to do what you want. You're the one in mourning."

"Funny, I thought we were both grieving our loss."

The last remark was surprisingly thoughtful of him, to think of *her* loss in *his* hour of grief. Maybe the next nine or ten months with him wouldn't be as difficult as Brigitte feared. She was not seeing him at his best. This was a difficult time for both of them.

Oliver put his arm around Brigitte and pulled her close. She might have objected another time, but she knew he needed the comfort. As his hand slipped from her shoulder to her hip she could tell that comfort wasn't all he wanted.

She told herself that this was okay. He was in a difficult place at the moment and his feelings were confused. Actually she recalled reading that it was a natural part of the grieving process to feel strong desire soon after losing a partner.

She was also aware that she had an obligation to Oliver and Miriam. An obligation that, once fulfilled, would ensure the lives of everyone on St Ignatius. Brigitte rested her head on Oliver's shoulder and gazed out of the window. Her mind went back over her first months in the city.

BRIGITTE HAD FIRST met Oliver Chevalier in a trailer park for evacuees in the Lower Ninth Ward of New Orleans. She was staying with a group of ex-pats from St Ignatius who had all lost their homes in the flood.

Oliver had been helping with the reconstruction of the Lower Ninth.

This area of the city had been hit hardest by the hurricanes, and he had set up a foundation to raise money to restore and rebuild it. The people she was staying with knew Oliver's family came from St Ignatius and he still had an interest in the island. They were also aware that his wife was very sick.

Oliver did not serve the Loa. He was Catholic, but he had a great respect for the religion of his ancestors. He had been raised by his grandmother, who'd grown up on St Ignatius and told him stories of the Voodoo ceremonies of her youth.

Brigitte was introduced to Oliver as a Mambo, a powerful Voodoo priestess. Her fellow islanders were sure she could help with Oliver's wife Miriam. Oliver was very wealthy. He had paid for the best medical care available, but nothing was working. He was ready to try anything, including the Voodoo his grandmother had told him so much about.

Brigitte agreed to help Miriam but she was keen to limit both Miriam and Oliver's expectations. Oliver said he understood and offered Brigitte a guest cottage on his estate in the Garden District. This was how Brigitte came to meet Miriam Chevalier, the woman whose body and identity she would eventually assume.

They did not hit it off straight away. Miriam was a devout Catholic and did not want some "medicine woman" trying to cure her with "evil spirits." Brigitte was careful to reassure her that she had no truck with evil forces. Instead she spoke about her own belief in God and her relationship with the saints.

Brigitte also provided a sympathetic ear to Miriam as she spoke of what troubled her most. Her anger at the disease that was killing her, her regret for all the things she wouldn't get to do. Her dismay that she would never be able to give Oliver what he wanted most of all from their marriage.

More than anything, Miriam confided, she was afraid of the months of pain and wasting that were to come. So afraid that she was strongly considering euthanasia. She knew of clinics in Europe that could provide the service simply and painlessly. Miriam wanted to die with dignity and without suffering, but she was afraid of how this would endanger her immortal soul. She could not reconcile her wishes with her belief that suicide was a sin.

A deep affection grew between them as they prayed and spoke and wept together. They shared stories of growing up and Miriam became as fascinated with Brigitte's heritage as her husband was with his grandmother's tales of Voodoo.

Brigitte also told Miriam of the dreadful plight that had befallen her fellow islanders. Miriam could not quite believe Brigitte at first. Nothing like that happened in the privileged world she lived in.

She knew that Brigitte wouldn't lie, though. And the Bible spoke of the dead returning to life, so she could believe that, if she stretched her imagination. What Miriam had most trouble accepting was the thought that someone could actually reduce an entire community to nothing more than walking corpses in order to enslave them. She couldn't conceive of human beings reduced to monstrosities so that that rich Westerners could study them and learn to become crueler and more exploitative.

In a way, Brigitte shared her disbelief. It was hard to believe that any human being was capable of such measures. But with patience and tact, Brigitte pointed out to Miriam that it wasn't so far removed from how the West already treated much of the Third World.

After all, Brigitte argued, the sweat shops that supply the West with cheap consumer goods reduce the men, women and children who work in them into disposable labour. Taking away someone's life and turning them into a zombie is simply the logical conclusion of that.

Miriam was uncertain about this. She thought Brigitte might have a point but it sounded to her like she was preaching socialism, so Brigitte let the matter drop. It wasn't until Brigitte broke down and spoke of the guilt she felt for the part she'd played in what happened that Miriam truly came around.

Brigitte had trained the man who'd enslaved her island and given him the tools he used to do it. What's more, she'd saved his life when he was first washed up on its shores, the only survivor of a dreadful accident. She'd nursed him back to health and they'd become lovers.

The idyll was broken when Brigitte was visited by the spirit of her ancestor who told her of the curse he'd placed on her lover's family. A curse that she was expected to fulfill.

Brigitte sought to break the curse through love. She went against the wills of both their ancestors and the Loa, and everyone she ever loved had paid the price.

Brigitte hadn't mentioned the magical artefact that her ancestor had entrusted to her, however. This was secret. Even when her lover had tricked and captured her she hadn't revealed where it was, desperate as her lover was to know. She would dearly have loved to confide this in Miriam, though, for the burden of the artefact weighed heavily on Brigitte's soul.

When Brigitte spoke of the horrors of her escape, the truth of it finally came home to Miriam. Brigitte told how she had been buried alive by her lover, who had started calling himself Doc Papa.

She described how, as the air in the coffin ran out, she had sent her soul out of her body and taken over one of the zombies, a strong young man who was also her second cousin. Inside the young man's walking corpse she had given her captors the slip and sought out her grave. With less than an hour left to live she had dug up the earth of the grave with the young man's dead hands. As she dug she had also neutralised the wards and spells Doc Papa had placed upon the grave.

When she was finally free, Brigitte's soul returned to her body and she sent the young zombie back to join the others so his absence wouldn't be spotted. Then she replaced all the earth and reset the spells so Doc Papa wouldn't realise she was gone.

She stole away from the island in an abandoned fishing boat and made her way to Haiti. From there she eventually found her way to the US, but no matter how far she traveled she couldn't shake her guilt. Guilt for escaping while the rest of her community still suffered, and guilt for having brought that suffering on them.

Miriam's bedside became a private space of absolution for both of them. Between the endless stream of specialists examining Miriam, she and Brigitte became the confessors each of them so badly needed. The bond of trust between them became so strong that Miriam finally felt able to ask Brigitte for the help of the Loa.

In the dead of night they held a rite. Brigitte called upon the Loa and Ayida Wédo mounted her. Brigitte lost all consciousness as the spirit took over her body. When she came around Miriam, was in tears.

She recounted her vision to Brigitte. Miriam said the Virgin Mary had visited and spoken to her through Brigitte. She'd told Miriam that God had a plan for her and that there was a place for her in heaven, with her father and her aunt. They had visited, too, and had told her she would soon be with them in her eternal reward.

The Virgin Mary had told Miriam there was a way to relieve her suffering and to save the people of Brigitte's island. Brigitte had to use the rites known to her as a Voodoo priestess to help Miriam's soul leave its dying body and make its way to heaven before the illness claimed her. With her soul gone, the illness would lose its hold on her.

Miriam's body would then become a living vessel for Brigitte's soul. She could send it out of her body and into Miriam's as she'd done when she possessed the young male zombie. This would allow her to pose as Miriam.

Brigitte could return to St Ignatius using Miriam's identity. Miriam would put her half of Oliver's fortune at Brigitte's disposal so she could buy her way onto the course and pretend to be one of Doc Papa's students. No-one would recognise her, so she would be free to infiltrate Doc Papa's organisation and save her people.

Brigitte did not know what to say. She recognised Ayida Wédo's hand in the plan. The Loa had appeared to Miriam in her aspect as Our Lady of the Immaculate Conception. Nevertheless, Brigitte was over-awed by the generosity and bravery Miriam showed, in offering to do this for her and her people.

She reached out and put her arms around Miriam and the two of them wept on the hospital bed, tears of grief mingled with joy. Grief for everything they had lost in their lives, and joy for the blessings they could bring one another. They wept with gratitude for having found a sister in each other. For the joy that sisterhood brought and the grief it would mean when they parted.

Brigitte had then left Miriam's side for the first time in weeks so Miriam could tell Oliver about her plans. Oliver was not pleased to begin with. When he saw how much it meant to Miriam, though, he began to come round. Miriam finally won him over when she explained how it would allow her to give him the one thing they'd always wanted.

BRIGITTE GAZED OUT of the limousine's window at the ornate Victorian houses of the Garden District, with their perfect lawns and wrought-iron fences. Her mind was still in the past, reliving her last days with Miriam.

"You've been quiet for a long time," said Oliver. "What are you thinking about?"

"Miriam," said Brigitte. "How much I'm going to miss her. How grateful I am to you and her, for everything you've done."

Oliver took her hands in his. "I'm grateful to you too. Watching Miriam lying there in that bed, dying a little more each day, felt like a part of me was dying with her. The part of me that could be happy and feel hope and enjoy life. I thought that would go forever when she went. But you're giving me something to live for again and I can't thank you enough."

Brigitte smiled a sad smile and squeezed Oliver's hands. They pulled past a mansion as Brigitte recalled the last time Oliver had said that to her.

IT WAS JUST before the final ceremony. Oliver had taken her hands, just as he did in the car, and thanked her. They were standing on the second storey landing outside the master bedroom. There were tears streaming down his cheeks. He had just said goodbye to his wife. Miriam had returned to the mansion; she wanted to spend her last earthly hours in the comfort and privacy of her home.

Brigitte had called on certain special traders down on South Rampart Street to buy the materials she needed for the ceremony. The room had been prepared in accordance with the Loa's wishes. Oliver left them alone.

The full ceremony took over two days to complete. There were so many gates Brigitte had to open to the afterlife. So many Loa had to be called on to ensure the safe passage of Miriam's soul and the health of her body when Brigitte entered it. Brigitte couldn't afford to let her concentration lapse for a second. Her life and Miriam's soul depended on it.

Finally, Brigitte opened Miriam's eyes and looked out of them for the first time. She saw her old body sitting in a chair next to the bed and called Oliver back in. They placed Brigitte's old body on the bed and called the undertaker and a priest. Then they set about planning Brigitte's funeral. A funeral that only they knew was secretly to honour Miriam.

"I DON'T KNOW about you, but I need a drink," said Oliver as Brigitte sank into a leather sofa in the library back at the mansion. "Here, take a look at this." He threw her a brochure for an exclusive hotel in the Maldives while he fixed them both a drink.

"What's this?"

"It's where we're going on vacation next week. I just ordered the tickets."

"And you didn't think to ask me?"

"I thought we needed a break. Don't you like the Maldives?"

"It would have been nice if you'd asked me whether I wanted to go before you booked the tickets."

Oliver sighed and looked at the floor. "Okay, there's going to be difficulties with this that I didn't foresee." He took a slug of his drink and handed Brigitte hers. "Miriam used to like it when I took charge. She liked surprises too, so I'd tend to spring things on her. I'm a take-charge kind of a guy and I like to move quickly. You have to be that way in my line of work. That's how I manage things and that's how I manage people."

"I'm not one of the people you manage."

"You're right," Oliver said, changing his tone. "Would you like to come away with me to the Maldives? You've been through a lot. We both have. I think the break would do us both some good."

Miriam flicked through the glossy brochure. The rooms were immense, the facilities incredible. It reeked of a luxury that made Brigitte uncomfortable.

"I don't know if I could relax in a place like this while so many people here are still homeless. While the people from my island are still suffering."

"You're suffering from too much guilt," said Oliver. "You still have survivor's guilt and you're adding new wealth guilt to that. It's natural to feel that way for a while, but you have to come to terms with it."

"How can you come to terms with it? How can you live like this when so many other people live in poverty?"

"By helping those people. By using the wealth and the talents I've been blessed with to tackle some of the problems they're facing."

"I thought rich people and their greed were the *main* problem the poor are facing."

"There's nothing wrong with being rich, Brigitte, any more than being poor. Rich people don't necessarily create poor ones. "

"If there were fewer rich people there'd be fewer poor."

"There's always going to be rich people, though. I'm totally in favour of equal opportunities for everyone. But not everyone is equal. That's the way the world is. Some people are just smarter than others or more driven. Some people can jump higher, run faster or draw better than most other people. It's only fair they should be rewarded for this. Any system that punishes them and stifles their talent isn't creating equality. It's just denying the world the benefit of those talents and the wealth they could have created. Being rich doesn't mean you have to be a bad person."

"No, but most rich people are. That's why they turn innocent people into monsters so they can learn to become worse monsters themselves."

"And most black people are poor, but that doesn't mean that every black person has to be poor and it doesn't mean every rich person has to be bad. I'm living proof of both those assertions. You don't have to brutalise and exploit other people in order to get rich. Even if some people do get rich that way – a lot of people don't. Their brutality and exploitation can be their undoing. It's not the only way to make or use a fortune. But come, I don't want to argue on a night like this."

"I don't know," she said, uncrossing her legs. "I find it quite stimulating."

"Good, finish your drink."

Oliver put his hand on her thigh and her heart beat faster. She felt a jolt of nervous anticipation and a deep yearning her new body had been waiting a long time to unleash. Did the passion belong entirely to Miriam's body? A body that knew Oliver's so well. If it didn't, was it wrong of Brigitte to desire him?

Oliver led her to the master bedroom. She found she rather liked him being masterful in this instance. He put his arm round her waist and pulled her to him. She could smell his aftershave and the fresh sweat breaking on his skin. His scent was as familiar as it was exciting and new to her.

He ran his hand over her breast. Brigitte flinched and stepped back from him.

"I'm sorry," Oliver said. "Miriam used to really like that."

"And so do I. But this is the first time I've done this with you. I need you to go a little slower."

"I'm sorry, of course you do."

Brigitte suddenly became aware of a warm golden light at the foot of the bed they were standing by. She turned her head to look at the source.

"What's the matter?" said Oliver. "Did I do something else wrong?"

"No, it's Miriam. She's with us. She's come to say her final goodbye."

"She's not mad at us is she?"

"No, she's happy. She's here to give us her blessing."

Brigitte could feel Miriam's happiness coming off her in waves and radiating through the room. She fancied even Oliver could feel it.

Miriam was overjoyed that she and Oliver would soon have what they'd always wanted from their marriage. A child.

CHAPTER THIRTY-ONE

Doc Papa thrived on crisis management. It was a circumstance to which his temperament and skill set were best suited. He always did best in those situations where other, weaker types failed.

So he wasn't the least bit fazed when Truffet and the rest of the shareholders stormed into his office on the top floor of the mansion.

"Just what the fuck is going on around here?" Lyon's growled in his deep southern drawl. He'd made his fortune selling arms and ammunition to the domestic market, and liked to portray himself as an old time gunslinger. At only five-foot-five, however, with balding ginger hair, he didn't cut too imposing a figure.

"One minute I'm getting blown in a hot tub. The next I'm lying on the floor and someone's giving me CPR," Lyons said. "Apparently, practically everyone on the island was knocked unconscious. If that Thai hooker hadn't dragged me out of the tub I would've drowned."

"There are some distressing rumours going around," Truffet said. He peered down at Doc Papa through his horn-rimmed spectacles. "I understand that our two biggest assets have been stolen."

"The assets are perfectly safe," said Doc Papa. "Someone did try to get the undead off the island but I dealt with the problem and my men are currently rounding them up."

"Someone, *who*?" said Lyons.

Doc Papa smiled. "A pitiful, little collection of wannabe terrorists calling themselves the Zombie Liberation Front."

The shareholders laughed with disbelief.

"Just when you think you've heard of every nut-job," said Simons.

"What about the soul bank?" said Frank Evans.

"All the Pot-tets are still in the soul bank and the area has been secured," said Doc Papa. "Everything is under control."

"So why do I feel so cold inside?" said Evans. "Why am I losing the feeling in my hands and feet? Why is my heart beating slower and slower?"

"The soul bank has been sabotaged," said Doc Papa. "As I said, all the Pot-tets are in our possession, but their seals have been corrupted."

"What does that mean?" barked Lyons.

"The souls are no longer fixed in their Pot-tets. The spells surrounding the containers have been reversed and the souls are slowly leaking out."

"Does that include *our* souls?"

"Yes it does. The unconsciousness that you all experienced was a side effect of this. When the spells were reversed this sent a psychic backlash across the island."

"Who did this and why?" said O'Shaugnessy.

"I believe it was one of the current crop of guests. A lady calling herself Miriam Chavalier."

"One of the guests," said Lyon. "How the fuck did she manage that?"

"Apparently she knows Voodoo, a fact our extensive background check failed to turn up. I believe she did it in order to create a diversion so she could escape from the Ounfó with the zombies."

"I thought you said your men were rounding the zombies up," said O'Shaugnessy. "Now you're saying they've escaped. Do you have the zombies or not?"

"It is merely a matter of time."

"Never mind about the zombies," said Evans. "What about our souls? What's going to happen to them? What's going to happen to us?"

"Without the correct vessel to hold them the souls will slowly fade out of existence. They are denied access to the afterlife and they can't remain intact unless they have something to house them."

"Can't you just put them back inside us?" said Lyons.

"I'm afraid the stars aren't in the right alignment to return the souls to their bodies. I can't perform that ceremony for a while."

"What does that mean to us?" said O'Shaugnessy. "If you can't put them back in us, what's going to happen?"

"The worst case scenario is that as your Gros Bon Ange, the part of your soul that's in the Pot-tet, slowly withers away, your Ti Bon Ange, the soul that's still with you, will also go. This will mean that your intelligence will disappear along with all vital signs of life and you'll become a zombie."

Evans banged his fist on the desk. His craggy face was even redder than usual. "God damn it! Do you mean to tell me that we're all going to become zombies because you can't organise proper fucking security?"

"No. That isn't what I mean to tell you at all." Doc Papa leaned back in his chair and smiled. His movements were precise and controlled. "You are all going to be fine. I have allowed for just such a contingency." He pressed the button on his intercom. "You can come in now."

The door opened and Palmer and Vincenzo entered. Palmer was carrying a briefcase which he handed to Doc Papa. Doc Papa opened the briefcase and showed the contents to the shareholders.

On a velvet cushion were five talismans carved in ivory and stained with blood. "These, gentlemen, are Bakas," said Doc Papa. "I think you'll remember them from the ceremony I performed. They're special talismans that hold your souls to the earthly plane. They are also beacons that light the way for your soul. You have but to place them on a suitable vessel and your soul will make its new home there."

"What suitable vessel?" said O'Shaugnessy. "I thought you said all the Pot-tets were corrupted."

"They are," said Doc Papa. "But they aren't the only vessel in which a dispossessed soul can live. A zombie is a perfect vessel for just such a soul, because they're nothing more than human bodies with no soul or intellect. All the guests will be issued with their Bakas and a zombie will be provided as soon as they are back in our custody."

"Why can't you just use the Bakas to put our souls back in our own bodies? Why do we have to stick it in some walking corpse?"

"While your soul is in your body it has the opportunity to move on to the afterlife. The Baka is designed to hold the soul to this plane of existence, so it can't transfer the soul into anything living that will allow the soul to move on. Don't worry, your soul will be completely safe in the zombie we find for it."

"Fuck that," said Lyons. "I'm not waiting around for you to round up some zombies while my life is on the line!"

"You won't have to wait around. In fact Palmer has five beautiful little zombies all tied up and waiting to house your souls right here in the centre."

Palmer turned bright red. "I, err... don't know what you're talking about."

"Oh, come now, Palmer," said Doc Papa. "Do you seriously think I don't know all about your little harem? Nothing that goes on here escapes my attention. Now kindly escort the shareholders to your underground lair so they can save their souls."

"But there's only five zombies down there," said Palmer. "What about *my* soul?"

"That's hardly one of my more pressing problems. I'll attend to that in time."

"But..."

"I said go!"

Palmer left with his tail between his legs, closely followed by the shareholders.

Doc Papa stood and walked to the window. Vincenzo remained standing quietly by the desk.

"You know what I learned from my days as a trader?" Doc Papa said. Vincenzo knew better than to answer. "That every catastrophe is an opportunity for great profit. Those men haven't the vision to see this, that's why I've got them just where I want them. Like all small-minded fools they see only a crisis, where I see greater forces at work – forces of opportunity. When these forces strike, it doesn't matter if they're a market correcting itself, an ecological disaster or the Loa exerting their will, there is always a great profit to be made. When people are panicked and uncertain of what's happening, they're vulnerable. And when they're vulnerable, you can profit from them."

"You were toying with them, weren't you?" said Vincenzo.

"I see you've been paying attention for once. They're not aware of it of course, but whoever sabotaged the soul bank did us a favour. With the souls released from their Pot-tets they're that much easier to reap and to dominate."

"Do you know who sabotaged the soul bank yet?"

"I have my suspicions, now I just have to go and confirm them. If I'm right, then Erzulie Zandor has made good on her word."

CHAPTER THIRTY-TWO

SAM MCKANE WAS fighting mad. He was ready to hog-tie that Doc Papa son-of-a-bitch and put one right between his eyes. As soon as he got off this God-forsaken island he was going to put together an army of lawyers so big these motherfuckers would be shitting writs for the rest of their lives.

Goddamn it, there was blood on his alligator boots. The cut on his hand was dripping again. Problem was, he couldn't hardly feel a thing in either of his hands anymore. He cut the hand this morning on a cologne bottle. Dropped it on the bathroom floor trying to get rid of the smell.

He was starting to stink like one of them damned walking corpses. Every one of the guests was. He didn't know what they'd done to him but, by God, they were going to pay.

He wrapped his kerchief round his hand. He really should go to the infirmary and get it seen to, but he couldn't afford to leave the mansion. They were about to make some sort of announcement and he needed to know what was going on.

All the guests were packed in there, as well as those cocksuckers they'd flown in who'd already done the course. No-one knew what was going on. Everyone was nervous and confused, milling around and waiting for something to happen. All of 'em looking like spare pricks at a party for unemployed whores. Finally Palmer appeared, looking in poor shape and obviously as pissed as the rest of them. He was flanked by a squadron of guards, who set up a podium for him. He was mobbed before he even opened his mouth.

Everyone charged him, shouting questions, waving fists, making demands. The guards shielded Palmer as he raised his hands to quiet the clamour of raised voices.

"All right, all right. That's enough," Palmer said. "Let's have a bit of order. I'm not going to take individual questions at this juncture. To begin with, the management on St Ignatius would like to apologise for the disruption in our services and any inconvenience this has caused you." There was a chorus of jeers and catcalls. Palmer shook his head. "Okay, if you want to find out what's going on, you're going to have to let me get through this. Now, some of you might have noticed some changes in the way you feel. This is a perfectly natural part of the process you're going through. It'll all become clear in a little while.

"We're always striving to increase the parameters of the course here on St Ignatius and to improve the scope of your learning. That's why I'm excited to announce the next stage in your journey along the Way of the Barefoot Zombie. This part of the course will be new to all of you. Due to the nature of what we had planned, and the timing in unveiling it, we couldn't make any pre-announcements. But we can now promise you an even greater degree of intimacy with your Inner Zombie and an increased level of power and understanding."

There were disgruntled murmurings among the guests. Sam knew bullshit when he smelled it, and he could smell it now. Palmer held up an ivory disk with some Voodoo markings on it.

"Now you should all remember this from the soul transference ceremony. It's a Baka. It's a Voodoo talisman that keeps your soul safe. You should think of it as a credit card for the soul bank. It allows you to deposit your soul and withdraw it. Now we've added a new facility which allows you to transfer your soul between vessels.

"Up until now we've only offered you the opportunity to store your soul in a Pot-tet. But now you can upgrade to one of the Living Dead. Once you've been issued with your personal Baka, we'll find a time in the next few days when you can choose a zombie from our colony to house your soul.

"Now some of you might have noticed they've left the compound at present. I also understand that our newest graduates encountered them at the Ounfó last night. This is all part of the process of readying them for your souls. To get the zombies properly receptive we had to allow them to roam free for a while. But let me assure you they have been under supervision at all times and will be returned to the compound shortly."

There was a huge uproar at this. Whatever it was Palmer was selling, no-one was buying it.

"I've already said I won't take individual questions. Now the guards are going to pass among you with your personalised Bakas. I suggest you try and receive them in as orderly a fashion as possible. Once you've been issued with your Baka, you merely have to place it on the forehead of a zombie, right between the eyes where the third eye is, to transfer your soul into it."

Two guards stepped around the front of the podium as Palmer beat a hasty retreat. They opened two security cases. Inside were the Bakas. Everyone rushed them.

"What do you think of what Palmer just said?" George Griffin asked Sam.

"I think it's horse shit, is what it is."

"I hear that terrorists have kidnapped the zombies," said Arthur Sonnenfeldt. "And they blew up the soul bank, used some kind of gas to knock us all out. That's why they're giving us these Bakas, because the soul bank doesn't work anymore."

"But why would terrorists want to kidnap the zombies?" said Bessie. "What are they going to do with them?"

"Let 'em loose in some public place, use 'em to torture prisoners," said Sam. "Who knows what these whack-jobs will get up to? They're motivated by envy and dogma. They hate us 'cause of the things we have and they don't."

"More importantly," said George, "what does this mean to us? What's going to happen to us if our souls aren't safe?"

"I think it's obvious, isn't it?" said Sam. "We're turning into one of them. We're becoming walking corpses."

"Oh my," said Bessie.

"How could we be this stupid?" said Arthur. "I mean to just hand over our souls to them. What were we thinking?"

"We weren't thinking," said George. "We were so caught up in what we could gain we didn't assess the risks properly. Why does anyone make a stupid investment? Because they don't want to lose out when it looks as though everyone else is profiting. If an investment keeps paying off, we all want to jump on. We don't want to think about what might happen if the bubble bursts, because no-one else is. We're a herd animal. We run with the pack, even when it's charging off a steep cliff. You've only got to look at the current financial crisis to see that."

"Yeah, well the current crisis is the least of my worries," said Sam. "How're we going to get our hands on a zombie to keep our souls safe?"

"Don't you trust the centre to round them up for us?" said Bessie.

"Not one bit. We're going to have to take matters into our own hands, before time runs out."

Without any warning, everyone started to pile out of the lobby, pushing past Sam and the others. Sam grabbed the arm of the young guy he'd seen taking a swing at a zombie back in the Ounfó. "Hey, buddy. Where's everyone going?"

"Into the jungle. Someone's found out where all the zombies are."

"Oh, yeah? And where's that?"

"There's an abandoned copper mine about twenty minutes down the track from the temple."

"Much obliged," said Sam and let the young guy go.

"Listen," said Arthur, getting antsy. "I don't mean to be rude or nothing, but I don't want to miss out on this."

"Me neither," said Bessie and followed Arthur.

"Just like I told you," said George. "We're a herd animal. Always will be. Be seeing you, Sam."

"'Bye, George. You take care going over them cliffs now."

Sam sauntered over to the guards posted by the entrance to the office suite.

"Sir," said one of the youngest to his superior. "Shouldn't we be doing something?"

"My orders are to guard the mansion," said his superior. "And that's what I'm doing. I wasn't told nothing 'bout keeping no guests in the building."

"Morning, boys," Sam said.

"Sir," said the guard. "We're not permitted to fraternise with guests of the establishment."

"Well, now, son, I appreciate that, but fraternising wasn't quite what I had in mind. I'll come straight to the point. I've got a business proposition for y'all."

CHAPTER THIRTY-THREE

"THIS NAIL ISN'T long enough," Benjamin said. "See, it only just goes though the plank? You need to get me some longer ones."

"There aren't any longer ones," Tatyana said. "We've got to make do with what we can find."

Benjamin punched the wall in frustration. He always got bullish and overbearing when he tried to do any kind of DIY. Maybe he thought it made him look more manly. Tatyana didn't care. He was pissing her off, acting like a brute.

"I still don't see why Miria – I mean, Brigitte couldn't get a bunch of the zombies to help out," he said.

"Because they wouldn't be any use to us. Can you image one of them trying to use a hammer?"

"Ow," he said, accidentally hitting his thumb. "Well, they couldn't do a much worse job than me."

Tatyana smiled. She liked him better when he kept his sense of humour.

They were both tense and exhausted. They hadn't slept since the night before. Their muscles ached from barricading the doors and windows of the old copper mine's offices. They smelled of damp and decay; bits of machinery and office supplies from the 'sixties lay in dusty corners.

"Does that look as though it'll hold?" asked Benjamin, looking at the last of the planks he'd nailed to the main window.

"I guess."

"Y'know. I can't work out whether this is more like the beginning of *Night of the Living Dead*, when Duane Jones and Judith O'Dea board up the windows of the house they're trapped in, or *Day of the Dead*, when everyone's holed up in that military bunker next to the abandoned mine."

"Oh, for God's sake, Benjamin, will you give it a rest with the zombie movies? What's up with you? This isn't some dumb movie, this is really happening to us."

"I know it's not a movie, okay? I am painfully aware there are men out there with guns that are coming to kill us and we're barricaded in here with a bunch of walking corpses that could tear us to pieces at any moment. And that is scaring me shitless right now. The only way I have of dealing with that is by viewing the whole thing as a movie. That way, I can kid myself that if anything goes wrong, I can just hit pause and rewind. Is that okay with you?"

Now it was Tatyana's turn to feel like a brute. "Yeah, that's just fine with me. We've all got our ways of coping. Sorry for busting your balls."

"It's okay. We're both on edge."

"I guess it's your way of sticking to the Third Rule of Interaction: 'It doesn't matter and you don't care.'"

"Or Rule Five." *Master yourself and nothing can threaten you.*

"Yeah, I wish that was the case. Right now everything seems threatening, no matter what side of the barricades we're on. Speaking of which, all we've got to do is block up that last door. We're out of planks. Do you think a couple of filing cabinets and a desk will hold it?"

"It's worth a try."

They'd just shoved the desk up against the two filing cabinets when they heard it.

"Does that sound like someone running to you?" said Benjamin.

Tatyana could hear several sets of footsteps in the undergrowth outside the office. Then she heard someone shout, although they were too far away for her to make out what they said.

"Is that the guards again?" Tatyana said. She walked round to one of the windows they'd just boarded up and peered through a gap in the planks.

Benjamin joined her. "Can't see anything. How 'bout you?"

A sudden sharp tap on the window pane made them both jump.

"Hey, Benjamin, is that you? It is. It is you. Hey, let me in, kid."

Tatyana looked at Benjamin, who just shrugged. It was Arthur Sonnenfeldt. He was red-faced from running and he was motioning to them to let him in.

"Err, Arthur, I think you ought to get out of here," Benjamin called out to him. "This place is full of zombies and the guards are on their way."

"I know, I know. That's why you've got to let me in quick. Hey, how'd you get in there with them anyway? You've got to tell me the way in."

Benjamin looked at Tatyana. "Do you think we should let him in?"

"I don't know. What if he's a spy or something? Maybe they've sent him to try and get in so he can let the guards in."

Benjamin called out to Arthur again. "I don't think that's a good idea. We're going to go now, Arthur. You really ought to get out of here."

"Hey, hey! Don't you walk away from me." Arthur shouted. "Don't you walk away from me, you little pissant! Come back here, you've got to let me in, you've got to. I don't have much longer, I can feel it. It's alright for you, you're young. Don't go, I said don't..."

"What the hell is he talking about?" said Benjamin.

"I have no idea," said Tatyana.

She heard more commotion in the jungle outside and Arthur called out: "Hey, hey, over here! They're in here! quick!"

Tatyana heard what sounded like a stampede charging towards them. Then the sound of thirty or forty pairs of hands began banging on the windows, the doors and the walls. The filing cabinets began to shake as someone battered on the door.

People were shouting. "Open up!" "Let us in!" "You get those boards down right now, you hear? Right now!"

The panes in the windows shattered and the planks over them started to shake. Someone found the board Benjamin hadn't entirely nailed in place and pushed it off, sending it crashing to the floor. Five or six arms reached through the gap, grasping at the air and tearing at the other boards.

It was the other guests; they were trying to get in, but why? Tatyana could see the expressions on their faces, desperate, angry, full of fear and need. These weren't marauding creatures, they were human beings, panicked and nearly hysterical. Even with everything she'd been through, it was one of the most frightening things she'd ever seen.

Brigitte came through from the next room where she'd been looking after the zombies. Tatyana could hear they were getting agitated.

"What's going on?" Brigitte said.

"I have no idea," Benjamin said. "They all turned up and demanded we let them in."

"Are they crazy?" Tatyana said. "Why would they want to get in here with all these zombies?"

"I think I know," said Brigitte.

They all looked up as they heard footsteps on the roof.

"Can they get in that way?" said Benjamin.

The noise of breaking glass reached them as the skylight in the other room broke.

"I think they just have," Tatyana said.

Tatyana followed the others in time to see three guests she didn't recognise jump down among the zombies. One of them had cut her hand on the skylight. She landed badly and yowled in pain.

Four zombies closed in. The woman got to her feet and held out her hands to ward them off. The smell of the blood drove them wild.

She backed away, stumbled and fell, and the zombies fell on her. The woman screamed in agony as their dead, decaying teeth tore into her.

Tatyana looked to Brigitte, who shook her head. "It's too late to intervene," she said. "It would just get more of them riled up."

The other two intruders fared better. They got to their feet and dropped straight into zombie mode, obeying the first two Rules of Interaction.

More and more of the zombies crowded round the body of the dead guest, trying to tear a scrap of flesh or bone loose. Brigitte couldn't push through the throng to get to the intruders.

Through the bustle of the zombies Tatyana saw one of the intruders pull out an ivory disk. He held it at arms length and moved slowly but eagerly towards one of the zombies scrabbling for the woman's flesh.

When he got close enough the man placed the ivory talisman on the zombie's forehead. Both of them shook as though electrocuted the moment the talisman touched the zombie.

This caused the man to stumble and fall over two of the feeding zombies, who dropped the bones they were gnawing and grabbed him. The man tried to wrestle them off, but jostled still more zombies, who moved in on him.

The man managed to sit upright before a young female zombie with beads in its hair sunk its teeth into his neck, coming away with a huge chunk of his flesh in its mouth. Blood pumped in great gouts from the ragged hole, spilling down his chest and soaking his shirt as he screamed and hyperventilated. Excited by the freshly spilled blood, the other zombies tore into him.

As this was happening the zombie he had touched with the talisman began to shout and scream in distress. It was the first time Tatyana had heard one of them try to speak. It was hard to understand at first; its vocal chords had not been used in a while and there wasn't much air coming from its lungs.

Tatyana was surprised when she realised it was shouting: "No! Stop it, stop it, get off, you're killing me!" The screaming zombie tried pulling the other zombies off the man but didn't succeed.

Brigitte waded into the middle of the undead and raised her arms. She shouted something in the tongue of the dead and the zombies became more docile. They parted to form a space around Brigitte and the screaming zombie, slinking off to chew on their stolen morsels like scolded children.

The other intruder hung back and watched as Brigitte bent down and picked up the ivory talisman the man had dropped. She glanced at it and shook her head in disgust.

"Get out of him!" she said to the screaming zombie.

"Please," said the zombie. "This is all I've got, please let me stay. I'll leave right away. I won't bother you."

"Get out now!" Brigitte raised her arm and made a sign in the air.

"But I've got nowhere to go. I can't pass over now. I'll die completely and totally."

"You already have," said Brigitte, clicking her fingers.

The zombie went rigid and fell, face first, to the ground.

Brigitte crouched and checked the unmoving body. She let out a wail of anguish and dismay. "You've killed him," she cried, beating the dead body with her fists. "I can't save him now you've killed him!"

Brigitte glanced up at the other intruder. She was shaking with anger as she stood and confronted him. "Give me the Baka."

"But..." said the man. "It's my only hope. It's all I've got."

"I wasn't asking you. I said give it to me!"

The man handed it over. Miriam held the talisman to her lips and whispered to it. The man clutched at his chest and his stomach as though something was missing from him. "What... did... you... what... did... you... do?"

"I sent your Gros Bon Ange on to the crossroads of the worlds, to wait with the souls of all the others. If I am successful it will be returned to you when all the others are reunited with theirs."

The man put his hands to his head as though he had a splitting headache. "I can't... think. Why... happen... that...?"

"Now your Gros Bon Ange is no longer on this plane, your Ti Bon Ange has gone to join it. You're changing."

The man's eyes rolled up into his head and his body shuddered. He had obviously died, but he didn't fall to the ground. His body twitched and jerked. It began to walk as though it didn't understand why it was still moving, going nowhere and bumping in to the other zombies.

"What's happened to him?" said Tatyana.

"He has become the same as the islanders." said Brigitte.

"A zombie?"

"If you want to call it that, yes. The souls of my people are trapped at the crossroads of the astral worlds. Their souls cannot carry on into the afterlife, so their bodies cannot rest. I have sent his soul to be with theirs. If I can return their souls to them, his will also be returned."

"How will you do that?"

"Tonight is the last night of the Festival of the Gédé, the one night of the year when I can perform the ceremony that will return their souls to them. I need to get them to a crossroads at the centre of St Ignatius to do this. Until then I need to keep them safe."

"What's with these weird disks they're carrying?" said Benjamin.

"Bakas. They were created for the ceremony Doc Papa performed last night. They hold the soul to the earthly plane and they can also direct it into other vessels. Now we've destroyed their soul bank, the only place they can store their souls is inside a living corpse."

"So that's what happened when he put his Baka thing on the zombie's forehead? He was transferring his soul into it? Then you drove his soul out of the zombie's body. But why did you get upset about killing him?"

"Way to go with the sensitive questions," said Tatyana.

"It's okay," said Brigitte. "I wasn't upset about killing him. What upset me was that the body he was possessing died."

"The body," said Tatyana. "Was that someone you knew well?"

"It was my brother. We were very close. And I failed him."

Tatyana couldn't think of anything else to say after that. Neither could Benjamin. They left Brigitte alone to mourn her loss.

Tatyana wanted to check the barricades in the office were still up. To her alarm, half of them were down and the guests outside were almost able to climb in.

"There's a large basement downstairs that connects to the mine shaft," Brigitte said. "It's one of the main entrances to the mine. It has a metal door we can bolt. We have to get down there quickly."

Brigitte led them through the room and down several flights of stairs. Watching the zombies' stumbling progress down the concrete steps was painful.

There were several falls with every flight. The zombies who fell had to be encouraged back to their feet. All the while they could hear the guests getting closer to finally breaking in.

Finally they got the last of the zombies into the basement and bolted the heavy iron door. They could hear the guests' feet clattering on the concrete steps as they did.

The basement was pitch black with the door closed; Tatyana couldn't see a thing. All she could hear was the sound of the zombies shuffling feet and their strange groaning breath.

She reached out for Benjamin and found him in the dark. She slipped her arms round his waist and pulled him close. He seemed a little surprised, but put his arms round her for comfort all the same.

Tatyana heard a match strike and saw a flickering light come closer. It was Brigitte, carrying an oil lamp.

"This was left behind here," she said. "Lucky I have good night vision."

"Can I talk zombie movies for a minute?" said Benjamin.

"Sure," said Tatyana. "Knock yourself out."

"Well, it just occurred to me that what's happening here is like the complete opposite of more or less any zombie movie. Sooner or later pretty much all of them boil down to a siege situation. A group of survivors find themselves trapped, surrounded by zombies trying to break in, to bite them so they'll die and come back as zombies."

"Okay, tell me something I don't know."

"Haven't you noticed it's the zombies who are under siege here? The living are the ones trying to break in and get to *them*. Not to kill them, but to bring them back to life by injecting their souls into them with those weird Baka things. It's a complete reversal of the formula."

"That's because there's no formula here, " said Tatyana. "This isn't fiction. Welcome to real life."

CHAPTER THIRTY-FOUR

"GOT YOU." THE little vixen was coming out from behind the trees. Palmer had her just where he wanted her.

He'd picked her up on the island's CCTV. He'd had a huge row with Doc Papa about getting the cameras installed around the island. Doc Papa had claimed he didn't need them. That he could access the "invisible world" using his Voodoo, and that was much better.

Palmer had pointed out that Doc Papa had better things to do with his time than monitor the entire island via the 'invisible world,' and that the people they'd have to pay to do the monitoring wouldn't know Voodoo. Doc Papa eventually conceded, but only after he found a way to make it look as though it had been his idea all along. Simply to remind Palmer who was really in control.

That's what Doc Papa was doing when he handed all of Palmer's lovelies over to those cocksucking shareholders. He was trying to put Palmer in his place. He was also trying to incentivise him, so that Palmer would ensure the zombies were rounded up at all costs in order to save his own soul.

Doc Papa had reckoned without Palmer's resourcefulness, though. None of the guests, or even the shareholders, were ever told, but there were a few stray zombies roaming the island, usually in the remoter areas.

The first thing Palmer did after handing his lovers over to the shareholders was head straight for the control room to check the CCTV cameras for these strays. After an hour of searching he finally saw something he liked. A hot little number wandering round the jungle on the other side of the island.

Which is how he came to be sitting in a jeep, stalking her a couple of hours later. As she came into view Palmer picked up the snare and slipped out of the jeep. He snuck up to a tree she was shambling towards and waited.

As she passed the tree Palmer stepped out behind her and slipped the snare around her neck. The zombie began to thrash about as soon he caught her, gnashing her teeth and grasping for him. Oh, she was a feisty little one indeed.

Probably hadn't eaten in a while, by the look of her. She wasn't in the best shape. Still he couldn't afford to be choosy in the circumstances. She was the closest thing to his type that he could find.

He pushed her up against a tree with the snare, then walked around back of her so she couldn't grab him. Holding the Baka in his free hand he placed it on her forehead right where her third eye ought to be.

What happened next felt a lot like an ejaculation that started several miles away and rushed right through him and into the zombie. Both of them shook so hard that Palmer dropped the snare and fell backwards. Strangely, he felt colder and more empty than ever when it was over, even though he had found a vessel for his dispossessed soul.

Palmer got to his feet and rested against the tree. He felt shaken and drained, as though he had just undergone a huge emotional outburst. He looked over at the zombie no longer flailing about like a wild creature, and caught its eyes.

They were alight with an awareness and intelligence she hadn't possessed before. A cold, prying intelligence that Palmer recognised as his own. It was a strange sensation to see himself staring out of someone else's eyes. He didn't care much for it; it made him feel judged. There was a silent condemnation coming from behind those newly awoken eyes.

"Alright," he said. "I presume you can understand me?"

The zombie made to speak but her mouth wasn't able make any words. She put her hand to her throat as though something was blocking it.

"You need to get in the jeep. We're getting off the island. Things are falling apart. It's time to cut our losses and run before the bottom falls out of the whole enterprise. Do you hear me?"

The zombie nodded and followed Palmer to the jeep.

"I've got to get you back inside me before I get off the island," said Palmer. "In spite of what Doc Papa told those idiot shareholders, this is the last day that souls *can* be transferred. He's obviously playing some power game with them, manipulating them like he does everyone else. But not me, oh, no. If he thinks he's got my measure, then he's sorely mistaken. He thinks he's the only one who really knows what's going on round here, but he's wrong. I've picked up a thing or two in my time on this island. I know we need to take you to a glade in the centre of the island. And we need to sacrifice a black goat and a black hen. That's why we've got to make a quick pit stop back at the compound to pick them up."

Palmer glanced over at the zombie. She was looking intently at him, almost through him. "For Christ's sake, will you stop staring like that? You're making me uncomfortable."

The zombie coughed violently. It looked like she was choking. Eventually she spat a great mouthful of soil and dead leaves into her hand. A giant, chestnut-brown beetle crawled out of her mouth, opened its carapace and flew away.

"I'm sorry," she said in a gravelly voice. "That was stopping me from talking."

Palmer turned away to concentrate on the track as he started up the jeep. He found the sight of the zombie coughing up soil and insects so repulsive that he was seriously turned on. He tried to ignore the huge erection he was getting as he drove off.

"It's not the staring."

"What?"

"It's not the staring that makes you uncomfortable," said the zombie, her voice sounding unusually masculine. "It's that fact that you can't ignore me any longer. You've been ignoring the existence of your soul for most of your life. Now you're faced with the incontrovertible proof that you have a soul, you don't like it. You can't neglect me anymore. I'm right in your face."

She really knew how to kill the mood.

"I know you exist," said Palmer. "I've seen too much in my time here to think otherwise."

"Yes but I'm an inconvenient truth to you. A guilty secret you have to keep hidden from others, like a weakness."

"Look, I'm doing everything in my power to get you back inside me. I can't be that ashamed of you."

"You're only hanging on to me because of what I mean to your survival. I'm just an asset to you, something to stop you turning into a zombie."

"You're the most precious asset I have. Isn't that obvious from the lengths I'm going to just to hang on to you?"

"I've got to argue your case before God when we die, you know?" said Palmer's soul. "Convince Him not to toss you into the abyss. That's what a Gros Bon Ange does. You haven't given me much to work with so far, though, have you? What am I going to say in your defence? That I was the most precious thing on your balance sheet? So that cancels out all the people you've hurt, with the things that you've done?"

Palmer stared straight ahead at the jungle. "You sound just like my father."

"Yes," said the zombie. "I suppose I do. That's why I judge you so harshly. Because that's how your father judged you. That's how you were taught to judge yourself. Nothing you ever did was good enough. That's how he made you feel all the time. And your mother, she may as well have been dead for all the comfort and love she showed. All of that was reserved for your sister, not you. Then, when you were twelve she did die. You got to spend a whole hour with the corpse, do you remember? That was the longest you'd spent in her company since you were a baby. Just before you had to go, when you knew no-one was looking, you bent and gave her cold lips a goodbye kiss, do you recall? You probably don't realise it, but that's where this whole necrophilia thing started."

"I don't know what you're talking about."

"Don't try putting me on. I'm you, remember. I know more of your guilty secrets than you do. Don't go pretending this doesn't turn you on. You've finally done what you've wanted to do your whole life. You've impregnated a corpse with your soul. Most men get to see bits of themselves inside the children they beget on women. But you, you got to impregnate the object of your desire with nothing more than your own life. When you look into the eyes of this corpse you see only yourself staring back. Isn't that what you dream of in a lover?"

Palmer put his foot down in annoyance. "You're just a tease. That's all you are. A filthy tease."

"I'm not stopping you, lover. I've never stopped you indulging your desires, have I? You wouldn't listen to me anyway. I know all about that hard-on you're trying to hide. I know where you'd like to put it. This corpse is pretty ripe isn't it, all rotting and decayed? I know what that smell's doing to you. Why resist anymore?"

"There isn't time."

"There won't be any time soon. This might be your only opportunity."

Palmer stopped the jeep. He leant over and put his hands on the zombie's hips. She moved closer to him. He pressed his lips to her cheek. The skin felt rotten and soft, on the point of putrefaction. He could see the maggots crawling around underneath it.

Palmer couldn't believe how much this aroused him. He slid his hand up the zombie's thigh, lifted her tattered dress and slipped his fingers into her fraying knickers.

Then he froze. He felt sickened and repulsed by what he felt inside her underwear. He pulled his hand away in revulsion. "You tricked me. You knew."

"Oh, did I forget to tell you?" said his soul laughing inside the zombie. She slipped down her knickers and revealed the largest penis Palmer had ever seen, on the living or the dead. "You just picked up the island's only zombie lady-boy."

CHAPTER THIRTY-FIVE

SAM MCKANE WAS ready to kick ass. This was where people started paying. He was taking control and he was getting his due.

The jeep was driving cross-country, swerving to avoid palm trees and rocks. He and the guards were thrown about in the back.

He seemed to be losing all sensation of pain. His back would usually be in agony after this much punishment, not to mention his ass, but it didn't bother him at all. He wondered if this was a drawback or a bonus of the changes he was going through. He didn't care to find out what would happen if he changed much further. That was why he was taking action.

The jeep pulled up in a clearing and the men jumped out. Sam climbed out after them. "Why are we stopping? he demanded. "This isn't the mine."

"No, sir," said Donovan, the Head Guard. "The mine's about ten minutes down that track. This is the best wi-fi connection in this part of the island."

"Wi-fi? I thought there wasn't any internet here?"

"Not for the private use of guests, there isn't, sir. But the guards and the management have access. There's a transmitter in the security post, behind us."

"Security post?"

"They're all over the island sir, tiny bases where two or three men can hole up, for security and defence purposes."

A thickset guard with a moustache handed Donovan a silver laptop, which he opened and gave to Sam. "Now, about the small matter of payment," Donovan said.

Sam grunted. "Playing hardball, huh? Where'd you get the laptop?"

"One of my men stole it, sir. You said you'd transfer two million dollars into an account we could all access. You'll be able to do that on this machine."

"We're getting a little ahead of ourselves, aren't we, son? I'm paying you to do a job. So far all you've done is get my ass sore by driving me into the middle of nowhere."

"Sir, the mine is just around the corner. We're ahead of any other troops they've sent. But my men need assurances if they're going to disobey direct orders and put their lives in danger."

"You'll get paid, soon as you've got me a zombie. Don't you worry about that."

"Sir, we need to get paid now or you can take your chances getting your own damn zombie."

Sam logged on to one of his three private banks and brought up his account details. "I'm going to create an account for you. I'll transfer a million into it now and I'll transfer the rest once I'm off the island."

"Make it a million and a half."

"Make it 'suck my dick.'" Sam handed the laptop back to Donovan. "That's the account I've created for you, all the security and access details are on the screen and you can see the balance."

"One million dollars," said Donovan. A guard looking over his shoulder whistled. Donovan put his elbow in the guard's ribs. "Shut up, Kavanaugh."

Kavanaugh was as tall as Donovan, but not as broad and, judging from his pizza face, a decade younger. He sloped off.

"Yates, stick this back in the truck." Donovan handed the laptop to the guard with the moustache.

"Now, this is what you're going to do," said Sam. "Two of you will stay and guard me in the jeep, the rest of you will break into the that mine and get me the three fittest male zombies you can find. When I've transferred my soul into the zombie I want you're going to drive me to the harbour, commandeer a boat to escort me to mainland Haiti. When I'm safe, and I've got hold of my own witchdoctor who can get me back my soul, you can have the rest of the money."

"Sir, what about zombies for myself and my men?" said Donovan. "Our souls were in that bank too."

"There won't be room in the jeep for that many zombies, and there won't be time for all of you to cherry pick your favourite ones. You go straight in, get my zombies and come straight out. Is that clear?"

"With respect sir, time is of the essence for all of us. If I send men to Haiti with you they won't get a chance to save their souls. And judging from the rate we're all changing that means they won't be of much use to you when you hit Haiti."

"That's your problem, son, not mine. When I pay someone to do a job, I don't expect to have to hold their hand every damn step of the way. That's something you've got to sort out in your own time, not while you're working for me."

"Thanks, Sam," said Donovan. "That makes this a lot easier." He pulled out his pistol.

"What the fuck? Boy, do you want me to take that thing off you and shove it up your ass?"

"Old man, you're too frail to even shove it up your own ass."

"Hey, Donovan, man," said Yates. "Are you sure you know what you're doing?"

"I know exactly what I'm doing."

"You ain't gonna shoot him now, are ya?" said Kavanaugh. "'Cause if you do, then we won't get paid t'other million."

"We ain't ever going to get paid the other million," Donovan said. "This wily old cunt'd fuck us six ways to Sunday before he ever paid us that. We've got all we're going to get out of him."

"Now, son, that ain't exactly true," Sam said. "Why, I've always been strictly honest and above board in all my dealings. You ask anyone I've done business with. I'm a man of my word, and when I give it, by heck I keep it."

"Like fuck you do," said Donovan. "I'm sorry Sam but I'm just not buying your act."

Sam felt his heart start to beat faster. He could even feel sweat on his brow. He was wrangling for his life and soul now.

"Now, hold on a moment. You're turning down a lot of money here, boys. You could all be set up for life with what I'm offering. You guys like to bargain hard, I respect that. I tell you what, as a show of good faith I'll even throw in an extra half million when we get to Haiti. What do you say?"

"Not interested, Sam," said Donovan.

Yates stepped up to him. "Whoa, whoa. Hold on, Donovan. You didn't consult us about this. What if we want to take him up on his offer?"

"He's right, boys," said Sam. "You ought to listen to this man."

"Shut your fucking face, Sam," said Donovan. "I'm your commanding officer, Yates. Since when did I consult you about what I'm going to do?"

"I'm just saying we could make a lot more money if you don't shoot him now. We might not get a chance at this much money ever again in our lives."

"I'm with Yates," said Kavanaugh.

"Another word from you, dickwad," said Donovan, "and you're next for a bullet. We can make a lot more money than he's offering, or probably even got. Here's what we're going to do. When I've shot him we're going to go down to that mine and take control of all those zombies. We're going to hole up with them nice and secure so no-one can get in and then we're going to auction them off, one at time, to those bastards. If he's prepared to pay us two million for one of 'em, then they all will. There's at least fifty of them on this island. You do the math."

"Now that's just plain crazy, boy," said Sam. "There's a hundred guards on this island they'll never let you get away with that."

"If we take the zombies down into the mine they won't be able to find us. We'll control the one thing on the island everyone wants, including the guards. They'll *have* to do business with us."

"Look son, let me give you a piece of business advice. I've been in business a long time and I've learned a thing or two. You stick with the deal you've got in your hand; you don't go endangering it by chasing off after some half-baked, cockamamie scheme. I'm prepared to go higher if the price is an issue. How does three and a half million sound?"

"Not interested."

"Why don't we make it four million?"

"Why don't we make it 'suck my dick.'" Donovan said and fired three times.

Sam felt like he'd been punched three times in the stomach and back. He looked down at the holes the bullet had left in his gut and wondered why it didn't hurt as much as it ought to. Blood began to trickle out, but not as fast or as much as he expected. His body was even getting slow at dying now.

"He's still standing," said Kavanaugh. "Why is he standing?"

Donovan raised his pistol and aimed at Sam's head.

Sam cowered and held out his hand to protect his face. The last thing he saw, in the split second before his brains blew out of the back of his head, was the bullet slicing off his middle finger.

CHAPTER THIRTY-SIX

"That's impossible," said Vincenzo.

Doc Papa looked at the freshly dug soil of the grave and the long empty box at the bottom of it. "Apparently not."

"But you put her in that box," Vincenzo said. "I saw you nail it shut. I helped you bury her. We did the ceremony, the wards and charms are all still working. How did she get out if they're all still working? They should have warned us."

"And yet they didn't. It seems we underestimated her. And babbling like an idiot isn't going to help."

"What *is* going to help?"

"Following my orders to the letter. Giving yourself over entirely to my will. I am divinely ordained by the Loas. To follow me is to follow them."

"Right now I'm following you down the road to ruin."

Doc Papa drew himself up and glowered at Vincenzo. The sheer force of his stare was enough to make the other man wilt.

Doc Papa dismissed the two acolytes who had dug up the grave, and they went back to wait by the vehicle. The light was dimming, evening was coming on. The clock was ticking and he had much to achieve before the Festival of the Gédé drew to a close.

"Describing our current situation as 'the road to ruin' only shows how little you understand," said Doc Papa. "This is confirmation that the Loa have blessed my plans. For a start we've settled the little matter of who our rouge Mambo is. I should have recognised her handiwork the minute all this started."

"You can't seriously be suggesting that Brigitte Laveau is back on St Ignatius? We created a living death for her. How did she escape that? How did she get back on the island without us knowing about it?"

"My guess is that she never died. She found some way to circumvent our spell and got off the island without us finding out. Then she either created an entirely new identity, complete with a new body and a new fortune, or she found a way to borrow one. You have to admire her prowess if nothing else."

"You still have feelings for her," said Vincenzo, with a smirk.

Doc Papa drew a symbol in the air and Vincenzo collapsed in agony. He had been overstepping himself a lot lately, and needed to be reminded just how in thrall he was to Doc Papa. With a supreme effort of will, Vincenzo held up a hand in surrender. As he was in a good mood Doc Papa only let him suffer a little while longer.

"Can I get up now?" said Vincenzo.

"Why don't you try?"

Vincenzo shook as he got to his feet. He stared down at the empty grave so as not to look Doc Papa in the eye. "You really think Brigitte Laveau is back on the island?"

"I'm certain of it. Erzulie Zandor is putting all the pieces into place for me, just as she promised."

"By sending this accursed woman back to stop you?"

"Not to stop me. To help me."

"Help you?"

"She's the only one who knows where the Gateway of the Souls is."

"You really think it exists?" Vincenzo held up his hands in deference. "I don't mean any disrespect, but we've looked everywhere in the Invisible World and we never found even a trace of it. The only proof we've found of its existence are a few rumours and the word of a woman we tried to kill."

"I know it exists. Don't mistake your ignorance for lack of proof. You know only as much as I allow you to; that's why I'm permanently ahead of you. You can't even see the pattern here. At the very moment when I need the Gateway most, Erzulie Zandor sends me the one person who knows its location, just as she said she would."

"How are you going to get it from her? She wouldn't tell you the last time, even to save herself from a living death. Now we're not even sure where *she* is, let alone the Gateway of the Souls. All we know is she's down a mine somewhere."

"I am disappointed that you show so little faith in my abilities, Vincenzo. Maybe I was wrong to give you so much responsibility. Perhaps another of my acolytes would assist me better."

"I wasn't saying I don't have faith in you. I just wanted to know what you were planning so I could assist you in the best possible way."

"The best way you can assist me is to do exactly as you're told when you're told. I don't need to know her exact physical location. Now I know who she is, I can find her through the Invisible World. I can tear the knowledge from her mind. As I'm fairly certain she doesn't know I've discovered who she really is, which gives me the element of surprise; an advantage I intend to fully exploit."

Doc Papa turned his back on Vincenzo and walked back to the jeep. Vincenzo followed at a respectful distance. Doc Papa wasn't buying his fake deference. Vincenzo was asking too many questions. Why was he so keen to know Doc Papa's plans and motives all of a sudden? It smacked of duplicity.

Doc Papa didn't think Vincenzo had the intelligence or the initiative to challenge him alone. Someone else must have made him a counter offer, and Doc Papa knew just who. It stood to reason really. Doc Papa would have done the same thing in their position. It was simply good business sense and he would have been disappointed in his associates if they hadn't attempted something. That's why he hadn't let Vincenzo out of his sight since the shareholders had stormed into his office.

He was even a little impressed by Vincenzo's treacherousness. Still, they had all made the mistake of underestimating him. Doc Papa was more than prepared for them when they made their move.

He stopped when they reached the jeep and let Vincenzo get in first, smiling innocently to hide his true thoughts. Vincenzo smiled humbly back, hiding his true feelings almost as well. He hadn't realised he'd been rumbled yet.

"To the mansion," Doc Papa instructed the driver. It was time to visit his ceremony room, the most secret and heavily guarded room of the mansion, where the endgame would be played out.

CHAPTER THIRTY-SEVEN

Two Years Ago

Doc stood at the bottom of the stone steps. Above him, the burnt-out shell of Mangrove Hall caught the crimson twilight of the setting sun. Moss and lichen covered the steps, and tufts of grass pushed their way out of the cracks. The terraced lawns were given over to weeds and creepers.

This was a palace once. Look at what they've done to it. This is why they have to pay, Emil. You have to make them pay and you have to rebuild it. Restore this estate to its former glory, Emil.

Emil, the name didn't feel appropriate anymore. That was the name of another man from another world. A man of wealth and influence. The man he had nearly forgotten he once was.

'Doc' was the name of the person who had stood in for that man when he had no memory. Neither name sat comfortably with him anymore. Neither of them represented what he had become. He needed a better mantle. One that befitted a man uniquely placed to re-make the world.

The name Doc came from his title. He couldn't be a Hougan in spite of his accomplishments, so they'd called him Doctor as was customary.

As no-one knew his real name, the islanders shortened Doctor to Doc, and that's how he became known.

You're a Papamal Emil, any new name you choose must take that into account.

Doc shook his head to quiet the voice. It was becoming tiresome now. The spirit knew this, and clung to him tighter as a consequence. That was how ghosts were, when they got their claws into you.

He had to admit she'd been useful to him, though. She knew where his lost memories lay. She could trace them along the ancestral bloodlines. She re-taught him his whole past, and much more besides.

Doc had known nothing of his past before that. His memories started when he was washed ashore on the small beach. He knew now that his charter plane, on its way to Rio, had crashed into the waters off St Ignatius. The engines failed, according to the pilot; it was the last thing he'd said. Doc wondered if there weren't other forces at work.

Doc had total amnesia when the natives found him and brought him to Brigitte. Brigitte tended his wounds, brought his fever down and nursed him back to health. But every time she touched him she set off a different fever, deep inside him, and he saw it burn in her eyes too. As his health returned, this fever grew hotter in both of them. Eventually they were forced to succumb and it claimed them.

It wasn't the only thing to claim Doc. When he was well enough, Doc asked to be taken to a Voodoo ceremony. Brigitte was happy to oblige, and introduced him to her congregation at the Ounfó. As the ceremony reached its peak, to everyone's surprise, the Loa Baron Samedi, ruler of the Gédé, chose to mount Doc and ride him.

As he lurched, macabre and obscene, Baron Samedi told the congregation that Doc had a special significance to the Loa. Baron Samedi commanded that Doc be initiated into the deepest mysteries of Voodoo.

So Doc became Brigitte's student as well as her lover. Under her tutelage he rose up through the stages of initiation faster than anyone had ever seen. He was joined with his Met-tet, Baron Samedi, in the ritual of the lave tet. Then he walked through fire in the kanzo rite. Finally he became a houn'ior and took the asson, his mystic rattle and badge of office, after walking the Poun'goueh – the waters of the abyss.

With no recollections of his former life, he was an empty vessel, ready to be filled with the knowledge of Voodoo. He went from being a broken castaway to a powerful Vodouisant, second only to Brigitte in the standing of the Ounfó, loved, feared and respected by the inhabitants of the island that had become his home.

Even then, there was an aching hole in his life, like a wound that wouldn't heal. Nothing about his life or personality seemed fixed or permanent until he could anchor it to his past, but that past was missing. Without memories, he felt insubstantial and insufficient. So much of him remained a question, so little provided answers.

It pained Brigitte to see her lover so troubled. To help him, she suggested a special rite in which they would invoke his ancestors, as his memories were now like lost family members.

They had watched over him all his life. They knew the man he'd been, was and would be. They held all his memories in trust, so they could return them at the point of death. Your life does indeed flash before your eyes just before you die; your ancestors see to that.

Two weeks ago they'd held the rite inside the Djévo, the private chamber of the Ounfó. It had not gone as planned. Someone had come through, but not who they expected. Brigitte had been visited, not Doc.

She seemed confused as the spirit of her own ancestor came upon her. She wouldn't tell Doc what the ancestor was saying, but it troubled her greatly. She fled the Ounfó without speaking to him and disappeared into the night.

He hadn't seen her since.

You're better off without her. You lost her but you gained me, and I can teach you so much more.

Doc had won the attention of perhaps his most famous ancestor. As soon as Brigitte left the temple, his ancestor came upon him and revealed herself. She'd been waiting for his lover to leave.

His ancestor brought his lost memories with her, and something even more valuable. A new sense of purpose.

Experiencing his memories once more was like living his life all over again, but as a different person. He had to introduce the person he'd become to the person he used to be. And in spite of the giant gulf between their worlds, he had to integrate them into one working personality.

His old self was appalled and amused to discover that he'd been living like a peasant on a tiny island near a third-world country. The occult power that his new self wielded impressed him, though.

His new self was astounded to find he used to own and control more wealth than he knew existed. The sheer number of material possessions he used to have overwhelmed him. He liked the influence and control this wealth could buy, however.

One thing that united both selves was a lust for power. It was around this trait that he built his new character.

And I brought you power, didn't I? I showed you a way to rule this island and to raise a fortune bigger than anything your forefathers dreamed.

Doc was careful to hide the thought that he found his ancestor's ambitions to be hopelessly limited, next to his own.

While Brigitte was away, he took the time to plot his next move. He made covert contacts and new allies and waited for the right time to strike. That time had now arrived.

She'd sent word to him earlier today that she wanted to speak. He was to meet her in the ruins of Mangrove hall.

So now he climbed the steps of a building that had meant so much to his forefathers, that he had seen practically every day since coming to the island, and yet had never once explored.

He thought it fitting that Brigitte had chosen to meet him here. In this crumbling ruin that haunted the skyline of the entire island. He wondered if she was aware of the irony.

Despite all the things he planned to do, he was excited about seeing her again. There was a primordial attraction between them, an unstoppable natural force.

Pah, men! Stop thinking with your cock and start thinking with your head for a change. She's a pathetic peasant girl, descended from slave stock. You could do a lot better. I admit I enjoyed a few of them myself, that's what they're there for. But I never got attached to one.

Doc walked between the pillars that held up the stone porch, and through the burnt archway from which the doors had once hung. His footsteps echoed round the blackened stone walls as he crossed the tiled floor. Good thing he wasn't trying to sneak up on her.

Brigitte was standing in front of a window at the rear of the property. He could see her silhouette against the fading evening light. She turned as she heard him coming, and shot him a welcoming smile. Her face was half in shadow and twice as lovely for it.

"You came," she said.

"How could I stay away?"

Brigitte was wearing a simple pink dress and had tucked a blossom behind her ear. She couldn't have looked more desirable.

"Look who's all dressed up?"

"I thought I'd make an effort," she said. "I haven't seen you in a while."

"I missed you," he said, slipping his arm around her waist almost without thinking. She put her hand on his chest, to stop him moving closer, but he could see that she liked touching him.

Pull yourself together, you're like a dog on heat. You catch one whiff of cunny and you fall to pieces.

Doc let go of Brigitte.

"I'm sorry that I haven't been in touch," she said. "I had a lot to think about, and now I've got a lot to tell you."

"I'm all ears."

"You've probably guessed by now that it was me who was visited by an ancestor. The rite didn't go wrong; there was a good reason for it. It concerns your ancestors and mine. I was contacted by my ancestor, Toussaint Laveau, whose daughter Millicent was my great-great-grandmother. He told me your name. You're Emil Papamal, and your ancestor is the woman who used to live in this house, Mary April Papamal. Before he died, Toussaint placed a curse on Mary's bloodline: one of her ancestors would suffer a hideous death at the hands of a Laveau. That's you, my love."

"Go on."

"You're not shocked by this?"

You're the one who has the shock coming, my dear.

"I'm still processing it. Why did he place the curse on my ancestor? What was so bad about her?"

"You've heard the stories. You must know."

"Rumours and legends. The things mothers make up to scare their children."

"No, they're all true. Toussaint showed me everything. How she married Jean Papamal for his money and then murdered him. Then, after she inherited everything, this house and his sugar plantation, she discovered he was bankrupt."

The man was a fool who lived beyond his means. He would have lost the whole estate if I hadn't acted when I did.

Be quiet, Doc thought. *She has powers. She'll hear you. You'll ruin everything.*

"Are you alright, my love?" Brigitte put her hand on his shoulder. "You seem distant. Distracted."

"This is a lot to take in. I'm having a bit of trouble. I wanted to regain my past, and you're telling me you're going to kill me because of things that happened over a century ago."

"I'm sorry, I know it's a lot to take in. It took me a while to come to terms with it all. But it's important that you know this."

"Okay. So, if her husband went bankrupt, is that how this place became a ruin?"

"No, that was much later, she saved the plantation by marrying a rich Admiral about a year later. She didn't like him any better than her first husband, though. That's when she started taking lovers from among her slaves. When her new husband found out, he threatened to divorce her and dispossess her of everything, his money and the plantation, which he now legally owned."

"What did she do?"

"She hid three of her lovers in his bedroom. When he retired, she had one of them hold him down while another throttled him and the third took her right there on the bed in front of him. He died watching his wife coupling with one of the slaves. She spent the night with all three of them while her husband's corpse lay next to them in the bed.

"That's when your great-grandfather was conceived. She never knew who his true father was. For reasons known only to herself, she carried the baby to term and handed him over to her slaves to rear. She let him keep her name, though, which is why you now bear it."

"I still don't see what all this has to do with you and me?"

"It has everything to do with you and me. What happened to our ancestors continues to affect us today. There was a settlement of free islanders on the south side of the island, a small fishing village where the harbour is. Toussaint was their Houngan. Mary wanted his power and tried to join his Ounfó. He resisted at first, but she held a lot of power. In the end, for the sake of his congregation, he thought it better to be allied to her than against her so he let her join."

That's a lie! He lusted after me from the minute he saw me. He was as eager for my body as you are for this bitch's flesh. He would have done anything to get me and, after leading him on for a while, I obliged.

"They were lovers?"

"Yes. How did you know that?" Brigitte was silent for a moment and looked about her. "Is there something here with us? I'm sure I can detect something."

"It's this place. It must be filled with ghosts. You were telling me about our ancestors."

"That's right. Mary used all her feminine wiles to seduce Toussaint. She was very beautiful and very cunning and, in spite of his wisdom, Toussaint gave in. But she took against my great-great-grandmother. Millicent was betrothed to a young man who had caught Mary's eye. When the young man spurned her, Mary was determined to have her revenge.

"Mary kidnapped Millicent and planned to sacrifice her in a hideous ceremony she had planned. She'd come across a spell that would steal the souls of every one of her slaves and turn them all into walking corpses that would do her absolute bidding. She planned to set them to work on the plantation."

It was an economic decision. It would have slashed my overheads. Do you have any idea how much it costs to feed and clothe the amount of slaves needed to run a plantation that size? A third of my profits went to looking after them. Think of how rich I'd have been if not for her stinking ancestor.

"Toussaint only discovered her plans once the ceremony was underway. He confronted her as she began to siphon off the souls of the slaves. To save the slaves and his daughter, Toussaint invoked and opened the Gateway of the Souls."

"The Gateway of the Souls," said Doc. "That's like some sort of black hole isn't it? An artefact that draws lost souls to it from anywhere in the Invisible World. That really exists?"

"It exists and Toussaint opened it. He drew the souls of the slaves back from the crossroads where they were trapped and returned them to their bodies. But once created, the Gateway can never be destroyed and Mary hungered for its power. Toussaint was too exhausted from conjuring up the Gateway to fight Mary for control of it. To stop her from seizing it he transported it inside himself."

"That can be done? How? You must tell me."

"There are things that you must wait to learn."

"So what happened to Toussaint, then?"

"In a fit of anger Mary tried to finish the sacrifice and stab Toussaint's daughter. He threw himself in the way and was killed instead. As he died he uttered the curse that we've now got to deal with."

Curse? More like a pathetic grudge. Feeble sorcery that won't come to anything, I'll see to that.

"I'm guessing the Gateway of the Souls didn't disappear when Toussaint died. Does that mean it still exists?"

"It does."

"Where is it? You have to tell me."

"It is safe. That's all you need to know."

"And what about Mary Papamal? What did your ancestor say happened to her?"

"There was a revolt. The slaves grabbed their farm tools and stormed the house as Toussaint died; they murdered Mary and her henchmen and set light to the plantation."

"And they got away with that? Why didn't the authorities do anything?"

"I don't know. Things were pretty volatile on mainland Haiti then, I suppose."

"What about the plantation?"

"Well, neither Mary or Jean Papamal had any relatives, so the slaves took it over, turned most of it into small holdings and farmed it."

"Incredible that no-one exploited the potential in such a huge estate. That they let it go to waste."

"That's a strange thing to say."

"Sorry. I was just thinking aloud." Doc took Brigitte's hands and looked into her eyes. "So what about this curse, am I going to suffer a hideous death at your hands?"

Doc's tone was playful and mocking, but Brigitte's expression was serious.

"That's what I've been thinking about while I was away," she said. "That's why I ran that night in the Djevo and hid from you. I didn't want you to be that woman's ancestor. I didn't want the curse hanging over our heads for the rest of our lives. I didn't want to kill you."

"But the curse is there and we both know about it now. We can't avoid that."

"We can't avoid it, but we don't need to fulfill it. It doesn't have to rule our lives. It was dark, hateful Voodoo, spoken by a dying man who wanted to make his murderer pay. She did pay, so why should I have to suffer because of his death? I'm not a murderer and you're innocent. Why should you have to pay for something your ancestor did?"

"So how do you suggest we get around this?"

"Love."

"Love?"

"Yes, it's that simple."

"We've never spoken about love before."

"You're not a man who speaks about his emotions. You never tell me what you're feeling."

"But love?"

"It doesn't have to be romantic love, if that scares you. It can be the love you have for your friends or for a companion. Love is how you beat hate and dispel dark Voodoo like this." Brigitte's became flirtatious. "I've certainly loved you with my body many times."

Doc grinned. She'd given him an idea. She was playing to her strengths to win him over, but she'd betrayed her weakness and, if he used it right, this would all go a lot quicker and easier.

"I have to admit I *do* love your body," he said. "I've had an idea. If love dispels dark Voodoo, then what about a love spell? Why don't we forge a love knot?"

"A love knot? That's for binding a couple together forever. That's a big step."

"One that will save us both. You said so yourself. You're not afraid of commitment, are you?"

"No, but I... I mean, you never..."

"Speak about my feelings? Perhaps it's time I did, especially when my life depends on it." Doc produced a nylon scarf from his pocket. "I believe we need one of these for the spell. And a small clipping from an intimate area." He took a penknife from his pocket, reached into the front of his trousers and cut some of his public hair.

Brigitte looked surprised. "Why are you carrying a knife and scarves around?"

"I just had a feeling that I might need them. I think the Loa were guiding my actions. I'll need a clipping from you as well, if this is going to work." Doc placed his hand on Brigitte's thigh and gently lifted her dress.

Brigitte held his wrist and stopped him. "You're getting rather forward, aren't you?"

"And you're getting rather coy. That isn't like you."

"Maybe I like to be asked properly."

"Would you be so kind?"

"Maybe I will." She slipped her panties off. He took a clipping of her hair. He was close enough to smell her body. Her scent was intoxicating. He was completely hard. Did he have time for one last tryst?

Don't be an idiot! Strike now before she realises, while she's vulnerable.

However much she annoyed him, his ancestor was right. Palming his own hair, he split Brigitte's into two clippings and tied the scarf around them. Then he tied seven more knots, each one more intricate than the last.

"Be careful," Brigitte said. "If you make a mistake with one of the knots you could..."

"Paralyse you?" Doc said.

Brigitte sat, rigid, on the crumbling window sill. Only her eyes showed any sign of life.

"That was the whole idea. I wasn't making a love knot. I was creating a spell to snare you. Of course the effect is only temporary, as you know. Unless the knots are sealed with goofer dust and burned."

Doc took a snakeskin pouch from his pocket. It contained the goofer dust, a fine powder of ground rattlesnake skulls and graveyard dust mixed with salt and brimstone. He sprinkled the dust over the knotted scarf then placed the scarf in the pouch.

This is the Mambo who trained you? I'm not impressed. I thought you said she had power, yet you tricked her so easily.

Brigitte's eyes widened in alarm as she finally felt the presence of Doc's ancestor.

"Yes, she's been with me for quite a while," Doc said. "You weren't the only one to get visited that night. She's taught me a lot as well. Not only have I regained my past, I've also planned out my future. I'm afraid you're not in it. I already knew about the curse, but I have a different solution. I'm going to take you out of the picture. You can't inflict a hideous death on me if I get to you first. A living death, though. If I killed you outright, your spirit could wreak vengeance on me. If I trap your soul in the grave with your corpse, there's nothing you can do.

"You see, I've realised there's a huge natural resource on this island that's ripe for exploitation. You may not be aware of this, but I'm rather wealthy, and keen to find new ventures to invest in. Thanks to Mary Papamal, I now know how to conduct the ceremony she attempted so many years ago, and she's very keen for me to try it again. That's the other reason I can't let you live. I was certain you'd try to stop me, and you may be the only person who could. However, once I've taken care of that eventuality, I stand to profit heavily from my actions."

Doc began to collect twigs and logs to start a fire. He piled them up and put a match to them. As the moon came up and the flames lit the shell of the old house, Brigitte's eyes darted to a figure who stepped out of the shadows.

"I think you remember Vincenzo," said Doc. "He used to be your rival for the head of the Ounfó, until his liking for secret Petro rituals and his traffic with malevolent Loa got him exiled to Haiti. I invited him back and offered him a very good position in my new organisation. He's going to assist me in disposing of you." Doc turned to Vincenzo. "You got what I asked you for?"

Vincenzo handed him another pouch, and Doc looked inside at the ground human bones. He emptied them into the snakeskin pouch, then tossed it on the fire.

What are you doing? What was in that pouch?

"Ground human bones," said Doc. "To seal the paralysis spell."

There's more to it than that. What are you up to?

"A simple rite to sever the connection with an ancestor who's plaguing you. You grind her bones to a fine powder and then you burn them.

You what!?

"You didn't think we could find your grave, did you? It has no marker and your bones don't lie in any cemetery, but the Loa told Vincenzo where your remains were buried. He dug you up and ground your bones for me."

Why?

"I'm afraid I don't have room for partners in this new venture, and you simply don't have the vision to understand it. The market has moved on too much since your day. So I'm dissolving our merger as of this moment."

The temperature in the ruined house dropped in spite of the fire. There was a sound like a huge wind rushing by and Mary Papamal was dragged back to the afterlife.

She let out a bitter scream of fury, which even Vincenzo and Brigitte heard. The flames of the fire leapt as it roared with her anger and frustration.

Then she was gone.

"Well she certainly had spirit," said Doc. "If you'll pardon the pun. Mary's grave, did you dig it deep enough to house Brigitte?"

"I did," said Vincenzo. "Do we bury her tonight?"

"We do." Doc turned and spoke to Brigitte. "After trapping you in the house of your ancestor's bitter enemy, we're going to inter you in her grave. I hope you appreciate all the trouble we've gone to on your behalf.

"Do we move her now, Doc?"

"Don't call me Doc. As of this moment that's no longer my name."

"What should I call you? Doctor Emil?"

"Doc Papamal perhaps. No that doesn't sound right. Doc Papa. That's who I've become. Call me Doc Papa."

CHAPTER THIRTY-EIGHT

TATYANA JUMPED AS gunshots sounded outside the metal door. The zombies around her became aware of her heart beating faster. Tatyana backed slowly away from them.

She joined Benjamin, with his ear pressed up against the door.

"What's happening?" she said.

"I think some of the guards have arrived," Benjamin said. "They told the guests to get out of the way, but the guests weren't budging. They're too desperate to get their hands on the zombies. That must have been when they opened fire."

"Did they shoot anyone?"

"I don't know. I didn't hear any screams. They're probably just firing into the air to scare them."

Tatyana put her ear against the door, but couldn't hear anything. "What do you think is happening?"

"I don't know. It's gone quiet now. I heard footsteps and some cries. That might have been the guests moving. They were more bothered about grabbing a zombie than getting shot. I don't understand it."

"They're changing," said Brigitte. "The longer their Gros Bon Ange goes without a proper vessel, the closer they get to being one of the zombies. It's what happens when you tear the soul out of something."

"And you knew this when you sabotaged all the Pot-tets?" said Tatyana.

Brigitte looked affronted. "Yes, I did. Is it any more than they deserve? You've seen what they're capable of doing. They studied so hard to be like zombies and now their wish has been granted. I don't see how you can judge me. I recall seeing you sink to murder with the rest of them."

Tatyana dropped Brigitte's gaze and stared at the floor in shame. The memory of the man she had helped to kill stung her to the very core.

"I'm sorry," said Brigitte. "That was a low blow."

"You're right, though," said Tatyana. "I wasn't being judgmental. I was just surprised. It's not like you to do something that would harm someone else. When everyone was tearing that poor man apart, for instance, you used your Voodoo to hide yourself so no-one could see you weren't joining in."

"You could see that?" Brigitte was astonished.

"Erm, well, yeah. You made me forget, didn't you? But it just came back. It's happened before as well. You made me forget in the lecture hall, but then I felt this presence and the memory came back. I hope you don't mind, but I followed you when you left the lecture theatre. Your field has this, like, blind spot. I hid in it so no-one saw me, not even you. That's how I knew where the secret entrance to the compound was."

"That's where you went," said Benjamin. "Why didn't you tell me?"

"I don't know. It just seemed like something that I shouldn't talk about. It was all kind of strange. I thought you might not believe me. I'd always thought I was this sceptical atheist, and then I start to see and experience all these weird things."

"Sceptical atheist?" said Benjamin. "You came here to take part in Voodoo rituals and free zombies. How sceptical is that?"

"Okay, when you put it like that, I don't sound too sceptical, but that seemed different somehow. I don't think I really believed in any of it except for the zombies. Now I'm not so sure, though."

"The Loa are calling you, my child," said Brigitte. "You have a gift and a feeling for this. You might pretend to be a sceptic, but your soul knows different. It is hungry, and it calls for sustenance."

"We have to feed our souls?" said Tatyana.

"Of course we do. How else will they grow?"

"How do you feed your soul?"

"With prayer, and devotion to God, with pure thoughts and deeds and with service to the Loa. That's why you're right about what I did to the guests and their Pot-tets. That will impoverish my soul, not feed it. When we die, our Gros Bon Ange has to argue our case before God and that action will not go in my favour."

"Well, I don't know about my soul," said Benjamin. "But my stomach is famished. I haven't had anything to eat since yesterday morning."

Before she could say anything, Tatyana was knocked off her feet. The ground shook and the metal door buckled as something exploded outside it.

"What the hell was that?" Tatyana said.

"A grenade I think," said Benjamin, picking himself up. "Or a rocket or something. I don't think we should wait around to find out."

"No," said Brigitte helping a rotund male zombie get to its feet. "They'll be through that door any moment. We'll have to go further into the mines to escape them."

As she spoke Tatyana heard the guards start battering the badly buckled door. They were minutes from getting inside.

"Follow me," Brigitte said.

She led them down a darkened tunnel carrying the lamp. At the end of the tunnel was an old electric lift that could hold about twenty or thirty people. Brigitte threw a switch to get the power on, then started up the lift and sent it down without anyone inside.

"What did you do that for?" said Benjamin. "How are we going to get down now?"

"There's a steep tunnel just along from here," said Brigitte. "I want them to think we've taken the lift. That way they'll descend to a different network of tunnels."

"Oh right," said Benjamin. "Good plan."

As they entered the tunnel Tatyana heard the door give way. This was followed by sounds of gunfire and shouted commands. She prayed they had enough of a lead to evade the guards.

Prayed? Maybe Brigitte was right. Perhaps her fascination really was a hunger. But there wasn't time to think on this.

CHAPTER THIRTY-NINE

PALMER HAD GOTTEN out of the dot com bubble before it burst. He'd dumped his shares in both Enron and Bear Stearns before the scandals broke. He was damned if he wasn't going to get out of St Ignatius before it all turned to shit.

"Damned is the right word," said his soul.

"What?" shouted Palmer. The jeep's engine was making an awful racket and the black goat tethered in the back was bleating its head off, probably sensing its impending death.

"I said 'damned' is the right word," said his soul. "Unless you get off this island, repent your ways and start making amends."

Palmer glanced from the dirt track ahead of him to the lady-boy zombie that housed his soul. It was wearing that sanctimonious expression that infuriated him.

"You know what?" Palmer said. "You are one almighty pain in the ass. That's what you are. An almighty pain in the ass."

"That's all I've ever been to you. A tiny wizened appendage, like a stunted Siamese twin you couldn't wait to have removed and pickled in a jar."

"I thought I had removed you."

"You did indeed. Then fate took a hand and suddenly you're forced to confront me and every terrible crime that I know about. Do you think you'll be able to ignore me if you do manage to reunite us?"

"Well I've been fairly successful so far, if you're to be believed."

"Of course I'm to be believed. I don't lie to you, Samuel. I know every lie you've ever told yourself and others, but I never repeat or believe them. That's why I'm so valuable to you."

"Don't flatter yourself. You're only valuable to me because I don't want to become like that thing you're currently inside."

"What, this old thing?" said his soul in a mocking tone. "Why, Samuel, you picked this out specially for me. Don't tell me you've gone off my outfit."

"It's strictly last season," said Palmer, pulling up right next to the hidden glade. "And it's time to slip into something more comfortable – namely me."

Palmer climbed out of the jeep, untied the goat and lifted the bamboo cage with the black hen inside it. "Grab that bag in the back and come with me. I want you inside me, as soon as possible."

Palmer led the goat and the zombie into the glade. It contained seven citron trees, which were sacred to Baron Samedi, the head of the Gédé, the Loa of the dead. It was also right next to an abandoned burial ground, which made it ideal for the ceremony Palmer wanted to perform.

He tied the goat to a tree, put the cage down and took the bag off the zombie. He pulled some flour and a diagram of a Vèvè out of the bag, and tried to draw the Vèvè on the ground with the flour.

"Does that look anything like this to you?" he asked, holding the diagram up to his soul when he was done.

His soul shook the zombie's head. "Not a bit, I'm afraid. I don't think this is your forté."

"Thanks for the encouragement."

"I said I'd never lie to you, Samuel. I'm the only thing in your life that won't."

"Never mind, it's the best I can do."

"Are you sure you want to go ahead with this? These are ancient, primal forces. The Houngans and Mambos who commune with them train for years before summoning one."

"This is the only way," Palmer said, lighting the black candles he'd got from the bag. "I'm running out of time, and I haven't got anyone else to do this for me. Besides I've watched Doc Papa and Vincenzo do this enough times. How difficult can it be?"

Palmer opened the bamboo cage and took the black hen out. It immediately tried to fly away, flapping at him and trying to attack him. He held it at arms length and lifted it up to what he hoped were the four points of the compass, muttering the incantations he'd memorised.

Now how did this go? That's right, he had to break its neck first, then the wings, then the legs. Every time he reached for the bird's neck it pecked at him. In his annoyance he squeezed it until it ribcage cracked. The bird squawked in pain but he was finally able to despatch it in the way he intended.

Now he had to bite its head off. Palmer put the limp head in his mouth and bit down. His stomach turned over as its spine cracked and he choked on blood and feathers. He spat the head out onto the *Vèvè* he'd drawn and dropped the body next to it. He produced a hip flask and poured rum over the hen as he picked the feathers out of his teeth.

Next, he took a knife from the bag and cut the rope tethering the goat. He grabbed the goat by the horns but it could sense what he was up to and dug its heels in, bleating and kicking. Palmer put his arm around the goat's neck and tried to drag it back.

"A little help wouldn't go amiss."

"Trust me," said his soul. "In the long run, you will not appreciate my help with this."

"Well, in the short term, you can go fuck yourself. Ow!" Palmer cried out as the goat bit him. Without thinking he rammed the knife into its eyeball. It stopped kicking and started to spasm.

Palmer dragged the dying goat over to the Vèvè and slit its throat. Its blood gushed onto the ground, soaking the badly-drawn symbol and splashing his handmade leather shoes. He uttered the last of the invocations to Baron Samedi and waited.

Nothing happened.

The flames of the black candles guttered. The glade was still and silent. Palmer felt an intense anti-climax.

Why was nothing easy today? Why wouldn't anything go his way? Once, just once, couldn't he catch a fucking break?

Unable to control his anger, he kicked the goat. Then he kicked it again and again in a blind fury.

"Cocksucking, motherfucking asshole!" he shouted, waving his fists at the empty air. "Why didn't you come, you asshole? Why didn't you fucking come?!" Palmer turned to the zombie. He was panting and his shoulders were slumped with defeat. "Go on, then, aren't you going to say it, you sanctimonious bastard? Aren't you going to say 'I told you so'?"

Palmer's soul didn't say anything. In fact, it didn't seem to be inside the zombie anymore. The smug, pitying look had been replaced with a vacant stare. Palmer didn't know why, but he was suddenly quite nervous.

The zombie began to shake and twitch. Then its face burst into a huge lascivious grin. It started to gyrate its hips then threw back its head and let out a raucous laugh.

"Baron Samedi," said Palmer. "Is that you? Look, I'm sorry about calling you a... I mean about what I said. I'm sort of new to this and I didn't know, you know, how long I should wait, or if you were coming or anything."

"You certainly are new to this. And quite terrible, judging from the mess you made of the ceremony," said the zombie. It didn't sound like Baron Samedi; the voice was deep and husky, but decidedly feminine.

"Err, you are Baron Samedi, aren't you?"

"No, my dear, you got his wife, Le Gran Brigitte. I told you you were terrible at this, didn't I? Nonetheless, I've been waiting to speak to you for a long time."

"You have?" Now he felt really nervous.

"Oh yes, I've been receiving a lot of complaints from my daughters about your activities."

"Your daughters?"

"The dead, my dear, I'm a mother to all of them. Especially those who feel they've been wronged. Who can't protect themselves and want retribution."

"I don't know what you're talking about."

"Oh don't be ridiculous, you foolish little man. You don't think you can hide anything from the dead, do you? Most of them have nothing better to do than watch the living all day. They know everything that goes on. Particularly when it concerns their newly dead bodies and what happens to them. Just because they're dead doesn't mean they've granted you consent, you know. It's still rape, my dear."

"Look, if it's a question of money..."

"Money, my silly little darling? And pray tell me, what would we do with money where we live? Buy ourselves a new house, or some expensive jewelry? Invest it in the stock market, perhaps? I don't think so. You can't buy your way out of this little problem."

"If you don't want me to pay, then what do you want?"

"Oh I want you to pay, my sweet, but not with money."

"I don't understand."

"You've wronged so many of my daughters. Violated their bodies over and over again while they were forced to watch, unable to do anything. You've visited grieving families and gloated over what you were going to do to the loved ones they'd lost. Now you must be punished."

Palmer picked up the sacrificial knife and held it out in front of him. "I'm warning you. Don't come any closer."

"And just what are you going to do with that, my dear? I'm an immortal being inside an animated corpse. Do you think a little bit of sharpened metal is going to hurt me? Incidentally, I don't envy your poor soul having to live inside this little thing. She's a bit far gone, isn't she? Should I use the word *she*? Isn't that how they like to be referred to? Transsexuals, that is, not walking corpses. Anyway, she's been out in the wild rather a long time, hasn't she? Her flesh is crawling with maggots. But that rather suits my purpose."

Palmer glanced back at the jeep, wondering if he could outrun the Loa. "Don't even think it, sweetie," said Gran Brigitte. "It doesn't work that way."

A bony hand broke though the earth by Palmer's foot and grasped his ankle, digging its fleshless fingers into him. He howled in pain and tried to pry the fingers apart but he couldn't.

"This *is* a burial ground, or did you forget?" Gran Brigitte said. "This is where I hold dominion. I control everything here, and not just the dead. Death has a gravity, you see. It draws everything to it eventually. If I increase that gravity I can accelerate life cycles. Take the maggots squirming inside this corpse. I can turn them into flies in an instant."

Palmer watched as the maggots began to writhe and thrash under the skin of the lady-boy zombie. Then, to his horror, he saw them burrow out and turn into a swarm of flies. The flies swirled around the zombie like a buzzing black aura.

"I can snatch their tiny souls," Gran Brigitte said clicking her fingers. The flies dropped out of the air and formed a carpet of tiny corpses at her feet. "And I can return them again, as undead as this poor shell."

The flies began to wave their legs in the air, and gradually flipped themselves over and took to the air around the zombie again. There was something unnatural, almost otherworldly, about the drone of their wings as they returned from death.

"Why are you doing this? What are you playing at?"

"Well, seeing as you like raping corpses so much, my sweet, I thought you might like to find out what it's like from the other side."

The undead flies landed on the zombie's midriff and began to crawl back under its rotting skin. The zombie's abdomen bulged as they forced their way inside it. Gran Brigitte lifted the zombie's tattered skirt to reveal where all the reanimated flies were going.

The zombie's gargantuan member no longer hung flaccid between its legs. It was standing stiff and proud, with all the undead insects burrowing into it. The glans bulged and rippled obscenely from the zombified flies crawling about inside.

Palmer tried once again to free his leg from the skeletal grasp of the dead hand, but before he could get anywhere the zombie was on him. It knocked him, face first, to the ground and placed a rotting hand between his shoulders. He struggled as hard as he could but he couldn't shake it off.

"What was it you called your soul when it was in this body?" said Gran Brigitte. "Oh yes, that's right, an 'almighty pain in the ass.' Well, honey, you don't know the half of it."

"Stop it! What are you doing?"

Palmer felt the zombie's fingers slip down the back of his trousers and take hold of the belt and the waist band. With one unnaturally strong tug, his trousers were torn off.

Gran Brigitte let out a throaty chuckle. "You did say it's time to slip into something more comfortable – namely, you."

"Please... Oh, God, no, please..."

"Oh, come now, Samuel. You just said you wanted it inside you, as soon as possible."

PALMER'S SOUL DRIFTED back to the zombie it had been inhabiting. Gran Brigitte was long gone. Palmer was still on the ground at the zombie's feet. He was lying in a pool of blood and faeces with what was left of his trousers round his ankles, sobbing quietly.

Palmer's soul couldn't think of anything to say to comfort its owner. To be truthful, which was its nature, it didn't really want to comfort him.

The soul looked down at the mangled remains of the zombie's penis. It hung in tatters like the fraying dress it wore. The flies of the living dead had left it. They'd swarmed into Palmer on the point of climax.

Palmer suddenly jerked and held his stomach, writhing in pain. He coughed and a trickle of blood spilled down his chin. His eyes were full of pain and fear.

"The flies. They're inside me. They're trying to get out. They're... oh, God, they're feeding on me!"

Palmer screamed with unimaginable agony as a thousand ravenous little mouths consuming his innards.

Palmer's soul shook the zombie's head in contradiction.

"Not flies, Palmer, guilt. You see that's the thing about guilt; sooner or later it eats you all up inside."

CHAPTER FORTY

"I HAVE TO attack her from the inside," said Doc Papa. "Her magical defences are primed for an external attack. She still thinks I don't know who she is. So she won't expect me to get up close and personal, won't have shielded her core, at least not where I intend to strike."

"What if her astral form gets loose?" said Vincenzo, drawing the last of the protection charms around Doc Papa in fine ground bone dust and gunpowder.

"It won't, that's what the binding spell is for."

Doc Papa was lying on the floor of his ceremony room. It was hidden behind his office on the top floor of Mangrove Hall. He'd had it specially built when he'd renovated the estate. Only he and a handful of his acolytes knew about it.

It was everything his office wasn't. The magical Id to the Super Ego that was his place of work. Taken as a whole, the two rooms symbolised the duality of his nature as a successful businessman and a powerful Houngan. The office displayed the trappings of his wealth to show the scale of his success, the ceremony room betrayed the strength of his Voodoo and the degree to which the Loa favoured him.

The ceremony room was not a traditional space like the Ounfó. Doc Papa had brought his vast resources to bear on it, creating a modern, technological approach to the mysteries of the Loa. He was taking Voodoo into the twenty-first century.

Instead of a bare earthen floor, Doc Papa was lying on a toughened LCD screen. It generated a series of holographic symbols that combined to make a living Vévé which could alter and adapt itself to the exact nature of the ritual at any moment. The precision this gave Doc Papa's psychic will, combined with the traditional charms Vincenzo had drawn, made it an impenetrable magical barrier.

The speaker system played a series of pre-programmed ceremonial drumbeats, each one looped and intercut with the others to intensify its powerful rhythm. The hi-tech speaker system turned the walls and floors into speakers, with the result that the listener could bathe in the sonic waves of the Voodoo rhythms.

To bind Brigitte's astral form, Doc Papa had prepared a black bottle lamp, an antique glass bottle filled with castor oil, piment-chien, Guinea-pepper, powdered lizard, the powder of a decomposed corpse, and soot. Tied to the wick was a tiny bag containing samples of Brigitte's hair, a tooth she'd lost and a snipping from her dress.

Doc Papa had gathered these last items from the old hut by the shore where Brigitte used to live. No-one had been back there since the night they buried her alive; the place was exactly as she left it. It woke long-suppressed feelings in him.

The tooth he had taken from an old charm he had found over a door. The dress clipping from her closet. And the hair he'd collected from the bed where they had lain. It lay on sheets they'd stained with their passions and marked with their scent, in another lifetime, when they were other people.

He knew her true name and he had touched her essence. She was his helpless prey. He would trap her spirit and he would wrest the Gateway of the Souls from her.

Doc Papa let the life go from his body. The rhythm of the drums bathed his whole being, and the living holographic Vévé pulsed and shifted in accordance with his soul's vibrations. He released his astral form and shuffled off his mortal body.

Doc Papa was just orienting himself and preparing to leave the room in search of Brigitte when Vincenzo surprised him, rubbing away two of the powder-drawn charms with his foot and dropping another wick into the black bottle lamp and lighting it. This wick also had a tiny pouch tied to it. Doc Papa knew exactly whose personal effects were in the pouch.

Vincenzo was trying to trap him. Thanks to the new wick in the black bottle lamp, Doc Papa's astral form was now bound to the room. His body was seemingly defenceless. He would have to wait to see how this one played out.

He didn't have to wait long. Vincenzo opened the secret door that connected the ceremony room to his office and the five shareholders walked in with their zombie soul vessels.

So that was his game.

"Now you're sure this cocksucker's out cold?" said O'Shaugnessey. "He can't hurt us?"

"His astral form has left his body and I hold it captive," said Vincenzo. "He is powerless against us."

"Is he here in the room?" said Walden Truffet. "Can he hear us?"

"Yes," said Vincenzo. "He can hear."

Doc Papa watched as O'Shaugnessey walked over to his body and prodded it with his toe.

"Sorry, feller," said O'Shaugnessey. "But we're mounting a hostile takeover. It's not that we don't appreciate everything you've given the corporation, we just don't trust you to run it for us anymore. You have to admit that your recent actions haven't done much to inspire confidence in your decision-making."

"You've lost control," said Lyons. "And the whole thing has fallen to shit. So you're out of the picture as of now."

So that was their game. Doc Papa's suspicions were right, which was why he'd taken precautions. Of course they'd waited until he was vulnerable before they struck, which was only good tactical sense. They weren't totally incompetent, he'd give them that.

Vincenzo had impressed him. It was a shame that his cunning and deviousness would have to be punished. Doc Papa nearly admired them. His major failing, however, was his arrogance. He thought himself invulnerable to attack. While he was shielding himself from Doc Papa's astral form, he hadn't covered his Met-tet, the invisible route by which his Patron Loa could enter his body and ride him. Before he had time to realise this, Doc Papa struck.

He shot into Vincenzo's body and Vincenzo shook violently.

"What's happening?" said Frank Evans. "Is he meant to be doing that?"

"No," said O'Shaugnessey. "I don't think he is, and I don't think I like it."

"I wouldn't, if I was you," said Doc Papa, taking full control of Vincenzo.

"That's not Vincenzo," said Walden "Why does he sound like that? Who is it?

"Can't you guess? I'm afraid Vincenzo is a little indisposed at the moment. You'll have to go through me instead."

"Doc Papa?" said O'Shaugnessey. "Now wait a minute, let's not do anything hasty. This is business, after all. No-one's getting personal here. If you've got a counter-offer then we're prepared to listen to it."

"The only offer I'm going to make you is a quick but painful death."

Doc Papa walked over to the black bottle lamp and removed the still-burning wick, then took a small paper disk with some markings on it out of glass jar on the altar.

The shareholders were muttering amongst themselves the whole while. One of their zombie-bound souls was trying to make itself heard.

"You pipe down or you'll get worse than last time," Lyons threatened. Then he turned to Doc Papa.

"Now look here, Papa. Don't think you can intimidate us with all your Hoodoo bullshit. We put good money into your operation and in the last couple of days all you've done is put our lives and our fortunes at risk. We're taking control of this outfit for everyone's benefit, and there's nothing you can do to stop us."

"I wouldn't be so sure of that," said Doc Papa, setting light to the disk of paper. "You see, I anticipated that you might attempt a little coup, so I took some precautions."

As one the zombies began to scream. Their flesh began to liquefy and drip off them in great, foul smelling gobs.

"What have you done?" said O'Shaugnessey.

"I've activated the necrotising spell that I put on your Bakas," said Doc Papa. O'Shaugnessey stared at him non-plussed. "The what?"

"Necrotising spell. You see, the Bakas I gave you were corrupted. If you think of them as a portal and your souls as information, then you'll understand the dangers inherent into downloading them into new machines, in this case the zombies. I impregnated your Bakas with a magical virus that rode into the zombies on the backs of your souls. When I burnt the paper I activated the virus. It causes the zombies to rot away to nothing in a mater of minutes."

The zombies were now little more than skeletons standing in puddles of rancid flesh.

"As you are linked to the zombies via your souls, the virus will also affect you," Doc Papa said. "Taking effect almost immediately."

The shareholders tried pleading, threatening and bargaining with him, but it did them no good. In short order, they all – zombie and shareholder alike – ran together into a fetid pool of bubbling flesh.

Doc Papa lamented what it was going to cost him to clean this up. He was going to have to get rid of the carpet, take up the floorboards and get the whole room refitted. And that was after he'd had the place fumigated. Still, that was for later. There were more pressing things to deal with.

Doc Papa used Vincenzo's fingers to redraw the protection charms around his still motionless body. Then he took a large sacrificial dagger off the wall. Held the dagger over Vincenzo's left breast. Some distance away he was aware of Vincenzo's Gros Bon Ange pleading with him not to strike. He ignored it.

Doc Papa plunged the dagger into Vincenzo's heart. As his body fell to the floor Doc Papa discarded it like an old set of clothes. His astral form hovered in the air and looked down at Vincenzo, lying next to the putrid slop that had once been the shareholders and their zombies. Blood was pouring out of Vincenzo's chest where the dagger had pierced it. More cleaning bills to think of; this had been an expensive exercise in maintaining power.

Doc Papa put this out of his mind and returned to the matter at hand. He still had to get Brigitte to give up the Gateway of the Souls. He concentrated on the rhythm of the drums and tried to forget that all the melted flesh was deadening the sound.

He pictured Brigitte at her most intimate and vulnerable, then he reached out with his mind and went looking for her.

CHAPTER FORTY-ONE

BENJAMIN WAS LOOKING for Brigitte. He'd stopped to look at an arrangement of skulls in the wall and they'd turned a corner and left him.

After trying to feel his way along the tunnel in pitch darkness, Benjamin keyed into the zombies' group mind and followed them. He was slowly working his way to the front of the group, where Tatyana and Brigitte were, but it wasn't easy.

He had to sidestep and slip past the zombies in the pitch dark. One wrong move and they might pounce on him. He couldn't see Brigitte's lamp up ahead, so she probably wasn't close enough to save him if the zombies did decide to start feeding.

In the distance, he heard the insistent tramp of the guards' feet getting closer. They'd never quite lost the guards. They'd come close several times, but the guards always seemed to pick up their trail.

To throw the guards off, Brigitte had led them into a series of natural tunnels connected to the mine. She told them the whole island was crisscrossed with underground caves and catacombs. Most of them were naturally occurring, but a few had been specially excavated by the natives, like the ossuary where they now found themselves.

The walls and ceilings of these long tunnels were entirely covered with human bones. Skulls, mainly, but there were also intricate arrangements of other bones embedded in the stone walls. This was where the islanders had come to honour their dead and commune with their ancestors.

Benjamin hoped the ancestors would look out for the zombies as the guards got closer. He tried not to think about how slow the zombies' dead muscles and atrophied limbs made them. Or how fast the guards could move.

He had to fight rising panic all the time. If he didn't, his heart would start racing, he'd break out in a sweat and begin hyperventilating. Any one of those things would give him away to the zombies.

He'd been in fear of his life for so long now, he couldn't imagine not being in a state of constant terror. His old life of comfort and privilege seemed so far away. He couldn't imagine what it would be like to do simple things anymore, like fixing a snack, watching cable or just calling up friends.

He clung to the Rules of Interaction like a lifeline. Each one had become like a mantra to him. He repeated them over and over in his mind. It was the only way to ensure his survival. They felt like spells, charms cast to ensure he would come out of this ordeal alive.

It doesn't matter and you don't care.

Master yourself and nothing can threaten you.

He wished he had a little more mastery over himself right now.

Finally he saw a glimmer of light up ahead as he drew closer to Brigitte and Tatyana. The lamp Brigitte was carrying lit up the ceiling above her and a host of skulls stared down, their sockets wide with terror, their jaws open in a silent cry of warning.

Benjamin was getting really close to the other two, but the zombies directly in front of him were too tightly packed together to squeeze past. He could almost tap Brigitte on the shoulder, but he didn't want to risk it in case he accidentally hit a zombie and his fingers were bitten off.

They stopped at a crossroads. The tunnel directly ahead of them led out of the ossuary. It wasn't covered with bones, but the roads to their left and right were. The zombies started milling about as Brigitte deliberated over which way to go. Benjamin was able to slip past them and grab hold of Tatyana's hand.

She turned to him with a look of relief and squeezed his hand to show she was pleased to see him. There was comfort and reassurance in their physical closeness, but there was no longer any passion. It seemed like their fear had chased all that away.

It also felt like they were learning too much about themselves and each other to carry on as before. They just couldn't live inside the dreams that had propped up their relationship before they came here.

"Which way now?" asked Tatyana.

Brigitte seemed indecisive. "The route ahead of us comes out near the crossroads where I have to take my people. That's where I can open the invisible crossroads between the three worlds of the Loa and our own. Their souls are held captive there. "

"Well let's go," said Tatyana. "We don't have much time."

"But I don't want to lead the guards there. We need to shake them before we can get there. It'll be too dangerous otherwise."

"How long have we got?"

"Until sunrise."

"Guys, I don't want to worry you," said Benjamin. "But we haven't got until sunrise until those guards catch us. We've got five minutes or less. We need to make a decision now. Do we stay underground or try and lose them in the jungle above?"

Before Brigitte could answer, she shuddered and almost lost control of her body. Benjamin caught her and Tatyana took the lamp.

"What's the matter?" Tatyana said.

Brigitte was rolling her eyes. "I carry a great weight inside me. I was given it by my ancestor for safe keeping. I need it to help my people, but the burden is too great. He wants it. He wants it so badly. He's inside me, looking for it."

"Who?' said Tatyana. "Who is it?"

"I can't fight him," said Brigitte, She looked as though she was struggling to stay conscious. "You've got to protect them. Please look after them."

Brigitte's face went blank. Her eyes rolled up into her head and her body went limp. Benjamin struggled to hold her up.

"What's up with her?" said Tatyana. "Is she still alive?"

"She's still breathing. But she's gone into some kind of coma."

"What are we going to do?"

"Well, we can't stay here."

"Can you carry her?"

"I don't think so. I'm going to have to put her down."

"We can't just leave her here for the guards to find. We're completely lost without her."

Just how lost became apparent when the zombies around them started to notice their presence. Their hearts were beating faster from the shock of seeing Brigitte keel over.

A young female zombie reached out and ran her fingers along Benjamin's cheek. It put her fingers unsteadily in her mouth and ran them along her dried up tongue. It could taste Benjamin's sweat on the tips.

Tatyana started to back away, not seeing the rotund male zombie come up behind her. She backed right into it and only just managed to get away before it closed its arms about her. She dropped the lamp as she dodged it, and it went out.

Rule Number One, Benjamin heard in his head. *Show no signs of life*. They'd already blown that. Now Rule Number Two – *Move in slow motion* – seemed totally inappropriate too. All Benjamin wanted to do was get away as fast as he could.

In the distance he heard a voice call out: "Boys! Hey, boys, over here! Donovan, they're over here."

The guards had finally caught up to them.

He and Tatyana were trapped underground, in the pitch dark with an uncontrollable horde of the living dead. The only person who could keep them alive had fallen into a coma. They had to avoid being torn apart and eaten long enough to keep the zombies safe from the guards, who were also coming to kill them.

There didn't seem to be a way out.

CHAPTER FORTY-TWO

BRIGITTE COULDN'T FIND a way out. She was trapped. Her astral form had been plucked from her body and she wasn't able to return.

She was on the second astral plane of the Loas. All around her, planetary forces, expressed in strange geometries, intersected with one another to create shapes her earthly eyes couldn't understand and her earthly brain couldn't process.

She hadn't entered this plane voluntarily, and she wasn't prepared for the shock of being here. That was what a ritual was for, to prepare the initiate to experience this kind of heightened reality. Without that vital preparation, she was reeling from the shock of finding herself in a space that wasn't anything like the reality she was used to.

She knew who'd brought her here. She'd been so careful to fly under his radar, to remain undetected inside Miriam's body. Nevertheless, it was inevitable that he would discover who she really was. She'd hoped he wouldn't realise until she'd gotten all the islanders to the crossroads and returned their souls. But, as her grandmother used to say, "the Loa teach us more through the hopes they deny than the desires they grant."

As soon as she thought of Doc Papa, he appeared. Thought had power on this plane. He came in the body of a serpent with a human head, wearing a top hat that had the eight of spades tucked into the brim.

She felt his coils wrap themselves around her before she saw him. He slithered round her and thrust his face into hers.

Remembering how to alter her form in this space, she transformed herself into the golden apple of Erzulie. This had repelled Ogou Fer when he took the serpent form in Eden, which was why he had Eve pick it for him. As soon as she shifted into this shape Doc Papa was himself repelled and shot away.

He reverted into the human shape of his Ti Bon Ange, and so did Brigitte. Strangely, though she knew his physical body, had explored every inch of it with her own, she had never seen the astral body of his Ti Bon Ange.

Even under the circumstances, she still felt a huge desire for him, and could tell that he felt it too. It crackled though his astral body like a flame and it sang in the vibrations it was giving off.

"I'm impressed," he said. "You threw me off quicker than I anticipated. I should know not to underestimate you."

"Something you do at your peril."

"Yes, as I learned when I unearthed your grave. But you were tricked so easily when I put you there, I was quite surprised. I became complacent. I didn't think you'd escape."

"Seems I'm not the only one who's easily tricked. But it wasn't your complacency that undid you, it was your arrogance. You didn't think anyone could circumvent your magic."

"For old times sake, as one magician to another, tell me how you managed to escape? I'm guessing you possessed one of the zombies and dug yourself up. But how did your soul get past all the spells I set to keep it trapped with your corporeal form?"

"As I said, it was your arrogance that undid you. You forgot that magic, especially in Voodoo, is all about the letter of the law. You have to specify the outcome you want and allow for all possible interpretations. This means, unless you allow for everything that could happen, one spell can always get around another. You set the traps to catch my dead soul, not my living one. So as long as I was still alive in the coffin the traps wouldn't catch my soul."

Doc Papa tilted his top hat to her. "Exceptional. I am ashamed to say I hadn't thought of that. You won't escape so easily this time, however. You know what I want. The location of the Gateway of the Souls."

"As I told you two years ago, it's safe. That's all you need to know."

"I'm afraid that's nowhere near what I need to know. I am only giving you the opportunity to tell me out of sentimentality. I'm quite prepared to take it from you."

"I assume that's what this is all about."

"Of course."

"It still doesn't have to be this way, you know."

"Oh really? Are you still suggesting we can love it all better? That a two-hundred-year-old blood curse can be brushed aside by simply holding hands and gazing into each other's eyes? I've come too far to throw it all away now. I stand on the verge of dominating the entire planet. Do you think I'm just going to throw my hands in the air and say: 'You know what, you're right. Let's have a big hug and kiss it all better'?"

"I've seen things just as miraculous."

"Not with me, you haven't."

"You've been lusting after the Gateway of the Souls since I first mentioned it," said Brigitte. "Why are you so fascinated with such a dangerous artefact?"

"Because of the power it will bring."

"It's a portal for drawing souls from one place into another, often against their will. How is that going to bring you power?"

"You expect me to reveal my whole plan to you, like some bad movie villain in the last reel?"

"Humour me. What can I do about it? I'm not going anywhere, you've seen to that."

"I have on St Ignatius the souls of the most rich and powerful people in the world. Having them in my possession gives me a great deal of leverage with these people, but not as much as I want.

"If I take the Gateway of the Souls inside me, as your ancestor did, and then open it, I will have complete and utter dominion over them. I will be the receptacle for their souls. I will own their single most valuable commodities. They will be a part of me. If anything happens to me, their eternal futures will be void. They'll have no choice but to put my wellbeing and survival above their own. I will be like a god to them, and they will have to do everything I tell them. They control nine-tenths of the world's resources and I will control them."

Brigitte was aghast. "You know there's no way I can tell you where the Gateway to the Souls is now you've told me that."

"There's no way you can resist telling me," Doc Papa said. He shifted shape again.

The second astral plane of the Loas was where everything that had been born on the first plane found its shape, prior to being given form on the third plane. Shape was everything here. To think something was to become it. The shapes that held the most power were those that mirrored the divine mysteries of the Loa.

Doc Papa became a serpent once more, but a different Loa, Dambala Wédo, whose serpentine form represents the path of descent taken by the gift of life and secrets of the Holy Spirit as they come from God down to man. Because of his great age, Dambala never speaks and so is the great confessor to whom all secrets are confided.

Brigitte could not afford to confess the secret of the Gateway's location to Doc Papa. As he prepared to strike, she became the rainbow of Ayida Wédo, the heavenly form through which the gifts that Dambala brings are dispersed and distributed to the world.

Doc Papa's energies were dispersed and disempowered as he struck, like the rays of the sun refracted by the rain. He slid harmlessly down her rainbow but found no pot of gold at the end.

"Well played," Doc Papa said. "But you realise you are simply delaying the inevitable. The best you can hope for is a quick demise."

"That remains to be seen. I have much of your work to undo and I can't afford a quick demise."

"Then you'll have to settle for a painful one." Doc Papa took the shape of Baron Zaraguin, the Scorpion Loa whose insect body is impermeable metal and expands across unimaginable dimensions. He arched his tail, ready to sting, and reached for her with his unbreakable claws. Brigitte became Sim'bi d'l'eau, countering his unyielding and relentless form with the fluid permeability of water. She trickled through his claws and ran down his spine, rusting them as she went, which brought him to a halt.

In a move Brigitte would never have anticipated, Doc Papa became a simple Govi, a clay pot used for holding otherworldly spirits. As Sim'bi d'l'eau she spilled into the container and he brought a stopper down on the top. She was trapped.

"This is your last chance to die with a little dignity," Doc Papa said.

He began to alter the shape of the Govi. As Brigitte was trapped inside his shape she couldn't do anything to stop him. The earthenware Govi became a clear glass container in the shape of a heart. Doc Papa manifested a giant dagger above her. He was becoming the sacred attribute of Erzulie Zandor – a bloodied heart pierced with the dagger of the Ogou.

As Brigitte was inside him she was at his heart, so the dagger would pierce her Ti Bon Ange and slowly kill her. From out of nowhere she heard a voice say: "Stop. If your pierce me, you harm the Gateway." It sounded exactly like her voice, but she hadn't said those words or even thought them. They came from somewhere else, but where?

Doc Papa chuckled. "Of course," he said. "Toussaint would have hidden it in the one place I wouldn't think to look, inside his own ancestor. You have been carrying it inside you all this time. He passed it on to you; he knew that if I thought you dead I would never suspect that the Gateway lay inside you."

"You'll have to cut it out of me to get it," said the voice that sounded like hers.

How had he coaxed her to say that? How could she have given away the location of the Gateway? How was she able to speak without even realising it?

Shh, little sister. It wasn't you, it was me.

Toussaint? How was her ancestor able to speak to her here?

It's Erzulie Zandor's doing. As soon as Doc Papa took her shape he gave her the power to place me inside here. It's time for me to take back what I gave you for safe keeping.

"Cut it out of you," said Doc Papa. "What an excellent idea."
Brigitte felt Toussaint reach into her and take the burden from her core. He was reclaiming the Gateway of the Souls. He was taking it to safety before she died.

No, little sister, you will not die. I am taking your place and I am sending you back to help our people.

But that meant Doc Papa would kill Toussaint.

Just as he is supposed to. I am taking your place just as I took your great-great-grandmother's.

Doc Papa would take the Gateway of the Souls if Toussaint did that.

Exactly as I plan him to. This is my curse coming to fruition.

But how would Brigitte help her people without the Gateway? How would she draw them back from the crossroads as Toussaint had done if she couldn't open it? She felt her astral form begin to flow out of the great glass heart as Toussaint's spirit poured in to take its place.

Hush, little sister, you already have the solution. You just applied it to the wrong problem.

What did that mean? There wasn't time for Toussaint to answer as the last of Brigitte left the heart and the dagger descended. She heard Toussaint scream as he died a second time at the hands of a Papamal. Even in death beyond death, Toussaint disguised his voice to sound like hers. *That's what I would sound like if I were murdered*, she thought.
Brigitte felt herself pulled back to her body, along a path Doc Papa couldn't see. She could still see him, though.
She watched as he sliced the Gateway of the Souls out of Toussaint, without ever realising who he had truly killed. He held up the Gateway and let out a bitter laugh of victory. The Gateway was almost too bright

to look at. It had an immense gravity that bent everything around it and seemed to refract both time and space.

Doc Papa took the Gateway of Souls and disappeared back to his body.

He had won, completely and irrevocably.

CHAPTER FORTY-THREE

THEY WERE LOST, completely and irrevocably. Tatyana couldn't get her breathing and heart beat under control and the zombies had noticed. They were shambling towards her. Her eyes had adjusted to the dark and she could see a little, but she wished she couldn't.

"Benjamin," she called out. She needed him close to her. She didn't want to die alone.

He was struggling with Brigitte's body. "Here, give me a hand." He propped the body up on its feet and huddled behind it, pulling Tatyana to him.

The zombies stopped advancing; some vestigial memory inside them still responded to the sight of Brigitte.

"We're going to drag her to the tunnel behind us," Benjamin said pulling Brigitte towards the tunnel that led to the surface.

Further down the tunnel, Tatyana could hear the guards approaching. "We're going to die, aren't we?" she said. "It's all over."

"Do you hear the fat lady singing?"

"No." Tatyana had no idea what he was talking about.

"Neither do I. And that means it's far from over."

"What are we going to do?"

"We're going to take the fight to the guards."

"But they've got guns and rockets and God knows what."

"Yeah, and we've got an army of zombies. I know who I'd put my money on."

"An army of zombies that's about to eat us."

"No, it's not," said Benjamin. She'd never seen him like this before. So focused and determined. "Look, Tatyana, I know it's all over between us, but I still love you. I always will. And I'm not going to let you die like this, down here in this tunnel on some foreign island. We can do this. It's time to stop hiding behind Brigitte. Okay, so she stopped them from attacking us once before. But we rounded them up for her. We've spent longer in the company of bloodthirsty, flesh-eating zombies than probably any human who's ever lived and we're still alive. That's not just Brigitte. It's also us. We're good at this.

"What's gotten into you?" said Tatyana. "I've never seen you like this before."

"Maybe I've been backed into too many corners not to come out fighting."

Tatyana put her arms round him and pulled him close. She couldn't keep the tears out of her eyes, however soppy that made her feel. Was he right about it being over between them? She hadn't thought about it until now. He was being so brave and mature about it and she wasn't sure if she wanted to let him go yet. Even if he was right.

Benjamin took hold of her by the shoulders and looked her straight in the eyes. God, he had beautiful eyes. Even in the pitch dark they sparkled.

"Listen to me," he said. "We're going to use ourselves as bait and lure the zombies back down the tunnel on the right. It leads down to another crossroads at the start of the ossuary, I'm sure of it."

"What good will that do?"

"They're expecting to take the zombies from the rear. They won't anticipate the zombies coming up behind them. They'll be caught in a... what do you call it? A pincer movement. They'll be trapped in the tunnel and they'll have to fight on both sides. They won't have a chance."

"But what if they outnumber the zombies?"

"I've been listening to the footsteps of the guards chasing us. I was at the back of the zombies for quite a while, don't forget. I'm sure there's only about seven or eight of them on our tail. That means the zombies outnumber them by more than twenty to one."

"What about Brigitte?"

"We can't carry her, she's too heavy. She'll be safe if we leave her here. No-one's going to look for her in this tunnel. We can come back for her later." Benjamin took Tatyana's hand and squeezed it. "Look. You're one of the coolest and most together people I know. I can't do this without you. Are you with me?"

"Of course." She wiped the tears from her eyes and brought his hand up to her lips. His beautiful fingers were interlaced with hers. She kissed each one. "Just say the word."

Benjamin sat Brigitte up against the wall of the tunnel, tucked behind a convenient outcrop.

"The word," he said and ran back out to the crossroads. "Hey, over here!" Benjamin called out to the zombies. "Look, it's a moving buffet." He motioned to Tatyana to follow him. "All you can eat, so long as you catch me."

Tatyana ran out and stood behind him. The rotund male zombie and the female zombie who'd tasted his sweat were lumbering after him, followed by another female zombie dressed in a maid's outfit. They were gnashing their decayed teeth and grabbing for him with their rotten fingers.

More zombies began to follow as Benjamin led them down the tunnel which, just as he guessed, began to curve round so it ran parallel to the tunnel they'd left. Tatyana stayed behind Benjamin as he taunted the zombies. He'd put himself almost within their reach and then jump back as they lunged for him.

If Benjamin put one foot wrong, he'd be dead. They'd both seen what the zombies could do to a person. Hell, they'd even tried to copy it. It took a lot of guts to do what he was doing.

She'd been about to go to pieces back there at the crossroads. Hunger, lack of sleep and too much stress had gotten the better of her. Benjamin had really stepped up to the mark just when she needed him. He was probably right about them being over, but right now she wanted to think of him as her man. Her big, brave man who was looking out for her.

As they walked backwards down the tunnel Tatyana could hear the guards more clearly.

"Listen," Benjamin said. "I want you to start your zombie breathing now, get your heartbeat down too. As soon as we get to the crossroads we've got to drop back into zombie mode and hang back. Can you do that?"

"I think so."

"Brilliant."

They hit the crossroads and did just that. Tatyana ducked around a corner to get out of the way and compose herself. Benjamin backed right into the guard on point. The guard swung round, but Benjamin took the initiative, pushing the guard right into the hands of the zombies chasing them.

Tatyana saw at least six pairs of undead hands and teeth latch onto the guard before he had time to react. His screams brought two more guards running down to the crossroads. They were met with a mass of starving zombies lurching around the corner of the tunnel. The guards tried to run back up the tunnel and one of them made it, but the other was too slow. He went down under the tide of ravenous undead.

The guards were now trapped between two flanks of zombies. There were several burst of gunfire. Two bullets struck the wall inches from Tatyana's head, showering her with shards of bone and rock. She flinched and fought to keep her heart rate under control.

"Don't shoot you fucking idiots!" shouted one of the guards. "You'll just damage the merchandise. Besides it doesn't stop them, use the fucking flamethrower!"

"The piece of shit flamethrower's not working."

"Where's my talisman thing? Oh shit, I've dropped it. Can I get a light over here?"

"There's too many of them, we can't pull out."

"What do we do now eh, Donovan? C'mon, you got us into this, what do we do now?"

The question went unanswered as the zombies overwhelmed them. Tatyana stood very still and hardly breathed. She concentrated on reducing her vital signs. All to block out the sounds of the guard's screams and curses.

She tried not to think about their suffering, or whether they had wives and children who'd mourn them but never recover or bury their remains. She tried especially hard not to think about her part in their death or the other deaths in which she was complicit.

She wondered how she was going to atone for all the things she'd done. One of the main things that fascinated her about religion was the opportunity it offered for absolution.

If the Loa were calling her, as Brigitte said, should she answer the call? Would that be her opportunity to make good for all the bad things she'd done?

CHAPTER FORTY-FOUR

Doc Papa was about to make good on everything he'd done since founding the Way of the Barefoot Zombie. He'd returned to his ceremony room and was hovering above his body. It was still lying on the floor surrounded by the living Vévé.

He held up the Gateway of the Souls and savoured his victory. It was an artefact of rare and unimaginable beauty. Fashioned from a perfect blend of solar energy and dark mass, it had an undeniable gravity about it, even when closed as it was now.

The Gateway was to the soul what a black hole was to light, inescapable. Even in his astral form he could feel his soul beating at his body's breast to be free to enter it. What a burden it must have been to Brigitte to have carried it within her all this time. Yet she put up such a fight to hang on to it.

The living Vévé shifted into a new shape so that Doc Papa could return to his body with the Gateway. He descended with exceptional care into his corporeal form. It felt like clambering down a gigantic pile of broken glass carrying several pounds of live gelignite. One wrong move and his mind, body and soul would be torn to pieces.

He marveled again at the brilliance and ingenuity of Brigitte's ancestor for not only opening the Gateway, but finding a way to carry it inside himself and later to hide it in Brigitte. He was relieved to be free of the curse that Toussaint had placed on his bloodline.

Doc Papa's astral form finally found its way carefully back inside his body, and brought the Gateway with it. He came back to consciousness with a start, sat bolt upright and vomited. He emptied the entire contents of his stomach over Vincenzo's still cooling corpse. That was something else that would have to be cleaned up in the morning.

Still, he shouldn't focus on tiny details like that at such an auspicious moment. He got to his feet, but couldn't stop himself from swaying. He felt drained and unsteady. He didn't want to admit it, but the battle with Brigitte had taken more out of him than he realised.

The Gateway was also having an effect on him. He could feel an immense inward pull at the centre of himself that was contracting his whole being. So much power and so little time left to use it.

Doc Papa reached inside himself and opened the Gateway.

It felt like an infinite unfolding, taking place forever and in the space of one moment. The finite nature of his being was now host to an endlessly expanding opening that it shouldn't be able to accommodate but could.

As the Gateway opened he started to feel its pull. A huge vortex was unleashed within him. It hollowed him out inside and drew every untethered human soul to him.

He felt the first of them dragged to him, mewling and afraid: George Griffin the investment banker and the real estate tycoon Arthur Sonnenfeldt. More followed. He enveloped them as they entered him, in a confused and vulnerable state. They were totally subject to his consciousness. He had never had such power over other humans. It was beyond intoxicating.

Every part of their essential being belonged to him. Within an instant he knew every guilty secret they harboured, every weakness they hid. Their whole being was annexed to his. Like puddles draining into a great pool, they were engulfed by him.

He was swollen by them as their thoughts, hopes and fears swam through him and became his to command. This was domination beyond the dreams of any despot. It was subjugation to which no police state could ever aspire. No implanted micro-chip, twenty-four hour CCTV coverage or illegal wire tap had ever stripped a citizen of this much privacy or individuality.

And still more souls flooded into him. Everyone who'd ever entrusted their soul to his bank was drawn into him. He glutted himself on their greed and lusts, their needs and hunger, all of them his now, all of them part of him.

He became the central nexus point for all the souls. They could have no desperate longing, no vengeful urge or boiling hatred that didn't run through him first.

Every whim or desire he had was filtered down to the hundreds of souls under his dominion and would bring hundreds of responses as the other souls processed it. His tiniest impulse brought a wall of feedback that was almost too much to take in.

He was surrounded by a symphony of being. He had hundreds of other consciousnesses to consider, hundreds of desperate, clingy appetites grasping at his attention. There was no longer any separation between his own will and that of every other will he'd married to him.

The barriers between himself and the others began to crumble. There were too many of them in too little space. It was too much to bear. He couldn't find himself any more. Stripped of their uniqueness and identity, none of the souls could tell themselves apart and neither could Doc Papa.

Who was who? Who was he? What was his anymore? Was this his thought or theirs? Was it his confusion or theirs? Who were they, weren't they him now? Where was he?

Didn't he own them? Didn't he? All of them his. All of them on top of him. Needing. Wanting. Taking. Taking. Taking.

Stop. Stop it. Stop them. Who them? Them or us? Isn't them us? I am them, but who is I? They are here, but where is me? What am I? I am Legion...

...and lost...

stifled

suffocated

drowning.

Wait, get a grip. A grip on this. How to stop this? What caused this? The Gateway. Yes, the Gateway! Got to close it. Got to remember how to close it. But how? So many memories to go through, so many memories that are now his. Which one holds what's needed?

Can't think. Can't stop thinking. Too much thinking. Move. Get out. Fresh air, we all need fresh air. Take me out. Take me out to the ball game.

Ball game, there's a ball game?

No stupid, it's a song.

Who are you calling stupid?

I don't know, who are you?

Don't you know?

Doesn't who know?

Who's in charge here?

Who has hold of the reins?

Reins, are there any?

Where are we going?

Out to the ballgame.

This is a whole new ballgame.

This is madness.

This is
This

From the furthest reaches of the afterlife, the last remnants of the man who was Toussaint looked down on Doc Papa, the last of the Papamals, as he ran from that hateful house he'd rebuilt.

Doc Papa screamed as he ran. He laughed and gibbered and cried. He tore his clothes and he pulled his hair. He scraped his skin and he bit his tongue until they both bled. But nothing he did would silence the clamour inside him. Nothing would get them all out.

This was just as Toussaint had planned it. The curse had come to fruition. Erzulie Zandor had granted Doc Papa's wish; and as she had said, it would be a lesson to many. Toussaint could rest now.

CHAPTER FORTY-FIVE

Brigitte couldn't rest now, though she desperately longed to. Her body ached and her soul was weary. It had been a long route back from the astral plane to her body. Or at least it felt that way.

She came to in complete darkness. She was sitting up against the jagged wall of a tunnel. In the distance she could hear the sound of shuffling feet and flesh being rent as bodies were torn apart and chewed by lifeless jaws.

Oh, God. She hoped that wasn't Benjamin and Tatyana. Brigitte tried to get to her feet. She banged her elbow on the wall and fell back down. The sound of shuffling got closer and she felt something bump against her leg. There was a scuffle and the sound of someone falling.

"Ouch," said a voice. "I think I've found her." It was Tatyana. Legba be praised, she was alive.

"Are you all right?" said another voice, Benjamin's. "Let me give you a hand."

"I could do with a hand as well," said Brigitte. She heard Tatyana gasp.

"You're okay," said Tatyana. "Thank goodness."

"I was thinking the same thing," said Miriam as they helped her to her feet. "What happened to the guards?"

"The err... zombies got them," said Benjamin. He sounded contrite.

"Oh," said Brigitte, unable to hide the disappointment in her voice.

"You asked us to look after them for you," said Benjamin. "It was the only way we could stop the guards from capturing them and killing us."

"I'm sure it was," said Brigitte, sighing with tiredness. "It's just that they've been used as violent monsters for so long, I get upset when it happens again. I take it that's the guards they're feeding on?"

"Yes," said Tatyana. "I'm sorry, we couldn't stop them."

"No, I don't suppose you could. But it makes them harder to control when they've tasted blood. Where are they?"

"They're in the tunnel just down here," said Tatyana. "We'll lead you if you like. Our eyes have kind of got used to the dark now."

"I thought we had a lamp."

"Yeah, that got broke when I dropped it, sorry. I was avoiding one of the zombies."

"It was trying to eat her," Benjamin said by way of explanation.

"Do you mind us calling them zombies?" said Tatyana. "I mean I know that's what they are, but they're your friends and relations, aren't they? Should we call them by their names or something?"

"That's okay. You can call them zombies if you like. I don't like to think of them as monsters, but I don't want to think of them as the people they were. Not when they're in this state."

Benjamin and Tatyana led Brigitte to the crossroads in the tunnel. She readied herself to take control of the zombies one last time. She reached out with her mind and pieced together a group mind for them, teasing out each tiny piece of consciousness they possessed and weaving it into a collective mind; one that she could communicate with and instruct.

It was harder after they had just killed. There was little to them but savage instinct, and it took a bit of effort to get them all to focus on her. Especially as they hadn't been fed in a while and there was plenty of fresh meat left on the guards. She was tired and hungry and hardly had the strength for the extra effort. She pushed herself all the same.

Eventually they all came round. She felt light-headed from expending so much energy. She swayed and nearly lost her footing. Benjamin caught her and stopped her from falling.

"Are you okay?" he said. "Do you want to sit down and rest?"

"There isn't time. It'll be sunrise in just under an hour and then the Festival of the Gédé will have passed. We can't afford to wait another year for this chance."

As her islanders stood and chewed over the bones or other scraps they'd torn from the guards' bodies, Benjamin pointed to several beams of light on the floor.

"Hey, look," he said. "They had those torch things on their helmets There's one for each of us."

Brigitte led them out of the ossuary and along the tunnel that took them back to the surface, coming out of a cave entrance that her ancestors had carved to look like a skull. In times gone past, they would light candles in the eyes and leave offerings to Baron Samedi and Le Gran Brigitte during the Festival of the Gédé.

A short walk from the cave entrance was the crossroads. When they arrived, Brigitte arranged the islanders around the crossroads in a circle. This took some doing. Some of them were still vicious and savage from the blood they'd tasted and needed coaxing. When she had them all in position, she led Benjamin and Tatyana into the centre of the crossroads with her.

"This crossroads sits at the very centre of St Ignatius," Brigitte said. "For that reason it is a very sacred site. This is where I'm going to open a portal to the Celestial Crossroads that lies between the three worlds of the Loa and the world of the humans. When you pass on, your soul comes to the Celestial Crossroads; when you arrive you can choose to follow the roads to eternal damnation or eternal salvation, to re-enter the cycle of birth and death in another life or even to return to the life you've just left."

"Hold on a minute," said Tatyana. "Didn't you say that when you died your Gros Bon Ange argued your case before God and that's how He decided what was going to happen to your soul? But now you seem to be saying that we can just choose? How can that be?"

"Sooner or later you'll meet God on the road you've chosen to follow. That is when your Gros Bon Ange will argue your case. Ultimately, however, it is God's decision whether your choice of road is the correct one and if it will lead you where you want to go."

"Wow."

"Indeed," said Brigitte. "Sometimes a Houngan can trap a soul at the Celestial Crossroads so they can't choose a road. When a person's soul is no longer part of their body and unable to move to the next life, then they're no longer alive but they can't properly die either."

"They become a zombie," said Benjamin, as the penny dropped. "That's what happened to your islanders. And it's also what's happening to the other guests."

"Exactly," said Brigitte. "I need to open a portal to the Celestial Crossroads so that I can free my people from the spell they're under and give them the opportunity to make the choice they've been denied all this time."

"How are you going to do that?"

"To be honest," said Brigitte. "I'm not entirely sure. I'm going to have to wing it. I was given a magical artefact that my ancestor used to free his people from the crossroads. But Doc Papa stole it from me when I was out of my body. It's very powerful and I'm afraid of what he'll do with it. We have to free my people before he tries to stop us."

"What do you need us to do?" said Tatyana.

"More than anything, I need you to believe. The world only continues to be the way it is, and operate according to certain laws, because we believe it will. This goes for everything from gravity to money or the rules of high finance. Magic, in Voodoo, is the same. We only get the outcome we want because we *believe* the Loa will grant it. If you want to alter reality, your belief in this change has to be stronger than the belief of everyone who's keeping reality the way it currently is. You need to defy their belief in order to change the way things are. Do you understand what I'm saying?"

"I think so," said Tatyana.

"Opening this portal involves strong magic because it goes against most people's view of what reality is. If you have any scepticism or doubt about the outcome, it could jeopardise the whole spell. I'm hoping that after everything you've seen, this won't be the case, but I need to know you believe in what I'm about to do?"

"I want to believe in this more than anything in the world," said Tatyana. "In fact I need to."

"I thought that might be the case," said Brigitte. She turned to Benjamin. "How about you, do you have faith?"

"Yeah, you know what, I do have faith."

"Good, because we need to invoke Papa Legba, the most powerful of all the Loa, to make this work, and he demands complete faith from his servants."

"Who is Papa Legba?"

"The Master of the Crossroads and the Gatekeeper between the worlds. It is only through his permission that the other Loa are allowed to cross over into our world. That's why he's the first Loa to be invoked at the beginning of every ceremony. Only he can open the portal and lift the spell on my people."

"Is there anything we need to do?"

"Usually it would take a big ceremony with a sacrifice to summon him. We don't have the time or the tools for that, though. So I'm going to improvise. Kick off your shoes, and then join me in the circle."

Brigitte held out her hands to Tatyana and Benjamin. She reached out to the group mind of her people and sent an impulse out to all of them. They all lifted their left leg and brought it down. Then, concentrating hard, she got them to do the same with their right leg. Most of them did this in unison. She got them to repeat the actions, stamping first their left foot then their right until they had a workable rhythm going.

"We don't have any drums," said Brigitte. "So we're going to use our feet instead. We're each going to take a ritual drum and stamp out the part ourselves. Tatyana, I want you to be the Ka-Tha-Bou drum. I'm going to stamp out your part then I want you to repeat it." Brigitte stamped it out for her and Tatyana tried to copy the rhythm. After two attempts she got it right.

"Benjamin, you're going to be the Manman drum. This is your part." Benjamin got it first time and stamped in counterpoint to Tatyana's rhythm. "I'm going to be the Grondez drum."

The whole ground shook to the slap and the stomp of living and undead feet. "As I can't draw a Vévé we're going to have to picture Papa Legba in our minds. You can visualise him as a crooked old man with a walking stick and a small pipe. Or you can think of him as St Peter carrying a holy book and a set of keys. This is the Catholic saint he's associated with. He is very charming but a great trickster, so be careful in his presence."

Brigitte closed her eyes and pictured herself drawing Papa Legba's Vévé on the floor of her Ounfó. Then she summoned up her memories of every time she had ever encountered the Master of the Crossroads, laying them over the Vévé she had drawn in her mind.

"Now I want you to sing this invocation with me." Brigitte sang them the invocation line by line, and after a few attempts they were word perfect. They repeated the invocation over and over again, singing:

"Papa Legba ouvri bayè-a pou mwen

"Pou mwen pase

"Lè ma tounen, ma salyié Loa yo."

The moon was low in the sky but a sudden shaft of her light fell on Tatyana. She began to shake and flail as Papa Legba entered her, letting go of their hands as though she had been dragged away. Her limbs and back began to twist and bend into the posture of an old, old man.

"Greetings to you, Papa Legba," said Brigitte. "I didn't expect you to honour us with your presence."

"Ah, no," said Papa Legba. "You expected me to hear you treaties from afar and grant your request. It's always the same. I'm the first up and the last to bed, opening the way so the younger ones can rush out and mount their horses while I wait patiently at the gate."

"I have a request, Papa Legba."

"I know, I know, you always have requests. No-one calls me up just to chew the fat, or ask me how my day went. No-one offers me a glass of rum or a comfortable seat by the fire. No, no it's always 'can you put my name on the guest list? Can I get a backstage pass? Which Loas are playing tonight, could you introduce me?' It's a wonder I ever leave my bed."

"Papa Legba, if I have offended you..."

"You'd be wearing your innards as a necklace, little sister. I am having fun with you. There's no need for this sobriety."

"But there's every need for care."

"Indeed, little sister, watch where you tread. I am old, but not toothless."

"If I may ask of you a favour...?"

"Ah, yes, your request. Don't waste your breath, little sister, I know what you want. Quite a few of the Loa have been watching your progress. I had already decided if you got this far you would earn my favour."

"Papa Legba, I don't know what to say."

"Oh, hush, shush, you haven't heard my conditions yet. I like this horse that I'm riding. She is fine and supple and bends well beneath me. I will have her stay here on the island and I will be her Met-tet. You will train her and teach her to serve the Loa."

"What if she doesn't want to stay?"

"Oh, *pshaw!* I think we both know what she is secretly planning to do, even if she hasn't admitted it to herself yet."

"Then you'll grant my request?"

"Step aside, little sister, your people are coming home."

Normal space seemed to warp around Papa Legba as the Loa reached out much further than Tatyana's arm should ever stretch and took hold of the night sky like a curtain. With a movement that defied the mind, he pulled aside the fabric of this world to reveal the worlds beyond.

From the corner of her eye Brigitte saw Benjamin shake his head as his mind tried to deny what he was seeing. She placed a hand on his shoulder. "Don't close yourself off from what you're seeing. Allow yourself to believe this, and you will grow in more ways than you can imagine."

Brigitte saw the Celestial Crossroads, and she saw her people at the centre of it. They looked beaten, dejected and oppressed. They were huddled together in such a tight space that Brigitte was reminded of a picture she had once seen in a book, showing prisoners jammed into a cattle truck. She reached out to them with her soul but as she got close she ran into the force that was holding them captive.

It was the essence of barbed wire and steel bayonets. It was powered by the force that inspires concentrations camps, detention centres and secret military prisons for terrorist suspects. Brigitte recoiled in pain and fear.

"Oh, come now, little sister," said Papa Legba. "Are you going to let the residue of a defeated Houngan's spell deter you?"

Defeated Houngan? But Brigitte had been beaten by Doc Papa. She had seen him snatch the Gateway of the Souls from Toussaint's dead breast. Was Papa Legba playing a trick on her? Or had Toussaint played one on Doc Papa?

Brigitte put that from her mind. What mattered right now was freeing her people. What was it Toussaint had said? She already had the solution. She'd just applied it to the wrong problem. Was he talking about the curse? She'd tried to beat that with love and the consequences had been disastrous.

Would love be any more effective now?

"Love is how you beat hate and dispel dark Voodoo," she'd told Doc Papa. This spell was the worst sort of dark, hateful Voodoo. She had to try it.

She reached out to the force that held her people and she tried to find some love for it. She concentrated on the things she loved about Doc Papa, the man who had tried to condemn her and all the islanders to a living death. But she needn't be beaten by that.

She thought of the things she loved about him. She loved his hands and the way they'd touched her. And his mind, so quick and brilliant, she loved that too. She loved the taste of his skin, especially when it was speckled with sweat from the sun. She loved the expression on his face when he came.

She took this love and she sent it into the dark force around her people. All at once the pain and fear were banished. The barbed wire wilted and the barriers crumbled. Her people were captive no longer.

They could hardly believe they were free. They didn't dare move. Then a few of the bravest tested the ground around them and found there was nothing holding them in place. When the others saw this, they were overjoyed.

"Brothers and sisters," Brigitte said to the souls at the Celestial Crossroads. "Your ordeal is over. It is time to come home, or to continue into the next life."

The souls didn't know how to react to this news. They looked out from the Crossroads at their empty, shambling bodies.

The youngest souls were the first to venture back to the world they had left. Other souls looked with dismay at the state of their bodies and the things they must have done and decided they could no longer live inside them. They turned with a heavy heart and followed the road to the next life. Most chose salvation, a tiny few judged their sins too great and took the road to damnation.

Brigitte was surprised to see that one of these was the guest whose soul she had sent to the crossroads when he broke into the mine.

Still others searched in vain for their bodies. They looked from face to face among the zombies and never found their own. Having nowhere else to go, they too eventually turned and went with reluctance along another road.

When the last of the souls had chosen a road, the portal closed and the Celestial Crossroads faded from view. It felt like waking from a dream that has just slipped your mind.

Papa Legba let out a wild laugh and disappeared. Tatyana dropped to the floor. Benjamin rushed over to her. All around them the islanders were having convulsions, throwing up or shuddering uncontrollably. After spending two years outside of their bodies they were now having difficulty adjusting to being flesh and bone once again.

Brigitte never found it a pleasant experience when her soul returned to her body after she'd sent it out. It felt like putting on clothes caked with blood and filth after stepping out of a warm cleansing bath. And that was returning to a live body after only a few hours. She could only imagine the horror and revulsion the islanders must be feeling returning to bodies that had been walking corpses for two years.

Benjamin was supporting Tatyana in his lap and cradling her head as she came round. "What happened?" she said. "God, my arms and legs ache."

"Aw man it was awesome," said Benjamin. "I wish you could have seen it. You were possessed by Papa Legba. He was old and really funny, but kind of wise and dangerous with it. He parted the night sky like a curtain and showed this other world underneath, and Brigitte freed all the souls there. And hey, he also said that you..."

Brigitte put her hand gently on Benjamin's shoulder to stop him. "Wait. That's something she has to come to herself."

"Oh, so now you're both going to go all cryptic on me," said Tatyana. "It worked though right? The ceremony I mean."

"Yes it worked," said Brigitte. "Thanks be to Papa Legba."

"So what now?"

"Now we begin rebuilding our lives," said Brigitte. "But first we must find out what's happening with the guests and the others who have lost their souls. For that we must find Doc Papa."

CHAPTER FORTY-SIX

MUST FIND DOC Papa. Him have their souls. Him suck them all up like greedy belly. Bessie join others in hunt him.

Bessie get worse and worse now. Legs not work good no more. Brain not think right no more. Everything not work good no more. Others not good neither. Look like zombies and stink bad. They all hunt Doc Papa now. His fault they not work good.

Doc Papa try run away from them but them feel where him is. Empty hole in all of them feel where Doc Papa is. Empty hole aches from no soul. Souls in Doc Papa now. Pull them to him. Doc Papa no escape them.

Them all go in grounds of big house now. Doc Papa try hide there. No good. Empty soul holes feel him out.

Them nearly catch Doc Papa earlier. Him on road, run from big house. Them come for him. Him scream like him laughing at them and laugh like him screaming. Him pull his trousers off and try piss at them.

Then him do shit and throw at them. When them not stop coming for Doc Papa, him smear shit on him body. Him not want them eat him. Him think shit make him taste bad and them not eat him.

Them not mind. Them have no taste no more. Them have no feelings no more. Bessie fall on steps when she come up to big house. Her leg go smack. Her bone go crack and poke through skin. Little blood come out. Her no bleed much no more.

Bessie no feel thing. Leg no walk right no more. Bessie stop and look at leg. George Griffin stop too. Him look at Bessie leg. Him sniff Bessie's leg. Them still smell good even if them no feel.

George want eat Bessie leg. Him lick Bessie blood then try bite leg. Bessie hit George and hit him again. George nose go crack. Bessie knuckle go pop. George stop trying to eat Bessie leg. Bessie hand not work good now with knuckle popped.

Bessie walk slower as them come into big house. Bessie leg keep slipping and Bessie fall lots. Others pass her as them go in door. Them get better morsels than Bessie.

Bessie feel so hungry as her get close to Doc Papa. Soul hole ache like Bessie been stabbed. Bessie feel soul calling to her from Doc Papa body. Soul crying like little baby in trouble. Soul dying in there. Soul go rotten like Bessie's body.

Doc Papa on stairs as them find him. Him want run from them but they souls inside him want back in they bodies. Bessie see Doc Papa have fight with himself. Him argue with himself, then plead then burst out laughing and shout. Bessie try get closer to him on stairs but fall down when leg slip. Stupid leg! Bessie angry. Bessie hit leg and then fall down again.

First of them get hold of Doc Papa on stairs. Him swear at them and tell them him will choke and kill them if them eat him. Bessie get more hungry when him talk of eating. She try stand on stupid leg again. She walk five steps without falling. That good record for stupid leg. Bessie not hit it so hard when her fall this time.

Doc Papa start screaming as them get their teeth in him. Them feel hungry for their souls too. Bessie feel her teeth start chewing by themselves her get so hungry at thought of eating Doc Papa.

Bessie try get closer as them start to chew on him whole body. Him blood start to pour down stairs like red waterfall. Bessie stop to look at blood. Her think it pretty 'til her skid in it as her try get at Doc Papa. Then her fall in it. Blood on her hand. Bessie lick him blood and want more.

Others have big mouth full of him, with blood drip down them chin. Bessie is jealous and wants mouth full too when she sees them chins with blood on. She starts to push through others to get near him and others push back. Them start to fight over him when not all of them can have bite of him flesh.

Doc Papa him scream and scream with pain as them eat him and fight. Some of them start to pull on him arms like a tug of war. Doc Papa shouts at them as him arms come off and some blood hits Bessie in her face. Bessie licks blood and her stomach growls.

Some of them grab for arms and push each other to get bite of them. Some pull at Doc Papa's head and legs. Doc Papa's head comes off but still him scream and shout even when one man bite him tongue out. Him legs split apart and him guts fall out on stairs with wet splat sound.

Bessie like that. Her grab for guts and get him liver. Moira Jacobs try and take liver from her. Bessie put hand on Moira Jacobs' head and smash her face into stairs. Moira Jacobs teeth come out and her leave Bessie alone.

Bessie bite warm liver. Taste good. Bessie hear liver scream. Bessie feel it in teeth as her chew him liver. Liver scream as it go down Bessie's throat and into Bessie stomach.

Doc Papa so full of souls that every part of him alive. Him not die when them tear him into pieces. Every piece still feel pain. Every piece scream and scream and scream. All them hear it and feel good to make Doc Papa scream.

Him feel it as they chew him guts and bite him flesh and crack him bones and lick him marrow. Even him marrow feel the pain and scream. Him screams are closest Bessie come to feel her soul again.

Souls them going now. No more left of Doc Papa to keep them in. With them souls gone them not have life now. Them stop breath and heart stop beat.

Bessie feel tired. Others start lie down and not get up. Others fall down with him screaming blood dribbling from them mouths. Them bodies not work no more. Some twitch, some kick, some don't.

Bessie stop think.

Body stop move.

Bessie sto...

CHAPTER FORTY-SEVEN

A Week Later

TATYANA FOUND ANOTHER spot on the stair. She sprayed it with the stain remover and scrubbed it with the brush, trying not to think how it got there in the first place.

"Only another forty steps to go," said Brigitte, coming down the stairs.

Tatyana grinned. "Are you sure this is an essential part of my spiritual training?"

"Anything your Mambo tells you to do is an essential part of your training. Besides, I need all the slave labour I can get to clean this mess up."

"It feels kind of weird, though. I'm not being funny, but when I scrub at a patch of blood that's still kind of fresh, it feels like it's... well it almost sounds like it's..."

"Screaming?"

"Yeah, how'd you know?"

"It's still alive."

"It is? Oh, my God, that's gross. How can it be alive if it's week-old blood?"

"Every part of Doc Papa was alive. When he opened the Gateway of Souls inside himself he became suffused with all the souls that were loose. That was more than anyone could accommodate or even bear. The souls couldn't all reside in his core so they spread out and filled every part of his body. It would most probably have driven him mad. I didn't realise it at the time, but that's why my ancestor Toussaint gave him the Gateway."

"And the guests tore him apart and ate him?"

"They were trying to get their souls back, I imagine. They would have been more or less zombies at that point."

"So if every part of him was alive from the souls inside him, would he still have felt it even after they tore him apart?"

"Every shred of his flesh and bone would have been in unimaginable pain throughout the whole ordeal."

"Gross."

"It was Toussaint's curse coming to pass. Mary Papamal's descendant died a hideous and bloody death at the hands of a Laveau. It just wasn't the Laveau I imagined."

Tatyana heard a clatter behind her and turned to see Benjamin dropping his spade as he tried to lean it against the wall. He'd been helping to bury the guest's bodies. He was in his vest; his muscles were taught and firm from all the digging he'd been doing. His skin had a sheen of sweat from working in the sun and his arms were smeared with dried mud.

Tatyana felt a pang of desire and loss at the same time. She loved Benjamin, and she still found him attractive, but she'd chosen a different future for herself.

"That's pretty much the last of them done," he said.

"You made certain they marked every grave with the right name, didn't you?" said Brigitte. "Because at some point, their families are going to want to come and dig them up again."

"I checked every name against the register and whatever ID we found in their wallets."

"What are we going to do when the authorities start asking questions about what happened?" said Tatyana.

"My guess is, the people who set up the course were so connected to everyone in power that the authorities will want the whole thing covered up," said Brigitte. "Too many of them would be embarrassed if it all came out."

"What about you and the islanders?" said Benjamin.

"We're going to carry on rebuilding our lives."

That's pretty much what they'd all been doing since they came to Mangrove Hall and found the bodies of the dead guests on the stairs. Everyone was trying to find a bit of normality after the bloodshed. The horror was over and they had to pick themselves up and deal with the business of everyday life.

Tatyana found it rather comforting to worry about mundane things again, like what she was going to have for breakfast and where she was going to be sleeping from now on. That's why she didn't mind scrubbing the stairs. It felt good to do a household chore, something that wouldn't lead to a violent death if she didn't keep her wits about her. It was a far cry from the privileged lifestyle she was used to, but it felt more honest and real.

While she and Benjamin helped clear away the bodies and clean up the hall, the rest of the islanders repaired their old homes and started looking for food and other necessities. There was a sense of optimism in everyone, in spite of what they'd been through. The very worst had happened, but they'd survived and were getting on with their lives.

Faces that had been blank and feral now wore smiles and winked at Tatyana. Hands she once feared might tear her apart, patted her on the back and helped her whenever they could. Suddenly the islanders were people again. With personalities and memories and opinions. They weren't some monstrous threat anymore.

In many ways, she thought, that's what a zombie represented: humans without their humanity. The same was true of any enemy. They were people you couldn't identify with, so they weren't human, and if your opponent's not human then it doesn't feel so wrong to hurt or kill them. That's probably what Doc Papa intended when he started preaching the Way of the Barefoot Zombie. That's what turning people into zombies was all about.

"So, you're really going to stay and join the Ounfó, then?" said Benjamin, joining her on the stairs.

Tatyana nodded and made sure he didn't get dirt on her clean step. "Yes, I am. In fact I'm kind of honoured they've accepted me, seeing as I don't come from the island or anything."

"I don't think we had any choice about accepting you," said Brigitte, sitting on the step above them. "As servants of the Loa, we have to heed their wishes, and Papa Legba was pretty adamant that you stay. You have a talent for this and you might not realise, but you've had the calling for a long time."

"Who'd have thought?" said Benjamin.

"Yeah," said Tatyana. "But I think I've been looking for something to believe in my whole life. That's probably what drew me to the ZLF. I wanted to have faith in something, and I thought taking up a cause would give me that. Of course, there were other things that attracted me too." She took Benjamin's hand as she said that. He squeezed it in a friendly fashion and let go. He was withdrawing from her emotionally. She knew he had to, but she missed being close to him. And she missed the sex. She was probably going to have to go without it for a while.

Benjamin nodded. "I think we all hoped the cause would give us something we were looking for."

"What were you looking for, Benjamin?" Brigitte asked.

"I think I was looking for somewhere to belong. And I think I was really trying to piss my stepdad off."

"That's the first time I ever heard you call Richard your stepdad," said Tatyana.

"I know. I guess that's what he is, though. I need to accept that if I'm going to get on better with him and my Mom."

"This is a really mature side that you're showing," said Tatyana. "I rather like it."

"Thanks," said Benjamin. "Coming here has put a lot of things into perspective for me. Doing this course showed me how much I wanted to belong and the things I was capable of doing to feel I belonged. I think that's what my fascination with zombie movies was all about."

"Really?" said Tatyana.

"Yeah. It was the tension between being an individual or fitting in. The human survivors in these movies were like the individuals resisting the mindless herd of the zombie conformists. I always identified with them at the beginning of the movie, but towards the end when they all start becoming zombies I couldn't help thinking it would be easier to just lie down and get it over with. To get bitten, become a zombie and then they couldn't hurt you anymore."

"So you secretly wanted to conform," said Brigitte.

"Exactly, even though all the dressing up and stuff made me stand out."

"I find the West's fascination with zombies quite baffling, actually," said Brigitte. "Is that what it's all about, individuality versus conformity?"

"Not entirely," said Benjamin. "I think the zombie is sort of how we secretly see ourselves and our society. Our culture's all about mindlessly consuming material things, a bit like a zombie.

"Modern zombie films are always about the breakdown of society due to some calamity that brings the dead back to life. And we don't want to admit it, but we know that if we carry on this way our society's going to break down and that's the kind of world we'll be living in."

"Wow," said Tatyana. "You have been getting things into perspective, haven't you?"

"Yeah, I guess I have. You know, I'm reminded of something my granddad once told me. He wasn't my real granddad, he was Richard's dad, but he's the closest I ever got to a real granddad. He was a broker during the stock market crash of 1929. He saw all his money wiped out in one afternoon. The only thing he could think of doing was to open the window of his top floor office and walk out onto the ledge. When he got out there he just froze. He couldn't get back inside and he couldn't jump.

He was trapped there for eight hours until the fire fighters got him down.

"While he was up there, facing death, he said his whole life suddenly fell into perspective. He saw all the wrong choices he'd made, like cheating on his wife and lying to his bosses. He saw the reasons why he'd made those choices and the things he could do to put things right. When it looked as though his life was over, he saw all the ways that he could fix it."

"I know exactly what you mean," said Tatyana. "It just cuts through all the bullshit. Being so close to death for so long has convinced me that there's got to be something else beyond it. I'm not entirely certain what that is but I'd like to learn more about it. I know this probably sounds a bit strange coming from a former atheist, but Voodoo just makes sense of the way that I've always experienced the world. Do you know what I mean?"

"Yeah, I think I do. And trust me, nothing sounds strange after what we've just been through,"

"I've always known there was this other invisible world going on all around us but I never wanted to admit it. Mainly because of my father, I guess. I mean he told me and my mother we were atheists and so we were. I was too frightened of him to argue. I was frightened of being disloyal to him, that if I started believing in things he didn't, then I'd stop loving him, which I don't want to do, in spite of all his faults. I think I was also afraid that if I started to believe in religion, it would take over my life and I'd stop being the person I was. Now, of course, I realise that having a faith allows me to be the person I really am."

"Now look who's getting some perspective," Benjamin said.

"So you understand then? Why I'm doing this, I mean? And you're not mad at me?"

Benjamin shook his head and rolled his eyes in mock exasperation. "Are you kidding? I'm so impressed by what you're doing. Why would I be mad?"

"Well, you know, because of you and me, and the way things have turned out."

"Listen, we've grown up loads together and now I guess we've gotten to a stage where we going to have to grow some more apart from each other. I won't stop loving you, though, no matter what happens."

"I can see what you saw in him now," said Brigitte.

Tatyana put her hand on Benjamin's knee. "He's lovely, isn't he?"

"And what about you, Benjamin?" said Brigitte. "What are you going to do next?"

"Well, first, I'm going to grab a shower, get my stuff together and catch the launch this afternoon," he said. The islanders had got a boat together to take all the people left alive who'd worked for Doc Papa over to Haiti. Benjamin was joining them.

"After that," Benjamin continued. "I think as soon as I get home, I'm going to have to get in touch with the families of our friends and explain what happened to them here."

"Are you okay to do that?" Tatyana said.

Benjamin shrugged. "Someone's got to, and I guess it ought to be me. I got them involved in the first place, so I suppose it's my fault." Tatyana and Benjamin's moods suddenly fell as they thought about the friends they'd lost.

Brigitte put her hand on Benjamin's shoulder. "What you did was foolish, ill considered and reckless, but you can't hold yourself responsible for what happened to your friends. I've been holding myself responsible for what happened to my fellow islanders since I left the island two years ago, and I realise now that I was wrong to do that. There's only one person who's ultimately responsible, and he paid the ultimate price."

"Yeah, I still get creeped out when I think about what happened to him," said Benjamin. "I guess your ancestor really knew how to place a curse."

"Yes. He certainly did."

"So you're really going to try and get on better with your folks?" said Tatyana.

"Well my Mom mainly. But Richard, too, I guess. First I've got to face the music and explain what happened to Richard's yacht and the five million he put up for me to come here."

"How do you think they'll take it?"

"Richard will be a dick. My Mom will play peacemaker, and I'll have to eat a lot of shit and make a lot of compromises to get back in with them. But I figure it'll be worth it, to patch things up with my Mom."

"That's kind of a big step for you."

"It is, but out in the jungle, when Brigitte did that Voodoo healing on me, it lifted so much anger off me. I see now how so much of it came from my relationship with my Mom. We both miss each other and the way it used to be between us, and I want to put that right now. I never properly thanked you for that, Brigitte."

"No thanks are needed," said Brigitte. "In fact, I should really be thanking you. You've made me realise how important the bond between a mother and a son is. I haven't told anyone, but before I came back here I gave birth to a son. It was part of the agreement I had with Miriam and Oliver Chevalier. I carried him for nine months, but I told myself that he wasn't my child. I was inhabiting another woman's body and the baby inside me belonged to Miriam and his father, not me. I felt so guilty about what happened to everyone on St Ignatius that I was fixated on getting back here and doing what I thought was my duty to them. I forgot about my duty to my son. He might not have been conceived in the womb I was born with, but I'm still the only mother he has. I need to become the mother he deserves."

"How are things with your own Mom?" said Tatyana.

"They've been worse," said Brigitte. "At least she's talking to me now."

"'Cause she's forgiven you or 'cause she's not a zombie anymore?" said Benjamin.

"Probably the latter."

"This is incredible," said Tatyana. "The past week or so I've been more intimate with you guys than anyone else in my life. But I've learned more about you in the last thirty minutes than the whole time I've known you. It's like we're suddenly spilling our guts."

"That's what happens when you think you might not see someone for a long while," said Benjamin. "You suddenly think of all the things you want to tell them before you go. That reminds me, I need to shower and pack."

TATYANA STOOD ON the jetty and waved goodbye. Benjamin was fooling around at the back of the boat, pulling faces to stop her from crying. It didn't work.

She'd pulled Benjamin to her for one last kiss just before the boat left. He was a little surprised and hesitant at first but she wasn't going to let him go without one. That meeting of lips spoke more about how they felt than they'd said in their whole awkward farewells.

She watched until the boat disappeared over the horizon, taking all those people away to carry on with the rest of their lives, while she stayed here to continue hers.

Is this where the adventure ends? thought Tatyana. She remembered Benjamin telling her his Uncle Brian once said that there were no beginnings or endings in real life. Just a sequence of events from which we draw our own significance.

Tatyana was sure of one thing, no sequence of events would ever hold more significance than those she'd just lived through.

THE END

JASPER BARK is a novelist, children's author and script writer specialising in comics and graphic novels. He's written three previous novels, *A Fistful of Strontium* (Black Flame, 2005 with Steve Lyons) *Sniper Elite: Spear of Destiny* (Abaddon, 2006) and *The Afterblight Chronicles: Dawn Over Doomsday* (Abaddon, 2008). His all-ages book, *Inventions, Leonardo Da Vinci*, has been translated into five different languages and his *Battle Cries* series of graphic novels are used in schools throughout to improve literacy for 12 to 16 year old readers. He's written comics for just about every publisher in the British comics industry, from *2000 AD* to *The Beano*, and an increasing number of American and international publishers. Prior to this he worked as a film journalist and cable TV presenter by day and a stand-up poet and playwright by night. In 1993 he released an anthology of poetry and a spoken word album both called *Bark Bites*. In 1999 he was awarded a Fringe First at the Edinburgh International Festival.

A COLLECTION OF THREE TERRIFYING ZOMBIE TALES

FEATURING MATTHEW SMITH, AL EWING & REBECCA LEVENE

THE BEST OF

TOMES OF THE DEAD

 ISBN (UK): 978-1-907519-34-5   (US): 978-1-907519-35-2
UK £9.99   US $12.99   CAN $14.99

TOMES of the DEAD

ANNO MORTIS

Rebecca Levene

ISBN: 978-1-905437-85-6
UK £.6.99   US $7.99

Abaddon
Books

Follow us on twitter: www.twitter.com/abaddonbooks

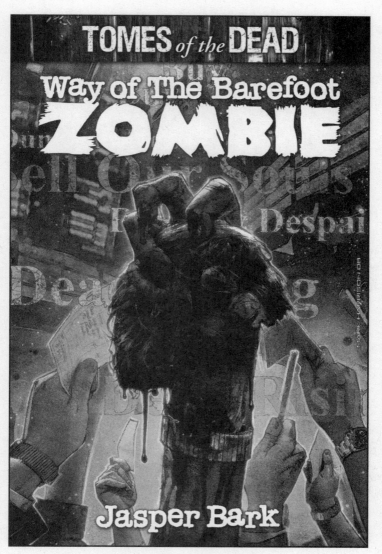

Visit www.abaddonbooks.com for information on our titles,
interviews, news and exclusive content.

ISBN: 978-1-906735-06-7
UK £6.99   US $7.99

Abaddon
Books

Follow us on twitter: www.twitter.com/abaddonbooks

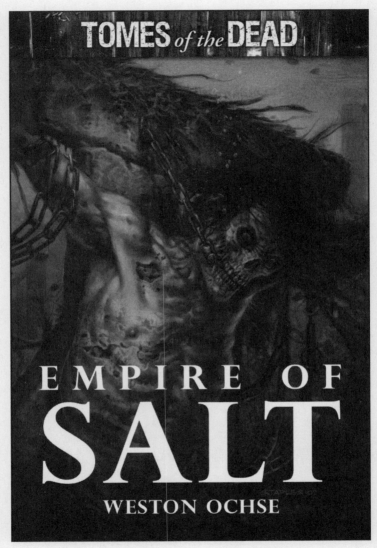

TOMES *of the* DEAD

EMPIRE OF
SALT

WESTON OCHSE

Visit www.abaddonbooks.com for information on our titles,
interviews, news and exclusive content.

ISBN: 978-1-906735-32-6
UK £.6.99   US $7.99

Abaddon
Books

Follow us on twitter: www.twitter.com/abaddonbooks

Visit www.abaddonbooks.com for information on our titles,
interviews, news and exclusive content.

ISBN: 978-1-906735-26-5
UK £.6.99   US $7.99

Abaddon
Books

Follow us on twitter: www.twitter.com/abaddonbooks

TOMES *of the* DEAD

I, Zombie

Al Ewing

ISBN: 978-1-905437-72-6
UK £.6.99   US $7.99

Abaddon
Books

Follow us on twitter: www.twitter.com/abaddonbooks

TOMES *of the* DEAD

TIDE OF SOULS

SIMON BESTWICK

Visit www.abaddonbooks.com for information on our titles,
interviews, news and exclusive content.

ISBN: 978-1-906735-14-2
UK £.6.99   US $7.99

Abaddon
Books

Follow us on twitter: www.twitter.com/abaddonbooks